THE PENGUIN BOOKS OF

HORROR STORIES

J. A. Cuddon was born in 1928. He was educated at Douai School and at Brasenose College, Oxford, where, after taking a degree, he did postgraduate work on the concept of evil and the devil in medieval and Renaissance literature. He also represented the university at cricket, rugby and hockey, though without gaining a 'blue'. For ten years he wrote only plays, before turning to other forms. Apart from numerous essays, short stories, articles, contributions to encyclopedias, a dozen plays and three libretti, he also published a number of novels, notably *A Multitude of Sins*, *Testament of Iscariot*, *Acts of Darkness*, *The Six Wounds* and *The Bride of Battersea*, which have been translated into several languages. His two travel books, *The Owl's Watchsong: A Study of Istanbul* and the *Companion Guide to Jugoslavia*, have also been translated. *A Dictionary of Literary Terms* was begun while he was on a fellowship at Cambridge in 1968 and it was completed seven years later. It is now available as *The Penguin Dictionary of Literary Terms and Literary Theory* and is currently in its third edition. In 1971 Cuddon received an award from the Goldsmiths' Company to make a study of medieval frescoes in Serbia and Macedonia. In 1980 he published *A Dictionary of Sport and Games*, a two-million word account of most of the sports and games of the world since 5200 BC, which came out in paperback in 1981. He edited both *The Penguin Book of Ghost Stories* and *The Penguin Book of Horror Stories* in 1984, and James Hogg's *The Private Memoirs and Confessions of a Justified Sinner* in 1995. A compulsive traveller, with a special interest in the Balkan and the Near East, his main recreations were going to the theatre, watching sport and pursuing an amateur interest in zoology.

J. A. Cuddon died in March 1996. In its obituary *The Times* described him as 'one of the great polymaths of his day . . . learned and erudite . . . [he was] always a pleasure to read'.

THE PENGUIN BOOK OF
HORROR STORIES

EDITED BY J. A. CUDDON

PENGUIN BOOKS

PENGUIN BOOKS

Published by the Penguin Group
Penguin Books Ltd, 27 Wrights Lane, London W8 5TZ, England
Penguin Putnam Inc., 375 Hudson Street, New York, New York 10014, USA
Penguin Books Australia Ltd, Ringwood, Victoria, Australia
Penguin Books Canada Ltd, 10 Alcorn Avenue, Toronto, Ontario, Canada M4V 3B2
Penguin Books (NZ) Ltd, Private Bag 102902, NSMC, Auckland, New Zealand

Penguin Books Ltd, Registered Offices: Harmondsworth, Middlesex, England

This collection first published 1984
15 17 19 20 18 16

Introduction and selection copyright © J. A. Cuddon, 1984
All rights reserved

The acknowledgements on pages 9–10 constitute an extension of this copyright page.

Set in Bembo VIP
Printed in England by Clays Ltd, St Ives plc

Contents

6 CONTENTS

What is the sickly smell, the vapour? the dark green light from a cloud on a withered tree? The earth is heaving to parturition of issue of hell. What is the sticky dew that forms on the back of my hand?

T. S. Eliot: *Murder in the Cathedral*, Act I

Acknowledgements

For permission to reprint the stories specified we are indebted to:

Penguin Books Ltd for 'Who Knows?' by Guy de Maupassant from *Miss Harriet and Other Stories*, trans. H. N. P. Sloman (Penguin, 1951), copyright 1951 by H. N. P. Sloman; Elizabeth McNally for her translation of 'The Death of Olivier Bécaille' by Emile Zola, copyright © Elizabeth McNally, 1984; Edward Arnold Ltd for 'Lost Hearts' by M. R. James from *The Ghost Stories of M. R. James* (1931), copyright 1931 by M. R. James; The Literary Executors of the Estate of H. G. Wells for 'The Sea-Raiders' by H. G. Wells from *The Short Stories of H. G. Wells* (1927; first published in the *Weekly Sun Literary Supplement*, December 1896), copyright 1896 by H. G. Wells; Martin Secker & Warburg Ltd and Schocken Books, Inc., for 'In the Penal Colony' by Franz Kafka, trans. Willa and Edwin Muir, from *In the Penal Settlement* (1948), copyright 1948, 1976 by Schocken Books, Inc.; The Executors of the Estate of K. S. P. McDowell for 'Mrs Amworth' by E. F. Benson from *Visible and Invisible* (1923; first published in *Hutchinson's Magazine*, June 1922), copyright 1922 by E. F. Benson; J. M. Dent & Sons Ltd for 'The Beast with Five Fingers' by W. F. Harvey from *The Beast with Five Fingers and Other Midnight Tales*, copyright © W. F. Harvey; Alfred A. Knopf, Inc., Random House, Inc., and Curtis Brown Ltd, London, for 'Dry September' by William Faulkner from *Collected Stories of William Faulkner*, copyright 1930 by William Faulkner, renewed 1958; William Heinemann Ltd for 'Couching at the Door' by D. K. Broster from *Cornhill Magazine* (1933) and 'Comrade Death' by Gerald Kersh from *The Horrible Dummy*; Curtis Brown Ltd on behalf of John Child-Villiers and Valentine Lamb as literary executors of Lord Dunsany for 'The Two Bottles of Relish' by Lord Dunsany from *Tales to be Told in the Dark*, ed. Basil Davenport (1953); A. D. Peters & Co. Ltd and Little, Brown & Company for 'The Man Who Liked Dickens' by Evelyn Waugh from *A Handful of Dust* (Chapman Hall, 1934), copyright 1934 by Evelyn Waugh, copyright renewed 1964 by Evelyn Waugh; A. M. Heath and Co. Ltd for 'Taboo' by Geoffrey Household from *The Salvation of Pisco Gabar and Other Stories* (Jonathan Cape, 1939), copyright 1939 by Geoffrey Household; Hamish Hamilton Ltd and the Executors of the Estate of L. P. Hartley for 'The Thought' from *The Complete Short Stories of L. P. Hartley* (first published in *The Travelling Grave*, 1951), copyright © The Executors of the Estate, 1973; Ohio University Press for 'The Brink of Darkness' by Yvor Winters from *Anchor in the Sea: An Anthology of Psychological Fiction*, ed. Alan Swallow (Swallow Press, 1947), copyright by Yvor Winters; Miss Monica Dickens for 'Activity Time', copyright © Monica Dickens, 1981; Robert Graves for 'Earth to Earth' from *Punch* (February 1955), copyright © Robert Graves, 1955; Anthony Sheil Associates Ltd and Don Congdon Associates Ltd for 'The Dwarf' by Ray Bradbury from *The October Country* (Rupert Hart Davis, 1956), copyright © Ray Bradbury, 1954, 1982; Harold Ober Associates, Inc., for 'The Portobello Road' by Muriel Spark from *The Go-away Bird* (Macmillan London Ltd, 1958), copyright © Copyright Administration Ltd, 1958; Jonathan Cape Ltd and Simon and Schuster, Inc., for 'No Flies on Frank' by John Lennon from *In His Own Write* (1964), copyright © John Lennon, 1964; Miss Dorothy K. Haynes for 'Thou Shalt Not Suffer a Witch . . .', copyright © Dorothy K. Haynes; William Heinemann Ltd and Doubleday & Co., Inc., for 'The Terrapin' by Patricia Highsmith from *Eleven* (Penguin, 1972), copyright 1945 by Patricia Highsmith; Alfred A. Knopf, Inc., and Murray Pollinger for 'Man from the South' by Roald Dahl from *Someone Like You*, copyright 1948 by Roald Dahl, Michael Joseph Ltd (Publishers), and Penguin Books Ltd; The author and Scott Meredith Literary Agency Inc., 845 Third Avenue, New York, New York 10022 for 'Uneasy Home-coming' by Will F. Jenkins (first published in *Weird Tales*, April, 1935), copyright 1935 by Will F. Jenkins, copyright renewed 1963; J. N. Allan for 'The Aquarist' from the *London Magazine* (August/September, 1981), copyright © J. N. Allan.

Despite extensive inquiries over many months it has, unfortunately, not been possible to trace who holds the rights for: 'The Waxwork' by A. M. Burrage; 'Mr Meldrum's Mania' by John Metcalfe (first published in *Judas and Other Stories*, Constable, 1935); 'Leiningen Versus the Ants' by Carl Stephenson; 'Sister Coxall's Revenge' by Dawn Muscillo; 'An Interview with M. Chakko' by Vilas Sarang (published in the *London Magazine*, December, 1982/January, 1983).

Nor has it been possible to find who holds the USA and Canadian rights for 'Couching at the Door' by D. K. Broster and 'Comrade Death' by Gerald Kersh.

Introduction

Bacon remarked of the essay that 'the thing is ancient but the word is late'. The same, with a certain amount of truth, might be said of the horror story which, like the ghost story, is often taken to be a sub-species of the short story. However, the term may also cover stories of novella and novel length.

It is not clear when the term first came into use or was first applied to fiction.[1] Nor, often enough, will people agree in their definition of what precisely the thing is. Inability to do so is not surprising since the term appears to subsume a considerable variety of fiction, ranging from, say, Charles Maturin's *Melmoth the Wanderer* to the more macabre tales in Roald Dahl's *Kiss, Kiss*, or from, say, William Burroughs's *The Naked Lunch* to Poe's *The Masque of the Red Death*. Other works, among the hundreds that might qualify, which have been put into this genre are, for example, Nathaniel Hawthorne's *Young Goodman Brown*, Wilkie Collins's *A Terribly Strange Bed*, F. Marion Crawford's *The Dead Smile*, Bram Stoker's *The Squaw*, W. W. Jacobs's *The Monkey's Paw*, Conrad Aiken's *Silent Snow, Secret Snow*, Anthony Burgess's *A Clockwork Orange*, J. G. Ballard's *The Atrocity Exhibition* and some of the stories in Robert Coover's *Pricksongs and Descants*.

For the purposes of this Introduction I have taken a 'horror story' to be a piece of fiction in prose of variable length (but tending to be between, say, 2,000 words and 100,000 words) which shocks or even frightens the reader, or perhaps induces a feeling of repulsion or loathing.[2] There appears to be a considerable range of possible responses. And it should be added at once that some horror stories are serio-comic or comic/grotesque, but they may be none the less alarming or frightening for that.

As for the materials of the horror story, these are extensive and diverse.

1. The OED Supplement cites only one usage – and it is clearly an eccentric, metaphorical one – from Edgar Snow's *Red Star over China* (1937). The OED cites a number of uses of 'horror' in the tradition of the sublime (notably from Hazlitt's observations on dramatic literature). It is possible that the coinage is a late nineteenth-century modulation in that tradition.

2. The stories that comprise this anthology are all short, or fairly short, averaging 5,000–6,000 words.

Whether or not it is a literary form (or can be accepted as such) it seems
to be a kind of Gladstone bag of literature. Apart from being about
murder, suicide, torture, fear and madness, horror stories are also
concerned with ghosts, vampires, *Doppelgängers*, succubae, incubi, pol-
tergeists, demonic pacts, diabolic possession, exorcism, witchcraft,
spiritualism, black magic, voodoo and lycanthropy, plus such miscellaneous occult or quasi-occult practices as telekinesis and hylomancy.

In the hands of a serious and genuinely imaginative writer the horror
story, whatever length it may be, explores the limits of what people are
capable of doing and the limits of what they are capable of experiencing.
Thus he ventures (as he does in the tale of terror and the ghost story: all three
are closely related) into the realms of psychological chaos, emotional waste-
lands, psychic trauma, abysses opened up by the imagination, the capacity
for experiencing fear, hysteria and madness, all that lies on the dark side of
the mind and the near side of barbarism, on and beyond the shifting
frontiers of consciousness, where some kind of precarious vigilance and
control are kept by convention and taboo and by the repressive censors of
feelings; and where, perhaps, there dwell ultimate horrors or concepts of
horror[1] (e.g. Room 101 in *1984*) which are paradigms, images and figures
of suffering and chaos, and thus of various kinds of 'hell' – taking 'hell' to be
a more or less universal symbol of an extreme condition (e.g. intense grief,
an overwhelming feeling of loss, acute fear, irrational foreboding or physical pain). There is, I believe, what may be described as a residual concept of
hell which exemplifies the worst possible conditions to which a human
being may be exposed, often expressed in clichés: 'hell on earth', 'I went
through hell', 'a hell of a time', and so on.

It seems to me that the horror story (like the tale of terror[2] and the
ghost story) is part of a long process by which we have tried to come to
terms with and find adequate descriptions and symbols for deeply rooted,
primitive and powerful forces, energies and fears which are related to
death, afterlife, punishment, darkness, evil, violence and destruction.

1. The word 'horror' derives from Latin *horrere*, 'to make the hair stand on end, tremble,
shudder'.

2. There has been some discussion of the terms terror and horror ('tale of terror', 'horror
story') and attempts to make distinctions. Boris Karloff, as gentle and benign a man as one
could wish to meet, might occasionally be persuaded to offer an opinion on such matters.
It is worth recording that in his view horror is a response to a physical reality such as
murder and torture, whereas terror (a more intense form of fear) is awakened in the presence
of the supernatural, the unknown, the invisible threat. I find this distinction persuasive. It
should be added that Boris Karloff preferred to talk about cricket, of which he was a
lifelong, devoted, globe-trotting watcher and about whose arcane rites he was very
knowledgeable.

They are also, no doubt, part of a need (instinctual, perhaps) to discover or imagine something incomparably worse than already exists, or may come into some form of existence.

At a basic level an experience of the horrific is a likelihood of everyday life. Fortunate indeed is the person who lives his biblical span and is not part of an event or experience which curdles his blood, makes the hair on his neck stand up, puts fear in his heart and terror in his soul, turns his bowels to water or makes his gorge rise in nausea.

Nowadays, so efficient are the media, one can participate daily and vicariously in the horrific misfortunes which befall others. As one sits comfortably sipping a drink, pictures of death, agony and catastrophe, bounced off satellites between commercials, are skilfully presented on the tragic lantern. The results of the latest famine, earthquake, war or bomb outrage blend into weather forecasts, football scores and advertisements for cat food and breakfast cereals. The newspapers flourish on the offal of other people's disasters. It has become easy to satisfy a fundamental, human, ghoulish instinct and appetite.

If the horror is not so readily accessible people will seek it out. Some years ago there was a plane crash near a British airport. Many people were killed and pieces of their bodies were scattered over a wide area. Within an hour there were traffic jams caused by sightseers. There followed the weird and unseemly spectacle of suburban dwellers scrambling about in the undergrowth of the airport's hinterland in search of 'souvenirs'.

I have little doubt that if you hired Wembley Stadium and advertised a public execution the event would be a sell-out; and the touts would have a field-day on the black market.

It is an aspect of 'the human condition' (in Malraux's terms) that a percentage of people tend to be drawn towards and perhaps even fascinated by that which basically repels them. Taboo, convention and the 'voices of education' erect barriers, but the urge to look over those barriers or get past them is strong. This contradictory behaviour creates conflict and tension which is not unpleasing. Violence, the gory and gruesome, death itself, pluck at, twitch, some dark orectic nerve; perhaps, too, some dark, aphrodisiac nerve.

Writers seem to have been well aware of such tendencies – I don't say all along, but certainly at various stages – and have seen how to exploit or appeal to particular inclinations and appetites. One might cite hundreds of instances; here there is space for only a few indications.

*

In classical Greek drama there was no violence on stage. For aesthetic reasons (and perhaps also for residual religious reasons, since the drama derived from and was associated with religious practices) horrific events were reported by a messenger. A notable instance occurs in Sophocles' *Trachiniae* when Hyllus describes Heracles' agonies from the poisoned shirt.

The Roman dramatist who specialized in describing the horrific in lurid detail was Seneca, whose tragedies (intended for recitation, and thus a form of closet drama) were to have extensive influence on Elizabethan playwrights, especially after they were translated into English between 1559 and 1581.

Crime, the criminal, murder, suicide, cruelty, revenge, pain, insanity and physical torture are notable features of his extant tragedies. Like the Jacobean practitioners of revenge tragedy – who learnt much from Seneca – the Roman was profoundly interested in extremes of human suffering. Horror is piled on horror in the most sensational fashion.

In classical epic numerous scenes are concerned with violence and not a few qualify as horrific. Some passages have become celebrated, such as Virgil's description, in the *Aeneid*, of the death of Laocoön and his sons when they are crushed by snakes. In epic, too, occur the well-known descriptions of the Underworld which, in conjunction with comparable descriptions in the Old Testament and the Apocrypha, were to have a long-term influence on later Christian 'visions' of hell throughout the Middle Ages; that is to say, for at least a thousand years.

Few Latin authors had a better eye and ear for the horrific episode and effect than the prodigy Lucan who, unhappily, incurred the jealousy of Nero in literary matters and was commanded to take his life when only twenty-six, in AD 65. In *Pharsalia* there are a number of vivid and bloodcurdling passages. Sometimes he displays a good deal of poetic licence, but it works. For instance, there is the celebrated account of the sea battle in Book III, and the description of Scaeva's lone stand against Pompey's army. Scaeva is hit in the eye by a Cretan arrow: 'He tore the stubborn steel with ligaments of muscle, and, unterrified, having plucked the arrow out with his eyeball attached to it, he trampled the weapon and his own eye into the ground . . . Rage had ruined his face, his features were disfigured with bloody rain.'

In Book VI there is a powerful description of the Thessalian witches, and Erictho in particular. This haggard and loathsome crone inhabited rifled tombs from which the ghosts had been driven. Her breath poisoned the air and her tread destroyed what lay beneath it. She would eat the burning bones of children and rip out the stiffened eyeballs of the dead.

Crucified corpses were a speciality for her. She gnawed the flesh and bones and sucked up the clotted filth and 'black humour' of corruption that oozed out of them. When a kinsman was buried it was her habit to mutilate the head, force open the dead lips and then chew the tongue, meanwhile sending a message 'of mysterious horror down to the shades of hell'.

In the ninth book of *Pharsalia* Lucan devotes a long passage to the hideous poisonous snakes that may be encountered in Libya, especially the tiny *seps*. A bite from this reptile causes the disintegration of the body. The limbs are soaked with blood, calves and legs melt away, knees are stripped and a black discharge issues from the groin. The belly gapes open and the bowels gush out. Destruction is so comprehensive that the body of a whole man is reduced to a little puddle of putrescent matter. Rather what happened to M. Valdemar in Edgar Allan Poe's weird story.

Lucan elaborates in a manner which would have certainly appealed to Poe in his more bizarre moods. Statius, Silicus Italicus and Valerius Flaccus all showed a comparable knack and tendency to make the most of a gruesome episode. In the use of episode Ovid's example was a major influence for at least a century and his exploitation of the bloody scene involving cruelty and violence is occasionally outstanding.

For instance there is that scene in *Metamorphoses IV* when Pyramus commits suicide. Having lavished tears and kisses on Thisbe's veil, he thrusts his sword deep into his side and falls back, dying:

> His blood shot high in the air, very much as when a pipe bursts because the lead has been flawed, and through the narrow hissing crack a high jet of water is flung up and pulses on the air. The leaves of the tree were sprayed with his blood and turned a dark colour; and its roots, saturated with blood, tinged the pendent berries a dark red.

The somewhat clinical detachment here is highly effective, and the realism is enhanced by the fine simile of the burst pipe.

In *Metamorphoses XI* there is the horrible description of the destruction of Orpheus by the Maenads. Elsewhere in the same work he describes the silencing of Philomela. Bound and manacled by her murderer, she is powerless. But her tongue still moves. With it she reviles her murderer and calls her father's name. The murderer grasps the tongue with forceps and slices it off with his sword: 'The stump of her tongue flickered in her throat, while the tongue itself lay wriggling and muttering to the black earth; and, as the tail of a snake writhes after it has been chopped off, it fluttered . . .'

Such excerpts might come into the category of 'purple passage' (or purple patch) and it is perhaps worth mentioning that reciters of poetry in public were wont to use what is known as the *deinosis* effect: a rhetorical method or technique for emphasizing 'strangeness'. Broadly speaking, *deinosis* denoted exaggeration or exacerbation; it implied the new, clever and strange, even, perhaps, the terrible. It was brought into use for bloody deeds, battles, storms and so forth; in short, where something extra was called for. It was a way of raising the emotional temperature and charging certain passages with additional force and vigour in order to impinge on audiences more effectively.

So far as I can discover there is no such thing as a fully fledged 'horror story' in classical literature of the kind that we have today, but there are certainly stories which approach the modern sort. For instance, in Lucian's *Philopseudes* there are some exaggerated bogeyman stories, and in Petronius's *Satyricon* there are a couple of anecdotes which, in little, contain the components of the fully developed thing. They are comic/grotesque, somewhat in the Rabelaisian manner, and one can easily see how they might have been expanded into something much more substantial.

During the famous banquet of Trimalchio, Niceros tells a tale of a werewolf (a regular theme for practitioners of horror stories). He goes out into the countryside with his host for an evening walk:

The Moon shone bright as Day, and about Cock-crowing we fell in with a Burying-place, and certain Monuments of the Dead: my Man loitered behind me a star-gazing, and I sitting expecting him, fell a singing and numbering them; when looking round me what should I see but mine Host stript stark-naked, and his Cloaths lying by the High-way-side. The sight struck me every where, and I stood as if I had been dead; but he Piss'd round his Cloaths, and of a sudden was turned to a Wolf . . . He set up a Howl and fled to the Woods. At first I knew not where I was, till going to take up his Cloaths, I found them also turn'd to Stone.[1]

Very frightened, Niceros eventually runs to the place where his employer's wife has gone to stay. She tells him that a wolf has raided the farm and 'made Butchers work enough among the Cattle' and a servant has run the beast through the neck with a pitchfork. Niceros returns home the next day and when he passes the place where the 'Cloaths were turned to Stone' he sees nothing but a puddle of blood. At home he finds his host in bed while a surgeon dresses his neck.

Trimalchio attempts to cap this yarn with one of his own about the

1. This version is taken from the translation ascribed to William Burnaby (1694).

corpse of a child that was snatched from its cradle by marauding witches. In its stead they left a bolster of straw.

Better examples than these are to be found in that witty and exuberant book *The Golden Ass* by Apuleius (who flourished in the second century A.D., c. 155) who has a penchant for the supernatural and the grotesque and combines the comical/absurd with the horrific. He has, too, a knack for the tall story which takes some beating.

Early in *The Golden Ass* he relates the tale of Aristomenes who is sharing a room with his old friend Socrates in an inn. The innkeeper is a witch and a practitioner of the black arts. In the middle of the night the bedroom door is hurled open and two hideous crones enter. One hag bears a lighted torch, the other a sponge and a drawn sword. Aristomenes, terrified, takes refuge under his collapsed bed. Standing over Socrates, the hags discuss how to punish him for various misdemeanours:

Panthia said to Meroë – she could only have been Meroë [i.e., the innkeeper]: 'Sister, shall we tear him to pieces at once, or shall we first tie strong twine around his privates and haul him up to a rafter and watch them being slowly cut through?'

'No, no, dear, nothing of the sort! [replied Meroë] Let him be for a while. My darling Socrates will be needing a sexton tomorrow to dig a little hole for him somewhere or other.' Still speaking, she turned Socrates' head on the pillow and I watched her drive the sword up to the hilt through the left side of his neck. Blood spurted out, but she had a small bladder ready and caught every drop as it fell. Socrates' windpipe had been sliced through, but he uttered a sort of cry or indistinct gurgle, and then was silent.

To complete the sacrificial rite Meroë thrusts her hand into the wound, gropes about inside and at length pulls out the heart. Panthia then stops the gaping wound with a sponge. Then they cross the room to Aristomenes, lift away the bed and piss long and vigorously in his face.

Aristomenes fears that he will be accused of murdering Socrates. He panics, thinks of running away and then decides to commit suicide. His attempt is a fiasco. He ties a rope to a rafter, puts his head in the noose and kicks away the bed. The rope, being rotten, breaks under his weight and he crashes on to Socrates on his mattress. The porter runs in wondering what the noise is. Socrates springs up, apparently unharmed. Aristomenes is overjoyed and hugs and kisses him. Socrates shoves him away saying: 'Ugh, you stink like the bottom of a sewer!'

The friends decide to leave town at once. En route Socrates divulges that he has had a terrible nightmare in which he dreamt he was having his throat cut and then that his heart was pulled out. There are no signs of any wounds on Socrates. There follows an unexpected sequel.

This bizarre and slightly macabre tale runs to about 2,000 words. Later in *The Golden Ass* there is a considerably longer story in which there features no fantastic or bawdy element.

It is about the Lady Charitë who marries Tlepolemus. The latter's rival, Thrasyllus, is furious at being rejected and elects to murder her husband. In the course of a boar hunt he contrives an 'accident' in which Tlepolemus is unhorsed and Thrasyllus kills him with his lance. The Lady Charitë is driven to distraction by her anguish. Thrasyllus bides his time and then begins to importune her. Tlepolemus's ghost appears to her and tells her what actually happened. To get her revenge she agrees to sleep with Thrasyllus. He is given a powerful sleeping draught by Charitë's old nurse. While he lies in drugged stupor Charitë takes a bronze pin from her hair and plunges it repeatedly into his eyes. She then runs to her husband's tomb and kills herself by thrusting a sword into her breast. Her relatives lay her beside Tlepolemus. When Thrasyllus hears what has happened he is overcome with guilt and remorse. He gives orders to be carried to the tomb where, contrite, he allows himself to starve to death.

This crude summary makes the thing sound melodramatic. But it is a skilfully constructed tale in which some care is given to the development of character (especially that of Thrasyllus) and the descriptions of feeling and action are vivid and convincing. In fact it is no more melodramatic than some stories by recent purveyors of horror; for example, Edgar Allan Poe, F. Marion Crawford, Arthur Machen, H. P. Lovecraft and Marjorie Bowen.

The literature of Byzantium, of Constantinople, is rich in copious quantities of history, biography, philosophy, theology, miscellaneous didactic works, critical exegeses and commentaries, religious poetry, hymns and even ballads; but there are no drama, no fiction and no horror stories.

During what old-fashioned historians were wont to call 'the Dark Ages' not much literature was produced in Western Europe; or, if it was, it has not survived. All the extant Old English literature fits into one fairly small book. No doubt, war, plague, fire, earthquake, flood and famine – the mere task of survival – were enough for most people to contend with.

Later, in the Icelandic *sagas* and the Old Norse *Eddas* we find – as we would expect in epic – passages of horror and violence comparable with those to be found in *Gilgamesh* and in the poems of Homer, Virgil and

Lucan. In *Beowulf*, too, there are some nasty moments – to say the least of them. The description of Grendel's onslaught on Heorot, followed by the vengeful attack of his mother, are sufficiently hair-raising for most people's taste. In most such narratives the supernatural or quasi-supernatural element (usually manifested by the powers of evil, hell and darkness) is often strong. By the time we reach the beginning of the late Middle Ages these powers are receiving close attention. By the age of Chaucer (1340?–1400) a very considerable body of horror literature had accumulated.

One of the best short stories of the late Middle Ages is Chaucer's *Pardoner's Tale* (of which there were several European analogues), a cautionary horror story and *exemplum* which is all the more successful for its 'low' tone (what Northrop Frye would probably classify as 'low mimetic') and almost matter-of-fact style.

The scene is set in Flanders in a permissive society which indulged in excessive drinking, gambling and whoring and in general led a debauched and godless life, tells of three 'riotoures' (i.e. drunken layabouts) who were drinking in a tavern very early one morning ('Long erst er prime rong'). They hear a funeral bell toll in the street and one of them calls a servant-boy to go and see whose corpse is being carried away. 'It nedeth neveradeel,' the lad answers, the body is that of an old friend of yours who died suddenly this very night. A secret thief whom men call Death 'smoot his herte atwo'.

The publican confirms that in a nearby village this thief has done great slaughter that year. Full of arrogant and drunken bravado the 'riotoures' set forth to find this 'false traytour Deeth' and slay him. En route they meet an old man by a stile (this encounter is one of Chaucer's finest scenes) who, in response to their request, directs them to a particular tree in a nearby wood. The three men immediately run to the tree and there they find:

> Of floryns fyne of gold ycoyned rounde
> Wel ny an eighte busshels, as hem thoughte.

At once losing interest in their search for Death, they plan how they can make away with the treasure trove. They decide to transport it under cover of darkness. Meanwhile they will need food and drink, so they draw lots and it falls to the youngest to go to the town and buy food and wine while the other two guard the money. The two who remain plot to kill the third on his return so that they can divide the cash between them. Avarice so consumes the third that he decides to buy some deadly rat poison and doctor the wine with it.

> What nedeth it to sermone of it moore?

The climax is abrupt. When the youngest returns he is murdered and the murderers drink the poisoned wine.

> For which anon they storven bothe two.

During the twentieth century, in civilized countries, death has become a secret and hygienic business. In time of peace one might live a whole life and see but three or four corpses. In the fourteenth and fifteenth centuries it was very different. The spectacle of death, especially during the terrible plagues which ravaged Europe, was ubiquitous. One might think that its actual omnipresence would have been sufficient reminder of mortality, and thus that any form of *memento mori* would have been superfluous.

This was not so. The horrors of death, when man would become mere 'wormes fode', were persistently emphasized. Preachers, moralists and compilers of works of spiritual edification exploited the fact and the idea to reinforce their admonitions. 'Horror' stories, *exempla*, of what might or would befall one if one died in a state of mortal sin (or *not* in a state of grace) were abundant. A great many *exempla* in theological handbooks told thoroughly nasty stories of what might happen to one in life, never mind in dying and death, which became something of an obsession in the fourteenth and fifteenth centuries (though not, perhaps, quite such an obsession as Huizinga suggested in *The Waning of the Middle Ages*). As chiliastic doom-mongers roamed Europe,[1] once again the end of the world seemed nigh and the bubonic rats proliferated through village, town and city in terrifying numbers.

It was the poets and artists of the late medieval period who figured out and expressed some of the innermost fears and some of the ultimate horrors, real and imaginary, of human consciousness. Fear created horrors enough and the eschatological order seems never to have been far from people's minds. Poets dwelt on and amplified the *ubi sunt* motif and artists depicted the spectre of death in paint, through sculpture and by means of the woodcut.

The *ubi sunt* theme laments the brevity of life and the transience of beauty. We find it in Greek poetry, in the literature of the Fathers of the Church, in medieval Latin verse and in medieval Persian poetry.

Ubi sunt are the opening words of a number of medieval Latin poems.

---

1. A scholarly, interesting and highly readable account of chiliastic movements in Europe from the eleventh to the sixteenth century is to be found in Norman Cohn's *The Pursuit of the Millennium* (1957).

Sometimes they begin a stanza; sometimes they serve as a refrain. A fairly well-known thirteenth-century lyric is titled *Ubi Sount Qui Ante Nos Fuerount*. Several French poets made considerable use of the motif. In the fourteenth century Eustache Deschamps composed several *ballades* on the theme. In the following century Georges Chastellain elaborated it in a long poem called *Le Pas de la mort*, and in the same period Olivier de la Marche worked it through the allegorical *Parement et triumphes des dames*. Probably the best known of all is Villon's *Ballade des dames du temps jadis* (also fifteenth century). The motif was to recur regularly in Tudor, Elizabethan and seventeenth-century lyric poetry. Outstanding instances are Dunbar's magnificent *Lament for the Makaris* with its resounding and knell-like refrain *Timor Mortis Conturbat Me*, and Thomas Nashe's beautiful and poignant *In Time of Pestilence*.

It is apparent that during the fifteenth century the elegiac and mournful strain begins to give place to a somewhat morbid and materialistic emphasis on senility, death and decay. The ghastly spectacle of the rotting corpse is evoked, the gleam of the skull beneath the skin. The tendency is discernible in, for example, Chastellain's *Le Pas de la mort* and in Villon's *Ballades*. In the latter, the poet's sardonic humour sharpens the images.

Increasingly, too, in funerary sculpture, the processes of decomposition were stressed. Tombs were adorned by skeletal figures and semblances of hideous corpses out of whose skulls, breasts, guts and bowels there writhed energetic maggots and worms.

The tendency also becomes explicit in the work of Guyot Marchant who published the *Danse macabre*[1] in 1485. The excellent wood engravings of this were accompanied by verses in dialogue-form between the dead and the living. This was so successful that he followed it up with a second edition the next year, plus a volume including a *Danse macabre des femmes* for which the verses were written by Martial d'Auvergne.

The *danse macabre* (also known as the 'Dance of Death') is a phenomenon of some importance in art and literature from late in the fourteenth century until well on into the sixteenth century. It depicted a procession or dance in which the dead lead the living to the grave. It was a reminder of mortality, of the ubiquity of death and of the equality of all men. It was also a reminder of the need for repentance and that the wages of sin is death.

Apart from its moral and allegorical elements it was very often satirical in tone. The dead might be represented by a number of figures (usually skeletons) or by a single personification of death. The living were usually

1. It seems likely that the first use of the word *macabre* dates from 1376 when it appeared in a poem by Jehan Le Fèvre called *Respit de la mort*: 'Je fis de macabre la danse.'

arranged in some kind of order of precedence: Pope, cardinal, archbishop; emperor, king, duke, etc. All classes might be represented from the greatest to the humblest, thus illustrating the doctrine of social equality in death which was later to be finely expressed by James Shirley in his dirge at the end of *The Contention of Ajax and Ulysses* (1659):

> Death lays his icy hand on kings:
>> Sceptre and crown
>> Must tumble down,
> And in the dust be equal made
> With the poor crooked scythe and spade.

Many different media were employed: verse, prose, manuscript illustrations, printed books, paintings on canvas, wood and stone, engravings on stone and metal, woodcuts, sculpture, tapestry, embroidery, stained glass and so on. Its many and various versions were also widespread geographically – chiefly in France, Spain, Germany, Switzerland, Italy, Austria and Britain – and were shaped and altered by numerous classes of people in a variety of social milieux: by printers, publishers, artists, merchants, friars, scribes, lay- and churchmen.

The theme or subject appealed particularly to artists. The two major works were Holbein's engravings, and the pictures and verses in the cloisters of the church of the Holy Innocents in Paris. The frescoes there were executed in 1425 but were destroyed by fire in the seventeenth century. It was these frescoes that Guyot Marchant freely imitated for his engravings. Holbein's 'Dance of Death' was done in 1523/4 and his 'Alphabet of Death' in 1524. The former was published in Lyons and went into ten editions in twelve years.

In Britain there survive the stone screen in the parish church of Newark-on-Trent and the paintings in Hexham Priory. On the Continent the best known are at Lübeck, Basel, La Chaise Dieu, Kemaria and Beram. The frescoes at La Chaise Dieu and Beram seem to me to be exceptionally well done. There is a curious absence of pictures in Spain but a multitude in Italy. In Germany and Switzerland especially there are many poems in block-books and on woodcuts and frescoes.

There is an early suggestion of the *danse macabre* in a late twelfth-century poem, *Les Vers de la mort* (c. 1195), written by Helinand, a monk of Fiordmont, in which death is encouraged to travel about visiting different people in order to warn them of their end. Other predecessors were the twelfth-century *Debat du corps et de l'âme*, the thirteenth-century *Vado Mori* poems and the *Dit des trois mors et des trois vifs* (c. 1280) – a macabre tale of three living men being told by three dead men of their future decay. It is possible that in the fourteenth century the *danse* took the form of a mimed sermon or liturgical drama in which various characters representing different classes presented themselves and were then taken away by a figure representing a corpse.

From the fifteenth century there survive the *Ballo della morte* from Italy, the Spanish *Danza general de la muerte*, a Catalan 'Dance of Death' translated from the French, Lydgate's version in *The Falles of Princes* (1494), and Marchant's works already referred to.

In its various forms it was a way of dealing with, of coming to terms with, the unknown, the fearful and the horrific. Contemplating it in, say, the sombre parish church of La Chaise Dieu, the spectator, to this day, may well experience an authentic shudder. But the shudder may be mitigated by a smile. There is often a serio-comic element in *danse macabre* frescoes. Sometimes there is deliberate wit and mordant humour on the part of the artists. Besides, the skeletons themselves, because of their grinning skulls, look as if they have job satisfaction in haling off the living to the grave. They look jaunty, to the point of executing a skittish caper, as they snatch an obese and gluttonous bishop, bestow a bony embrace on a noblewoman richly dressed in the height of fashion or stoop to a cowering child.[1]

However, in the late Middle Ages and until well into the sixteenth century there was a much more potent and frightening image of horror than anything depicted or suggested in the 'Dance of Death': namely, Hell. The worst horror stories of all were concerned with the abode of eternal loss, pain and damnation.

To acquire a clearer understanding of the importance of Hell during that period we need to remember that over some 800 to 900 years the geocentric system of the universe as propounded by Ptolemy had a profound influence on Christendom and on how man saw himself in relation to God and the world.

According to the cosmology the sun revolved round the earth, and there were then successive 'spheres' of planets which became more sublime the further away they were from earth. In the seventh and last sphere lay the Empyrean – the abode of pure, spiritual existence, pure essences.

The poets of classical antiquity were agreed that Hades was subterranean. Some places were thought to be entrances to it, especially Lake Avernus, near Puteoli. Virgil, Strabo, Lucretius and Livy all thought that

1. Since the late nineteenth century at least the term *macabre* has acquired comic connotations and is associated with black comedy, sick verse and the sick joke. Some of the best modern horror stories, which fall into the comic/grotesque category, have a distinctly macabre tone.

this volcanic crater was a way in. Almost as famous was the cave of Taenarus, in the southern Peloponnese. In the Old Testament there are numerous references to a subterranean Hell, the Pit, Sheol . . . The orthodox teaching of the Church on the whereabouts of Hell was cautious, though there was general agreement in matters of demonology. St Bernard, Peter Lombard, Albert the Great and St Thomas Aquinas were all in accord as to the activities of evil spirits and where they resided.

By the twelfth century, if not earlier, a popular conception prevailed that Hell was in the centre of the earth. So, as A. O. Lovejoy pointed out in his classic work *The Great Chain of Being*, the world/universe was not only geocentric, it was *diabolocentric*. At the bottom of Hell – the lowest possible point in the cosmological scheme, plumb in the middle of the abode of eternal pain, torture, loss and terror, was Satan, the Devil himself, accompanied by hosts of fiends.

The horror stories of the Middle Ages are mostly to be found in the numerous 'visions' of Hell and Purgatory (there were also not a few 'visions' of Paradise). Vision literature was a popular form of entertainment and edification. A standard storyteller's device was for the narrator or principal character in the story to have a dream or fall into a trance in the course of which he was haled by supernatural agency to another world. If it was to Hell (and Hell was not always a nether world in these visions) or to Purgatory he was there given a ghastly introduction to the agonies and tortures of everlasting perdition or to the excoriating pains of those souls who must be cleansed before they were fit to enter Heaven. Moralists and preachers made extensive use of such experiences for admonitory and didactic purposes.

One of the earliest was the so-called *Vision of St Paul* (which M. R. James, that expert in supernatural matters, included in his translations of *The Apocryphal New Testament*). It dates from perhaps as early as the third century in its Greek form and had an enormously wide influence in the centuries that followed. Versions of the story appeared in many European languages (at least eight in Middle English) and *Redaction IV* survives in at least twenty-seven *codices*. The horrors of Hell are depicted in dreadful detail. Some sinners are immersed in ice, others in molten metal; the vain and proud are hanged by their hair and eyebrows; adulterers are hanged by their genitals.[1]

---

1. There are earlier instances, such as the *Apocalypse of Peter* (of the second or perhaps even the first century A.D.). Apocalyptic literature is rich in horrors. Also very early was the *Vision of Thespesius* in Plutarch's *Moralia* in the essay *Concerning Such Whom God is Slow to Punish*. Another vision described by Plutarch is that of Timarchus in the *Discourse concerning Socrates' Daemon*. Plutarch lived *c.* A.D. 46–*c.* 120.

In the twelfth-century *Vision of Alberic* the spectacles of infinite punishment are no less appalling. On the sword-like branches of a forest sinners are impaled. Elsewhere, uncharitable women who refused to nurse orphans swing from trees while reptiles slither over their bodies and suck their breasts dry.

Much more important than either of these (and many others) was the twelfth-century *Vision of Tundale*, the best known of all medieval visions during the Middle Ages and later (though now, of course, Dante's is the most famous). Tundale's vision was most likely published in Latin originally but before the end of the fifteenth century it had spread all over Europe with translations in German, Dutch, Italian and French (there were even versions in Old Norse and Gaelic).

Tundale, a wealthy landowner, falls into a trance while trying to extract rent from a backsliding tenant. His soul, separated from his body, finds itself in a gloomy place, where it is surrounded by threatening demons. A bright star then appears in the distance and reveals itself as Tundale's guardian angel. Together they set out to explore Hell and eventually reach the pit of Satan. The infernal topography is similar to that in many other visions. In the very lowest region of Hell they come to a terrifying and static monster with a thousand hands, on each of which there were twenty fingers with sharp nails. Each finger was the 'leynthe of an hundryt sponne' and 'ten sponne aboute of thykness'. He was about a hundred cubits long (a cubit was about two feet) and twenty cubits broad.

This monstrous figure lay on a gridiron (over burning coals) to which he was bound by immense chains. His sole occupation was the consumption of vast quantities of damned spirits which he seized in his giant hands and squashed like grapes before thrusting them into his cavernous mouth. After this treatment they were regurgitated, a thousand at a time, and scattered once more into the surrounding fire, only to be consumed again, without end, in the same manner. Thus the lord of Hell was self-dedicated to perpetual ignominy and pain.

Tundale's description is considerably more detailed than Dante's. The latter's Satan is portrayed as three-faced and gigantic, standing waist-deep in ice and possessing three wings, six eyes and a triple chin. His mountainous body is shaggy and in order to sustain this frame he has a modest diet of but three sinners at a time: Judas, Brutus and Cassius.

In all but one of the medieval visions of Hell, Satan, when portrayed in his own dominions (by writer or painter), is a hideously grotesque, terrifying and malevolent monster (usually of vast proportions), a symbol of all that is foul, ugly, perverted and violent.

Chaucer's view (late in the fourteenth century) is the exception. His Satan is monstrous and hairy enough; but he also makes him ludicrous: a shaggy dog with (one may reasonably deduce from the details) an anus the size of a football stadium.

The description occurs in the *Prologue* to *The Summoner's Tale*. The Summoner is furious at the story the Friar has just related (wittily and elegantly, at the expense of 'summonours'), and is set on revenge. The account is a satire on visions of Hell and Satan as well as friars for, as the Summoner says, 'Freres and feendes been but lyte asonder.'

The particular friar in this incident is led down to Hell by an angel and there they find Satan, who, according to the angel (who slips easily into the conventional patter of the experienced guide), has 'a tayl brodder than of a carryk is the sayl'. Then, like a performing animal, at the guide's command to show his arse 'and let the frere se where is the nest of freres in this place', behold, the canine Devil's tail is lifted:

> And er that half a furlong way of space,
> Right so as bees out swarmen from an hyve
> Out of the develes ers ther gonne dryve
> Twenty thousand freres on a route,
> And thurghout helle swarmed al aboute,
> And comen agayn as faste as they may gon,
> And in his ers they crepten everychon.
> He clapte his tayl agayn and lay ful stille.

Here the scatological and eschatological 'orders' meet, so to speak, as they do elsewhere in medieval literature and, frequently, in representations of Hell depicted by painters.

In most of the descriptions of Hell, as I have suggested, there is detailed emphasis on the terrifying environment, the hideousness and ferocity of the demons who are resident torturers, and the dreadfulness of the agonies of the lost souls – agonies necessarily shown in physical terms; and authors showed considerable ingenuity in devising punishments which, of course, were based on what human beings were wont to do to each other: an additional irony.

However, Hell as described in numerous visions prior to the thirteenth century is usually rather a crude affair as compared with Dante's *Inferno* (which, incidentally, appeared some 170 years earlier than Chaucer's *Summoner's Tale*).

The scheme, the topography, the 'architecture' of the *Inferno* (and the *Purgatorio*) are so well known they need little comment here. The whole, amazing, funnel-shaped terraced underworld (beyond which lies, ultimately, the Mount of Purgatory) represents an encyclopedic, punitive system in the creation of which the powers of intellect and imagination have combined to an extraordinary degree.

Hell is voluntary (like super tax, love and sin). Hell is also sin; not its similitude but *sin itself*. The lost souls exemplify the spiritual diseases which predominated in their earthly lives and which, by so doing, corrupted them. Dante's punishments fit the crimes. The gluttonous wallow in filth and are drenched by bitterly cold rain; the lustful are harried by howling winds; the heretics reside in burning tombs; the counsellors of fraud are wrapped in plumes of fire; flatterers are immersed in liquid excrement and traitors are embedded to their necks in ice . . .

As Dante and Virgil move, with difficulty, sometimes in peril, down the gradations of punishment and through the declensions of turpitude, the horrors intensify. The modern horror story is, often enough, a puny and timid affair when set alongside what is happening in one of the Circles of the *Inferno*.

Take, for example, the Wood of the Suicides (Circle VII, Canto XIII). The Dark Wood or Forest is a common feature and symbol in visions of Hell and Dante's wood contains the souls of those who wantonly destroyed their own lives. Because they have insulted their bodies Dante deprives them even of the semblance of human form. They are become withered and sterile trees. Throughout the wood there is a sound of mournful wailing. Dante breaks off a twig from a thorn-tree and at once the trunk cries out: 'Why tear my limbs away?' The trunk darkens with blood and cries out again: 'Why do you rend my bones? Have you no pity in your breast?'

The description continues (in Dorothy Sayers's translation):

> As when you burn one end of a green brand,
>   Sap at the other oozes from the wood,
>   Sizzling as the imprisoned airs expand,
>
> So from that broken splint came words and blood
>   At once: I dropped the twig, and like to one
>   Rooted to the ground with terror, there I stood.

For a period of some 400 years Hell was a motif and subject in many parts of Europe in the hands of numerous artists and craftsmen. It appears over and over again, in carvings of stone and wood, in capitals, door-knockers, doors, in lintels and tympanums, in tapestries, woodcuts, panels, polyptychs, in engravings, psalters and miniatures, in manuscript illuminations and in illustrations to Books of Hours, in fresco paintings and in oil paintings.

In Byzantine mosaic work Hell is a traditional feature of scenes depicting the 'Last Judgement', but it is invariably subsidiary, discreet and, of course, stylized. In the wonderful basilical church at Torcello, for instance, a small area of the 'Last Judgement' scene (twelfth century) depicts aspects of Hell. A slightly Neptunish Satan, holding Antichrist on his knee, presides over a collection of distinguished sinners who are just keeping their heads above the flames. Below, naked figures are portrayed in a stylized choreography of pain, and at the very bottom there is a *memento mori* motif of skulls out of whose eye-sockets there wriggle worms (or snakes). An interesting feature is that a 'river' of fire flows down from Christ's *mandorla* to Hell, indicating that the flames are kept going by the will of God.

In the twelfth-, thirteenth- and fourteenth-century Serbian and Macedonian monastic churches of the Raška, Central Serbian and Morava 'schools', frescoes done by itinerant court painters (mostly from Constantinople) also give a traditional treatment to Hell in 'Last Judgement' programmes. Again it is modest and subsidiary.

From the thirteenth century onwards, in Western Europe, Hell, in art, assumes magnitude (several artists were quite clearly influenced by *The Vision of Tundale* and by Dante's *Inferno*) and not a few of the paintings are terrifying. There is no other word for them. Here were totally appropriate illustrations to the horror stories of the visions, of *exempla* and anecdote in theological handbooks, the stories related in works of moral and spiritual edification, and the eschatological reminders and admonitions so frequently delivered from the pulpit. Those many who could not read could see – and be afraid.

Hell, *ipso facto*, is chaos; anarchy without limit or definition, the absolute opposite of Heaven; a grotesque distortion and mutilated obverse of paradisal order and harmony. The task of the painter (as of the writer) was to present a credible, plausible and, as it were, legible vision. An abstract pandaemonium would hardly do. The artists, like the writers, settled for a kind of parody. Everything was inverted. God was at the top of Heaven; Satan was at the bottom of Hell. Thus Hell became organized chaos; a series of carefully composed images of destruction, aggression, violence, pain, hatred and evil.

Hell inspired some notable works of art and here it is possible only to remind the reader of the existence of a few of them. Apart from Orcagna's rather tantalizing fragments of Hell fresco (all that survives) in Florence, a major work early in the fourteenth century is Taddeo di Bartolo's fresco at San Gimignano. Monstrous devils, winged, horned and hairy, mete out suitable punishments: a miser is strangled, a bloated usurer lies supine, gaping, while a leering fiend excretes gold coins into his open mouth, gluttons are forced to consume inedible food, the lustful are cruelly flogged, while a sodomite is impaled on a stake from anus to mouth (a devil turns one end of the stake and the other end is held in the mouth of a fellow sodomite). Other outstanding instances are Traini's fresco in the Camposanto, Pisa, which is a part of the 'Universal Judgement' scene, and Nardo di Cione's fresco in Santa Maria Novella, Florence. This is the only major fresco which follows closely Dante's programme in the *Inferno*. Of the early fourteenth century there is also Giotto's 'Last Judgement' in the Scrovegni Chapel, Padua. A fine example of an illustration of *The Vision of Tundale* is Pol de Limbourg's in the *Très Riches Heures du Duc de Berry*. In the Museo Lazaro, Madrid, there is another 'Tundale' painting (actually inscribed *Visio Tondaly*) done by an imitator of Hieronymus Bosch. Some of the details come straight from the Vision and the Irish knight Tundale is actually depicted in the painting. At Orvieto there is a superb fresco of the tortures of the damned by Luca Signorelli; and on the façade of that cathedral Lorenzo depicted the damned in Hell. The contorted figures, coiled about by reptiles and lacerated by demons, display extreme states of grief and agony.

To my mind one of the most horrific of all images is Grünewald's 'Damnation of Lovers', in the Strasbourg Cathedral Museum. It depicts a man and a woman semi-naked, grinning and hideously emaciated as if they are suffering from some form of dreadful terminal cancer. Their wizened and decaying flesh is wreathed and penetrated by snakes and disfigured by running sores on which large black flies have settled to sip the blood and pus and to lay their eggs. A huge toad (traditional witch's familiar and harbourer of evil spirits) is battened to the woman's genitals.

During the twentieth century the 'Hells' of Hieronymus Bosch and Pieter Bruegel (and their followers) have become famous and are now familiar to most people. Their infernal landscapes, luridly lit, reveal an encyclopedic vision of pain and suffering in many forms, often bizarre and fantastic, which is very different from other (and earlier) artists. There is much less feeling of a subterranean Hell. It is as if Hell has 'surfaced'. It is 'exterior'. It is, in a sense, Hell on earth. It displays the crimes and inhumanity of mankind, the horrors of a worldly existence. Later, and in very different ways, both Jacques Callot and Goya were to record the horrors of life before death; Callot in *Les Grandes Misères de la guerre* (1633), and Goya in his *Desastres* (1810–14).

Many of the horror stories of the Middle Ages and the Renaissance are associated with and involve demonic activity on the surface of the earth, and the powers of evil and their manifestations were a fecund source of inspiration to storytellers, as indeed they still are.

A corresponding interest in diabolic activity outside Hell is discernible in the work of artists (and architects and stonemasons). A favourite theme or subject for artists was 'The Temptations of St Anthony', events which inspired some terrifying nightmare scenes, such as those of Pieter Huys (in the Louvre), Jan Mandyn (Galleria Barberini, Rome), Pietro Gerini (Castellani Chapel, Santa Croce, Florence), Sassetta (Pinacoteca, Siena), Grünewald (Colmar Museum), Andrea Parentino (Galleria Doria, Rome) and Jacques Callot (British Museum). In these and other such phantasmagoria it is as if hosts of demonic creatures have materialized out of the air and the malevolent violence and hatred which they express is another version of what was portrayed in Hell. They are surrealistic, and the surreal is often a part of horror. They are from outer darkness or, perhaps, inner darkness; in either case from a domain of total barbarism.

Michelangelo's 'Last Judgement' (begun in 1536 and unveiled in 1541) in the Sistine Chapel is different from anything earlier or, for that matter, later. In this vast, magnificent, sombre and profoundly pessimistic painting the mouth of Hell gapes over the altar and the muscle-bound damned (some being whacked out of a boat by Charon) blunder confusedly over a dark shore. All the traditional horrors have gone and indeed the lost souls are a subsidiary part of the picture.

In earlier paintings of the Last Judgement there were signs of joy, of rejoicing, glimpses of beatific splendour (for example, in Fra Angelico's marvellous version in the Museo di San Marco, Florence); and the scenes in Hell might reveal a certain cruelly sardonic and ironic humour. In Michelangelo's painting the predominant mood is pessimistic disillusionment expressed on a grandiose scale. There is but one touch of laconic wit, and this needs an historical footnote by way of explanation.[1]

As Robert Hughes has rightly observed, Michelangelo's 'Last Judgement' 'is the first modern Hell. It is tragically subjective.' Here, the keyword is 'subjective'. From some not easily determinable point – I would locate it at round about the turn of the sixteenth century – Hell was becoming subjective, personal, within. And so, in many respects, it still is.

During the latter part of the sixteenth century and for much of the

1. At the far bottom left of the picture (right as you view it) is the figure of a man, Biagio de Cesena, Pope Paul III's master of ceremonies. Before the fresco was complete Biagio criticized the nude figures as indecent. Michelangelo promptly got his own back by painting Biagio (with ass's ears and a snake coiled round him) as Minos, judge of Hell. Biagio implored the Pope to have the portrait deleted. With admirable wit and presence of mind the Pope replied: 'I might have released you from Purgatory, but over Hell I have no power.' In any case, the Pope thoroughly approved of the fresco.

seventeenth century the traditional concepts of Hell (and the concepts of Satan and evil) were undergoing many changes and modifications. Hell and the Devil were virtually to disappear from art and architecture and to undergo a series of metamorphoses in literature, changes which were to receive a form of grand synthesis in Milton's epic vision of *Paradise Lost*, the last great 'statement' on Hell and the Devil (and all his progeny) in European literature.

The Copernican revolution (Copernicus published *De Revolutionibus* in 1543) eventually had the effect of displacing Hell from the centre of the earth; the universe became heliocentric (it is now acentric), and anthropocentric humanism brought about a very different view of mankind (at any rate in Europe) in relationship to God and the universe, and a very different view of man himself.

The realization that Hell was no longer in the centre of the earth and that the earth could no longer be regarded as diabolocentric naturally had a profound influence over a period of many years; as profound as if we today were to discover the *actual* whereabouts of Hell. The earth was, as it were, 'released' from the effects of the impregnation and corruption of all evil. The natural order, which had for so long been thought to be infected or contaminated by evil, was viewed in a new light. But, the questions remained: Where were the Devil and his demons? And where was Hell? Where the hell was it? so to speak. Nobody could be sure.

Debate on such issues continued steadily during the second half of the sixteenth century and during the seventeenth century (periods of intensive interest in witchcraft, diabolism, possession and the occult sciences) and remained unresolved. As late as 1714 Tobias Swinden was propounding, in *An Enquiry into the Nature and Place of Hell*, that Hell was in the sun. The sun was very hot and it was very large. What more suitable place to accommodate those vast numbers of lost souls for whom there could be no space in the middle of the earth? Besides, it was then regarded as the lowest created place in the universe and therefore the most appropriate abode for the Devil and the rebel angels, plus all those (reckoned by Swinden to be far in excess of 100,000,000,000) who had finally and irrevocably turned their faces from God.

However, the idea of a solar Hell did not catch on. The sun was the source of light and life, and there were too many ancient associations with it as a symbol of God. As Sir Thomas Browne had put it in a magnificent sentence in *The Garden of Cyrus*: 'The sun itself is but the dark *simulacrum*, and light but the shadow of God.'

Milton, in his depiction of Hell, amalgamated many of the ancient and traditional ideas and presented Satan as the polymorphous and ubiquitous spirit of evil that he traditionally was – at any rate, from the eleventh century onwards.[1]

Milton does not locate Hell. After the Council of Pandaemonium, Satan sets forth on his epic journey to the new world of Earth. Having gone through Hell Gates he passes *upward* through the realm of Chaos. He alights on the outer convex of the universe, finds the stairs leading *up* to Heaven and then *descends* to the Sun. From there he travels to Earth and, by dint of assuming various shapes (he had already disguised himself as an angel of light to deceive Uriel in the Sun) he arrives in the Garden of Eden. He penetrates by stealth to the very bower of 'our first parents' and there he is discovered:

> Squat like a toad, close at the ear of Eve.

Milton's Hell is terrible enough, though not as frightening, I think, as those of Dante and some of the medieval and Renaissance painters. But long before *Paradise Lost* was first published in 1667, altogether different views of Hell and evil and the horrors that go with them had begun to develop; views which indicate the beginning of the growth of the idea of a subjective, inner Hell, a psychological Hell; a personal and individual source of terror and horror, such as the chaos of a disturbed and tormented mind, the pandaemonium (a word invented by Milton) of psychopathic conditions, rather than the abode of *lux atra* and everlasting pain with its definite location in a measurable cosmological system.

Such a concept is suggested, with momentous simplicity, by Mephistopheles in Marlowe's *Dr Faustus* (*c.* 1588) when, in the guise of a Friar, he says:

> Hell hath no limits, nor is circumscrib'd
> In one selfe place, for where we are is hell,
> And where hell is, must we ever be.

Towards the end of his life, Sir Walter Ralegh in a long passage of sombre and resonant eloquence (in his *Historie of the World*, 1614) suggests a comparable idea. It begins: 'Now the Devil, because he cannot play upon the open stage of this world; (as in those daies)[2] and being still as industrious as ever, finds it more for his advantage to creep into the minds of men; and inhabiting in the Temples of their hearts, works them to a more effectual adoration of himself than ever.'

There are several powerful echoes of these ideas in Sir Thomas

---

1. There is a basic paradox involved here. That the Devil was static at the base of Hell and also capable of being anywhere he wished to be were not mutually exclusive ideas.
2. Ralegh has been discussing Heathenism and Judaism.

Browne's writings, especially in a well-known passage in *Religio Medici* (1642), where he elaborates the concept of a cerebral Devil, one working from within; one who has breached the defences of 'The Castle of Mansoul' and conducts his operations on the spirit from an intellectual stronghold. At the same time, here, Browne has not entirely shed traditional notions:

Surely, though we place Hell under Earth, the Devil's walk and purlue is about it: men speak too popularly who place it in those flaming mountains, which to grosser apprehensions represent Hell. The heart of man is the place Devils dwell in; I feel sometimes a Hell within myself; Lucifer keeps his court in my breast. Legion is revived in me. There are as many Hells, as Anaxagoris conceited worlds. There was more than one Hell in Magdalene, when there were seven Devils, for every Devil is an Hell unto himself; he holds enough torture in his own *ubi*, and needs not the misery of circumference to afflict him; and thus a distracted Conscience here, is a shadow or introduction unto Hell hereafter.

Later, in *Paradise Lost*, Milton has Satan express a similar point of view:

> The mind is in its own place, and in itself
> Can make a Heav'n of Hell, a Hell of Heav'n.
>
> (Book I)

In Book IV he soliloquizes in agony:

> Me miserable! which way shall I fly
> Infinite wrath, and infinite despair?
> Which way I fly is Hell; myself am Hell;

The basic idea was to be expressed in many different ways by numerous writers, especially dramatists.

The horror stories of the late sixteenth and early seventeenth centuries, like the ghost stories, are provided for us by playwrights.[1] The Tudor (or Elizabethan) and Jacobean tragedians were deeply interested in evil, crime, murder, suicide and violence. They were also very interested in

1. Hell and the Devil had important roles in the Mystery Play Cycles through the late Middle Ages and also in the Tudor Moralities. Hell mouth was part of certain stage settings (e.g. *The Harrowing of Hell* scenes) and demons played a conspicuous part in drama until quite late in the sixteenth century. The Devil was developed as a character and personality in the later Mystery Plays and then in Moralities until, in the mature psychological drama of the late Tudor and Jacobean periods, the Devil was 'humanized' and the villain 'diabolized'. This was a lengthy, complex and sophisticated process of transmogrification. After *c.* 1590 the Devil disappears as a character except in some comedy. Hell, too, was dispensed with.

extreme states of suffering: fear, pain and madness. They found new modes, new metaphors and images for presenting the horrific and in doing so they created *simulacra* of Hell. Were there space one might cite perhaps a thousand or more instances from plays in the period *c.* 1580 to *c.* 1642 in which Hell is a variable, all-purpose and diachronic image of horror whether as a place of punishment or as a state of mind and spirit. And horrific episodes – the representation of bloodcurdling and hair-raising action – are to be found in abundance in the tragedy of the age and particularly in revenge tragedy. Again one might cite scores of these from the plays of Kyd, Marlowe, Shakespeare, Chapman, Middleton, Rowley, Chettle, Ford, Shirley, Marston, Massinger, Fletcher, Webster and Tourneur – to name several from among the sixty or so dramatists who were then active.

There are the horrible murders in *Arden of Feversham* and *The Yorkshire Tragedy* (events in both plays were based on actual events), the scarcely tolerable cruelty, tortures and bloodshed of *Titus Andronicus*, the brief but awful scene in *Macbeth* when Lady Macduff and her children are stabbed, and the blinding of Gloucester in *King Lear* – to cite only a handful of instances.

The practitioners of revenge tragedy were inclined to take things as far as they could. Death was the main subject on the syllabus of the revenge villains; torture and murder their specialities; the quainter, the more ingenious and bizarre the better. They studied their techniques with professional expertise. When decadence set in in the shape of gratuitous sensationalism the horrors began to verge on the absurd.

Thereafter, violence and horror on stage was rare and not to be seen again regularly until towards the end of the eighteenth century, when Gothic novels were dramatized, and during the vogue for melodrama in the nineteenth century. By then a new form of horror story was becoming well established.[1]

Interest in demonology, ghosts, vampires, witchcraft, the black arts,

---

1. In the twentieth century there have been various theatrical experiments in devising means of presenting the horrific. A pioneer was Antonin Artaud who published an influential essay, *Le Théâtre de la cruauté*, in 1932. His kind of theatre seeks to present an awareness of pain and suffering and the presence of evil, mainly through non-verbal means. His ideas were widely discussed in the 1960s and his concept of the theatre explored, particularly by Jerzy Grotowski with his company Theatre Laboratory. Grotowski's experiments in turn influenced the radical Living Theatre founded by Julian Beck in 1972. Total Theatre (as presented by such directors as Peter Brook and Jean-Louis Barrault) has also been concerned with horror and violence. In the 1960s and 1970s numerous dramatists experimented with horrific themes. Well-known examples are Weiss's *Marat/Sade* and *The Investigation*, Edward Bond's *Lear* and Peter Shaffer's *Equus*.

devils, diabolic possession and the occult sciences (all of which are fruitful sources of horror stories) persisted until late in the seventeenth century, during which period, incidentally, there was intensive witch-hunting and burning of witches in Europe;[1] but by the closing years of the century neoclassicism was becoming well established in Europe and England (the movement was under way earlier in France). The Augustan Age was beginning, the 'age of reason' during which the prime literary, artistic and aesthetic virtues were decorum, harmony, order, elegance, good manners, restraint and good sense. Violence, bloodshed, cruelty, the depiction of evil, the operations of the supernatural orders, horrors and excesses of any kind, had little place in art and literature.

By the mid-1740s the Augustan Age was coming to an end. There began to develop a discernible change or 'shift' in sensibility. The advent of this was signalled by, among other events, the works of the 'graveyard poets' who wrote what came to be called 'graveyard poetry': verse which was preoccupied with death and suffering, with the necropolitan, with corpses and charnel-houses. The *danse macabre* would have appealed to the graveyard poets.

This poetry challenged rationalism and was very different indeed from anything that Addison, Steele, Swift, Pope and Fielding and their fellow Augustans would have approved of.[2] In some ways it was foreshadowed by Thomas Parnell's *Night-Piece* which appeared in 1722. The main poems came out in the 1740s and were Edward Young's *Night Thoughts* (1742–5), Blair's *The Grave* (1743) and James Hervey's *Meditations among the Tombs* (1745–7). Some would add Gray's *Elegy*. There was also Thomas Warton's work on *The Pleasures of Melancholy* (1747).[3]

Such writings had a pronounced influence on the Gothic novel which was shortly to appear and with it the ghost and the horror story in fiction. It also had a profound influence on German writers of 'terror fiction' and what was called the *Schaurroman* or 'shudder novel' at the turn of the eighteenth century.

Most Gothic novels are tales of mystery and horror (or terror) intended to chill the blood and make the reader's hair stand on end. The

1. Even in the second half of the twentieth century misconceptions about witch-hunting and witch-burning were being perpetuated by relatively intelligent people, such as the late Sir Julian Huxley who allowed his prejudices to convince him that those activities were characteristic of the Middle Ages, whereas they were a product of the Renaissance period, the 'age of enlightenment'.

2. Addison died in 1719, Steele in 1729, Pope in 1744, Swift in 1745, Fielding in 1754. Oliver Goldsmith lived later, 1730–74. Dr Johnson straddled the century from 1709 to 1784.

3. William Blake was to produce some notable illustrations for Blair's *Grave* and Young's *Night Thoughts*.

supernatural element is often strong and they have all or most of the now-familiar topography, sites, props, presences and happenings: wild and desolate landscapes, dark forests, ruined abbeys, feudal halls and medieval castles with dungeons, secret passages, *oubliettes*, sliding panels and torture chambers; monstrous spectres and curses; heroes and heroines in the direst of imaginable straits, wicked tyrants, malevolent witches, demonic powers of unspeakably hideous aspect, and so on . . . The whole apparatus, in fact, that has kept the cinema and much third-rate fiction going for years, is to be found in these tales. They were read avidly.

One of the earliest examples of the genre was *Ferdinand Count Fathom* (1753), by Tobias Smollett. This was probably the first novel (a form then in its infancy) to propose terror and cruelty as its main themes. Much better known than this, and incomparably more influential, was Horace Walpole's *The Castle of Otranto* (1764), which he wrote in his house at Strawberry Hill, Twickenham. This gruesome tale of passion, bloodshed and villainy (it includes a monstrous ghost) was an immensely popular book and is believed to have gone through no fewer than 115 editions since it first appeared. Walpole's intention was to scare the daylights out of his readers. No doubt he succeeded. Today it is usually read as a bizarre curiosity.

In the next fifty years or so there came a succession of such novels of variable quality, many of which were dramatized (as was *The Castle of Otranto*). Some of the major examples of the genre were Clara Reeve's *The Old English Baron* (1778), William Beckford's *Vathek* (1786), Ann Radcliffe's *Mysteries of Udolpho* (1794), M. G. ('Monk') Lewis's *Ambrosio* and *The Monk* (1796), C. R. Maturin's *The Fatal Revenge* (1807) and his *Melmoth the Wanderer* (1820) and Mary Shelley's *Frankenstein* (1818). Godwin's *Caleb Williams* (1794) is often classed as Gothic, but has a special importance as an early instance of the propaganda novel and the novel of crime and its detection.

Over the same period German writers were developing their own brand of sensational and Gothic fiction. During the eighteenth century considerable interest in English literature arose in German literary circles. Klopstock, Gellert and Wieland, for instance, were much influenced by Shakespeare, Milton, Edward Young and James Hervey (and, it seems curious now, by Richardson). Goethe even considered Young to be in the same league as Milton.

In England there was a corresponding interest in German literature. 'Monk' Lewis, for example, was well read in German, was a gifted translator and was to influence E. T. A. Hoffmann. Translation of the *Schaurroman* and German 'terror fiction' began in the 1790s with the publication of an English rendering of Benedikte Naubert's *Hermann von Unna*. A series of translations followed. They included works by Karl Grosse, Leonhard Wachter, C. H. Spiess and Heinrich Zschokke. C. A. Vulpius's *Rinaldo Rinaldini* proved very popular. Ann Radcliffe was influenced by Schiller's strange and powerful story *Der Geisterseher* (1789); and Schiller's play *Die Räuber* (1777–80), translated in 1792, was perhaps most important of all. Coleridge, among many others, was enraptured by Schiller.

In passing it should be noted that there was a difference between the German and English conceptions of the function of the Gothic story. Many of the German writers were politically committed. Their fictional heroes were 'political'. Critical social comment (e.g. anti-clericalism) was implicit and explicit in the stories. Schiller, particularly, expressed the point of view of the individual against social convention and taboo. The *Ritter- und Räuberroman* which, with the *Schaurroman*, were a kind of counterpart of English Gothic, were aspects of the *Sturm und Drang* revolutionary literary movement.

Tragedians of the period had no inhibitions about displaying horrors on stage. Dramatized versions of Gothic novels set out to frighten audiences and these were what can only be described as 'horror plays'. For example, *Le Comte de Comminges* (1764) by the French writer François Baculard D'Arnaud (1716–1805): this horrific drama was set, for good measure, in the burial crypt of a Trappist monastery. So ghastly were the deeds represented that the management laid on restorative cordials for members of the audience who passed out.

Another example of the same period was H. W. Von Gerstenberg's *Ugolino* (1768), which was based on the story of Ugolino recounted by Dante in the *Inferno* (Canto XXXIII). Ugolino and his three sons are starving in a dungeon in Pisa. One son escapes, but his body is soon brought back in a coffin together with the corpse of Ugolino's wife. The survivors continue to starve. Ugolino becomes insane for a while and kills one of his sons. The last son dies of starvation and Ugolino eventually commits suicide.

In their own rather crude and melodramatic way D'Arnaud and Von Gerstenberg (like other playwrights then and later) created microcosmic images of Hell – a place where horror, evil and pain rule – which are comparable to those found in, say, *The Spanish Tragedy*, *Macbeth*, *The White Devil* and *The Atheist's Tragedy*.

During the eighteenth and nineteenth centuries, in orthodox doctrine as taught by the various 'churches' and sects, Hell remained a place of eternal fire and punishment and the abode of the Devil. Writers of the Romantic period and thereafter did not recreate Hell as a visitable place. There are exceptions, the most notable being Beckford. In *Vathek* (1786) the Caliph becomes a servant of the Devil (Eblis) and, having sacrificed fifty children by way of gaining the necessary credentials, eventually has passport to the subterranean halls of Eblis, a luxurious and Mammonian inferno, resplendent with riches and wonders, where his punishment was to be eternal torture.

However, a few artists were drawn to 'illustrate' earlier conceptions of Hell. Three were prominent and remain well known: William Blake (1757–1827), John ('Mad') Martin (1789–1854) and Gustave Doré (1832–83). Blake produced 102 engravings for Dante's *Inferno* in 1826. His vision is highly idiosyncratic and individual. It is memorable, but it must be admitted that the victims look tolerably at ease when you compare their lot with that of those being skewered, impaled, racked, whipped, garotted, strangled, bastinadoed, lacerated, disembowelled, squashed, hanged, boiled, fried, roasted and flayed *et semper in aeternam* in the paintings of Taddeo di Bartolo and Traini.

Martin and Doré (whose work was very popular in their day) were more concerned with the scenery and topography than with the occupants of Hell. Martin illustrated *Paradise Lost* and Doré applied himself to Dante and Milton. Unhappily, the results were melodramatic, shallow and jejune. One might think that between them they had attained a level of banality which it would be difficult to surpass. However, in the 1950s it was surpassed by Robert Rauschenberg, an exponent of 'combine-painting' and collage who was ill-advised enough to attempt a series of illustrations to the *Inferno*.

The *actual* Hells of the eighteenth and nineteenth centuries were the jails, the madhouses, the slums and bedlams and those lanes and alleys where vice, squalor, depravity and unspeakable misery created a social and moral chaos: terrestrial counterparts to the horrors of Dante's Circles. The sardonic and mercilessly truthful recorder of those scenes in the eighteenth century was William Hogarth.

Very nearly contemporaneously another and very different artist, namely Piranesi, was creating an extraordinary nightmare world, the idea for which is said to have come to him while he was suffering delirium in the course of a fever. Piranesi's 'Prisons' (*Carceri d'Invenzione*) were, and are, the grandiose visual equivalent images of Kafka's castles and penal colonies, of panoptic gaols, of labour and concentration camps, indeed of all those megalomaniac punitive establishments designed by men to try and break and destroy men. They are also the visual equivalents of a metaphysical and mental Hell.

They comprise a kind of insane Pythagorean geometry of colossal and superb architecture; monumental dungeons of Cyclopean proportions in which bastions, piers, buttresses tower up, merging into vaults and arches, and yet more arches and vaults . . . The eye is led on through chiaroscuric vistas of curves and perpendiculars which go on to nowhere. Among them run galleries, stairways and balconies. From the walls hang contraptions, cables, ropes. On the floors stand other contraptions, sinister machines and apparatus which have the appearance of instruments of torture.

The whole point about the prisons is that they are totally and utterly pointless. Nothing serves any purpose. The arches, buttresses and vaults support nothing; the galleries and stairways go nowhere. The sinister contraptions are functionless. And, in this huge, austere, beautiful, architectonic and mathematical desolation, dimly perceptible in the penumbras, are what appear to be human figures: tiny, lost, solitary and faceless. They, too, are going nowhere.

The prisons are timeless. They might have been etched last year. It comes as something of a shock to remember he began them *c.* 1745.

Piranesi's vision, the way he sees human beings in relationship to their environment and the world, prefigures the horrors of the psychological and subjective 'hell' and the state of metaphysical anguish which many writers were to explore in the nineteenth and twentieth centuries. For example, there are the novels and short stories of Dostoyevsky, Gogol and Kafka, the beautiful but deeply pessimistic and despairing lyrics of Leopardi, Lautréamont's extraordinary lyrical fragments in prose in *Les Chants de Maldoror* (1868), Rimbaud's equally extraordinary 'fragments' of prose and poetry in *Une Saison en enfer* (1873), James Thomson's terrifying poem *The City of Dreadful Night* (1874), and so on. One might cite many instances. The logic and 'illogic' of Sartre's *tour de force Huis clos* was one of the more recent and certainly one of the most brilliantly conceived forms of 'hell'. A drawing-room in Second Empire style. No racks, no red-hot pincers, no resident torturers . . . Just other people. By comparison, the torments, bloodshed and screams of Grand Guignol theatre seem uncouth.

In passing we should also mention what might be described as the secular and worldly 'hell' as depicted in the more disturbing anti-utopian (or dystopian) visions: the world of Zamyatin's *We* (1924), Huxley's *Brave New World* (1932), Orwell's *Nineteen Eighty-Four* (1949) and David

Karp's *One* (1953). In the corridors of totalitarian power the rule of fear is absolute, 'wrong' thinking is ruthlessly punished and love and truth are grossly perverted.

One can hardly dissociate Hell and the Devil. Towards the end of the eighteenth century Satan received a new lease of life and was to become a dominant figure in literature in the nineteenth century, more particularly in tales of horror.

Until that period the last devil of any note in European literature (if we except one or two quasi-comic figures such as the demon of Lesage's *Le Diable boiteux* (1707) was the Satan of Milton's *Paradise Regained* (1671). In that poem Satan's traditional capacity for dissemblance is maintained. He first appears to Christ in the desert in the guise of an aged man in 'Rural weeds'. Later, he becomes a 'gray dissimulation'. When he reappears before Christ he is 'seemlier clad' as one 'in City, or Court, or Palace bred'.

At his renaissance during the Romantic period the Devil is as polymorphous and ubiquitous as ever. In Goethe's *Faust* (1808, 1832) Mephistopheles appears as a man, a poodle and an old woman. In Chamisso's extraordinary story *Peter Schlemihl* (1814) he is a gentleman in grey. And in Johann Apel's *Der Freischutz* (1823) he is an old soldier with a wooden leg, while in Baron Fouqué's *The Field of Terror* (c. 1830) he is a dark-visaged collier. Elsewhere he is found in miscellaneous roles and shapes, not infrequently sinister and often frightening. C. R. Maturin, James Hogg, Hoffmann, Walter Scott, Dostoyevsky, Gogol, Turgenev and Barbey d'Aurevilly presented the father of lies and murder in a variety of guises.

Satan's 'rebirth' during the Romantic period, and his burgeoning long after, led to other and more surprising views of him: the beautiful Lucifer, the angel of light (Blake, incidentally, painted him as an angel of light), the Romantic hero and rebel. Byron, for example, in *Cain* (1821), saw him as a proud and indomitable figure, a sort of freedom-fighter against oppression and capable of the sort of bombast and tub-thumping rhetoric which Shakespeare put into Hotspur's mouth. Carducci addressed a hymn to him:

> Salute, o Satana,
> o ribellione
> o forza vindice
> della ragione!

Rapisardi, the Sicilian poet of the social revolution, in his epic, *Il Lucifero*

(1877) sees Lucifer as gaining a final victory over God. And Baudelaire, in a famous poem, invoked his aid and compassion:

> O toi, le plus savant et le plus beau des Anges,
> Dieu trahi par le sort et privé de louanges,
> O Satan, prends pitié de ma longue misère!

There were yet other metamorphoses devised for the traditional exemplar of all evil. George Sand, in her *Consuelo* (1842) conceives of a Satan who is converted and redeemed. The Italian poet Montanelli put forward a similar idea in his dramatic poem *La Tentazione* (1856). In a poem which he planned but never wrote Alfred de Vigny intended to relate the story of Satan's salvation, while Victor Hugo, in his unfinished poem *La Fin de Satan*, proposed to bring about the reconciliation of God with Satan, which would have been a summit meeting and treaty of a conclusive nature. All this was a long, long way indeed from the image of the horned and malignant monster chewing the cud of traitors while embedded in perpetuity in the ice-bound sump of the universe.

In view of the resurgence of interest in the Devil it is in no way surprising to discover that the Faust legend and theme (more or less dormant since Marlowe) should be revived in the latter half of the eighteenth century; and that, having been revived, it should become of great interest. From Lessing (whose scene for a Faust-play was printed in *Literaturbriefe* in 1759) to Thomas Mann whose *Doktor Faustus* was published in 1947, the theme was very nearly a German monopoly. It must be more than likely that a renewed interest in the Faust theme was in great part responsible for the 'reappearance' of the Devil.

In turn this motif was to inspire a succession of short stories, novellas and novels the bases of whose plots were variations on the idea of the demonic pact. There were at least ninety treatments of this by writers in the nineteenth century and not a few of them were horror stories. The authors range from the Ettrick shepherd James Hogg to, somewhat surprisingly perhaps, Max Beerbohm.

Closely associated with the recrudescence of the Devil as a 'character' is that major theme of the Romantic period, the divisibility of the human identity; the ancient duality; the good man and the bad man; the two souls coexistent; the divided self. It seems that this came into literature (or, some would maintain, returned to literature since it had been inherent in the Morality plays and in allegory) via German folklore. However it arrived, the *Doppelgänger* ('double-goer, double-walker') is German in origin. As a theme it was to prove of persistent interest through the nineteenth century and was to be the source and mainspring of some of the most powerful psychological horror stories; stories in which mental and spiritual states are examined and exposed, in which fear, madness, cruelty and evil predominate; stories, in fact, in which the kind of subjective Hell posited by Sir Walter Ralegh and Sir Thomas Browne are explored.

Chamisso was one of the first to exploit the possibilities of the *Doppelgänger* idea in depth in his story of *Peter Schlemihl* (1814), the man who sold his shadow. Hoffmann treated it in *Die Elixiere des Teufels* (1815–16) and in *Fräulein von Scuderi* (1819), the tale of the goldsmith who was so obsessed by the works he had created with his own hands that he murdered his clients in order to recover the artefacts. In fact, Cardillac the goldsmith is a Jekyll-and-Hyde figure. Much more terrifying was James Hogg's *The Private Memoirs and Confessions of a Justified Sinner* (1824). Wringham is haunted by a demon whose features initially resemble his own and he is persuaded by the demon that he may do anything he wishes. Ultimately (and too late) Wringham awakens to reality. 'I have two souls [he says] . . . the one being all unconscious of what the other performs.' Edgar Allan Poe, who was considerably influenced by Hoffmann, wrought variations on the double theme in his short stories *William Wilson* (1839) and a *Tale of the Ragged Mountains* (1844). Dostoyevsky's *The Double* (1846) and Storm's *Ein Doppelgänger* (1887) display other possibilities. In English literature easily the most original and most famous *Doppelgänger* stories are Robert Louis Stevenson's *Dr Jekyll and Mr Hyde* (1886) and Oscar Wilde's *The Picture of Dorian Gray* (1891). Conrad's strange tale *The Secret Sharer* (1912) was yet another version of the 'double' idea, though not a horror story.

Vampirism, a subject with a copious literature and a voluminous accumulation of legend and lore of worldwide proportions, also became of interest during the Romantic period and, during the last 150 years or so, has proved a fruitful topic for the makers of horror stories – and, since the 1930s, movies.

Vampires are usually associated with Eastern Europe and, more particularly, with Hungary and Transylvania. But few regions of the world, it seems, lack vampires and vampire tales. They flourish from China to Peru and the more scientific scholars adopt a taxonomic method in classifying them.

Thus: LOCALITY: Albania. SPECIES: *Liugat – Sampiro*. CHARACTERISTICS: Goes around at night, wrapped up in its shroud and wears shoes with very high heels; its tomb is indicated by a will-o'-the-wisp. HOW IT

BECOMES A VAMPIRE: Natural causes; being an Albanian of Turkish blood. SPECIAL ACTIVITIES: Spreads death and destruction.

Or, thus: LOCALITY: Brazil. SPECIES: *Lobishomen*. CHARACTERISTICS: Small stature, stumpy and hunch-backed, resembling a monkey, but with a yellow face, bloodless lips, black teeth, bushy beard and plush-covered feet. SPECIAL ACTIVITIES: Makes its victims (all women) into nymphomaniacs. CURE: Let it get drunk on blood in order to catch it more easily, then crucify it on a tree while stabbing it.

Perusal of a field-guide to vampires reveals a remarkable range of species, of various appearances and habits, as well as cures for their attentions. One species peculiar to Vietnam, for instance, sometimes consists only of a head with red antennae coming out of the nose. These it sucks with.

John Polidori, for a while secretary and companion to Byron, was one of the first to write a fictional or semi-fictional vampire story in the nineteenth century. It was called quite simply *The Vampyre* and was published in 1818, the same year as *Frankenstein*. There is little about bloodsucking in it; it is mostly concerned with sex, as are most vampire stories. However, the protagonist, Lord Ruthven, had a vampire's curious habits and was to become the model for the English vampire in fiction.

By this stage the vampire was becoming a prominent symbol among Romantic writers. For example: Geraldine in Coleridge's *Christabel* (1797); the spectral bloodsucker in Byron's *The Giaour* (1813); the figure of Misery in Shelley's *Invocation to Misery* (1818); and, most striking of all, Keats's beautiful and merciless dame who sucked the blood from the knight – and everybody and everything else.

In due course the vampire was to become a standby for writers of horror stories and also for playwrights who practised melodrama. As early as 1820 Charles Nodier produced *Le Vampire*. One of the earliest stories remains one of the best, namely Gogol's *Viy* (1835). In the same year Poe published *Berenice* which has implications of vampirism. Poe, being a necrophile and a thanatophile, could hardly fail to be interested in vampires. In 1836 Théophile Gautier published *La Morte amoureuse*, generally regarded as the most famous vampire story in French literature. Sheridan Le Fanu wrote one good one, namely *Carmilla* (1872). Much later, E. F. Benson, something of an expert in the bloodcurdling, produced *Mrs Amworth*, a memorable account of a sturdy, bridge-playing blood-drinker in the erstwhile stockbroker belt. Luigi Capuana's *A Vampire* (1907) constituted another original variation on a hackneyed theme. And F. G. Loring's *The Tomb of Sarah* (*c.* 1930) achieved originality by virtue of the author's style and narrative structure.

The one vampire story that everyone knows is Bram Stoker's *Dracula* (1897), a tale of horror which has produced numerous imitations and has been responsible for a form of sub-culture in what E. M. Forster was wont to call the cinemaphote.

There are also inset vampire stories in Lawrence Durrell's *Balthazar* (Durrell is witty and ingenious), and in Simon Raven's *Doctors Wear Scarlet* (1960). *The Adventure of the Sussex Vampire* by Conan Doyle is a kind of 'anti-vampire' tale. All the evidence suggests vampirism; Holmes (very nearly on his best form) shows the truth to be otherwise.

There are some stories in which a 'creature' (akin, say, to a *lamia* or a *succubus*) haunts characters and feeds off them emotionally and psychologically. The parasitical roles of these evil beings suggest that in some respects they are a kind of ghostly presence. De Maupassant's extraordinary story *Le Horla* (1887) is a notable example. In English literature outstanding instances are *How Love Came to Professor Guildea* (1900) by Robert Hichens and *The Beckoning Fair One* (1911) by Oliver Onions. All three are tales of horror. The victims are debilitated and driven to insanity and death. D. K. Broster's *Couching at the Door* (1933), a sinister and excellent story, if somewhat mannered in style, uses the idea of a 'familiar' which grows in size.

The werewolf theme also became of interest from early in the nineteenth century and has been taken up in some successful horror stories. Belief in werewolves is ancient and is found in numerous regions of the world.[1] Many languages have a word for such a creature and our word is the Old English *werewulf*. The fairy tale *Beauty and the Beast*[2] is clearly related to this werewolf theme. One of the best-known tales is Marryat's *The White Wolf of the Hartz Mountains* (1839). G. W. M. Reynolds used the idea in *Wagner, the Wehr-wolf* (1846–7). Later, Robert Louis Stevenson, Kipling and Algernon Blackwood tried out its possibilities with some success, Stevenson with *Olalla* (1887), Kipling with *The Mark of the Beast* (1887) and Blackwood with *The Camp of the Dog* (1908). Later variations are to be found in Ambrose Bierce's *The Eyes of the Panther* and C. H. B. Kitchin's *The Beauty and the Beast*. Two other well-known stories are Garnett's *Lady into Fox* (1923) and Peter Fleming's *The Kill* (1942). The best and most horrible of lycanthropic tales still seems to me to be Geoffrey Household's *Taboo* (*c.* 1939).

1. Elliot O'Donnell, in his book *Werewolves*, takes the subject seriously enough to assert that such creatures not only have existed but actually do exist.

2. The best-known version appears in the French *contes* of Mme de Villeneuve (1744). A similar story is included in Straparola's *Piacevoli Notte* (1550).

Thus far, this cursory resumé may suggest that in the last thirty-odd years of the eighteenth century and the first twenty to thirty years of the nineteenth century there took place quite important changes in the ways people thought and felt about the metaphysical and preternatural. It is as if, after a long period of rationalism and apparent mental, spiritual and psychological stability, the rediscovery of 'old worlds' and, more especially, the rediscovery of the world of supernatural or quasi-supernatural evil, had a strong disruptive influence. A whole bag of tricks was opened up, a veritable Pandora's box. Out of it came devils, wizards and witches, trolls, hobgoblins, werewolves, vampires, *Doppelgängers* – and what not? None had had any place in the 'Age of Reason'. Nor, for that matter, had satanism, possession, black magic, sorcery, exorcism or diabolic pacts. Most conspicuous of all was the ghost, 'revived', after an absence of a great many years, as a figure and 'character'.

The advent of the ghost story as a short story at the beginning of the nineteenth century coincided with the arrival of the short story, which rapidly became a highly evolved form. It seems more than likely that the ghost story was a natural development or growth from the Gothic novel and from Gothic tales in general, not a few of which were a form of short story.[1]

By the turn of the eighteenth century scores of Gothic novels and tales (many of them hackwork now sunk without trace except in the vaults of the major libraries) were being published. The demand for cheap, sensational literature was high. Publishers, scenting large profits, exerted themselves. So did the authors of such stories; they wrote fast.

To us they are curiosities, 'period pieces' (I have included a couple in this anthology) with resonant titles designed to cause a delightful shudder of apprehension: *The Anaconda* (by 'Monk' Lewis); *The Monk of Horror, or The Conclave of Corpses* (anonymous); *The Black Spider* (anonymous); *The Unknown! or The Knight of the Blood-Red Plume* (by Anne of Swansea); *The Astrologer's Prediction, or The Maniac's Fate* (anonymous). Shelley, Byron and De Quincey all made contributions. In fact, De Quincey's short story *The Dice* (1823), on the old theme of a contract with the Devil, is excellent.[2]

1. For the evolution of the ghost story see the introduction to *The Penguin Book of Ghost Stories* (1984).

2. Study of the long-term and pervasive influence of Gothic on nineteenth-century novelists needs a book. Apart from Scott and Dickens, four in particular, popular in their day, are well worth examining. They are G. P. R. James (1799–1860), Bulwer Lytton (1803–73), William Harrison Ainsworth (1805–82) and G. W. M. Reynolds (1814–79).

As implied above, the vogue for Gothic was to continue for quite a few years, until *c.* 1820–25. By that stage the need for something different and rather more sophisticated was starting to be felt. Jane Austen had suggested this in *Northanger Abbey* (published in 1818, but begun in 1798 and prepared for the press in 1803). In 1818, too, Peacock published *Nightmare Abbey* which pokes fun at Gothic excesses. And in 1819 Leigh Hunt observed ruefully in his preamble to *A Tale for a Chimney Corner*: '. . . a man who does not contribute his quota of grim story nowadays, seems hardly to be free of the republic of letters. He is bound to wear a death's head as part of his insignia. If he does not frighten everybody, he is nobody. If he does not shock the ladies, what can be expected of him?' Later he takes 'Monk' Lewis to task: 'When his spectral nuns go about bleeding, we think they ought in decency to have applied to some ghost of a surgeon. His little Grey Men, who sit munching hearts, are of a piece with fellows who eat cats for a wager.' After some other happily phrased observations he relates a short ghost-cum-horror story of his own.

In fact, the ghost and the horror story (*as short stories*) emerged more or less simultaneously and were given impetus and distinction by two major writers, both German: Kleist and Hoffmann. Both were better and more profound writers than those predecessors or contemporaries, in Europe or elsewhere, who were practitioners in the Gothic genre or its derivatives. Kleist's *Das Bettelweib von Locarno* ('The Beggarwoman of Locarno') was published in *Berliner Abendblätter* in 1810 and in *Erzählungen* in 1811. It is a very short ghost story (some 800 words) and might equally well be regarded as a horror story. But then it is true to say that many of the best ghost stories are horrific; and not a few of the best horror stories involve ghosts. Kleist's *Das Erdbeben in Chili* was first published in 1807; a terrifying version of the earthquake which took place at Santiago in 1647.

In 1817 Hoffmann published his lengthy ghost story, *Das Majorat* ('The Entail'). Complex, subtle and carefully wrought, it is thirty times longer than Kleist's *Das Bettelweib von Locarno*. From approximately the same period date some of his outstanding horror stories: *Die Elixiere des Teufels* (1815–16), *Ignaz Denner* (1816), *Der Sandmann* (1816–17) and *Das Fräulein von Scuderi* (1818–21).[1]

Using the short-story and the *Novellen* forms Kleist and Hoffmann

1. A minor influence on the development of the ghost story was Johann Apel, a contemporary of Kleist and Hoffmann, who published a large collection in *Gespensterbuch* (1810–17). Schiller's *Der Geisterseher* (1789), fine story though it be, is not, I feel, a ghost story. The 'ghost' produced by the Sicilian con-man is bogus and the enigmatic and sinister Armenian looks to be based on the Wandering Jew (a figure who became of considerable interest during the Romantic period).

between them set standards for ghost and horror stories which have seldom been equalled, except by other masters such as Edgar Allan Poe, de Maupassant, Henry James, M. R. James and Walter de la Mare, to name a handful of the foremost.

Unhappily, Hoffmann died of an illness, aged only forty-six, in 1822. Kleist stage-managed his own death and that of Henritte Vogel on the shore of the Wannsee in 1811. He shot her and then immediately killed himself. In its own right it was a kind of horror story.

Curiously enough, neither the ghost story nor the horror story (in short-story form) flourished subsequently in German literature. The influence of Gothic was to prevail for some time and this is discernible in Fouqué and Tieck. As suggested earlier, demonic agency and supernatural forces featured in a number of novels and *Novellen*. Here and there one finds a story which might be put into the 'horror' category. For instance, Gotthelf's *Die schwarze Spinne* (1842) and Gustav Meyrink's *Der Golem* (1915), a weird and eerie tale of the Prague ghetto. More recently Hans Ewers (1871–1943) wrote some horror novels and short stories which are somewhat melodramatic and sensational in the manner of Poe, though nothing like as good.

English Gothic novels were much read and imitated in France in the nineteenth century. Their influence, plus the influences of German Gothic, the *Schauerroman* and especially Hoffmann's stories, becomes apparent in French literature. Some of Nodier's work (e.g. *La fée aux miettes* and *Smarra ou les Démons de la nuit* (1821)) ventures into the horror genre. The same is true of some of Balzac's stories, such as *El Verdugo*, *La Grande Bretêche* and *Melmoth réconcilié* (1835). This last was one of his 'Études philosophiques' (much under the influence of Maturin) and is a remarkable and frightening reworking of the Wanderer theme: the selling of one's soul – on the principle of the transferable bargain – to the Devil in return for long life.

Gérard de Nerval produced one very fine comic/grotesque horror story in the shape of *La Main enchantée* (1832): the 'adventures' of a hand, newly severed from a corpse, which performs a series of bloodcurdling antics.[1]

Several of Prosper Mérimée's *nouvelles* are highly original horror stories, especially *Mateo Falcone* (1833), *La Vénus d'Ille* (1841) and *Lokis*

1. There are several sinister tales of the horror phylum to which a hand is central. De Maupassant wrote two: *The Hand* and *The Withered Hand*. There are also Le Fanu's *The Narrative of a Ghost of a Hand*, Louis Golding's *The Call of the Hand*, Theodore Dreiser's *The Hand*, Conan Doyle's *The Brown Hand* and W. F. Harvey's *The Beast with Five Fingers*. To these it is appropriate to add W. W. Jacobs's classic spine-chiller *The Monkey's Paw*.

(1873). His precise, objective style and somewhat laconic tone make an agreeable change after the rodomontade of overblown Gothic.

At a lower level were the melodramatic horror stories of Petrus Borel (he, de Nerval and Gautier were friends), especially *Champavert, contes immoraux* (1833) and *Madame Putiphar* (1839).

Other French writers to experiment with horror themes were Barbey d'Aurevilly who published *Les Diaboliques* in 1874 and Villiers de l'Isle-Adam who wrote *Contes cruels* (1883) and *Nouveaux Contes cruels* (1888). Zola, who had a morbid fear of death (as is evident in, for instance, the macabre scenes in the morgue in *Thérèse Raquin* and the frightening description of the flooded coalmine in *Germinal*), produced one excellent story on the theme of premature burial, namely, *La Mort d'Olivier Bécaille*.

Of all the nineteenth-century French writers the one who had the keenest insights into fear, neuroses, madness and the apprehension of evil was de Maupassant. A number of his stories are sinister and frightening. There are two in particular of nightmarish vision which fall very readily into the horror category: *Le Horla* (1887), which is also a kind of ghost story, and *Who Knows?* (1890).

Gothic also travelled to America where Isaac Mitchell achieved some reputation with *The Asylum* (1811) and Charles Brockden Brown attained something approaching fame with a succession of Gothic romances: *Wieland* (1798), *Arthur Mervyn* (1799), *Ormond* (1799) and *Edgar Huntly* (1799). Some of the main influences on Brown were Richardson, Godwin and Ann Radcliffe. In turn Brown was to influence Hawthorne and Poe and several English writers, including Mary Shelley. Hoffmann's stories were soon known in America and Washington Irving was the first American to write ghost stories. He published two in 1820, which suggests the speed with which the new kind of story was developing. As communications steadily improved during the nineteenth century so cross-pollination in literature burgeoned.

In the 1830s Edgar Allan Poe began to write the short stories for which he has ever since been famous. Some have become classics which most schoolboys may be expected to know and Poe remains one of the most frequently anthologized of all writers of short stories. His first collection, *Tales of the Grotesque and Arabesque* appeared in 1839. He had already shown a gift for writing about the horrific in *The Narrative of Arthur Gordon Pym* (1838). The tales are short, intense, sensational (sometimes luridly melodramatic) and have the power to inspire horror and terror. Like de Maupassant, but by very different methods, he depicts extremes of fear, suffering and insanity and, through the operations of evil, gives us glimpses of hell. His most notable horror stories are *The Fall of the House of Usher* (1839), *The Murders in the Rue Morgue* (1841), *A Descent into the Maelstrom* (1841), *The Masque of the Red Death* (1842), *The Pit and the Pendulum, The Black Cat* and *The Tell-tale Heart* (all 1843), *The Case of M. Valdemar* (1845) and *The Cask of Amontillado* (1846).

Poe's long-term influence was immeasurable – and in the case of some writers not altogether for their good: one can detect it persisting through the nineteenth century; in, for example, the French *Symbolistes* (Baudelaire published translations of his tales in 1856 and 1857), in such English writers as Rossetti, Swinburne, Dowson and Stevenson, and in such Americans as Ambrose Bierce, Hart Crane and H. P. Lovecraft. Poe has, perhaps, been somewhat overrated – though it is surely heresy to say so. He did have a tendency to over-write.

In Britain the ghost story began to develop in the 1820s when Walter Scott wrote a number of very good ones and also published his important essay *On the Supernatural in Fictitious Composition* (1827). R. H. Barham produced several in the 1830s, later to be incorporated in *The Ingoldsby Legends* (1840). But it was Dickens who really established the ghost story between 1837 and the 1860s. Apart from his own outstanding contributions, he commissioned writers to supply them for his periodicals; among them Wilkie Collins, Charles Collins, Bulwer Lytton and Sheridan Le Fanu.

The growth of the ghost story and that of the horror story in this mid-century period tended to coalesce; indeed, it is difficult to establish objective criteria by which to distinguish between the two. A taxonomical approach invariably begins to break down at an early stage. There are scores of supernatural 'horror' stories ('crawlers' as R. L. Stevenson called them) from the last hundred years or so which are very difficult to classify. Having said this, however, it might be argued that Wilkie Collins's *A Terribly Strange Bed* (1856) is a horror story, Elizabeth Gaskell's *The Old Nurse's Tale* (1852) is a ghost story, and that Sheridan Le Fanu's *Green Tea* (1869) is a combination of both. On balance it is probable that a ghost story will contain an element of horror.

When Le Fanu died in 1873 the ghost story had become firmly established as a distinct genre. Over a century later there is still no sign of diminution in its popularity, though there may have been some decline in the quality of writing. The vast majority of ghost stories (around 98 per cent) are in English and roughly 70 per cent of those are written by English men and women. Since the 1880s the horror story has proliferated and, it seems, has never been more popular than it is now. Again, most horror stories are in English (about 90 per cent) and perhaps 70 per cent of those are by British men and women.

Towards the end of the nineteenth century a number of British writers were experimenting with different modes of horror story and this was at a time when there had been steadily growing interest in psychic phenomena, in psychotherapy and extreme psychological states and also in spiritualism. The Society for Psychical Research was founded by F. W. H. Myers and there was increasing interest in drugs and their effects as well as in dreams and insanity.

A notable practitioner of the horror story in the 1890s and later was Arthur Machen. In 1895 he published *The Great God Pan* and *The Inmost Light*. In 1896 came *The Novel of the White Powder*, one of the most repulsive of horror tales. During the next forty years he became a prominent specialist in the horrific and was a considerable influence on the American H. P. Lovecraft who had a strong predilection for abominable physical horrors. Both writers had the same shortcoming: they would overdo the sensationalism, sometimes to such an extent that their stories became ludicrous when they were meant to instil terror.

F. Marion Crawford also specialized in sensational novels and short stories and was prolific in output. Among his short horror stories the best known are *The Dead Smile*, *The Upper Berth* and *The Screaming Skull* (all 1911). Like Machen and Lovecraft he had a detrimental tendency to over-write.

I mentioned R. L. Stevenson earlier in connection with the *Doppelgänger* theme and *Dr Jekyll and Mr Hyde*. He produced some other excellent horror stories (as well as ghost stories) which were to become famous; particularly *Markheim* (1887), *Olalla* (1887), a werewolf tale, *The Bottle Imp* (1892–3) and *The Body Snatcher*.

Dreams, delirium, derangement of the senses, the activity of the mind under intense pressure – these areas were of much interest to Kipling who, besides penning a quantity of very good ghost stories, wrote some notable horror stories (often anthologized). Among the widest read are *The Strange Ride of Morrowbie Jukes* (1885), *Beyond the Pale*, *The Mark of the Beast* (1891), a kind of werewolf story, and *At the End of the Passage* (1891).

Henry James's sense of the past and his acute sensitivity to the spirit and atmosphere of places were important factors in his creation of some of the finest ghost stories that exist. Over a period of some forty years he wrote vast numbers. The most famous is *The Turn of the Screw* (1898) which, it seems to me, is so sinister and so compelling in its depiction of evil that it is also, *ipso facto*, a horror story. Much less well known is *The*

Romance of Certain Old Clothes (1868) which has a surprise and horrific ending. In this, as in other 'supernatural' tales, James achieved his most powerful effects by stealth, hint and understatement, by 'the process of adumbration' as he put it. The reader is allowed, persuaded, to create his own fear and apprehension; he is enabled to 'think the evil'.

Very different styles and techniques were used by Ambrose Bierce (1842–1914?), almost an exact contemporary of Henry James (1843–1916) and also an American. He wrote a handful of first-class ghost stories and his black, sardonic humour was very well suited to the making of horror stories, several of which have withstood the long-distance tests of taste and time. Several collections of his stories were published, including *Tales of Soldiers and Civilians* (1891) and *Can Such Things Be?* (1893). Some of his most successful horror stories are *The Man and the Snake*, *A Watcher by the Dead*, *The Damned Thing*, *The Boarded Window*, *A Horseman in the Sky*.

In the same year that *Can Such Things Be?* was published, another American, Robert W. Chambers, produced a collection of original horror stories titled *The King in Yellow*. Though his style is exotic to the point of extravagance (these were not typical of his work), some of the tales are powerful descriptions of mental breakdown. One of the most effective is *The Repairer of Reputations*, a study of megalomaniac insanity.

It may be argued that many of M. R. James's ghost stories are also horror stories. Certainly the best of them contain that moment of deadly chill, the icy touch of fear, which is so much more effective and memorable than the rather shrill and strenuous elaborations of Machen, F. Marion Crawford, H. P. Lovecraft and others. He is particularly successful at arousing physical revulsion: the unclean thing of decaying flesh hinted at in *Lost Hearts*, the toad-like being in *The Treasure of Abbot Thomas*, the spiders in *The Ash-Tree*, and, in *Mr Humphreys and his Inheritance*, the nightmarish manifestation: 'It took shape as a face – a human face – a *burnt* human face: and with the odious writhings of a wasp creeping out of a rotten apple there clambered out the appearance of a form.'

His *Ghost Stories of an Antiquary* were first published under that title in 1904. In 1911 there came *More Ghost Stories of an Antiquary*, and the collected stories were finally published in 1931.

Algernon Blackwood was almost an exact contemporary of M. R. James, though he lived several years longer. Unlike James, he was deeply interested in and learned in the occult and in psychic phenomena and was the author of some outstanding stories about supernatural evil and supernatural forces which are totally indifferent to man. Few writers have

understood the psychology of fear better. Among his well-known stories
are *Ancient Sorceries* and *Secret Worship* (1906), *The Willows*, *The Insanity
of Jones*, *The Dance of Death* (1907) and *The Camp of the Dog* (1908). He
also wrote a number of ghost stories.

Another near contemporary was William Hope Hodgson, who, besides
a quantity of ghost stories, produced such flesh-creeping tales as *The
Island of the Ud*, *The Whistling Room* and *The Derelict*.

One may not immediately associate Conan Doyle with the horror story
but he did try his hand at a variety of tales which might well be put into
this category. Most of them were written between 1890 and 1920, and
collections were published in 1922, titled *Tales of Twilight and the Unseen*
and *Tales of Terror and Mystery*. They included *The Brown Hand*
(mentioned earlier), *The New Catacomb*, *The Case of Lady Sannox*, *The
Brazilian Cat*, *The Terror of Blue John Gap* and *The Horror of the Heights*.

'Saki' (H. H. Munro) was the author of several sinister stories. Three
of them have been regarded as horror stories; namely, *The Music on the
Hill*, *The Open Window* (which is in fact a spoof ghost story) and *Sredni
Vashtar*. There are also *Gabriel-Ernest*, a werewolf tale about a naked
savage boy who lives off child-flesh, and *The Easter Egg*, which has a very
nasty climax.

Yet another outstanding practitioner of the short story during the same
period was H. G. Wells. Some of his best depend on suspense and an
element of the horrific, especially the threat to man by some non-human
creature, as in *The Abyss* and *The Sea-Raiders* (both 1897), *The Valley of
Spiders* (1903) and *The Empire of the Ants* (1911). Others are concerned
with aspects of hallucination and obsession: for example, *The Remarkable
Case of Davidson's Eyes* and *The Flowering of the Strange Orchid* (both
1895), and *The Moth* (1895), a weird horror-cum-ghost story. *Pollock and
the Porroh Man* (1897) has a voodoo theme. Both *The Lord of the Dynamos*
(1895) and *The Cone* (1897) are horror stories carrying a similar idea:
vengeance in the form of 'sacrifice' of a human being. *The Red Room*
(1896) is a spinechiller about a room haunted by an evil presence, and this
is more obviously in the Gothic tradition.

E. F. Benson was a specialist in ghost stories and these have remained
popular since his first collection *The Room in the Tower* (1912). He also
produced some excellent horror stories, including *Mrs Amworth* and *The
Confession of Charles Linkworth*.

During the 1920s and 1930s many well-crafted short horror stories
were published by such writers as A. J. Alan, Elizabeth Bowen, A. M.
Burrage, John Collier, A. E. Coppard, Lord Dunsany, L. P. Hartley, W.
F. Harvey, C. E. Montague, Evelyn Nesbit, L. A. G. Strong, H. Russell

Wakeford, Dennis Wheatley, Alexander Woollcot *et al*. Of these, Hartley is the one most often mentioned in connection with the genre. His *Night Fears and Other Stories* was published in 1924. In 1951 another collection appeared: *The Travelling Grave*, which contains *The Killing Bottle*, *Conrad and the Dragon* and *The Thought*. The title story is a particularly good example of the macabre and comic/grotesque type of tale – macabre applying to not a few of his stories. In that inter-war period Walter de La Mare was the most notable writer of ghost stories, but he is not usually reckoned to be an exponent of horrors.

During these same years the long-term influences of the Gothic novel were still discernible and Gothic received another lease of life, as it were, in the horror film – a well-documented subject which has received much erudite attention on the university campus as well as elsewhere. The horror film may have had some effect (difficult to measure) on the horror story in literature; but it would be plausible to surmise that writers have been encouraged to write horror stories because of the popularity of the films.

From the early days of the cinema the horror film was well established. There were a series of German masterpieces during the silent era and the movement of Expressionism in the arts certainly affected the film-makers. Some of the German directors were to become famous (e.g. Wegener, Wiene, Lang and Murnau). In the early 1930s came a succession of American horror films now particularly associated with the directors Tod Browning and James Whale and with the acting of Boris Karloff as Frankenstein and Bela Lugosi as Dracula.

In the period 1931–33 there not only appeared Browning's *Dracula* and Whales's *Frankenstein*, but also Rouben Mamoulian's version of *Dr Jekyll and Mr Hyde*, Schoedsack and Pichel's *The Most Dangerous Game*, Erle C. Kenton's *Island of Lost Souls*, Victor Halperin's *White Zombie*, Karl Freund's *The Mummy* and Schoedsack and Pichel's *King Kong*.

Since then there have been numerous versions of *Dr Jekyll and Mr Hyde* and of *Frankenstein*. These two, plus *King Kong*, have become quasi myths and the source of cults, yet a surprising number of people have no idea that Frankenstein films derive from a book by Mary Shelley published in 1818.

The 1950s saw the making of many (too many) horror-cum-science-fiction films, for the most part crudely sensational and simplistic. However, in the 1960s Hammer Studios produced a series of good films which were basically investigations in psychopathology. The best were *Taste of Fear* (1960), *Maniac* (1962), *Paranoiac* (1963), *Fanatic* (1965) and *The Anniversary* (1967). In the 1960s, too, Roger Corman made a remarkable contribution to the horror genre with his 'Poe cycle'. These films are permanently linked with the exceptional acting of Vincent Price.

Three major films that explore the pathology of terror are Hitchcock's *Psycho* (1960), Michael Powell's *Peeping Tom* (1960) and Polanski's *Repulsion* (1965). These reveal the horror which may lie not far below the surfaces of mundane life. By comparison, the full-blooded Gothic extravagances of *The Exorcist* (1973) are trite and not much more than a tribute to the skills of the special-effects department.

Since the 1950s short horror stories (and what purport to be horror stories) have proliferated. In fact, one could say that they have *tended* to proliferate for about 100 years. Certainly since the turn of the nineteenth century it is a form which has shown remarkable diversification. A great many professional writers have turned their hand to it at least once as indeed they have to the ghost story. Besides those already mentioned, any list of names would be bound to include the following (in alphabetical order): Sir Charles Birkin, Robert Bloch, Heinrich Böll, Marjorie Bowen, E. F. Bozman, Ray Bradbury, Thomas Burke, Truman Capote, Mark Channing, Sir Hugh Clifford, Richard Connell, Isak Dinesen, Guy Endore, Paul Gallico, Thomas Hardy, E. and H. Heron, Patricia Highsmith, E. W. Hornung, Richard Hughes, John Jasper, Will F. Jenkins, F. Tennyson Jesse, Gerald Kersh, Vernon Lee, Daphne du Maurier, Richard Middleton, Fitz-James O'Brien, Vincent O'Sullivan, Roger Pater, V. S. Pritchett, William Sansom, W. B. Seabrook, Elizabeth Walter, Edward Lucas White, Angus Wilson and John Wyndham.

Such a list might easily be doubled. There are many now neglected who have, for a few minutes at least, chilled the blood of their readers. Nor does the above list include the names of a complete generation of younger writers.

The advent of science fiction on a massive scale (often now displayed in bookshops en bloc under the legend HORROR) has diversified horror fiction even more than one might at first suppose. New maps of Hell have been drawn and are being drawn; new dimensions of the horrific exposed and explored; new simulacra and *exempla* created. Fear, pain, suffering, guilt and madness (what we have already seen in miscellaneous hells) remain powerful and emotive elements in horror stories. Through the cracks, the 'faults in reality', we and our writers catch other vertiginous glimpses of chaos, fissiparating images of death and destruction.

The work of some modern novelists (as well as that of practitioners of short horror stories) recreates internal and external microcosms of hell: dislocated worlds seen through dislocative visions. One might call it modern Gothic, an increasingly portmanteau term.[1] The fiction of J. G. Ballard is an obvious instance, particularly *The Terminal Beach* (1964) and *The Atrocity Exhibition* (1970), and some of his short stories (e.g. *The Billenium* (1964)). Other horror novelists – though not perhaps quite so well known as Ballard – are John Hawkes (author of *The Cannibal* (1962) and *The Blood Oranges* (1971)); Joyce Carol Oates (*A Garden of Earthly Delights* (1967) and *Expensive People* (1968)); Thomas Pynchon (*The Crying of Lot 49* (1966) and *Gravity's Rainbow* (1973)); and James Purdy (*Eustace Chisholm and the Works* (1967)). I would also include Mervyn Peake's novels, some of William Burroughs's work (especially *The Naked Lunch* (1959)) and Anthony Burgess's *A Clockwork Orange* (1962). The American, Stephen King, has also written some horror stories which are indebted to Gothic modes and styles, as has Angela Carter (e.g. *Heroes and Villains* (1969)).

Such fiction constitutes what Mr Punter assesses as 'perceptions of modern barbarism'. What they depict has counterparts on the terraces of the *Inferno* and in the visual images of painters already referred to.

Unfortunately there is not space to represent any of the authors just mentioned. Here are only short stories of which twenty-odd (out of the hundreds available and of which I have read probably fewer then half) stand for attitudes, feelings and personal visions expressed between late in the eighteenth century and the mid-twentieth century.

What is noticeable about horror stories of more recent times (especially the short stories) is that they set out to shock in ways which are quite often crude or even somewhat obvious. The shock effect is perhaps comparable to seeing a cobra slithering up through a hole in the kitchen skirting of one's semi-detached in London, or, on opening the front door to bring in the milk, finding a beheaded cat on the step. The stories are often inventive, skilful, slick or efficient (perhaps with half an eye on television or cinematic possibilities?), but not so many have much psychological depth or display any real attempt to explain and come to terms with the subversive and complex nature of the human personality. The best ones tend to be concerned with the nature of evil as a force within man and about him.

From among the many hundreds available that have been published in the last thirty to forty years (I have read just on 500 of them taken from this period), I have chosen a dozen or so to represent the more recent horror story. They range from Patricia Highsmith's *The Terrapin*, a

1. In his excellent book *The Literature of Terror* (1980) a scholarly investigation into the evolution of the Gothic tale and its various progeny, David Punter devotes a chapter to what he describes as 'Modern Perceptions of the Barbaric'.

sinister tale of maternal cruelty, to J. N. Allan's serio-comic and grotesque fantasy *The Aquarist*.

Within the general framework I have sought to present a selection of authors ranging from the famous (e.g. Henry James) to the obscure or, as I believe, hardly known (e.g. Dawn Muscillo). Within those polarities there come the very well known (e.g. Monica Dickens), the well known (e.g. Lord Dunsany) and the fairly well known (e.g. Gerald Kersh). To these loose categories perhaps one should add the 'forgotten' (or almost forgotten), of whom there are several: for instance, John Russell, A. M. Burrage and D. K. Broster.

In making the whole selection I have been guided by a few other straightforward, self-imposed rules. From the outset I opted for a rough chronological representation covering the greater part of the last two hundred years. So I begin with *The Monk of Horror, or The Conclave of Corpses* (1798) and finish with Vilas Sarang's *An Interview with M. Chakko* (*London Magazine*, December 1983). *The Monk of Horror . . .* is an anonymous tale which appeared in an anonymous chapbook titled *Tales of the Crypt – in the style of The Monk*. One could not claim that it is typical of Gothic fiction but it gives an impression of the kind of thing that was popular then. As I suggested earlier, it is a period-piece. So is *The Astrologer's Prediction, or The Maniac's Fate* (1826). Hogg's *The Expedition to Hell* (1836) is more interesting because it combines dream and reality in a way which was very unusual at the time. Vilas Sarang's clever and macabre fantasy is much more improbable than any of these three.

At all stages I looked for originality of content and ideas and excellence of form and style (many a good horror story has been marred by poor or indifferent writing), and in doing so I have tried to present a range of stories which vary in tone and mood as much as they do in technique and style. Thus, at one extreme, we have, for instance, Robert Louis Stevenson's slightly 'old-fashioned' melodramatic spinechiller *The Body Snatcher*, and at the other the subtle and naturalistic evocation of the presence of evil in Yvor Winters's beautifully written *The Brink of Darkness*.

Insanity, fear, obsessional neurosis, terror of death, vampirism, torture, revenge, lycanthropy, cruelty, diabolic infiltration, witchcraft, the power of evil – all these are represented in various ways by the authors in this anthology.

I have picked some stories partly because of their 'humour'. The comic/grotesque or black-comedy horror story incorporates its own antidote, as it were: the therapeutic serum to combat the poison and perhaps induce mirth. Not that the humour is likely to make one laugh aloud. It is more likely to cause a grim inward smile: an uneasy combination of a wince and a laconic rictus. Lord Dunsany's *The Two Bottles of Relish* and John Lennon's *No Flies on Frank*, among others, seem to me to come into this category.

I do not suppose there is much in this selection which will be new to the connoisseurs but there may well be some stories which are unfamiliar to the general reader – and it is that person whom I have had primarily in mind.

Some renowned writers of horror stories are not represented. They include Hoffmann, Gautier, Gogol, Sheridan Le Fanu, Conan Doyle, Arthur Machen, Algernon Blackwood and H. P. Lovecraft. I would very much have liked to include Hoffmann's *Fräulein von Scuderi* and Gogol's *Viy*, but they are too long for collections of this kind. Work by the others has been omitted on preference and to leave space for stories of merit by authors much less well known. On the whole, I have sedulously avoided ghost stories, largely because there is already *The Penguin Book of Ghost Stories*.

Some of the stories included have appeared in other anthologies whose thematic *raison d'être* is, variously, horror/terror/suspense/mystery/supernatural. There are three principal reasons for reprinting them: (a) they are stories which will stand reprinting; (b) they are necessary for the balance and variety of this selection; (c) they are by authors who *ought* to appear in an anthology which seeks to be regionally and chronologically representative.

Finally, when all is said and done, there is a limit to the number of stories which can be included in any anthology and it is the compiler's unenviable task to decide what must be omitted. It is axiomatic that no anthology is going to please, let alone satisfy, everyone.

That satiety which Macbeth claimed to have experienced when he said

> . . . I have supp'd full with horrors;
> Direness, familiar to my slaughterous thoughts,
> Cannot once start me . . .

seems not to be the condition of the reading public whose appetite for horror appears unabated. Why do people go on reading horror stories? I suspect that a likely answer is that at a basic and, perhaps, somewhat childish level they rather enjoy being frightened, or even being scared stiff.

Long ago (in 1773) Mrs Anne Letitia Barbauld, the wife of a clergyman and one of the female pioneers in the skills of freezing comparatively modern blood, published a story titled *Sir Bertrand* (it was part of a projected novel) in a collection of Gothic tales.

Sir Bertrand, 'ere he had proceeded half his journey', loses his way on dreary moors. Benighted, he comes upon an antique mansion strongly marked by the injuries of time. Undaunted, he enters the mansion and pursues a weird, will-o'-the-wisp blue flame. Further and further he goes until:

He was now in total darkness, and with his arms extended, began to ascend the second staircase. A dead cold hand met his left hand, and firmly grasped it, drawing him forcibly backwards – he endeavoured to disengage himself, but could not – he made a furious blow with his sword, and instantly a loud shriek pierced his ears, and the dead hand was left powerless with his – He dropped it, and rushed forward with a desperate valour . . . The staircase grew narrower and narrower, and at length terminated in a low iron gate. Sir Bertrand pushed it open – it led to an intricate winding passage, just large enough to admit a person upon his hands and knees . . .

And so on.

The collection of bloodcurdlers in which this appeared was prefaced by an essay: *On the Pleasure Derived from Objects of Terror.*

Lastly I would like to thank several people who have been generous with their time, resources and knowledge: Mr Michael Charlesworth who supplied much valuable material and advice; Miss Geraldine Cooke, my patient, sympathetic and enthusiastic editor; Mr Harry Jackson for advice on Franz Kafka; Mrs Elizabeth McNally for her translation of Zola's story *La Mort d'Olivier Bécaille*; Mr Paul Moreland for a number of valuable suggestions on classical literature and the loan of books; Dr David Singmaster and Mrs Deborah Singmaster for numerous suggestions, continual interest and the loan of a lot of books; Professor J. P. Stern of Cambridge University for most helpful advice on German literature; Dr William Thom for many suggestions and the loan of a large number of books; Mr Clive Wilmer for introducing me to the work of the late Professor Yvor Winters.

The Monk of Horror,

or

The Conclave of Corpses

Anonymous

Some three hundred years since, when the convent of Kreutzberg was in its glory, one of the monks who dwelt therein, wishing to ascertain something of the hereafter of those whose bodies lay all undecayed in the cemetery, visited it alone in the dead of night for the purpose of prosecuting his inquiries on that fearful subject. As he opened the trap-door of the vault a light burst from below; but deeming it to be only the lamp of the sacristan, the monk drew back and awaited his departure concealed behind the high altar. The sacristan emerged not, however, from the opening; and the monk, tired of waiting, approached, and finally descended the rugged steps which led into the dreary depths. No sooner had he set foot on the lower-most stair, than the well-known scene underwent a complete transformation in his eyes. He had long been accustomed to visit the vault, and whenever the sacristan went thither, he was almost sure to be with him. He therefore knew every part of it as well as he did the interior of his own narrow cell, and the arrangement of its contents was perfectly familiar to his eyes. What, then, was his horror to perceive that this arrangement, which even but that morning had come under his observation as usual, was altogether altered, and a new and wonderful one substituted in its stead.

A dim lurid light pervaded the desolate abode of darkness, and it just sufficed to give to his view a sight of the most singular description.

On each side of him the dead but imperishable bodies of the long-buried brothers of the convent sat erect in their lidless coffins, their cold, starry eyes glaring at him with lifeless rigidity, their withered fingers locked together on their breasts, their stiffened limbs motionless and still. It was a sight to petrify the stoutest heart; and the monk's quailed before it, though he was a philosopher, and a sceptic to boot. At the upper end of the vault, at a rude table formed of a decayed coffin, or something which once served the same purpose, sat three monks. They were the oldest corpses in the charnel house, for the inquisitive brother knew their faces well; and the cadaverous hue of their cheeks seemed still more cadaverous in the dim light shed upon them, while their hollow eyes gave forth what looked to him like flashes of flame. A large book lay open before one of them, and the others bent over the rotten table as if in intense pain, or in deep and fixed attention. No word was said; no sound was heard; the vault was as silent as the grave, its awful tenants still as statues.

Fain would the curious monk have receded from this horrible place; fain would he have retraced his steps and sought again his cell, fain would he have shut his eyes to the fearful scene; but he could not stir from the spot, he felt rooted there; and though he once succeeded in turning his eyes to the entrance of the vault, to his infinite surprise and dismay he could not discover where it lay, nor perceive any possible means of exit. He stood thus for some time. At length the aged monk at the table beckoned him to advance. With slow tottering steps he made his way to the group, and at length stood in front of the table, while the other monks raised their heads and glanced at him with fixed, lifeless looks that froze the current of his blood. He knew not what to do; his senses were fast forsaking him; Heaven seemed to have deserted him for his incredulity. In this moment of doubt and fear he bethought him of a prayer, and as he proceeded he felt himself becoming possessed of a confidence he had before unknown. He looked on the book before him. It was a large volume, bound in black, and clasped with bands of gold, with fastenings of the same metal. It was inscribed at the top of each page.

'*Liber Obedientiae.*'

He could read no further. He then looked, first in the eyes of him before whom it lay open, and then in those of his fellows. He finally glanced around the vault on the corpses who filled every visible coffin in its dark and spacious womb. Speech came to him, and resolution to use it. He addressed himself to the awful beings in whose presence he stood, in the words of one having authority with them.

'*Pax vobis,*' twas thus he spake – 'Peace be to ye.'

'*Hic nulla pax,*' replied an aged monk, in a hollow, tremulous tone, baring his breast the while – 'Here is no peace.'

He pointed to his bosom as he spoke, and the monk, casting his eye upon it, beheld his heart within surrounded by living fire, which seemed to feed on it but not consume it. He turned away in affright, but ceased not to prosecute his inquiries.

'*Pax vobis, in nomine Domini,*' he spake again – 'Peace be to ye, in the name of the Lord.'

'*Hic non pax,*' the hollow and heartrending tones of the ancient monk who sat at the right of the table were heard to answer.

On glancing at the bared bosom of this hapless being also the same sight was exhibited – the heart surrounded by a devouring flame, but still remaining fresh and unconsumed under its operation. Once more the monk turned away and addressed the aged man in the centre.

'*Pax vobis, in nomine Domini,*' he proceeded.

At these words the being to whom they were addressed raised his head, put forward his hand and, closing the book with a loud clap, said –

'Speak on. It is yours to ask, and mine to answer.'

The monk felt reassured, and his courage rose with the occasion.

'Who are ye?' he inquired; 'who may ye be?'

'We know not!' was the answer, 'alas! we know not!'

'We know not; we know not!' echoed in melancholy tones the denizens of the vault.

'What do ye here?' pursued the querist.

'We await the last day, the day of the last judgement! Alas for us! woe! woe!'

'Woe! woe!' resounded on all sides.

The monk was appalled, but still he proceeded.

'What did ye to deserve such doom as this? What may your crime be that deserves such dole and sorrow?'

As he asked the question the earth shook under him, and a crowd of skeletons uprose from a range of graves which yawned suddenly at his feet.

'These are our victims,' answered the old monk. 'They suffered at our hands. We suffer now, while they are at peace; and we shall suffer.'

'For how long?' asked the monk.

'For ever and ever!' was the answer.

'For ever and ever, for ever and ever!' died along the vault.

'May God have mercy on us!' was all the monk could exclaim.

The skeletons vanished, the graves closing over them. The aged men disappeared from his view, the bodies fell back in their coffins, the light fled, and the den of death was once more enveloped in its usual darkness.

On the monk's revival he found himself lying at the foot of the altar. The grey dawn of a spring morning was visible, and he was fain to retire to his cell as secretly as he could, for fear he should be discovered.

From thenceforth he eschewed vain philosophy, says the legend, and, devoting his time to the pursuit of true knowledge, and the extension of the power, greatness, and glory of the Church, died in the odour of sanctity, and was buried in that holy vault, where his body is still visible.

The Astrologer's Prediction

or

The Maniac's Fate

Anonymous

Reginald, sole heir of the illustrious family of Di Venoni, was remarkable, from his earliest infancy, for a wild enthusiastic disposition. His father, it was currently reported, had died of an hereditary insanity; and his friends, when they marked the wild mysterious intelligency of his eye, and the determined energy of his aspect, would often assert that the dreadful malady still lingered in the veins of young Reginald. Whether such was the case or not, certain it is, that his mode of existence was but ill calculated to eradicate any symptoms of insanity. Left at an early age to the guidance of his mother, who since the death of her husband had lived in the strictest seclusion, he experienced but little variety to divert or enliven his attention. The gloomy château in which he resided was situated in Swabia on the borders of the Black Forest. It was a wild isolated mansion, built after the fashion of the day in the gloomiest style of Gothic architecture. At a distance rose the ruins of the once celebrated Castle of Rudstein, of which at present but a mouldering tower remained; and, beyond, the landscape was terminated by the deep shades and impenetrable recesses of the Black Forest.

Such was the spot in which the youth of Reginald was immured. But his solitude was soon to be relieved by the arrival of an unexpected resident. On the anniversary of his eighteenth year, an old man, apparently worn down with age and infirmity, took up his abode at the ruined tower of Rudstein. He seldom stirred out during the day; and from the singular circumstance of his perpetually burning a lamp in the tower, the villagers naturally enough concluded that he was an emissary of the devil. This report soon acquired considerable notoriety; and having at last reached the ears of Reginald through the medium of a gossiping gardener, his curiosity was awakened, and he resolved to introduce himself into the presence of the sage, and ascertain the motives of his singular seclusion.

Impressed with this resolution he abruptly quitted the château of his mother, and bent his steps towards the ruined tower, which was situated at a trifling distance from his estate. It was a gloomy night, and the spirit of the storm seemed abroad on the wings of the wind. As the clock from the village church struck twelve, he gained the ruin; and ascending the time-worn staircase, that tottered at each step he took, reached with some labour the apartment of the philosopher. The door was thrown open, and the old man was seated by the grated casement. His appearance was awfully impressive. A long white beard depended from his chin, and his feeble frame with difficulty sustained a horoscope that was directed to the heavens. Books, written in unknown characters of cabalism, were promiscuously strewed about the floor; and an alabaster vase, engraved with the sign of the Zodiac, and circled by mysterious letters, was stationed on the table. The appearance of the Astrologer himself was equally impressive. He was habited in a suit of black velvet, fancifully embroidered with gold, and belted with a band of silver. His thin locks hung streaming in the wind, and his right hand grasped a wand of ebony. On the entrance of a stranger he rose from his seat, and bent a scrutinizing glance on the anxious countenance of Reginald.

'Child of ill-starred fortunes!' he exclaimed in a hollow tone, 'dost thou come to pry into the secrets of futurity? Avoid me, for thy life, or, what is dearer still, thine eternal happiness! for I say unto thee, Reginald Di Venoni, it is better that thou hadst never been born, than permitted to seal thy ruin in a spot which, in after years, shall be the witness of thy fall.'

The countenance of the Astrologer as he uttered these words was singularly terrific, and rung in the ears of Reginald like his death-knell. 'I am innocent, father!' he falteringly replied, 'nor will my disposition suffer me to perpetrate the sins you speak of.' – 'Hah!' resumed the prophet, 'man is indeed innocent, till the express moment of his damnation; but the star of thy destiny already wanes in the heaven, and the fortunes of the proud family of Venoni must decline with it. Look to the west! Yon planet that shines so brightly in the night-sky, is the star of thy nativity. When next thou shalt behold it, shooting downward like a meteor through the hemisphere, think on the words of the prophet and tremble. A deed of blood will be done, and thou art he that shall perpetrate it!'

At this instant the moon peeped forth from the dun clouds that lagged slowly in the firmament, and shed a mild radiance upon the earth. To the west, a single bright star was visible. It was the star of Reginald's nativity. He gazed with eyes fixed in the breathless intensity of expectation, and watched it till the passing clouds concealed its radiance from his view. The Astrologer, in the meantime, had resumed his station at the window. He raised the horoscope to heaven. His frame seemed trembling with convulsion. Twice he passed his hand across his brow, and shuddered as he beheld the aspect of the heavens. 'But a few days,' he said, 'are yet left me on earth, and then shall my spirit know the eternal repose of the grave. The star of my nativity is dim and pale. It will never be bright again, and the aged one will never know comfort more. Away!' he continued, motioning Reginald from his sight, 'disturb not the last moments of a dying man; in three days return, and under the base of this ruin inter the corpse that you will find mouldering within. Away!'

Impressed with a strange awe, Reginald could make no reply. He remained as it were entranced; and after the lapse of a few minutes rushed from the tower, and returned in a state of disquietude to the gloomy château of his mother.

The three days had now elapsed, and, faithful to his promise, Reginald pursued his route back to the tower. He reached it at nightfall, and tremblingly entered the fatal apartment. All within was silent, but his steps returned a hollow echo as he passed. The wind sighed around the ruin, and the raven from the roofless turrets had already commenced his death-song. He entered. The Astrologer, as before, was seated by the window, apparently in profound abstraction, and the horoscope was placed by his side. Fearful of disturbing his repose, Reginald approached with caution. The old man stirred not. Emboldened by so unexpected a silence, he advanced and looked at the face of the Astrologer. It was a corpse he gazed on, – the relic of what had once been life. Petrified with horror at the sight, the memory of his former promise escaped him, and he rushed in agony from the apartment.

For many days the fever of his mind continued unabated. He frequently became delirious, and in the hour of his lunacy was accustomed to talk of an evil spirit that had visited him in his slumbers. His mother was shocked at such evident symptoms of derangement. She remembered the fate of her husband; and implored Reginald, as he valued her affection, to recruit the agitation of his spirits by travel. With some difficulty he was induced to quit the home of his infancy. The expostulations of the countess at last prevailed, and he left the Chateau Di Venoni for the sunny climes of Italy.

Time rolled on; and a constant succession of novelty had produced so beneficial an effect, that scarcely any traces remained of the once mysterious and enthusiastic Venoni. Occasionally his mind was disturbed and gloomy, but a perpetual recurrence of amusement diverted the influence of past recollection, and rendered him at least as tranquil as it was in the power of his nature to permit. He continued for years abroad, during which time he wrote frequently to his mother, who still continued at the Chateau Di Venoni, and at last announced his intention of settling finally at Venice. He had remained but a few months in the city, when, at the gay period of the Carnival, he was introduced, as a foreign nobleman, to the beautiful daughter of the Doge. She was amiable, accomplished, and endowed with every requisite to ensure permanent felicity. Reginald was charmed with her beauty, and infatuated with the excelling qualities of her mind. He confessed his attachment, and was informed with a blush that the affection was mutual. Nothing, therefore, remained but application to the Doge; who was instantly addressed on the subject, and implored to consummate the felicity of the young couple. The request was attended with success, and the happiness of the lovers was complete.

On the day fixed for the wedding, a brilliant assemblage of beauty thronged the ducal palace of St Mark. All Venice crowded to the festival; and, in the presence of the gayest noblemen of Italy, Reginald Count Di Venoni received the hand of Marcelia, the envied daughter of the Doge. In the evening, a masqued festival was given at the palace; but the young couple, anxious to be alone, escaped the scene of revelry, and hurried in their gondola to the château that was prepared for their reception.

It was a fine moonlight night. The mild beams of the planets sparkled on the silver bosom of the Adriatic, and the light tones of music, 'by distance made more sweet', came wafted on the western gale. A thousand lamps, from the illuminated squares of the city, reflected their burnished hues along the wave, and the mellow chaunt of the gondoliers kept time to the gentle splashing of their oars. The hearts of the lovers were full, and the witching spirit of the hour passed with all its loveliness into their souls. On a sudden a deep groan escaped the overcharged heart of Reginald. He had looked to the western hemisphere, and the star which, at that moment, flashed brightly in the horizon, reminded him of the awful scene which he had witnessed at the tower of Rudstein. His eye sparkled with delirious brilliancy; and had not a shower of tears come opportunely to his relief, the consequence might have been fatal. But the affectionate caresses of his young bride succeeded for the present in soothing his agitation, and restoring his mind to its former tranquil temperament.

A few months had now elapsed from the period of his marriage, and the heart of Reginald was happy. He loved Marcelia, and was tenderly beloved in return. Nothing, therefore, remained to complete his felicity but the presence of his mother, the Countess. He wrote accordingly to intreat that she would come and reside with him at Venice, but was informed by her confessor in reply, that she was dangerously ill, and requested the immediate attendance of her son. On the receipt of this afflicting intelligence he hurried with Marcelia to the Château Di Venoni. The countess was still alive when he entered, and received him with an affectionate embrace. But the exertion of so unexpected an interview with her son, was too great for the agitated spirits of the parent, and she expired in the act of folding him to her arms.

From this moment the mind of Reginald assumed a tone of the most confirmed dejection. He followed his mother to the grave, and was observed to smile with unutterable meaning as he returned home from the funeral. The Chateau Di Venoni increased the native depression of his spirits, and the appearance of the ruined tower never failed to imprint a dark frown upon his brow. He would wander for days from his home, and when he returned, the moody expression of his countenance alarmed the affection of his wife. She did all in her power to assuage his anguish, but his melancholy remained unabated. Sometimes, when the fit was on him, he would repulse her with fury; but, in his gentler moments, would gaze on her as on a sweet vision of vanished happiness.

He was one evening wandering with her through the village, when his conversation assumed a more dejected tone than usual. The sun was slowly setting, and their route back to the chateau lay through the churchyard where the ashes of the countess reposed. Reginald seated himself with Marcelia by the grave, and plucking a few wild flowers from the turf, exclaimed, 'Are you not anxious to join my mother, sweet girl? She has gone to the land of the blest – to the land of love and sunshine! If we are happy in this world, what will be our state of happiness in the next? Let us fly to unite our bliss with hers, and the measure of our joy will be full.' As he uttered these words his eye glared with delirium, and his hand seemed searching for a weapon. Marcelia, alarmed at his appearance, hurried him from the spot, and clasping his hand in hers, drew him gently onward.

The sun in the meantime had sunk, and the stars of evening came out in their glory. Brilliant above all shone the fatal western planet, the star of Reginald's nativity. He observed it with horror, and pointed it out to the notice of Marcelia. 'The hand of heaven is in it!' he mentally exclaimed, 'and the proud fortunes of Venoni hasten to a close.' At this instant the ruined tower of Rudstein appeared in sight, with the moon shining full upon it. 'It is the place,' resumed the maniac, 'where a deed of blood must be done, and I am he that must perpetrate it! But fear not,

my poor girl,' he added, in a milder tone, while the tears sprang to his
eyes, 'thy Reginald cannot harm thee; he may be wretched, but he never
shall be guilty!' With these words he reached the château, and threw
himself on his couch in restless anxiety of mind.

Night waned, morning dawned on the upland hills of the scenery, and
with it came a renewal of Reginald's disorder. The day was stormy, and
in unison with the troubled feeling of his spirit. He had been absent from
Marcelia since day break, and had given her no promise of return. But as
she was seated at twilight near the lattice, playing on her harp a favourite
Venetian canzonet, the folding doors flew open, and Reginald made his
appearance. His eye was red, with the deepest – the deadliest madness,
and his whole frame seemed unusually convulsed. ' 'Twas not a dream,'
he exclaimed, 'I have seen her and she has beckoned us to follow.' 'Seen
her, seen who?' said Marcelia, alarmed at his phrenzy. 'My mother,'
replied the maniac. 'Listen while I repeat the horrid narrative. Methought
as I was wandering in the forest, a sylph of heaven approached, and
revealed the countenance of my mother, I flew to join her but was
withheld by a sage who pointed to the western star. On a sudden loud
shrieks were heard, and the sylph assumed the guise of a demon. Her
figure towered to an awful height, and she pointed in scornful derision to
thee; yes, to thee, my Marcelia. With rage she drew thee towards me. I
seized – I murdered thee; and hollow groans broke on the midnight gale.
The voice of the fiendish Astrologer was heard shouting as from a charnel
house, "The destiny is accomplished, and the victim may retire with
honour." Then, methought, the fair front of heaven was obscured, and
thick gouts of clotted, clammy blood showered down in torrents from
the blackened clouds of the west. The star shot through the air, and – the
phantom of my mother again beckoned me to follow.'

The maniac ceased, and rushed in agony from the apartment. Marcelia
followed and discovered him leaning in a trance against the wainscot of
the library. With gentlest motion she drew his hand in hers, and led him
into the open air. They rambled on, heedless of the gathering storm,
until they discovered themselves at the base of the tower of Rudstein.
Suddenly the maniac paused. A horrid thought seemed flashing across his
brain, as with giant grasp he seized Marcelia in his arms, and bore her to
the fatal apartment. In vain she shrieked for help, for pity. 'Dear Reginald,
it is Marcelia who speaks, you cannot surely harm her.' He heard – he
heeded not, nor once staid his steps, till he reached the room of death. On
a sudden his countenance lost its wildness, and assumed a more fearful,
but composed look of determined madness. He advanced to the window,
and gazed on the stormy face of heaven. Dark clouds flitted across the

horizon, and hollow thunder echoed awfully in the distance. To the west the fatal star was still visible, but shone with sickly lustre. At this instant a flash of lightning re-illuminated the whole apartment, and threw a broad red glare upon a skeleton, that mouldered upon the floor. Reginald observed it with affright, and remembered the unburied Astrologer. He advanced to Marcelia, and pointing to the rising moon, 'A dark cloud is sailing by,' he shudderingly exclaimed, 'but ere the full orb again shines forth, thou shalt die, I will accompany thee in death, and hand in hand will we pass into the presence of our mother.' The poor girl shrieked for pity, but her voice was lost in the angry ravings of the storm. The cloud in the meantime sailed on, – it approached – the moon was dimmed, darkened, and finally buried in its gloom. The maniac marked the hour, and rushed with a fearful cry towards his victim. With murderous resolution he grasped her throat, while the helpless hand and half strangled articulation, implored his compassion. After one final struggle the hollow death rattle announced that life was extinct, and that the murderer held a corpse in his arms. An interval of reason now occurred, and on the partial restoration of his mind, Reginald discovered himself the unconscious murderer of Marcelia. Madness – deepest madness again took possession of his faculties. He laughed – he shouted aloud with the unearthly yellings of a fiend, and in the raging violence of his delirium, hurled himself headlong from the summit of the tower.

In the morning the bodies of the young couple were discovered, and buried in the same tomb. The fatal ruin of Rudstein still exists; but is now commonly avoided as the residence of the spirits of the departed. Day by day it slowly crumbles to earth, and affords a shelter for the night raven, or the wild beasts of the forests. Superstition has consecrated it to herself, and the tradition of the country has invested it with all the awful appendages of a charnel house. The wanderer who passes at night-fall, shudders while he surveys its utter desolation, and exclaims as he journies on, 'Surely this is a spot where guilt may thrive in safety, or bigotry weave a spell to enthrall her misguided votaries.'

The Expedition to Hell

James Hogg

There is no phenomenon in nature less understood, and about which greater nonsense is written than dreaming. It is a strange thing. For my part I do not understand it, nor have I any desire to do so; and I firmly believe that no philosopher that ever wrote knows a particle more about it than I do, however elaborate and subtle the theories he may advance concerning it. He knows not even what sleep is, nor can he define its nature, so as to enable any common mind to comprehend him; and how, then, can he define that ethereal part of it, wherein the soul holds intercourse with the external world? – how, in that state of abstraction, some ideas force themselves upon us, in spite of all our efforts to get rid of them; while others, which we have resolved to bear about with us by night as well as by day, refuse us their fellowship, even at periods when we most require their aid?

No, no; the philosopher knows nothing about either; and if he says he does; I entreat you not to believe him. He does not know what mind is; even his own mind, to which one would think he has the most direct access: far less can he estimate the operations and powers of that of any other intelligent being. He does not even know, with all his subtlety, whether it be a power distinct from his body, or essentially the same, and only incidentally and temporarily endowed with different qualities. He sets himself to discover at what period of his existence the union was established. He is baffled; for Consciousness refuses the intelligence, declaring, that she cannot carry him far enough back to ascertain it. He tries to discover the precise moment when it is dissolved, but on this Consciousness is altogether silent; and all is darkness and mystery; for the origin, the manner of continuance, and the time and mode of breaking up of the union between soul and body, are in reality undiscoverable by our natural faculties – are not patent,· beyond the possibility of mistake:

but whosoever can read his Bible, and solve a dream, can do either, without being subjected to any material error.

It is on this ground that I like to contemplate, not the theory of dreams, but the dreams themselves; because they prove to the unlettered man, in a very forcible manner, a distinct existence of the soul, and its lively and rapid intelligence with external nature, as well as with a world of spirits with which it has no acquaintance, when the body is lying dormant, and the same to the soul as if sleeping in death.

I account nothing of any dream that relates to the actions of the day; the person is not sound asleep who dreams about these things; there is no division between matter and mind, but they are mingled together in a sort of chaos – what a farmer would call compost – fermenting and disturbing one another. I find that in all dreams of that kind, men of every profession have dreams peculiar to their own occupations; and, in the country, at least, their import is generally understood. Every man's body is a barometer. A thing made up of the elements must be affected by their various changes and convulsions; and so the body assuredly is. When I was a shepherd, and all the comforts of my life depended so much on good or bad weather, the first thing I did every morning was strictly to overhaul the dreams of the night; and I found that I could calculate better from them than from the appearance and changes of the sky. I know a keen sportsman who pretends that his dreams never deceive him. If the dream is of angling, or pursuing salmon in deep waters, he is sure of rain; but if fishing on dry ground, or in waters so low that the fish cannot get from him, it forebodes drought; hunting or shooting hares is snow, and moorfowl wind, &c. But the most extraordinary professional dream on record is, without all doubt, that well-known one of George Dobson, coach-driver in Edinburgh, which I shall here relate; for though it did not happen in the shepherd's cot, it has often been recited there.

George was part proprietor and driver of a hackneycoach in Edinburgh, when such vehicles were scarce; and one day a gentleman, whom he knew, came to him and said: 'George, you must drive me and my son here out to —,' a certain place that he named, somewhere in the vicinity of Edinburgh.

'Sir,' said George, 'I never heard tell of such a place, and I cannot drive you to it unless you give me very particular directions.'

'It is false,' returned the gentleman; 'there is no man in Scotland who knows the road to that place better than you do. You have never driven on any other road all your life; and I insist on you taking us.'

'Very well, sir,' said George, 'I'll drive you to hell, if you have a mind; only you are to direct me on the road.'

'Mount and drive on, then,' said the other; 'and no fear of the road.'

George did so, and never in his life did he see his horses go at such a noble rate; they snorted, they pranced, and they flew on; and as the whole road appeared to lie down-hill, he deemed that he should soon come to his journey's end. Still he drove on at the same rate, far, far down-hill – and so fine an open road he never travelled – till by degrees it grew so dark that he could not see to drive any farther. He called to the gentleman, inquiring what he should do; who answered that this was the place they were bound to, so he might draw up, dismiss them, and return. He did so, alighted from the dickie, wondered at his foaming horses, and forthwith opened the coach-door, held the rim of his hat with the one hand and with the other demanded his fare.

'You have driven us in fine style, George,' said the elder gentleman, 'and deserve to be remembered; but it is needless for us to settle just now, as you must meet us here again tomorrow precisely at twelve o'clock.'

'Very well, sir,' said George; 'there is likewise an old account, you know, and some toll-money;' which indeed there was.

'It shall be all settled tomorrow, George, and moreover, I fear there will be some toll-money today.'

'I perceived no tolls today, your honour,' said George.

'But I perceived one, and not very far back neither, which I suspect you will have difficulty in repassing without a regular ticket. What a pity I have no change on me!'

'I never saw it otherwise with your honour,' said George, jocularly; 'what a pity it is you should always suffer yourself to run short of change!'

'I will give you that which is as good, George,' said the gentleman; and he gave him a ticket written with red ink, which the honest coachman could not read. He, however, put it into his sleeve, and inquired of his employer where that same toll was which he had not observed, and how it was that they did not ask from him as he came through? The gentleman replied, by informing George that there was no road out of that domain, and that whoever entered it must either remain in it, or return by the same path; so they never asked any toll till the person's return, when they were at times highly capricious; but that the ticket he had given him would answer his turn. And he then asked George if he did not perceive a gate, with a number of men in black standing about it.

'Oho! Is yon the spot?' says George; 'then, I assure your honour, yon is no toll-gate, but a private entrance into a great man's mansion; for do not I know two or three of the persons yonder to be gentlemen of the law, whom I have driven often and often? and as good fellows they are too as any I know – men who never let themselves run short of change! Good day – Twelve o'clock tomorrow?'

'Yes, twelve o'clock noon, precisely;' and with that, George's employer vanished in the gloom, and left him to wind his way out of that dreary labyrinth the best way he could. He found it no easy matter, for his lamps were not lighted, and he could not see a yard before him – he could not even perceive his horses' ears; and what was worse, there was a rushing sound, like that of a town on fire, all around him, that stunned his senses, so that he could not tell whether his horses were moving or standing still. George was in the greatest distress imaginable, and was glad when he perceived the gate before him, with his two identical friends, men of the law, still standing. George drove boldly up, accosted them by their names, and asked what they were doing there; they made him no answer, but pointed to the gate and the keeper. George was terrified to look at this latter personage, who now came up and seized his horses by the reins, refusing to let him pass. In order to introduce himself, in some degree, to this austere toll-man, George asked him, in a jocular manner, how he came to employ his two eminent friends as assistant gate-keepers?

'Because they are among the last comers,' replied the ruffian, churlishly. 'You will be an assistant here tomorrow.'

'The devil I will, sir.'

'Yes, the devil you will, sir.'

'I'll be d—d if I do then – that I will!'

'Yes, you'll be d—d if you do – that you will.'

'Let my horses go in the meantime, then, sir, that I may proceed on my journey.'

'Nay.'

'Nay! – Dare you say nay to me, sir? My name is George Dobson, of the Pleasance, Edinburgh, coach-driver, and coach-proprietor too; and no man shall say *nay* to me, as long as I can pay my way. I have his Majesty's licence, and I'll go and come as I choose – and that I will. Let go my horses there, and tell me what is your demand.'

'Well, then, I'll let your horses go,' said the keeper: 'But I'll keep yourself for a pledge.' And with that he let go the horses, and seized honest George by the throat, who struggled in vain to disengage himself, and swore, and threatened, according to his own confession, most bloodily. His horses flew off like the wind so swiftly, that the coach seemed flying in the air and scarcely bounding on the earth once in a quarter of a mile. George was in furious wrath, for he saw that his grand coach and harness would all be broken to pieces, and his gallant pair of horses maimed or destroyed; and how was his family's bread now to be won! – He struggled, threatened, and prayed in vain; – the intolerable toll-man was deaf to all remonstrances. He once more appealed to his two genteel acquaintances of the law, reminding them how he had of late driven them to Roslin on a Sunday, along with two ladies, who he supposed, were their sisters, from their familiarity, when not another coachman in town would engage with them. But the gentlemen, very ungenerously, only shook their heads, and pointed to the gate. George's circumstances now became desperate, and again he asked the hideous toll-man what right he had to detain him, and what were his charges.

'What right have I to detain you, sir, say you? Who are you that make such a demand here? Do you know where you are, sir?'

'No, faith, I do not,' returned George; 'I wish I did. But I *shall* know, and make you repent your insolence too. My name, I told you, is George Dobson, licensed coach-hirer in Pleasance, Edinburgh; and to get full redress of you for this unlawful interruption, I only desire to know where I am.'

'Then, sir, if it can give you so much satisfaction to know where you are,' said the keeper, with a malicious grin, 'you *shall* know, and you may take instruments by the hands of your two friends there instituting a legal prosecution. Your redress, you may be assured, will be most ample, when I inform you that you are in HELL! and out at this gate you pass no more.'

This was rather a damper to George, and he began to perceive that nothing would be gained in such a place by the strong hand, so he addressed the inexorable toll-man, whom he now dreaded more than ever, in the following terms: 'But I must go home at all events, you know, sir, to unyoke my two horses, and put them up, and to inform Chirsty Halliday my wife, of my engagement. And, bless me! I never recollected till this moment, that I am engaged to be back here tomorrow at twelve o'clock, and see, here is a free ticket for my passage this way.'

The keeper took the ticket with one hand, but still held George with the other. 'Oho! were you in with our honourable friend, Mr R— of L—y?' said he. 'He has been on our books for a long while; – however, this will do, only you must put your name to it likewise; and the engagement is this – You, by this instrument, engage your soul, that you will return here by tomorrow at noon.'

'Catch me there, billy!' says George. 'I'll engage no such thing, depend on it; – that I will not.'

'Then remain where you are,' said the keeper, 'for there is no other alternative. We like best for people to come here in their own way – in the way of their business;' and with that he flung George backwards, heels-over-head down hill, and closed the gate.

George finding all remonstrance vain, and being desirous once more to see the open day, and breathe the fresh air, and likewise to see Chirsty Halliday, his wife, and set his house and stable in some order, came up again, and in utter desperation signed the bond, and was suffered to depart. He then bounded away on the track of his horses with more than ordinary swiftness, in hopes to overtake them; and always now and then uttered a loud Wo! in hopes they might hear and obey, though he could not come in sight of them. But George's grief was but beginning; for at a well-known and dangerous spot, where there was a tan-yard on the one hand, and a quarry on the other, he came to his gallant steeds overturned, the coach smashed to pieces, Dawtie with two of her legs broken, and Duncan dead. This was more than the worthy coachman could bear, and many degrees worse than being in hell. There, his pride and manly spirit bore him up against the worst of treatment; but here his heart entirely failed him, and he laid himself down, with his face on his two hands, and wept bitterly, bewailing, in the most deplorable terms, his two gallant horses, Dawtie and Duncan.

While lying in this inconsolable state, some one took hold of his shoulder, and shook it; and a well-known voice said to him, 'Geordie! what is the matter wi' ye, Geordie?' George was provoked beyond measure at the insolence of the question, for he knew the voice to be that of Chirsty Halliday, his wife. 'I think you needna ask that, seeing what you see,' said George. 'O, my poor Dawtie, where are a' your jinkings and prancings now, your moopings and your wincings? I'll ne'er be a proud man again – bereaved o' my bonny pair!'

'Get up, George; get up, and bestir yourself,' said Chirsty Halliday, his wife. 'You are wanted directly to bring the Lord President to the Parliament House. It is a great storm, and he must be there by nine o'clock – Get up – rouse yourself, and make ready – his servant is waiting for you.'

'Woman, you are demented!' cried George. 'How can I go and bring in the Lord President, when my coach is broken in pieces, my poor Dawtie lying with twa of her legs broken, and Duncan dead? And, moreover, I have a previous engagement, for I am obliged to be in hell before twelve o'clock.'

Chirsty Halliday now laughed outright, and continued long in a fit of laughter; but George never moved his head from the pillow, but lay and groaned – for, in fact, he was all this while lying snug in his bed; while the tempest without was roaring with great violence, and which circumstance may perhaps account for the rushing and deafening sound which astounded him so much in hell. But so deeply was he impressed with the idea of the reality of his dream, that he would do nothing but lie and moan, persisting and believing in the truth of all he had seen. His wife now went and informed her neighbours of her husband's plight, and of his singular engagement with Mr R— of L—y at twelve o'clock. She persuaded one friend to harness the horses, and go for the Lord President; but all the rest laughed immoderately at poor coachy's predicament. It was, however, no laughing matter to him; he never raised his head, and his wife becoming uneasy about the frenzied state of his mind, made him repeat every circumstance of his adventure to her (for he would never believe or admit that it was a dream), which he did in the terms above narrated; and she perceived or dreaded that he was becoming somewhat feverish. She went out, and told Dr Wood of her husband's malady, and of his solemn engagement to be in hell at twelve o'clock.

'He maunna keep it, dearie. He maunna keep that engagement at no rate,' said Dr Wood. 'Set back the clock an hour or twa, to drive him past the time, and I'll ca' in the course of my rounds. Are ye sure he hasna been drinking hard?' She assured him he had not. 'Weel, weel, ye maun tell him that he maunna keep that engagement at no rate. Set back the clock, and I'll come and see him. It is a frenzy that maunna be trifled with. Ye maunna laugh at it, dearie – maunna laugh at it. Maybe a nervish fever, wha kens.'

The Doctor and Chirsty left the house together, and as their road lay the same way for a space, she fell a telling him of the two young lawyers whom George saw standing at the gate of hell, and whom the porter had described as two of the last comers. When the Doctor heard this, he stayed his hurried, stooping pace in one moment, turned full round on the woman, and fixing his eyes on her, that gleamed with a deep unstable lustre, he said, 'What's that ye were saying, dearie? What's that ye were saying? Repeat it again to me, every word.' She did so. On which the Doctor held up his hands, as if palsied with astonishment, and uttered some fervent ejaculations. 'I'll go with you straight,' said he, 'Before I visit another patient. This is wonderfu'! it is terrible! The young gentlemen are both at rest – both lying corpses at this time! Fine young men – I attended them both – died of the same exterminating disease – Oh, this is wonderful; this is wonderful!'

The Doctor kept Chirsty half running all the way down the High Street and St Mary's Wynd, at such a pace did he walk, never lifting his eyes from the pavement, but always exclaiming now and then, 'It is wonderfu' most wonderfu'!' At length, prompted by woman's natural curiosity,

Chirsty inquired at the Doctor if he knew any thing of their friend Mr R— of L—y. But he shook his head, and replied, 'Na, na, dearie – ken naething about him. He and his son are baith in London – ken naething about him; but the tither is awfu' – it is perfectly awfu'!'

When Dr Wood reached his patient he found him very low, but only a little feverish; so he made all haste to wash his head with vinegar and cold water, and then he covered the crown with a treacle plaster, and made the same application to the soles of his feet, awaiting the issue. George revived a little, when the Doctor tried to cheer him up by joking him about his dream; but on mention of that he groaned, and shook his head. 'So you are convinced, dearie, that it is nae dream?' said the Doctor.

'Dear sir, how could it be a dream?' said the patient. 'I was there in person, with Mr R— and his son; and see, here are the marks of the porter's fingers on my throat.' Dr Wood looked, and distinctly saw two or three red spots on one side of his throat, which confounded him not a little. 'I assure you, sir,' continued George, 'it was no dream, which I know to my sad experience. I have lost my coach and horses – and what more have I? – signed the bond with my own hand, and in person entered into the most solemn and terrible engagement.'

'But ye're no to keep it, I tell ye,' said Dr Wood; 'ye're no to keep it at no rate. It is a sin to enter into a compact wi' the deil, but it is a far greater ane to keep it. Sae let Mr R— and his son bide where they are yonder, for ye sanna stir a foot to bring them out the day.'

'Oh, oh, Doctor!' groaned the poor fellow, 'this is not a thing to be made a jest o'! I feel that it is an engagement that I cannot break. Go I must, and that very shortly. Yes, yes, go I must, and go I will, although I should borrow David Barclay's pair.' With that he turned his face towards the wall, groaned deeply, and fell into a lethargy, while Dr Wood caused them to let him alone, thinking if he would sleep out the appointed time, which was at hand, he would be safe; but all the time he kept feeling his pulse and by degrees showed symptoms of uneasiness. His wife ran for a clergyman of famed abilities, to pray and converse with her husband, in hopes by that means to bring him to his senses; but after his arrival, George never spoke more, save calling to his horses, as if encouraging them to run with great speed; and thus in imagination driving at full career to keep his appointment, he went off in a paroxysm, after a terrible struggle, precisely within a few minutes of twelve o'clock.

A circumstance not known at the time of George's death made this singular professional dream the more remarkable and unique in all its parts. It was a terrible storm on the night of the dream, as has been already mentioned, and during the time of the hurricane, a London smack went down off Wearmouth about three in the morning. Among the sufferers were the Hon. Mr R— of L—y, and his son! George could not know aught of this at break of day, for it was not known in Scotland till the day of his interment; and as little knew he of the deaths of the two young lawyers, who both died of the small-pox the evening before.

Mateo Falcone

Prosper Mérimée

On leaving Porto-Vecchio from the northwest and directing his steps towards the interior of the island, the traveller will notice that the land rises rapidly, and after three hours' walking over tortuous paths obstructed by great masses of rock and sometimes cut by ravines, he will find himself on the border of a great mâquis. The mâquis is the domain of the Corsican shepherds and of those who are at variance with justice. It must be known that, in order to save himself the trouble of manuring his field, the Corsican husbandman sets fire to a piece of woodland. If the flame spread farther than is necessary, so much the worse! In any case he is certain of a good crop from the land fertilized by the ashes of the trees which grow upon it. He gathers only the heads of his grain, leaving the straw, which it would be unnecessary labour to cut. In the following spring the roots that have remained in the earth without being destroyed send up their tufts of sprouts, which in a few years reach a height of seven or eight feet. It is this kind of tangled thicket that is called a mâquis. They are made up of different kinds of trees and shrubs, so crowded and mingled together at the caprice of nature that only with an axe in hand can a man open a passage so thick and bushy that the wild sheep themselves cannot penetrate them.

If you have killed a man, go into the mâquis of Porto-Vecchio. With a good gun and plenty of powder and balls, you can live there in safety. Do not forget a brown cloak furnished with a hood, which will serve you for both cover and mattress. The shepherds will give you chestnuts, milk and cheese, and you will have nothing to fear from justice nor the relatives of the dead except when it is necessary for you to descend to the city to replenish your ammunition.

When I was in Corsica in 18—, Mateo Falcone had his house half a league from this mâquis. He was rich enough for that country, living in noble style – that is to say, doing nothing – on the income from his flocks, which the shepherds, who are a kind of nomads, lead to pasture here and there on the mountains. When I saw him, two years after the event that I am about to relate, he appeared to me to be about fifty years old or more. Picture to yourself a man, small but robust, with curly hair, black as jet, an aquiline nose, thin lips, large, restless eyes, and a complexion the colour of tanned leather. His skill as a marksman was considered extraordinary even in his country, where good shots are so common. For example, Mateo would never fire at a sheep with buckshot; but at a hundred and twenty paces, he would drop it with a ball in the head or shoulder, as he chose. He used his arms as easily at night as during the day. I was told this feat of his skill, which will, perhaps, seem impossible to those who have not travelled in Corsica. A lighted candle was placed at eighty paces, behind a paper transparency about the size of a plate. He would take aim, then the candle would be extinguished, and, at the end of a moment, in the most complete darkness, he would fire and hit the paper three times out of four.

With such a transcendent accomplishment, Mateo Falcone had acquired a great reputation. He was said to be as good a friend as he was a dangerous enemy; accommodating and charitable, he lived at peace with all the world in the district of Porto-Vecchio. But it is said of him that in Corte, where he had married his wife, he had disembarrassed himself very vigorously of a rival who was considered as redoubtable in war as in love; at least, a certain gun-shot which surprised this rival as he was shaving before a little mirror hung in his window was attributed to Mateo. The affair was smoothed over and Mateo was married. His wife Giuseppa had given him at first three daughters (which infuriated him), and finally a son, whom he named Fortunato, and who became the hope of his family, the inheritor of the name. The daughters were well married: their father could count at need on the poignards and carbines of his sons-in-law. The son was only ten years old, but he already gave promise of fine attributes.

On a certain day in autumn, Mateo set out at an early hour with his wife to visit one of his flocks in a clearing of the mâquis. The little Fortunato wanted to go with them, but the clearing was too far away; moreover, it was necessary some one should stay to watch the house; therefore the father refused: it will be seen whether or not he had reason to repent.

He had been gone some hours, and the little Fortunato was tranquilly stretched out in the sun, looking at the blue mountains, and thinking that the next Sunday he was going to dine in the city with his uncle, the

Caporal, when he was suddenly interrupted in his meditations by the firing of a musket. He got up and turned to that side of the plain whence the noise came. Other shots followed, fired at irregular intervals, and each time nearer; at last, in the path which led from the plain to Mateo's house, appeared a man wearing the pointed hat of the mountaineers, bearded, covered with rags, and dragging himself along with difficulty by the support of his gun. He had just received a wound in his thigh.

This man was an outlaw, who, having gone to the town by night to buy powder, had fallen on the way into an ambuscade of Corsican light-infantry. After a vigorous defence he was fortunate in making his retreat, closely followed and firing from rock to rock. But he was only a little in advance of the soldiers, and his wound prevented him from gaining the mâquis before being overtaken.

He approached Fortunato and said: 'You are the son of Mateo Falcone?' – 'Yes.'

'I am Gianetto Saupiero. I am followed by the yellow-collars. Hide me, for I can go no farther.'

'And what will my father say if I hide you without his permission?'

'He will say that you have done well.'

'How do you know?'

'Hide me quickly; they are coming.'

'Wait till my father gets back.'

'How can I wait? Malediction! They will be here in five minutes. Come, hide me, or I will kill you.'

Fortunato answered him with the utmost coolness:

'Your gun is empty, and there are no more cartridges in your belt.'

'I have my stiletto.'

'But can you run as fast as I can?'

He gave a leap and put himself out of reach.

'You are not the son of Mateo Falcone! Will you then let me be captured before your house?'

The child appeared moved.

'What will you give me if I hide you?' said he, coming nearer.

The outlaw felt in a leather pocket that hung from his belt, and took out a five-franc piece, which he had doubtless saved to buy ammunition with. Fortunato smiled at the sight of the silver piece; he snatched it, and said to Gianetto:

'Fear nothing.'

Immediately he made a great hole in a pile of hay that was near the house. Gianetto crouched down in it and the child covered him in such a way that he could breathe without it being possible to suspect that the hay concealed a man. He bethought himself further, and, with the subtlety of a tolerably ingenious savage, placed a cat and her kittens on the pile, that it might not appear to have been recently disturbed. Then, noticing the traces of blood on the path near the house, he covered them carefully with dust, and, that done, he again stretched himself out in the sun with the greatest tranquillity.

A few moments afterwards, six men in brown uniforms with yellow collars, and commanded by an Adjutant, were before Mateo's door. This Adjutant was a distant relative of Falcone's. (In Corsica the degrees of relationship are followed much further than elsewhere.) His name was Tiodoro Gamba; he was an active man, much dreaded by the outlaws, several of whom he had already entrapped.

'Good day, little cousin,' said he, approaching Fortunato; 'how tall you have grown. Have you seen a man go past here just now?'

'Oh! I am not yet so tall as you, my cousin,' replied the child with a simple air.

'You soon will be. But haven't you seen a man go by here, tell me?'

'If I have seen a man go by?'

'Yes, a man with a pointed hat of black velvet, and a vest embroidered with red and yellow.'

'A man with a pointed hat, and a vest embroidered with red and yellow?'

'Yes, answer quickly, and don't repeat my questions?'

'This morning the curé passed before our door on his horse, Piero. He asked me how papa was, and I answered him –'

'Ah, you little scoundrel, you are playing sly! Tell me quickly which way Gianetto went? We are looking for him, and I am sure he took this path.'

'Who knows?'

'Who knows? It is I know that you have seen him.'

'Can any one see who passes when they are asleep?'

'You were not asleep, rascal; the shooting woke you up.'

'Then you believe, cousin, that your guns make so much noise? My father's carbine has the advantage of them.'

'The devil take you, you cursed little scapegrace! I am certain that you have seen Gianetto. Perhaps, even, you have hidden him. Come, comrades, go into the house and see if our man is there. He could only go on one foot, and the knave has too much good sense to try to reach the mâquis limping like that. Moreover, the bloody tracks stop here.'

'And what will papa say?' asked Fortunato with a sneer; 'what will he say if he knows that his house has been entered while he was away?'

'You rascal!' said the Adjutant, taking him by the ear, 'do you know that it only remains for me to make you change your tone? Perhaps you will speak differently after I have given you twenty blows with the flat of my sword.'

Fortunato continued to sneer.

'My father is Mateo Falcone,' said he with emphasis.

'You little scamp, you know very well that I can carry you off to Corte or to Bastia. I will make you lie in a dungeon, on straw, with your feet in shackles, and I will have you guillotined if you don't tell me where Gianetto is.'

The child burst out laughing at this ridiculous menace. He repeated: 'My father is Mateo Falcone.'

'Adjutant,' said one of the soldiers in a low voice, 'let us have no quarrels with Mateo.'

Gamba appeared evidently embarrassed. He spoke in an undertone with the soldiers who had already visited the house. This was not a very long operation, for the cabin of a Corsican consists only of a single square room, furnished with a table, some benches, chests, housekeeping utensils and those of the chase. In the meantime, little Fortunato petted his cat and seemed to take a wicked enjoyment in the confusion of the soldiers and of his cousin.

One of the men approached the pile of hay. He saw the cat, and gave the pile a careless thrust with his bayonet, shrugging his shoulders as if he felt that his precaution was ridiculous. Nothing moved; the boy's face betrayed not the slightest emotion.

The Adjutant and his troop were cursing their luck. Already they were looking in the direction of the plain, as if disposed to return by the way they had come, when their chief, convinced that menaces would produce no impression on Falcone's son, determined to make a last effort, and try the effect of caresses and presents.

'My little cousin,' said he, 'you are a very wide-awake little fellow. You will get along. But you are playing a naughty game with me; and if I wasn't afraid of making trouble for my cousin, Mateo, the devil take me! but I would carry you off with me.'

'Bah!'

'But when my cousin comes back I shall tell him about this, and he will whip you till the blood comes for having told such lies.'

'You don't say so!'

'You will see. But hold on! – be a good boy and I will give you something.'

'Cousin, let me give you some advice; if you wait much longer Gianetto will be in the mâquis and it will take a smarter man than you to follow him.'

The Adjutant took from his pocket a silver watch worth about ten crowns, and noticing that Fortunato's eyes sparkled at the sight of it, said, holding the watch by the end of its steel chain:

'Rascal! you would like to have such a watch as that hung around your neck, wouldn't you, and to walk in the streets of Porto-Vecchio proud as a peacock? People would ask you what time it was, and you would say: "Look at my watch." '

'When I am grown up, my uncle, the Caporal, will give me a watch.'

'Yes; but your uncle's little boy has one already; not so fine as this either. But then, he is younger than you.'

The child sighed.

'Well! Would you like this watch, little cousin?'

Fortunato, casting sidelong glances at the watch, resembled a cat that has been given a whole chicken. It feels that it is being made sport of, and does not dare to use its claws; from time to time it turns its eyes away so as not to be tempted, licking its jaws all the while, and has the appearance of saying to its master, 'How cruel your joke is!'

However, the Adjutant seemed in earnest in offering his watch. Fortunato did not reach out his hand for it, but said with a bitter smile:

'Why do you make fun of me?'

'Good God! I am not making fun of you. Only tell me where Gianetto is and the watch is yours.'

Fortunato smiled incredulously, and fixing his black eyes on those of the Adjutant tried to read there the faith he ought to have had in his words.

'May I lose my epaulets,' cried the Adjutant, 'if I do not give you the watch on this condition. These comrades are witnesses; I can not deny it.'

While speaking he gradually held the watch nearer till it almost touched the child's pale face, which plainly showed the struggle that was going on in his soul between covetousness and respect for hospitality. His breast swelled with emotion; he seemed about to suffocate. Meanwhile the watch was slowly swaying and turning, sometimes brushing against his cheek. Finally, his right hand was gradually stretched towards it; the ends of his fingers touched it; then its whole weight was in his hand, the Adjutant still keeping hold of the chain. The face was light blue; the cases newly burnished. In the sunlight it seemed to be all on fire. The temptation was too great. Fortunato raised his left hand and pointed over his shoulder with his thumb at the hay against which he was reclining. The Adjutant understood him at once. He dropped the end of the chain and Fortunato felt himself the sole possessor of the watch. He sprang up with the agility of a deer and stood ten feet from the pile, which the soldiers began at once to overturn.

There was a movement in the hay, and a bloody man with a poignard in his hand appeared. He tried to rise to his feet, but his stiffened leg would not permit it and he fell. The Adjutant at once grappled with him and took away his stiletto. He was immediately secured, notwithstanding his resistance.

Gianetto, lying on the earth and bound like a faggot, turned his head towards Fortunato, who had approached.

'Son of —!' said he, with more contempt than anger.

The child threw him the silver piece which he had received, feeling that he no longer deserved it; but the outlaw paid no attention to the movement, and with great coolness said to the Adjutant:

'My dear Gamba, I cannot walk; you will be obliged to carry me to the city.'

'Just now you could run faster than a buck,' answered the cruel captor; 'but be at rest. I am so pleased to have you that I would carry you a league on my back without fatigue. Besides, comrade, we are going to make a litter for you with your cloak and some branches, and at the Crespoli farm we shall find horses.'

'Good,' said the prisoner. 'You will also put a little straw on your litter that I may be more comfortable.'

While some of the soldiers were occupied in making a kind of stretcher out of some chestnut boughs and the rest were dressing Gianetto's wound, Mateo Falcone and his wife suddenly appeared at a turn in the path that led to the mâquis. The woman was staggering under the weight of an enormous sack of chestnuts, while her husband was sauntering along, carrying one gun in his hands, while another was slung across his shoulders, for it is unworthy of a man to carry other burdens than his arms.

At the sight of the soldiers Mateo's first thought was that they had come to arrest him. But why this thought? Had he then some quarrels with justice? No. He enjoyed a good reputation. He was said to have a particularly good name, but he was a Corsican and a highlander, and there are few Corsican highlanders who, in scrutinizing their memory, can not find some peccadillo, such as a gun-shot, dagger-thrust, or similar trifles. Mateo more than others had a clear conscience; for more than ten years he had not pointed his carbine at a man, but he was always prudent, and put himself into a position to make a good defence if necessary. 'Wife,' said he to Giuseppa, 'put down the sack and hold yourself ready.'

She obeyed at once. He gave her the gun that was slung across his shoulders, which would have bothered him, and, cocking the one he held in his hands, advanced slowly towards the house, walking among the trees that bordered the road, ready at the least hostile demonstration, to hide behind the largest, whence he could fire from under cover. His wife followed closely behind, holding his reserve weapon and his cartridge-box. The duty of a good housekeeper, in case of a fight, is to load her husband's carbines.

On the other side the Adjutant was greatly troubled to see Mateo advance in this manner, with cautious steps, his carbine raised, and his finger on the trigger.

'If by chance,' thought he, 'Mateo should be related to Gianetto, or if he should be his friend and wish to defend him, the contents of his two guns would arrive amongst us as certainly as a letter in the post; and if he should see me, notwithstanding the relationship!'

In this perplexity he took a bold step. It was to advance alone towards Mateo and tell him of the affair while accosting him as an old acquaintance, but the short space that separated him from Mateo seemed terribly long.

'Hello! old comrade,' cried he. 'How do you do, my good fellow? It is I, Gamba, your cousin.'

Without answering a word, Mateo stopped, and in proportion as the other spoke, slowly raised the muzzle of his gun so that it was pointing upward when the Adjutant joined him.

'Good day, brother,' said the Adjutant, holding out his hand. 'It is a long time since I have seen you.'

'Good day, brother.'

'I stopped while passing, to say good day to you and to cousin Pepa here. We have had a long journey today, but have no reason to complain, for we have captured a famous prize. We have just seized Gianetto Saupiero.'

'God be praised!' cried Giuseppa. 'He stole a milch goat from us last week.'

These words reassured Gamba.

'Poor devil!' said Mateo, 'he was hungry.'

'The villain fought like a lion,' continued the Adjutant, a little mortified. 'He killed one of my soldiers, and not content with that, broke Caporal Chardon's arm; but that matters little, he is only a Frenchman. Then, too, he was so well hidden that the devil couldn't have found him. Without my little cousin, Fortunato, I should never have discovered him.'

'Fortunato!' cried Mateo.

'Fortunato!' repeated Giuseppa.

'Yes, Gianetto was hidden under the hay-pile yonder, but my little cousin showed me the trick. I shall tell his uncle, the Caporal, that he may send him a fine present for his trouble. Both his name and yours will be in the report that I shall send to the Attorney-general.'

'Malediction!' said Mateo in a low voice.

They had rejoined the detachment. Gianetto was already lying on the litter ready to set out. When he saw Mateo and Gamba in company he smiled a strange smile, then, turning his head towards the door of the house, he spat on the sill, saying:

'House of a traitor.'

Only a man determined to die would dare pronounce the word traitor to Falcone. A good blow with the stiletto, which there would be no need of repeating, would have immediately paid the insult. However, Mateo made no other movement than to place his hand on his forehead like a man who is dazed.

Fortunato had gone into the house when his father arrived, but now he reappeared with a bowl of milk which he handed with downcast eyes to Gianetto.

'Get away from me!' cried the outlaw, in a loud voice. Then, turning to one of the soldiers, he said:

'Comrade, give me a drink.'

The soldier placed his gourd in his hands, and the prisoner drank the water handed to him by a man with whom he had just exchanged bullets. He then asked them to tie his hands across his breast instead of behind his back.

'I like,' said he, 'to lie at my ease.'

They hastened to satisfy him; then the Adjutant gave the signal to start, said adieu to Mateo, who did not respond, and descended with rapid steps towards the plain.

Nearly ten minutes elapsed before Mateo spoke. The child looked with restless eyes, now at his mother, now at his father, who was leaning on his gun and gazing at him with an expression of concentrated rage.

'You begin well,' said Mateo at last with a calm voice, but frightful to one who knew the man.

'Oh, father!' cried the boy, bursting into tears, and making a forward movement as if to throw himself on his knees. But Mateo cried, 'Away from me!'

The little fellow stopped and sobbed, immovable, a few feet from his father.

Giuseppa drew near. She had just discovered the watchchain, the end of which was hanging out of Fortunato's jacket.

'Who gave you that watch?' demanded she in a severe tone.

'My cousin, the Adjutant.'

Falcone seized the watch and smashed it in a thousand pieces against a rock.

'Wife,' said he, 'is this my child?'

Giuseppa's cheeks turned a brick-red.

'What are you saying, Mateo? Do you know to whom you speak?'

'Very well, this child is the first of his race to commit treason.'

Fortunato's sobs and gasps redoubled as Falcone kept his lynx-eyes upon him. Then he struck the earth with his gunstock, shouldered the weapon, and turned in the direction of the mâquis, calling to Fortunato to follow. The boy obeyed. Giuseppa hastened after Mateo and seized his arm.

'He is your son,' said she with a trembling voice, fastening her black eyes on those of her husband to read what was going on in his heart.

'Leave me alone,' said Mateo, 'I am his father.'

Giuseppa embraced her son, and bursting into tears entered the house. She threw herself on her knees before an image of the Virgin and prayed ardently. In the meanwhile Falcone walked some two hundred paces along the path and only stopped when he reached a little ravine which he descended. He tried the earth with the butt-end of his carbine, and found it soft and easy to dig. The place seemed to be convenient for his design.

'Fortunato, go close to that big rock there.'

The child did as he was commanded, then he kneeled.

'Say your prayers.'

'Oh, father, father, do not kill me!'

'Say your prayers!' repeated Mateo in a terrible voice.

The boy, stammering and sobbing, recited the Pater and the Credo. At the end of each prayer the father loudly answered, 'Amen!'

'Are those all the prayers you know?'

'Oh! father, I know the Ave Maria and the litany that my aunt taught me.'

'It is very long, but no matter.'

The child finished the litany in a scarcely audible tone.

'Are you finished?'

'Oh! my father, have mercy! Pardon me! I will never do so again. I will beg my cousin, the Caporal, to pardon Gianetto.'

He was still speaking. Mateo raised his gun, and, taking aim, said:

'May God pardon you!'

The boy made a desperate effort to rise and grasp his father's knees, but there was not time. Mateo fired and Fortunato fell dead.

Without casting a glance on the body, Mateo returned to the house for a spade with which to bury his son. He had gone but a few steps when he met Giuseppa, who, alarmed by the shot, was hastening hither.

'What have you done?' cried she.

'Justice.'

'Where is he?'

'In the ravine. I am going to bury him. He died a Christian. I shall have a mass said for him. Have my son-in-law, Tiodoro Bianchi, sent for to come and live with us.'

The Case of M. Valdemar

Edgar Allan Poe

Of course I shall not pretend to consider it any matter for wonder, that the extraordinary case of M. Valdemar has excited discussion. It would have been a miracle had it not – especially under the circumstances. Through the desire of all parties concerned, to keep the affair from the public, at least for the present, or until we had further opportunities for investigation – through our endeavours to effect this – a garbled or exaggerated account made its way into society, and became the source of many unpleasant misrepresentations, and, very naturally, of a great deal of disbelief.

It is now rendered necessary that I give the *facts* – as far as I comprehend them myself. They are, succinctly, these:

My attention, for the last three years, had been repeatedly drawn to the subject of Mesmerism; and, about nine months ago, it occurred to me, quite suddenly, that in the series of experiments made hitherto, there had been a very remarkable and most unaccountable omission: – no person had as yet been mesmerized *in articulo mortis*. It remained to be seen, first, whether, in such condition, there existed in the patient any susceptibility to the magnetic influence; secondly, whether, if any existed, it was impaired or increased by the condition; thirdly, to what extent, or for how long a period, the encroachments of Death might be arrested by the process. There were other points to be ascertained, but these most excited my curiosity – the last one especially, from the immensely important character of its consequences.

In looking around me for some subject by whose means I might test these particulars, I was brought to think of my friend, M. Ernest Valdemar, the well-known compiler of the *Bibliotheca Forensica*, and author (under the *nom de plume* of Issachar Marx) of the Polish versions of *Wallenstein* and *Gargantua*. M. Valdemar, who has resided principally at Haarlem, N.Y., since the year 1839, is (or was) particularly noticeable for the extreme spareness of his person – his lower limbs much resembling those of John Randolph; and, also, for the whiteness of his whiskers, in violent contrast to the blackness of his hair – the latter, in consequence, being very generally mistaken for a wig. His temperament was markedly nervous, and rendered him a good subject for mesmeric experiment. On two or three occasions I had put him to sleep with little difficulty, but was disappointed in other results which his peculiar constitution had naturally led me to anticipate. His will was at no period positively, or thoroughly, under my control, and in regard to *clairvoyance*, I could accomplish with him nothing to be relied upon. I always attributed my failure at these points to the disordered state of his health. For some months previous to my becoming acquainted with him, his physicians had declared him in a confirmed phthisis. It was his custom, indeed, to speak calmly of his approaching dissolution, as of a matter neither to be avoided nor regretted.

When the ideas to which I have alluded first occurred to me, it was of course very natural that I should think of M. Valdemar. I knew the steady philosophy of the man too well to apprehend any scruples from *him*; and he had no relatives in America who would be likely to interfere. I spoke to him frankly upon the subject; and, to my surprise, his interest seemed vividly excited. I say to my surprise; for, although he had always yielded his person freely to my experiments, he had never before given me any tokens of sympathy with what I did. His disease was of that character which would admit of exact calculation in respect to the epoch of its termination in death; and it was finally arranged between us that he would send for me about twenty-four hours before the period announced by his physicians as that of his decease.

It is now rather more than seven months since I received, from M. Valdemar himself, the subjoined note:

My Dear P—,

You may as well come now. D— and F— are agreed that I cannot hold out beyond tomorrow midnight; and I think they have hit the time very nearly.

Valdemar

I received this note within half an hour after it was written, and in fifteen minutes more I was in the dying man's chamber. I had not seen him for ten days, and was appalled by the fearful alteration which the brief interval had wrought in him. His face wore a leaden hue; the eyes were utterly lustreless; and the emaciation was so extreme that the skin had been broken through by the cheek-bones. His expectoration was excessive. The pulse was barely perceptible. He retained, nevertheless, in a very remarkable manner, both his mental power and a certain degree of physical strength. He spoke with distinctness – took some palliative medicines without aid – and, when I entered the room was occupied in pencilling memoranda in a pocket-book. He was propped up in the bed by pillows. Doctors D— and F— were in attendance.

After pressing Valdemar's hand, I took these gentlemen aside, and obtained from them a minute account of the patient's condition. The left lung had been for eighteen months in a semi-osseous or cartilaginous state, and was, of course, entirely useless for all purposes of vitality. The right, in its upper portion, was also partially, if not thoroughly, ossified, while the lower region was merely a mass of purulent tubercles, running one into another. Several extensive perforations existed; and, at one point, permanent adhesion to the ribs had taken place. These appearances in the right lobe were of comparatively recent date. The ossification had proceeded with very unusual rapidity; no sign of it had been discovered a month before, and the adhesion had only been observed during the three previous days. Independently of the phthisis, the patient was suspected of aneurism of the aorta; but on this point the osseous symptoms rendered an exact diagnosis impossible. It was the opinion of both physicians that M. Valdemar would die about midnight on the morrow (Sunday). It was then seven o'clock on Saturday evening.

On quitting the invalid's bedside to hold conversation with myself, Doctors D— and F— had bidden him a final farewell. It had not been their intention to return; but, at my request, they agreed to look in upon the patient about ten the next night.

When they had gone, I spoke freely with M. Valdemar on the subject of his approaching dissolution, as well as, more particularly, of the experiment proposed. He still professed himself quite willing and even anxious to have it made, and urged me to commence it at once. A male and a female nurse were in attendance; but I did not feel myself altogether at liberty to engage in a task of this character with no more reliable witnesses than these people, in case of sudden accident, might prove. I therefore postponed operations until about eight the next night, when the arrival of a medical student with whom I had some acquaintance (Mr Theodore L—l), relieved me from further embarrassment. It had been my design, originally, to wait for the physicians; but I was induced to proceed, first by the urgent entreaties of M. Valdemar, and secondly, by my conviction that I had not a moment to lose, as he was evidently sinking fast.

Mr L—l was so kind as to accede to my desire that he would take notes of all that occurred; and it is from his memoranda that what I now have to relate is, for the most part, either condensed or copied *verbatim*.

It wanted about five minutes to eight when, taking the patient's hand, I begged him to state, as distinctly as he could, to Mr L—l, whether he (M. Valdemar) was entirely willing that I should make the experiment of mesmerizing him in his then condition.

He replied feebly, yet quite audibly, 'Yes, I wish to be mesmerized' – adding immediately afterwards, 'I fear you have deferred it too long.'

While he spoke thus, I commenced the passes which I had already found most effectual in subduing him. He was evidently influenced with the first lateral stroke of my hand across his forehead; but although I exerted all my powers, no further perceptible effect was induced until some minutes after ten o'clock, when Doctors D— and F— called, according to appointment. I explained to them, in a few words, what I designed, and as they opposed no objection, saying that the patient was already in the death agony, I proceeded without hesitation – exchanging, however, the lateral passes for downward ones, and directing my gaze entirely into the right eye of the sufferer.

By this time his pulse was imperceptible and his breathing was stertorous, and at intervals of half a minute.

This condition was nearly unaltered for a quarter of an hour. At the expiration of this period, however, a natural although a very deep sigh escaped the bosom of the dying man, and the stertorous breathing ceased – that is to say, its stertorousness was no longer apparent; the intervals were undiminished. The patient's extremities were of an icy coldness.

At five minutes before eleven I perceived unequivocal signs of the mesmeric influence. The glassy roll of the eye was changed for that expression of uneasy *inward* examination which is never seen except in cases of sleep-waking, and which it is quite impossible to mistake. With a few rapid lateral passes I made the lids quiver, as in incipient sleep, and with a few more I closed them altogether. I was not satisfied, however, with this, but continued the manipulation vigorously, and with the fullest exertion of the will, until I had completely stiffened the limbs of the slumberer, after placing them in a seemingly easy position. The legs were at full length; the arms were nearly so, and reposed on the bed at a moderate distance from the loins. The head was very slightly elevated.

When I had accomplished this, it was fully midnight, and I requested the gentlemen present to examine M. Valdemar's condition. After a few experiments, they admitted him to be in an unusually perfect state of mesmeric trance. The curiosity of both the physicians was greatly excited. Dr D— resolved at once to remain with the patient all night, while Dr

F— took leave with a promise to return at daybreak. Mr L—l and the nurse remained.

We left M. Valdemar entirely undisturbed until about three o'clock in the morning, when I approached him and found him in precisely the same condition as when Dr F— went away – that is to say, he lay in the same position; the pulse was imperceptible; the breathing was gentle (scarcely noticeable, unless through the application of a mirror to the lips); the eyes were closed naturally; and the limbs were as rigid and as cold as marble. Still, the general appearance was certainly not that of death.

As I approached M. Valdemar I made a kind of half effort to influence his right arm into pursuit of my own, as I passed the latter gently to and fro above his person. In such experiments with this patient I had never perfectly succeeded before, and assuredly I had little thought of succeeding now; but to my astonishment, his arm very readily, although feebly, followed every direction I assigned it with mine. I determined to hazard a few words of conversation.

'M. Valdemar,' I said, 'are you asleep?' He made no answer, but I perceived a tremor about the lips, and was thus induced to repeat the question, again and again. At its third repetition, his whole frame was agitated by a very slight shivering; the eyelids unclosed themselves so far as to display a white line of the bell; the lips moved sluggishly, and from between them, in a barely audible whisper, issued the words:

'Yes; asleep now. Do not wake me – let me die so!'

I here felt the limbs and found them as rigid as ever. The right arm, as before, obeyed the direction of my hand. I questioned the sleep-waker again:

'Do you still feel pain in the breast, M. Valdemar?'

The answer now was immediate, but even less audible than before:

'No pain – I am dying.'

I did not think it advisable to disturb him further just then, and nothing more was said or done until the arrival of Dr F—, who came a little before sunrise, and expressed unbounded astonishment at finding the patient still alive. After feeling the pulse and applying a mirror to the lips, he requested me to speak to the sleep-waker again. I did so, saying:

'M. Valdemar, do you still sleep?'

As before, some minutes elapsed ere a reply was made; and during the interval the dying man seemed to be collecting his energies to speak. At my fourth repetition of the question, he said very faintly, almost inaudibly:

'Yes; still asleep – dying.'

It was now the opinion, or rather the wish, of the physicians that M.

Valdemar should be suffered to remain undisturbed in his present apparently tranquil condition, until death should supervene – and this, it was generally agreed, must now take place within a few minutes. I concluded, however, to speak to him once more, and merely repeated my previous question.

While I spoke, there came a marked change over the countenance of the sleep-waker. The eyes rolled themselves slowly open, the pupils disappearing upwardly; the skin generally assumed a cadaverous hue, resembling not so much parchment as white paper; and the circular hectic spots which, hitherto, had been strongly defined in the centre of each cheek, *went out* at once. I use this expression, because the suddenness of their departure put me in mind of nothing so much as the extinguishment of a candle by a puff of the breath. The upper lip, at the same time, writhed itself away from the teeth, which it had previously covered completely; while the lower jaw fell with an audible jerk, leaving the mouth widely extended, and disclosing in full view the swollen and blackened tongue. I presumed that no member of the party then present had been unaccustomed to death-bed horrors; but so hideous beyond conception was the appearance of M. Valdemar at this moment that there was a general shrinking back from the region of the bed.

I now feel that I have reached a point of this narrative at which every reader will be startled into positive disbelief. It is my business, however, simply to proceed.

There was no longer the faintest sign of vitality in M. Valdemar; and concluding him to be dead, we were consigning him to the charge of the nurses, when a strong vibratory motion was observable in the tongue. This continued for perhaps a minute. At the expiration of this period, there issued from the distended and motionless jaws a voice – such as it would be madness in me to attempt describing. There are, indeed, two or three epithets which might be considered as applicable to it in parts; I might say, for example, that the sound was harsh, and broken, and hollow; but the hideous whole is indescribable, for the simple reason that no similar sounds have ever jarred upon the ear of humanity. There were two particulars, nevertheless, which I thought then, and still think, might fairly be stated as characteristic of the intonation – as well adapted to convey some idea of its unearthly peculiarity. In the first place, the voice seemed to reach our ears – at least mine – from a vast distance, or from some deep cavern within the earth. In the second place, it impressed me (I fear, indeed, that it will be impossible to make myself comprehended) as gelatinous or glutinous matters impress the sense of touch.

I have spoken both of 'sound' and of 'voice'. I mean to say that the sound was one of distinct – of even wonderfully, thrillingly distinct – syllabification. M. Valdemar *spoke* – obviously in reply to the question I had propounded to him a few minutes before. I had asked him, it will be remembered, if he slept. He now said:

'Yes; no; I *have been* sleeping – and now – now – *I am dead.*'

No person present even affected to deny, or attempted to repress, the unutterable shuddering horror which these few words, thus uttered, were so calculated to convey. Mr L—l (the student) swooned. The nurses immediately left the chamber, and could not be induced to return. My own impressions I would not pretend to render intelligible to the reader. For nearly an hour we busied ourselves, silently – without the utterance of a word – in endeavours to revive Mr L—l. When he came to himself, we addressed ourselves again to an investigation of M. Valdemar's condition.

It remained in all respects as I have last described it, with the exception that the mirror no longer afforded evidence of respiration. An attempt to draw blood from the arm failed. I should mention, too, that this limb was no further subject to my will. I endeavoured in vain to make it follow the direction of my hand. The only real indication, indeed, of the mesmeric influence was now found in the vibratory movement of the tongue whenever I addressed M. Valdemar a question. He seemed to be making an effort to reply, but had no longer sufficient volition. To queries put to him by any other person than myself he seemed utterly insensible – although I endeavoured to place each member of the company in mesmeric *rapport* with him. I believe that I have now related all that is necessary to an understanding of the sleep-waker's state at this epoch. Other nurses were procured, and at ten o'clock I left the house in company with the two physicians and Mr L—l.

In the afternoon we all called again to see the patient. His condition remained precisely the same. We had now some discussion as the propriety and feasibility of awakening him; but we had little difficulty in agreeing that no good purpose would be served by so doing. It was evident that, so far, death (or what is usually termed death) had been arrested by the mesmeric process. It seemed clear to us all that to awaken M. Valdemar would be merely to insure his instant, or at least his speedy dissolution.

From this period until the close of last week – *an interval of nearly seven months* – we continued to make daily calls at M. Valdemar's house, accompanied now and then by medical and other friends. All this time the sleep-waker remained *exactly* as I have last described him. The nurses' attentions were continual.

It was on Friday last that we finally resolved to make the experiment of awakening, or attempting to awaken him; and it is the (perhaps) unfortunate result of this latter experiment which has given rise to so much discussion in private circles – to so much of what I cannot help thinking unwarranted popular feeling.

For the purpose of relieving M. Valdemar from the mesmeric trance, I made use of the customary passes. These, for a time, were unsuccessful. The first indication of revival was afforded by a partial descent of the iris. It was observed, as especially remarkable, that this lowering of the pupil was accompanied by the profuse outflowing of a yellowish ichor (from beneath the lids) of a pungent and highly offensive odour.

It was now suggested that I should attempt to influence the patient's arm, as heretofore. I made the attempt and failed. Dr F— then intimated a desire to have me put a question. I did so, as follows:

'M. Valdemar, can you explain to us what are your feelings or wishes now?'

There was an instant return of the hectic circles on the cheeks; the tongue quivered, or rather rolled violently in the mouth (although the jaws and lips remained rigid as before); and at length the same hideous voice which I have already described broke forth:

'For God's sake! – quick! – quick! – put me to sleep – or, quick! – waken me! – quick! *I say to you that I am dead!*'

I was thoroughly unnerved, and for an instant remained undecided what to do. At first I made an endeavour to re-compose the patient; but, failing in this through total abeyance of the will, I retraced my steps and as earnestly struggled to awaken him. In this attempt I soon saw that I should be successful – or at least I soon fancied that my success would be complete – and I am sure that all in the room were prepared to see the patient awaken.

For what really occurred, however, it is quite impossible that any human being could have been prepared.

As I rapidly made the mesmeric passes, amid ejaculations of 'dead! dead!' absolutely *bursting* from the tongue and not from the lips of the sufferer, his whole frame at once – within the space of a single minute, or even less, shrunk – crumbled – absolutely *rotted* away beneath my hands. Upon the bed, before that whole company, there lay a nearly liquid mass of loathsome – of detestable putridity.

La Grande Bretêche

Honoré de Balzac

'Ah! madame,' replied the doctor, 'I have some appalling stories in my collection. But each one has its proper hour in a conversation – you know the pretty jest recorded by Chamfort, and said to the Duc de Fronsac: "Between your sally and the present moment lie ten bottles of champagne." '

'But it is two in the morning, and the story of Rosina has prepared us,' said the mistress of the house.

'Tell us, Monsieur Bianchon!' was the cry on every side.

The obliging doctor bowed, and silence reigned.

'At about a hundred paces from Vendôme, on the banks of the Loire,' said he, 'stands an old brown house, crowned with very high roofs, and so completely isolated that there is nothing near it, not even a fetid tannery or a squalid tavern, such as are commonly seen outside small towns. In front of this house is a garden down to the river, where the box shrubs, formerly clipped close to edge the walks, now straggle at their own will. A few willows, rooted in the stream, have grown up quickly like an enclosing fence, and half hide the house. The wild plants we call weeds have clothed the bank with their beautiful luxuriance. The fruit-trees, neglected for these ten years past, no longer bear a crop, and their suckers have formed a thicket. The espaliers are like a copse. The paths, once gravelled, are overgrown with purslane; but, to be accurate, there is no trace of a path.

'Looking down from the hill-top, to which cling the ruins of the old castle of the Dukes of Vendôme, the only spot whence the eye can see into this enclosure, we think that at a time, difficult now to determine, this spot of earth must have been the joy of some country gentleman devoted to roses and tulips, in a word, to horticulture, but above all a lover of choice fruit. An arbour is visible, or rather the wreck of an arbour, and under it a table still stands, not entirely destroyed by time. From the aspect of this garden that is no more, the negative joys of the peaceful life of the provinces may be divined as we divine the history of a worthy tradesman when we read the epitaph on his tomb. To complete the mournful and tender impressions which seize the soul, on one of the walls there is a sundial graced with this homely Christian motto, "Ultimam cogita".

'The roof of this house is dreadfully dilapidated; the outside shutters are always closed; the balconies are hung with swallows' nests; the doors are for ever shut. Straggling grasses have outlined the flagstones of the steps with green; the ironwork is rusty. Moon and sun, winter, summer, and snow have eaten into the wood, warped the boards, peeled off the paint. The dreary silence is broken only by birds and cats, pole-cats, rats, and mice, free to scamper round, and fight, and eat each other. An invisible hand has written over it all: "Mystery".

'If, prompted by curiosity, you go to look at this house from the street, you will see a large gate, with a round-arched top; the children have made many holes in it. I learned later that this door had been blocked for ten years. Through these irregular breaches you will see that the side towards the courtyard is in perfect harmony with the side towards the garden. The same ruin prevails. Tufts of weeds outline the paving stones; the walls are scored by enormous cracks, and the blackened coping is laced with a thousand festoons of pellitory. The stone steps are disjointed; the bell-cord is rotten; the gutter-spouts broken. What fire from heaven can have fallen there? By what decree has salt been sown on this dwelling? Has God been mocked here? Or was France betrayed? These are the questions we ask ourselves. Reptiles crawl over it, but give no reply. This empty and deserted house is a vast enigma of which the answer is known to none.

'It was formerly a little domain, held in fief, and is known as La Grande Bretêche. During my stay at Vendôme, where Despleins had left me in charge of a rich patient, the sight of this strange dwelling became one of my keenest pleasures. Was it not far better than a ruin? Certain memories of indisputable authenticity attach themselves to a ruin; but this house, still standing, though being slowly destroyed by an avenging hand, contained a secret, an unrevealed thought. At the very least it testified to a caprice. More than once in the evening I attacked the hedge, run wild, which surrounded the enclosure. I braved scratches, I got into this ownerless garden, this plot which was no longer public or private; I lingered there for hours gazing at the disorder. I would not, as the price of the story to which this strange scene no doubt was due, have asked a single question of any gossiping native. On that spot I wove delightful romances, and abandoned myself to little debauches of melancholy which enchanted me. If I had known the reason – perhaps quite commonplace – of this neglect, I should have lost the unwritten poetry which intoxicated me. To me this refuge represented the most various phases of human life, shadowed by misfortune; sometimes the calm of a cloister without the monks; sometimes the peace of the graveyard without the dead, who speak in the language of epitaphs; one day I saw in it the home of lepers; another, the house of the Atridae; but above all, I found there provincial life, with its contemplative ideas, its hour-glass existence. I often wept there, I never laughed.

'More than once I felt involuntary terrors as I heard overhead the dull hum of the wings of some hurrying wood-pigeon. The earth is dank; you must be on the watch for lizards, vipers, and frogs, wandering about with the wild freedom of nature; above all, you must have no fear of cold, for in a few minutes you feel an icy cloak settle on your shoulders, like the Commendatore's hand on Don Giovanni's neck.

'One evening I felt a shudder; the wind had turned an old rusty weathercock, and the creaking sounded like a cry from the house, at the very moment when I was finishing a gloomy drama to account for this monumental embodiment of woe. I returned to my inn, lost in gloomy thoughts. When I had supped, the hostess came into my room with an air of mystery, and said, "Monsieur, here is Monsieur Regnault."

' "Who is Monsieur Regnault?"

' "What, sir, don't you know Monsieur Regnault? – Well, that's odd," said she, leaving the room.

'Suddenly I saw a man appear, tall, slim, dressed in black, hat in hand, who came in like a ram ready to butt his opponent, showing a receding forehead, a small pointed head, and a colourless face of the hue of a glass of dirty water. You would have taken him for an usher. The stranger wore an old coat, much worn at the seams; but he had a diamond in his shirt frill, and gold rings in his ears.

' "Monsieur," said I, "whom have I the honour of addressing?" – He took a chair, placed himself in front of my fire, put his hat on my table, and answered while he rubbed his hands: "Dear me, it is very cold – Monsieur, I am Monsieur Regnault."

'I was encouraging myself by saying to myself, '*Il bondo cani!* Seek!'

' "I am," he went on, "the notary at Vendôme."

' "I am delighted to hear it, Monsieur," I exclaimed. "But I am not in a position to make a will for reasons best known to myself."

' "One moment!" said he, holding up his hand as though to gain silence. "Allow me, Monsieur, allow me! I am informed that you sometimes go to walk in the garden of la Grande Bretêche."

' "Yes, Monsieur."

' "One moment!" said he, repeating his gesture. "That constitutes a misdemeanour. Monsieur, as executor under the will of the late Comtesse de Merret, I come in her name to beg you to discontinue the practice. One moment! I am not a Turk, and do not wish to make a crime of it. And besides, you are probably ignorant of the circumstances which compel me to leave the finest mansion in Vendôme to fall into ruin. Nevertheless, Monsieur, you must be a man of education, and you should know that the laws forbid, under heavy penalties, any trespass on enclosed property. A hedge is the same as a wall. But, the state in which the place is left may be an excuse for your curiosity. For my part, I should be quite content to make you free to come and go in the house; but being bound to respect the will of the testatrix, I have the honour, Monsieur, to beg that you will go into the garden no more. I myself, Monsieur, since the will was read, have never set foot in the house, which, as I had the honour of informing you, is part of the estate of the late Madame de Merret. We have done nothing there but verify the number of doors and windows to assess the taxes I have to pay annually out of the funds left for that purpose by the late Madame de Merret. Ah! my dear sir, her will made a great commotion in the town."

'The good man paused to blow his nose. I respected his volubility, perfectly understanding that the administration of Madame de Merret's estate had been the most important event of his life, his reputation, his glory, his Restoration. As I was forced to bid farewell to my beautiful reveries and romances, I now hoped to learn the truth on official authority.

' "Monsieur," said I, "would it be indiscreet if I were to ask you the reasons for such eccentricity?"

'At these words an expression, which revealed all the pleasure which men feel who are accustomed to ride a hobby, overspread the lawyer's countenance. He pulled up the collar of his shirt with an air, took out his snuffbox, opened it, and offered me a pinch; on my refusing, he took a large one. He was happy! A man who has no hobby does not know all the good to be got out of life. A hobby is the happy medium between a passion and a monomania. At this moment I understood the whole bearing of Sterne's charming passion, and had a perfect idea of the delight with which my Uncle Toby, encouraged by Trim, bestrode his hobby-horse.

' "Monsieur," said Monsieur Regnault, "I was head clerk in Monsieur Roguin's office, in Paris. A first-rate house, which you may have heard mentioned? No! An unfortunate bankruptcy made it famous. – Not having money enough to purchase a practice in Paris at the price to which they were run up in 1816, I came here and bought my predecessor's business. I had relations in Vendôme; among others, a wealthy aunt, who allowed me to marry her daughter. – Monsieur," he went on after a little pause, "three months after being licensed by the Keeper of the Seals, one evening, as I was going to bed – it was before my marriage – I was sent for by Madame la Comtesse de Merret, to her Château of Merret. Her maid, a good girl, who is now a servant in this inn, was waiting at my door with the Countess's own carriage. Ah! one moment! I ought to tell you that Monsieur le Comte de Merret had gone to Paris to die two months before I came here. He came to a miserable end, flinging himself into every kind of dissipation. You understand?

' "On the day he left, Madame la Comtesse had quitted la Grande Bretêche, having dismantled it. Some people even say that she had burnt all the furniture, the hangings – in short, all the chattels and furniture whatever used in furnishing the premises now let by the said M.— (Dear! what am I saying? I beg your pardon, I thought I was dictating a lease) – in short, that she burnt everything in the meadow at Merret. Have you been to Merret, Monsieur? – No," said he, answering himself. "Ah, it is a very fine place."

' "For about three months previously," he went on, with a jerk of his head, "the Count and Countess had lived in a very eccentric way; they admitted no visitors; Madame lived on the ground floor, and Monsieur on the first floor. When the Countess was left alone, she was never seen except at church. Subsequently, at home, at the château, she refused to see the friends, whether gentlemen or ladies, who went to call on her. She was already very much altered when she left la Grande Bretêche to go to Merret. That dear lady – I say dear lady, for it was she who gave me this diamond, but indeed I saw her but once – that kind lady was very ill; she had, no doubt, given up all hope, for she died without choosing to send for a doctor; indeed, many of our ladies fancied she was not quite right in her head. Well, sir, my curiosity was strangely excited by hearing that Madame de Merret had need of my services. Nor was I the only person who took an interest in the affair. That very night, though it was already late, all the town knew that I was going to Merret.

' "The waiting-woman replied but vaguely to the questions I asked her on the way; nevertheless, she told me that her mistress had received the Sacrament in the course of the day at the hands of the Curé of Merret, and seemed unlikely to live through the night. It was about eleven when I reached the château. I went up the great staircase. After crossing some large, lofty, dark rooms, diabolically cold and damp, I reached the state bedroom where the Countess lay. From the rumours that were current concerning this lady (Monsieur, I should never end if I were to repeat all the tales that were told about her), I had imagined her a coquette. Imagine, then, that I had great difficulty in seeing her in the great bed where she was lying. To be sure, to light this enormous room, with old-fashioned heavy cornices, and so thick with dust that merely to see it was enough to make you sneeze, she had only an old Argand lamp. Ah! but you have not been to Merret. Well, the bed is one of those old-world beds, with a high tester hung with flowered chintz. A small table stood by the bed, on which I saw an 'Imitation of Christ', which, by the way, I bought for my wife, as well as the lamp. There were also a deep arm-chair for her confidential maid, and two small chairs. There was no fire. That was all the furniture; not enough to fill ten lines in an inventory.

' "My dear sir, if you had seen, as I then saw, that vast room, papered and hung with brown, you would have felt yourself transported into a scene of romance. It was icy, nay more, funereal," and he lifted his hand with a theatrical gesture and paused.

' "By dint of seeking, as I approached the bed, at last I saw Madame de Merret, under the glimmer of the lamp, which fell on the pillows. Her face was as yellow as wax, and as narrow as two folded hands. The Countess wore a lace cap, showing abundant hair, but as white as linen thread. She was sitting up in bed, and seemed to keep upright with great difficulty. Her large black eyes, dimmed by fever, no doubt, and half-dead already, hardly moved under the bony arch of her eyebrows – There," he added, pointing to his own brow. "Her forehead was clammy; her fleshless hands were like bones covered with soft skin; the veins and muscles were perfectly visible. She must have been very handsome; but at this moment I was startled into an indescribable emotion at the sight. Never, said those who wrapped her in her shroud, had any living creature been so emaciated and lived. In short, it was awful to behold! Sickness had so consumed that woman, that she was no more than a phantom. Her lips, which were pale violet, seemed to me not to move when she spoke to me.

' "Though my profession has familiarized me with such spectacles, by calling me not unfrequently to the bedside of the dying to record their last wishes, I confess that families in tears and the agonies I have seen were as nothing in comparison with this lonely and silent woman in her vast château. I heard not the least sound, I did not perceive the movement which the sufferer's breathing ought to have given to the sheets that covered her, and I stood motionless, absorbed in looking at her in a sort of stupor. In fancy I am there still – At last her large eyes moved; she tried to raise her right hand, but it fell back on the bed, and she uttered these words, which came like a breath, for her voice was no longer a voice: 'I have waited for you with the greatest impatience.' A bright flush rose to her cheeks. It was a great effort for her to speak.

' "Madame," I began. She signed to me to be silent. At that moment the old housekeeper rose and said in my ear, 'Do not speak; Madame la Comtesse is not in a state to bear the slightest noise, and what you would say might agitate her.'

' "I sat down. A few instants after, Madame de Merret collected all her remaining strength to move her right hand, and slipped it, not without infinite difficulty, under the bolster; she then paused a moment. With a last effort she withdrew her hand; and when she brought out a sealed paper, drops of perspiration rolled from her brow. 'I place my will in your hands – Oh! God! Oh!' and that was all. She clutched a crucifix that lay on the bed, lifted it hastily to her lips, and died.

' "The expression of her eyes still makes me shudder as I think of it. She must have suffered much! There was joy in her last glance, and it remained stamped on her dead eyes.

' "I brought away the will, and when it was opened I found that Madame de Merret had appointed me her executor. She left the whole of her property to the hospital of Vendôme, excepting a few legacies. But these were her instructions as relating to la Grande Bretêche: she ordered me to leave the place, for fifty years counting from the day of her death, in the state in which it might be at the time of her decease, forbidding anyone, whoever he might be, to enter the apartments, prohibiting any repairs whatever, and even setting a salary to pay watchmen if it were needful to secure the absolute fulfilment of her intentions. At the expiration of that term, if the will of the testatrix has been duly carried out, the house is to become the property of my heirs, for, as you know, a notary cannot take a bequest. Otherwise la Grande Bretêche reverts to the heirs-at-law, but on condition of fulfilling certain conditions set forth in a codicil to the will, which is not to be opened till the expiration of the said term of fifty years. The will has not been disputed, so—" and without finishing his sentence, the lanky notary looked at me with an air of triumph; I made him quite happy by offering him my congratulations.

' "Monsieur," I said in conclusion, "you have so vividly impressed me that I fancy I see the dying woman whiter than her sheets; her glittering eyes frighten me; I shall dream of her tonight. – But you must have formed some idea as to the instructions contained in that extraordinary will."

' "Monsieur," said he, with comical reticence, "I never allow myself to criticize the conduct of a person who honours me with the gift of a diamond."

'However, I soon loosened the tongue of the discreet notary of Vendôme, who communicated to me, not without long digressions, the opinions of the deep politicians of both sexes whose judgements are law in Vendôme. But these opinions were so contradictory, so diffuse, that I was near falling asleep in spite of the interest I felt in this authentic history. The notary's ponderous voice and monotonous accent, accustomed no doubt to listen to himself and to make himself listened to by his clients or fellow-townsmen, were too much for my curiosity. Happily, he soon went away.

' "Ah, ha, Monsieur," said he on the stairs, "a good many persons would be glad to live five-and-forty years longer; but – one moment!" and he laid the first finger of his right hand to his nostril with a cunning look, "Mark my words! – To last as long as that – as long as that, you must not be past sixty now."

'I closed my door, having been roused from my apathy by this last speech, which the notary thought very funny; then I sat down in my arm-chair, with my feet on the fire-dogs. I had lost myself in a romance à la Radcliffe, constructed on the juridical base given me by Monsieur Regnault, when the door, opened by a woman's cautious hand, turned on the hinges. I saw my landlady come in, a buxom, florid dame, always good-humoured, who had missed her calling in life. She was a Fleming, who ought to have seen the light in a picture by Teniers.

' "Well, Monsieur," said she, "Monsieur Regnault has no doubt been giving you his history of la Grande Bretêche?"

' "Yes, Madame Lepas."

' "And what did he tell you?"

'I repeated in a few words the creepy and sinister story of Madame de Merret. At each sentence my hostess put her head forward, looking at me with an innkeeper's keen scrutiny, a happy compromise between the instinct of a police constable, the astuteness of a spy, and the cunning of a dealer.

' "My good Madame Lepas," said I as I ended, "you seem to know more about it. Heh? If not, why have you come up to me?"

' "On my word, as an honest woman –"

' "Do not swear; your eyes are big with a secret. You knew Monsieur de Merret; what sort of man was he?"

' "Monsieur de Merret – well, you see he was a man you never could see the top of, he was so tall! A very good gentleman, from Picardy, and who had, as we say, his head close to his cap. He paid for everything down, so as never to have difficulties with anyone. He was hot-tempered, you see! All our ladies liked him very much."

' "Because he was hot-tempered?" I asked her.

' "Well, maybe," said she; "and you may suppose, sir, that a man had to have something to show for a figure-head before he could marry Madame de Merret, who, without any reflection on others, was the handsomest and richest heiress in our parts. She had about twenty thousand francs a year. All the town was at the wedding; the bride was pretty and sweet-looking, quite a gem of a woman. Oh, they were a handsome couple in their day!"

' "And were they happy together?"

' "Hm, hm! so-so — so far as can be guessed, for, as you may suppose, we of the common sort were not hail-fellow-well-met with them. — Madame de Merret was a kind woman and very pleasant, who had no doubt sometimes to put up with her husband's tantrums. But though he was rather haughty, we were fond of him. After all, it was his place to behave so. When a man is a born nobleman, you see —"

' "Still, there must have been some catastrophe for Monsieur and Madame de Merret to part so violently?"

' "I did not say there was any catastrophe, sir. I know nothing about it."

' "Indeed. Well, now, I am sure you know everything."

' "Well, sir, I will tell you the whole story — When I saw Monsieur Regnault go up to see you, it struck me that he would speak to you about Madame de Merret as having to do with la Grande Bretêche. That put it into my head to ask your advice, sir, seeming to me that you are a man of good judgement and incapable of playing a poor woman like me false — for I never did anyone a wrong, and yet I am tormented by my conscience. Up to now I have never dared to say a word to the people of these parts; they are all chatterers, with tongues like knives. And never till now, sir, have I had any traveller here who stayed so long in the inn as you have, and to whom I could tell the history of the fifteen thousand francs —"

' "My dear Madame Lepas, if there is anything in your story of a nature to compromise me," I said, interrupting the flow of her words, "I would not hear it for all the world."

' "You need have no fears," said she; "you will see."

'Her eagerness made me suspect that I was not the only person to whom my worthy landlady had communicated the secret of which I was to be a sole possessor, but I listened.

' "Monsieur," said she, "when the Emperor sent the Spaniards here, prisoners of war and others, I was required to lodge at the charge of the Government a young Spaniard sent to Vendôme on parole. Notwithstanding his parole, he had to show himself every day to the sub-prefect. He was a Spanish grandee – neither more nor less. He had a name in *os* and *dia*, something like Bagos de Férédia. I wrote his name down in my books, and you may see it if you like. Ah! he was a handsome young fellow for a Spaniard, who are ugly, they say. He was not more than five feet two or three in height, but so well made; and he had little hands that he kept so beautifully! Ah! you should have seen them. He had as many brushes for his hands as a woman has for her toilet. He had thick, black hair, a flame in his eye, a somewhat coppery complexion, but which I admired all the same. He wore the finest linen I have ever seen, though I have had princesses to lodge here, and, among others, General Bertrand, the Duc and Duchesse d'Abrantés, Monsieur Descazes, and the King of Spain. He did not eat much, but he had such polite and amiable ways that it was impossible to owe him a grudge for that. Oh! I was very fond of him, though he did not say four words to me in a day, and it was impossible to have the least bit of talk with him; if he was spoken to, he did not answer; it is a way, a mania they all have, it would seem.

' "He read his breviary like a priest, and went to Mass and all the services quite regularly. And where did he post himself? – we found this out later – Within two yards of Madame de Merret's chapel. As he took that place the very first time he entered the church, no one imagined that there was any purpose in it. Besides, he never raised his nose above his book, poor young man! And then, Monsieur, of an evening he went for a walk on the hill among the ruins of the old castle. It was his only amusement, poor man; it reminded him of his native land. They say that Spain is all hills!

' "One evening, a few days after he was sent here, he was out very late. I was rather uneasy when he did not come in till just on the stroke of midnight; but we all got used to his whims; he took the key of the door, and we never sat up for him. He lived in a house belonging to us in the Rue des Casernes. Well, then, one of our stable-boys told us one evening that, going down to wash the horses in the river, he fancied he had seen the Spanish grandee swimming some little way off, just like a fish. When he came in, I told him to be careful of the weeds, and he seemed put out at having been seen in the water.

' "At last, Monsieur, one day, or rather one morning, we did not find him in his room; he had not come back. By hunting through his things, I found a written paper in the drawer of his table, with fifty pieces of

Spanish gold of the kind they call doubloons, worth about five thousand francs; and in a little sealed box ten thousand francs' worth of diamonds. The paper said that in case he should not return, he left us this money and these diamonds in trust to found Masses to thank God for his escape and for his salvation.

' "At that time I still had my husband, who ran off in search of him. And this is the queer part of the story: he brought back the Spaniard's clothes, which he had found under a big stone on a sort of breakwater along the river bank, nearly opposite la Grande Bretêche. My husband went so early that no one saw him. After reading the letter, he burnt the clothes, and, in obedience to Count Férédia's wish, we announced that he had escaped.

' "The sub-prefect set all the constabulary at his heels; but, pshaw! he was never caught. Lepas believed that the Spaniard had drowned himself. I, sir, have never thought so; I believe, on the contrary, that he had something to do with the business about Madame de Merret, seeing that Rosalie told me that the crucifix her mistress was so fond of that she had it buried with her, was made of ebony and silver; now in the early days of his stay here, Monsieur Férédia had one of ebony and silver which I never saw later – And now, Monsieur, do not you say that I need have no remorse about the Spaniard's fifteen thousand francs? Are they not really and truly mine?"

' "Certainly – But have you never tried to question Rosalie?" said I.

' "Oh, to be sure I have, sir. But what is to be done? That girl is like a wall. She knows something, but it is impossible to make her talk."

'After chatting with me for a few minutes, my hostess left me a prey to vague and sinister thoughts, to romantic curiosity, and a religious dread not unlike the deep emotion which comes upon us when we go into a dark church at night and discern a feeble light glimmering under a lofty vault – a dim figure glides across – the sweep of a gown or of a priest's cassock is audible – and we shiver! La Grande Bretêche, with its rank grasses, its shuttered windows, its rusty ironwork, its locked doors, its deserted rooms, suddenly rose before me in fantastic vividness. I tried to get into the mysterious dwelling to search out the heart of this solemn story, this drama which had killed three persons.

'Rosalie became in my eyes the most interesting being in Vendôme. As I studied her, I detected signs of an inmost thought, in spite of the blooming health that glowed in her dimpled face. There was in her soul some element of truth or of hope; her manner suggested a secret, like the expression of devout souls who pray in excess, or of a girl who has killed her child and for ever hears its last cry. Nevertheless, she was simple and clumsy in her ways; her vacant smile had nothing criminal in it, and you would have pronounced her innocent only from seeing the large red and blue checked kerchief that covered her stalwart bust, tucked into the tight-laced square bodice of a lilac- and white-striped gown. "No," said I to myself, "I will not quit Vendôme without knowing the whole history of la Grande Bretêche. To achieve this end, I will make love to Rosalie if it proves necessary."

' "Rosalie!" said I one evening.

' "Your servant, sir?"

' "You are not married?" She started a little.

' "Oh! there is no lack of men if ever I take a fancy to be miserable!" she replied laughing. She got over her agitation at once; for every woman, from the highest lady to the inn-servant inclusive, has a native presence of mind.

' "Yes; you are fresh and good-looking enough never to lack lovers! But tell me, Rosalie, why did you become an inn-servant on leaving Madame de Merret? Did she not leave you some little annuity?"

' "Oh yes, sir. But my place here is the best in all the town of Vendôme."

'This reply was such a one as judges and attorneys call evasive. Rosalie, as it seemed to me, held in this romantic affair the place of a middle square of the chess-board; she was at the very centre of the interest and of the truth; she appeared to me to be tied into the knot of it. It was not a case for ordinary love-making; this girl contained the last chapter of a romance, and from that moment all my attentions were devoted to Rosalie. By dint of studying the girl, I observed in her, as in every woman whom we make our ruling thought, a variety of good qualities; she was clean and neat; she was handsome, I need not say; she soon was possessed of every charm that desire can lend to a woman in whatever rank of life. A fortnight after the notary's visit, one evening, or rather one morning, in the small hours, I said to Rosalie:

' "Come, tell me all you know about Madame de Merret."

' "Oh!" she cried in terror, "do not ask me that, Monsieur Horace!"

'Her handsome features clouded over, her bright colouring grew pale, and her eyes lost their artless, liquid brightness.

' "Well," she said, "I will tell you; but keep the secret carefully."

' "All right, my child; I will keep all your secrets with a thief's honour, which is the most loyal known."

' "If it is all the same to you," said she, "I would rather it should be with your own."

'Thereupon she set her head-kerchief straight, and settled herself to tell the tale; for there is no doubt a particular attitude of confidence and security is necessary to the telling of a narrative. The best tales are told at a certain hour – just as we are all here at table. No one ever told a story well standing up, or fasting.

'If I were to reproduce exactly Rosalie's diffuse eloquence, a whole volume would scarcely contain it. Now, as the event of which she gave me a confused account stands exactly midway between the notary's gossip and that of Madame Lepas, as precisely as the middle term or a rule-of-three sum stands between the first and third, I have only to relate it in as few words as may be. I shall therefore be brief.

'The room at la Grande Bretêche in which Madame de Merret slept was on the ground floor; a little cupboard in the wall, about four feet deep, served her to hang her dresses in. Three months before the evening of which I have to relate the events, Madame de Merret had been seriously ailing, so much so that her husband had left her to herself, and had his own bedroom on the first floor. By one of those accidents which it is impossible to foresee, he came in that evening two hours later than usual from the club, where he went to read the papers and talk politics with the residents in the neighbourhood. His wife supposed him to have come in, to be in bed and asleep. But the invasion of France had been the subject of a very animated discussion; the game of billiards had waxed vehement; he had lost forty francs, an enormous sum at Vendôme, where everybody is thrifty, and where social habits are restrained within the bounds of a simplicity worthy of all praise, and the foundation perhaps of a form of true happiness which no Parisian would care for.

'For some time past Monsieur de Merret had been satisfied to ask Rosalie whether his wife was in bed; on the girl's replying always in the affirmative, he at once went to his own room, with the good faith that comes of habit and confidence. But this evening, on coming in, he took it into his head to go to see Madame de Merret, to tell her of his ill-luck, and perhaps to find consolation. During dinner he had observed that his wife was very becomingly dressed; he reflected as he came home from the club that his wife was certainly much better, that convalescence had improved her beauty, discovering it, as husbands discover everything, a little too late. Instead of calling Rosalie, who was in the kitchen at the moment watching the cook and the coachman playing a puzzling hand at cards, Monsieur de Merret made his way to his wife's room by the light of his lantern, which he set down on the lowest step of the stairs. His step, easy to recognize, rang under the vaulted passage.

'At the instant when the gentleman turned the key to enter his wife's room, he fancied he heard the door shut of the closet of which I have spoken; but when he went in, Madame de Merret was alone, standing in front of the fireplace. The unsuspecting husband fancied that Rosalie was in the cupboard; nevertheless, a doubt, ringing in his ears like a peal of bells, put him on his guard; he looked at his wife, and read in her eyes an indescribably anxious and haunted expression.

' "You are very late," said she – Her voice, usually so clear and sweet, struck him as being slightly husky.

'Monsieur de Merret made no reply, for at this moment Rosalie came in. This was like a thunderclap. He walked up and down the room, going from one window to another at a regular pace, his arms folded.

' "Have you had bad news, or are you ill?" his wife asked him timidly, while Rosalie helped her to undress. He made no reply.

' "You can go, Rosalie," said Madame de Merret to her maid; 'I can put in my curl-papers myself." – She scented disaster at the mere aspect of her husband's face, and wished to be alone with him. As soon as Rosalie was gone, or supposed to be gone, for she lingered a few minutes in the passage, Monsieur de Merret came and stood facing his wife, and said coldly, "Madame, there is someone in your cupboard!" She looked at her husband calmly, and replied quite simply, "No, Monsieur."

'This "No" wrung Monsieur de Merret's heart; he did not believe it; and yet his wife had never appeared purer or more saintly than she seemed to be at this moment. He rose to go and open the closet door. Madame de Merret took his hand, stopped him, looked at him sadly, and said in a voice of strange emotion, "Remember, if you should find no one there, everything must be at an end between you and me."

'The extraordinary dignity of his wife's attitude filled him with deep esteem for her, and inspired him with one of those resolves which need only a grander stage to become immortal.

' "No, Josephine," he said, "I will not open it. In either event we should be parted for ever. Listen; I know all the purity of your soul, I know you lead a saintly life, and would not commit a deadly sin to save your life." – At these words Madame de Merret looked at her husband with a haggard stare – "See, here is your crucifix," he went on. "Swear to me before God that there is no one in there; I will believe you – I will never open that door."

'Madame de Merret took up the crucifix and said, "I swear it."

' "Louder," said her husband; "and repeat: 'I swear before God that there is nobody in that closet.' " She repeated the words without flinching.

' "That will do," said Monsieur de Merret coldly. After a moment's silence: "You have there a fine piece of work which I never saw before,"

said he, examining the crucifix of ebony and silver, very artistically
wrought.

' "I found it at Duvivier's; last year when that troop of Spanish prisoners
came through Vendôme, he bought it of a Spanish monk."

' "Indeed," said Monsieur de Merret, hanging the crucifix on its nail;
and he rang the bell.

'He had not to wait for Rosalie. Monsieur de Merret went forward
quickly to meet her, led her into the bay of the window that looked on to
the garden, and said to her in an undertone:

' "I know that Gorenflot wants to marry you, that poverty alone
prevents your setting up house, and that you told him you would not be
his wife till he found means to become a master mason. – Well, go and
fetch him; tell him to come here with his trowel and tools. Contrive to
wake no one in his house but himself. His reward will be beyond your
wishes. Above all, go out without saying a word – or else!" and he
frowned.

'Rosalie was going, and he called her back. "Here, take my latch-key,"
said he.

' "Jean!" Monsieur de Merret called in a voice of thunder down the
passage. Jean, who was both coachman and confidential servant, left his
cards and came.

' "Go to bed, all of you," said his master, beckoning him to come
close; and the gentleman added in a whisper, "When they are all asleep
– mind, *asleep* – you understand? – come down and tell me."

Monsieur de Merret, who had never lost sight of his wife while giving
his orders, quietly came back to her at the fireside, and began to tell her
the details of the game of billiards and the discussion at the club. When
Rosalie returned she found Monsieur and Madame de Merret conversing
amiably.

'Not long before this Monsieur de Merret had had new ceilings made
to all the reception-rooms on the ground floor. Plaster is very scarce at
Vendôme; the price is enhanced by the cost of carriage; the gentleman
had therefore had a considerable quantity delivered to him, knowing that
he could always find purchasers for what might be left. It was this
circumstance which suggested the plan he carried out.

' "Gorenflot is here, sir," said Rosalie in a whisper.

' "Tell him to come in," said her master aloud.

'Madame de Merret turned paler when she saw the mason.

' "Gorenflot," said her husband, "go and fetch some bricks from the
coachhouse; bring enough to wall up the door of this cupboard; you can
use the plaster that is left for cement." Then, dragging Rosalie and the

workman close to him – "Listen, Gorenflot," said he, in a low voice, "you are to sleep here tonight; but tomorrow morning you shall have a passport to take you abroad to a place I will tell you of. I will give you six thousand francs for your journey. You must live in that town for ten years; if you find you do not like it, you may settle in another, but it must be in the same country. Go through Paris and wait there till I join you. I will there give you an agreement for six thousand francs more, to be paid to you on your return, provided you have carried out the conditions of the bargain. For that price you are to keep perfect silence as to what you have to do this night. To you, Rosalie, I will secure ten thousand francs, which will not be paid you till your wedding day, and on condition of your marrying Gorenflot; but, to get married, you must hold your tongue. If not, no wedding gift!"

' "Rosalie," said Madame de Merret, "come and brush my hair."

'Her husband quietly walked up and down the room, keeping an eye on the door, on the mason, and on his wife, but without any insulting display of suspicion. Gorenflot could not help making some noise. Madame de Merret seized a moment when he was unloading some bricks, and when her husband was at the other end of the room, to say to Rosalie: "My dear child, I will give you a thousand francs a year if only you will tell Gorenflot to leave a crack at the bottom." Then she added aloud quite coolly: "You had better help him."

'Monsieur and Madame de Merret were silent all the time while Gorenflot was walling up the door. This silence was intentional on the husband's part; he did not wish to give his wife the opportunity of saying anything with a double meaning. On Madame de Merret's side it was pride or prudence. When the wall was half built up, the cunning mason took advantage of his master's back being turned to break one of the two panes in the top of the door with a blow of his pick. By this Madame de Merret understood that Rosalie had spoken to Gorenflot. They all three then saw the face of a dark, gloomy-looking man, with black hair and flaming eyes.

'Before her husband turned round again the poor woman had nodded to the stranger, to whom the signal was meant to convey, "Hope."

'At four o'clock, as day was dawning, for it was the month of September, the work was done. The mason was placed in charge of Jean, and Monsieur de Merret slept in his wife's room.

'Next morning when he got up he said with apparent carelessness, "Oh, by the way, I must go to the Mairie for the passport." He put on his hat, took two or three steps towards the door, paused, and took the crucifix. His wife was trembling with joy.

' "He will go to Duvivier's," thought she.

'As soon as he had left, Madame de Merret rang for Rosalie, and then in a terrible voice she cried: "The pick! Bring the pick! and set to work. I saw how Gorenflot did it yesterday; we shall have time to make a gap and build it up again."

'In an instant Rosalie had brought her mistress a sort of cleaver; she, with a vehemence of which no words can give an idea, set to work to demolish the wall. She had already got out a few bricks, when, turning to deal a stronger blow than before, she saw behind her Monsieur de Merret. She fainted away.

' "Lay Madame on her bed," said he coldly.

'Foreseeing what would certainly happen in his absence, he had laid this trap for his wife; he had merely written to the Mairie and sent for Duvivier. The jeweller arrived just as the disorder in the room had been repaired.

' "Duvivier," asked Monsieur de Merret, "did not you buy some crucifixes of the Spaniards who passed through the town?"

' "No, Monsieur."

' "Very good; thank you," said he, flashing a tiger's glare at his wife. "Jean," he added, turning to his confidential valet, "you can serve my meals here in Madame de Merret's room. She is ill, and I shall not leave her till she recovers."

'The cruel man remained in his wife's room for twenty days. During the earlier time, when there was some little noise in the closet, and Josephine wanted to intercede for the dying man, he said, without allowing her to utter a word, "You swore on the Cross that there was no one there." '

After this story all the ladies rose from table, and thus the spell under which Bianchon had held them was broken. But there were some among them who had almost shivered at the last words.

The Romance of Certain Old Clothes

Henry James

I

Towards the middle of the eighteenth century there lived in the Province of Massachusetts a widowed gentlewoman, the mother of three children, by name Mrs Veronica Wingrave. She had lost her husband early in life, and had devoted herself to the care of her progeny. These young persons grew up in a manner to reward her tenderness and to gratify her highest hopes. The first-born was a son, whom she had called Bernard, after his father. The others were daughters – born at an interval of three years apart. Good looks were traditional in the family, and this youthful trio were not likely to allow the tradition to perish. The boy was of that fair and ruddy complexion and that athletic structure which in those days (as in these) were the sign of good English descent – a frank, affectionate young fellow, a deferential son, a patronizing brother, a steadfast friend. Clever, however, he was not; the wit of the family had been apportioned chiefly to his sisters. The late Mr Wingrave had been a great reader of Shakespeare, at a time when this pursuit implied more freedom of thought than at the present day, and in a community where it required much courage to patronize the drama even in the closet: and he had wished to call attention to his admiration of the great poet by calling his daughters out of his favourite plays. Upon the elder he had bestowed the romantic name of Rosalind, and the younger he had called Perdita, in memory of a little girl born between them, who had lived but a few weeks.

When Bernard Wingrave came to his sixteenth year his mother put a brave face upon it and prepared to execute her husband's last injunction. This had been a formal command that, at the proper age, his son should be sent out to England, to complete his education at the university of

Oxford, where he himself had acquired his taste for elegant literature. It was Mrs Wingrave's belief that the lad's equal was not to be found in the two hemispheres, but she had the old traditions of literal obedience. She swallowed her sobs, and made up her boy's trunk and his simple provincial outfit, and sent him on his way across the seas. Bernard presented himself at his father's college, and spent five years in England, without great honour, indeed, but with a vast deal of pleasure and no discredit. On leaving the university he made the journey to France. In his twenty-fourth year he took ship for home, prepared to find poor little New England (New England was very small in those days) a very dull, unfashionable residence. But there had been changes at home, as well as in Mr Bernard's opinions. He found his mother's house quite habitable, and his sisters grown into two very charming young ladies, with all the accomplishments and graces of the young women of Britain, and a certain native-grown originality and wildness, which, if it was not an accomplishment, was certainly a grace the more. Bernard privately assured his mother that his sisters were fully a match for the most genteel young women in the old country; whereupon poor Mrs Wingrave, you may be sure, bade them hold up their heads. Such was Bernard's opinion, and such, in a tenfold higher degree, was the opinion of Mr Arthur Lloyd. This gentleman was a college-mate of Mr Bernard, a young man of reputable family, of a good person and a handsome inheritance; which latter appurtenance he proposed to invest in trade in the flourishing colony. He and Bernard were sworn friends; they had crossed the ocean together, and the young American had lost no time in presenting him at his mother's house, where he had made quite as good an impression as that which he had received and of which I have just given a hint.

The two sisters were at this time in all the freshness of their youthful bloom; each wearing, of course, this natural brilliancy in the manner that became her best. They were equally dissimilar in appearance and character. Rosalind, the elder – now in her twenty-second year – was tall and white, with calm grey eyes and auburn tresses; a very faint likeness to the Rosalind of Shakespeare's comedy, whom I imagine a brunette (if you will), but a slender, airy creature, full of the softest, quickest impulses. Miss Wingrave, with her slightly lymphatic fairness, her fine arms, her majestic height, her slow utterance, was not cut out for adventures. She would never have put on a man's jacket and hose; and, indeed, being a very plump beauty, she may have had reasons apart from her natural dignity. Perdita, too, might very well have exchanged the sweet melancholy of her name against something more in consonance with her aspect and disposition. She had the cheek of a gypsy and the eye of an eager child, as well as the smallest waist and lightest foot in all the country of the Puritans. When you spoke to her she never made you wait, as her handsome sister was wont to do (while she looked at you with a cold fine eye), but gave you your choice of a dozen answers before you had uttered half your thought.

The young girls were very glad to see their brother once more; but they found themselves quite able to spare part of their attention for their brother's friend. Among the young men their friends and neighbours, the *belle jeunesse* of the Colony, there were many excellent fellows, several devoted swains, and some two or three who enjoyed the reputation of universal charmers and conquerors. But the homebred arts and somewhat boisterous gallantry of these honest colonists were completely eclipsed by the good looks, the fine clothes, the punctilious courtesy, the perfect elegance, the immense information, of Mr Arthur Lloyd. He was in reality no paragon; he was a capable, honourable, civil youth, rich in pounds sterling, in his health and complacency and his little capital of uninvested affections. But he was a gentleman; he had a handsome person; he had studied and travelled; he spoke French, he played the flute, and he read verses aloud with very great taste. There were a dozen reasons why Miss Wingrave and her sister should have thought their other male acquaintance made but a poor figure before such a perfect man of the world. Mr Lloyd's anecdotes told our little New England maidens a great deal more of the ways and means of people of fashion in European capitals than he had any idea of doing. It was delightful to sit by and hear him and Bernard talk about the fine people and fine things they had seen. They would all gather round the fire after tea, in the little wainscoted parlour, and the two young men would remind each other, across the rug, of this, that and the other adventure. Rosalind and Perdita would often have given their ears to know exactly what adventure it was, and where it happened, and who was there, and what the ladies had on; but in those days a well-bred young woman was not expected to break into the conversation of her elders, or to ask too many questions; and the poor girls used therefore to sit fluttering behind the more languid – or more discreet – curiosity of their mother.

II

That they were both very fine girls Arthur Lloyd was not slow to discover; but it took him some time to make up his mind whether he liked the big sister or the little sister best. He had a strong presentiment – an emotion of a nature entirely too cheerful to be called a foreboding – that he was destined to stand up before the parson with one of them; yet he was unable to arrive at a preference, and for such a consummation a preference was certainly necessary, for Lloyd had too much young blood in his veins to make a choice by lot and be cheated of the satisfaction of falling in love. He resolved to take things as they came – to let his heart speak. Meanwhile he was on very pleasant footing. Mrs Wingrave showed a dignified indifference to his 'intentions', equally remote from a carelessness of her daughter's honour and from that sharp alacrity to make him come to the point, which, in his quality of young man of property, he had too often encountered in the worldly matrons of his native islands. As for Bernard, all that he asked was that his friend should treat his sisters as his own; and as for the poor girls themselves, however each may have secretly longed that their visitor should do or say something 'marked', they kept a very modest and contented demeanour.

Towards each other, however, they were somewhat more on the offensive. They were good friends enough, and accommodating bed-fellows (they shared the same four-poster), betwixt whom it would take more than a day for the seeds of jealousy to sprout and bear fruit; but they felt that the seeds had been sown on the day that Mr Lloyd came into the house. Each made up her mind that, if she should be slighted, she would bear her grief in silence, and that no one should be any the wiser; for if they had a great deal of ambition, they had also a large share of pride. But each prayed in secret, nevertheless, that upon *her* the selection, the distinction, might fall. They had need of a vast deal of patience, of self-control, of dissimulation. In those days a young girl of decent breeding could made no advances whatever, and barely respond, indeed, to those that were made. She was expected to sit still in her chair, with her eyes on the carpet, watching the spot where the mystic handkerchief should fall. Poor Arthur Lloyd was obliged to carry on his wooing in the little wainscoted parlour, before the eyes of Mrs Wingrave, her son, and his prospective sister-in-law. But youth and love are so cunning that a hundred signs and tokens might travel to and fro, and not one of these three pairs of eyes detect them in their passage. The two maidens were almost always together, and had plenty of chances to betray themselves. That each knew she was being watched, made not a grain of difference in the little offices they mutually rendered, or in the various household tasks they performed in common. Neither flinched nor fluttered beneath the silent battery of her sister's eyes. The only apparent change in their habits was that they had less to say to each other. It was impossible to talk about Mr Lloyd, and it was ridiculous to talk about anything else. By tacit agreement they began to wear all their choice finery, and to devise such little implements of conquest, in the way of ribbons and top-knots and kerchiefs, as were sanctioned by indubitable modesty. They executed in the same inarticulate fashion a contract of fair play in this exciting game. 'Is it better so?' Rosalind would ask, tying a bunch of ribbons on her bosom, and turning about from her glass to her sister. Perdita would look up gravely from her work and examine the decoration. 'I think you had better give it another loop,' she would say, with great solemnity, looking hard at her sister with eyes that added, 'upon my honour!' So they were for ever stitching and turning their petticoats, and pressing out their muslins, and contriving washes and ointments and cosmetics, like the ladies in the household of the vicar of Wakefield. Some three or four months went by; it grew to be midwinter, and as yet Rosalind knew that if Perdita had nothing more to boast of than she, there was not much to be feared from her rivalry. But Perdita by this time – the charming Perdita – felt that her secret had grown to be tenfold more precious than her sister's.

One afternoon Miss Wingrave sat alone – that was a rare accident – before her toilet-glass, combing out her long hair. It was getting too dark to see; she lit the two candles in their sockets, on the frame of her mirror, and then went to the window to draw her curtains. It was a grey December evening; the landscape was bare and bleak, and the sky heavy with snow-clouds. At the end of the large garden into which her window looked was a wall with a little postern door, opening into a lane. The door stood ajar, as she could vaguely see in the gathering darkness, and moved slowly to and fro, as if someone were swaying it from the lane without. It was doubtless a servant-maid who had been having a tryst with her sweetheart. But as she was about to drop her curtain Rosalind saw her sister step into the garden and hurry along the path which led to the house. She dropped the curtain, all save a little crevice for her eyes. As Perdita came up the path she seemed to be examining something in her hand, holding it close to her eyes. When she reached the house she stopped a moment, looked intently at the object, and pressed it to her lips.

Poor Rosalind slowly came back to her chair and sat down before her glass where, if she had looked at it less abstractly, she would have seen her handsome features sadly disfigured by jealousy. A moment afterwards the door opened behind her and her sister came into the room, out of breath, her cheeks aglow with the chilly air.

Perdita started. 'Ah,' said she, 'I thought you were with our mother.' The ladies were to go to a tea-party, and on such occasions it was the habit of one of the girls to help their mother to dress. Instead of coming in, Perdita lingered at the door.

'Come in, come in,' said Rosalind. 'We have more than an hour yet. I should like you very much to give a few strokes to my hair.' She knew that her sister wished to retreat, and that she could see in the glass all her movements in the room. 'Nay, just help me with my hair,' she said, 'and I will go to mamma.'

Perdita came reluctantly, and took the brush. She saw her sister's eyes, in the glass, fastened hard upon her hands. She had not made three passes when Rosalind clapped her own right hand upon her sister's left, and started out of her chair. 'Whose ring is that?' she cried, passionately, drawing her towards the light.

On the young girl's third finger glistened a little gold ring, adorned with a very small sapphire. Perdita felt that she need no longer keep her secret, yet that she must put a bold face on her avowal. 'It's mine,' she said proudly.

'Who gave it to you?' cried the other.

Perdita hesitated a moment. 'Mr Lloyd.'

'Mr Lloyd is generous, all of a sudden.'

'Ah no,' cried Perdita, with spirit, 'not all of a sudden! He offered it to me a month ago.'

'And you needed a month's begging to take it?' said Rosalind, looking at the little trinket, which indeed was not especially elegant, although it was the best that the jeweller of the Province could furnish. 'I wouldn't have taken it in less than two.'

'It isn't the ring,' Perdita answered, 'it's what it means!'

'It means that you are not a modest girl!' cried Rosalind. 'Pray, does your mother know of your intrigue? does Bernard?'

'My mother has approved my "intrigue", as you call it. Mr Lloyd has asked for my hand, and mamma has given it. Would you have had him apply to you, dearest sister?'

Rosalind gave her companion a long look, full of passionate envy and sorrow. Then she dropped her lashes on her pale cheeks and turned away. Perdita felt that it had not been a pretty scene; but it was her sister's fault. However, the elder girl rapidly called back her pride, and turned herself about again. 'You have my very best wishes,' she said, with a low curtsey. 'I wish you every happiness, and a very long life.'

Perdita gave a bitter laugh. 'Don't speak in that tone!' she cried. 'I would rather you should curse me outright. Come, Rosy,' she added, 'he couldn't marry both of us.'

'I wish you very great joy,' Rosalind repeated, mechanically, sitting down to her glass again, 'and a very long life, and plenty of children.'

There was something in the sound of these words not at all to Perdita's taste. 'Will you give me a year to live at least?' she said. 'In a year I can have one little boy – or one little girl at least. If you will give me your brush again I will do your hair.'

'Thank you,' said Rosalind. 'You had better go to mamma. It isn't becoming that a young lady with a promised husband should wait on a girl with none.'

'Nay,' said Perdita good-humouredly, 'I have Arthur to wait upon me. You need my service more than I need yours.'

But her sister motioned her away, and she left the room. When she had gone poor Rosalind fell on her knees before her dressing-table, buried her head in her arms, and poured out a flood of tears and sobs. She felt very much the better for this effusion of sorrow. When her sister came back she insisted on helping her to dress – on her wearing her prettiest things. She forced upon her acceptance a bit of lace of her own, and declared that now that she was to be married she should do her best to appear worthy of her lover's choice. She discharged these offices in stern silence; but, such as they were, they had to do duty as an apology and an atonement; she never made any other.

Now that Lloyd was received by the family as an accepted suitor nothing remained but to fix the wedding-day. It was appointed for the following April, and in the interval preparations were diligently made for the marriage. Lloyd, on his side, was busy with his commercial arrangements, and with establishing a correspondence with the great mercantile house to which he had attached himself in England. He was therefore not so frequent a visitor at Mrs Wingrave's as during the months of his diffidence and irresolution, and poor Rosalind had less to suffer than she had feared from the sight of the mutual endearments of the young lovers. Touching his future sister-in-law Lloyd had a perfectly clear conscience. There had not been a particle of love-making between them, and he had not the slightest suspicion that he had dealt her a terrible blow. He was quite at his ease; life promised so well, both domestically and financially. The great revolt of the Colonies was not yet in the air, and that his connubial felicity should take a tragic turn it was absurd, it was blasphemous, to apprehend. Meanwhile, at Mrs Wingrave's, there was a greater rustling of silks, a more rapid clicking of scissors and flying of needles, than ever. The good lady had determined that her daughter should carry from home the genteelest outfit that her money could buy or that the country could furnish. All the sage women in the Province were convened, and their united taste was brought to bear on Perdita's wardrobe. Rosalind's situation, at this moment, was assuredly not to be envied. The poor girl had an inordinate love of dress, and the very best taste in the world, as her sister perfectly well knew. Rosalind was tall, she was stately and sweeping, she was made to carry stiff brocade and masses of heavy lace, such as belong to the toilet of a rich man's wife. But Rosalind sat aloof, with her beautiful arms folded and her head averted, while her mother and sister and the venerable women aforesaid worried and wondered over their materials, oppressed by the multitude of their resources. One day there came in a beautiful piece of white silk, brocaded with heavenly blue and silver sent by the bridegroom himself – it not being thought amiss in those days that the husband-elect should contribute to the bride's trousseau. Perdita could think of no form or fashion which would do sufficient honour to the splendour of the material.

'Blue's your colour, sister, more than mine,' she said, with appealing eyes. 'It is a pity it's not for you. You would know what to do with it.'

Rosalind got up from her place and looked at the great shining fabric, as it lay spread over the back of a chair. Then she took it up in her hands and felt it – lovingly, as Perdita could see – and turned about towards the mirror with it. She let it roll down to her feet, and flung the other end over her shoulder, gathering it in about her waist with her white arm, which was bare to the elbow. She threw back her head, and looked at her image, and a hanging tress of her auburn hair fell upon the gorgeous surface of the silk. It made a dazzling picture. The women standing about uttered a little 'Look, look!' of admiration. 'Yes, indeed,' said Rosalind, quietly, 'blue is my colour.' But Perdita could see that her fancy had been stirred, and that she would now fall to work and solve all their silken riddles. And indeed she behaved very well, as Perdita, knowing her insatiable love of millinery, was quite ready to declare. Innumerable yards of lustrous silk and satin, of muslin, velvet and lace, passed through her cunning hands, without a jealous word coming from her lips. Thanks to her industry, when the wedding-day came Perdita was prepared to espouse more of the vanities of life than any fluttering young bride who had yet received the sacramental blessing of a New England divine.

It had been arranged that the young couple should go out and spend the first days of their wedded life at the country-house of an English gentleman – a man of rank and a very kind friend to Arthur Lloyd. He was a bachelor; he declared he should be delighted to give up the place to the influence of Hymen. After the ceremony at church – it had been performed by an English clergyman – young Mrs Lloyd hastened back to her mother's house to change her nuptial robes for a riding-dress. Rosalind helped her to effect the change, in the little homely room in which they had spent their undivided younger years. Perdita then hurried off to bid farewell to her mother, leaving Rosalind to follow. Then parting was short; the horses were at the door, and Arthur was impatient to start. But Rosalind had not followed, and Perdita hastened back to her room, opening the door abruptly. Rosalind, as usual, was before the glass, but in a position which caused the other to stand still, amazed. She had dressed herself in Perdita's cast-off wedding veil and wreath, and on her neck she had hung the full string of pearls which the young girl had received from her husband as a wedding-gift. These things had been hastily laid aside, to await their possessor's disposal on her return from the country. Bedizened by this unnatural garb Rosalind stood before the mirror, plunging a long look into its depths and reading heaven knows what audacious visions. Perdita was horrified. It was a hideous image of their old rivalry come to life again. She made a step towards her sister, as if to pull off the veil and the flowers. But catching her eyes in the glass, she stopped.

'Farewell, sweetheart,' she said. 'You might at least have waited till I had got out of the house!' And she hurried away from the room.

Mr Lloyd had purchased in Boston a house which to the taste of those days appeared as elegant as it was commodious; and here he very soon established himself with his young wife. He was thus separated by a distance of twenty miles from the residence of his mother-in-law. Twenty miles, in that primitive era of roads and conveyances, were as serious a matter as a hundred at the present day, and Mrs Wingrave saw but little of her daughter during the first twelvemonth of her marriage. She suffered in no small degree from Perdita's absence; and her affliction was not diminished by the fact that Rosalind had fallen into terribly low spirits and was not to be roused or cheered but by change of air and company. The real cause of the young lady's dejection the reader will not be slow to suspect. Mrs Wingrave and her gossips, however, deemed her complaint a mere bodily ill, and doubted not that she would obtain relief from the remedy just mentioned. Her mother accordingly proposed, on her behalf, a visit to certain relatives on the paternal side, established in New York, who had long complained that they were able to see so little of their New England cousins. Rosalind was despatched to these good people, under a suitable escort, and remained with them for several months. In the interval her brother Bernard, who had begun the practice of the law, made up his mind to take a wife. Rosalind came home to the wedding, apparently cured of her heartache, with bright roses and lilies in her face and a proud smile on her lips. Arthur Lloyd came over from Boston to see his brother-in-law married, but without his wife, who was expecting very soon to present him with an heir. It was nearly a year since Rosalind had seen him. She was glad – she hardly knew why – that Perdita had stayed at home. Arthur looked happy, but he was more grave and important than before his marriage. She thought he looked 'interesting' – for although the word, in its modern sense, was not then invented, we may be sure that the idea was. The truth is, he was simply anxious about his wife and her coming ordeal. Nevertheless, he by no means failed to observe Rosalind's beauty and splendour, and to note how she effaced the poor little bride. The allowance that Perdita had enjoyed for her dress had now been transferred to her sister, who turned it to wonderful account. On the morning after the wedding he had a lady's saddle put on the horse of the servant who had come with him from town, and went out with the young girl for a ride. It was a keen, clear morning in January; the ground was bare and hard, and the horses in good condition – to say nothing of Rosalind, who was charming in her hat and plume, and her dark blue riding coat, trimmed with fur. They rode all the morning, lost their way and were obliged to stop for dinner at a farm-house. The early winter dusk had fallen when they got home. Mrs Wingrave met them with a long face. A messenger had arrived at noon from Mrs Lloyd; she was beginning to be ill, she desired her husband's immediate return. The young man, at the thought that he had lost several hours, and that by hard riding he might already have been with his wife, uttered a passionate oath. He barely consented to stop for a mouthful of supper, but mounted the messenger's horse and started off at a gallop.

He reached home at midnight. His wife had been delivered of a little girl. 'Ah, why weren't you with me?' she said, as he came to her bedside.

'I was out of the house when the man came. I was with Rosalind,' said Lloyd, innocently.

Mrs Lloyd made a little moan, and turned away. But she continued to do very well, and for a week her improvement was uninterrupted. Finally, however, through some indiscretion in the way of diet or exposure, it was checked, and the poor lady grew rapidly worse. Lloyd was in despair. It very soon became evident that she was breathing her last. Mrs Lloyd came to a sense of her approaching end, and declared that she was reconciled with death. On the third evening after the change took place she told her husband that she felt she should not get through the night. She dismissed her servants, and also requested her mother to withdraw

– Mrs Wingrave having arrived on the preceding day. She had had her infant placed on the bed beside her, and she lay on her side, with the child against her breast, holding her husband's hands. The night-lamp was hidden behind the heavy curtains of the bed, but the room was illuminated with a red glow from the immense fire of logs on the hearth.

'It seems strange not to be warmed into life by such a fire as that,' the young woman said, feebly trying to smile. 'If I had but a little of it in my veins! But I have given all *my* fire to this little spark of mortality.' And she dropped her eyes on her child. Then raising them she looked at her husband with a long, penetrating gaze. The last feeling which lingered in her heart was one of suspicion. She had not recovered from the shock which Arthur had given her by telling her that in the hour of her agony he had been with Rosalind. She trusted her husband very nearly as well as she loved him; but now that she was called away forever she felt a cold horror of her sister. She felt in her soul that Rosalind had never ceased to be jealous of her good fortune; and a year of happy security had not effaced the young girl's image, dressed in her wedding-garments, and smiling with simulated triumph. Now that Arthur was to be alone, what might not Rosalind attempt? She was beautiful, she was engaging; what arts might she not use, what impression might she not make upon the young man's saddened heart? Mrs Lloyd looked at her husband in silence. It seemed hard, after all, to doubt of his constancy. His fine eyes were filled with tears; his face was convulsed with weeping; the clasp of his hands was warm and passionate. How noble he looked, how tender, how faithful and devoted! 'Nay,' thought Perdita, 'he's not for such a one as Rosalind. He'll never forget me. Nor does Rosalind truly care for him; she cares only for vanities and finery and jewels.' And she lowered her eyes on her white hands, which her husband's liberality had covered with rings, and on the lace ruffles which trimmed the edge of her nightdress. 'She covets my rings and my laces more than she covets my husband.'

At this moment the thought of her sister's rapacity seemed to cast a dark shadow between her and the helpless figure of her little girl. 'Arthur,' she said, 'you must take off my rings. I shall not be buried in them. One of these days my daughter shall wear them – my rings and my laces and silks. I had them all brought out and shown me today. It's a great wardrobe – there's not such another in the Province; I can say it without vanity, now that I have done with it. It will be a great inheritance for my daughter when she grows into a young woman. There are things there that a man never buys twice, and if they are lost you will never again see the like. So you will watch them well. Some dozen things I have left to Rosalind; I have named them to my mother. I have given her that blue and silver; it was meant for her; I wore it only once, I looked ill in it. But the rest are to be sacredly kept for this little innocent. It's such a providence that she should be my colour; she can wear my gowns; she has her mother's eyes. You know the same fashions come back every twenty years. She can wear my gowns as they are. They will lie there quietly waiting till she grows into them – wrapped in camphor and rose-leaves, and keeping their colours in the sweet-scented darkness. She shall have black hair, she shall wear my carnation satin. Do you promise me, Arthur?'

'Promise you what, dearest?'

'Promise me to keep your poor little wife's old gowns.'

'Are you afraid I shall sell them?'

'No, but that they may get scattered. My mother will have them properly wrapped up, and you shall lay them away under a double-lock. Do you know the great chest in the attic, with the iron bands? There is no end to what it will hold. You can put them all there. My mother and the housekeeper will do it, and give you the key. And you will keep the key in your secretary, and never give it to anyone but your child. Do you promise me?'

'Ah, yes, I promise you,' said Lloyd, puzzled at the intensity with which his wife appeared to cling to this idea.

'Will you swear?' repeated Perdita.

'Yes, I swear.'

'Well – I trust you – I trust you,' said the poor lady, looking into his eyes with eyes in which, if he had suspected her vague apprehensions, he might have read an appeal quite as much as an assurance.

Lloyd bore his bereavement rationally and manfully. A month after his wife's death, in the course of business, circumstances arose which offered him an opportunity of going to England. He took advantage of it, to change the current of his thoughts. He was absent nearly a year, during which his little girl was tenderly nursed and guarded by her grandmother. On his return he had his house again thrown open, and announced his intention of keeping the same state as during his wife's lifetime. It very soon came to be predicted that he would marry again, and there were at least a dozen young women of whom one may say that it was by no fault of theirs that, for six months after his return, the prediction did not come true. During this interval he still left his little daughter in Mrs Wingrave's hands, the latter assuring him that a change of residence at so tender an age would be full of danger for her health. Finally, however, he declared that his heart longed for his daughter's presence and that she must be brought up to town. He sent his coach and his housekeeper to fetch her home. Mrs Wingrave was in terror lest something should befall her on the road; and, in accordance with this feeling, Rosalind offered to accompany her. She could return the next day. So she went up to town with her little niece, and Mr Lloyd met her on the threshold of his house, overcome with her kindness and with paternal joy. Instead of returning the next day Rosalind stayed out the week; and when at last she reappeared, she had only come for her clothes. Arthur would not hear of her coming home, nor would the baby. That little person cried and choked if Rosalind left her; and at the sight of her grief Arthur lost his wits, and swore that she was going to die. In fine, nothing would suit them but that the aunt should remain until the little niece had grown used to strange faces.

It took two months to bring this consummation about; for it was not until this period had elapsed that Rosalind took leave of her brother-in-law. Mrs Wingrave had shaken her head over her daughter's absence; she had declared that it was not becoming, that it was the talk of the whole country. She had reconciled herself to it only because, during the girl's visit, the household enjoyed an unwonted term of peace. Bernard Wingrave had brought his wife home to live, between whom and her sister-in-law there was as little love as you please. Rosalind was perhaps no angel; but in the daily practice of life she was a sufficiently good-natured girl, and if she quarrelled with Mrs Bernard, it was not without provocation. Quarrel, however, she did, to the great annoyance not only of her antagonist, but of the two spectators of these constant altercations. Her stay in the household of her brother-in-law, therefore, would have been delightful, if only because it removed her from contact with the object of her antipathy at home. It was doubly – it was ten times – delightful, in that it kept her near the object of her early passion. Mrs Lloyd's sharp suspicions had fallen very far short of the truth. Rosalind's sentiment had been a passion at first, and a passion it remained – a passion of whose radiant heat, tempered to the delicate state of his feelings, Mr Lloyd very soon felt the influence. Lloyd, as I have hinted, was not a modern Petrarch; it was not in his nature to practise an ideal constancy. He had not been many days in the house with his sister-in-law before he began to assure himself that she was, in the language of that day, a devilish fine woman. Whether Rosalind really practised those insidious arts that her sister had been tempted to impute to her it is needless to inquire. It is enough to say that she found means to appear to the very best advantage. She used to seat herself every morning before the big fireplace in the dining-room, at work upon a piece of tapestry, with her little niece disporting herself on the carpet at her feet, or on the train of her dress, and playing with her woollen balls. Lloyd would have been a very stupid fellow if he had remained insensible to the rich suggestions of this charming picture. He was exceedingly fond of his little girl, and was never weary of taking her in his arms and tossing her up and down, and making her crow with delight. Very often, however, he would venture upon greater liberties than the young lady was yet prepared to allow, and then she would suddenly vociferate her displeasure. Rosalind, at this, would drop her tapestry, and put out her handsome hands with the serious smile of the young girl whose virgin fancy has revealed to her all a mother's healing arts. Lloyd would give up the child, their eyes would meet, their hands would touch, and Rosalind would extinguish the little girl's sobs upon the snowy folds of the kerchief that crossed her bosom. Her dignity was perfect, and nothing could be more discreet than the manner in which she accepted her brother-in-law's hospitality. It may almost be said, perhaps, that there was something harsh in her reserve. Lloyd had a provoking feeling that she was in the house and yet was unapproachable. Half-an-hour after supper, at the very outset of the long winter evenings, she would light her candle, make the young man a most respectful curtsey, and march off to bed. If these were arts, Rosalind was a great artist. But their effect was so gentle, so gradual, they were calculated to work upon the young widower's fancy with a *crescendo* so finely shaded, that, as the reader has seen, several weeks elapsed before Rosalind began to feel sure that her returns would cover her outlay. When this became morally certain she packed up her trunk and returned to her mother's house. For three days she waited: on the fourth Mr Lloyd made his appearance – a respectful but pressing suitor. Rosalind heard him to the end, with great humility, and accepted him with infinite modesty. It is hard to imagine that Mrs Lloyd would have forgiven her husband; but if anything might have disarmed her resentment it would have been the ceremonious continence of this interview. Rosalind imposed upon her lover but a short probation. They were married, as was becoming, with great privacy – almost with secrecy – in the hope perhaps, as was waggishly remarked at the time, that the late Mrs Lloyd wouldn't hear of it.

The marriage was to all appearance a happy one, and each party obtained what each had desired – Lloyd 'a devilish fine woman', and Rosalind – but Rosalind's desires, as the reader will have observed, had remained a good deal of a mystery. There were, indeed, two blots upon their felicity, but time would perhaps efface them. During the first three years of her marriage Mrs Lloyd failed to become a mother, and her husband on his side suffered heavy losses of money. This latter circumstance compelled a material retrenchment in his expenditure, and Rosalind was perforce less of a fine lady than her sister had been. She contrived, however, to carry it like a woman of considerable fashion. She had long since ascertained that her sister's copious wardrobe had been sequestrated for the benefit of her daughter, and that it lay languishing in thankless gloom in the dusty attic. It was a revolting thought that these exquisite fabrics should await the good pleasure of a little girl who sat in a high chair and ate bread-and-milk with a wooden spoon. Rosalind had the good taste, however, to say nothing about the matter until several months had expired. Then, at last, she timidly broached it to her husband. Was it not a pity that so much finery should be lost? – for lost it would be, what with colours fading, and moths eating it up, and the change of fashions. But Lloyd gave her so abrupt and peremptory a refusal, that she saw, for the present, her attempt was vain. Six months went by, however, and brought with them new needs and new visions. Rosalind's thoughts hovered lovingly about her sister's relics. She went up and looked at the chest in which they lay imprisoned. There was a sullen defiance in its three great padlocks and its iron bands which only quickened her cupidity. There was something exasperating in its incorruptible immobility. It was like a grim and grizzled old household servant, who locks his jaws over a family secret. And then there was a look of capacity in its vast extent, and a sound as of dense fullness, when Rosalind knocked its side with the toe of her little shoe, which caused her to flush with baffled longing. 'It's absurd,' she cried; 'it's improper, it's wicked'; and she forthwith resolved upon another attack upon her husband. On the following day, after dinner, when he had had his wine, she boldly began it. But he cut her short with great sternness.

'Once for all, Rosalind,' said he, 'it's out of the question. I shall be gravely displeased if you return to the matter.'

'Very good,' said Rosalind. 'I am glad to learn the esteem in which I am held. Gracious heaven,' she cried, 'I am a very happy woman! It's an agreeable thing to feel one's self sacrificed to a caprice!' And her eyes filled with tears of anger and disappointment.

Lloyd had a good-natured man's horror of a woman's sobs, and he attempted – I may say he condescended – to explain. 'It's not a caprice, dear, it's a promise,' he said – 'an oath.'

'An oath? It's a pretty matter for oaths! and to whom, pray?'

'To Perdita,' said the young man, raising his eyes for an instant, and immediately dropping them.

'Perdita – ah, Perdita!' and Rosalind's tears broke forth. Her bosom heaved with stormy sobs – sobs which were the long-deferred sequel of the violent fit of weeping in which she had indulged herself on the night when she discovered her sister's betrothal. She had hoped, in her better moments, that she had done with her jealousy; but her temper, on that occasion, had taken an ineffaceable hold. 'And pray, what right had Perdita to dispose of my future?' she cried. 'What right had she to bind you to meanness and cruelty? Ah, I occupy a dignified place, and I make a very fine figure! I am welcome to what Perdita has left! And what has she left? I never knew till now how little! Nothing, nothing, nothing.'

This was very poor logic, but it was very good as a 'scene'. Lloyd put his arm around his wife's waist and tried to kiss her, but she shook him off with magnificent scorn. Poor fellow! he had coveted a 'devilish fine woman', and he had got one. Her scorn was intolerable. He walked away with his ears tingling – irresolute, distracted. Before him was his secretary, and in it the sacred key which with his own hand he had turned in the triple lock. He marched up and opened it, and took the key from a secret drawer, wrapped in a little packet which he had sealed with his own honest bit of glazonry. *Je garde*, said the motto – 'I keep.' But he was ashamed to put it back. He flung it upon the table beside his wife.

'Put it back!' she cried. 'I want it not. I hate it!'

'I wash my hands of it,' cried her husband. 'God forgive me!'

Mrs Lloyd gave an indignant shrug of her shoulders, and swept out of the room, while the young man retreated by another door. Ten minutes later Mrs Lloyd returned, and found the room occupied by her little step-daughter and the nursery-maid. The key was not on the table. She glanced at the child. Her little niece was perched on a chair, with the packet in her hands. She had broken the seal with her own small fingers. Mrs Lloyd hastily took possession of the key.

At the habitual supper-hour Arthur Lloyd came back from his counting-room. It was the month of June, and supper was served by daylight. The meal was placed on the table, but Mrs Lloyd failed to make her appearance. The servant whom his master sent to call her came back with the assurance that her room was empty, and that the women informed him that she had not been seen since dinner. They had, in truth, observed her to have been in tears, and, supposing her to be shut up in her chamber, had not disturbed her. Her husband called her name in various parts of the house, but without response. At last it occurred to him that he might find her by taking the way to the attic. The thought gave him a strange feeling of discomfort, and he bade his servants remain behind, wishing no witness in his quest. He reached the foot of the staircase leading to the topmost flat, and stood with his hands on the banisters, pronouncing his wife's name. His voice trembled. He called again louder and more firmly. The only sound which disturbed the absolute silence was a faint echo of his own tones, repeating his question under the great eaves. He nevertheless felt irresistibly moved to ascend the staircase. It opened upon a wide hall, lined with wooden closets, and terminating in a window which looked westward, and admitted the last rays of the sun. Before the window stood the great chest. Before the chest, on her knees, the young man saw with amazement and horror the figure of his wife. In an instant he crossed the interval between them, bereft of utterance. The lid of the chest stood open, exposing, amid their perfumed napkins, its treasure of stuffs and jewels. Rosalind had fallen backward from a kneeling posture, with one hand supporting her on the floor and the other pressed to her heart. On her limbs was the stiffness of death, and on her face, in the fading light of the sun, the terror of something more than death. Her lips were parted in entreaty, in dismay, in agony; and on her blanched brow and cheeks there glowed the marks of ten hideous wounds from two vengeful ghostly hands.

Who Knows?

Guy de Maupassant

. . . . .

I

Thank God! At last I've made up my mind to put my experiences on record! But shall I ever be able to do it, shall I have the courage? It's all so mysterious, so inexplicable, so unintelligible, so crazy!

If I were not sure of what I've seen, certain that there has been no flaw in my reasoning, no mistake in my facts, no gap in the strict sequence of my observations, I should consider myself merely the victim of a hallucination, the sport of some strange optical delusion. After all, who knows?

Today I am in a Mental Home, but I went there of my own free will as a precaution, because I was afraid. Only one man knows my story, the House Doctor. Now I'm going to put it on paper, I really don't quite know why. Perhaps in the hope of shaking off the obsession, which haunts me like some ghastly nightmare.

Anyhow, here it is:

I have always been a lonely man, a dreamer, a kind of solitary, good-natured, easily satisfied, harbouring no bitterness against mankind and no grudge against Heaven. I have always lived alone, because of a sort of uneasiness, which the presence of others sets up in me. How can I explain it? I can't. It's not that I shun society; I enjoy conversation and dining with my friends, but when I am conscious of them near me, even the most intimate, for any length of time, I feel tired, exhausted, on edge, and I am aware of a growing and distressing desire to see them go away or to go away myself and be alone.

This desire is more than a mere craving, it is an imperative necessity. And if I had to remain in their company, if I had to go on, I do not say listening to, but merely hearing their conversation, I am sure something dreadful would happen. What? Who knows? Possibly, yes, probably, I should simply collapse.

I am so fond of being alone that I cannot even endure the proximity of other human beings sleeping under the same roof; I cannot live in Paris; to me it is a long drawn-out fight for life. It is spiritual death; this huge swarming crowd living all round me, even in their sleep, causes me physical and nervous torture. Indeed other people's sleep is even more painful to me than their conversation. And I can never rest, when I know or feel that there are living beings, on the other side of the wall, suffering this nightly suspension of consciousness.

Why do I feel like this? Who knows? Perhaps the reason is quite simple: I get tired very quickly of anything outside myself. And there are many people like me.

There are two kinds of human beings. Those who need others, who are distracted, amused, soothed by company, while loneliness, such as the ascent of some forbidding glacier or the crossing of a desert, worries them, exhausts them, wears them out: and those whom, on the contrary, the society of their fellows wearies, bores, irritates, cramps, while solitude gives them peace and rest in the free world of phantasy.

It is, in fact, a recognized psychological phenomenon. The former are equipped to lead the life of the extrovert, the latter that of the introvert. In my own case my ability to concentrate on things outside myself is limited and quickly exhausted, and as soon as this limit is reached, I am conscious of unbearable physical and mental discomfort. The result of this has been that I am, or rather I was, very much attached to inanimate objects, which take on for me the importance of human beings, and that my house has, or rather had, become a world in which I led a lonely but purposeful life, surrounded by things, pieces of furniture and ornaments that I knew and loved like friends. I had gradually filled my home and decorated it with them, and in it I felt at peace, contented, completely happy as in the arms of a loving wife, the familiar touch of whose caressing hand has become a comforting, restful necessity.

I had had this house built in a beautiful garden, standing back from the roads, not far from a town, where I could enjoy the social amenities, of which I felt the need from time to time. All my servants slept in a building at the far end of a walled kitchen-garden. In the silence of my home, deep hidden from sight beneath the foliage of tall trees, the enveloping darkness of the nights was so restful and so welcome that every evening I put off going to bed for several hours in order to prolong my enjoyment of it.

That evening there had been a performance of *Sigurd* at the local theatre. It was the first time I had heard this beautiful fairy play with music and I had thoroughly enjoyed it.

I was walking home briskly, with scraps of melody running in my head and the entrancing scenes still vivid in my memory. It was dark, pitch dark, and when I say that I mean I could hardly see the road and several times I nearly fell headlong into the ditch. From the toll-gate to my house is a little more than half a mile or about twenty minutes slow walking. It was one o'clock in the morning, one o'clock or half-past one; suddenly the sky showed slightly luminous in front of me, and the crescent moon rose, the melancholy crescent of the waning moon. The moon in its first quarter, when it rises at four or five o'clock in the evening, is bright, with cheerful, silvery light; but in the last quarter, when it rises after midnight, it is copper-coloured, suggesting gloomy foreboding, a real Witches' Sabbath moon. Anyone given to going out much at night might have noticed this. The first quarter's crescent, even when slender as a thread, sheds a faint but cheering gleam, at which the heart lifts, and throws clearly defined shadows on the ground; the last quarter's crescent gives a feeble, fitful light, so dim that it casts almost no shadow.

The dark silhouette of my garden loomed ahead and for some reason I felt an odd disinclination to go in. I slackened my pace. The night was very mild. The great mass of trees looked like a tomb, in which my house lay buried.

I opened the garden gate and entered the long sycamore drive leading to the house with the trees meeting overhead; it stretched before me like a lofty tunnel through the black mass of the trees and past lawns, on which the flower-beds showed up in the less intense darkness as oval patches of no particular colour.

As I approached the house I felt curiously uneasy. I paused. There was not a sound, not a breath of air stirring in the leaves. 'What has come over me?' I thought. For ten years I had been coming home like this without the least feeling of nervousness. I was not afraid. I have never been afraid in the dark. The sight of a man, a thief or a burglar, would merely have thrown me into a rage and I should have closed with him unhesitatingly. Moreover, I was armed; I had my revolver. But I did not put my hand on it, for I wanted to resist this feeling of fear stirring within me.

What was it? A presentiment? That unaccountable presentiment which grips a man's mind at the approach of the supernatural? Perhaps. Who knows?

As I went on, I felt shivers running down my spine, and when I was close to the wall of my great shuttered house I felt I must pause for a few moments before opening the door and going in. So I sat down on a garden seat under my drawing-room windows. I stayed there, my heart thumping, leaning my head against the wall, staring into the blackness of the foliage. For the first few minutes I noticed nothing unusual. I *was* aware of a kind of rumbling in my ears, but that often happens to me. I sometimes think I can hear trains passing, bells ringing or the tramp of a crowd.

But soon the rumbling became more distinct, more definite, more unmistakable. I had been wrong. It was not the normal throbbing of my arteries, which was causing this buzzing in my ears, but a quite definite, though confused, noise coming, without any question, from inside my house. I could hear it through the wall, a continuous noise, a rustling rather than a noise, a faint stirring, as of many objects being moved about, as if someone were shifting all my furniture from its usual place and dragging it about gently.

Naturally, for some time I thought I must be mistaken. But after putting my ear close to the shutters in order to hear the strange noises in the house more clearly, I remained quite firmly convinced that something abnormal and inexplicable was going on inside. I was not afraid, but – how can I express it? – startled by the sheer surprise of the thing. I did not slip the safety-catch of my revolver, somehow feeling certain it would be of no use. I just waited.

I waited a long while, unable to come to any decision, with my mind perfectly clear but deeply disturbed. I waited motionless, listening all the time to the growing noise, which swelled at times to a violent crescendo before turning into an impatient, angry rumble, which made me feel that some outburst might follow at any minute.

Then suddenly, ashamed of my cowardice, I seized my bunch of keys, picked out the one I wanted, thrust it into the lock, turned it twice, and pushing the door with all my force hurled it back against the wall inside.

The bang echoed like a gunshot and immediately the crash was answered by a terrific uproar from cellar to attic. It was so sudden, so terrifying, so deafening, that I stepped back a few paces and, though I realized it was useless, I drew my revolver from its holster.

I waited again, but not for long. I could now distinguish an extraordinary sound of trampling on the stairs, parquet floors and carpets, a trampling not of human feet or shoes, but of crutches, wooden crutches and iron crutches, that rang with the metallic insistence of cymbals. Suddenly, on the threshold of the front door, I saw an armchair, my big reading chair, come waddling out; it moved off down the drive. It was followed by others from the drawing-room; next came the sofas, low on the ground and crawling along like crocodiles on their stumpy legs, then all the rest of my chairs, leaping like goats, and the little stools loping along like rabbits.

Imagine my feelings! I slipped into a clump of shrubs, where I crouched, my eyes glued all the time to the procession of my furniture, for it was all on the way out, one piece after the other, quickly or slowly according to their shape and weight. My piano, my concert grand, galloped past like a runaway horse with a faint jangle of wires inside; the smaller objects, brushes, cut-glass and goblets, slid over the gravel like ants, gleaming like glow-worms in the moonlight. The carpets and hangings crawled away, sprawling for all the world like devil-fish. I saw my writing-desk appear, a rare eighteenth-century collector's piece, containing all my letters, the whole record of anguished passion long since spent. And in it were also my photographs.

Suddenly all fear left me; I threw myself upon it and grappled with it, as one grapples with a burglar; but it went on its way irresistibly, and, in spite of my utmost efforts, I could not even slow it up. As I wrestled like a madman against this terrible strength, I fell to the ground in the struggle. It rolled me over and over and dragged me along the gravel, and already the pieces of furniture behind were beginning to tread on me, trampling and bruising my legs; then, when I let go, the others swept over me, like a cavalry charge over an unhorsed soldier.

At last, mad with terror, I managed to drag myself off the main drive and hide again among the trees, watching the disappearance of the smallest, tiniest, humblest pieces that I had ever owned, whose very existence I had forgotten.

Presently I heard, in the distance, inside the house, which was full of echoes like an empty building, a terrific din of doors being shut. They banged from attic to basement and last of all the hall door slammed, which I had foolishly opened myself to allow the exodus.

At that I fled, and ran towards the town and I didn't pull myself together till I got to the streets and met people going home late. I went and rang the door of a hotel where I was known. I had beaten my clothes with my hands to shake the dust out of them, and I made up a story that I had lost my bunch of keys with the key of the kitchen-garden, where my servants slept in a house by itself, behind the garden wall which protected my fruit and vegetables from thieves.

I pulled the bed-clothes up to my eyes in the bed they gave me; but I couldn't sleep and I waited for dawn, listening to the violent beating of my heart. I had given orders for my servants to be informed as soon as it was light, and my valet knocked at my door at seven o'clock in the morning. His face showed how upset he was.

'An awful thing has happened during the night, Sir,' he said.

'What is it?'

'All your furniture has been stolen, Sir, absolutely everything, down to the smallest things.'

Somehow I was relieved to hear this. Why? I don't know.

I had complete control of myself; I knew I could conceal my feelings, tell no one what I had seen, hide it, bury it in my breast like some ghastly secret. I replied:

'They are the same people who stole my keys. The police must be informed at once. I'm getting up and I'll be with you in a few minutes at the police station.'

The inquiry lasted five months. Nothing was brought to light. Neither the smallest of my ornaments nor the slightest trace of the thieves was ever found. Good Heavens! If I had told them what I knew . . . If I had told . . . they would have shut up, not the thieves, but me, the man who could have seen such a thing.

Of course, I knew how to keep my mouth shut. But I never furnished my house again. It was no good. The same thing would have happened. I never wanted to go back to it again. I never did go back. I never saw it again. I went to a hotel in Paris and consulted doctors about the state of my nerves, which had been causing me considerable anxiety since that dreadful night.

They prescribed travel and I took their advice.

II

I began with a trip to Italy. The sun did me good. For six months I wandered from Genoa to Venice, from Venice to Florence, from Florence to Rome, from Rome to Naples. Next I toured Sicily, an attractive country, both from the point of view of scenery and monuments, the remains left by the Greeks and the Normans. I crossed to Africa and travelled at my leisure through the great sandy, peaceful desert, where camels, gazelles and nomad Arabs roam and where in the clear, dry air no obsession can persist either by day or night.

I returned to France via Marseilles and, in spite of the gaiety of Provence, the diminished intensity of the sunlight depressed me. On my return to Europe I had the odd feeling of a patient who thinks he is cured, but is suddenly warned by a dull pain that the source of the trouble is still active.

I went back to Paris, but after a month I got bored. It was autumn, and I decided to take a trip, before the winter, through Normandy, which was new ground to me.

I began with Rouen, of course, and for a week I wandered about, intrigued, charmed, thrilled, in this medieval town, this amazing museum of rare specimens of Gothic art.

Then one evening, about four o'clock, as I was entering a street that seemed too good to be true, along which flows an inky black stream called the Eau de Robec, my attention, previously centred on the unusual, old-fashioned aspect of the houses, was suddenly arrested by a number of second-hand furniture shops next door to one another.

They had, indeed, chosen their haunt well, these seedy junk dealers, in this fantastic alley by the side of this sinister stream, under pointed roofs of tile or slate, on which the weather-vanes of a vanished age still creaked.

Stacked in the depths of the cavernous shops could be seen carved chests, china from Rouen, Nevers and Moustiers, statues, some painted, some in plain oak, crucifixes, Madonnas, Saints, church ornaments, chasubles, copes, even chalices, and an old tabernacle of gilded wood, now vacated by its Almighty tenant. What astonishing store-rooms there were in these great, lofty houses, packed from cellar to attic with pieces of every kind, whose usefulness seemed finished and which had outlived their natural owners, their century, their period, their fashion, to be bought as curios by later generations!

My passion for old things was reviving in this collector's paradise. I went from shop to shop, crossing in two strides the bridges made of four rotten planks thrown over the stinking water of the Eau de Robec. And then – Mother of God! My heart leapt to my mouth. I caught sight of one of my finest cabinets at the edge of a vault crammed with junk, that looked like the entrance to the catacombs of some cemetery of old furniture. I went towards it trembling all over, trembling to such an extent that I did not dare touch it. I stretched out my hand, then I hesitated. It *was* mine, there was no question about it, a unique Louis XIII cabinet, unmistakable to anyone who had ever seen it. Suddenly, peering further into the sombre depths of this gallery, I noticed three of my arm-chairs covered with 'petit point' embroidery, and farther off my two Henri II tables, which were so rare that people came specially from Paris to see them.

Imagine, just imagine my feelings!

Then I went forward, dazed and faint with excitement, but I went in, for I am no coward; I went in like a knight in the dark ages entering a witches' kitchen. As I advanced, I found all my belongings, my chandeliers, my books, my pictures, my hangings and carpets, my weapons, everything except the writing-desk containing my letters, which I could not discover anywhere.

I went on, downstairs, along dark passages, and up again to the floors above. I was alone. I called but there was no answer. I was alone; there was no one in this huge winding labyrinth of a house.

Night came on and I had to sit down in the dark on one of my own chairs, for I wouldn't go away. At intervals I shouted: 'Hullo! Hullo! Anybody there!'

I had been there, I am sure, more than an hour, when I heard footsteps, light, slow steps; I could not tell where they came from. I nearly ran away, but, pulling myself together, I called again and I saw a light in the next room.

'Who's there?' said a voice.

I answered:

'A customer.'

The answer came:

'It's very late, we're really closed.'

I retorted:

'I've been waiting for you an hour.'

'You could have come back tomorrow.'

'Tomorrow I shall have left Rouen.'

I did not dare to move and he did not come to me. All this time I saw the reflection of his light shining on a tapestry, in which two angels were flying above the dead on a battlefield. That, too, belonged to me.

I said:

'Well, are you coming?'

He replied:

'I'm waiting for you.'

I got up and went towards him.

In the centre of a large room stood a very short man, very short and very fat, like the fat man at a show, and hideous into the bargain. He had a sparse, straggling, ill-kept, dirty-yellow beard, and not a hair on his head, not a single one! As he held his candle raised at arm's length in order to see me, the dome of his bald head looked like a miniature moon in this huge room stacked with old furniture. His face was wrinkled and bloated, his eyes mere slits.

After some bargaining I bought three chairs that were really mine and paid a large sum in cash, merely giving the number of my room at the hotel. They were to be delivered next morning before nine o'clock. Then I left the shop. He showed me to the door most politely.

I went straight to the Head Police station, where I told the story of the theft of my furniture and the discovery I had just made.

The Inspector telegraphed, on the spot, for instructions to the Public Prosecutor's Office, where the investigation into the theft had been held, asking me to wait for the answer. An hour later it was received, completely confirming my story.

'I'll have this man arrested and questioned at once,' he said, 'for he may have become suspicious and he might move your belongings. I suggest you go and dine, and come back in two hours' time; I'll have him here and I'll put him through a second examination in your presence.'

'Excellent, Inspector! I'm more than grateful to you.'

I went and dined at my hotel, and my appetite was better than I should have thought possible. But I was pretty well satisfied. They had got him.

Two hours later I was back at the Police Station, where the officer was waiting for me.

'Well, Sir,' he said, when he saw me, 'we haven't got your friend. My men haven't been able to lay hands on him.'

'Do you mean . . . ?'

A feeling of faintness came over me.

'But . . . you *have* found the house?' I asked.

'Oh yes! And it will, of course, be watched and guarded till he comes back. But he has disappeared.'

'Disappeared?'

'Yes, disappeared. He usually spends the evening with his next door neighbour, a queer old hag, a widow called Mme Bidoin, a second-hand dealer like himself. She hasn't seen him this evening and can't give any information about him. We shall have to wait till tomorrow.'

I went away. The streets of Rouen now seemed sinister, with the disturbing effect of a haunted house.

I slept badly, with nightmares every time I dropped off.

As I didn't want to seem unduly anxious, or in too much of a hurry, I waited next morning till ten o'clock before going round to the Police Station.

The dealer had not reappeared; his shop was still closed.

The Inspector said to me:

'I've taken all the necessary steps. The Public Prosecutor's Department has been informed; we'll go together to the shop and have it opened; you can show me what belongs to you.'

We drove to the place. Policemen were on duty, with a locksmith, in front of the door, which had been opened.

When I went in I saw neither my cabinet nor my arm-chairs nor my tables, not a single one of all the contents of my house, though the evening before I could not take a step without running into something of mine.

The Chief Inspector, in surprise, at first looked at me suspiciously.

'Well, I must say, Inspector, the disappearance of this furniture coincides oddly with that of the dealer,' I commented.

He smiled:

'You're right! You made a mistake in buying and paying for your pieces yesterday. It was that gave him the tip.'

I replied:

'What I can't understand is that all the space occupied by my furniture is now filled with other pieces.'

'Oh well!' answered the Inspector, 'he had the whole night before him, and accomplices, too, no doubt. There are sure to be means of communication with the houses on either side. Don't be alarmed, Sir, I shall leave no stone unturned. The thief won't elude us for long, now we've got his hide-out.'

My heart was beating so violently that I thought it would burst.

I stayed on in Rouen for a fortnight. The man did not come back. God knows, nobody could outwit or trap a man like that!

Then on the following morning I got this strange letter from my gardener, who was acting as caretaker of my house, which had been left unoccupied since the robbery:

DEAR SIR,

I beg to inform you that something happened last night, which we can't explain, nor the Police neither. All the furniture has come back, absolutely everything down to the smallest bits. The house is now just as it was the evening before the burglary. It's fit to send you off your head. It all happened on the night between Friday and Saturday. The paths are cut up as if everything had been dragged from the garden gate to the front door. It was just the same the day it all disappeared.

I await your return and remain,

Yours respectfully,

PHILIP RAUDIN

No! No! No! I will *not* return there!

I took the letter to the Chief Inspector of Rouen.

'It's a very neat restitution,' he said. 'We'll lie doggo and we'll nab the fellow one of these days.'

But he has not been nabbed. No! They've never got him, and now I'm afraid of him, as if a wild animal were loose on my track.

He can't be found! He'll never be found, this monster with the bald head like a full moon. They'll never catch him. He'll never go back to his shop. Why should he? Nobody but me *can* meet him, and I won't. I won't! I won't! I won't!

And if he does go back, if he returns to his shop, who will be able to prove that my furniture was ever there? There's only my evidence and I've a feeling that is becoming suspect.

No! My life was getting impossible. And I couldn't keep the secret of what I had seen. I couldn't go on living like everyone else, with the fear that this sort of thing might begin again at any moment.

I went and consulted the doctor who keeps this Mental Home, and told him the whole story.

After putting me through a lengthy examination, he said:

'My dear Sir, would you be willing to stay here for a time?'

'I should be very glad to.'

'You're not short of money?'

'No, Doctor.'

'Would you like a bungalow to yourself?'

'Yes, I should.'

'Would you like your friends to come and see you?'

'No, Doctor, no one. The man from Rouen might venture to follow me here to get even with me.'

And I have been here alone for three months, absolutely alone. I have practically no anxieties. I am only afraid of one thing . . . Supposing the second-hand dealer went mad . . . and suppose he was brought to this Home . . . Even prisons are not absolutely safe . . .

The Body Snatcher

Robert Louis Stevenson

Every night in the year, four of us sat in the small parlour of the George at Debenham – the undertaker, and the landlord, and Fettes, and myself. Sometimes there would be more; but blow high, blow low, come rain or snow or frost, we four would be each planted in his own particular armchair. Fettes was an old drunken Scotsman, a man of education obviously, and a man of some property, since he lived in idleness. He had come to Debenham years ago, while still young, and by a mere continuance of living had grown to be an adopted townsman. His blue camlet cloak was a local antiquity, like the church-spire. His place in the parlour at the George, his absence from church, his old, crapulous, disreputable vices, were all things of course in Debenham. He had some vague Radical opinions and some fleeting infidelities, which he would now and again set forth and emphasize with tottering slaps upon the table. He drank rum – five glasses regularly every evening; and for the greater portion of his nightly visit to the George sat, with his glass in his right hand, in a state of melancholy alcoholic saturation. We called him the Doctor, for he was supposed to have some special knowledge of medicine and had been known, upon a pinch, to set a fracture or reduce a dislocation; but beyond these slight particulars, we had no knowledge of his character and antecedents.

One dark winter night – it had struck nine some time before the landlord joined us – there was a sick man in the George, a great neighbouring proprietor suddenly struck down with apoplexy on his way to Parliament; and the great man's still greater London doctor had been telegraphed to his bedside. It was the first time that such a thing had happened in Debenham, for the railway was but newly open, and we were all proportionately moved by the occurrence.

'He's come,' said the landlord, after he had filled and lighted his pipe.

'He?' said I. 'Who? – not the doctor?'

'Himself,' replied our host.

'What is his name?'

'Dr Macfarlane,' said the landlord.

Fettes was far through his third tumbler, stupidly fuddled, now nodding over, now staring mazily around him; but at the last word he seemed to awaken and repeated the name 'Macfarlane' twice, quietly enough the first time, but with sudden emotion at the second.

'Yes,' said the landlord, 'that's his name, Doctor Wolfe Macfarlane.'

Fettes became instantly sober; his eyes awoke, his voice became clear, loud and steady, his language forcible and earnest. We were all startled by the transformation, as if a man had risen from the dead.

'I beg your pardon,' he said, 'I am afraid I have not been paying much attention to your talk. Who is this Wolfe Macfarlane?' And then, when he had heard the landlord out, 'It cannot be, it cannot be,' he added; 'and yet I would like well to see him face to face.'

'Do you know him, Doctor?' asked the undertaker, with a gasp.

'God forbid!' was the reply. 'And yet the name is a strange one; it were too much to fancy two. Tell me, landlord, is he old?'

'Well,' said the host, 'he's not a young man, to be sure, and his hair is white; but he looks younger than you.'

'He is older, though; years older. But,' with a slap upon the table, 'it's the rum you see in my face – rum and sin. This man, perhaps, may have an easy conscience and a good digestion. Conscience! Hear me speak. You would think I was some good, old, decent Christian, would you not? But no, not I; I never canted. Voltaire might have canted if he'd stood in my shoes; but the brains' – with a rattling fillip on his bald head – 'the brains were clear and active and I saw and made no deductions.'

'If you know this doctor,' I ventured to remark, after a somewhat awful pause, 'I should gather that you do not share the landlord's good opinion.'

Fettes paid no regard to me.

'Yes,' he said, with sudden decision, 'I must see him face to face.'

There was another pause and then a door was closed rather sharply on the first floor and a step was heard upon the stair.

'That's the doctor,' cried the landlord. 'Look sharp and you can catch him.'

It was but two steps from the small parlour to the door of the old George inn; the wide oak staircase landed almost in the street; there was room for a Turkey rug and nothing more between the threshold and the last round of the descent; but this little space was every evening brilliantly lit up, not only by the light upon the stair and the great signal-lamp below the sign, but by the warm radiance of the bar-room window. The George thus brightly advertised itself to passers-by in the cold street. Fettes walked steadily to the spot and we, who were hanging behind, beheld the two men meet, as one of them had phrased it, face to face. Dr Macfarlane was alert and vigorous. His white hair set off his pale and placid, although energetic, countenance. He was richly dressed in the finest of broadcloth and the whitest of linen, with a great gold watch-chain, and studs and spectacles of the same precious material. He wore a broad-folded tie, white and speckled with lilac, and he carried on his arm a comfortable driving-coat of fur. There was no doubt but he became his years, breathing, as he did, of wealth and consideration; and it was a surprising contrast to see our parlour sot – bald, dirty, pimpled and robed in his old camlet cloak – confront him at the bottom of the stairs.

'Macfarlane!' he said somewhat loudly, more like a herald than a friend.

The great doctor pulled up short on the fourth step, as though the familiarity of the address surprised and somewhat shocked his dignity.

'Toddy Macfarlane!' repeated Fettes.

The London man almost staggered. He stared for the swiftest of seconds at the man before him, glanced behind him with a sort of scare, and then in a startled whisper, 'Fettes!' he said, 'you!'

'Ay,' said the other, 'me! Did you think I was dead too? We are not so easy shut of our acquaintance.'

'Hush, hush!' exclaimed the doctor. 'Hush, hush! this meeting is so unexpected – I can see you are unmanned. I hardly knew you, I confess, at first, but I am overjoyed – overjoyed to have this opportunity. For the present it must be how-d'ye-do and good-bye in one, for my fly is waiting and I must not fail the train; but you shall – let me see – yes – you shall give me your address and you can count on early news of me. We must do something for you, Fettes. I fear you are out at elbows; but we must see to that for auld lang syne, as once we sang at suppers.'

'Money!' cried Fettes; 'money from you! The money that I had from you is lying where I cast it in the rain.'

Dr Macfarlane had talked himself into some measure of superiority and confidence, but the uncommon energy of this refusal cast him back into his first confusion.

A horrible, ugly look came and went across his almost venerable countenance. 'My dear fellow,' he said, 'be it as you please; my last thought is to offend you. I would intrude on none. I will leave you my address, however –'

'I do not wish it – I do not wish to know the roof that shelters you,' interrupted the other. 'I heard your name; I feared it might be you; I wished to know if, after all, there were a God; I know now that there is none. Begone!'

He still stood in the middle of the rug, between the stair and the doorway; and the great London physician, in order to escape, would be forced to step to one side. It was plain that he hesitated before the thought of this humiliation. White as he was, there was a dangerous glitter in his spectacles; but while he still paused uncertain, he became aware that the driver of his fly was peering in from the street at this unusual scene and caught a glimpse at the same time of our little body from the parlour, huddled by the corner of the bar. The presence of so many witnesses decided him at once to flee. He crouched together, brushing on the wainscot, and made a dart like a serpent, striking for the door. But his tribulation was not yet entirely at an end, for even as he was passing Fettes clutched him by the arm and these words came in a whisper, and yet painfully distinct, 'Have you seen it again?'

The great rich London doctor cried out aloud with a sharp, throttling cry; he dashed his questioner across the open space, and, with his hands over his head, fled out of the door like a detected thief. Before it had occurred to one of us to make a movement, the fly was already rattling towards the station. The scene was over like a dream, but the dream had left proofs and traces of its passage. Next day the servant found the fine gold spectacles broken on the threshold, and that very night we were all standing breathless by the bar-room window, and Fettes at our side, sober, pale, and resolute in look.

'God protect us, Mr Fettes!' said the landlord, coming first into possession of his customary senses. 'What in the universe is all this? These are strange things you have been saying.'

Fettes turned towards us; he looked us each in succession in the face. 'See if you can hold your tongues,' said he. 'That man Macfarlane is not safe to cross; those that have done so already have repented it too late.'

And then, without so much as finishing his third glass, far less waiting for the other two, he bade us good-bye and went forth, under the lamp of the hotel, into the black night.

We three turned to our places in the parlour, with the big red fire and four clear candles; and as we recapitulated what had passed the first chill of our surprise soon changed into a glow of curiosity. We sat late; it was the latest session I have known in the old George. Each man, before we parted, had his theory that he was bound to prove; and none of us had any nearer business in this world than to track out the past of our condemned companion, and surprise the secret that he shared with the great London doctor. It was no great boast, but I believe I was a better hand at worming out a story than either of my fellows at the George; and perhaps there is now no other man alive who could narrate to you the following foul and unnatural events.

In his young days Fettes studied medicine in the schools of Edinburgh. He had talent of a kind, the talent that picks up swiftly what it hears and readily retails it for its own. He worked little at home; but he was civil, attentive, and intelligent in the presence of his masters. They soon picked him out as a lad who listened closely and remembered well; nay, strange as it seemed to me when I first heard it, he was in those days well favoured, and pleased by his exterior. There was, at that period, a certain extramural teacher of anatomy, whom I shall here designate by the letter K. His name was subsequently too well known. The man who bore it skulked through the streets of Edinburgh in disguise, while the mob that applauded at the execution of Burke called loudly for the blood of his employer. But Mr K— was then at the top of his vogue; he enjoyed a popularity due partly to his own talent and address, partly to the incapacity of his rival, the university professor. The students, at least, swore by his name, and Fettes believed himself, and was believed by others, to have laid the foundations of success when he had acquired the favour of this meteorically famous man. Mr K— was a *bon vivant* as well as an accomplished teacher; he liked a sly allusion no less than a careful preparation. In both capacities Fettes enjoyed and deserved his notice, and by the second year of his attendance he held the half-regular position of second demonstrator or sub-assistant in his class.

In this capacity, the charge of the theatre and lecture room developed in particular upon his shoulders. He had to answer for the cleanliness of the premises and the conduct of the other students, and it was a part of his duty to supply, receive, and divide the various subjects. It was with a view to this last – at that time very delicate – affair that he was lodged by Mr K— in the same wynd, and at last in the same building, with the dissecting rooms. Here, after a night of turbulent pleasures, his hand still tottering, his sight still misty and confused, he would be called out of bed in the black hours before the winter dawn by the unclean and desperate interlopers who supplied the table. He would open the door to these men, since infamous throughout the land. He would help them with their tragic burthen, pay them their sordid price, and remain alone, when they were gone, with the unfriendly relics of humanity. From such a scene he would return to snatch another hour or two of slumber, to repair the abuses of the night, and refresh himself for the labours of the day.

Few lads could have been more insensible to the impressions of a life thus passed among the ensigns of mortality. His mind was closed against all general considerations. He was incapable of interest in the fate and fortunes of another, the slave of his own desires and low ambitions. Cold, light and selfish in the last resort, he had that modicum of prudence, miscalled morality, which keeps a man from inconvenient drunkenness or punishable theft. He coveted, besides, a measure of consideration from his masters and his fellow-pupils, and he had no desire to fail conspicuously in the external parts of life. Thus he made it his pleasure to gain some distinction in his studies, and day after day rendered unimpeachable eye-service to his employer, Mr K—. For his day of work he indemnified himself by nights of roaring, blackguardly enjoyment; and when that balance had been struck, the organ that he called his conscience declared itself content.

The supply of subjects was a continual trouble to him as well as to his master. In that large and busy class, the raw material of the anatomists kept perpetually running out; and the business thus rendered necessary was not only unpleasant in itself, but threatened dangerous consequences to all who were concerned. It was the policy of Mr K— to ask no questions in his dealings with the trade. 'They bring the body, and we pay the price,' he used to say, dwelling on the alliteration – '*quid pro quo*'. And again, and somewhat profanely, 'Ask no questions,' he would tell his assistants, 'for conscience' sake'. There was no understanding that the subjects were provided by the crime of murder. Had that idea been broached to him in words, he would have recoiled in horror; but the lightness of his speech upon so grave a matter was, in itself, an offence against good manners, and a temptation to the men with whom he dealt. Fettes, for instance, had often remarked to himself upon the singular freshness of the bodies. He had been struck again and again by the hang-dog, abominable looks of the ruffians who came to him before the dawn; and, putting things together clearly in his private thoughts, he perhaps attributed a meaning too immoral and too categorical to the unguarded counsels of his master. He understood his duty, in short, to have three branches: to take what was brought, to pay the price, and to avert the eye from any evidence of crime.

One November morning this policy of silence was put sharply to the test. He had been awake all night with a racking toothache – pacing his room like a caged beast or throwing himself in fury on his bed – and had fallen at last into that profound, uneasy slumber that so often follows on a night of pain, when he was awakened by the third or fourth angry repetition of the concerted signal. There was a thin, bright moonshine: it was bitter cold, windy, and frosty; the town had not yet awakened, but an indefinable stir already preluded the noise and business of the day. The ghouls had come later than usual, and they seemed more than usually eager to be gone. Fettes, sick with sleep, lighted them upstairs. He heard their grumbling Irish voices through a dream; and as they stripped the sack from their sad merchandise he leaned dozing with his shoulder propped against the wall; he had to shake himself to find the men their money. As he did so his eyes lighted on the dead face. He started; he took two steps nearer, with the candle raised.

'God Almighty!' he cried. 'That is Jane Galbraith!'

The men answered nothing, but they shuffled nearer the door.

'I know her, I tell you,' he continued. 'She was alive and hearty yesterday. It's impossible she can be dead; it's impossible you should have got this body fairly.'

'Sure, sir, you're mistaken entirely,' asserted one of the men.

But the other looked Fettes darkly in the eyes, and demanded the money on the spot.

It was impossible to misconceive the threat or to exaggerate the danger. The lad's heart failed him. He stammered some excuses, counted out the sum, and saw his hateful visitors depart. No sooner were they gone than he hastened to confirm his doubts. By a dozen unquestionable marks he identified the girl he had jested with the day before. He saw, with horror, marks upon her body that might well betoken violence. A panic seized him, and he took refuge in his room. There he reflected at length over the discovery that he had made; considered soberly the bearing of Mr K—'s instructions and the danger to himself of interference in so serious a business, and at last, in sore perplexity, determined to wait for the advice of his immediate superior, the class assistant.

This was a young doctor, Wolfe Macfarlane, a high favourite among all the restless students, clever, dissipated, and unscrupulous to the last degree. He had travelled and studied abroad. His manners were agreeable and a little forward. He was an authority on the stage, skilful on the ice or the links with skate or golf-club; he dressed with nice audacity, and, to put the finishing touch upon his glory, he kept a gig and a strong trotting-horse. With Fettes he was on terms of intimacy; indeed their relative positions called for some community of life; and when subjects were scarce the pair would drive far into the country in Macfarlane's gig, visit and desecrate some lonely graveyard, and return before dawn with their booty to the door of the dissecting room.

On that particular morning Macfarlane arrived somewhat earlier than his wont. Fettes heard him, and met him on the stairs, told him his story, and showed him the cause of his alarm. Macfarlane examined the marks on her body.

'Yes,' he said with a nod, 'it looks fishy.'

'Well, what should I do?' asked Fettes.

'Do?' repeated the other. 'Do you want to do anything? Least said soonest mended, I should say.'

'Someone else might recognize her,' objected Fettes. 'She was as well known as the Castle Rock.'

'We'll hope not,' said Macfarlane, 'and if anybody does – well you didn't, don't you see, and there's an end. The fact is, this has been going on too long. Stir up the mud, and you'll get K— into the most unholy trouble; you'll be in a shocking box yourself. So will I, if you come to that. I should like to know how any one of us would look, or what the devil we should have to say for ourselves, in any Christian witness-box. For me, you know there's one thing certain – that, practically speaking, all our subjects have been murdered.'

'Macfarlane!' cried Fettes.

'Come now!' sneered the other. 'As if you hadn't suspected it yourself!'

'Suspecting is one thing –'

'And proof another. Yes, I know; and I'm as sorry as you are this should have come here,' tapping the body with his cane. 'The next best thing for me is not to recognize it; and,' he added coolly, 'I don't. You may, if you please. I don't dictate, but I think a man of the world would do as I do; and I may add, I fancy that is what K— would look for at our hands. The question is, why did he choose us two for his assistants? And I answer, because he didn't want old wives.'

This was the tone of all others to affect the mind of a lad like Fettes. He agreed to imitate Macfarlane. The body of the unfortunate girl was duly dissected, and no one remarked or appeared to recognize her.

One afternoon, when his day's work was over, Fettes dropped into a popular tavern and found Macfarlane sitting with a stranger. This was a small man, very pale and dark, with coal-black eyes. The cut of his features gave a promise of intellect and refinement which was but feebly realized in his manners, for he proved, upon a nearer acquaintance, coarse, vulgar, and stupid. He exercised, however, a very remarkable control over Macfarlane; issued orders like the Great Bashaw; became inflamed at the least discussion or delay, and commented rudely on the servility with which he was obeyed. This most offensive person took a fancy to Fettes on the spot, plied him with drinks, and honoured him with unusual confidences on his past career. If a tenth part of what he confessed were true, he was a very loathsome rogue; and the lad's vanity was tickled by the attention of so experienced a man.

'I'm a pretty bad fellow myself,' the stranger remarked, 'but Macfarlane

is the boy – Toddy Macfarlane I call him. Toddy, order your friend
another glass.' Or it might be, 'Toddy, you jump up and shut the door.'
'Toddy hates me,' he said again. 'Oh, yes, Toddy, you do!'

'Don't call me that confounded name,' growled Macfarlane.

'Hear him! Did you ever see the lads play knife? He would like to do
that all over my body,' remarked the stranger.

'We medicals have a better way than that,' said Fettes. 'When we dislike
a dead friend of ours, we dissect him.'

Macfarlane looked up sharply, as though this jest was scarcely to his
mind.

The afternoon passed. Gray, for that was the stranger's name, invited
Fettes to join them at dinner, ordered a feast so sumptuous that the tavern
was thrown in commotion, and when all was done commanded Macfarlane to settle the bill. It was late before they separated; the man Gray was
incapably drunk. Macfarlane, sobered by his fury, chewed the cud of the
money he had been forced to squander and the slights he had been obliged
to swallow. Fettes, with various liquors singing in his head, returned
home with devious footsteps and a mind entirely in abeyance. Next day
Macfarlane was absent from the class, and Fettes smiled to himself as he
imagined him still squiring the intolerable Gray from tavern to tavern. As
soon as the hour of liberty had struck he posted from place to place in
quest of his last night's companions. He could find them, however,
nowhere; so returned early to his rooms, went early to bed, and slept the
sleep of the just.

At four in the morning he was awakened by the well-known signal.
Descending to the door, he was filled with astonishment to find
Macfarlane with his gig, and in the gig one of those long and ghastly
packages with which he was so well acquainted.

'What?' he cried. 'Have you been out alone? How did you manage?'

But Macfarlane silenced him roughly, bidding him turn to business.
When they had got the body upstairs and laid it on the table, Macfarlane
made at first as if he were going away. Then he paused and seemed to
hesitate; and then, 'You had better look at the face,' said he, in tones of
some constraint. 'You had better,' he repeated, as Fettes only stared at
him in wonder.

'But where, and how, and when did you come by it?' cried the other.

'Look at the face,' was the only answer.

Fettes was staggered; strange doubts assailed him. He looked from the
young doctor to the body, and then back again. At last, with a start, he
did as he was bidden. He had almost expected the sight that met his eyes,
and yet the shock was cruel. To see, fixed in the rigidity of death and

naked on that coarse layer of sack-cloth, the man whom he had left well-clad and full of meat and sin upon the threshold of a tavern, awoke, even in the thoughtless Fettes, some of the terrors of the conscience. It was a *cras tibi* which re-echoed in his soul, that two whom he had known should have come to lie upon these icy tables. Yet these were only secondary thoughts. His first concern regarded Wolfe. Unprepared for a challenge so momentous, he knew not how to look his comrade in the face. He durst not meet his eye, and he had neither words nor voice at his command.

It was Macfarlane himself who made the first advance. He came up quietly behind and laid his hand gently but firmly on the other's shoulder.

'Richardson,' said he, 'may have the head.'

Now Richardson was a student who had long been anxious for that portion of the human subject to dissect. There was no answer, and the murderer resumed: 'Talking of business, you must pay me; your accounts, you see, must tally.'

Fettes found a voice, the ghost of his own: 'Pay you!' he cried. 'Pay you for that?'

'Why, yes, of course you must. By all means and on every possible account, you must,' returned the other. 'I dare not give it for nothing, you dare not take it for nothing; it would compromise us both. This is another case like Jane Galbraith's. The more things are wrong the more we must act as if all were right. Where does old K— keep his money –'

'There,' answered Fettes hoarsely, pointing to a cupboard in the corner.

'Give me the key, then,' said the other, holding out his hand.

There was an instant's hesitation, and the die was cast. Macfarlane could not suppress a nervous twitch, the infinitesimal mark of an immense relief, as he felt the key turn between his fingers. He opened the cupboard, brought out pen and ink and a paper-book that stood in one compartment, and separated from the funds in a drawer a sum suitable to the occasion.

'Now, look here,' he said, 'there is the payment made – first proof of your good faith: first step to your security. You have now to clinch it by a second. Enter the payment in your book, and then you for your part may defy the devil.'

The next few seconds were for Fettes an agony of thought; but in balancing his terrors it was the most immediate that triumphed. Any future difficulty seemed almost welcome if he could avoid a present quarrel with Macfarlane. He set down the candle which he had been carrying all the time, and with a steady hand entered the date, the nature, and the amount of the transaction.

'And now,' said Macfarlane, 'it's only fair that you should pocket the lucre. I've had my share already. By-the-by, when a man of the world falls into a bit of luck, he has a few shillings extra in his pocket – I'm ashamed to speak of it, but there's a rule of conduct in the case. No treating, no purchase of expensive class-books, no squaring of old debts; borrow, don't lend.'

'Macfarlane,' began Fettes, still somewhat hoarsely. 'I have put my neck in a halter to oblige you.'

'To oblige me?' cried Wolfe. 'Oh, come! You did, as near as I can see the matter, what you downright had to do in self defence. Suppose I got into trouble, where would you be? This second little matter flows clearly from the first. Mr Gray is the continuation of Miss Galbraith. You can't begin and then stop. If you begin, you must keep on beginning; that's the truth. No rest for the wicked.'

A horrible sense of blackness and the treachery of fate seized hold upon the soul of the unhappy student.

'My God!' he cried, 'but what have I done? and when did I begin? To be made a class assistant – in the name of reason, where's the harm in that? Service wanted the position; Service might have got it. Would *he* have been where *I* am now?'

'My dear fellow,' said Macfarlane, 'what a boy you are! What harm *has* come to you? What harm *can* come to you if you hold your tongue? Why, man, do you know what this life is? There are two squads of us – the lions and the lambs. If you're a lamb, you'll come to lie upon these tables like Gray or Jane Galbraith; if you're a lion, you'll live and drive a horse like me, like K——, like all the world with any wit or courage. You're staggered at the first. But look at K——! My dear fellow, you're clever, you have pluck. I like you, and K—— likes you. You were born to lead the hunt: and I tell you, on my honour and my experience of life, three days from now you'll laugh at all these scarecrows like a high school boy at a farce.'

And with that Macfarlane took his departure and drove off up the wynd in his gig to get under cover before daylight. Fettes was thus left alone with his regrets. He saw the miserable peril in which he stood involved. He saw, with inexpressible dismay, that there was no limit to his weakness, and that, from concession to concession, he had fallen from the arbiter of Macfarlane's destiny to his paid and helpless accomplice. He would have given the world to have been a little braver at the time, but it did not occur to him that he might still be brave. The secret of Jane Galbraith and the cursed entry in the daybook closed his mouth.

Hours passed; the class began to arrive; the members of the unhappy Gray were dealt out to one and to another, and received without remark. Richardson was made happy with the head; and before the hour of freedom rang Fettes trembled with exultation to perceive how far they had already gone towards safety.

For two days he continued to watch, with increasing joy, the dreadful process of disguise.

On the third day Macfarlane made his appearance. He had been ill, he said; but he made up for lost time by the energy with which he directed the students. To Richardson in particular he extended the most valuable assistance and advice, and that student, encouraged by the praise of the demonstrator, burned high with ambitious hopes, and saw the medal already in his grasp.

Before the week was out Macfarlane's prophecy had been fulfilled. Fettes had outlived his terrors and had forgotten his baseness. He began to plume himself upon his courage, and had so arranged the story in his mind that he could look back on these events with an unhealthy pride. Of his accomplice he saw but little. They met, of course, in the business of the class; they received their orders together from Mr K—. At times they had a word or two in private, and Macfarlane was from first to last particularly kind and jovial. But it was plain that he avoided any reference to their common secret; and even when Fettes whispered to him that he had cast in his lot with the lions and forsworn the lambs, he only signed to him smilingly to hold his peace.

At length an occasion arose which drew the pair once more into a closer union. Mr K— was again short of subjects; pupils were eager, and it was a part of this teacher's pretensions to be always well supplied. At the same time there came the news of a burial in the rustic graveyard of Glencorse. Time has little changed the place in question. It stood then, as now, upon the crossroad, out of call of human habitations, and buried fathom deep in the foliage of six cedar trees. The cries of the sheep upon the neighbouring hills, the streamlets upon either hand, one loudly singing among pebbles, the other dripping furtively from pond to pond, the stir of the wind in mountainous old flowering chestnuts, and once in seven days the voice of the bell and the old tunes of the precentor, were the only sounds that disturbed the silence around the rural church. The Resurrection Man – to use a by-name of the period – was not to be deterred by any of the sanctities of customary piety. It was part of his trade to despise and desecrate the scrolls and trumpets of old tombs, the paths worn by the feet of worshippers and mourners, and the offerings and the inscriptions of bereaved affection. To rustic neighbourhoods, where love is more than commonly tenacious, and where some bonds of blood or fellowship unite the entire society of a parish, the body snatcher, far from being repelled by natural respect, was attracted by the ease and safety of the task. To bodies that had been laid in earth, in joyful expectation of a far different awakening, there came that hasty, lamp-lit, terror-haunted resurrection of the spade and mattock. The coffin was forced, the cerements torn, and the melancholy relics, clad in sackcloth, after being rattled for hours on moonless by-ways, were at length exposed to uttermost indignities before a class of gaping boys.

Somewhat as two vultures may swoop upon a dying lamb, Fettes and Macfarlane were to be let loose upon a grave in that green and quiet resting place. The wife of a farmer, a woman who had lived for sixty years, and been known for nothing but good butter and a godly conversation, was to be rooted from her grave at midnight and carried, dead and naked, to that far away city that she had always honoured with her Sunday best; the place beside her family was to be empty till the crack of doom; her innocent and almost venerable members to be exposed to that last curiosity of the anatomist.

Late one afternoon the pair set forth, well wrapped in cloaks and furnished with a formidable bottle. It rained without remission – a cold, dense, lashing rain. Now and again there blew a puff of wind, but these sheets of falling water kept it down. Bottle and all, it was a sad and silent drive as far as Penicuik, where they were to spend the evening. They stopped once, to hide their implements in a thick bush not far from the churchyard, and once again at the Fisher's Tryst, to have a toast before the kitchen fire and vary their nips of whisky with a glass of ale. When they reached their journey's end the gig was housed, the horse was fed and comforted, and the two young doctors in a private room sat down to the best dinner and the best wine the house afforded. The lights, the fire, the beating rain upon the window, the cold, incongruous work that lay before them, added zest to their enjoyment of the meal. With every glass their cordiality increased. Soon Macfarlane handed a little pile of gold to his companion.

'A compliment,' he said. 'Between friends these little damned accommodations ought to fly like pipe-lights.'

Fettes pocketed the money, and applauded the sentiment to the echo. 'You are a philosopher,' he cried. 'I was an ass till I knew you. You and K— between you, by the Lord Harry! but you'll make a man of me.'

'Of course we shall,' applauded Macfarlane. 'A man? I tell you, it required a man to back me up the other morning. There are some big, brawling, forty-year-old cowards who would have turned sick at the look of the damned thing; but not you – you kept your head. I watched you.'

'Well, and why not?' Fettes thus vaunted himself. 'It was no affair of mine. There was nothing to gain on the one side but disturbance, and on the other I could count on your gratitude, don't you see?' And he slapped his pocket till the gold pieces rang.

Macfarlane somehow felt a certain touch of alarm at these unpleasant words. He may have regretted that he had taught his young companion so successfully, but he had no time to interfere, for the other noisily continued in this boastful strain:

'The great thing is not to be afraid. Now, between you and me, I don't want to hang – that's practical; but for all cant, Macfarlane, I was born with a contempt. Hell, God, Devil, right, wrong, sin, crime, and all the old gallery of curiosities – they may frighten boys, but men of the world, like you and me, despise them. Here's to the memory of Gray!'

It was by this time growing somewhat late. The gig, according to order, was brought round to the door with both lamps brightly shining, and the young men had to pay their bill and take the road. They announced that they were bound for Peebles, and drove in that direction till they were clear of the last houses of the town; then, extinguishing the lamps, returned upon their course, and followed a by-road towards Glencorse. There was no sound but that of their own passage, and the incessant, strident pouring of the rain. It was pitch dark; here and there a white gate or a white stone in the wall guided them for a short space across the night; but for the most part it was at a foot pace, and almost groping, that they picked their way through that resonant blackness to their solemn and isolated destination. In the sunken woods that traverse the neighbourhood of the burying ground the last glimmer failed them, and it became necessary to kindle a match and re-illumine one of the lanterns of the gig. Thus, under the dripping trees, and environed by huge and moving shadows, they reached the scene of their unhallowed labours.

They were both experienced in such affairs, and powerful with the spade; and they had scarce been twenty minutes at their task before they were rewarded by a dull rattle on the coffin lid. At the same moment Macfarlane, having hurt his hand upon a stone, flung it carelessly above his head. The grave, in which they now stood almost to the shoulders, was close to the edge of the plateau of the graveyard; and the gig lamp had been propped, the better to illuminate their labours, against a tree, and on the immediate verge of the steep bank descending to the stream. Chance had taken a sure aim with the stone. Then came a clang of broken glass; night fell upon them; sounds alternately dull and ringing announced the bounding of the lantern down the bank, and its occasional collision with the trees. A stone or two, which it had dislodged in its descent rattled behind it into the profundities of the glen; and then silence, like night, resumed its sway; and they might bend their hearing to its utmost pitch, but naught was to be heard except the rain, now marching to the wind, now steadily falling over miles of open country.

They were so nearly at an end of their abhorred task that they judged it wisest to complete it in the dark. The coffin was exhumed and broken open; the body inserted in the dripping sack and carried between them to the gig; one mounted to keep it in its place, and the other, taking the horse by the mouth, groped along by the wall and bush until they reached the wider road by the Fisher's Tryst. Here was a faint disused radiancy, which they hailed like daylight; by that they pushed the horse to a good pace and began to rattle along merrily in the direction of the town.

They had both been wetted to the skin during their operations, and now, as the gig jumped among the deep ruts, the thing that stood propped between them fell now upon one and now upon the other. At every repetition of the horrid contact each instinctively repelled it with greater haste; and the process, natural although it was, began to tell upon the nerves of the companions. Macfarlane made some ill-favoured jest about the farmer's wife, but it came hollowly from his lips, and was allowed to drop in silence. Still their unnatural burthen bumped from side to side; and now the head would be laid, as if in confidence, upon their shoulders, and now the drenching sackcloth would flap icily about their faces. A creeping chill began to possess the soul of Fettes. He peered at the bundle, and it seemed somehow larger than at first. All over the countryside, and from every degree of distance, the farm dogs accompanied their passage with tragic ululations; and it grew and grew upon his mind that some unnatural miracle had been achieved, that some nameless change had befallen the dead body, and that it was in fear of their unholy burthen that the dogs were howling.

'For God's sake,' said he, making a great effort to arrive at speech, 'for God's sake, let's have a light!'

Seemingly Macfarlane was affected in the same direction; for though he made no reply, he stopped the horse, passed the reins to his companion, got down, and proceeded to kindle the remaining lamp. They had by that time got no farther than the crossroad down to Auchendinny. The rain still poured as though the deluge were returning, and it was no easy matter to make a light in such a world of wet and darkness. When at last the flickering blue flame had been transferred to the wick and began to expand and clarify, and shed a wide circle of misty brightness round the gig, it became possible for the two young men to see each other and the thing they had along with them. The rain had moulded the rough sacking to the outlines of the body underneath; the head was distinct from the trunk, the shoulders plainly modelled; something at once spectral and human riveted their eyes upon the ghastly comrade of their drive.

For some time Macfarlane stood motionless, holding up the lamp. A nameless dread was swathed, like a wet sheet, above the body, and tightened the white skin upon the face of Fettes; a fear that was meaningless, a horror of what could not be, kept mounting to his brain. Another beat of the watch, and he had spoken. But his comrade forestalled him.

'That is not a woman,' said Macfarlane, in a hushed voice.

'It was a woman when we put her in,' whispered Fettes.

'Hold that lamp,' said the other. 'I must see her face.'

And as Fettes took the lamp his companion untied the fastenings of the sack and drew down the cover from the head. The light fell very clear upon the dark, well-moulded features and smooth-shaven cheeks of a too familiar countenance, often beheld in dreams of both of these young men. A wild yell rang up into the night; each leaped from his own side into the roadway; the lamp fell, broke, and was extinguished; and the horse, terrified by this unusual commotion, bounded and went off towards Edinburgh at a gallop, bearing along with it, sole occupant of the gig, the body of the dead and long-dissected Gray.

The Death of Olivier Bécaille

Emile Zola

I

It was a Saturday morning, at six o'clock, that I died. I had been ill for three days. My poor wife had just been rummaging through a trunk, looking for some clean linen, and when she turned, she saw me lying there stiff, eyes staring, not breathing; she rushed over to me, thinking that I must have fainted; she touched my hands, bent down to look at my face. Terror-stricken, she burst into tears, repeating in broken tones: 'Dear God, he's dead, Olivier's dead.'

I could hear everything, although the sounds were muffled, as it they were coming from a long way off . . . With my left eye I could just distinguish a dull glimmer of light, a white haze into which all the objects in the room merged; my right eye was totally paralysed. My entire body had been affected by the fit; it was as though a thunderbolt had struck me down. My will-power had died, and there was not a nerve in my body which would respond. The only thing that remained in this state of non-being, above my lifeless limbs, was my ability to think, somewhat dull and sluggish, but still intact.

Poor Marguerite was on her knees at my bedside, weeping and wailing, 'He's dead, oh God, he's dead.'

Was this, then, death? this strange state of torpor, the flesh suddenly condemned to immobility, while the mind remained as active as ever? Or was it that my soul was still lingering in my body, and about to fly off? I had been a prey to nervous attacks since childhood. Twice when I was still very young, I had nearly died of an acute fever. So people had become used to my being sickly; it had indeed been I who had told Marguerite not to fetch a doctor on the day we arrived in Paris, when I had had to take to my bed in the boarding house in the rue Dauphine. What I needed was a little rest, I was just worn out after the journey. In fact, though, I was extremely worried. We had left our country home very suddenly; we were poor and had scarcely enough to cope before we'd receive the first month's pay for the clerical job I had taken on. And on top of all those worries, now this attack looked as though it was going to carry me off!

Was it really death? I had thought it would be darker, that the silence would be heavier. I had been scared of death since I was a child. Because I was weakly, people were always pitying me, and I was permanently afraid that I did not have long to live, that they'd have to bury me at an early age. The idea of the earth terrified me, and although it obsessed my waking and my sleeping hours, I had never been able to accept it. As I grew older I never outgrew the obsession. From time to time, after long days spent thinking of nothing else, I could almost believe that I had finally conquered my fear. After all, each one of us died; everything came to an end; there was an end to everything; we all had to die sooner or later; there was nothing more appropriate, nothing better. I would even manage to laugh at it; I could look death in the face. But then an icy shudder would run down my spine and my terror would return in full, just as though some giant hand had picked me up and swung me over a bottomless black hole. It was always the thought of the earth that came back to me and prevented me thinking straight. How many times, at night, have I woken up with a start, not knowing what ghostly breath had brushed over me as I slept, and clasped my hands in despair, jabbering that we all have to die. Fear tightened my chest; the inevitability of death was even more inhuman in this half-sleeping state. It was hard, after that, to go back to sleep; sleep itself scared me, because it was so akin to death. Supposing I were to sleep for ever! Supposing I were to close my eyes never to open them again!

I do not know if other people experience this anguish. It had certainly made my life a lonely one. Death has come between me and everything I have ever loved. I can recall now the happiest moments of my life with Marguerite. During the first few months of our marriage, when she lay sleeping alongside me at night; and as I thought of her, while dreaming of the future, inevitably the idea of being separated from her would spoil my joy and ruin all my dreams. We would have to leave each other maybe the following day, maybe in just an hour's time. An unbearable hopelessness would overcome me; I'd wonder what was the point of ever being happy together, since it was bound to end in so tragic a separation. My imagination would indulge itself in the morbid. Who would be the first to go, she or I? At both possibilities, my eyes would fill with tears of self-pity, as the scene of our broken lives would unfold before me. At each one of the best moments of my life, I have had similar attacks of melancholy, which no one has ever been able to understand. Whenever I had a piece of good luck, people would be surprised at how gloomily I would react. It was because I would suddenly be struck, in the middle of my joy, with the thought of being no longer. The awful words 'What's the point?' would ring out in my ears like the voice of doom. The worst thing about such suffering is that it has to be endured like a secret vice. You can't tell anyone else about it. Frequently husband and wife must lie side by side in a darkened room, feeling the same fear, yet neither of them speaking about it, because one cannot talk about death any more readily than one can use obscene words. We are so afraid of it that we dare not name it; we hide it, just as we hide our sexual organs.

Such were the thoughts that went through my mind, as Marguerite continued her sobbing beside me. It hurt me not to be able to soothe her and tell her that I was not in pain. If death were merely this numbing of the body, I had been quite mistaken to dread it so. There was a feeling of personal well-being, a total calm in which I could cast my worries aside. My memory, in particular, seemed to have become extraordinarily acute. The whole of my past life rushed past me like a show in which I was no longer an actor. The feeling was a bizarre one, and somewhat amusing; it was as though some distant speaker was telling me the story of my own life.

The memory of the countryside near Guérande, on the Piriac road, kept coming back to me. The road bends, and a pine wood sprawls over the rocky slopes. When I was seven, I used to go there with my father to a tumbledown old house where we would partake of pancakes with Marguerite's family. They were having a hard time trying to make a living out of the nearby salt works. Then I recalled the school in Nantes where I grew up in the restriction of the old walls, constantly longing for the open spaces of Guérande with its endless salt marshes just below the town, and the vast expanses of the sea and sky. At that point, darkness descended on my life – my father died, and I got a clerical job in the local hospital; I began a wretched life in which the only bright spot was the Sunday visits I would make to the old house on the Piriac road. Things were going from bad to worse there, as the salt marshes were not producing much and the whole area was increasingly poverty-stricken. Marguerite was still just a child. She liked me because I used to give her wheelbarrow rides. Later, when I asked her to marry me, I realized from the movement of repulsion she made that she found me unprepossessing. Her parents gave her to me immediately; they were better off without her. She was a dutiful daughter, and didn't complain. As she got used to the idea of becoming my wife, she did not seem too upset. On our wedding day at Guérande, I remember how it poured with rain and how, when we got home, she had to stay in her petticoats because her dress had been soaked.

That, then, was my youth. We went on living there for a while, till one day, when I got home from work, I came across my wife in floods of tears. She was apparently unhappy, wanted to move somewhere else. After six months, I had managed to scrimp and save some money by doing extra work, and an old family friend found me a job; I was able to take my little love off to Paris to stop her shedding any more tears. In the train, she laughed. The third-class benches were hard and I sat her on my lap so that she could sleep more comfortably.

That is the past. And now I have just died, on this narrow bed in the boarding house, and my wife is kneeling there, bemoaning her fate. The white blur I could see with my left eye was growing hazier but I could still remember the room clearly. The chest of drawers to the left; to the right the fireplace, with, in the centre, the clock which no longer told the right time because its pendulum was broken; it stood at six minutes past ten. The window looked out over the dark street. The whole of Paris seemed to pass by and with so much clatter that I could hear the window-panes creaking.

We did not know a soul in Paris. As we had left earlier than intended, I was not expected in the office till the following Monday. Ever since I had taken to my bed I had had the strange feeling of being imprisoned in this room where our journey had led us, still bemused by our fifteen hours in the train, and bewildered by the bustle of the streets of Paris. My wife had looked after me in her usual gentle, smiling way, but I sensed how perturbed she must be. From time to time, she would go over to the window, look out at the street, and come back pale and upset by the sheer size of Paris, which she did not know at all and which constantly made so terrifying a noise. What could she do, if I didn't wake up? What would become of her in this huge city, alone, without help, not knowing anyone or anything?

Marguerite had now taken one of my hands in hers, as it lay there lifeless on the edge of the bed. She kissed it over and over again, imploring me thus: 'Oh, say something . . . Dear God, he's dead . . .'

Death, then, couldn't be nothingness, since I could still hear and think. But not being had terrified me since I was a child. I couldn't conceive of myself disappearing; the total suppression of all that I was, for ever, for all eternity, without my life ever being able to begin again. I sometimes used to tremble if I came across a date in some newspaper of a future century; I would no longer be alive at that time, and the idea of a year in a future that I would not know and when I would no longer be filled me with anguish. Was not I the world, and wouldn't everything end when I left it?

I had always hoped to dream of life in death. But this probably wasn't death, after all. I would doubtless wake up in an hour or two. Yes, that was it; I would soon be able to bend over Marguerite and take her into my arms, and dry her tears. What bliss to be together again! and how we would love each other more deeply than ever! I would take two more days off, then I'd go to work. A new life would begin for us, happier, more open. Though I wasn't in a hurry for it yet. In a while; for the time being I was too tired. Marguerite was wrong to despair, and I didn't have the energy to turn my head and give her a smile. In a minute, when she again lamented 'He's dead', I would kiss her and murmur in her ear, so as not to frighten her too much, 'It's all right, my love. I was just asleep. See! I'm alive and I love you.'

II

Because of all Marguerite's wailing, the door suddenly opened and someone's voice said: 'What's the matter? Has he had another attack?'

I recognized the voice. It was an old lady, Mme Gabin, who had a room on the same landing as us. As soon as we had arrived, she had been very kind to us, and sorry for our plight. She had told us her story immediately. Some wretch of a landlord had sold her furniture the previous winter, since which she had been living in the boarding house with her daughter Adèle who was ten. They both cut out lampshades and scraped together about forty sous.

'Dear God, it's all over, then?' she asked in a whisper.

I realized that she was coming over to me. She looked at me, touched me, then said, in a hushed tone, 'You poor little thing.'

At the end of her tether now, Marguerite burst into tears like a child. Mme Gabin picked her up and made her sit down in the rickety armchair next to the fireplace; she did her best to comfort her.

'Well, if you go on like that you'll do yourself an injury. You don't have to kill yourself just because your husband has died. Of course, I felt just like you do when I lost Gabin; three days, I was, without being able to swallow a morsel of food. But it didn't get me anywhere; quite the

opposite, it just made matters worse . . . Come along, now, for goodness'
sake. Be a good girl.'

Gradually, Marguerite calmed down. She was exhausted, and from
time to time another burst of sobbing would rack her. Meanwhile the old
woman took control of the whole room with stern determination.

'Don't you bother about anything,' she said. 'Dédé has gone off with
some lampshades and anyway neighbours ought to help each other. Now
then, your trunks aren't all unpacked, are they? but there should be some
linen in the cupboard, shouldn't there?'

I heard her opening the cupboard. She must have got out a towel, and
came over and laid it out on the table. She then struck a match, which
made me think she must be lighting one of the candles on the fireplace.
I was able to follow every one of the movements she made in the room,
every one of her actions.

'Poor man,' she muttered. 'It's a good job I heard you, my dear.'

Suddenly, the white light that I had been able to see with my left eye
disappeared. Mme Gabin had closed my eyes, although I had not felt the
touch of her finger on my lids. When I realized what had happened, a
chill ran down my spine.

The door opened again. Dédé, the ten-year-old daughter, came in,
saying, in her high-pitched voice: 'Mummy, mummy, ah, I knew you
must be here! Here's the money, three francs forty. I've brought back
twenty dozen lampshades.'

'Sh! be quiet, will you,' her mother tried to stop her.

When her daughter still went on, she pointed to the bed. Dédé stopped
and I could feel how worried she was, as she moved backwards towards
the door.

'Is the gentleman asleep?' she whispered.

'Yes, so just you go off and play,' answered Mme Gabin.

The child, however, did not go off. She must have been watching me
wide-eyed, scared and only half understanding what was happening.
Suddenly, she was panic-stricken and ran off, knocking a chair on her
way.

The silence was total. Marguerite, huddled in a chair, was no longer
crying. Mme Gabin was walking to and fro about the room. She started
muttering through her teeth again. 'Children always know everything
nowadays. Just look at her. God knows, I bring her up as best I can.
When she goes out on an errand for me, or if I send her off to bring some
work back, I count the minutes so that I can be sure she's not up to
anything bad. It doesn't make any difference, she always knows everything. She saw it then, she realized in a second what was the matter. Yet

she's only ever seen one dead person; that was her Uncle François, and she was only four when that happened. Children aren't children any longer, are they?'

She broke off and went on immediately on a different tack. 'Now then, my dear, you'll have to start thinking about all the formalities, registering the death, and then the funeral. You really aren't in any fit state to bother about all that. And I don't want to leave you by yourself. I'll just go and see if M. Simoneau is in, if you don't mind.'

Marguerite did not reply. I watched all this as though I was many miles away. Sometimes I felt as though I was flying, like a will-o'-the-wisp, through the room while some foreign body was lying on the bed. I should, however, have preferred Marguerite to refuse the offer of M. Simoneau's services. I had had three or four glimpses of him during my illness. He had one of the neighbouring rooms and seemed kind enough. Mme Gabin had told us that he was just passing through Paris, sorting out the financial affairs of his father, who lived in the country and had recently died. He was a tall, good-looking, well-built fellow. I loathed him, perhaps because of his rude health. He had been in the evening before, and it had hurt to see him so close to Marguerite. She was so pretty and so fair next to him!

He looked at her so closely and she had smiled up at him, telling him how kind it was of him to come and see how I was!

'Here is M. Simoneau,' said Mme Gabin, as she came back in.

He pushed the door open carefully and, as soon as she saw him, Marguerite burst into tears. Seeing this friend, the only person she knew, brought back her grief. He did not attempt to comfort her. I could not see him, but, in the shadows engulfing me, I could recall his face and imagine it clearly, upset and concerned to find my wife suffering. She must have looked so beautiful, with her fair hair loose, her pale face and her tiny little hands feverish.

'I'll do anything I can,' Simoneau murmured, 'anything. Just let me take charge.'

She could only reply in broken sentences. As the young man withdrew, Mme Gabin accompanied him, and I could hear them mentioning money as they passed by me. It was always so expensive and she didn't think the poor little thing could have a penny to her name; they'd have to ask her. Simoneau told the old woman to be quiet. He didn't want Marguerite to be upset; he would go himself to the town hall and sort out the funeral arrangements.

When the silence began again, I wondered whether the nightmare was going to last long. I was alive, since I was aware of the least significant external fact. And I was beginning to understand more exactly what my state was. It was doubtless one of these cases of catalepsy of which I had heard. Even when I was a child I had been subject to fits which could last several hours. It was presumably something of a similar nature which was holding me thus, stiff as a corpse, and which was misleading everyone around me. But surely my heart would start beating again, and my blood would pump through my veins; I would awaken and be able to comfort Marguerite. By such arguments I managed to encourage myself to keep calm.

Hours passed. Mme Gabin had brought her food in. Marguerite refused to eat anything. The afternoon went by. Through the window, which had been left open, the noises rose from the rue Dauphine. The faint sound of the copper candlestick chinking against the marble table indicated that the candle had been changed. Finally Simoneau came back.

'Well?' the old lady inquired softly.

'Everything is organized,' he replied. 'The funeral will start tomorrow at eleven o'clock. Don't worry yourself about anything, and don't start talking about it in front of this poor lady.'

Mme Gabin replied nevertheless. 'The death doctor hasn't come yet.'

Simoneau went and sat down beside Marguerite, comforted her, then fell quiet. The procession was to start the next day at eleven; the news resounded in my head like a death knell. What with that and the death doctor, as Mme Gabin called him, not coming! He would be sure to see immediately that I was simply in a deep sleep. He would do everything that was necessary; he would know how to rouse me. I awaited him in an agony of worry.

Meanwhile, the day went on. Mme Gabin had brought up her lampshades, so as not to waste any time. She had even got Dédé to come up, once she had asked Marguerite's permission, because, she said, she didn't like leaving a child alone for too long at a time.

'Come along, come in,' she said to the girl, 'and don't be silly. Don't look away like that or you'll be having me to deal with.'

She would not let her look at me; she felt it would not be fitting. Dédé obviously took a peep from time to time, because I could hear her mother slapping her arm. She would then say, angrily, 'Work, or you'll have to go out. And then the gentlemen will come and pester you tonight.'

Mother and daughter were settled at our table. The sound of their scissors slitting the material of the lampshades came to me clearly; it·was delicate work and the cutting had to be done very carefully; they couldn't rush it. I began counting them one by one, my despair increasing.

In the room the only sound was that of the scissors. Marguerite, overcome with exhaustion, must have gone to sleep. Twice, Simoneau got up. The awful suspicion that he was taking advantage of her being asleep to brush her hair with his lips tormented me. I did not know the man, yet I felt that he was in love with her. The sound of Dédé's laughter annoyed me.

'What are you laughing for, silly?' asked her mother. 'Come along, tell me, why are you laughing?'

The child blurted out that she hadn't been laughing, she'd just been coughing. I imagined that what she had seen was Simoneau leaning over Marguerite, and that she'd found it funny.

The light was lit. Someone knocked.

'Ah, the doctor at last,' said the old lady.

It was, indeed, the doctor. He did not bother to apologize for arriving so late. He had doubtless had many steps to climb during his day's work. The light was very dim, and he asked: 'The body is here?'

'Yes, sir,' Simoneau replied.

Marguerite had stood up, shivering. Mme Gabin had made Dédé go out to the landing because children should not be present at such a scene. She made my wife go over to the window, so as to spare her the sight.

The doctor came over towards me quickly. I knew he was tired, in a hurry, anxious to be off. Did he touch me? Did he place his hand on my heart? I could not tell. But he did seem to have bent over me in a somewhat negligent manner.

'Would you like me to hold the lamp closer for you?' asked Simoneau.

'No, it's not worth it,' the doctor replied calmly.

What! Not worth it? This man had my life in his hands and didn't think it worth while taking a careful look at me. But I wasn't dead! I would have given anything to shout out that I wasn't dead.

'When did he die?' he asked.

'At six this morning,' replied Simoneau.

A surge of revolt rose through me, from within the dreadful rigidity that bound me. Oh! The terror of not being able to utter a word, or move a muscle.

The doctor added, 'The weather is very heavy. There's nothing so tiring as these early spring days.'

He moved away. It was my life that was moving away. Shouts, tears, insults rose in me, tore at my stricken throat – from which not even the slightest breath came. The wretch! The habit of his profession had turned him into a machine and he could turn up at someone's deathbed with the mere thought of a formality to go through. He knew nothing, the idiot.

All his learning was a lie – he couldn't even tell the difference between life and death. And he was going away, going away.

'Good night, doctor,' Simoneau said.

There was a silence. The doctor was probably taking his leave of Marguerite, who had moved from the window which Mme Gabin was now closing. He then went from the room and I could hear him going down the stairs.

So it was all over. I was a condemned man. My last hope had disappeared along with the doctor. If I didn't come to before tomorrow at eleven I would be buried alive. The idea was so terrifying that I lost all consciousness of what was going on around me. It was like fainting within death. The last noise I heard was that of Mme Gabin's and Dédé's scissors. The funeral wake began. No one spoke. Marguerite had refused to go to bed in the next room; she remained there, half lying in the chair, with her lovely pale face, her eyes closed and her lashes still wet with tears; meanwhile, seated in front of her, silent in the darkness, Simoneau watched.

III

I cannot find words to describe my anguish of the following morning. It has remained with me like some nightmarish dream; my feelings were so bizarre, so confused that it would be almost impossible for me to recount them accurately. What made my agony so dreadful was that I was constantly hoping to awake. As the time of the funeral procession drew nearer, my terror increased.

It was only towards dawn that I became aware of people and things around me again. The creaking of the bolt awoke me. Mme Gabin had opened the window. It was about seven o'clock, for I could hear the shopkeepers in the street below, the high voice of the girl selling chickweed and the deeper one of the carrot seller. The noise of Paris waking up soothed me for a moment or two; it seemed impossible that I could be buried underground while all this life was going on around me. Something I recalled made me even calmer. I remembered having seen a case similar to mine when I worked at the hospital in Guérande. A man had slept for a full twenty-eight hours and his sleep had been so deep that the doctors had been unable to come to any decision; suddenly the man had sat up on his backside and been able to leave his bed immediately. I had now been asleep for twenty-five hours; if I were to awake before ten, there would still be time.

I attempted to work out who was in the room and what they were all doing. Little Dédé was doubtless playing, because the door was open and a child's voice could be heard. Simoneau was probably no longer about, at least, no sound I could hear indicated that he was there. Mme Gabin's clogs clattered across the tiled floor. At last someone spoke.

'My dear,' the old lady said, 'you are wrong not to have some while it's still hot, it will do you good.'

She was talking to Marguerite and the drip, drip from the filter, on the mantelpiece, told me she was making coffee.

'I needed that, I can tell you,' she went on. 'I can't take these long nights at my age. It's worse at night-time, too, when there's a death in the house. Just have a drop of this coffee, there's a good girl.'

She made Marguerite have a cup.

'There, it's nice and hot, you can feel the good it's doing you. You'll need all your strength today. Now, if you were really good, you'd go and wait in my room.'

'No,' replied Marguerite, firmly. 'I want to stay here.'

Her voice, which I hadn't heard since the evening before, touched me to the quick. It had changed, it was grief-stricken. Ah, my love; I could feel her close to me, my final comfort. I knew her eyes were constantly fixed on me and that she was weeping her heart out.

The minutes, meanwhile, were ticking by. There was a noise at the door which I did not at first recognize. It sounded like a piece of furniture being banged against the walls of the narrow staircase. Then I understood. I heard Marguerite's sobbings. It was the coffin.

'You're too early,' said Mme Gabin crossly. 'Put it down by the bed.'

What time could it be? Nine, perhaps. And the coffin was already here. I could see it through the shadows, bright and shiny, the wood still rough from the saw. Dear God, was everything going to end now? Was I really going to be carried off in this box that I could feel at my feet?

I did however have one great pleasure left. Marguerite, despite her exhaustion, was determined to lay out my body. It was she, aided by the old woman, who dressed me, with the gentleness of a sister and wife. I could feel that I was in her arms again as she put on each of my clothes. She stopped, overcome with emotion; she hugged me to her, bathed me in her tears. I longed to return her embrace, to tell her I was alive; but I was powerless, I had to lie there, an inert mass.

'Don't do that. It's useless,' chided Mme Gabin.

Marguerite replied, her voice choked with tears, 'Let me be. I want him to have the best things we had.'

I realized that she was dressing me up as I had been for our wedding day. I still had the clothes which I intended to use in Paris only on high days and holidays. She fell back in the chair, exhausted by her efforts.

Suddenly I heard Simoneau's voice. He must have just come in.

'They are downstairs,' he said.

'Just as well, not too soon,' said Mme Gabin, lowering her voice as he had. 'Tell them to come up, we must get this over with.'

'I am worried about how much it will upset this poor lady.'

The old lady thought for a minute. She then went on, 'Listen, M. Simoneau, you make her go into my room. I don't want her to stay here. It's a kindness we'll be doing her. While you do that, we'll get everything sewn up here as quick as a flash.'

The words were like a knife in my heart. Worse still, as I listened to the struggle that then ensued, Simoneau went over to Marguerite imploring her not to stay in the room.

'For pity's sake,' he said. 'Come along with me, spare yourself any unnecessary suffering.'

'No, no,' said my wife. 'I am staying here, I want to stay till the last possible moment. Just imagine, he is all I have in the world. When he is no longer here, I shall be quite alone.'

Mme Gabin, just by the bed, whispered in the young man's ear: 'Go off, take her by the arm, carry her if needs be.'

Would Simoneau take Marguerite in his arms and carry her off? I heard her sudden cry. Filled with fury I wanted to leap to my feet. There wasn't an ounce of strength left in my body. I had to stay there, stiff, not able even to lift an eyelid to see what was happening there, in front of me. The struggle went on. My wife was clutching the furniture, saying again and again, 'Please don't. Leave me, leave me.'

He must now have taken her in his strong arms, and her only cries were the whimpers of a child. He carried her away, the sobs became fainter and I imagined the two of them, he so strong and tall, bearing her off, her arms round his neck; she in tears, shattered, letting herself go, ready to follow him anywhere he wished.

'Goodness, that took some doing,' murmured Mme Gabin. 'Well, now they are out of the way, I can get things done.'

I was consumed with jealousy and could only see his act as a despicable intrusion. I hadn't been able to see Marguerite since the previous evening but at least I could hear her. Now even that was over: she had been taken from me; a man had captured her, even before I was under the ground. And he was with her, just on the other side of the wall; he alone could comfort her, even kiss her . . .

The door had opened again, heavy steps moved round the room.

'Hurry up now, get a move on,' urged Mme Gabin. 'Before the poor lady comes back.'

She was speaking to strangers who replied only in grunts.

'After all, I'm not one of the family. I'm only a neighbour. I haven't got anything to gain from all this. It's out of the kindness of my heart I'm doing it. And it's not much fun I can tell you. Yes, I spent the whole night here. And it wasn't very warm at four in the morning. But then I've always been a bit soft-hearted. I'm too kind for my own good.'

At that point, the coffin was pulled into the centre of the room and I understood. I was condemned; I wasn't going to wake up. My thoughts became muddled; everything turned into a fuzzy darkness; I felt so tired that it was almost a comfort no longer to hope for anything.

'They were generous with the wood,' croaked one of the undertakers. 'The box is too long.'

'Well, he'll be travelling in comfort,' said another, cheerfully.

I didn't weigh too much, which they were pleased about because there were three flights of stairs to go down. When they took me by the elbows and feet, Mme Gabin suddenly started shouting, 'You wretched child! Has to put her nose round every corner, doesn't she? I'll teach you to peep and pry, just you wait.'

Dédé had pushed the door half open and poked her tousled head through. She wanted to see the gentleman put in the box. A couple of slaps rang out, followed by the sound of tears. When her mother returned, she started chatting to the men about her daughter as they arranged me in the coffin.

'Ten years old, she is. A good girl, but too nosy by half. I don't often smack her, but she must learn to do what she's told.'

'Oh,' replied one of the men, 'little girls are all the same. As soon as someone dies, they're there nosing around.'

I was now lying down comfortably and it was almost as though I was still in my bed, apart from my left arm hurting a bit where it was squashed against the wood. Just as they had said, I fitted quite easily because I wasn't too big.

'Wait a minute,' said Mme Gabin. 'I promised his wife I'd put a cushion under his head.'

The men were in a hurry, however, and stuffed the pillow in, without thought for me. One was looking for the hammer, swearing away; they had left it downstairs and had to go and get it. The lid was put in place and I felt a shudder throughout my body as two blows of the hammer nailed it down. It had happened, I had lived. The nails went in, one after the other, and the hammer banged away rhythmically. It was like packers nailing up a box of dried fruits, with thoughtless efficiency . . . From then on, the noises from above were muffled and indistinct, echoing in a curious way as if the pine coffin had become a sound box. The last words to reach me in the room in rue Dauphine were those of Mme Gabin: 'Go down carefully, mind the banister on the second floor. It's giving way.'

I was being carried; it felt like drifting over a stormy sea . . .

From that time on, my memories are shrouded in a mist. I can, though, remember that the sole thought which occupied my mind – a senseless, automatic one – was to work out the route we were taking to the cemetery. I didn't know a single road in Paris and was totally ignorant of where the main cemeteries were, though I had heard their names often enough, but none of this prevented me from concentrating all my mental efforts on working out whether we were turning right or left. The hearse bumped me around over the cobbled streets. All around me, the noise of traffic and passing feet made a sort of rumbling noise which echoed in the coffin. At first I was able to follow the way we took quite clearly. Then we stopped and I was lifted out; I thought we must be at the church. When the hearse set off again, I lost consciousness of where we were. Bells ringing meant we had passed a church; a softer more continuous sound made me think we were going along a wide avenue. I was a condemned man being taken to his execution, my senses dulled, awaiting the final blow which was slow in coming . . .

We stopped and I was taken out of the hearse. It was all over. All sound ceased, I knew I was in some deserted place, beneath the trees, the open sky above my head. Obviously there were several people following the hearse, people from the boarding house, Simoneau and others, because I could hear their muffled voices. There was a psalm, and the priest muttered away in Latin. They stood around for several seconds. Suddenly I was aware that I was being lowered; ropes were rubbing against the sides of the coffin, scraping like the bow of a cracked 'cello. It was the end. A dreadful noise like the rumbling of a cannon burst over my head to the left; another one came from around my feet; a third, even worse, over my belly; I thought the coffin had split in two. I fainted.

IV

I don't know how long I remained like this. An eternity and a second are the same in nothingness. I was no longer. Gradually, confusedly, the awareness of life came back to me. I was still asleep, but I had begun to dream. A nightmare started to emerge in the dark, blocking the horizon of my thoughts. The dream I had was a strange fantasy, one that had often tormented me before when, eyes open, with my tendency to conjure up the most dreadful pictures, I used to indulge in the morbid pleasure of inventing disasters.

I thus started dreaming that my wife was expecting me somewhere – in Guérande, I think – and that I had taken the train to go and meet her. As the train was going through a tunnel, suddenly a dreadful noise thundered out. Two falls of earth had occurred. Our train hadn't been touched by a single stone and the coaches were still intact; but at each end of the tunnel, behind us and in front, the roof had caved in and we were in the middle of a mountain, walled in by blocks of rock. A long and terrible wait then began. There was no hope of help; it would have taken a month to unblock the tunnel and would have required extremely powerful machines and great care. We were prisoners in a cave with no way out. Our death was only a matter of hours.

I had often, as I said, imagined this scene. I used to concoct different variations on the theme. I'd create men, women and children as actors in the drama, more than a hundred people, a great crowd, and they would provide me with all sorts of different episodes. There were a few provisions in the train, but they soon ran out and, although they didn't actually end up eating each other, they had the most vicious arguments about who would have the last crumb of bread. Should it be an old man, pushed aside, already half dead, or a mother who fought like a dragon to keep a few morsels for her child? In my compartment, a young newly wed couple suffered in agony in each other's arms, no hope left, till they died. The track was empty and people got out, prowled along the length of the train, like wild animals on the run, desperate for food. The different classes mixed together, a wealthy man, possibly some high-up civil servant, would weep on the shoulders of a labourer, calling him brother. The lights had gone out very shortly after the disaster, and the engine fires had died. As people passed from one coach to the next, they had to feel their way along, so as not to bump into anything; they knew when they got to the engine because of the ice-cold connecting rod, the huge, sleeping flanks; all that energy gone to waste, still and motionless under the ground, as though buried alive with its passengers all dying off one by one.

I revelled in dreaming up the most lurid of details. Screams rending the dark. All of a sudden, someone you had not realized was there and whom you could not see fell against you. This time, however, what was worst was the cold and the lack of air. I had never in my life felt so cold; a blanket of ice was covering me, heavy dankness wrapping my head. I couldn't breathe properly and it seemed as if the stone ceiling was falling on my chest, the whole mountain weighing me down and crushing me. Suddenly, a shout of joy rang out. For some time we had been imagining that we could hear a distant sound, comforting ourselves that someone was working close by to us. Help did not, however, arrive. One of us had found a shaft within the tunnel and we all ran there to see it – at the top flickered a blue light, scarcely bigger than a piece of sealing wax. What joy it gave us. It was the sky; we reached out to breathe it in; we could make out little black dots moving, probably workmen setting up a winch to try to get us out. A frantic cry went up – 'We're safe, we're safe.' We all cried, our arms stretching out towards the tiny blue spot.

The loudness of this shout woke me up. Where could I be? Still in the tunnel, maybe. I was lying flat out and could feel on either side something hard imprisoning me. I tried to get up but bumped my head. Was the rock all around me? The blue spot had disappeared, and the sky was no more. I was being smothered, my teeth chattering with cold, shaking in all my limbs.

Suddenly it all came back to me. My hair stood on end and I felt the whole of the terror shudder through me from top to toe, icy. Had I finally come out of the fit which had imprisoned me for so many long hours in a corpse-like trance? Yes, I could move, I could run my hands along the edges of the coffin. One last test remained – I opened my mouth and started talking, calling on Marguerite, instinctively. But I had in fact shouted aloud, and my voice, within the pine box, took on so terrifying a tone that I frightened myself. Dear God, so it was true! I could talk, I could shout out loud that I was alive, but my voice would not be heard; I was shut in, crushed under the earth.

I made a superhuman effort to calm down and think. Was there no way of escaping? My dream came back; I did not yet have the all-too-solid coffin; I started mixing the fantasy of the shaft of air and the spot of sunlight with the reality of the hole in which I was suffocating. My eyes wide open, I watched the shadows. Perhaps I would see some hole, a crack of light, a glimpse of day! But only sparks of flame passed through the night – red lights blazing and dying away. Nothing – a black void – impenetrable. Finally, I recovered my sanity and pushed aside the nightmare; I needed to be completely clear-headed if I wanted to escape.

At first, the greatest danger seemed to be that of suffocating to death. I had probably been able to last so long without air because of the fit which had meant that all my functions had slowed down. Now that my heart had begun beating again, however, and that my lungs were gulping in air, I would die of asphyxia if I didn't get out soon. I was also acutely aware of how cold I was and was afraid lest numbness proved fatal, as happens when someone slips in the snow, never to rise again.

Although I kept telling myself to keep calm, at the same time waves of fear kept rising in me. So I summoned all my strength, attempting to recall what I knew of burial procedures. I was probably in a private five-year plot. This deprived me of one hope; I had noticed years ago at Nantes that in the public graves, because of the constant coming and going, the feet of the most recently buried biers often could be seen. If that had been my case, I could simply have broken a plank or two and got out; whereas if I were in a properly filled hole, there would be a complete layer of earth over me, which would probably prove an insurmountable obstacle. Hadn't I heard someone saying that in Paris people were buried under six feet of earth? How would I ever be able to get through? Even were I able to pierce through the lid of my coffin, the earth would filter through, seep through like sand, filling my eyes and mouth. And there would be death, another dreadful death, drowning in mud.

Nevertheless, I felt around me carefully. The coffin was wide and I could move my arms quite freely. I couldn't feel any crack in the lid. To my right and left, the planks were roughly planed, but they were strong and tough. I bent my arm inwards over my chest and felt towards my head. There I found a knot of wood in the end plank which gave a little if I pushed; I worked away carefully and pressed out the knot; on the other side I could feel the earth, rich, damp clay. It didn't help me at all. I even regretted having pushed out the knot, as though the earth was going to start coming through the hole. I then tried something else – tapping at the edges of the coffin to find out whether there was by any remote chance a gap somewhere. It sounded exactly the same all over. When I tried tapping with my toes, it did seem, though, that the sound at the end was different. Though it could just have been the sound effects in the box.

I then started pushing gently with clenched fists, arms braced. The wood did not give. I next used my knees, arching my back. Not the slightest crack. I finally put all my strength into such a push that all the bones in my body seemed to screech with pain. It was then that I went mad.

Till that moment, I had not succumbed to panic, nor to the force of anger which coursed through my veins like drink. I was particularly careful to restrain my shouts; I realized that were I to shout I would be lost. But suddenly, now, I started screaming my head off. It was stronger than I; the cries came from my throat, using all the breath in my body. I yelled for help in a voice which I did not recognize, becoming more and more panic-stricken with each shout, screaming that I did not want to die. I scratched at the wood with my nails, twisted and turned like some wild animal in a cage. I do not know how long this went on, but I can still remember the hard feel of the unbending wood as I struggled, still hear the storm of shouts and tears which filled my four walls. A final flash of reason told me to restrain myself, but I could not.

I was overcome with tiredness. I awaited death in a painful half-consciousness. The coffin was made of stone; I should never be able to open it; convinced of my impending doom, I lay there motionless, incapable of making the slightest movement. I had now begun suffering the pangs of hunger in addition to those of cold and being suffocated. I weakened fast. The agony soon became intolerable. I tried to finger out bits of earth through the knot of wood I had loosened and eat them; this only increased my torment. I bit my arms, but not till they bled, and sucked my skin, longing to plunge my teeth into it.

How I longed to die, now. I had feared not being all my life, now I wanted it, I called for it – nothing could be black enough for me. How childish I had been to fear this dreamless sleep, this eternity of silence and shadows. Death was good only if it stopped being in one fell swoop, for ever. Oh to sleep like the stones, to disappear into the clay, to be no longer!

Meanwhile my hands went on mechanically feeling the wood. Suddenly I pinched my left thumb, and the pain shook me from my numbness. What could it be? I felt again, found a nail which the undertakers had not knocked in straight and which was loose in the wood of the coffin. It was very long and sharp. The head was fast in the lid but I could move it. From that moment onward, I had but one idea in my head: to get hold of this nail. I moved my right hand over my stomach and began shaking it. It was incredibly hard to loosen it. I often had to change hands, and my left hand, which I couldn't position very well, got tired very quickly. As I worked away, a plan started forming in my head. The nail was my salvation. I needed it. But would I be in time? I was famished and I had to stop when I became so dizzy that my hands wouldn't obey me and my mind was wandering. I had sucked the drops of blood from my thumb. I then bit my arm and drank my blood. Encouraged by my pain and warmed by this bitter taste of tepid wine in my mouth, I went back to tackle the nail with both hands and finally managed to get it out.

From then on, I believed I would be successful. My plan was quite simple. I dug the tip of the nail into the lid, and ran it down in a long straight line so as to make a crack. My hands were getting stiff but I went on stubbornly. When I reckoned I had made a deep enough hole in the wood, I turned over on to my stomach then, raising myself on my knees and my elbows, I pushed my back against the lid. It split but still did not come open. The hole was not deep enough. I had to turn over on to my back once more and start all over again, which sapped my strength. A final effort and the lid cracked from one end to the other.

I had not yet escaped but hope filled my heart. I stopped pushing, didn't move for fear of disturbing the earth and having it cave in on me. I wanted to be able to use the lid as a shield while I made a shaft in the clay. Unfortunately, this turned out to be hard work; the clods of earth got in the way of the planks of wood and I couldn't manipulate them easily; I would never get to ground level; the earth was already falling in and pressing against my spine and almost burying my face. Fear overcame me again when suddenly, as I stretched out to find some support, I thought I felt the plank holding the coffin at the feet give way. I kicked with all my might, hoping there might be some kind of hole being dug.

My feet kicked into nothingness. My idea had been right. A new grave was being dug and there was only a thin layer of earth to kick away before I was able to wriggle over into it. Great God! I was saved!

I lay there for a second, my eyes raised, at the bottom of the hole. It was dark. Stars were twinkling in the velvet blue of the sky above. An occasional breeze wafted the warmth of spring over me, and the scent of the trees. Dear God, I had escaped, I was breathing. I was warm, I could cry and offer my thanks, hands raised to infinity. How good it was to be alive!

V

The first idea I had was to go to see the cemetery-keeper and ask him to take me home. But some vague presentiment held me back. I would frighten everyone. Why hurry, since I was in control of everything? I felt my body; all that was wrong with me was the bite on my left arm; even the slight temperature I had pleased me, gave me an unexpected strength. I should certainly be able to walk unaided.

So I took my time. All kinds of vague thoughts crossed my mind. I had felt the gravediggers' tools next to me and wanted to make good the damage I had done, and fill up the hole again so that no one would know anything about my rising from the dead. At that particular time I had no precise idea in my head as to what I was going to do; I simply thought that it was not a good idea to advertise the incident too widely, feeling somewhat ashamed to be alive when everyone believed me to be dead. After half an hour's work I had completely covered any trace of what had happened. And I jumped out of the ditch.

What a lovely evening it was! The cemetery was in total silence. The black trees cast motionless shadows among the white tombs. As I attempted to get my bearings, I noticed that one half of the sky seemed to be ablaze with light. Paris was over there. I walked towards it along a path, through the shadows of the branches. After only fifty paces I had to stop for breath. I sat down on a gravestone. I looked down at myself and realized that I was fully dressed, only lacking a hat. How grateful I was for the pious care with which Marguerite had dressed me! The sudden thought of Marguerite made me get to my feet again. I wanted to see her.

At the end of the lane, there was a wall in the way. I climbed up on to a gravestone, hung on to the coping on the other side and let myself drop. The jolt was hard. I then walked for a few minutes down a deserted road which encircled the cemetery. I had no idea where I was but I kept telling myself obsessively that I would soon be back in Paris and be able to find the rue Dauphine. People passed but I did not question them; I was too suspicious and refused to trust anyone. I now know that I was already racked with fever and my mind was wandering. As I turned into a wider road, I lost consciousness and fell heavily to the pavement.

The next three weeks of my life are a blank; I remained unconscious. When I finally came to I found myself in some unknown room. A man was there, looking after me. He told me how he had picked me up one morning on the Boulevard Montparnasse and taken me to his home. He was a doctor but no longer practising. When I thanked him, he answered shortly that he had found my case interesting and wanted the chance of studying it further. For the early days of my convalescence, he refused to allow me to ask him any questions. Later on, he asked me none. I had to stay in bed for another week and continued to feel very weak, not wishing to try to remember anything, because the effort hurt too much. I felt timid and diffident. I'd see when I was able to get about. I might have mentioned a name during my fever but the doctor never once alluded to anything I might have said. He was discreet in his kindness.

Meanwhile, summer had come. One June day I finally obtained permission to take a short walk. It was a lovely morning, with one of those bright suns which liven up the old streets of Paris. I walked slowly, asking people at each crossroads the whereabouts of the rue Dauphine. I reached it, but scarcely recognized the old boarding house where we had been. A childish fear held me back. If I were to show myself without warning to Marguerite the shock could well kill her. It might be preferable to tell our old neighbour, Mme Gabin, first. But I didn't like the idea of someone coming between us. I couldn't make up my mind. Deep down, I felt a great emptiness, as though I had made the sacrifice long ago.

The house shone yellow in the sun. I knew which one it was because of a somewhat seedy restaurant on the ground floor from which they sent us up food. I looked up at the third-floor window on the left. It was wide open. Suddenly a young woman, hair tousled and with her camisole awry, came and leant at the window. Behind her came a young man, he bent over and kissed her neck. It was not Marguerite. I felt no surprise. It seemed to me as if I had dreamt it all, this and other things I was to learn.

I stayed there for a while, in the street, unable to make up my mind whether or not to go up and talk to the young couple who were still there, laughing in the sun. Then I decided to go into the restaurant below. I could not be recognized; my beard had grown during my illness and my face had got much thinner. As I sat down, I saw Mme Gabin bringing across a cup to buy herself a drop of coffee; she stood at the counter and began gossiping with the women behind the counter. I listened hard.

'So,' asked the woman, 'has that poor little thing on the third floor come to a decision yet?'

'What do you expect?' replied Mme Gabin. 'It was best for her. M. Simoneau has been so kind to her. He's finished his business here, something to do with coming into a fortune and he was proposing to take her away with him to live with his aunt who needs "someone she can trust".'

The lady at the counter laughed. I had buried my face in a paper, pale-faced, and my hands were trembling.

'It will probably end up with them getting married,' Mme Gabin continued. 'But I can honestly say to you that things have been all clean and above board. She was very upset about her husband and that young man has behaved like a perfect gentleman. Anyway, they went off yesterday. As soon as she's come out of mourning, they'll be able to do as they please.'

At that point, the door of the restaurant opened wide and Dédé came in.

'Mum, aren't you coming up? I've been waiting for you. Hurry up.'

'I'll come in a minute. You get on my nerves,' said her mother.

The child stayed there, listening to the two women with that look she had of a precocious child who had to grow up on the streets of Paris.

'Gracious me!' said Mme Gabin. 'After all, the late husband wasn't a patch on M. Simoneau. I didn't take to him at all, such a runt of a man! Always moaning! And not a penny to his name. No, having a husband like that is no fun for a woman with red blood in her veins. But M. Simoneau, now, he's a wealthy man and as strong as a horse.'

'I saw him one day,' interjected Dédé, 'when he was washing. He's got such hairy arms!'

'Will you leave us alone,' shouted the old woman, pushing her daughter out. 'You always have to poke your nose into business that doesn't concern you.'

Then she went on: 'The first one did her a good turn, dying when he did.'

When I was back out in the street, I walked slowly, my legs almost giving way beneath me. Yet I wasn't suffering too much. I even managed a smile when I saw my shadow in the sun. Yes, I wasn't much of a figure of a man; it had been an odd idea to marry Marguerite. I thought of all her problems in Guérande, how upset she'd got, how miserable and tiring her life was. She had been good to me. But I had never been a lover to her; it was more of a brother whom she had mourned. Why upset her life again? A dead man can't be jealous. I looked up and saw the Jardins du Luxembourg in front of me; I went in and sat there in the sun, dreaming peacefully. The thought of Marguerite filled me with tenderness. I envisaged her in the country, a lady in a small town, happy, loved, cosseted; getting more and more beautiful, bearing three sons and two daughters. Yes, it had been nice of me to die and I wasn't prepared to be fool enough to rise from the dead.

I have travelled a lot since that time, lived here, there and everywhere. I am a normal man, working and eating like everyone else. Death no longer frightens me; but it doesn't seem to want me any more, whereas I have no reason to go on living; I am afraid that it may pass me by . . .

The Boarded Window

Ambrose Bierce

In 1830, only a few miles away from what is now the great city of Cincinnati, lay an immense and almost unbroken forest. The whole region was sparsely settled by people of the frontier – restless souls who no sooner had hewn fairly habitable homes out of the wilderness and attained to that degree of prosperity which today we should call indigence than, impelled by some mysterious impulse of their nature, they abandoned all and pushed farther westward, to encounter new perils and privations in the effort to regain the meagre comforts which they had voluntarily renounced. Many of them had already forsaken that region for the remoter settlements, but among those remaining was one who had been of those first arriving. He lived alone in a house of logs surrounded on all sides by the great forest, of whose gloom and silence he seemed a part, for no one had ever known him to smile nor speak a needless word. His simple wants were supplied by the sale or barter of skins of wild animals in the river town, for not a thing did he grow upon the land which, if needful, he might have claimed by right of undisturbed possession. There were evidences of 'improvement' – a few acres of ground immediately about the house had once been cleared of its trees, the decayed stumps of which were half concealed by the new growth that had been suffered to repair the ravage wrought by the axe. Apparently the man's zeal for agriculture had burned with a failing flame, expiring in penitential ashes.

The little log house, with its chimney of sticks, its roof of warping clapboards weighted with traversing poles and its 'chinking' of clay, had a single door and, directly opposite, a window. The latter, however, was boarded up – nobody could remember a time when it was not. And none knew why it was so closed; certainly not because of the occupant's dislike of light and air, for on those rare occasions when a hunter had passed that lonely spot the recluse had commonly been seen sunning himself on his doorstep if heaven had provided sunshine for his need. I fancy there are few persons living today who ever knew the secret of that window, but I am one, as you shall see.

The man's name was said to be Murlock. He was apparently seventy years old, actually about fifty. Something besides years had had a hand in his aging. His hair and long, full beard were white, his grey, lustreless eyes sunken, his face singularly seamed with wrinkles which appeared to belong to two intersecting systems. In figure he was tall and spare, with a stoop of the shoulders – a burden bearer. I never saw him; these particulars I learned from my grandfather, from whom also I got the man's story when I was a lad. He had known him when living near by in that early day.

One day Murlock was found in his cabin, dead. It was not a time and place for coroners and newspapers, and I suppose it was agreed that he had died from natural causes or I should have been told, and should remember. I know only that with what was probably a sense of the fitness of things the body was buried near the cabin, alongside the grave of his wife, who had preceded him by so many years that local tradition had retained hardly a hint of her existence. That closes the final chapter of this true story – excepting, indeed, the circumstances that many years afterwards, in company with an equally intrepid spirit, I penetrated to the place and ventured near enough to the ruined cabin to throw a stone against it, and ran away to avoid the ghost which every well-informed boy thereabout knew haunted the spot. But there is an earlier chapter – that supplied by my grandfather.

When Murlock built his cabin and began laying sturdily about with his axe to hew out a farm – the rifle, meanwhile, his means of support – he was young, strong and full of hope. In that eastern country whence he came he had married, as was the fashion, a young woman in all ways worthy of his honest devotion, who shared the dangers and privations of his lot with a willing spirit and light heart. There is no known record of her name; of her charms of mind and person tradition is silent and the doubter is at liberty to entertain his doubt; but God forbid that I should share it! Of their affection and happiness there is abundant assurance in every added day of the man's widowed life; for what but the magnetism of a blessed memory could have chained that venturesome spirit to a lot like that?

One day Murlock returned from gunning in a distant part of the forest to find his wife prostrate with fever, and delirious. There was no physician within miles, no neighbour; nor was she in a condition to be left, to summon help. So he set about the task of nursing her back to health, but at the end of the third day she fell into unconsciousness and so passed away, apparently, with never a gleam of returning reason.

From what we know of a nature like his we may venture to sketch in some of the details of the outline picture drawn by my grandfather. When convinced that she was dead, Murlock had sense enough to remember that the dead must be prepared for burial. In performance of this sacred duty he blundered now and again, did certain things incorrectly, and others which he did correctly were done over and over. His occasional failures to accomplish some simple and ordinary act filled him with astonishment, like that of a drunken man who wonders at the suspension of familiar natural laws. He was surprised, too, that he did not weep – surprised and a little ashamed; surely it is unkind not to weep for the dead. 'Tomorrow,' he said aloud, 'I shall have to make the coffin and dig the grave; and then I shall miss her, when she is no longer in sight; but now – she is dead, of course, but it is all right – it *must* be all right, somehow. Things cannot be so bad as they seem.'

He stood over the body in the fading light, adjusting the hair and putting the finishing touches to the simple toilet, doing all mechanically, with soulless care. And still through his consciousness ran an undersense of conviction that all was right – that he should have her again as before, and everything explained. He had had no experience in grief; his capacity had not been enlarged by use. His heart could not contain it all, nor his imagination rightly conceive it. He did not know he was so hard struck; *that* knowledge would come later, and never go. Grief is an artist of powers as various as the instruments upon which he plays his dirges for the dead, evoking from some the sharpest, shrillest notes, from others the low, grave chords that throb recurrent like the slow beating of a distant drum. Some natures it startles; some it stupefies. To one it comes like the stroke of an arrow, stinging all the sensibilities to a keener life; to another as the blow of a bludgeon which, in crushing, benumbs. We may conceive Murlock to have been that way affected, for (and here we are upon surer ground than that of conjecture) no sooner had he finished his pious work than, sinking into a chair by the side of the table upon which the body lay, and noting how white the profile showed in the deepening gloom, he laid his arms upon the table's edge, and dropped his face into them, tearless yet and unutterably weary. At that moment came in through the open window a long, wailing sound like the cry of a lost child in the far deeps of the darkening wood! But the man did not move. Again, and nearer than before, sounded that unearthly cry upon his failing sense. Perhaps it was a wild beast; perhaps it was a dream. For Murlock was asleep.

Some hours later, as it afterwards appeared, this unfaithful watcher awoke, and lifting his head from his arms intently listened – he knew not why. There in the black darkness by the side of the dead, recalling all without a shock, he strained his eyes to see – he knew not what. His senses were all alert, his breath was suspended, his blood had stilled its tides as if to assist the silence. Who – what had waked him, and where was it?

Suddenly the table shook beneath his arms, and at the same moment he heard, or fancied that he heard, a light, soft step – another – sounds as of bare feet upon the floor!

He was terrified beyond the power to cry out or move. Perforce he waited – waited there in the darkness through seeming centuries of such dread as one may know, yet live to tell. He tried vainly to speak the dead woman's name, vainly to stretch forth his hand across the table to learn if she were there. His throat was powerless, his arms and hands were like lead. Then occurred something most frightful. Some heavy body seemed hurled against the table with an impetus that pushed it against his breast so sharply as nearly to overthrow him, and at the same instant he heard and felt the fall of something upon the floor with so violent a thump that the whole house was shaken by the impact. A scuffling ensued, and a confusion of sounds impossible to describe. Murlock had risen to his feet. Fear had by excess forfeited control of his faculties. He flung his hands upon the table. Nothing was there!

There is a point at which terror may turn to madness; and madness incites to action. With no definite intent, from no motive but the wayward impulse of a madman, Murlock sprang to the wall, with a little groping seized his loaded rifle, and without aim discharged it. By the flash which lit up the room with a vivid illumination, he saw an enormous panther dragging the dead woman towards the window, its teeth fixed in her throat! Then there were darkness blacker than before, and silence; and when he returned to consciousness the sun was high and the wood vocal with songs of birds.

The body lay near the window, where the beast had left it when frightened away by the flash and report of the rifle. The clothing was deranged, the long hair in disorder, the limbs lay anyhow. From the throat, dreadfully lacerated, had issued a pool of blood not yet entirely coagulated. The ribbon with which he had bound the wrists was broken; the hands were tightly clenched. Between the teeth was a fragment of the animal's ear.

Lost Hearts

M. R. James

It was, as far as I can ascertain, in September of the year 1811 that a post-chaise drew up before the door of Aswarby Hall, in the heart of Lincolnshire. The little boy who was the only passenger in the chaise, and who jumped out as soon as it had stopped, looked about him with the keenest curiosity during the short interval that elapsed between the ringing of the bell and the opening of the hall door. He saw a tall, square, red-brick house, built in the reign of Anne; a stone-pillared porch had been added in the purer classical style of 1790; the windows of the house were many, tall and narrow, with small panes and thick white woodwork. A pediment, pierced with a round window, crowned the front. There were wings to right and left, connected by curious glazed galleries, supported by colonnades, with the central block. These wings plainly contained the stables and offices of the house. Each was surmounted by an ornamental cupola with a gilded vane.

An evening light shone on the building, making the window-panes glow like so many fires. Away from the Hall in front stretched a flat park studded with oaks and fringed with firs, which stood out against the sky. The clock in the church-tower, buried in trees on the edge of the park, only its golden weathercock catching the light, was striking six, and the sound came gently beating down the wind. It was altogether a pleasant impression, though tinged with the sort of melancholy appropriate to an evening in early autumn, that was conveyed to the mind of the boy who was standing in the porch waiting for the door to open to him.

The post-chaise had brought him from Warwickshire, where, some six months before, he had been left an orphan. Now, owing to the generous offer of his elderly cousin, Mr Abney, he had come to live at Aswarby. The offer was unexpected, because all who knew anything of Mr Abney looked upon him as a somewhat austere recluse, into whose steady-going household the advent of a small boy would import a new and, it seemed, incongruous element. The truth is that very little was known of Mr Abney's pursuits or temper. The Professor of Greek at Cambridge had been heard to say that no one knew more of the religious beliefs of the later pagans than did the owner of Aswarby. Certainly his library contained all the then available books bearing on the Mysteries, the Orphic poems, the worship of Mithras, and the Neo-Platonists. In the marble-paved hall stood a fine group of Mithras slaying a bull, which had been imported from the Levant at great expense by the owner. He had contributed a description of it to the *Gentleman's Magazine* and he had written a remarkable series of articles in the *Critical Museum* on the superstitions of the Romans of the Lower Empire. He was looked upon, in fine, as a man wrapped up in his books, and it was a matter of great surprise among his neighbours that he should even have heard of his orphan cousin, Stephen Elliott, much more that he should have volunteered to make him an inmate of Aswarby Hall.

Whatever may have been expected by his neighbours, it is certain that Mr Abney – the tall, the thin, the austere – seemed inclined to give his young cousin a kindly reception. The moment the front door was opened he darted out of his study, rubbing his hands with delight.

'How are you, my boy? – how are you? How old are you?' said he – 'that is, you are not too much tired, I hope, by your journey to eat your supper?'

'No, thank you, sir,' said Master Elliott; 'I am pretty well.'

'That's a good lad,' said Mr Abney. 'And how old are you, my boy?'

It seemed a little odd that he should have asked the question twice in the first two minutes of their acquaintance.

'I'm twelve years old next birthday, sir,' said Stephen.

'And when is your birthday, my dear boy? Eleventh of September, eh? That's well – that's very well. Nearly a year hence, isn't it? I like – ha, ha! – I like to get these things down in my book. Sure it's twelve? Certain?'

'Yes, quite sure, sir.'

'Well, well! Take him to Mrs Bunch's room, Parkes, and let him have his tea – supper – whatever it is.'

'Yes, sir,' answered the staid Mr Parkes; and conducted Stephen to the lower regions.

Mrs Bunch was the most comfortable and human person whom Stephen had as yet met in Aswarby. She made him completely at home; they were great friends in a quarter of an hour; and great friends they remained. Mrs Bunch had been born in the neighbourhood some fifty-five years before the date of Stephen's arrival, and her residence at the

Hall was of twenty years' standing. Consequently, if anyone knew the ins and outs of the house and the district, Mrs Bunch knew them; and she was by no means disinclined to communicate her information.

Certainly there were plenty of things about the Hall and the Hall gardens which Stephen, who was of an adventurous and inquiring turn, was anxious to have explained to him. 'Who built the temple at the end of the laurel walk? Who was the old man whose picture hung on the staircase, sitting at a table, with a skull under his hand?' These and many similar points were cleared up by the resources of Mrs Bunch's powerful intellect. There were others, however, of which the explanations furnished were less satisfactory.

One November evening Stephen was sitting by the fire in the housekeeper's room reflecting on his surroundings.

'Is Mr Abney a good man, and will he go to heaven?' he suddenly asked, with the peculiar confidence which children possess in the ability of their elders to settle these questions, the decision of which is believed to be reserved for other tribunals.

'Good? – bless the child!' said Mrs Bunch. 'Master's as kind a soul as ever I see! Didn't I never tell you of the little boy as he took in out of the street, as you may say, this seven years back? and the little girl, two years after I first come here?'

'No. Do tell me all about them, Mrs Bunch – now this minute!'

'Well,' said Mrs Bunch, 'the little girl I don't seem to recollect so much about. I know master brought her back with him from his walk one day, and give orders to Mrs Ellis, as was housekeeper then, as she should be took every care with. And the pore child hadn't no one belonging to her – she told me so her own self – and here she lived with us a matter of three weeks it might be; and then, whether she were somethink of a gipsy in her blood or what not, but one morning she out of her bed afore any of us had opened a eye, and neither track nor yet trace of her have I set eyes on since. Master was wonderful put about, and had all the ponds dragged; but it's my belief she was had away by them gipsies, for there was singing round the house for as much as an hour the night she went, and Parkes, he declare as he heard them a-calling in the woods all that afternoon. Dear, dear! a hodd child she was, so silent in her ways and all, but I was wonderful taken up with her, so domesticated she was – surprising.'

'And what about the little boy?' said Stephen.

'Ah, that pore boy!' sighed Mrs Bunch. 'He were a foreigner – Jevanny he called hisself – and he come a-tweaking his 'urdy-gurdy round and about the drive one winter day, and master 'ad him in that minute, and ast all about where he came from, and how old he was, and how he made his way, and where was his relatives, and all as kind as heart could wish. But it went the same way with him. They're a hunruly lot, them foreign nations, I do suppose, and he was off one fine morning just the same as the girl. Why he went and what he done was our question for as much as a year after; for he never took his 'urdy-gurdy, and there it lays on the shelf.'

The remainder of the evening was spent by Stephen in miscellaneous cross-examination of Mrs Bunch and in efforts to extract a tune from the hurdy-gurdy.

That night he had a curious dream. At the end of the passage at the top of the house, in which his bedroom was situated, there was an old disused bathroom. It was kept locked, but the upper half of the door was glazed, and, since the muslin curtains which used to hang there had long been gone, you could look in and see the lead-lined bath affixed to the wall on the right hand, with its head towards the window.

On the night of which I am speaking, Stephen Elliott found himself, as he thought, looking through the glazed door. The moon was shining through the window, and he was gazing at a figure which lay in the bath.

His description of what he saw reminds me of what I once beheld myself in the famous vaults of St Michan's Church in Dublin, which possess the horrid property of preserving corpses from decay for centuries. A figure inexpressibly thin and pathetic, of a dusty leaden colour, enveloped in a shroud-like garment, the thin lips crooked into a faint and dreadful smile, the hands pressed tightly over the region of the heart.

As he looked upon it, a distant, almost inaudible moan seemed to issue from its lips, and the arms began to stir. The terror of the sight forced Stephen backwards, and he awoke to the fact that he was indeed standing on the cold boarded floor of the passage in the full light of the moon. With a courage which I do not think can be common among boys of his age, he went to the door of the bathroom to ascertain if the figure of his dream were really there. It was not, and he went back to bed.

Mrs Bunch was much impressed next morning by his story, and went so far as to replace the muslin curtain over the glazed door of the bathroom. Mr Abney, moreover, to whom he confided his experiences at breakfast, was greatly interested, and made notes of the matter in what he called 'his book'.

The spring equinox was approaching, as Mr Abney frequently reminded his cousin, adding that this had been always considered by the ancients to be a critical time for the young: that Stephen would do well to take care of himself, and to shut his bedroom window at night, and that Censorinus had some valuable remarks on the subject. Two incidents that occurred about this time made an impression upon Stephen's mind.

The first was after an unusually uneasy and oppressed night that he had passed – though he could not recall any particular dream that he had had.

The following evening Mrs Bunch was occupying herself in mending his nightgown.

'Gracious me, Master Stephen!' she broke forth rather irritably, 'how do you manage to tear your nightdress all to flinders this way? Look here, sir, what trouble you do give to poor servants that have to darn and mend after you!'

There was indeed a most destructive and apparently wanton series of slits or scorings in the garment, which would undoubtedly require a skilful needle to make good. They were confined to the left side of the chest – long, parallel slits, about six inches in length, some of them not quite piercing the texture of the linen. Stephen could only express his entire ignorance of their origin: he was sure they were not there the night before.

'But,' he said, 'Mrs Bunch, they are just the same as the scratches on the outside of my bedroom door; and I'm sure I never had anything to do with making *them*.'

Mrs Bunch gazed at him open-mouthed, then snatched up a candle, departed hastily from the room, and was heard making her way upstairs. In a few minutes she came down.

'Well,' she said, 'Master Stephen, it's a funny thing to me how them marks and scratches can 'a' come there – too high up for any cat or dog to 'ave made 'em, much less a rat: for all the world like a Chinaman's finger-nails, as my uncle in the tea-trade used to tell us of when we was girls together. I wouldn't say nothing to master, not if I was you, Master Stephen, my dear; and just turn the key of the door when you go to your bed.'

'I always do, Mrs Bunch, as soon as I've said my prayers.'

'Ah, that's a good child: always say your prayers, and then no one can't hurt you.'

Herewith Mrs Bunch addressed herself to mending the injured night-gown, with intervals of meditation, until bed-time. This was on a Friday night in March, 1812.

On the following evening the usual duet of Stephen and Mrs Bunch was augmented by the sudden arrival of Mr Parkes, the butler, who as a rule kept himself rather *to* himself in his own pantry. He did not see that Stephen was there: he was, moreover, flustered, and less slow of speech than was his wont.

'Master may get up his own wine, if he likes, of an evening,' was his first remark. 'Either I do it in the daytime or not at all, Mrs Bunch. I don't know what it may be: very like it's the rats, or the wind got into cellars; but I'm not so young as I was, and I can't go through with it as I have done.'

'Well, Mr Parkes, you know it is a surprising place for the rats, is the Hall.'

'I'm not denying that, Mrs Bunch; and, to be sure, many a time I've heard the tale from the men in the shipyards about the rat that could speak. I never laid no confidence in that before; but tonight, if I'd demeaned myself to lay my ear to the door of the further bin, I could pretty much have heard what they was saying.'

'Oh, there, Mr Parkes, I've no patience with your fancies! Rats talking in the wine-cellar indeed!'

'Well, Mrs Bunch, I've no wish to argue with you: all I say is, if you choose to go to the far bin, and lay your ear to the door, you may prove my words this minute.'

'What nonsense you do talk, Mr Parkes – not fit for children to listen to! Why, you'll be frightening Master Stephen there out of his wits.'

'What! Master Stephen?' said Parkes, awaking to the consciousness of the boy's presence. 'Master Stephen knows well enough when I'm a-playing a joke with you, Mrs Bunch.'

In fact, Master Stephen knew much too well to suppose that Mr Parkes had in the first instance intended a joke. He was interested, not altogether pleasantly, in the situation; but all his questions were unsuccessful in inducing the butler to give any more detailed account of his experiences in the wine-cellar.

We have now arrived at March 24, 1812. It was a day of curious experiences for Stephen: a windy, noisy day, which filled the house and the gardens with a restless impression. As Stephen stood by the fence of the grounds, and looked out into the park, he felt as if an endless procession of unseen people were sweeping past him on the wind, borne on resistlessly and aimlessly, vainly striving to stop themselves, to catch at something that might arrest their flight and bring them once again into contact with the living world of which they had formed a part. After luncheon that day Mr Abney said:

'Stephen, my boy, do you think you could manage to come to me tonight as late as eleven o'clock in my study? I shall be busy until that time, and I wish to show you something connected with your future life which it is most important that you should know. You are not to mention this matter to Mrs Bunch nor to anyone else in the house; and you had better go to your room at the usual time.'

Here was a new excitement added to life: Stephen eagerly grasped at the opportunity of sitting up till eleven o'clock. He looked in at the library door on his way upstairs that evening, and saw a brazier, which he had often noticed in the corner of the room, moved out before the fire; an old silver-gilt cup stood on the table, filled with red wine, and some written sheets of paper lay near it. Mr Abney was sprinkling some incense on the brazier from a round silver box as Stephen passed, but did not seem to notice his step.

The wind had fallen, and there was a still night and a full moon. At about ten o'clock Stephen was standing at the open window of his bedroom, looking out over the country. Still as the night was, the mysterious population of the distant moonlit woods was not yet lulled to rest. From time to time strange cries as of lost and despairing wanderers sounded from across the mere. They might be the notes of owls or water-birds, yet they did not quite resemble either sound. Were not they coming nearer? Now they sounded from the nearer side of the water, and in a few moments they seemed to be floating about among the shrubberies. Then they ceased; but just as Stephen was thinking of shutting the window and resuming his reading of *Robinson Crusoe*, he caught sight of two figures standing on the gravelled terrace that ran along the garden side of the Hall – the figures of a boy and girl, as it seemed; they stood side by side, looking up at the windows. Something in the form of the girl recalled irresistibly his dream of the figure in the bath. The boy inspired him with more acute fear.

Whilst the girl stood still, half smiling, with her hands clasped over her heart, the boy, a thin shape, with black hair and ragged clothing, raised his arms in the air with an appearance of menace and of unappeasable hunger and longing. The moon shone upon his almost transparent hands, and Stephen saw that the nails were fearfully long and that the light shone through them. As he stood with his arms thus raised, he disclosed a terrifying spectacle. On the left side of his chest there opened a black and gaping rent; and there fell upon Stephen's brain, rather than upon his ear, the impression of one of those hungry and desolate cries that he had heard resounding over the woods of Aswarby all that evening. In another moment this dreadful pair had moved swiftly and noiselessly over the dry gravel, and he saw them no more.

Inexpressibly frightened as he was, he determined to take his candle and go down to Mr Abney's study, for the hour appointed for their meeting was near at hand. The study or library opened out of the front hall on one side, and Stephen, urged on by his terrors, did not take long in getting there. To effect an entrance was not so easy. The door was not locked, he felt sure, for the key was on the outside of it as usual. His repeated knocks produced no answer. Mr Abney was engaged: he was speaking. What! why did he try to cry out? and why was the cry choked in his throat? Had he, too, seen the mysterious children? But now everything was quiet, and the door yielded to Stephen's terrified and frantic pushing.

On the table in Mr Abney's study certain papers were found which explained the situation to Stephen Elliott when he was of an age to understand them. The most important sentences were as follows:

'It was a belief very strongly and generally held by the ancients – of whose wisdom in these matters I have had such experience as induces me to place confidence in their assertions – that by enacting certain processes, which to us moderns have something of a barbaric complexion, a very remarkable enlightenment of the spiritual faculties in man may be attained: that, for example, by absorbing the personalities of a certain number of his fellow-creatures, an individual may gain a complete ascendancy over those orders of spiritual beings which control the elemental forces of our universe.

'It is recorded of Simon Magus that he was able to fly in the air, to become invisible, or to assume any form he pleased, by the agency of the soul of a boy whom, to use the libellous phrase employed by the author of the *Clementine Recognitions*, he had "murdered". I find it set down, moreover, with considerable detail in the writings of Hermes Trismegistus, that similar happy results may be produced by the absorption of the hearts of not less than three human beings below the age of twenty-one years. To the testing of the truth of this receipt I have devoted the greater part of the last twenty years, selecting as the *corpora vilia* of my experiment such persons as could conveniently be removed without occasioning a sensible gap in society. The first step I effected by the removal of one Phoebe Stanley, a girl of gipsy extraction, on March 24, 1792. The second, by the removal of a wandering Italian lad, named Giovanni Paoli, on the night of March 23, 1805. The final "victim" – to employ a word repugnant in the highest degree to my feelings – must be my cousin, Stephen Elliott. His day must be this March 24, 1812.

'The best means of effecting the required absorption is to remove the heart from the *living* subject, to reduce it to ashes, and to mingle them with about a pint of some red wine, preferably port. The remains of the first two subjects, at least, it will be well to conceal: a disused bathroom or wine-cellar will be found convenient for such a purpose. Some annoyance may be experienced from the psychic portion of the subjects, which popular language dignifies with the name of ghosts. But the man of philosophic temperament – to whom alone the experiment is appropriate – will be little prone to attach importance to the feeble efforts of these beings to wreak their vengeance on him. I contemplate with the liveliest satisfaction the enlarged and emancipated existence which the experiment, if successful, will confer on me; not only placing me beyond the reach of human justice (so-called), but eliminating to a great extent the prospect of death itself.'

Mr Abney was found in his chair, his head thrown back, his face stamped with an expression of rage, fright, and mortal pain. In his left side was a terrible lacerated wound, exposing the heart. There was no blood on his hands, and a long knife that lay on the table was perfectly clean. A savage wild-cat might have inflicted the injuries. The window of the study was open, and it was the opinion of the coroner that Mr Abney had met his death by the agency of some wild creature. But Stephen Elliott's study of the papers I have quoted led him to a very different conclusion.

The Sea-Raiders

H. G. Wells

Until the extraordinary affair at Sidmouth, the peculiar species *Haploteuthis ferox* was known to science only generically, on the strength of a half-digested tentacle obtained near the Azores, and a decaying body pecked by birds and nibbled by fish, found early in 1896 by Mr Jennings, near Land's End.

In no department of zoological science, indeed, are we quite so much in the dark as with regard to the deep-sea cephalopods. A mere accident, for instance, it was that led to the Prince of Monaco's discovery of nearly a dozen new forms in the summer of 1895, a discovery in which the before-mentioned tentacle was included. It chanced that a cachalot was killed off Terceira by some sperm whalers, and in its last struggles charged almost to the Prince's yacht, missed it, rolled under, and died within twenty yards of his rudder. And in its agony it threw up a number of large objects, which the Prince, dimly perceiving they were strange and important, was, by a happy expedient, able to secure before they sank. He set his screws in motion, and kept them circling in the vortices thus created until a boat could be lowered. And these specimens were whole cephalopods and fragments of cephalopods, some of gigantic proportions, and almost all of them unknown to science!

It would seem, indeed, that these large and agile creatures, living in the middle depths of the sea, must, to a large extent, for ever remain unknown to us, since under water they are too nimble for nets, and it is only by such rare unlooked-for accidents that specimens can be obtained. In the case of *Haploteuthis ferox*, for instance, we are still altogether ignorant of its habitat, as ignorant as we are of the breeding-ground of the herring or the sea-ways of the salmon. And zoologists are altogether at a loss to account for its sudden appearance on our coast. Possibly it was the stress of a hunger migration that drove it hither out of the deep. But it will be, perhaps, better to avoid necessarily inconclusive discussion, and to proceed at once with our narrative.

The first human being to set eyes upon a living *Haploteuthis* – the first human being to survive, that is, for there can be little doubt now that the wave of bathing fatalities and boating accidents that travelled along the coast of Cornwall and Devon in early May was due to this cause – was a retired tea-dealer of the name of Fison, who was stopping at a Sidmouth boarding house. It was in the afternoon, and he was walking along the cliff path between Sidmouth and Ladram Bay. The cliffs in this direction are very high, but down the red face of them in one place a kind of ladder staircase has been made. He was near this when his attention was attracted by what at first he thought to be a cluster of birds struggling over a fragment of food that caught the sunlight, and glistened pinkish-white. The tide was right out, and this object was not only far below him, but remote across a broad waste of rock reefs covered with dark sea-weed and interspersed with silvery shining tidal pools. And he was, moreover, dazzled by the brightness of the further water.

In a minute, regarding this again, he perceived that his judgement was in fault, for over this struggle circled a number of birds, jackdaws and gulls for the most part, the latter gleaming blindingly when the sunlight smote their wings and they seemed minute in comparison with it. And his curiosity was, perhaps, aroused all the more strongly because of his first insufficient explanations.

As he had nothing better to do than amuse himself, he decided to make this object, whatever it was, the goal of his afternoon walk, instead of Ladram Bay, conceiving it might perhaps be a great fish of some sort, stranded by some chance, and flapping about in its distress. And so he hurried down the long steep ladder, stopping at intervals of thirty feet or so to take breath and scan the mysterious movement.

At the foot of the cliff he was, of course, nearer his object than he had been; but, on the other hand, it now came up against the incandescent sky, beneath the sun, so as to seem dark and indistinct. Whatever was pinkish of it was now hidden by a skerry of weedy boulders. But he perceived that it was made up of seven rounded bodies, distinct or connected, and that the birds kept up a constant croaking and screaming, but seemed afraid to approach it too closely.

Mr Fison, torn by curiosity, began picking his way across the wave-worn rocks, and, finding the wet seaweed that covered them thickly rendered them extremely slippery, he stopped, removed his shoes and socks, and coiled his trousers above his knees. His object was, of course, merely to avoid stumbling into the rocky pools about him, and perhaps he was rather glad, as all men are, of an excuse to resume, even for a moment, the sensations of his boyhood. At any rate, it is to this, no doubt, that he owes his life.

He approached his mark with all the assurance which the absolute security of this country against all forms of animal life gives its inhabitants. The round bodies moved to and fro, but it was only when he surmounted the skerry of boulders I have mentioned that he realized the horrible nature of the discovery. It came upon him with some suddenness.

The rounded bodies fell apart as he came into sight over the ridge, and displayed the pinkish object to be the partially devoured body of a human being, but whether of a man or woman he was unable to say. And the rounded bodies were new and ghastly-looking creatures, in shape somewhat resembling an octopus, and with huge and very long and flexible tentacles, coiled copiously on the ground. The skin had a glistening texture, unpleasant to see, like shiny leather. The downward bend of the tentacle-surrounded mouth, the curious excrescence at the bend, the tentacles, and the large intelligent eyes, gave the creatures a grotesque suggestion of a face. They were the size of a fair-sized swine about the body, and the tentacles seemed to him to be many feet in length. There were, he thinks, seven or eight at least of the creatures. Twenty yards beyond them, amid the surf of the now returning tide, two others were emerging from the sea.

Their bodies lay flatly on the rocks, and their eyes regarded him with evil interest; but it does not appear that Mr Fison was afraid, or that he realized that he was in any danger. Possibly his confidence is to be ascribed to the limpness of their attitudes. But he was horrified, of course, and intensely excited and indignant at such revolting creatures preying upon human flesh. He thought they had chanced upon a drowned body. He shouted to them, with the idea of driving them off, and, finding they did not budge, cast about him, picked up a big rounded lump of rock, and flung it at one.

And then, slowly uncoiling their tentacles, they all began moving towards him – creeping at first deliberately, and making a soft purring sound to each other.

In a moment Mr Fison realized that he was in danger. He shouted again, threw both his boots and started off, with a leap, forthwith. Twenty yards off he stopped and faced about, judging them slow, and behold! the tentacles of their leader were already pouring over the rocky ridge on which he had just been standing!

At that he shouted again, but this time not threatening, but a cry of dismay, and began jumping, striding, slipping, wading across the uneven expanse between him and the beach. The tall red cliffs seemed suddenly at a vast distance, and he saw, as though they were creatures in another world, two minute workmen engaged in the repair of the ladder-way, and little suspecting the race for life that was beginning below them. At one time he could hear the creatures splashing in the pools not a dozen feet behind him, and once he slipped and almost fell.

They chased him to the very foot of the cliffs, and desisted only when he had been joined by the workmen at the foot of the ladder-way up the cliff. All three of the men pelted them with stones for a time, and then hurried to the cliff top and along the path towards Sidmouth, to secure assistance and a boat, and to rescue the desecrated body from the clutches of these abominable creatures.

And, as if he had not already been in sufficient peril that day, Mr Fison went with the boat to point out the exact spot of his adventure.

As the tide was down, it required a considerable detour to reach the spot, and when at last they came off the ladder-way, the mangled body had disappeared. The water was now running, submerging first one slab of slimy rock and then another, and the four men in the boat – the workmen, that is, the boatman, and Mr Fison – now turned their attention from the bearings off-shore to the water beneath the keel.

At first they could see little below them, save a dark jungle of laminaria, with an occasional darting fish. Their minds were set on adventure, and they expressed their disappointment freely. But presently they saw one of the monsters swimming through the water seaward, with a curious rolling motion that suggested to Mr Fison the spinning roll of a captive balloon. Almost immediately after, the waving streamers of laminaria were extraordinarily perturbed, parted for a moment, and three of these beasts became darkly visible, struggling for what was probably some fragment of the drowned man. In a moment the copious olive-green ribbons had poured over this writhing group.

At that all four men, greatly excited, began beating the water with oars and shouting, and immediately they saw a tumultuous movement among the weeds. They desisted to see more clearly, and as soon as the water was smooth, they saw, as it seemed to them, the whole sea bottom among the weeds set with eyes.

'Ugly swine!' cried one of the men. 'Why, there's dozens!' And forthwith the things began to rise through the water about them. Mr Fison has since described to the writer this startling eruption out of the waving laminaria meadows. To him it seemed to occupy a considerable time, but it is probable that really it was an affair of a few seconds only.

For a time nothing but eyes, and then he speaks of tentacles streaming out and parting the weed fronds this way and that. Then these things, growing larger, until at last the bottom was hidden by their intercoiling forms, and the tips of tentacles rose darkly here and there into the air above the swell of the waters.

One came up boldly to the side of the boat, and, clinging to this with three of its sucker-set tentacles, threw four others over the gunwale, as if with the intention either of over-setting the boat or of clambering into it. Mr Fison at once caught up the boathook, and jabbing furiously at the soft tentacles, forced it to desist. He was struck in the back and almost pitched overboard by the boatman, who was using his oar to resist a similar attack on the other side of the boat. But the tentacles on either side at once relaxed their hold at this, slid out of sight, and splashed into the water.

'We'd better get out of this,' said Mr Fison, who was trembling violently. He went to the tiller, while the boatman and one of the workmen seated themselves, and began rowing. The other workman stood up in the fore part of the boat, with the boathook, ready to strike any more tentacles that might appear. Nothing else seems to have been said. Mr Fison had expressed the common feeling beyond amendment. In a hushed, scared mood, with faces white and drawn, they set about escaping from the position into which they had so recklessly blundered.

But the oars had scarcely dropped into the water before dark, tapering, serpentine ropes had bound them, and were about the rudder; and creeping up the sides of the boat with a looping motion came the suckers again. The men gripped their oars and pulled, but it was like trying to move a boat in a floating raft of weeds. 'Help here!' cried the boatman, and Mr Fison and the second workman rushed to help lug at the oar.

Then the man with the boathook, his name was Ewan, or Ewen – sprang up with a curse, and began striking downward over the side, as far as he could reach, at the bank of tentacles that now clustered along the boat's bottom. And, at the same time, the two rowers stood up to get a better purchase for the recovery of their oars. The boatman handed his to Mr Fison, who lugged desperately, and, meanwhile, the boatman opened a big clasping knife, and, leaning over the side of the boat, began hacking at the spiring arms upon the oar shaft.

Mr Fison staggering with the quivering rocking of the boat, his teeth set, his breath coming short, and the veins starting on his hands as he pulled at his oar, suddenly cast his eyes seaward. And there, not fifty yards off, across the long rollers of the incoming tide, was a large boat standing in towards them, with three women and a little child in it. A boatman was rowing, and a little man in a pink-ribboned straw hat and whites stood in the stern, hailing them. For a moment, of course, Mr Fison thought of help, and then he thought of the child. He abandoned his oar forthwith, threw up his arms in a frantic gesture, and screamed to the party in the boat to keep away 'for God's sake!' It says much for the modesty and courage of Mr Fison that he does not seem to be aware that there was any quality of heroism in his action at this juncture. The oar he had abandoned was at once drawn under, and presently reappeared floating about twenty yards away.

At the same moment Mr Fison felt the boat under him lurch violently, and a hoarse scream, a prolonged cry of terror from Hill, the boatman, caused him to forget the party of excursionists altogether. He turned, and saw Hill crouching by the forward rowlock, his face convulsed with terror, and his right arm over the side and drawn tightly down. He gave now a succession of short sharp cries, 'Oh! oh! oh! – oh!' Mr Fison believes that he must have been hacking at the tentacles below the water-line, and have been grasped by them, but, of course, it is quite impossible to say now certainly what had happened. The boat was heeling over, so that the gunwale was within ten inches of water, and both Ewan and the other labourer were striking down into the water, with oar and boathook, on either side of Hill's arm. Mr Fison instinctively placed himself to counterpoise them.

Then Hill, who was a burly, powerful man, made a strenuous effort, and rose almost to a standing position. He lifted his arm, indeed, clean out of the water. Hanging to it was a complicated tangle of brown ropes; and the eyes of one of the brutes that had hold of him, glaring straight and resolute, showed momentarily above the surface. The boat heeled more and more, and the green-brown water came pouring in a cascade over the side. Then Hill slipped and fell with his ribs across the side, and his arm and the mass of tentacles about it splashed back in the water. He rolled over; his boot kicked Mr Fison's knee as the gentleman rushed forward to seize him, and in another moment fresh tentacles had whipped about his waist and neck, and after a brief, convulsive struggle, in which the boat was nearly capsized, Hill was lugged overboard. The boat righted with a violent jerk that all but sent Mr Fison over the other side, and hid the struggle in the water from his eyes.

He stood staggering to recover his balance for a moment, and as he did so, he became aware that the struggle and the inflowing tide had carried them close upon the weedy rocks again. Not four yards off a table of rock still rose in rhythmic movements above the inwash of the tide. In a moment Mr Fison seized the oar from Ewan, gave one vigorous stroke, then, dropping it, ran to the bows and leapt. He felt his feet slide over the rock, and, by a frantic effort, leapt again towards a further mass. He stumbled over this, came to his knees and rose again.

'Look out!' cried someone, and a large drab body struck him. He was knocked flat into a tidal pool by one of the workmen, and as he went down he heard smothered, choking cries that he believed at the time came from Hill. Then he found himself marvelling at the shrillness and variety of Hill's voice. Someone jumped over him, and a curving rush of foamy water poured over, and passed. He scrambled to his feet, dripping, and, without looking seaward, ran as fast as his terror would let him shoreward. Before him, over the flat space of scattered rocks, stumbled the two workmen – one a dozen yards in front of the other.

He looked over his shoulder at last, and, seeing that he was not pursued, faced about. He was astonished. From the moment of the rising of the cephalopods out of the water, he had been acting too swiftly to fully comprehend his actions. Now it seemed to him as if he had suddenly jumped out of an evil dream.

For there were the sky, cloudless and blazing with the afternoon sun, the sea weltering under its pitiless brightness, the soft creamy foam of the breaking water, and the low, long, dark ridges of rock. The righted boat floated, rising and falling gently on the swell about a dozen yards from shore. Hill and the monsters, all the stress and tumult of that fierce fight for life, had vanished as though they had never been.

Mr Fison's heart was beating violently; he was throbbing to the finger-tips, and his breath came deep.

There was something missing. For some seconds he could not think clearly enough what this might be. Sun, sky, sea, rocks – what was it? Then he remembered the boatload of excursionists. It had vanished. He wondered whether he had imagined it. He turned, and saw the two workmen standing side by side under the projecting masses of the tall pink cliffs. He hesitated whether he should make one last attempt to save the man Hill. His physical excitement seemed to desert him suddenly, and leave him aimless and helpless. He turned shoreward, stumbling and wading towards his two companions.

He looked back again, and there were now two boats floating, and the one farthest out at sea pitched clumsily, bottom upward.

So it was *Haploteuthis ferox* made its appearance upon the Devonshire coast. So far, this has been its most serious aggression. Mr Fison's account, taken together with the wave of boating and bathing casualties to which I have already alluded, and the absence of fish from the Cornish coasts that year, points clearly to a shoal of these voracious deep-sea monsters prowling slowly along the sub-tidal coast-line. Hunger migration has, I know, been suggested as the force that drove them hither; but, for my own part, I prefer to believe the alternative theory of Hemsley. Hemsley holds that a pack or shoal of these creatures may have become enamoured of human flesh by the accident of a foundered ship sinking among them, and have wandered in search of it out of their accustomed zone; first waylaying and following ships, and so coming to our shores in the wake of the Atlantic traffic. But to discuss Hemsley's cogent and admirably stated arguments would be out of place here.

It would seem that the appetites of the shoal were satisfied by the catch of eleven people – for so far as can be ascertained, there were ten people in the second boat, and certainly these creatures gave no further signs of their presence off Sidmouth that day. The coast between Seaton and Budleigh Salterton was patrolled all that evening and night by four Preventive Service boats, the men in which were armed with harpoons and cutlasses, and, as the evening advanced, a number of more or less similarly equipped expeditions, organized by private individuals, joined them. Mr Fison took no part in any of these expeditions.

About midnight excited hails were heard from a boat about a couple of miles out to sea to the south-east of Sidmouth, and a lantern was seen waving in a strange manner to and fro and up and down. The nearer boats at once hurried towards the alarm. The venturesome occupants of the boat, a seaman, a curate, and two schoolboys, had actually seen the monsters passing under their boat. The creatures, it seems, like most deep-sea organisms, were phosphorescent and they had been floating, five fathoms deep or so, like creatures of moonshine through the blackness of the water, their tentacles retracted and as if asleep, rolling over and over, and moving slowly in a wedge-like formation towards the south-east.

These people told their story in gesticulated fragments, as first one boat drew alongside and then another. At last there was a little fleet of eight or nine boats collected together, and from them a tumult, like the chatter of a marketplace, rose into the stillness of the night. There was little or no disposition to pursue the shoal, the people had neither weapons nor experience for such a dubious chase, and presently – even with a certain relief, it may be – the boats turned shoreward.

And now to tell what is perhaps the most astonishing fact in this whole astonishing raid. We have not the slightest knowledge of the subsequent movements of the shoal, although the whole south-west coast was now alert for it. But it may, perhaps, be significant that a cachalot was stranded off Sark on June 3. Two weeks and three days after this Sidmouth affair, a living *Haploteuthis* came ashore in Calais sands. It was alive, because several witnesses saw its tentacles moving in a convulsive way. But it is probable that it was dying. A gentleman named Pouchet obtained a rifle and shot it.

That was the last appearance of a living *Haploteuthis*. No others were seen on the French coast. On the 15th of June a dead body, almost complete, was washed ashore near Torquay, and a few days later a boat from the Marine Biological station, engaged in dredging off Plymouth, picked up a rotting specimen, slashed deeply with a cutlass wound. How the former specimen had come by its death it is impossible to say. And on the last day of June, Mr Egbert Caine, an artist, bathing near Newlyn, threw up his arms, shrieked, and was drawn under. A friend bathing with him made no attempt to save him, but swam at once for the shore. This is the last fact to tell of this extraordinary raid from the deeper sea. Whether it is really the last of these horrible creatures it is as yet premature to say. But it is believed, and certainly it is to be hoped, that they have returned now, and returned for good, to the sunless depths of the middle seas, out of which they have so strangely and so mysteriously arisen.

The Derelict

William Hope Hodgson

'It's the *Material*,' said the old ship's doctor . . . 'The *Material*, plus the conditions; and, maybe,' he added slowly, 'a third factor – yes, a third factor; but there, there . . .' He broke off his half-meditative sentence, and began to charge his pipe.

'Go on, Doctor,' we said encouragingly, and with more than a little expectancy. We were in the smoke-room of the *Sand-a-lea*, running across the North Atlantic; and the doctor was a character. He concluded the charging of his pipe, and lit it; then settled himself, and began to express himself more fully:

'The *Material*,' he said, with conviction, 'is inevitably the medium of expression of the Life-Force – the fulcrum, as it were; lacking which, it is unable to exert itself, or, indeed, to express itself in any form or fashion that would be intelligible or evident to us.

'So potent is the share of the *Material* in the production of that thing which we name Life, and so eager the Life-Force to express itself, that I am convinced it would, if given the right conditions, make itself manifest even through so hopeless-seeming a medium as a simple block of sawn wood; for I tell you, gentlemen, the Life-Force is both as fiercely urgent and as indiscriminate as Fire – the Destructor; yet which some are now growing to consider the very essence of Life rampant . . . There is a quaint seeming paradox there,' he concluded, nodding his old grey head.

'Yes, Doctor,' I said. 'In brief, your argument is that Life is a thing, state, fact, or element, call-it-what-you-like, which requires the *Material* through which to manifest itself, and that given the *Material*, plus the conditions, the result is Life. In other words, that Life is an evolved product, manifested through Matter and bred of conditions – eh?'

'As we understand the word,' said the old doctor. 'Though, mind you, there *may* be a third factor. But, in my heart, I believe that it is a matter of chemistry; conditions and a suitable medium; but given the conditions, the Brute is so almighty that it will seize upon anything through which to manifest itself. It is a force generated by conditions; but nevertheless this does not bring us one iota nearer to its *explanation*, any more than to the explanation of electricity or fire. They are, all three, of the Outer Forces – Monsters of the Void. Nothing we can do will *create* any one of them; our power is merely to be able, by providing the conditions, to make each one of them manifest to our physical senses. Am I clear?'

'Yes, Doctor, in a way you are,' I said. 'But I don't agree with you; though I think I understand you. Electricity and fire are both what I might call natural things; but life is an abstract something – a kind of all-permeating wakefulness. Oh, I can't explain it; who could? But it's spiritual; not just a thing bred out of a condition, like fire, as you say, or electricity. It's a horrible thought of yours. Life's a kind of spiritual mystery . . .'

'Easy, my boy!' said the old doctor, laughing gently to himself; 'or else I may be asking you to demonstrate the spiritual mystery of life of the limpet, or the crab, shall we say?'

He grinned at me, with ineffable perverseness. 'Anyway,' he continued, 'as I suppose you've all guessed, I've a yarn to tell you in support of my impression that life is no more a mystery or a miracle than fire or electricity. But, please to remember, gentlemen, that because we've succeeded in naming and making good use of these two forces, they're just as much mysteries, fundamentally, as ever. And, anyway, the thing I'm going to tell you, won't explain the mystery of life; but only give you one of my pegs on which I hang my feeling that life is, as I have said, a force made manifest through conditions (that is to say, natural chemistry), and that it can take for its purpose and need, the most incredible and unlikely matter; for without matter, it cannot come into existence – it cannot become manifest . . .'

'I don't agree with you, Doctor,' I interrupted. 'Your theory would destroy all belief in life after death. It would . . .'

'Hush, sonny,' said the old man, with a quiet little smile of comprehension. 'Hark to what I've to say first; and, anyway, what objection have you to material life, after death; and if you object to a material framework, I would still have you remember that I am speaking of life, as we understand the word in this our life. Now do be a quiet lad, or I'll never be done:

'It was when I was a young man, and that is a good many years ago, gentlemen. I had passed my examination; but was so run down with overwork, that it was decided that I had better take a trip to sea. I was by no means well off, and very glad, in the end, to secure a nominal post as doctor in a sailing passenger-clipper, running out to China.

'The name of the ship was the *Bheotpte*, and soon after I had got all my gear aboard, she cast off, and we dropped down the Thames, and next day were well away out in the Channel.

'The captain's name was Gannington, a very decent man; though quite illiterate. The first mate, Mr Berlies, was a quiet, sternish, reserved man, very well read. The second mate, Mr Selvern, was, perhaps, by birth and upbringing, the most socially cultured of the three; but he lacked the stamina and indomitable pluck of the two others. He was more of a sensitive; and emotionally and even mentally, the most alert man of the three.

'On our way out, we called at Madagascar, where we landed some of our passengers; then we ran eastward, meaning to call at North-West Cape; but about a hundred degrees east, we encountered very dreadful weather, which carried away all our sails and sprung the jib-boom and fore t'gallant mast.

'The storm carried us northward for several hundred miles, and when it dropped us finally, we found ourselves in a very bad state. The ship had been strained, and had taken some three feet of water through her seams; the main topmast had been sprung, in addition to the jib-boom and fore t'gallant mast; two of our boats had gone, as also one of the pigsties (with three fine pigs), this latter having been washed overboard but some half-hour before the wind began to ease, which it did quickly; though a very ugly sea ran for some hours after.

'The wind left us just before dark, and when morning came, it brought splendid weather; a calm, mildly undulating sea, and a brilliant sun, with no wind. It showed us also that we were not alone; for about two miles away to the westward was another vessel, which Mr Selvern, the second mate, pointed out to me.

' "That's a pretty rum-looking packet, Doctor," he said, and handed me his glass. I looked through it, at the other vessel, and saw what he meant; at least, I thought I did.

' "Yes, Mr Selvern," I said, "she's got a pretty old-fashioned look about her."

'He laughed at me, in his pleasant way.

' "It's easy to see you're not a sailor, Doctor," he remarked. "There's a dozen rum things about her. She's a derelict, and has been floating round, by the look of her, for many a score of years. Look at the shape of her counter, and the bows and cut-water. She's as old as the hills, as you might say, and ought to have gone down to Davy Jones a long time ago.

Look at the growths on her, and the thickness of her standing rigging; that's all salt encrustations, I fancy, if you notice the white colour. She's been a small barque; but don't you see she's not a yard left aloft. They've all dropped out of the slings; everything rotted away; wonder the standing rigging hasn't gone too. I wish the Old Man would let us take the boat, and have a look at her; she'd be well worth it."

'There seemed little chance, however, of this; for all hands were turned-to and kept hard at it all day long, repairing the damage to the masts and gear, and this took a long while, as you may think. Part of the time I gave a hand, heaving on one of the deck-capstans; for the exercise was good for my liver. Old Captain Gannington approved, and I persuaded him to come along and try some of the same medicine, which he did; and we grew very chummy over the job.

'We got talking about the derelict, and he remarked how lucky we were not to have run full tilt on to her, in the darkness; for she lay right away to leeward of us, according to the way that we had been drifting in the storm. He also was of the opinion that she had a strange look about her, and that she was pretty old but on this latter point, he plainly had far less knowledge than the second mate; for he was, as I have said, an illiterate man, and he knew nothing of sea-craft beyond what experience had taught him. He lacked the book knowledge, which the second mate had, of vessels previous to his day, which it appeared the derelict was.

' "She's an old 'un, Doctor," was the extent of his observations in this direction.

'Yet, when I mentioned to him that it would be interesting to go aboard, and give her a bit of an overhaul, he nodded his head, as if the idea had been already in his mind, and accorded with his own inclinations.

' "When the work's over, Doctor," he said. "Can't spare the men now, ye know. Got to get all shipshape an' ready as smart as we can. But we'll take my gig, an' go off in the Second Dog Watch. The glass is steady, an' it'll be a bit of jam for us."

'That evening, after tea, the captain gave orders to clear the gig and get overboard. The second mate was to come with me, and the skipper gave him word to see that two or three lamps were put into the boat, as it would soon fall dark. A little later, we were pulling across the calmness of the sea with a crew of six at the oars, and making very good speed of it.

'Now, gentlemen, I have detailed to you with great exactness, all the facts, both big and little, so that you can follow step by step each incident in this extraordinary affair; and I want you now to pay the closest attention.

'I was sitting in the stern-sheets, with the second mate and the captain, who was steering; and as we drew nearer and nearer to the stranger, I studied her with an ever-growing attention, as, indeed, did Captain Gannington, and the second mate. She was, as you know, to the westward of us, and the sunset was making a great flame of red light to the back of her, so that she showed a little blurred and indistinct, by reason of the halation of the light, which almost defeated the eye in any attempt to see her rotting spars and standing rigging, submerged as they were in the fiery glory of the sunset.

'It was because of this effect of the sunset, that we had come quite close, comparatively, to the derelict before we saw that she was surrounded by a sort of curious scum, the colour of which was difficult to decide upon, by reason of the red light that was in the atmosphere; but which afterwards we discovered to be brown. This scum spread all about the old vessel for many hundreds of yards, in a huge, irregular patch, a great stretch of which reached out to the eastward, upon our starboard side, some score, or so, fathoms away.

' "Queer stuff," said Captain Gannington, leaning to the side, and looking over. "Something in the cargo as 'as gone rotten an' worked out through 'er seams."

' "Look at her bows and stern," said the second mate; "just look at the growth on her."

'There were, as he said, great clumpings of strange-looking sea-fungi under the bows and the short counter astern. From the stump of her jib-boom and her cutwater, great beards of rime and marine growths hung downward into the scum that held her in. Her blank starboard side was presented to us, all a dead, dirtyish white, streaked and mottled vaguely with dull masses of heavier colour.

' "There's a steam of haze rising off her," said the second mate, speaking again; "you can see it against the light. It keeps coming and going. Look!"

'I saw then what he meant – a faint haze or steam, either suspended above the old vessel, or rising from her; and Captain Gannington saw it also:

' "Spontaneous combustion!" he exclaimed. "We'll 'ave to watch w'en we lift the 'atches; 'nless it's some poor devil that's got aboard of her; but that ain't likely."

'We were now within a couple of hundred yards of the old derelict, and had entered into the brown scum. As it poured off the lifted oars, I heard one of the men mutter to himself – "dam treacle!" and indeed, it was something like it. As the boat continued to forge nearer and nearer to the old ship, the scum grew thicker and thicker; so that, at last, it perceptibly slowed us.

‘ "Give way, lads! Put some beef to it!" sung out Captain Gannington; and thereafter there was no sound, except the panting of the men, and the faint, reiterated suck, suck, of the sullen brown scum upon the oars, as the boat was forced ahead. As we went, I was conscious of a peculiar smell in the evening air, and whilst I had no doubt that the puddling of the scum, by the oars, made it rise, I felt that in some way, it was vaguely familiar; yet I could give it no name.

‘We were now very close to the old vessel, and presently she was high above us, against the dying light. The captain called out then to – "in with the bow oars, and stand-by with the boat-hook", which was done.

‘ "Aboard there! Ahoy! Aboard there! Ahoy!" shouted Captain Gannington, but there came no answer, only the flat sound of his voice going lost into the open sea, each time he sang out.

‘ "Ahoy! Aboard there! Ahoy!" he shouted, time after time; but there was only the weary silence of the old hulk that answered us; and, somehow as he shouted, the while that I stared up half expectantly at her, a queer little sense of oppression, that amounted almost to nervousness, came upon me. It passed, but I remember how I was suddenly aware that it was growing dark. Darkness comes fairly rapidly in the tropics, though not so quickly as many fiction-writers seem to think; but it was not that the coming dusk had perceptibly deepened in that brief time, of only a few moments, but rather that my nerves had made me suddenly a little hyper-sensitive. I mention my state particularly; for I am not a nervy man, normally; and my abrupt touch of nerves is significant, in the light of what happened.

‘ "There's no one aboard there!" said Captain Gannington. "Give way, men!" For the boat's crew had instinctively rested on their oars, as the captain hailed the old craft. The men gave way again; and then the second mate called out excitedly – "Why, look there, there's our pigsty! See, it's got *Bheotpte* painted on the end. It's drifted down here, and the scum's caught it. What a blessed wonder!"

‘It was, as he had said, our pigsty that had been washed overboard in the storm, and most extraordinary to come across it there.

‘ "We'll tow it off with us, when we go," remarked the captain, and shouted to the crew to get down to their oars; for they were hardly moving the boat, because the scum was so thick, close in around the old ship, that it literally clogged the boat from going ahead. I remember that it struck me in a half-conscious sort of way, as curious that the pigsty, containing our three dead pigs, had managed to drift in so far, unaided, whilst we could scarcely manage to *force* the boat in now that we had come right into the scum. But the thought passed from my mind; for so many things happened within the next few minutes.

'The men managed to bring the boat in alongside, within a couple of feet of the derelict, and the man with the boat-hook hooked on.

' " 'Ave you got 'old there, forrard?" asked Captain Gannington.

' "Yessir!" said the bow man; and as he spoke there came a queer noise of tearing.

' "What's that?" asked the Captain.

' "It's tore, Sir. Tore clean away!" said the man; and his tone showed that he had received something of a shock.

' "Get a hold again then!" said Captain Gannington, irritably. "You don't s'pose this packet was built yesterday! Shove the hook into the main chains." The man did so gingerly, as you might say; for it seemed to me, in the growing dusk, that he put no strain on to the hook, though, of course, there was no need; you see, the boat could not go very far, of herself, in the stuff in which she was embedded. I remember thinking this, also, as I looked up at the bulging side of the old vessel. Then I heard Captain Gannington's voice:

' "Lord! but she's old! An' what a colour, Doctor! She don't half want paint, do she! . . . Now then, somebody – one of them oars."

'An oar was passed to him, and he leant it up against the ancient, bulging side, then he paused, and called to the second mate to light a couple of the lamps, and stand by to pass them up; for darkness had settled down now upon the sea.

'The second mate lit two of the lamps, and told one of the men to light a third, and keep it handy in the boat; when he stepped across, with a lamp in each hand, to where Captain Gannington stood by the oar against the side of the ship.

' "Now, my lad," said the captain, to the man who had pulled stroke, "up with you, an' we'll pass ye up the lamps."

'The man jumped to obey; caught the oar, and put his weight upon it, and as he did so, something seemed to give a little.

' "Look!" cried out the second mate, and pointed, lamp in hand . . . "It's sunk in!"

'This was true. The oar had made quite an indentation into the bulging, somewhat slimy side of the old vessel.

' "Mould, I reckon," said Captain Gannington, bending towards the derelict, to look. Then to the man:

' "Up you go, my lad, and be smart . . . Don't stand there waitin'!"

'At that, the man, who had paused a moment as he felt the oar give beneath his weight, began to shin up, and in a few seconds he was aboard, and leant out over the rail for the lamps. These were passed up to him, and the captain called to him to steady the oar. Then Captain Gannington went, calling to me to follow, and after me the second mate.

'As the captain put his face over the rail, he gave a cry of astonishment:

' "Mould, by gum! Mould . . . Tons of it! . . . Good Lord!"

'As I heard him shout that, I scrambled the more eagerly after him, and in a moment or two, I was able to see what he meant – everywhere that the light from the two lamps struck, there was nothing but smooth great masses and surfaces of a dirty-white mould.

'I climbed over the rail, with the second mate close behind, and stood upon the mould-covered decks. There might have been no planking beneath the mould, for all that our feet could feel. It gave under our tread with a spongy, puddingy feel. It covered the deck-furniture of the old ship, so that the shape of each article and fitment was often no more than suggested through it.

'Captain Gannington snatched a lamp from the other man, and the second mate reached for the other. They held the lamps high, and we all stared. It was most extraordinary, and somehow, most abominable. I can think of no other word, gentlemen, that so much describes the predominant feeling that affected me at the moment.

' "Good Lord!" said Captain Gannington, several times. "Good Lord!" But neither the second mate nor the man said anything, and for my part I just stared, and at the same time began to smell a little at the air, for there was again a vague odour of something half familiar, that somehow brought to me a sense of half-known fright.

'I turned this way and that, staring, as I have said. Here and there, the mould was so heavy as to entirely disguise what lay beneath, converting the deck-fittings into indistinguishable mounds of mould, all dirty-white, and blotched and veined with irregular, dull purplish markings.

'There was a strange thing about the mould, which Captain Gannington drew attention to – it was that our feet did not crush into it and break the surface, as might have been expected, but merely indented it.

' "Never seen nothin' like it before! . . . Never!" said the captain, after having stooped with his lamp to examine the mould under our feet. He stamped with his heel, and the stuff gave out a dull, puddingy sound. He stooped again, with a quick movement, and stared, holding the lamp close to the deck. "Blest if it ain't a reg'lar skin to it!" he said.

'The second mate and the man and I all stooped, and looked at it. The second mate progged it with his forefinger, and I remember I rapped it several times with my knuckles, listening to the dead sound it gave out, and noticing the close, firm texture of the mould.

' "Dough!" said the second mate. "It's just like blessed dough! . . . Pouf!" He stood up with a quick movement. "I could fancy it stinks a bit," he said.

'As he said this, I knew suddenly what the familiar thing was, in the vague odour that hung about us – it was that the smell had something animal-like in it; something of the same smell only *heavier*, that you will smell in any place that is infested with mice. I began to look about with a sudden very real uneasiness . . . There might be vast numbers of hungry rats on board . . . They might prove exceedingly dangerous, if in a starving condition, yet, as you will understand, somehow I hesitated to put forward my idea as a reason for caution, it was too fanciful.

'Captain Gannington had begun to go aft, along the mould-covered main-deck, with the second mate; each of them holding his lamp high up, so as to cast a good light about the vessel. I turned quickly and followed them, the man with me keeping close to my heels, and plainly uneasy. As we went, I became aware that there was a feeling of moisture in the air, and I remembered the slight mist, or smoke, above the hulk, which had made Captain Gannington suggest spontaneous combustion in explanation.

'And always, as we went, there was that vague animal smell; and suddenly I found myself wishing we were well away from the old vessel.

'Abruptly, after a few paces, the captain stopped and pointed at a row of mould-hidden shapes on either side of the main-deck . . . "Guns," he said. "Been a privateer in the old days, I guess; maybe worse! We'll 'ave a look below, doctor; there may be something worth touchin'. She's older than I thought. Mr Selvern thinks she's about three hundred years old; but I scarce think it."

'We continued our way aft, and I remember that I found myself walking as lightly and gingerly as possible; as if I were subconsciously afraid of treading through the rotten, mould-hid decks. I think the others had a touch of the same feeling, from the way that they walked. Occasionally the soft mould would grip our heels, releasing them with a little, sullen suck.

'The captain forged somewhat ahead of the second mate, and I know that the suggestion he had made himself, that perhaps there might be something below, worth the carrying away, had stimulated his imagination. The second mate was, however, beginning to feel somewhat the same way that I did; at least, I have that impression. I think if it had not been for what I might truly describe as Captain Gannington's sturdy courage, we should all of us have just gone back over the side very soon; for there was most certainly an unwholesome feeling abroad, that made one feel queerly lacking in pluck, and you will soon perceive that this feeling was justified.

'Just as the captain reached the few, mould-covered steps, leading up on to the short half-poop, I was suddenly aware that the feeling of moisture in the air had grown very much more definite. It was perceptible now, intermittently, as a sort of thin, moist, fog-like vapour, that came and went oddly, and seemed to make the decks a little indistinct to the view, this time and that. Once, an odd puff of it beat up suddenly from somewhere, and caught me in the face, carrying a queer, sickly, heavy odour with it, that somehow frightened me strangely, with a suggestion of a waiting and half-comprehended danger.

'We had followed Captain Gannington up the three mould-covered steps, and now went slowly aft along the raised after-deck.

'By the mizzen-mast, Captain Gannington paused, and held his lantern near to it . . .

' "My word, Mister," he said to the second mate, "it's fair thickened up with the mould; why, I'll g'antee it's close on four foot thick." He shone the light down to where it met the deck. "Good Lord!" he said, "look at the sea-lice on it!" I stepped up; and it was as he had said; the sea-lice were thick upon it, some of them huge, not less than the size of large beetles, and all a clear, colourless shade, like water, except where there were little spots of grey in them, evidently their internal organisms.

' "I've never seen the like of them, 'cept on a live cod!" said Captain Gannington, in an extremely puzzled voice. "My word! but they're whoppers!" Then he passed on, but a few paces farther aft, he stopped again, and held his lamp near to the mould-hidden deck.

' "Lord bless me, Doctor!" he called out, in a low voice, "did ye ever see the like of that? Why, it's a foot long, if it's a hinch!"

'I stooped over his shoulder, and saw what he meant; it was a clear, colourless creature, about a foot long, and about eight inches high, with a curved back that was extraordinary narrow. As we stared, all in a group, it gave a queer little flick, and was gone.

' "Jumped!" said the captain. "Well, if that ain't a giant of all the sea-lice that ever I've seen! I guess it jumped twenty-foot clear." He straightened his back, and scratched his head a moment, swinging the lantern this way and that with the other hand, and staring about us. "Wot are *they* doin' aboard 'ere?" he said. "You'll see 'em (little things) on fat cod, an' such like . . . I'm blowed, Doctor, if I understand."

'He held his lamp towards a big mound of the mould, that occupied part of the after portion of the low poop-deck, a little foreside of where there came a two-foot high "break" to a kind of second and loftier poop, that ran away aft to the taffrail. The mound was pretty big, several feet across, and more than a yard high. Captain Gannington walked up to it:

' "I reckon this 's the scuttle," he remarked, and gave it a heavy kick. The only result was a deep indentation into the huge, whitish hump of mould, as if he had driven his foot into a mass of some doughy substance. Yet, I am not altogether correct in saying that this was the only result; for a certain other thing happened – from a place made by the captain's foot, there came a little gush of a purplish fluid, accompanied by a peculiar smell, that was, and was not, half familiar. Some of the mould-like substance had stuck to the toe of the captain's boot, and from this, likewise, there issued a sweat, as it were, of the same colour.

' "Well!" said Captain Gannington, in surprise, and drew back his foot to make another kick at the hump of mould; but he paused, at an exclamation from the second mate:

' "Don't, Sir!" said the second mate.

'I glanced at him, and the light from Captain Gannington's lamp showed me that his face had a bewildered, half-frightened look, as if it were suddenly and unexpectedly half afraid of something, and as if his tongue had given way to his sudden fright, without any intention on his part to speak.

'The captain also turned and stared at him.

' "Why, Mister?" he asked, in a somewhat puzzled voice, through which there sounded just the vaguest hint of annoyance. "We've got to shift this muck, if we're to get below."

'I looked at the second mate, and it seemed to me that, curiously enough, he was listening less to the captain, than to some other sound.

'Suddenly, he said in a queer voice – "Listen, everybody!"

'Yet we heard nothing, beyond the faint murmur of the men talking together in the boat alongside.

' "I don't hear nothing",' said Captain Gannington, after a short pause. "Do you, Doctor?"

' "No," I said.

' "Wot was it you thought you heard?" asked the captain, turning again to the second mate. But the second mate shook his head, in a curious, almost irritable way; as if the captain's question interrupted his listening. Captain Gannington stared a moment at him, then held his lantern up, and glanced about him, almost uneasily. I know I felt a queer sense of strain. But the light showed nothing, beyond the greyish-dirty-white of the mould in all directions.

' "Mister Selvern," said the captain at last, looking at him, "don't get fancying things. Get hold of your bloomin' self. Ye know ye heard nothin'?"

' "I'm quite sure I heard something, Sir!" said the second mate. "I seemed to hear −" He broke off sharply, and appeared to listen, with an almost painful intensity.

' "What did it sound like?" I asked.

' "It's all right, Doctor," said Captain Gannington, laughing gently. "Ye can give him a tonic when we get back. I'm goin' to shift this stuff."

'He drew back and kicked for the second time at the ugly mass, which he took to hide the companion-way. The result of his kick was startling; for the whole thing wobbled sloppily, like a mound of unhealthy-looking jelly.

'He drew his foot out of it, quickly, and took a step backwards, staring, and holding his lamp towards it:

' "By gum!" he said, and it was plain that he was genuinely startled, "the blessed thing's gone soft!"

'The man had run back several steps from the suddenly flaccid mound, and looked horribly frightened. Though, of what, I am sure he had not the least idea. The second mate stood where he was, and stared. For my part, I know I had a most hideous uneasiness upon me. The captain continued to hold his light towards the wobbling mound, and stare.

' "It's gone squashy all through!" he said. "There's no scuttle there. There's no bally woodwork inside that lot! Phoo! what a rum smell!"

'He walked round to the after-side of the strange mound, to see whether there might be some signs of an opening into the hull at the back of the great heap of mould-stuff. And then:

' "*Listen!*" said the second mate, again, and in the strangest sort of voice.

'Captain Gannington straightened himself upright, and there succeeded a pause of the most intense quietness, in which there was not even the hum of talk from the men alongside in the boat. We all heard it − a kind of dull, soft Thud! Thud! Thud! Thud! somewhere in the hull under us, yet so vague that I might have been half doubtful I heard it, only that the others did so, too.

'Captain Gannington turned suddenly to where the man stood:

' "Tell them −" he began. But the fellow cried out something, and pointed. There had come a strange intensity into his somewhat unemotional face; so that the captain's glance followed his action instantly. I stared, also, as you may think. It was the great mound, at which the man was pointing. I saw what he meant.

'From the two gaps made in the mould-like stuff by Captain Ganning-ton's boot, the purple fluid was jetting out in a queerly regular fashion, almost as if it were being forced out by a pump. My word! but I stared. And even as I stared, a larger jet squirted out, and splashed as far as the man, spattering his boots and trouser-legs.

'The fellow had been pretty nervous before, in a stolid, ignorant sort of way, and his funk had been growing steadily; but, at this, he simply let out a yell, and turned about to run. He paused an instant, as if a sudden fear of the darkness that held the decks between him and the boat had taken him. He snatched at the second mate's lantern, tore it out of his hand, and plunged heavily away over the vile stretch of mould.

'Mr Selvern, the second mate, said not a word; he was just standing, staring at the strange-smelling twin streams of dull purple, that were jetting out from the wobbling mound. Captain Gannington, however, roared an order to the man to come back; but the man plunged on and on across the mould, his feet seeming to be clogged by the stuff, as if it had grown suddenly soft. He zigzagged as he ran, the lantern swaying in wild circles as he wrenched his feet free, with a constant plop, plop; and I could hear his frightened gasps, even from where I stood.

' "Come back with that lamp!" roared the captain again; but still the man took no notice, and Captain Gannington was silent an instant, his lips working in a queer, inarticulate fashion; as if he were stunned momentarily by the very violence of his anger at the man's insubordina-tion. And in the silence, I heard the sounds again: Thud! Thud! Thud! Thud! Quite distinctly now, beating, it seemed suddenly to me, right down under my feet, but deep.

'I stared down at the mould on which I was standing, with a quick, disgusting sense of the terrible all about me; then I looked at the captain, and tried to say something, without appearing frightened. I saw that he had turned again to the mound, and all the anger had gone out of his face. He had his lamp out towards the mound, and was listening. There was a further moment of absolute silence; at least, I know that I was not conscious of any sound at all, in all the world, except that extraordinary Thud! Thud! Thud! Thud! down somewhere in the huge bulk under us.

'The captain shifted his feet, with a sudden, nervous movement; and as he lifted them, the mould went plop! plop! He looked quickly at me, trying to smile, as if he were not thinking anything very much about it: "What do you make of it, Doctor!" he said.

' "I think –" I began. But the second mate interrupted with a single word; his voice pitched a little high, in a tone that made both stare instantly at him:

' "Look!" he said, and pointed at the mound. The thing was all of a slow quiver. A strange ripple ran outward from it, along the deck, like you will see a ripple run inshore out of a calm sea. It reached a mound a little fore-side of us, which I had supposed to be the cabin-skylight; and in a moment the second mound sank nearly level with the surrounding decks, quivering floppily in a most extraordinary fashion. A sudden quick tremor took the mould right under the second mate, and he gave out a hoarse little cry, and held his arms out on each side of him, to keep his balance. The tremor in the mould spread, and Captain Gannington swayed, and spread his feet with a sudden curse of fright. The second mate jumped across to him, and caught him by the wrist:

' "The boat, Sir!" he said, saying the very thing that I had lacked the pluck to say. "For God's sake –"

'But he never finished; for a tremendous hoarse scream cut off his words. They hove themselves round, and looked. I could see without turning. The man who had run from us, was standing in the waist of the ship, about a fathom from the starboard bulwarks. He was swaying from side to side and screaming in a dreadful fashion. He appeared to be trying to lift his feet, and the light from his swaying lantern showed an almost incredible sight. All about him the mould was in active movement. His feet had sunk out of sight. The stuff appeared to be *lapping* at his legs; and abruptly his bare flesh showed. The hideous stuff had rent his trouser-legs away, as if they were paper. He gave out a simply sickening scream, and, with a vast effort, wrenched one leg free. It was partly destroyed. The next instant he pitched face downward, and the stuff heaped itself upon him, as if it were actually alive, with a dreadful savage life. It was simply infernal. The man had gone from sight. Where he had fallen was now a writhing, elongated mound, in constant and horrible increase, as the mould appeared to move towards it in strange ripples from all sides.

'Captain Gannington and the second mate were stone silent, in amazed and incredulous horror; but I had begun to reach towards a grotesque and terrific conclusion, both helped and hindered by my professional training.

'From the men in the boat alongside, there was a loud shouting, and I saw two of their faces appear suddenly above the rail. They showed clearly a moment in the light from the lamp which the man had snatched from Mr Selvern; for strangely enough, this lamp was standing upright and unharmed on the deck, a little way fore-side of that dreadful, elongated, growing mound, that still swayed and writhed with an incredible horror. The lamp rose and fell on the passing ripples of the mould just – for all the world – as you will see a boat rise and fall on little swells. It is of some interest to me now, psychologically, to remember how that rising and falling lantern brought home to me, more than anything, the incomprehensible, dreadful strangeness of it all.

'The men's faces disappeared, with sudden yells, as if they had slipped or been suddenly hurt; and there was a fresh uproar of shouting from the boat. The men were calling to us to come away; to come away. In the same instant, I felt my left boot drawn suddenly and forcibly downward, with a horrible painful grip. I wrenched it free, with a yell of angry fear. Forrard of us, I saw that the vile surface was all a-move, and abruptly I found myself shouting in a queer frightened voice:

' "The boat, Captain! The boat, Captain!"

'Captain Gannington stared round at me, over his right shoulder, in a peculiar, dull way, that told me he was utterly dazed with bewilderment and the incomprehensibleness of it all. I took a quick, clogged, nervous step towards him, and gripped his arm and shook it fiercely.

' "The boat!" I shouted at him. "The boat! For God's sake, tell the men to bring the boat aft!"

'Then the mould must have drawn his feet down; for, abruptly, he bellowed fiercely with terror, his momentary apathy giving place to furious energy. His thick-set, vastly muscular body doubled and writhed with his enormous effort, and he struck out madly, dropping the lantern. He tore his feet free, something ripped as he did so. The *reality* and necessity of the situation had come upon him, brutishly real, and he was roaring to the men in the boat:

' "Bring the boat aft! Bring 'er aft! Bring 'er aft!"

'The second mate and I were shouting the same thing, madly.

' "For God's sake be smart, lads!" roared the captain, and stooped quickly for his lamp, which still burned. His feet were gripped again, and he hove them out, blaspheming breathlessly, and leaping a yard high with his effort. Then he made a run for the side, wrenching his feet free at each step. In the same instant, the second mate cried out something, and grabbed at the captain:

' "It's got hold of my feet! It's got hold of my feet!" he screamed. His feet had disappeared up to his boot-tops, and Captain Gannington caught him round the waist with his powerful left arm, gave a mighty heave, and the next instant had him free; but both his boot-soles had almost gone.

'For my part, I jumped madly from foot to foot, to avoid the plucking of the mould; and suddenly I made a run for the ship's side. But before I got there, a queer gap came in the mould, between us and the side, at least a couple of feet wide, and how deep I don't know. It closed up in an instant, and all the mould, where the gap had been, went into a sort of flurry of horrible ripplings, so that I ran back from it; for I did not dare to put my foot upon it. Then the captain was shouting at me:

' "Aft, Doctor! Aft, Doctor! This way, Doctor! Run!" I saw then that he had passed me, and was up on the after raised portion of the poop. He had the second mate thrown like a sack, all loose and quiet, over his left shoulder; for Mr Selvern had fainted, and his long legs flopped, limp and helpless, against the captain's massive knees as the captain ran. I saw, with a queer unconscious noting of minor details, how the torn soles of the second mate's boots flapped and jigged, as the captain staggered aft.

' "Boat ahoy! Boat ahoy! Boat ahoy!" shouted the captain; and then I was beside him, shouting also. The men were answering with loud yells of encouragement, and it was plain they were working desperately to force the boat aft, through the thick scum about the ship.

'We reached the ancient, mould-hid taffrail, and slewed about, breathlessly, in the half darkness, to see what was happening. Captain Gannington had left his lantern by the big mound, when he picked up the second mate; and as we stood gasping, we discovered suddenly that all the mould between us and the light was full of movement. Yet, the part on which we stood, for about six or eight feet forrard of us, was still firm.

'Every couple of seconds, we shouted to the men to hasten, and they kept on calling to us that they would be with us in an instant. And all the time, we watched the deck of that dreadful hulk, feeling, for my part, literally sick with mad suspense, and ready to jump overboard into that filthy scum all about us.

'Down somewhere in the huge bulk of the ship, there was all the time that extraordinary, dull, ponderous Thud! Thud! Thud! Thud! growing ever louder. I seemed to feel the whole hull of the derelict beginning to quiver and thrill with each dull beat. And to me, with the grotesque and monstrous suspicion of what made that noise, it was, at once, the most dreadful and incredible sound I have ever heard.

'As we waited desperately for the boat, I scanned incessantly so much of the grey-white bulk as the lamp showed. The whole of the decks seemed to be in strange movement. Forrard of the lamp I could see, indistinctly, the moundings of the mould swaying and nodding hideously, beyond the circle of the brightest rays. Nearer, and full in the glow of the lamp, the mound which should have indicated the skylight, was swelling steadily. There were ugly purple veinings on it, and as it swelled, it seemed to me that the veinings and mottling on it were becoming plainer – rising, as though embossed upon it, like you will see the veins stand out on the body of a powerful full-blooded horse. It was most extraordinary.

The mound that we had supposed to cover the companion-way had sunk flat with the surrounding mould, and I could not see that it jetted out any more of the purplish fluid.

'A quaking movement of the mould began, away forrard of the lamp, and came flurrying away aft towards us; and at the sight of that, I climbed up on to the spongy-feeling taffrail, and yelled afresh for the boat. The men answered with a shout, which told me they were nearer, but the beastly scum was so thick that it was evidently a fight to move the boat at all. Beside me, Captain Gannington was shaking the second mate furiously, and the man stirred and began to moan. The captain shook him awake.

' "Wake up! Wake up, Mister!" he shouted.

'The second mate staggered out of the captain's arms, and collapsed suddenly, shrieking: "My feet! Oh, God! My feet!" The captain and I lugged him off the mould, and got him into a sitting position upon the taffrail, where he kept up a continual moaning.

' "Hold 'im, Doctor," said the captain, and whilst I did so, he ran forrard a few yards, and peered down over the starboard quarter rail. "For God's sake, be smart, lads! Be smart! Be smart!" He shouted down to the men; and they answered him, breathless, from close at hand; yet still too far away for the boat to be any use to us on the instant.

'I was holding the moaning, half-unconscious officer, and staring forrard along the poop decks. The flurrying of the mould was coming aft, slowly and noiselessly. And then, suddenly, I saw something closer:

' "Look out, Captain!" I shouted; and even as I shouted, the mould near to him gave a sudden peculiar slobber. I had seen a ripple stealing towards him through the horrible stuff. He gave an enormous, clumsy leap, and landed near to us on the sound part of the mould, but the movement followed him. He turned and faced it, swearing fiercely. All about his feet there came abruptly little gapings, which made horrid sucking noises.

' "Come *back*, Captain!" I yelled. "Come back, *quick*!"

'As I shouted, a ripple came at his feet – lipping at them; and he stamped insanely at it, and leaped back, his boot torn half off his foot. He swore madly with pain and anger, and jumped swiftly for the taffrail.

' "Come on, Doctor! Over we go!" he called. Then he remembered the filthy scum, and hesitated, roaring out desperately to the men to hurry. I stared down, also.

' "The second mate?" I said.

' "I'll take charge, Doctor," said Captain Gannington, and caught hold of Mr Selvern. As he spoke, I thought I saw something beneath us, outlined against the scum. I leaned out over the stern, and peered. There was something under the port quarter.

' "There's something down there, Captain!" I called, and pointed in the darkness.

'He stooped far over, and stared.

' "A boat, by Gum! *A boat!*" he yelled, and began to wriggle swiftly along the taffrail, dragging the second mate after him. I followed.

' "A boat it is, sure!" he exclaimed, a few moments later, and, picking up the second mate clear of the rail, he hove him down into the boat, where he fell with a crash into the bottom.

' "Over ye go, Doctor!" he yelled at me, and pulled me bodily off the rail, and dropped me after the officer. As he did so, I felt the whole of the ancient, spongy rail give a peculiar sickening quiver, and begin to wobble. I fell on to the second mate, and the captain came after, almost in the same instant; but fortunately he landed clear of us, on to the fore thwart, which broke under his weight, with a loud crack and splintering of wood.

' "Thank God!" I heard him mutter. "Thank God! . . . I guess that was a mighty near thing to goin' to hell."

'He struck a match, just as I got to my feet, and between us we got the second mate straightened out on one of the after thwarts. We shouted to the men in the boat, telling them where we were, and saw the light of their lantern shining round the starboard counter of the derelict. They called back to us, to tell us they were doing their best, and then, while we waited, Captain Gannington struck another match, and began to over-haul the boat we had dropped into. She was a modern, two-oared boat, and on the stern there was painted *Cyclone Glasgow*. She was in pretty fair condition, and had evidently drifted into the scum and been held by it.

'Captain Gannington struck several matches, and went forrard towards the derelict. Suddenly he called to me, and I jumped over the thwarts to him.

' "Look, Doctor," he said; and I saw what he meant – a mass of bones, up in the bows of the boat. I stooped over them and looked. They were the bones of at least three people, all mixed together, in an extraordinary fashion, and quite clean and dry. I had a sudden thought concerning the bones; but I said nothing; for my thought was vague, in some ways, and concerned the grotesque and incredible suggestion that had come to me, as to the cause of that ponderous, dull Thud! Thud! Thud! Thud! that beat on so infernally within the hull, and was plain to hear even now that we had got off the vessel herself. And all the while, you know, I had a sick, horrible, mental picture of that frightful wriggling mound aboard the hulk.

'As Captain Gannington struck a final match I saw something that sickened me, and the captain saw it in the same instant. The match went out, and he fumbled clumsily for another, and struck it. We saw the thing again. We had not been mistaken . . . A great lip of grey-white was protruding in over the edge of the boat – a great lappet of the mould was coming stealthily towards us; a live mass of *the very hull itself*. And suddenly Captain Gannington yelled out, in so many words, the grotesque and incredible thing I was thinking:

' *"She's alive!"*

'I never heard such a sound of *comprehension* and terror in a man's voice. The very horrified assurance of it, made actual to me the thing that, before, had only lurked in my subconscious mind. I knew he was right; I knew that the explanation, my reason and my training, both repelled and reached towards, was the true one . . . I wonder whether anyone can possibly understand our feelings in that moment . . . the unmitigable horror of it, and the *incredibleness*.

'As the light of the match burned up fully, I saw that the mass of living matter, coming towards us, was streaked and veined with purple, the veins standing out, enormously distended. The whole thing quivered continuously to each ponderous Thud! Thud! Thud! Thud! of that gargantuan organ that pulsed within the huge grey-white bulk. The flame of the match reached the captain's fingers, and there came to me a little sickly whiff of burned flesh; but he seemed unconscious of any pain. Then the flame went out, in a brief sizzle, yet at the last moment, I had seen an extraordinary raw look, become visible upon the end of that monstrous, protruding lappet. It had become dewed with a hideous, purplish sweat. And with the darkness, there came a sudden charnel-like stench.

'I heard the match-box split in Captain Gannington's hands, as he wrenched it open. Then he swore, in a queer frightened voice; for he had come to the end of his matches. He turned clumsily in the darkness, and tumbled over the nearest thwart, in his eagerness, to get to the stern of the boat, and I after him; for he knew that thing was coming towards us through the darkness, reaching over that piteous mingled heap of human bones, all jumbled together in the bows. We shouted madly to the men, and for answer saw the bows of the boat emerge dimly into view, round the starboard counter of the derelict.

' "Thank God!" I gasped out; but Captain Gannington yelled to them to show a light. Yet this they could not do, for the lamp had just been stepped on, in their desperate efforts to force the boat round to us.

' "Quick! Quick!" I shouted.

' "For God's sake be smart, men!" roared the captain; and both of us faced the darkness under the port counter, out of which we knew (but could not see) the thing was coming towards us.

' "An oar! Smart now; pass me an oar!" shouted the captain; and reached out his hands through the gloom towards the oncoming boat. I saw a figure stand up in the bows, and hold something out to us, across the intervening yards of scum. Captain Gannington swept his hands through the darkness, and encountered it.

' "I've got it. Let go there!" he said, in a quick, tense voice.

'In the same instant, the boat we were in, was pressed over suddenly to starboard by some tremendous weight. Then I heard the captain shout: "Duck y'r head, Doctor," and directly afterwards he swung the heavy, fourteen-foot ash oar round his head, and struck into the darkness. There came a sudden squelch, and he struck again, with a savage grunt of fierce energy. At the second blow, the boat righted, with a slow movement, and directly afterwards the other boat bumped gently into ours.

'Captain Gannington dropped the oar, and springing across to the second mate, hove him up off the thwart, and pitched him with knee and arms clear in over the bows among the men; then he shouted to me to follow, which I did, and he came after me, bringing the oar with him. We carried the second mate aft, and the captain shouted to the men to back the boat a little; then they got her bows clear of the boat we had just left, and so headed out through the scum for the open sea.

' "Where's Tom 'Arrison?" gasped one of the men, in the midst of his exertions. He happened to be Tom Harrison's particular chum; and Captain Gannington answered him briefly enough:

' "Dead! Pull! Don't talk!"

'Now, difficult as it had been to force the boat through the scum to our rescue, the difficulty to get clear seemed tenfold. After some five minutes pulling, the boat seemed hardly to have moved a fathom, if so much; and a quite dreadful fear took me afresh; which one of the panting men put suddenly into words:

' "It's got us!" he gasped out; "same as poor Tom!" It was the man who had inquired where Harrison was.

' "Shut y'r mouth an' *pull*!" roared the captain. And so another few minutes passed. Abruptly, it seemed to me that the dull, ponderous Thud! Thud! Thud! Thud! came more plainly through the dark, and I stared intently over the stern. I sickened a little; for I could almost swear that the dark mass of the monster was actually *nearer* . . . that it was coming nearer to us through the darkness. Captain Gannington must have had the same thought; for after a brief look into the darkness, he made one jump to the stroke-oar, and began to double-bank it.

' "Get forrid under the thwarts, Doctor!" he said to me, rather breathlessly. "Get in the bows, an' see if you can't free the stuff a bit round the bows."

'I did as he told me, and a minute later I was in the bows of the boat, puddling the scum from side to side with the boat-hook, and trying to break up the viscid, clinging muck. A heavy, almost animal-like odour rose off it, and all the air seemed full of the deadening smell. I shall never find words to tell any one the whole horror of it all – the threat that seemed to hang in the very air around us; and, but a little astern, that incredible thing, coming, as I firmly believe, nearer, and the scum holding us like half-melted glue.

'The minutes passed in a deadly, eternal fashion, and I kept staring back astern into the darkness; but never ceased to puddle that filthy scum, striking at it and switching it from side to side, until I sweated.

'Abruptly, Captain Gannington sang out:

' "We're gaining, lads. Pull!" And I felt the boat forge ahead percepti-bly, as they gave way, with renewed hope and energy. There was soon no doubt of it; for presently that hideous Thud! Thud! Thud! Thud! had grown quite dim and vague somewhat astern, and I could no longer see the derelict! for the night had come down tremendously dark, and all the sky was thick overset with heavy clouds. As we drew nearer and nearer to the edge of the scum, the boat moved more and more freely, until suddenly we emerged with a clean, sweet, fresh sound, into the open sea.

' "Thank God!" I said aloud, and drew in the boat-hook, and made my way aft again to where Captain Gannington now sat once more at the tiller. I saw him looking anxiously up at the sky, and across to where the lights of our vessel burned, and again he would seem to listen intently; so that I found myself listening also.

' "What's that, Captain?" I said sharply; for it seemed to me that I heard a sound far astern, something between a queer whine and a low whistling. "What's that?"

' "It's wind, Doctor," he said, in a low voice. "I wish to God we were aboard."

'Then, to the men: "Pull! Put y'r backs into it, or ye'll never put y'r teeth through good bread again!"

'The men obeyed nobly, and we reached the vessel safely, and had the boat safely stowed, before the storm came, which it did in a furious white smother out of the west. I could see it for some minutes beforehand, tearing the sea, in the gloom, into a wall of phosphorescent foam; and as it came nearer, that peculiar whining, piping sound grew louder and louder, until it was like a vast steam-whistle, rushing towards us across the sea.

'And when it did come, we got it very heavy indeed; so that the morning showed us nothing but a welter of white seas; and that grim derelict was many a score of miles away in the smother, lost as utterly as our hearts could wish to lose her.

'When I came to examine the second mate's feet, I found them in a very extraordinary condition. The soles of them had the appearance of having been partly digested. I know of no other word that so exactly describes their condition; and the agony the man suffered, must have been dreadful.

'Now,' concluded the doctor, 'that is what I call a case in point. If we could know exactly what that old vessel had originally been loaded with, and the juxtaposition of the various articles of her cargo, plus the heat and time she had endured, plus one or two other only guessable quantities, we should have solved the chemistry of the Life-Force, gentlemen. Not necessarily the *origin*, mind you; but, at least, we should have taken a big step on the way. I've often regretted that gale, you know – in a way, that is, in a way! It was a most amazing discovery; but, at the time, I had nothing but thankfulness to be rid of it . . . A most amazing chance. I often think of the way the monster woke out of its torpor. And that scum . . . The dead pigs caught in it . . . I fancy that was a grim kind of net, gentlemen . . . It caught many things . . . It . . .'

The old doctor sighed and nodded.

'If I could have had her bill of lading,' he said, his eyes full of regret. 'If – It might have told me something to help. But, anyway . . .' He began to fill his pipe again . . . 'I suppose,' he ended, looking round at us gravely, 'I s'pose we humans are an ungrateful lot of beggars, at the best! . . . But . . . but what a chance! What a chance – eh?'

Thurnley Abbey

Perceval Landon

Three years ago I was on my way out to the East, and as an extra day in London was of some importance, I took the Friday evening mail train to Brindisi instead of the usual Thursday morning Marseilles express. Many people shrink from the long forty-eight-hour train journey through Europe, and the subsequent rush across the Mediterranean on the nineteen-knot *Isis* or *Osiris*; but there is really very little discomfort on either the train or the mail boat, and unless there is actually nothing for me to do, I always like to save the extra day and a half in London before I say good-bye to her for one of my longer tramps. This time – it was early, I remember, in the shipping season, probably about the beginning of September – there were few passengers, and I had a compartment in the P & O Indian express to myself all the way from Calais. All Sunday I watched the blue waves dimpling the Adriatic, and the pale rosemary along the cuttings; the plain white towns, with their flat roofs and their bold 'duomos', and the grey green olive orchards of Apulia. The journey was just like any other. We ate in the dining-car as often and as long as we decently could. We slept after luncheon; we dawdled the afternoon away with yellow-backed novels; sometimes we exchanged platitudes in the smoking-room, and it was there that I met Alastair Colvin.

Colvin was a man of middle height, with a resolute, well-cut jaw; his hair was turning grey; his moustache was sun-whitened, otherwise he was clean-shaven – obviously a gentleman, and obviously also a pre-occupied man. He had no great wit. When spoken to, he made the usual remarks in the right way, and I dare say he refrained from banalities only because he spoke less than the rest of us; most of the time he buried himself in the Wagon-lit Company's time-table, but seemed unable to concentrate his attention on any one page of it. He found that I had been over the Siberian railway, and for a quarter of an hour he discussed it with me. Then he lost interest in it, and rose to go to his compartment. But he came back again very soon, and seemed glad to pick up the conversation again.

Of course this did not seem to me to be of any importance. Most travellers by train become a trifle infirm of purpose after thirty-six hours' rattling. But Colvin's restless way I noticed in somewhat marked contrast with the man's personal importance and dignity; especially ill suited was it to his finely made large hand with strong, broad, regular nails and its few lines. As I looked at his hand I noticed a long, deep, and recent scar of ragged shape. However, it is absurd to pretend that I thought anything was unusual. I went off at five o'clock on Sunday afternoon to sleep away the hour or two that had still to be got through before we arrived at Brindisi.

Once there, we few passengers transhipped our hand baggage, verified our berths – there were only a score of us in all – and then, after an aimless ramble of half an hour in Brindisi, we returned to dinner at the Hotel International, not wholly surprised that the town had been the death of Virgil. If I remember rightly, there is a gaily painted hall at the International – I do not wish to advertise anything, but there is no other place in Brindisi at which to await the coming of the mails – and after dinner I was looking with awe at a trellis overgrown with blue vines, when Colvin moved across the room to my table. He picked up *Il Secolo*, but almost immediately gave up the pretence of reading it. He turned squarely to me and said:

'Would you do me a favour?'

One doesn't do favours to stray acquaintances on Continental expresses without knowing something more of them than I knew of Colvin. But I smiled in a non-committal way, and asked him what he wanted. I wasn't wrong in part of my estimate of him; he said bluntly:

'Will you let me sleep in your cabin on the *Osiris*?' And he coloured a little as he said it.

Now, there is nothing more tiresome than having to put up with a stable-companion at sea, and I asked him rather pointedly:

'But surely there is room for all of us?' I thought that perhaps he had been partnered off with some angry Levantine, and wanted to escape from him at all hazards.

Colvin, still somewhat confused, said: 'Yes; I am in a cabin by myself. But you would do me the greatest favour if you would allow me to share yours.'

This was all very well, but, besides the fact that I always sleep better when alone, there had been some recent thefts on board English liners, and I hesitated, frank and honest and self-conscious as Colvin was. Just then the mail-train came in with a clatter and a rush of escaping steam, and I asked him to see me again about it on the boat when we started. He answered me curtly – I suppose he saw the mistrust in my manner – 'I am a member of White's.' I smiled to myself as he said it, but I remembered in a moment that the man – if he were really what he claimed to be, and I make no doubt that he was – must have been sorely put to it before he urged the fact as a guarantee of his respectability to a total stranger at a Brindisi hotel.

That evening, as we cleared the red and green harbour-lights of Brindisi, Colvin explained. This is his story in his own words.

'When I was travelling in India some years ago, I made the acquaintance of a youngish man in the Woods and Forests. We camped out together for a week, and I found him a pleasant companion. John Broughton was a light-hearted soul when off duty, but a steady and capable man in any of the small emergencies that continually arise in that department. He was liked and trusted by the natives, and though a trifle over-pleased with himself when he escaped to civilization at Simla or Calcutta, Broughton's future was well assured in Government service, when a fair-sized estate was unexpectedly left to him, and he joyfully shook the dust of the Indian plains from his feet and returned to England. For five years he drifted about London. I saw him now and then. We dined together about every eighteen months, and I could trace pretty exactly the gradual sickening of Broughton with a merely idle life. He then set out on a couple of long voyages, returned as restless as before, and at last told me that he had decided to marry and settle down at his place, Thurnley Abbey, which had long been empty. He spoke about looking after the property and standing for his constituency in the usual way. Vivien Wilde, his *fiancée*, had, I suppose, begun to take him in hand. She was a pretty girl with a deal of fair hair and rather an exclusive manner; deeply religious in a narrow school, she was still kindly and high-spirited, and I thought that Broughton was in luck. He was quite happy and full of information about his future.

'Among other things, I asked him about Thurnley Abbey. He confessed that he hardly knew the place. The last tenant, a man called Clarke, had lived in one wing for fifteen years and seen no one. He had been a miser and a hermit. It was the rarest thing for a light to be seen at the Abbey after dark. Only the barest necessities of life were ordered, and the tenant himself received them at the side-door. His one half-caste manservant, after a month's stay in the house, had abruptly left without warning and had returned to the Southern States. One thing Broughton complained bitterly about: Clarke had wilfully spread the rumour among the villagers that the Abbey was haunted, and had even condescended to play childish tricks with spirit lamps and salt in order to scare trespassers away at night. He had been detected in the act of this tomfoolery, but the story spread, and no one, said Broughton, would venture near the house except in broad daylight. The hauntedness of Thurnley Abbey was now, he said with a grin, part of the gospel of the countryside, but he and his young wife were going to change all that. Would I propose myself any time I liked? I, of course, said I would, and equally, of course, intended to do nothing of the sort without a definite invitation.

'The house was put in thorough repair, though not a stick of the old furniture and tapestry was removed. Floors and ceilings were relaid: the roof was made watertight again, and the dust of half a century was scoured out. He showed me some photographs of the place. It was called an Abbey, though as a matter of fact it had been only the infirmary of the long-vanished Abbey of Closter some five miles away. The larger part of this building remained as it had been in pre-Reformation days, but a wing had been added in Jacobean times, and that part of the house had been kept in something like repair by Mr Clarke. He had in both the ground and first floors set a heavy timber door, strongly barred with iron, in the passage between the earlier and the Jacobean parts of the house, and had entirely neglected the former. So there had been a good deal of work to be done.

'Broughton, whom I saw in London two or three times about this period, made a deal of fun over the positive refusal of the workmen to remain after sundown. Even after the electric light had been put into every room, nothing would induce them to remain, though, as Broughton observed, electric light was death to ghosts. The legend of the Abbey's ghosts had gone far and wide, and the men would take no risks. They went home in batches of five and six, and even during the daylight hours there was an inordinate amount of talking between one and another, if either happened to be out of sight of his companion. On the whole, though nothing of any sort or kind had been conjured up even by their heated imaginations during their five months' work upon the Abbey, the belief in ghosts was rather strengthened than otherwise in Thurnley because of the men's confessed nervousness, and local tradition declared itself in favour of the ghost of an immured nun.

' "Good old nun!" said Broughton.

'I asked him whether in general he believed in the possibility of ghosts, and rather to my surprise, he said that he couldn't say he entirely disbelieved in them. A man in India had told him one morning in camp that he believed that his mother was dead in England, as her vision had come to his tent the night before. He had not been alarmed, but had said nothing, and the figure had vanished again. As a matter of fact, the next possible *dak-walla* brought on a telegram announcing the mother's death. "There the thing was," said Broughton. But at Thurnley he was practical enough. He roundly cursed the idiotic selfishness of Clarke, whose silly antics had caused all the inconvenience. At the same time, he couldn't refuse to sympathize to some extent with the ignorant workmen. "My own idea," said he, "is that if a ghost ever does come in one's way, one ought to speak to it."

'I agreed. Little as I knew of the ghost world and its conventions, I had always remembered that a spook was in honour bound to wait to be spoken to. It didn't seem much to do, and I felt that the sound of one's own voice would at any rate reassure oneself as to one's wakefulness. But there are few ghosts outside Europe – few, that is, that a white man can see – and I had never been troubled with any. However, as I have said, I told Broughton that I agreed.

'So the wedding took place, and I went to it in a tall hat which I bought for the occasion, and the new Mrs Broughton smiled very nicely at me afterwards. As it had to happen, I took the Orient Express that evening and was not in England again for nearly six months. Just before I came back I got a letter from Broughton. He asked if I could see him in London or come to Thurnley, as he thought I should be better able to help him than anyone else he knew. His wife sent a nice message to me at the end, so I was reassured about at least one thing. I wrote from Budapest that I would come and see him at Thurnley two days after my arrival in London, and as I sauntered out of the Pannonia into the Kerepesi Utcza to post my letters, I wondered of what earthly service I could be to Broughton. I had been out with him after tiger on foot, and I could imagine few men better able at a pinch to manage their own business. However, I had nothing to do, so after dealing with some small accumulations of business during my absence, I packed a kit-bag and departed to Euston.

'I was met by Broughton's great limousine at Thurnley Road station and after a drive of nearly seven miles we echoed through the sleepy streets of Thurnley village, into which the main gates of the park thrust themselves, splendid with pillars and spread-eagles and tom-cats rampant atop them. I never was a herald, but I know that the Broughtons have the right to supporters – Heaven knows why! From the gates a quadruple avenue of beech trees led inwards for a quarter of a mile. Beneath them a neat strip of fine turf edged the road and ran back until the poison of the dead beech leaves killed it under the trees. There were many wheel tracks on the road, and a comfortable little pony trap jogged past me laden with a country parson and his wife and daughter. Evidently there was some garden party going on at the Abbey. The road dropped away to the right at the end of the avenue, and I could see the Abbey across a wide pasture and a broad lawn thickly dotted with guests.

'The end of the building was plain. It must have been almost mercilessly austere when it was first built, but time had crumbled the edges and toned the stone down to an orange-lichened grey wherever it showed behind its curtain of magnolia, jasmine, and ivy. Farther on was the three-storeyed Jacobean house, tall and handsome. There had not been the slightest attempt to adapt the one to the other, but the kindly ivy had glossed over the touching-point. There was a tall flèche in the middle of the building, surmounting a small bell tower. Behind the house there rose the mountainous verdure of Spanish chestnuts all the way up the hill.

'Broughton had seen me coming from afar, and walked across from his other guests to welcome me before turning me over to the butler's care. This man was sandy-haired and rather inclined to be talkative. He could, however, answer hardly any questions about the house; he had, he said, only been there three weeks. Mindful of what Broughton had told me, I made no enquiries about ghosts, though the room into which I was shown might have justified anything. It was a very large low room with oak beams projecting from the white ceiling. Every inch of the walls, including the doors, was covered with tapestry, and a remarkably fine Italian four-post bedstead, heavily draped, added to the darkness and dignity of the place. All the furniture was old, well made and dark. Underfoot there was a plain green pile carpet, the only new thing about the room except the electric light fittings and the jugs and basins. Even the looking-glass on the dressing-table was an old pyramidal Venetian glass set in a heavy repoussé frame of tarnished silver.

'After a few minutes' cleaning up, I went downstairs and out upon the lawn, where I greeted my hostess. The people gathered there were of the usual country type, all anxious to be pleased and roundly curious as to the new master of the Abbey. Rather to my surprise, and quite to my pleasure, I rediscovered Glenham, whom I had known well in old days in Barotseland: he lived quite close, as, he remarked with a grin, I ought to have known. "But," he added, "I don't live in a place like this." He swept his hand to the long, low lines of the Abbey in obvious admiration, and then, to my intense interest, muttered beneath his breath, "Thank God!" He saw that I had overheard him, and turning to me said decidedly, "Yes, 'thank God' I said, and I meant it. I wouldn't live in the Abbey for all Broughton's money."

' "But surely," I demurred, "you know that old Clarke was discovered in the very act of setting light to his bug-a-boos?"

'Glenham shrugged his shoulders. "Yes, I know about that. But there is something wrong with the place still. All I can say is that Broughton is a different man since he has lived here. I don't believe that he will remain much longer. But – you're staying here? – well, you'll hear all about it tonight. There's a big dinner, I understand." The conversation turned off to old reminiscences, and Glenham soon after had to go.

'Before I went to dress that evening I had twenty minutes' talk with Broughton in his library. There was no doubt that the man was altered, gravely altered. He was nervous and fidgety, and I found him looking at me only when my eye was off him. I naturally asked him what he wanted of me. I told him I would do anything I could, but that I couldn't conceive what he lacked that I could provide. He said with a lustreless smile that there was, however, something, and that he would tell me the following morning. It struck me that he was somehow ashamed of himself, and perhaps ashamed of the part he was asking me to play. However, I dismissed the subject from my mind and went up to dress in my palatial room. As I shut the door a draught blew out the Queen of Sheba from the wall, and I noticed that the tapestries were not fastened to the wall at the bottom. I have always held very practical views about spooks, and it has often seemed to me that the slow waving in firelight of loose tapestry upon a wall would account for ninety-nine per cent of the stories one hears. Certainly the dignified undulation of this lady with her attendants and huntsmen – one of whom was untidily cutting the throat of a fallow deer upon the very steps on which King Solomon, a grey-faced Flemish nobleman with the order of the Golden Fleece, awaited his fair visitor – gave colour to my hypothesis.

'Nothing much happened at dinner. The people were very much like those of the garden party. A young woman next me seemed anxious to know what was being read in London. As she was far more familiar than I with the most recent magazines and literary supplements, I found salvation in being myself instructed in the tendencies of modern fiction. All true art, she said, was shot through and through with melancholy. How vulgar were the attempts at wit that marked so many modern books! From the beginning of literature it had always been tragedy that embodied the highest attainment of every age. To call such works morbid merely begged the question. No thoughtful man – she looked sternly at me through the steel rim of her glasses – could fail to agree with me. Of

course, as one would, I immediately and properly said that I slept with
Pett Ridge and Jacobs under my pillow at night, and that if *Jorrocks*
weren't quite so large and cornery, I would add him to the company. She
hadn't read any of them, so I was saved – for a time. But I remember
grimly that she said that the dearest wish of her life was to be in some
awful and soul-freezing situation of horror, and I remember that she dealt
hardly with the hero of Nat Paynter's vampire story, between nibbles at
her brown-bread ice. She was a cheerless soul, and I couldn't help thinking
that if there were many such in the neighbourhood, it was not surprising
that old Glenham had been stuffed with some nonsense or other about the
Abbey. Yet nothing could well have been less creepy than the glitter of
silver and glass, and the subdued lights and cackle of conversation all
round the dinner-table.

'After the ladies had gone I found myself talking to the rural dean. He
was a thin, earnest man, who at once turned the conversation to old
Clarke's buffooneries. But, he said, Mr Broughton had introduced such
a new and cheerful spirit, not only into the Abbey, but, he might say,
into the whole neighbourhood, that he had great hopes that the ignorant
superstitions of the past were from henceforth destined to oblivion.
Thereupon his other neighbour, a portly gentleman of independent means
and position, audibly remarked "Amen", which damped the rural dean,
and we talked of partridges past, partridges present, and pheasants to
come. At the other end of the table Broughton sat with a couple of his
friends, red-faced hunting men. Once I noticed that they were discussing
me, but I paid no attention to it at the time. I remembered it a few hours
later.

'By eleven all the guests were gone, and Broughton, his wife, and I
were alone together under the fine plaster ceiling of the Jacobean drawing-
room. Mrs Broughton talked about one or two of the neighbours, and
then, with a smile, said that she knew I would excuse her, shook hands
with me, and went off to bed. I am not very good at analysing things, but
I felt that she talked a little uncomfortably and with a suspicion of effort,
smiled rather conventionally, and was obviously glad to go. These things
seem trifling enough to repeat, but I had throughout the faint feeling that
everything was not square. Under the circumstances, this was enough to
set me wondering what on earth the service could be that I was to render
– wondering also whether the whole business were not some ill-advised
jest in order to make me come down from London for a mere shooting-
party.

'Broughton said little after she had gone. But he was evidently
labouring to bring the conversation round to the so-called haunting of

the Abbey. As soon as I saw this, of course I asked him directly about it. He then seemed at once to lose interest in the matter. There was no doubt about it: Broughton was somehow a changed man, and to my mind he had changed in no way for the better. Mrs Broughton seemed no sufficient cause. He was clearly fond of her, and she of him. I reminded him that he was going to tell me what I could do for him in the morning, pleaded my journey, lighted a candle, and went upstairs with him. At the end of the passage leading into the old house he grinned weakly and said, "Mind, if you see a ghost, do talk to it; you said you would." He stood irresolutely a moment and then turned away. At the door of his dressing-room he paused once more: "I'm here," he called out, "if you should want anything. Good night," and he shut his door.

'I went along the passage to my room, undressed, switched on a lamp beside my bed, read a few pages of *The Jungle Book*, and then, more than ready for sleep, turned the light off and went fast asleep.

'Three hours later I woke up. There was not a breath of wind outside. There was not even a flicker of light from the fireplace. As I lay there, an ash tinkled slightly as it cooled, but there was hardly a gleam of the dullest red in the grate. An owl cried among the silent Spanish chestnuts on the slope outside. I idly reviewed the events of the day, hoping that I should fall off to sleep again before I reached dinner. But at the end I seemed as wakeful as ever. There was no help for it. I must read my *Jungle Book* again till I felt ready to go off, so I fumbled for the pear at the end of the cord that hung down inside the bed, and I switched on the bedside lamp. The sudden glory dazzled me for a moment. I felt under my pillow for my book with half-shut eyes. Then, growing used to the light, I happened to look down to the foot of my bed.

'I can never tell you really what happened then. Nothing I could ever confess in the most abject words could even faintly picture to you what I felt. I know that my heart stopped dead, and my throat shut automatically. In one instinctive movement I crouched back up against the headboard of the bed, staring at the horror. The movement set my heart going again, and the sweat dripped from every pore. I am not a particularly religious man, but I had always believed that God would never allow any supernatural appearance to present itself to man in such a guise and in such circumstances that harm, either bodily or mental, could result to him. I can only tell you that at that moment both my life and my reason rocked unsteadily on their seats.'

The other *Osiris* passengers had gone to bed. Only he and I remained leaning over the starboard railing, which rattled uneasily now and then under the fierce vibration of the over-engined mail-boat. Far over, there were the lights of a few fishing smacks riding out the night, and a great rush of white combing and seething water fell out and away from us overside.

At last Colvin went on:

'Leaning over the foot of my bed, looking at me, was a figure swathed in a rotten and tattered veiling. This shroud passed over the head, but left both eyes and the right side of the face bare. It then followed the line of the arm down to where the hand grasped the bed-end. The face was not entirely that of a skull, though the eyes and the flesh of the face were totally gone. There was a thin, dry skin drawn tightly over the features, and there was some skin left on the hand. One wisp of hair crossed the forehead. It was perfectly still. I looked at it, and it looked at me, and my brains turned dry and hot in my head. I had still got the pear of the electric lamp in my hand, and I played idly with it; only I dared not turn the light out again. I shut my eyes, only to open them in a hideous terror the same second. The thing had not moved. My heart was thumping, and the sweat cooled me as it evaporated. Another cinder tinkled in the grate, and a panel creaked in the wall.

'My reason failed me. For twenty minutes, or twenty seconds, I was able to think of nothing else but this awful figure, till there came, hurtling through the empty channels of my senses, the remembrance that Broughton and his friends had discussed me furtively at dinner. The dim possibility of its being a hoax stole gratefully into my unhappy mind, and once there, one's pluck came creeping back along a thousand tiny veins. My first sensation was one of blind unreasoning thankfulness that my brain was going to stand the trial. I am not a timid man, but the best of us needs some human handle to steady him in time of extremity, and in the faint but growing hope that after all it might be only a brutal hoax, I found the fulcrum that I needed. At last I moved.

'How I managed to do it I cannot tell you, but with one spring towards the foot of the bed I got within arm's-length and struck out one fearful blow with my fist at the thing. It crumbled under it, and my hand was cut to the bone. With a sickening revulsion after the terror, I dropped half-fainting across the end of the bed. So it was merely a foul trick after all. No doubt the trick had been played many a time before: no doubt Broughton and his friends had had some large bet among themselves as to what I should do when I discovered the gruesome thing. From my state of abject terror I found myself transported into an insensate anger. I shouted curses upon Broughton. I dived rather than climbed over the bed-end on to the sofa. I tore at the robed skeleton – how well the whole thing had been carried out, I thought – I broke the skull against the floor, and stamped upon its dry bones. I flung the head away under the bed and rent the brittle bones of the trunk in pieces. I snapped the thin thigh–bones across my knee, and flung them in different directions. The shin–bones I set up against a stool and broke with my heel. I raged like a Berserker against the loathly thing, and stripped the ribs from the backbone and slung the breastbone against the cupboard. My fury increased as the work of destruction went on. I tore the frail rotten veil into twenty pieces and the dust went up over everything, over the clean blotting–paper and the silver inkstand. At last my work was done. There was but a raffle of broken bones and strips of parchment and crumbling wool. Then, picking up a piece of the skull – it was the cheek and the temple bone of the right side, I remember – I opened the door and went down the passage to Broughton's dressing-room. I remember still how my sweat dripping pyjamas clung to me as I walked. At the door I kicked and entered.

'Broughton was in bed. He had already turned the light on and seemed shrunken and horrified. For a moment he could hardly pull himself together. Then I spoke. I don't know what I said. Only I know that from a heart full and over-full with hatred and contempt, spurred on by shame of my own recent cowardice, I let my tongue run on. He answered nothing. I was amazed at my own fluency. My hair still clung lankily to my wet temples, my hand was bleeding profusely, and I must have looked a strange sight. Broughton huddled himself up at the head of the bed just as I had. Still he made no answer, no defence. He seemed preoccupied with something besides my reproaches, and once or twice moistened his lips with his tongue. But he could say nothing though he moved his hands now and then, just as a baby who cannot speak moves its hands.

'At last the door into Mrs Broughton's room opened and she came in, white and terrified. "What is it? What is it? Oh, in God's name! What is it?" she cried again and again, and then she went up to her husband and sat on the bed in her night–dress, and the two faced me. I told her what the matter was. I spared her husband not a word for her presence there. Yet he seemed hardly to understand. I told the pair that I had spoiled their cowardly joke for them. Broughton looked up.

' "I have smashed the foul thing into a hundred pieces," I said. Broughton licked his lips again and his mouth worked. "By God!" I shouted, "it would serve you right if I thrashed you within an inch of your life. I will take care that not a decent man or woman of my acquaintance ever speaks to you again. And there," I added, throwing the broken piece of the skull upon the floor beside his bed, "there is a souvenir for you, of your damned work tonight!"

'Broughton saw the bone, and in a moment it was his turn to frighten me. He squealed like a hare caught in a trap. He screamed and screamed till Mrs Broughton, almost as bewildered as myself, held on to him and coaxed him like a child to be quiet. But Broughton – and as he moved I thought that ten minutes ago I perhaps looked as terribly ill as he did – thrust her from him, and scrambled out of bed on to the floor, and still screaming put out his hand to the bone. It had blood on it from my hand. He paid no attention to me whatever. In truth I said nothing. This was a new turn indeed to the horrors of the evening. He rose from the floor with the bone in his hand and stood silent. He seemed to be listening. "Time, time, perhaps," he muttered, and almost at the same moment fell at full length on the carpet, cutting his head against the fender. The bone flew from his hand and came to rest near the door. I picked Broughton up, haggard and broken, with blood over his face. He whispered hoarsely and quickly, "Listen, listen!" We listened.

'After ten seconds' utter quiet, I seemed to hear something. I could not be sure, but at last there was no doubt. There was a quiet sound as of one moving along the passage. Little regular steps came towards us over the hard oak flooring. Broughton moved to where his wife sat, white and speechless, on the bed, and pressed her face into his shoulder.

'Then, the last thing that I could see as he turned the light out, he fell forward with his own head pressed into the pillow of the bed. Something in their company, something in their cowardice, helped me, and I faced the open doorway of the room, which was outlined fairly clearly against the dimly lighted passage. I put out one hand and touched Mrs Broughton's shoulder in the darkness. But at the last moment I too failed. I sank on my knees and put my face in the bed. Only we all heard. The footsteps came to the door, and there they stopped. The piece of bone was lying inside the door. There was a rustle of moving stuff, and the thing was in the room. Mrs Broughton was silent: I could hear Broughton's voice praying, muffled in the pillow: I was cursing my own cowardice. Then the steps moved out again on the oak boards of the passage, and I heard the sounds dying away. In a flash of remorse I went to the door and looked out. At the end of the corridor I thought I saw something that moved away. A moment later the passage was empty. I stood with my forehead against the jamb of the door almost physically sick.

' "You can turn the light on," I said, and there was an answering flare. There was no bone at my feet. Mrs Broughton had fainted. Broughton was almost useless, and it took me ten minutes to bring her to. Broughton only said one thing worth remembering. For the most part he went on muttering prayers. But I was glad afterwards to recollect that he had said that thing. He said in a colourless voice, half as a question, half as a reproach, "You didn't speak to her."

'We spent the remainder of the night together. Mrs Broughton actually fell off into a kind of sleep before dawn, but she suffered so horribly in her dreams that I shook her into consciousness again. Never was dawn so long in coming. Three or four times Broughton spoke to himself. Mrs Broughton would then just tighten her hold on his arm, but she could say nothing. As for me, I can honestly say that I grew worse as the hours passed and the light strengthened. The two violent reactions had battered down my steadiness of view, and I felt that the foundations of my life had been built upon the sand. I said nothing, and after binding up my hand with a towel, I did not move. It was better so. They helped me and I helped them, and we all three knew that our reason had gone very near to ruin that night. At last, when the light came in pretty strongly, and the birds outside were chattering and singing, we felt that we must do something. Yet we never moved. You might have thought that we should particularly dislike being found as we were by the servants: yet nothing of that kind mattered a straw, and an overpowering listlessness bound us as we sat, until Chapman, Broughton's man, actually knocked and opened the door. None of us moved. Broughton, speaking hardly and stiffly, said, "Chapman, you can come back in five minutes." Chapman was a discreet man, but it would have made no difference to us if he had carried his news to the "room" at once.

'We looked at each other and I said I must go back. I meant to wait outside till Chapman returned. I simply dared not re-enter my bedroom alone. Broughton roused himself and said that he would come with me. Mrs Broughton agreed to remain in her own room for five minutes if the blinds were drawn up and all the doors left open.

'So Broughton and I, leaning stiffly one against the other, went down to my room. By the morning light that filtered past the blinds we could see our way, and I released the blinds. There was nothing wrong in the room from end to end, except smears of my own blood on the end of the bed, on the sofa, and on the carpet where I had torn the thing to pieces.'

Colvin had finished his story. There was nothing to say. Seven bells stuttered out from the fo'c'sle and the answering cry wailed through the darkness. I took him downstairs.

'Of course I am much better now, but it is a kindness of you to let me sleep in your cabin.'

The Fourth Man

John Russell

The raft might have been taken for a swath of cut sedge or a drifting tangle of roots as it slid out of the shadowy river mouth at dawn and dipped into the first ground swell. But while the sky brightened and the breeze came fresh off shore it picked a way among shoals and swampy islets with purpose and direction, and when at last the sun leaped up and cleared his bright eye of the morning mist it had passed the wide entrance to the bay and stood to open sea.

It was a curious craft for such a venture, of a type that survives here and there in the obscure corners of the world. The coracle-maker would have scorned it. The first navigating pithecanthrope built nearly as well with his log and bush. A mat of pandanus leaves served for its sail and a pad of niaouli wood for its helm. But it had a single point of real seaworthiness. Its twin floats, paired as a catamaran, were woven of reed bundles and bamboo sticks upon triple rows of bladders. It was light as a bladder itself, elastic, fit to ride any weather. One other quality this raft possessed which recommended it beyond all comfort and all safety to its present crew. It was very nearly invisible. They had only to unstep its mast and lie flat in the cup of its soggy platform and they could not be spied half a mile away.

Four men occupied the raft. Three of them were white. Their bodies had been scored with brambles and blackened with dried blood, and on wrist and ankle they bore the dark and wrinkled stain of the gyves. The hair upon them was long and matted. They wore only the rags of blue canvas uniforms. But they were whites, members of the superior race – members of a highly superior race, according to those philosophers who rate the criminal aberration as a form of genius.

The fourth man was the man who had built the raft and was now sailing it. There was nothing superior about him. His skin was a layer of soot. His prognathous jaw carried out the angle of a low forehead. No line of beauty redeemed his lean limbs and knobby joints. Nature had set upon him her plainest stamp of inferiority, and his only attempts to relieve it were the twist of bark about his middle and the prong of pig ivory through the cartilage of his nose. Altogether a very ordinary specimen of one of the lowest branches of the human family – the Canaques of New Caledonia.

The three whites sat together well forward, and so they had sat in silence for hours. But at sunrise, as if some spell had been raised by the clang of that great copper gong in the east they stirred and breathed deep of the salt air and looked at one another with hope in their haggard faces, and then back towards the land which was now no more than a grey-green smudge behind them . . . 'Friends,' said the eldest, whose temples were bound with a scrap of crimson scarf, 'Friends – the thing is done.'

With a gesture like conjuring he produced from the breast of his tattered blouse three cigarettes, fresh and round, and offered them round.

'Nippers!' cried the one at his right. 'True nippers – name of a little good man! And here! Doctor, I always said you were a marvel. See if they be not new from the box!'

Dr Dubosc smiled. Those who had known him in very different circumstances about the boulevards, the lobbies, the clubs, would have known him again and in spite of all disfigurement by that smile. And here, at the bottom of the earth, it had set him still apart in the prisons, the cobalt mines, the chain-gangs of a community not much given to mirth. Many a crowded lecture-hall at Montpellier had seen him touch some intellectual firework with just such a twinkle behind his bristly grey brows, with just such a thin curl of lip.

'By way of celebration,' he explained. 'Consider. There are seventy-five evasions from Nouméa every six months, of which not more than one succeeds. I had the figures myself from Dr Pierre at the infirmary. He is not much of a physician, but a very honest fellow. Could anybody win on that percentage without dissipating? I ask you.'

'Therefore you prepared for this?'

'It is now three weeks since I bribed the night-guard to get these same nippers.'

The other regarded him with admiration. Sentiment came readily upon his beardless face, tender and languid, but overdrawn, with eyes too large and soft and oval too long. It was one of these faces familiar enough to the police which might serve as model for an angel were it not associated with some revolting piece of devilry. Fenayrou himself had been condemned 'to perpetuity' as an incorrigible.

'Is not our doctor a wonder?' he inquired as he handed a cigarette along to the third white man. 'He thinks of everything. You should be ashamed to grumble. See – we are free, after all. Free!'

The third was a gross, pock-marked man with hairless lids known sometimes as Niniche, Trois Huit, Le Tordeur, but chiefly among companions as Perroquet – a name derived perhaps from his beaked nose, or from some perception of his jail-bird character. He was a garrotter by profession, accustomed to rely upon his fists only for the exchange of amenities. Dubosc might indulge a fancy and Fenayrou seek to carry it as a pose, but The Parrot remained a gentleman of strictly serious turn. There is perhaps a tribute to the practical spirit of penal administration in the fact that while Dubosc was the most dangerous of these three and Fenayrou the most depraved Perroquet was the one with the official reputation, whose escape would be signalled first among the 'Wanted'. He accepted the cigarette because he was glad to get it, but he said nothing until Dubosc passed a tin box of matches and the first gulp of picadura filled his lungs . . .

'Wait till you've got your two feet on a *pavé*, my boy. That will be the time to talk of freedom. What? Suppose there came a storm.'

'It is not the season of storms,' observed Dubosc.

But The Parrot's word had given them a check. Such spirits as these, to whom the land had been a horror, would be slow to feel the terror of the sea. Back there they had left the festering limbo of a convict colony, oblivion. Out here they had reached the rosy threshold of the big round world again. They were men raised from the dead, charged with all the furious appetites of lost years, with the savour of life strong and sweet on their lips. And yet they paused and looked about in quickened perception, with the clutch at the throat that takes the landsman on big waters. The spaces were so wide and empty. The voices in their ears were so strange and murmurous. There was a threat in each wave that came from the depths, a sinister vibration. None of them knew the sea. None knew its ways, what tricks it might play, what traps it might spread – more deadly than those of the jungle.

The raft was running now before a brisk chop with alternate spring and wallow, while the froth bubbled in over the prow and ran down among them as they sat. 'Where is that cursed ship that was to meet us here?' demanded Fenayrou.

'It will meet us right enough.' Dubosc spoke carelessly, though behind the blown wisp of his cigarette he had been searching the outer horizon with keen glance. 'This is the day as agreed. We will be picked up from the mouth of the river.'

'You say,' growled Perroquet. 'But where is any river now? Or any mouth? Sacred name, this wind will blow us to China if we keep on.'

'We dare not lie in any closer. There is a Government launch at Torrien. Also the traders go armed hereabouts, ready for chaps like us. And don't imagine that the native trackers have given us up. They are likely to be following still in their proas.'

'So far?'

Fenayrou laughed, for The Parrot's dread of their savage enemies had a morbid tinge.

'Take care, Perroquet. They will eat you yet.'

'Is it true?' demanded the other, appealing to Dubosc. 'I have heard it is even permitted these devils to keep all runaways they can capture – name of God! – to fatten on.'

'An idle tale,' smiled Dubosc. 'They prefer the reward. But one hears of convicts being badly mauled. There was a forester who made a break from Baie du Sud and came back lacking an arm. Certainly these people have not lost the habit of cannibalism.'

'Piecemeal,' chuckled Fenayrou. 'They will only sample you, Perroquet. Let them make a stew of your brains. You would miss nothing.'

But The Parrot swore.

'Name of a name – what brutes!' he said, and by a gesture recalled the presence of that fourth man who was of their party and yet so completely separated from them that they had almost forgotten him.

The Canaque was steering the raft. He sat crouched at the stern, his body glistening like varnished ebony with spray. He held the steering paddle, immobile as an image, his eyes fixed upon the course ahead. There was no trace of expression on his face, no hint of what he thought or felt or whether he thought or felt anything. He seemed not even aware of their regard, and each one of them experienced somehow that twinge of uneasiness with which the white confronts his brother of colour – this enigma brown or yellow or black he is fated never wholly to understand or to fathom . . .

'It occurs to me,' said Fenayrou, in a pause, 'that our friend here who looks like a shiny boot is able to steer us God knows where. Perhaps to claim the reward.'

'Reassure yourself,' answered Dubosc. 'He steers by my order. Besides, it is a simple creature – an infant, truly, incapable of any but the most primitive reasoning.'

'Is he incapable of treachery?'

'Of any that would deceive us. Also, he is bound by his duty. I made a bargain with his chief up the river, and this one is sent to deliver us on board our ship. It is the only interest he has in us.'

'And he will do it?'

'He will do it. Such is the nature of the native.'

'I am glad you feel so,' returned Fenayrou, adjusting himself indolently among the drier reeds and nursing the last of his cigarette. 'For my part I wouldn't trust a figurehead like that for two sous. Mazette! What a monkey face!'

'Brute!' repeated Perroquet, and this man, sprung from some vile river-front slum of Argenteuil, whose home had been the dock pilings, the grog shop, and the jail, even this man viewed the black Canaque from an immeasurable distance with the look of hatred and contempt . . .

Under the heat of the day the two younger convicts lapsed presently into dozing. But Dubosc did not doze. His tormented soul peered out behind its mask as he stood to sweep the skyline again under shaded hand. His theory had been so precise, the fact was so different. He had counted absolutely on meeting the ship – some small schooner, one of those flitting, half-piratical traders of the copra islands that can be hired like cabs in a dark street for any questionable enterprise. Now there was no ship, and here was no cross-roads where one might sit and wait. Such a craft as the catamaran could not be made to lie to.

The doctor foresaw ugly complications for which he had not prepared and whereof he must bear the burden. The escape had been his own conception, directed by him from the start. He had picked his companions deliberately from the whole forced labour squad, Perroquet for his great strength, Fenayrou as a ready echo. He had made it plain since their first dash from the mine, during their skirmish with the military guards, their subsequent wanderings in the brush with bloodhounds and trackers on their trail – through every crisis – that he alone should be the leader.

For the others, they had understood well enough which of their number was the chief beneficiary. Those mysterious friends on the outside that were reaching half around the world to further their release had never heard of such individuals as Fenayrou and The Parrot. Dubosc was the man who had pulled the wires: that brilliant physician whose conviction for murder had followed so sensationally, so scandalously, upon his sweep of academic and social honours. There would be clacking tongues in many a Parisian salon, and white faces in some, when news should come of his escape. Ah, yes, for example, they knew the highflyer of the band, and they submitted – so long as he led them to victory. They submitted, while reserving a depth of jealousy, the inevitable remnant of caste persisting still in this democracy of stripes and shame.

By the middle of the afternoon the doctor had taken certain necessary measures.

'Ho!' said Fenayrou sleepily. 'Behold our colours at the masthead. What is that for, comrade?'

The sail had been lowered and in its place streamed the scrap of crimson scarf that had served Dubosc as a turban.

'To help them sight us when the ship comes.'

'What wisdom!' cried Fenayrou. 'Always he thinks of everything, our doctor, everything —'

He stopped with the phrase on his lips, and his hand outstretched towards the centre of the platform. Here, in a damp depression among the reeds, had lain the wicker-covered bottle of green glass in which they carried their water. It was gone.

'Where is that flask?' he demanded. 'The sun has grilled me like a bone.'

'You will have to grill some more,' said Dubosc grimly. 'This crew is put on rations.'

Fenayrou stared at him wide-eyed, and from the shadow of a folded mat The Parrot thrust his purpled face. 'What do you sing me there? Where is that water?'

'I have it,' said Dubosc.

They saw, in fact, that he held the flask between his knees, along with their single packet of food in its wrapping of coconut husk.

'I want a drink,' challenged Perroquet.

'Reflect a little. We must guard our supplies like reasonable men. One does not know how long we may be floating here . . .'

Fell a silence among them, heavy and strained, in which they heard only the squeaking of frail basketwork as their raft laboured in the wash. Slow as was their progress, they were being pushed steadily outward and onward, and the last cliffs of New Caledonia were no longer even a smudge in the west, but only a hazy line. And still they had seen no moving thing upon the great round breast of the sea that gleamed in its corselet of brass plates under a brazen sun. 'So that is the way you talk now?' began The Parrot, half choking. 'You do not know how long? But you were sure enough when we started.'

'I am still sure,' returned Dubosc. 'The ship will come. Only she cannot stay for us in one spot. She will be cruising to and fro until she intercepts us. We must wait.'

'Ah, good! We must wait. And in the meantime, what? Fry here in the

sacred heat with our tongues hanging out while you deal us drop by drop
– hein?'

'Perhaps.'

'But no!' The garrotter clenched his hands. 'Blood of God, there is no
man big enough to feed me with a spoon!'

Fenayrou's chuckle came pat, as it had more than once, and Dubosc
shrugged.

'You laugh!' cried Perroquet, turning in fury. 'But how about this
lascar of a captain that lets us put to sea unprovided? What? He thinks of
everything, does he? He thinks of everything! . . . Sacred farceur – let me
hear you laugh again!'

Somehow Fenayrou was not so minded.

'And now he bids us be reasonable,' concluded the Parrot. 'Tell that to
the devils in hell. You and your cigarettes, too. Bah – comedian!'

'It is true,' muttered Fenayrou, frowning. 'A bad piece of work for a
captain of runaways.'

But the doctor faced mutiny with his thin smile.

'All this alters nothing. Unless we would die very speedily, we must
guard our water.'

'By whose fault?'

'Mine,' acknowledged the doctor. 'I admit it. What then? We can't turn
back. Here we are. Here we must stay. We can only do our best with
what we have.'

'I want a drink,' repeated The Parrot, whose throat was afire since he
had been denied.

'You can claim your share, of course. But take warning of one thing.
After it is gone do not think to sponge on us – on Fenayrou and me.'

'He would be capable of it, the pig!' exclaimed Fenayrou, to whom this
thrust had been directed. 'I know him. See here, my old, the doctor is
right. Fair for one, fair for all.'

'I want a drink.'

Dubosc removed the wooden plug from the flask.

'Very well,' he said quietly.

With the delicacy that lent something of legerdemain to all his gestures,
he took out a small canvas wallet, the crude equivalent of the professional
black bag, from which he drew a thimble. Meticulously he poured a brimming measure, and Fenayrou gave a shout at the grumbler's fallen jaw as he
accepted that tiny cup between his big fingers. Dubosc served Fenayrou and
himself with the same amount before he recorked the bottle.

'In this manner we should have enough to last us three days – maybe
more – with equal shares among the three of us . . .'

Such was his summing of the demonstration, and it passed without comment, as a matter of course in the premises, that he should count as he did – ignoring that other who sat alone at the stern of the raft, the black Canaque, the fourth man.

Perroquet had been out-manoeuvred, but he listened sullenly while for the hundredth time Dubosc recited his easy and definite plan for their rescue, as arranged with his secret correspondents.

'That sounds very well,' observed The Parrot, at last. 'But what if these jokers only mock themselves of you? What if they have counted it good riddance to let you rot here? And us? Sacred name, that would be a famous jest! To let us wait for a ship and they have no ship!'

'Perhaps the doctor knows better than we how sure a source he counts upon,' suggested Fenayrou slyly.

'That is so,' said Dubosc, with great good humour. 'My faith, it would not be well for them to fail me. Figure to yourselves that there is a safety vault in Paris full of papers to be opened at my death. Certain friends of mine could hardly afford to have some little confessions published that would be found there . . . Such a tale as this, for instance –'

And to amuse them he told an indecent anecdote of high life, true or fictitious, it mattered nothing, so he could make Fenayrou's eyes glitter and The Parrot growl in wonder. Therein lay his means of ascendancy over such men, the knack of eloquence and vision. Harried, worn, oppressed by fears that he could sense so much more sharply than ever, he must expend himself now in vulgar marvels to distract these ruder minds. He succeeded so far that when the wind fell at sunset they were almost cheerful, ready to believe that the morning would bring relief. They dined on dry biscuit and another thimbleful of water apiece and took watch by amiable agreement. And through that long, clear night of stars whenever the one of the three who kept awake between his comrades chanced to look aft, he could see the vague blot of another figure – the naked Canaque, who slumbered there apart . . .

It was an evil dawning. Fenayrou, on the morning trick, was aroused by a foot as hard as a hoof, and started up at Perroquet's wrathful face, with the doctor's graver glance behind.

'Idler! Good-for-nothing! Will you wake at least before I smash your ribs? Name of God, here is a way to stand watch!'

'Keep off!' cried Fenayrou wildly. 'Keep off. Don't touch me.'

'Eh, and why not, fool? Do you know that the ship could have missed us? A ship could have passed us a dozen times while you slept?'

'Bourrique!'

'Vache!'

They spat the insults of the prison while Perroquet knotted his great
fist over the other, who crouched away cat-like, his mobile mouth twisted
to a snarl. Dubosc stood aside in watchful calculation until against the
angry red sunrise in which they floated there flashed the naked red gleam
of steel. Then he stepped between.

'Enough. Fenayrou, put up that knife.'

'The dog kicked me!'

'You were at fault,' said Dubosc sternly. 'Perroquet!'

'Are we all to die that he may sleep?' stormed The Parrot.

'The harm is done. Listen now, both of you. Things are bad enough
already. We may need all our energies. Look about.'

They looked and saw the far, round horizon and the empty desert of
the sea and their own long shadows that slipped slowly before them over
its smooth, slow heaving, and nothing else. The land had sunk away
from them in the night – some one of the chance currents that sweep
among the islands had drawn them none could say where or how far. The
trap had been sprung. 'Good God, how lonely it is!' breathed Fenayrou
in a hush.

No more was said. They dropped their quarrel. Silently they shared
their rations as before, made shift to eat something with their few drops
of water, and sat down to pit themselves one against another in the vital
struggle that each could feel was coming – a sort of tacit test of endur-
ance.

A calm had fallen, as it does between trades in this flawed belt, an
absolute calm. The air hung weighted. The sea showed no faintest crinkle,
only the maddening, unresting heave and fall in polished undulations on
which the lances of the sun broke and drove in under their eyelids as white,
hot splinters; a savage sun that kindled upon them with the power of a
burning glass, that sucked the moisture from poor human bits of jelly and
sent them crawling to the shelter of their mats and brought them out again,
gasping, to shrivel anew. The water, the world of water, seemed sleek and
thick as oil. They came to loathe it and the rotting smell of it, and when the
doctor made them dip themselves overside they found little comfort. It was
warm, sluggish, slimed. But a curious thing resulted . . .

While they clung along the edge of the raft they all faced inboard, and
there sat the black Canaque. He did not join them. He did not glance at
them. He sat hunkered on his heels in the way of the native, with arms
hugging his knees. He stayed in his place at the stern, motionless under
that shattering sun, gazing out into vacancy. Whenever they raised their
eyes they saw him. He was the only thing to see.

'Here is one who appears to enjoy himself quite well,' remarked Dubosc.

'I was thinking so myself,' said Fenayrou.

'The animal!' rumbled Perroquet.

They observed him, and for the first time with direct interest, with thought of him as a fellow-being – with the beginning of envy.

'He does not seem to suffer.'

'What is going on in his brain? What does he dream of there? One would say he despises us.'

'The beast!'

'Perhaps he is waiting for us to die,' suggested Fenayrou with a harsh chuckle. 'Perhaps he is waiting for the reward. He would not starve on the way home, at least. And he could deliver us – piecemeal.'

They studied him.

'How does he do it, doctor? Has he no feeling?'

'I have been wondering,' said Dubosc. 'It may be that his fibres are tougher – his nerves.'

'Yes, we have had water and he none.'

'But look at his skin, fresh and moist.'

'And his belly, fat as a football!'

The Parrot hauled himself aboard.

'Don't tell me this black beast knows thirst!' he cried with a strange excitement. 'Is there any way he could steal our supplies?'

'Certainly not.'

'Then, name of a dog, what if he has supplies of his own hidden about?'

The same monstrous notion struck them all, and the others swarmed to help. They knocked the black aside. They searched the platform where he had sat, burrowing among the rushes, seeking some secret cache, another bottle or a gourd. They found nothing.

'We are mistaken,' said Dubosc.

But Perroquet had a different expression for disappointment. He turned on the Canaque and caught him by the kinky mop of hair and proceeded to give him what is known as gruel in the cobalt mines. This was a little speciality of The Parrot's. He paused only when he himself was breathless and exhausted and threw the limp, unresisting body from him.

'There, lump of dirt! That will teach you. Maybe you're not so chipper now, my boy – hein? Not quite so satisfied with your luck. Pig! That will make you feel . . .'

It was a ludicrous, a wanton, a witless thing. But the others said nothing. The learned Dubosc made no protest. Fenayrou had none of his usual jests at the garrotter's stupidity. They looked on as at the satisfaction of a common grudge. The white trampled the black with or without cause, and that was natural. And the black crept away into his place with his hurts and his wrongs and made no sign and struck no blow. And that was natural, too.

The sun declined into a blazing furnace whereof the gates stood wide, and they prayed to hasten it and cursed because it hung enchanted. But when it was gone their blistered bodies still held the heat like things incandescent. The night closed down over them like a purple bow, glazed and impermeable. They would have divided the watches again, though none of them thought of sleep, but Fenayrou made a discovery.

'Idiots!' he rasped. 'Why should we look and look? A whole navy of ships cannot help us now. If we are becalmed, why so are they!'

The Parrot was singularly put out.

'Is this true?' he asked Dubosc.

'Yes, we must hope for a breeze first.'

'Then, name of God, why didn't you tell us so? Why did you keep on playing out the farce? You are wise, eh? You are very wise. You know things we do not and you keep them to yourself.' He leaned forward to peer into the doctor's face. 'Very good. But if you think you're going to use that cursed smartness to get the best of us in any way – see here, my zig, I pull your gullet out like the string of an orange . . . Like that. What?'

Fenayrou gave a nervous giggle and Dubosc shrugged, but it was perhaps about this time that he began to regret his intervention in the knife play.

For there was no breeze and there was no ship.

By the third morning each had sunk within himself, away from the rest. The doctor was lost in a profound depression, Perroquet in dark suspicion, and Fenayrou in bodily suffering which he supported ill. Only two effective ties still bound their confederacy. One was the flask which Dubosc had slung at his side by a strip of the wickerwork. Every move he made with it, every drop he poured, was followed by burning eyes. And he knew, and he had no advantage of them in knowing, that the will to live was working its relentless formula aboard that raft. Under his careful saving there still remained nearly half of their original store.

The other bond, as it had come to be by strange mutation, was the presence of the black Canaque.

There was no forgetting the fourth man now, no overlooking of him. He loomed upon their consciousness, more formidable, more mysterious, more exasperating with every hour. Their own powers were ebbing. The naked savage had yet to give the slightest sign of complaint or weakness.

During the night he had stretched himself out on the platform as before, and after a time he had slept. Through the hours of darkness and silence while each of the whites wrestled with despair, this black man had slept as placidly as a child, with easy, regular breathing. Since then he had resumed his place aft. And so he remained, unchanged, a fixed fact and a growing wonder.

The brutal rage of Perroquet, in which he had vented his distorted hate of the native, had been followed by superstitious doubts.

'Doctor,' he said at last, in awed huskiness, 'is this a man or a fiend?'

'It is a man.'

'A miracle,' put in Fenayrou.

But the doctor lifted a finger in a way his pupils would have remembered:

'It is a man,' he repeated, 'and a very poor and wretched example of a man. You will find no lower type anywhere. Observe his cranial angle, the high ears, the heavy bones of his skull. He is scarcely above the ape. There are educated apes more intelligent.'

'Ah! Then what?'

'He has a secret,' said the doctor.

That was a word to transfix them.

'A secret! But we see him – every move he makes, every instant. What a chance for a secret?'

The doctor rather forgot his audience, betrayed by chagrin and bitterness.

'How pitiful!' he mused. 'Here are we three – children of the century, products of civilization – I fancy none would deny that, at least. And here is this man who belongs before the Stone Age. In a set trial of fitness, of wits, or resource, is he to win! Pitiful!'

'What kind of secret!' demanded Perroquet, fuming.

'I cannot say,' admitted Dubosc, with a baffled gesture. 'Possibly some method of breathing, some peculiar posture that operates to cheat the sensations of the body. Such things are known among primitive peoples – known and carefully guarded – like the properties of certain drugs, the uses of hypnotism and complex natural laws. Then, again, it may be psychologic – a mental attitude persistently held. Who knows?

'To ask him? Useless. He will not tell. Why should he? We scorn him. We give him no share with us. We abuse him. He simply remains inscrutable – as he has always been and will always be. He never tells those innermost secrets. They are the means by which he has survived from the depth of time, by which he may yet survive when all our wisdom is dust.'

'I know several very excellent ways of learning secrets,' said Fenayrou as he passed his dry tongue over his lips. 'Shall I begin?'

Dubosc came back with a start and looked at him.

'It would be useless. He could stand any torture you could invent. No, that is not the way.'

'Listen to mine,' said Perroquet, with sudden violence. 'Me, I am wearied of the gab. You say he is a man? Very well. If he is a man, he must have blood in his veins. That would be, anyway, good to drink.'

'No,' returned Dubosc. 'It would be hot. Also it would be salt. For food – perhaps. But we do not need food.'

'Kill the animal, then, and throw him over!'

'We gain nothing.'

'Well, sacred name, what do you want?'

'To beat him!' cried the doctor, curiously agitated. 'To beat him at the game – that's what I want! For our own sakes, for our racial pride, we must, we must. To outlast him, to prove ourselves his masters. By better brain, by better organization and control. Watch him, watch him, friends – that we may ensnare him, that we may detect and defeat him in the end!'

But the doctor was miles beyond them.

'Watch?' growled The Parrot. 'I believe you, old windbag. It is all one watch. I sleep no more and leave any man alone with that bottle.'

To this the issue finally sharpened. Such craving among such men could not be stayed much longer by driblets. They watched. They watched the Canaque. They watched each other. And they watched the falling level in their flask – until the tension gave.

Another dawn upon the same dead calm, rising like a conflagration through the puddled air, cloudless, hopeless! Another day of blinding, slow-drawn agony to meet. And Dubosc announced that their allowance must be cut to half a thimbleful.

There remained perhaps a quarter of a litre – a miserable reprieve of bare life among the three of them, but one good swallow for a yearning throat.

At sight of the bottle, at the tinkle of its limpid contents, so cool and silvery green inside the glass, Fenayrou's nerve snapped . . .

'More!' he begged, with pleading hands. 'I die. More!'

When the doctor refused him he grovelled among the reeds, then rose suddenly to his knees and tossed his arms abroad with a hoarse cry:

'A ship! A ship!'

The others spun about. They saw the thin unbroken ring of this greater and more terrible prison to which they had exchanged: and that was all they saw, though they stared and stared. They turned back to Fenayrou and found him in the act of tilting the bottle. A cunning slash of his knife had loosed it from its sling at the doctor's side . . . Even now he was sucking at the mouth, spilling the precious liquid –

With the one sweep Perroquet caught up their paddle and flattened him, crushing him.

Springing across the prostrate man, Dubosc snatched the flask upright and put the width of the raft between himself and the big garrotter who stood wide-legged, his bloodshot eyes alight, rumbling in his chest.

'There is no ship,' said The Parrot. 'There will be no ship. We are done. Because of you and your rotten promises that brought us here – doctor, liar, ass!'

Dubosc stood firm.

'Come a step nearer and I break bottle and all over your head.'

They stood regarding each other, and Perroquet's brows gathered in a slow effort of thought.

'Consider,' urged Dubosc with his quaint touch of pedantry. 'Why should you and I fight? We are rational men. We can see this trouble through and win yet. Such weather cannot last for ever. Besides, here are only two of us to divide the water now.'

'That is true,' nodded The Parrot. 'That is true, isn't it? Fenayrou kindly leaves us his share. An inheritance – what? A famous idea. I'll take mine now.'

Dubosc probed him keenly.

'My share, at once, if you please,' insisted Perroquet, with heavy docility. 'Afterward, we shall see. Afterward.'

The doctor smiled his grim and wan little smile.

'So be it.'

Without relinquishing the flask he brought out his canvas wallet once more – the wallet which replaced the professional black bag – and rolled out the thimble by some swift sleight of his flexible fingers while he held Perroquet's glance with his own.

'I will measure it for you.'

He poured the thimbleful and handed it over quickly, and when Perroquet had tossed it off he filled again and again.

'Four – five,' he counted. 'That is enough.'

But The Parrot's big grip closed quietly around his wrist at the last offering and pinioned him and held him helpless.

'No, it is not enough. Now I will take the rest. Ha, wise man! Have I fooled you at last?'

There was no chance to struggle, and Dubosc did not try, only stayed smiling up at him, waiting.

Perroquet took the bottle.

'The best man wins,' he remarked. 'Eh, my zig? A bright notion – of yours. The – best –'

His lips moved, but no sound issued. A look of the most intense surprise spread upon his round face. He stood swaying a moment, and collapsed like a huge hinged toy when the string is cut.

Dubosc stooped and caught the bottle again, looking down at his big adversary, who sprawled in brief convulsion and lay still, a bluish scum oozing between his teeth . . .

'Yes, the best man wins,' repeated the doctor, and laughed as he in turn raised the flask for a draft.

'The best wins!' echoed a voice in his ear.

Fenayrou, writhing up and striking like a wounded snake, drove the knife home between his shoulders.

The bottle fell and rolled to the middle of the platform, and there, while each strove vainly to reach it, it poured out its treasure in a tiny stream that trickled away and was lost.

It may have been minutes or hours later – for time has no count in emptiness – when next a sound proceeded from that frail slip of a raft, hung like a mote between sea and sky. It was a phrase of song, a wandering strain in half tones and fluted accidentals, not unmelodious. The black Canaque was singing. He sang without emotion or effort, quite casually and softly to himself. So he might sing by his forest hut to ease some hour of idleness. Clasping his knees and gazing out into space, untroubled, unmoved, enigmatic to the end, he sang – he sang.

And after all, the ship came.

She came in a manner befitting the sauciest little tops'l schooner between Nukahiva and the Pelews – as her owner often averred and none but the envious denied – in a manner worthy, too, of that able Captain Jean Guibert, the merriest little scamp that ever cleaned a pearl bank or snapped a cargo of labour from a scowling coast. Before the first whiff out of the west came the *Petite Susanne*, curtsying and skipping along with a flash of white frill by her forefoot, and brought up startled and stood shaking her skirts and keeping herself quite daintily to windward.

'And 'ere they are sure enough, by dam'!' said the polyglot Captain Jean in the language of commerce and profanity. 'Zose passengers for us, hey? They been here all the time, not ten mile off – I bet you, Marteau. Ain't it 'ell? What you zink, my gar?'

The second, a tall and excessively bony individual of gloomy outlook, handed back the glasses.

'More bad luck. I never approved of this job. And now – see! – we have had our voyage for nothing. What misfortune!'

'Marteau, if that good Saint Pierre gives you some day a gold 'arp still you would holler bad luck – bad job!' retorted Captain Jean. 'Do I 'ire you to stand zere and cry about ze luck? Get a boat over, and quicker zan zat!'

M. Marteau aroused himself sufficiently to take command of the boat's crew that presently dropped away to investigate . . .

'It is even as I thought,' he called up from the quarter when he returned with his report. 'I told you how it would be, Captain Jean.'

'Hey?' cried the captain, bouncing at the rail. 'Have you got zose passengers yet, *enfant de salaud*?'

'I have not,' said Marteau in the tone of lugubrious triumph. There was nothing in the world that could have pleased him quite so much as this chance to prove Captain Jean the loser on a venture. 'We are too late. Bad luck, bad luck – that calm. What misfortune! They are all dead!'

'Will you mind your business?' shouted the skipper.

'But still, the gentlemen are dead –'

'What is zat to me? All ze better, they will cost nozing to feed.'

'But how –'

'Hogsheads, my gar,' said Captain Jean paternally. 'Zose hogsheads in the afterhold. Fill them nicely with brine, and zere we are!' And, having drawn all possible satisfaction from the other's amazement, he sprang the nub of his joke with a grin. 'Ze gentlemen's passage is all paid, Marteau. Before we left Sydney, Marteau. I contrac' to bring back three escape' convicts, and so by 'ell I do – in pickle! And now if you'll kindly get zose passengers aboard like I said an' bozzer less about ze goddam luck, I be much oblige'. Also, zere is no green on my eye, Marteau, and you can dam' well smoke it!'

Marteau recovered himself with difficulty in time to recall another trifling detail. 'There is a fourth man on board that raft, Captain Jean. He is a Canaque – still alive. What shall we do with him?'

'A Canaque?' snapped Captain Jean. 'A Canaque! I have no word in my contrac' about any Canaque . . . Leave him zere . . . He is only a dam' nigger. He'll do well enough where he is.'

And Captain Jean was right, perfectly right, for while the *Petite Susanne* was taking aboard her grisly cargo the wind freshened from the west, and just about the time she was shaping away for Australia the 'dam' nigger' spread his own sail of pandanus leaves and twirled his own helm of niaouli wood and headed the catamaran eastward, back towards New Caledonia.

Feeling somewhat dry after his exertion, he plucked at random from the platform a hollow reed with a sharp end, and, stretching himself at full length in his accustomed place, at the stern, he thrust the reed down into one of the bladders underneath and drank his fill of sweet water . . .

He had a dozen such storage bladders remaining, built into the floats at intervals above the water line — quite enough to last him safely home again.

In the Penal Colony

Franz Kafka

'It's a remarkable piece of apparatus,' said the officer to the explorer and surveyed with a certain air of admiration the apparatus which was after all quite familiar to him. The explorer seemed to have accepted merely out of politeness the Commandant's invitation to witness the execution of a soldier condemned to death for disobedience and insulting behaviour to a superior. Nor did the colony itself betray much interest in this execution. At least, in the small sandy valley, a deep hollow surrounded on all sides by naked crags, there was no one present save the officer, the explorer, the condemned man, who was a stupid-looking, wide-mouthed creature with bewildered hair and face, and the soldier who held the heavy chain controlling the small chains locked on the prisoner's ankles, wrists, and neck, chains that were themselves attached to each other by communicating links. In any case, the condemned man looked so like a submissive dog that one might have thought he could be left to run free on the surrounding hills and would only need to be whistled for when the execution was due to begin.

The explorer did not much care about the apparatus and walked up and down behind the prisoner with almost visible indifference while the officer made the last adjustments, now creeping beneath the structure, which was bedded deep in the earth, now climbing a ladder to inspect its upper parts. These were tasks that might well have been left to a mechanic, but the officer performed them with great zeal, whether because he was a devoted admirer of the apparatus or because of other reasons the work could be entrusted to no one else. 'Ready now!' he called at last and climbed down from the ladder. He looked uncommonly limp, breathed with his mouth wide open, and had tucked two fine ladies' handkerchiefs under the collar of his uniform. 'These uniforms are too heavy for the tropics, surely,' said the explorer, instead of making some inquiry about the apparatus, as the officer had expected. 'Of course,' said the officer, washing his oily and greasy hands in a bucket of water that stood ready, 'but they mean home to us; we don't want to forget about home. Now just have a look at this machine,' he added at once, simultaneously drying his hands on a towel and indicating the apparatus. 'Up till now a few things still had to be set by hand, but from this moment it works all by itself.' The explorer nodded and followed him. The officer, anxious to secure himself against all contingencies, said: 'Things sometimes go wrong, of course; I hope that nothing goes wrong today, but we have to allow for the possibility. The machinery should go on working continuously for twelve hours. But if anything does go wrong it will only be some small matter that can be set right at once.'

'Won't you take a seat?' he asked finally, drawing a cane chair out from among a heap of them and offering it to the explorer, who could not refuse it. He was now sitting at the edge of a pit, into which he glanced for a fleeting moment. It was not very deep. On one side of the pit the excavated soil had been piled up in a rampart, on the other side of it stood the apparatus. 'I don't know,' said the officer, 'if the Commandant has already explained this apparatus to you.' The explorer waved one hand vaguely; the officer asked for nothing better, since now he could explain the apparatus himself. 'This apparatus,' he said, taking hold of a crank handle and leaning against it, 'was invented by our former Commandant. I assisted at the very earliest experiments and had a share in all the work until its completion. But the credit of inventing it belongs to him alone. Have you ever heard of our former Commandant? No? Well, it isn't saying too much if I tell you that the organization of the whole penal colony is his work. We who were his friends knew even before he died that the organization of the colony was so perfect that his successor, even with a thousand new schemes in his head, would find it impossible to alter anything, at least for many years to come. And our prophecy has come true; the new Commandant has had to acknowledge its truth. A pity you never met the old Commandant! – But,' the officer interrupted himself, 'I am rambling on, and here stands his apparatus before us. It consists, as you see, of three parts. In the course of time each of these parts has acquired a kind of popular nickname. The lower one is called the "Bed", the upper one the "Designer", and this one here in the middle that moves up and down is called the "Harrow".'

'The Harrow?' asked the explorer. He had not been listening very attentively, the glare of the sun in the shadeless valley was altogether too strong, it was difficult to collect one's thoughts. All the more did he admire the officer, who in spite of his tight-fitting full-dress uniform coat, amply befrogged and weighed down by epaulettes, was pursuing his subject with such enthusiasm and, besides talking, was still tightening a screw here and there with a spanner. As for the soldier, he seemed to be in much the same condition as the explorer. He had wound the prisoner's chain around both his wrists, propped himself on his rifle, let his head hang, and was paying no attention to anything. That did not surprise the explorer, for the officer was speaking French, and certainly neither the soldier nor the prisoner understood a word of French. It was all the more remarkable, therefore, that the prisoner was none the less making an effort to follow the officer's explanations. With a kind of drowsy persistence he directed his gaze wherever the officer pointed a finger, and at the interruption of the explorer's question he, too, as well as the officer, looked around.

'Yes, the Harrow,' said the officer, 'a good name for it. The needles are set in like the teeth of a harrow and the whole thing works something like a harrow, although its action is limited to one place and contrived with much more artistic skill. Anyhow, you'll soon understand it. On the Bed here the condemned man is laid – I'm going to describe the apparatus first before I set it in motion. Then you'll be able to follow the proceedings better. Besides, one of the cogwheels in the Designer is badly worn; it creaks a lot when it's working; you can hardly hear yourself speak; spare parts, unfortunately, are difficult to get here – Well, here is the Bed, as I told you. It is completely covered with a layer of cotton wool; you'll find out why later. On this cotton wool the condemned man is laid, face down, quite naked, of course; here are straps for the hands, here for the feet, and here for the neck, to bind him fast. Here at the head of the Bed, where the man, as I said, first lays down his face, is this little gag of felt, which can be easily regulated to go straight into his mouth. It is meant to keep him from screaming and biting his tongue. Of course the man is forced to take the felt into his mouth, for otherwise his neck would be broken by the strap.' 'Is that cotton wool?' asked the explorer, bending forward. 'Yes, certainly,' said the officer, with a smile, 'feel it for yourself.' He took the explorer's hand and guided it over the Bed. 'It's specially prepared cotton wool, that's why it looks so different; I'll tell you presently what it's for.' The explorer already felt a dawning interest in the apparatus; he sheltered his eyes from the sun with one hand and gazed up at the structure. It was a huge affair. The Bed and the Designer were of the same size and looked like two dark wooden chests. The Designer hung about two metres above the Bed; each of them was bound at the corners with four rods of brass that almost flashed out rays in the sunlight. Between the chests shuttled the Harrow on a ribbon of steel.

The officer had scarcely noticed the explorer's previous indifference, but he was now well aware of his dawning interest; so he stopped explaining in order to leave a space of time for quiet observation. The condemned man imitated the explorer; since he could not use a hand to shelter his eyes he gazed upwards without shade.

'Well, the man lies down,' said the explorer, leaning back in his chair and crossing his legs.

'Yes,' said the officer, pushing his cap back a little and passing one hand over his heated face, 'now listen! Both the Bed and the Designer have an electric battery each; the Bed needs one for itself, the Designer for the Harrow. As soon as the man is strapped down, the Bed is set in motion. It quivers in minute, very rapid vibrations, both from side to side and up and down. You will have seen similar apparatus in hospitals; but in our Bed the movements are all precisely calculated; you see, they have to correspond very exactly to the movements of the Harrow. And the Harrow is the instrument for the actual execution of the sentence.'

'And how does the sentence run?' asked the explorer.

'You don't know that either?' said the officer in amazement, and bit his lips. 'Forgive me if my explanations seem rather incoherent. I do beg your pardon. You see, the Commandant always used to do the explaining; but the new Commandant shirks this duty; yet that such an important visitor' – the explorer tried to deprecate the honour with both hands, the officer, however, insisted – 'that such an important visitor should not even be told about the kind of sentence we pass is a new development, which –' He was just on the point of using strong language but checked himself and said only: 'I was not informed, it is not my fault. In any case, I am certainly the best person to explain our procedure, since I have here' – he patted his breast pocket – 'the relevant drawings made by our former Commandant.'

'The Commandant's own drawings?' asked the explorer. 'Did he combine everything in himself, then? Was he soldier, judge, mechanic, chemist, and draughtsman?'

'Indeed he was,' said the officer, nodding assent, with a remote, glassy look. Then he inspected his hands critically; they did not seem clean enough to him for touching the drawings; so he went over to the bucket and washed them again. Then he drew out a small leather wallet and said: 'Our sentence does not sound severe. Whatever commandment the prisoner has disobeyed is written upon his body by the Harrow. This prisoner, for instance' – the officer indicated the man – 'will have written on his body: HONOUR THY SUPERIORS!'

The explorer glanced at the man; he stood, as the officer pointed him

out, with bent head, apparently listening with all his ears in an effort to
catch what was being said. Yet the movement of his blubber lips, closely
pressed together, showed clearly that he could not understand a word.
Many questions were troubling the explorer, but at the sight of the
prisoner he asked only: 'Does he know his sentence?' 'No,' said the
officer, eager to go on with his exposition, but the explorer interrupted
him: 'He doesn't know the sentence that has been passed on him?' 'No,'
said the officer again, pausing a moment as if to let the explorer elaborate
his question, and then said: 'There would be no point in telling him.
He'll learn it on his body.' The explorer intended to make no answer, but
he felt the prisoner's gaze turned on him; it seemed to ask if he approved
such goings-on. So he bent forward again, having already leaned back in
his chair, and put another question: 'But surely he knows that he has been
sentenced?' 'Nor that either,' said the officer, smiling at the explorer as if
expecting him to make further surprising remarks. 'No,' said the explorer,
wiping his forehead, 'then he can't know either whether his defence was
effective?' 'He has had no chance of putting up a defence,' said the officer,
turning his eyes away as if speaking to himself and so sparing the explorer
the shame of hearing self-evident matters explained. 'But he must have
had some chance of defending himself,' said the explorer, and rose from
his seat.

The officer realized that he was in danger of having his exposition of
the apparatus held up for a long time; so he went up to the explorer, took
him by the arm, waved a hand towards the condemned man, who was
standing very straight now that he had so obviously become the centre of
attention – the soldier had also given the chain a jerk – and said: 'That is
how the matter stands. I have been appointed judge in this penal colony.
Despite my youth. For I was the former Commandant's assistant in all
penal matters and know more about the apparatus than anyone. My
guiding principle is this: Guilt is never to be doubted. Other courts cannot
follow that principle, for they consist of several opinions and have higher
courts to scrutinize them. That is not the case here, or at least, it was not
the case in the former Commandant's time. The new man has certainly
shown some inclination to interfere with my judgements, but so far I
have succeeded in fending him off and will go on succeeding. You wanted
to have the case explained; it is quite simple, like all of them. A captain
reported to me this morning that this man, who had been assigned to
him as a servant and sleeps before his door, had been asleep on duty. It is
his duty, you see, to get up every time the hour strikes and salute the
captain's door. Not an exacting duty, and very necessary, since he has to
be a sentry as well as a servant, and must be alert in both functions. Last

night the captain wanted to see if the man was doing his duty. He opened the door as the clock struck two and there was his man curled up asleep. He took his riding whip and lashed him across the face. Instead of getting up and begging pardon, the man caught hold of his master's legs, shook him, and cried: 'Throw that whip away or I'll eat you alive.' – That's the evidence. The captain came to me an hour ago, I wrote down his statement and appended the sentence to it. Then I had the man put in chains. That was all quite simple. If I had first called the man before me and interrogated him, things would have got into a confused tangle. He would have told lies, and had I exposed these lies he would have backed them up with more lies, and so on and so forth. As it is, I've got him and I won't let him go – Is that quite clear now? But we're wasting time, the execution should be beginning and I haven't finished explaining the apparatus yet.' He pressed the explorer back into his chair, went up again to the apparatus, and began: 'As you see, the shape of the Harrow corresponds to the human form; here is the harrow for the torso, here are the harrows for the legs. For the head there is only this one small spike. Is that quite clear?' He bent amiably forward towards the explorer, eager to provide the most comprehensive explanations.

The explorer considered the Harrow with a frown. The explanation of the judicial procedure had not satisfied him. He had to remind himself that this was in any case a penal colony where extraordinary measures were needed and that military discipline must be enforced to the last. He also felt that some hope might be set on the new Commandant, who was apparently of a mind to bring in, although gradually, a new kind of procedure which the officer's narrow mind was incapable of understanding. This train of thought prompted his next question: 'Will the Commandant attend the execution?' 'It is not certain,' said the officer, wincing at the direct question, and his friendly expression darkened. 'That is just why we have to lose no time. Much as I dislike it, I shall have to cut my explanations short. But of course tomorrow, when the apparatus has been cleaned – its one drawback is that it gets so messy – I can recapitulate all the details. For the present, then, only the essentials – When the man lies down on the Bed it begins to vibrate, the Harrow is lowered onto his body. It regulates itself automatically so that the needles barely touch his skin; once contact is made the steel ribbon stiffens immediately into a rigid band. And then the performance begins. An ignorant onlooker would see no difference between one punishment and another. The Harrow appears to do its work with uniform regularity. As it quivers, its points pierce the skin of the body which is itself quivering from the vibration of the Bed. So that the actual progress of the sentence

can be watched, the Harrow is made of glass. Getting the needles fixed
in the glass was a technical problem, but after many experiments we
overcame the difficulty. No trouble was too great for us to take, you see.
And now anyone can look through the glass and watch the inscription
taking form on the body. Wouldn't you care to come a little nearer and
have a look at the needles?'

The explorer got up slowly, walked across, and bent over the Harrow.
'You see,' said the officer, 'there are two kinds of needles arranged in
multiple patterns. Each long needle has a short one beside it. The long
needle does the writing, and the short needle sprays a jet of water to wash
away the blood and keep the inscription clear. Blood and water together
are then conducted here through small runnels into this main runnel and
down a waste pipe into the pit.' With his finger the officer traced the exact
course taken by the blood and water. To make the picture as vivid as
possible he held both hands below the outlet of the waste pipe as if to
catch the outflow, and when he did this the explorer drew back his head
and feeling behind him with one hand sought to return to his chair. To
his horror he found that the condemned man too had obeyed the officer's
invitation to examine the Harrow at close quarters and had followed him.
He had pulled forward the sleepy soldier with the chain and was bending
over the glass. One could see that his uncertain eyes were trying to
perceive what the two gentlemen had been looking at, but since he had
not understood the explanation he could not make head or tail of it. He
was peering this way and that way. He kept running his eyes along the
glass. The explorer wanted to drive him away, since what he was doing
was probably culpable. But the officer firmly restrained the explorer with
one hand and with the other took a clod of earth from the rampart and
threw it at the soldier. He opened his eyes with a jerk, saw what the
condemned man had dared to do, let his rifle fall, dug his heels into the
ground, dragged his prisoner back so that he stumbled and fell immediately, and then stood looking down at him, watching him struggling and
rattling in his chains. 'Set him on his feet!' yelled the officer, for he
noticed that the explorer's attention was being too much distracted by the
prisoner. In fact he was even leaning right across the Harrow, without
taking any notice of it, intent only on finding out what was happening to
the prisoner. 'Be careful with him!' cried the officer again. He ran around
the apparatus, himself caught the condemned man under the shoulders,
and with the soldier's help got him up on his feet, which kept slithering
from under him.

'Now I know all about it,' said the explorer as the officer came back to
him. 'All except the most important thing,' he answered, seizing the

explorer's arm and pointing upwards: 'In the Designer are all the cogwheels that control the movements of the Harrow, and this machinery is regulated according to the inscription demanded by the sentence. I am still using the guiding plans drawn by the former Commandant. Here they are' – he extracted some sheets from the leather wallet – 'but I'm sorry I can't let you handle them, they are my most precious possessions. Just take a seat and I'll hold them in front of you like this, then you'll be able to see everything quite well.' He spread out the first sheet of paper. The explorer would have liked to say something appreciative, but all he could see was a labyrinth of lines crossing and recrossing each other, which covered the paper so thickly that it was difficult to discern the blank spaces between them. 'Read it,' said the officer. 'I can't,' said the explorer. 'Yet it's clear enough,' said the officer. 'It's very ingenious,' said the explorer evasively, 'but I can't make it out.' 'Yes,' said the officer with a laugh, putting the paper away again, 'it's no calligraphy for school children. It needs to be studied closely. I'm quite sure that in the end you would understand it too. Of course the script can't be a simple one; it's not supposed to kill a man straight off, but only after an interval of, on an average, twelve hours; the turning point is reckoned to come at the sixth hour. So there have to be lots and lots of flourishes around the actual script; the script itself runs around the body only in a narrow girdle; the rest of the body is reserved for the embellishments. Can you appreciate now the work accomplished by the Harrow and the whole apparatus? – Just watch it!' He ran up the ladder, turned a wheel, called down: 'Look out, keep to one side!' and everything started working. If the wheel had not creaked, it would have been marvellous. The officer, as if surprised by the noise of the wheel, shook his fist at it, then spread out his arms in excuse to the explorer, and climbed down rapidly to peer at the working of the machine from below. Something perceptible to no one save himself was still not in order; he clambered up again, did something with both hands in the interior of the Designer, then slid down one of the rods, instead of using the ladder, so as to get down quicker, and with the full force of his lungs, to make himself heard at all in the noise, yelled in the explorer's ear: 'Can you follow it? The Harrow is beginning to write; when it finishes the first draft of the inscription on the man's back, the layer of cotton wool begins to roll and slowly turns the body over, to give the Harrow fresh space for writing. Meanwhile the raw part that has been written on lies on the cotton wool, which is specially prepared to staunch the bleeding and so makes all ready for a new deepening of the script. Then these teeth at the edge of the Harrow, as the body turns further around, tear the cotton wool away from the wounds, throw it into the pit, and there is more work for the Harrow. So it keeps on writing deeper and deeper for the whole twelve hours. The first six hours the condemned man stays alive almost as before, he suffers only pain. After two hours the felt gag is taken away, for he has no longer strength to scream. Here, into this electrically heated basin at the head of the Bed, some warm rice pap is poured, from which the man, if he feels like it, can take as much as his tongue can lap. Not one of them ever misses the chance. I can remember none, and my experience is extensive. Only about the sixth hour does the man lose all desire to eat. I usually kneel down here at that moment and observe what happens. The man rarely swallows his last mouthful, he only rolls it around his mouth and spits it out into the pit. I have to duck just then or he would spit it in my face. But how quiet he grows at just about the sixth hour! Enlightenment comes to the most dull-witted. It begins around the eyes. From there it radiates. A moment that might tempt one to get under the Harrow oneself. Nothing more happens than that the man begins to understand the inscription, he purses his mouth as if he were listening. You have seen how difficult it is to decipher the script with one's eyes; but our man deciphers it with his wounds. To be sure, that is a hard task; he needs six hours to accomplish it. By that time the Harrow has pierced him quite through and casts him into the pit, where he pitches down upon the blood and water and the cotton wool. Then the judgement has been fulfilled, and we, the soldier and I, bury him.'

The explorer had inclined his ear to the officer and with his hands in his jacket pockets watched the machine at work. The condemned man watched it too, but uncomprehendingly. He bent forward a little and was intent on the moving needles when the soldier, at a sign from the officer, slashed through his shirt and trousers from behind with a knife, so that they fell off; he tried to catch at his falling clothes to cover his nakedness, but the soldier lifted him into the air and shook the last remnants from him. The officer stopped the machine, and in the sudden silence the condemned man was laid under the Harrow. The chains were loosened and the straps fastened on instead; in the first moment that seemed almost a relief to the prisoner. And now the Harrow was adjusted a little lower, since he was a thin man. When the needle points touched him a shudder ran over his skin; while the soldier was busy strapping his right hand, he flung out his left hand blindly; but it happened to be in the direction towards where the explorer was standing. The officer kept watching the explorer sideways, as if seeking to read from his face the impression made on him by the execution, which had been at least cursorily explained to him.

The wrist strap broke; probably the soldier had drawn it too tight. The officer had to intervene, the soldier held up the broken piece of strap to show him. So the officer went over to him and said, his face still turned towards the explorer: 'This is a very complex machine, it can't be helped that things are breaking or giving way here and there; but one must not thereby allow oneself to be diverted in one's general judgement. In any case, this strap is easily made good; I shall simply use a chain; the delicacy of the vibrations for the right arm will of course be a little impaired.' And while he fastened the chains, he added: 'The resources for maintaining the machine are now very much reduced. Under the former Commandant I had free access to a sum of money set aside entirely for this purpose. There was a store, too, in which spare parts were kept for repairs of all kinds. I confess I have been almost prodigal with them, I mean in the past, not now as the new Commandant pretends, always looking for an excuse to attack our old way of doing things. Now he has taken charge of the machine money himself, and if I send for a new strap they ask for the broken old strap as evidence, and the new strap takes ten days to appear and then is of shoddy material and not much good. But how I am supposed to work the machine without a strap, that's something nobody bothers about.'

The explorer thought to himself: It's always a ticklish matter to intervene decisively in other people's affairs. He was neither a member of the penal colony nor a citizen of the state to which it belonged. Were he to denounce this execution or actually try to stop it, they could say to him: You are a foreigner, mind your own business. He could make no answer to that, unless he were to add that he was amazed at himself in this connection, for he travelled only as an observer, with no intention at all of altering other people's methods of administering justice. Yet here he found himself strongly tempted. The injustice of the procedure and the inhumanity of the execution were undeniable. No one could suppose that he had any selfish interest in the matter, for the condemned man was a complete stranger, not a fellow countryman or even at all sympathetic to him. The explorer himself had recommendations from high quarters, had been received here with great courtesy, and the very fact that he had been invited to attend the execution seemed to suggest that his views would be welcome. And this was all the more likely since the Commandant, as he had heard only too plainly, was no upholder of the procedure and maintained an attitude almost of hostility to the officer.

At that moment the explorer heard the officer cry out in rage. He had just, with considerable difficulty, forced the felt gag into the condemned man's mouth when the man in an irresistible access of nausea shut his eyes and vomited. Hastily the officer snatched him away from the gag and tried to hold his head over the pit; but it was too late, the vomit was running all over the machine. 'It's all the fault of that Commandant!' cried the officer, senselessly shaking the brass rods in front, 'the machine is befouled like a pigsty.' With trembling hands he indicated to the explorer what had happened. 'Have I not tried for hours at a time to get the Commandant to understand that the prisoner must fast for a whole day before the execution. But our new, mild doctrine thinks otherwise. The Commandant's ladies stuff the man with sugar candy before he's led off. He has lived on stinking fish his whole life long and now he has to eat sugar candy! But it could still be possible, I should have nothing to say against it, but why won't they get me a new felt gag, which I have been begging for the last three months. How should a man not feel sick when he takes a felt gag into his mouth which more than a hundred men have already slobbered and gnawed in their dying moments?'

The condemned man had laid his head down and looked peaceful, the soldier was busy trying to clean the machine with the prisoner's shirt. The officer advanced towards the explorer who in some vague presentiment fell back a pace, but the officer seized him by the hand, and drew him to one side. 'I should like to exchange a few words with you in confidence,' he said, 'may I?' 'Of course,' said the explorer, and listened with downcast eyes.

'This procedure and method of execution, which you are now having the opportunity to admire, has at the moment no longer any open adherents in our colony. I am its sole advocate, and at the same time the sole advocate of the old Commandant's tradition. I can no longer reckon on any further extension of the method, it takes all my energy to maintain it as it is. During the old Commandant's lifetime the colony was full of his adherents; his strength of conviction I still have in some measure, but not an atom of his power; consequently the adherents have skulked out of sight, there are still many of them but none of them will admit it. If you were to go into the teahouse today, on execution day, and listen to what is being said, you would perhaps hear only ambiguous remarks. These would all be made by adherents, but under the present Commandant and his present doctrines they are of no use to me. And now I ask you: because of this Commandant and the women who influence him, is such a piece of work, the work of a lifetime' – he pointed to the machine – 'to perish? Ought one to let that happen? Even if one has only come as a stranger to our island for a few days? But there's no time to lose, an attack of some kind is impending on my function as judge; conferences are already being held in the Commandant's office from which I am excluded;

even your coming here today seems to me a significant move; they are cowards and use you as a screen, you, a stranger. – How different an execution was in the old days! A whole day before the ceremony the valley was packed with people; they all came only to look on; early in the morning the Commandant appeared with his ladies; fanfares roused the whole camp; I reported that everything was in readiness; the assembled company – no high official dared to absent himself – arranged itself around the machine; this pile of cane chairs is a miserable survival from that epoch. The machine was freshly cleaned and glittering, I got new spare parts for almost every execution. Before hundreds of spectators – all of them standing on tiptoe as far as the heights there – the condemned man was laid under the Harrow by the Commandant himself. What is left today for a common soldier to do was then my task, the task of the presiding judge, and was an honour for me. And then the execution began! No discordant noise spoiled the working of the machine. Many did not care to watch it but lay with closed eyes in the sand; they all knew: Now Justice is being done. In the silence one heard nothing but the condemned man's sighs, half-muffled by the felt gag. Nowadays the machine can no longer wring from anyone a sigh louder than the felt gag can stifle; but in those days the writing needles let drop an acid fluid, which we're no longer permitted to use. Well, and then came the sixth hour! It was impossible to grant all the requests to be allowed to watch it from nearby. The Commandant in his wisdom ordained that the children should have the preference; I, of course, because of my office had the privilege of always being at hand; often enough I would be squatting there with a small child in either arm. How we all absorbed the look of transfiguration on the face of the sufferer, how we bathed our cheeks in the radiance of that justice, achieved at last and fading so quickly! What times these were, my comrade!' The officer had obviously forgotten whom he was addressing; he had embraced the explorer and laid his head on his shoulder. The explorer was deeply embarrassed, impatiently he stared over the officer's head. The soldier had finished his cleaning job and was now pouring rice pap from a pot into the basin. As soon as the condemned man, who seemed to have recovered entirely, noticed this action he began to reach for the rice with his tongue. The soldier kept pushing him away, since the rice pap was certainly meant for a later hour, yet it was just as unfitting that the soldier himself should thrust his dirty hands into the basin and eat out of it before the other's avid face.

The officer quickly pulled himself together. 'I didn't want to upset you,' he said, 'I know it is impossible to make those days credible now. Anyhow, the machine is still working and it is still effective in itself. It is effective in itself even though it stands alone in this valley. And the corpse still falls at the last into the pit with an incomprehensibly gentle wafting motion, even though there are no hundreds of people swarming around like flies as formerly. In those days we had to put a strong fence around the pit, it has long since been torn down.'

The explorer wanted to withdraw his face from the officer and looked around him at random. The officer thought he was surveying the valley's desolation; so he seized him by the hands, turned him around to meet his eyes, and asked: 'Do you realize the shame of it?'

But the explorer said nothing. The officer left him alone for a little; with legs apart, hands on hips, he stood very still, gazing at the ground. Then he smiled encouragingly at the explorer and said: 'I was quite near you yesterday when the Commandant gave you the invitation. I heard him giving it. I know the Commandant. I divined at once what he was after. Although he is powerful enough to take measures against me, he doesn't dare to do it yet, but he certainly means to use your verdict against me, the verdict of an illustrious foreigner. He has calculated it carefully: this is your second day on the island, you did not know the old Commandant and his ways, you are conditioned by European ways of thought, perhaps you object on principle to capital punishment in general and to such mechanical instruments of death in particular, besides, you will see that the execution has no support from the public, a shabby ceremony – carried out with a machine already somewhat old and worn – now, taking all that into consideration, would it not be likely (so thinks the Commandant) that you might disapprove of my methods? And if you disapprove, you wouldn't conceal the fact (I'm still speaking from the Commandant's point of view), for you are a man to feel confidence in your own well-tried conclusions. True, you have seen and learned to appreciate the peculiarities of many peoples, and so you would not be likely to take a strong line against our proceedings, as you might do in your own country. But the Commandant has no need of that. A casual, even an unguarded remark will be enough. It doesn't even need to represent what you really think, so long as it can be used speciously to serve his purpose. He will try to prompt you with sly questions, of that I am certain. And his ladies will sit around you and prick up their ears; you might be saying something like this: "In our country we have a different criminal procedure," or "In our country the prisoner is inter-rogated before he is sentenced," or "We haven't used torture since the Middle Ages." All these statements are as true as they seem natural to you, harmless remarks that pass no judgement on my methods. But how would the Commandant react to them? I can see him, our good

Commandant, pushing his chair away immediately and rushing onto the balcony, I can see his ladies streaming out after him, I can hear his voice – the ladies call it a voice of thunder – well, and this is what he says: "A famous Western investigator, sent out to study criminal procedure in all the countries of the world, has just said that our old tradition of administering justice is inhumane. Such a verdict from such a personality makes it impossible for me to countenance these methods any longer. Therefore from this very day I ordain . . .' and so on. You may want to interpose that you never said any such thing, that you never called my methods inhumane, on the contrary your profound experience leads you to believe they are most humane and most in consonance with human dignity, and you admire the machine greatly – but it will be too late; you won't even get onto the balcony, crowded as it will be with ladies; you may try to draw attention to yourself; you may want to scream out; but a lady's hand will close your lips – and I and the work of the old Commandant will be done for.'

The explorer had to suppress a smile; so easy, then, was the task he had felt to be so difficult. He said evasively: 'You overestimate my influence; the Commandant has read my letters of recommendation, he knows that I am no expert in criminal procedure. If I were to give an opinion, it would be as a private individual, an opinion no more influential than that of any ordinary person, and in any case much less influential than that of the Commandant, who, I am given to understand, has very extensive powers in this penal colony. If his attitude to your procedure is as definitely hostile as you believe, then I fear the end of your tradition is at hand, even without any humble assistance from me.'

Had it dawned on the officer at last? No, he still did not understand. He shook his head emphatically, glanced briefly around at the condemned man and the soldier, who both flinched away from the rice, came close up to the explorer, and without looking at his face but fixing his eye on some spot on his coat said in a lower voice than before: 'You don't know the Commandant; you feel yourself – forgive the expression – a kind of outsider so far as all of us are concerned; yet, believe me, your influence cannot be rated too highly. I was simply delighted when I heard that you were to attend the execution all by yourself. The Commandant arranged it to aim a blow at me, but I shall turn it to my advantage. Without being distracted by lying whispers and contemptuous glances – which could not have been avoided had a crowd of people attended the execution – you have heard my explanations, seen the machine, and are now in course of watching the execution. You have doubtless already formed your own judgement; if you still have some small uncertainties the sight of the execution will resolve them. And now I make this request to you: help me against the Commandant!'

The explorer would not let him go on. 'How could I do that,' he cried, 'it's quite impossible. I can neither help nor hinder you.'

'Yes, you can,' the officer said. The explorer saw with a certain apprehension that the officer had clenched his fists. 'Yes, you can,' repeated the officer, still more insistently. 'I have a plan that is bound to succeed. You believe your influence is insufficient. I know that it is sufficient. But even granted that you are right, is it not necessary, for the sake of preserving this tradition, to try even what might prove insufficient? Listen to my plan, then. The first thing necessary for you to carry it out is to be as reticent as possible today regarding your verdict on these proceedings. Unless you are asked a direct question you must say nothing at all; but what you do say must be brief and general; let it be remarked that you would prefer not to discuss the matter, that you are out of patience with it, that if you are to let yourself go you would use strong language. I don't ask you to tell any lies; by no means; you should only give curt answers, such as: "Yes, I saw the execution," or "Yes, I had it explained to me." Just that, nothing more. There are grounds enough for any impatience you betray, although not such as will occur to the Commandant. Of course, he will mistake your meaning and interpret it to please himself. That's what my plan depends on. Tomorrow in the Commandant's office there is to be a large conference of all the high administrative officials, the Commandant presiding. Of course the Commandant is the kind of man to have turned these conferences into public spectacles. He has had a gallery built that is always packed with spectators. I am compelled to take part in the conferences, but they make me sick with disgust. Now, whatever happens, you will certainly be invited to this conference; if you behave today as I suggest, the invitation will become an urgent request. But if for some mysterious reason you're not invited, you'll have to ask for an invitation; there's no doubt of your getting it then. So tomorrow you're sitting in the Commandant's box with the ladies. He keeps looking up to make sure you're there. After various trivial and ridiculous matters, brought in merely to impress the audience – mostly harbour works, nothing but harbour works! – our judicial procedure comes up for discussion too. If the Commandant doesn't introduce it, or not soon enough, I'll see that it's mentioned. I'll stand up and report that today's execution has taken place. Quite briefly, only a statement. Such a statement is not usual, but I shall make it. The Commandant thanks me, as always, with an amiable smile, and then he can't restrain himself, he seizes the excellent opportunity. "It has just been reported," he will say, or words to that effect, "that an execution has taken place. I should like merely to add that this execution was witnessed by the famous explorer who has, as you all know, honoured our colony so greatly by his visit to us. His presence at today's session of our conference also contributes to the importance of this occasion. Should we not now ask the famous explorer to give us his verdict on our traditional mode of execution and the procedure that leads up to it?" Of course there is loud applause, general agreement, I am more insistent than any one. The Commandant bows to you and says: "Then in the name of the assembled company, I put the question to you." And now you advance to the front of the box. Lay your hands where everyone can see them, or the ladies will catch them and press your fingers. – And then at last you can speak out. I don't know how I'm going to endure the tension of waiting for that moment. Don't put any restraint on yourself when you make your speech, publish the truth aloud, lean over the front of the box, shout, yes indeed, shout your verdict, your unshakable conviction, at the Commandant. Yet perhaps you wouldn't care to do that, it's not in keeping with your character, in your country perhaps people do these things differently, well, that's all right too, that will be quite as effective, don't even stand up, just say a few words, even in a whisper, so that only the officials beneath you will hear them, that will be quite enough, you don't even need to mention the lack of public support for the execution, the creaking wheel, the broken strap, the filthy gag of felt, no, I'll take all that upon me, and, believe me, if my indictment doesn't drive him out of the conference hall, it will force him to his knees to make the acknowledgement: Old Commandant, I humble myself before you. – That is my plan; will you help me to carry it out? But of course you are willing, what is more, you must.' And the officer seized the explorer by both arms and gazed, breathing heavily, into his face. He had shouted the last sentence so loudly that even the soldier and the condemned man were startled into attending; they had not understood a word but they stopped eating and looked over at the explorer, chewing their previous mouthfuls.

From the very beginning the explorer had no doubt about what answer he must give; in his lifetime he had experienced too much to have any uncertainty here; he was fundamentally honourable and unafraid. And yet now, facing the soldier and the condemned man, he did hesitate, for as long as it took to draw one breath. At last, however, he said, as he had to: 'No.' The officer blinked several times but did not turn his eyes away. 'Would you like me to explain?' asked the explorer. The officer nodded wordlessly. 'I do not approve of your procedure,' said the explorer then, 'even before you took me into your confidence – of course I shall never in any circumstances betray your confidence – I was already wondering whether it would be my duty to intervene and whether my intervention would have the slightest chance of success. I realized to whom I ought to turn: to the Commandant, of course. You have made that fact even clearer, but without having strengthened my resolution, on the contrary, your sincere conviction has touched me, even though it cannot influence my judgement.'

The officer remained mute, turned to the machine, caught hold of a brass rod, and then, leaning back a little, gazed at the Designer as if to assure himself that all was in order. The soldier and the condemned man seemed to have come to some understanding; the condemned man was making signs to the soldier, difficult though his movements were because of the tight straps; the soldier was bending down to him; the condemned man whispered something and the soldier nodded.

The explorer followed the officer and said: 'You don't know yet what I mean to do. I shall tell the Commandant what I think of the procedure, certainly, but not at a public conference, only in private; nor shall I stay here long enough to attend any conference; I am going away early tomorrow morning, or at least embarking on my ship.'

It did not look as if the officer had been listening. 'So you did not find the procedure convincing,' he said to himself and smiled, as an old man smiles at childish nonsense and yet pursues his own meditations behind the smile.

'Then the time has come,' he said at last, and suddenly looked at the explorer with bright eyes that held some challenge, some appeal for cooperation. 'The time for what?' asked the explorer uneasily, but got no answer.

'You are free,' said the officer to the condemned man in the native tongue. The man did not believe it at first. 'Yes, you are set free,' said the officer. For the first time the condemned man's face woke to real animation. Was it true? Was it only a caprice of the officer's, that might change again? Had the foreign explorer begged him off? What was it? One could read these questions on his face. But not for long. Whatever it might be, he wanted to be really free if he might, and he began to struggle so far as the Harrow permitted him.

'You'll burst my straps,' cried the officer, 'lie still! We'll soon loosen them.' And signing the soldier to help him, he set about doing so. The condemned man laughed wordlessly to himself, now he turned his face left towards the officer, now right towards the soldier, nor did he forget the explorer.

'Draw him out,' ordered the officer. Because of the Harrow this had to be done with some care. The condemned man had already torn himself a little in the back through his impatience.

From now on, however, the officer paid hardly any attention to him. He went up to the explorer, pulled out the small leather wallet again, turned over the papers in it, found the one he wanted, and showed it to the explorer. 'Read it,' he said. 'I can't,' said the explorer, 'I told you before that I can't make out these scripts.' 'Try taking a close look at it,' said the officer and came quite near to the explorer so that they might read it together. But when even that proved useless, he outlined the script with his little finger, holding it high above the paper as if the surface dared not be sullied by touch, in order to help the explorer to follow the script in that way. The explorer did make an effort, meaning to please the officer in this respect at least, but he was quite unable to follow. Now the officer began to spell it, letter by letter, and then read out the words. ' "BE JUST!" is what is written there,' he said, 'surely you can read it now.' The explorer bent so close to the paper that the officer feared he might touch it and drew it farther away; the explorer made no remark, yet it was clear that he still could not decipher it. ' "BE JUST!" is what is written there,' said the officer once more. 'Maybe,' said the explorer, 'I am prepared to believe you.' 'Well, then,' said the officer, at least partly satisfied, and climbed up the ladder with the paper; very carefully he laid it inside the Designer and seemed to be changing the disposition of all the cogwheels; it was a troublesome piece of work and must have involved wheels that were extremely small, for sometimes the officer's head vanished altogether from sight inside the Designer, so precisely did he have to regulate the machinery.

The explorer, down below, watched the labour uninterruptedly, his neck grew stiff and his eyes smarted from the glare of sunshine over the sky. The soldier and the condemned man were now busy together. The man's shirt and trousers, which were already lying in the pit, were fished out by the point of the soldier's bayonet. The shirt was abominably dirty and its owner washed it in the bucket of water. When he put on the shirt and trousers both he and the soldier could not help guffawing, for the garments were of course slit up behind. Perhaps the condemned man felt it incumbent on him to amuse the soldier, he turned around in his slashed garments before the soldier, who squatted on the ground beating his knees with mirth. All the same, they presently controlled their mirth out of respect for the gentlemen.

When the officer had at length finished his task aloft, he surveyed the machinery in all its details once more, with a smile, but this time shut the lid of the Designer, which had stayed open till now, climbed down, looked into the pit and then at the condemned man, noting with satisfaction that the clothing had been taken out, then went over to wash his hands in the water bucket, perceived too late that it was disgustingly dirty, was unhappy because he could not wash his hands, in the end thrust them into the sand – this alternative did not please him, but he had to put up with it – then stood upright and began to unbutton his uniform jacket. As he did this, the two ladies' handkerchiefs he had tucked under his collar fell into his hands. 'Here are your handkerchiefs,' he said, and threw them to the condemned man. And to the explorer he said in explanation: 'A gift from the ladies.'

In spite of the obvious haste with which he was discarding first his uniform jacket and then all his clothing, he handled each garment with loving care, he even ran his fingers caressingly over the silver lace on the jacket and shook a tassel into place. This loving care was certainly out of keeping with the fact that as soon as he had a garment off he flung it at once with a kind of unwilling jerk into the pit. The last thing left to him was his short sword with the sword belt. He drew it out of the scabbard, broke it, then gathered all together, the bits of the sword, the scabbard, and the belt, and flung them so violently down that they clattered into the pit.

Now he stood naked there. The explorer bit his lips and said nothing. He knew very well what was going to happen, but he had no right to obstruct the officer in anything. If the judicial procedure which the officer cherished were really so near its end – possibly as a result of his own intervention, as to which he felt himself pledged – then the officer was doing the right thing; in his place the explorer would not have acted otherwise.

The soldier and the condemned man did not understand at first what was happening, at first they were not even looking on. The condemned man was gleeful at having got the handkerchiefs back, but he was not allowed to enjoy them for long, since the soldier snatched them with a sudden, unexpected grab. Now the condemned man in turn was trying to twitch them from under the belt where the soldier had tucked them, but the soldier was on his guard. So they were wrestling, half in jest. Only when the officer stood quite naked was their attention caught. The condemned man especially seemed struck with the notion that some great change was impending. What had happened to him was now going to happen to the officer. Perhaps even to the very end. Apparently the foreign explorer had given the order for it. So this was revenge. Although he himself had not suffered to the end, he was to be revenged to the end. A broad, silent grin now appeared on his face and stayed there all the rest of the time.

The officer, however, had turned to the machine. It had been clear enough previously that he understood the machine well, but now it was almost staggering to see how he managed it and how it obeyed him. His hand had only to approach the Harrow for it to rise and sink several times till it was adjusted to the right position for receiving him; he touched only the edge of the Bed and already it was vibrating, the felt gag came to meet his mouth, one could see that the officer was really reluctant to take it but he shrank from it only a moment, soon he submitted and received it. Everything was ready, only the straps hung down at the sides, yet they were obviously unnecessary, the officer did not need to be fastened down. Then the condemned man noticed the loose straps, in his opinion the execution was incomplete unless the straps were buckled, he gestured eagerly to the soldier and they ran together to strap the officer down. The latter had already stretched out one foot to push the lever that started the Designer; he saw the two men coming up; so he drew his foot back and let himself be buckled in. But now he could not reach the lever; neither the soldier nor the condemned man would be able to find it, and the explorer was determined not to lift a finger. It was not necessary; as soon as the straps were fastened the machine began to work; the Bed vibrated, the needles flickered above the skin, the Harrow rose and fell. The explorer had been staring at it quite a while before he remembered that a wheel in the Designer should have been creaking; but everything was quiet, not even the slightest hum could be heard.

Because it was working so silently the machine simply escaped one's attention. The explorer observed the soldier and the condemned man. The latter was the more animated of the two, everything in the machine interested him, now he was bending down and now stretching up on tiptoe, his forefinger was extended all the time pointing out details to the soldier. This annoyed the explorer. He was resolved to stay till the end, but he could not bear the sight of these two. 'Go back home,' he said. The soldier would have been willing enough, but the condemned man took the order as a punishment. With clasped hands he implored to be allowed to stay, and when the explorer shook his head and would not relent, he even went down on his knees. The explorer saw that it was no use merely giving orders, he was on the point of going over and driving them away. At that moment he heard a noise above him in the Designer. He looked up. Was that cogwheel going to make trouble after all? But it was something quite different. Slowly the lid of the Designer rose up and then clicked wide open. The teeth of the cogwheel showed themselves and rose higher, soon the whole wheel was visible, it was as if some enormous force were squeezing the Designer so that there was no longer room for the wheel, the wheel moved up till it came to the very edge of the Designer, fell down, rolled along the sand a little on its rim, and then lay flat. But a second wheel was already rising after it, followed by many others, large and small and indistinguishably minute, the same thing happened to all of them, at every moment one imagined the Designer must now really be empty, but another complex of numerous wheels was already rising into sight, falling down, trundling along the sand, and lying flat. This phenomenon made the condemned man completely forget the explorer's command, the cogwheels fascinated him, he was already trying to catch one and at the same time urging the soldier to help, but always drew back his hand in alarm, for another wheel always came hopping along which, at least on its first advance, scared him off.

The explorer, on the other hand, felt greatly troubled; the machine was obviously going to pieces; its silent working was a delusion; he had a feeling that he must now stand by the officer, since the officer was no longer able to look after himself. But while the tumbling cogwheels absorbed his whole attention he had forgotten to keep an eye on the rest of the machine; now that the last cogwheel had left the Designer, however, he bent over the Harrow and had a new and still more unpleasant surprise. The Harrow was not writing, it was only jabbing, and the Bed was not turning the body over but only bringing it up quivering against the needles. The explorer wanted to do something, if possible, to bring the whole machine to a standstill, for this was no exquisite torture such as the officer desired, this was plain murder. He stretched out his hands. But at that moment the Harrow rose with the body spitted on it and moved to the side, as it usually did only when the twelfth hour had come. Blood was flowing in a hundred streams, not mingled with water, the water jets too had failed to function. And now the last action failed to fulfil itself, the body did not drop off the long needles, streaming with blood it went on hanging over the pit without falling into it. The Harrow tried to move back to its old position, but as if it had itself noticed that it had not yet got rid of its burden it stuck after all where it was, over the pit. 'Come and help!' cried the explorer to the other two, and himself seized the officer's feet. He wanted to push against the feet while the others seized the head from the opposite side and so the officer might be slowly eased off the needles. But the other two could not make up their minds to come; the condemned man actually turned away; the explorer had to go over to them and force them into position at the officer's head. And here, almost against his will, he had to look at the face of the corpse. It was as it had been in life; no sign was visible of the promised redemption; what the others had found in the machine the officer had not found; the lips were firmly pressed together, the eyes were open, with the same expression as in life, the look was calm and convinced, through the forehead went the point of the great iron spike.

As the explorer, with the soldier and the condemned man behind him, reached the first houses of the colony, the soldier pointed to one of them and said: 'There is the teahouse.'

In the ground floor of the house was a deep, low, cavernous space, its walls and ceiling blackened with smoke. It was open to the road all along its length. Although this teahouse was very little different from the other houses of the colony, which were all very dilapidated, even up to the Commandant's palatial headquarters, it made on the explorer the impression of a historic tradition of some kind, and he felt the power of past days. He went near to it, followed by his companions, right up between the empty tables that stood in the street before it, and breathed the cool, heavy air that came from the interior. 'The old man's buried here,' said the soldier, 'the priest wouldn't let him lie in the churchyard. Nobody knew where to bury him for a while, but in the end they buried him here. The officer never told you about that, for sure, because of course that's what he was most ashamed of. He even tried several times to dig the old man up by night, but he was always chased away.' 'Where is the grave?' asked the explorer, who found it impossible to believe the soldier. At once both of them, the soldier and the condemned man, ran before him pointing with outstretched hands in the direction where the grave should be. They led the explorer right up to the back wall, where guests were sitting at a few tables. They were apparently dock labourers, strong men with short, glistening, full black beards. None had a jacket, their shirts were torn, they were poor, humble creatures. As the explorer drew near, some of them got up, pressed close to the wall, and stared at him. 'It's a foreigner,' ran the whisper around him, 'he wants to see the grave.' They pushed one of the tables aside, and under it there was really a gravestone. It was a simple stone, low enough to be covered by a table. There was an inscription on it in very small letters, the explorer had to kneel down to read it. This was what it said: 'Here rests the old Commandant. His adherents, who now must be nameless, have dug this grave and set up this stone. There is a prophecy that after a certain number of years the Commandant will rise again and lead his adherents from this house to recover the colony. Have faith and wait!' When the explorer had read this and risen to his feet he saw all the bystanders around him smiling, as if they too had read the inscription, had found it ridiculous, and were expecting him to agree with them. The explorer ignored this, distributed a few coins among them, waiting till the table was pushed over the grave again, quitted the teahouse, and made for the harbour.

The soldier and the condemned man had found some acquaintances in the teahouse, who detained them. But they must have soon shaken them off, for the explorer was only halfway down the long flight of steps leading to the boats when they came rushing after him. Probably they wanted to force him at the last minute to take them with him. While he was bargaining below with a ferryman to row him to the steamer, the two of them came headlong down the steps, in silence, for they did not dare to shout. But by the time they reached the foot of the steps the explorer was already in the boat, and the ferryman was just casting off from the shore. They could have jumped into the boat but the explorer lifted a heavy knotted rope from the floor boards, threatened them with it, and so kept them from attempting the leap.

The Waxwork

A. M. Burrage

While the uniformed attendants of Marriner's Waxworks were ushering the last stragglers through the great glass-panelled double doors, the manager sat in his office interviewing Raymond Hewson.

The manager was a youngish man, stout, blond, and of medium height. He wore his clothes well and contrived to look extremely smart without appearing over-dressed. Raymond Hewson looked neither. His clothes, which had been good when new and which were still carefully brushed and pressed, were beginning to show signs of their owner's losing battle with the world. He was a small, spare, pale man, with lank, errant brown hair, and although he spoke plausibly and even forcibly he had the defensive and somewhat furtive air of a man who was used to rebuffs. He looked what he was, a man gifted somewhat above the ordinary, who was a failure through his lack of self-assertion.

The manager was speaking.

'There is nothing new in your request,' he said. 'In fact we refuse it to different people – mostly young bloods who have tried to make bets – about three times a week. We have nothing to gain and something to lose by letting people spend the night in our Murderers' Den. If I allowed it, and some young idiot lost his senses, what would be my position? But your being a journalist somewhat alters the case.'

Hewson smiled.

'I suppose you mean that journalists have no senses to lose.'

'No, no,' laughed the manager, 'but one imagines them to be responsible people. Besides, here we have something to gain; publicity and advertisement.'

'Exactly,' said Hewson, 'and there I thought we might come to terms.'

The manager laughed again.

'Oh,' he exclaimed, 'I know what's coming. You want to be paid twice, do you? It used to be said years ago that Madame Tussaud's would give a man a hundred pounds for sleeping alone in the Chamber of Horrors. I hope you don't think that we have made any such offer. Er – what is your paper, Mr Hewson?'

'I am free-lancing at present,' Hewson confessed, 'working on space for several papers. However, I should find no difficulty in getting the story printed. The *Morning Echo* would use it like a shot. "A Night with Marriner's Murderers". No live paper could turn it down.'

The manager rubbed his chin.

'Ah! And how do you propose to treat it?'

'I shall make it gruesome, of course; gruesome with just a saving touch of humour.'

The other nodded and offered Hewson his cigarette case.

'Very well, Mr Hewson,' he said. 'Get your story printed in the *Morning Echo*, and there will be a five-pound note waiting for you here when you care to come and call for it. But first of all, it's no small ordeal that you're proposing to undertake. I'd like to be quite sure about you, and I'd like you to be quite sure about yourself. I own I shouldn't care to take it on. I've seen those figures dressed and undressed. I know all about the process of their manufacture. I can walk about in company downstairs as unmoved as if I were walking among so many skittles. But I should hate having to sleep down there alone among them.'

'Why?' asked Hewson.

'I don't know. There isn't any reason. I don't believe in ghosts. If I did I should expect them to haunt the scene of their crimes or the spot where their bodies were laid, instead of a cellar which happens to contain their waxwork effigies. It's just that I couldn't sit alone among them all night, with their seeming to stare at me in the way they do. After all, they represent the lowest and most appalling types of humanity, and – although I would not own it publicly – the people who come to see them are not generally charged with the very highest motives. The whole atmosphere of the place is unpleasant, and if you are susceptible to atmosphere I warn you that you are in for a very uncomfortable night.'

Hewson had known that from the moment when the idea had first occurred to him. His soul sickened at the prospect, even while he smiled casually upon the manager. But he had a wife and family to keep, and for the past month he had been living on paragraphs, eked out by his rapidly dwindling store of savings. Here was a chance not to be missed – the price of a special story in the *Morning Echo*, with a five-pound note to add to it. It meant comparative wealth and luxury for a week, and freedom from the worst anxieties for a fortnight. Besides, if he wrote the story well, it might lead to an offer of regular employment.

'The way of transgressors – and newspaper men – is hard,' he said. 'I have already promised myself an uncomfortable night because your murderers' den is obviously not fitted up as a hotel bedroom. But I don't think your waxworks will worry me much.'

'You're not superstitious?'

'Not a bit.' Hewson laughed.

'But you're a journalist; you must have a strong imagination.'

'The news editors for whom I've worked have always complained that I haven't any. Plain facts are not considered sufficient in our trade, and the papers don't like offering their readers unbuttered bread.'

The manager smiled and rose.

'Right,' he said. 'I think the last of the people have gone. Wait a moment. I'll give orders for the figures downstairs not to be draped, and let the night people know that you'll be here. Then I'll take you down and show you round.'

He picked up the receiver of a house telephone, spoke into it and presently replaced it.

'One condition I'm afraid I must impose on you,' he remarked. 'I must ask you not to smoke. We had a fire scare down in the Murderers' Den this evening. I don't know who gave the alarm, but whoever it was it was a false one. Fortunately there were very few people down there at the time, or there might have been a panic. And now, if you're ready, we'll make a move.'

Hewson followed the manager through half a dozen rooms where attendants were busy shrouding kings and queens of England, the generals and prominent statesmen of this and other generations, all the mixed herd of humanity whose fame or notoriety had rendered them eligible for this kind of immortality. The manager stopped once and spoke to a man in uniform, saying something about an armchair in the Murderers' Den.

'It's the best we can do for you, I'm afraid,' he said to Hewson. 'I hope you'll be able to get some sleep.'

He led the way through an open barrier and down ill-lit stone stairs, which conveyed a sinister impression of giving access to a dungeon. In a passage at the bottom were a few preliminary horrors, such as relics of the Inquisition, a rack taken from a medieval castle, branding irons, thumbscrews and other mementoes of man's one-time cruelty to man. Beyond the passage was the Murderers' Den.

It was a room of irregular shape with a vaulted roof, and dimly lit by electric lights burning behind inverted bowls of frosted glass. It was, by design, an eerie and uncomfortable chamber – a chamber whose atmosphere invited its visitors to speak in whispers. There was something of the air of a chapel about it, but a chapel no longer devoted to the practice of piety and given over now for base and impious worship.

The waxwork murderers stood on low pedestals with numbered tickets at their feet. Seeing them elsewhere, and without knowing whom they represented, one would have thought them a dull-looking crew, chiefly remarkable for the shabbiness of their clothes.

Recent notorieties rubbed dusty shoulders with the old 'favourites'. Thurtell, the murderer of Weir, stood as if frozen in the act of making a shop-window gesture to young Bywaters. There was Lefroy, the poor half-baked little snob who killed for gain so that he might ape the gentleman. Charles Peace, the only member of that vile company who looked uncompromisingly and entirely evil, sneered across a gangway at Norman Thorne.

The manager, walking round with Hewson, pointed out several of the more interesting of these unholy notabilities.

'That's Crippen; I expect you recognize him. Insignificant little beast who looks as if he couldn't tread on a worm. That's Armstrong. Looks like a decent, harmless country gentleman, doesn't he? There's old Vaquier; you can't miss him because of his beard. And of course this –'

'Who's that?' Hewson interrupted in a whisper, pointing.

'Oh, I was coming to him,' said the manager in a light undertone. 'Come and have a good look at him. This is our star turn. He's the only one of the bunch that hasn't been hanged.'

The figure which Hewson had indicated was that of a small, slight man not much more than five feet in height. It wore little waxed moustaches, large spectacles and a caped coat. There was something so exaggeratedly French in its appearance that it reminded Hewson of a stage caricature. He could not have said precisely why the mild-looking face seemed to him so repellent, but he had already recoiled a step and, even in the manager's company, it cost him an effort to look again.

'But who is he?' he asked.

'That,' said the manager, 'is Dr Bourdette.'

Hewson shook his head doubtfully.

'I think I've heard the name,' he said, 'but I forget in connection with what.'

The manager smiled.

'You'd remember better if you were a Frenchman,' he said. 'For some long while that man was the terror of Paris. He carried on his work of healing by day, and of throat-cutting by night, when the fit was on him. He killed for the sheer devilish pleasure it gave him to kill, and always in the same way – with a razor. After his last crime he left a clue behind him which set the police upon his track. One clue led to another, and before very long they knew that they were on the track of the Parisian equivalent of our Jack the Ripper, and had enough evidence to send him to the madhouse or the guillotine on a dozen capital charges.

'But even then our friend was too clever for them. When he realized that the toils were closing about him he mysteriously disappeared, and ever since the police of every civilized country have been looking for him. There is no doubt that he managed to make away with himself, and by some means which has prevented his body coming to light. One or two crimes of a similar nature have taken place since his disappearance, but he is believed almost for certain to be dead. It's queer, isn't it, how every notorious murderer has imitators?'

Hewson shuddered and fidgeted with his feet.

'I don't like him at all,' he confessed. 'Ugh! What eyes he's got!'

'Yes, this figure's a little masterpiece. You find the eyes bite into you? Well, that's excellent realism, then, for Bourdette practised mesmerism, and was supposed to mesmerize his victims before dispatching them. Indeed, had he not done so, it is impossible to see how so small a man could have done his ghastly work. There were never any signs of a struggle.'

'I thought I saw him move,' said Hewson with a catch in his voice.

The manager smiled.

'You'll have more than one optical illusion before the night's out, I expect. You shan't be locked in. You can come upstairs when you've had enough of it. There are watchmen on the premises, so you'll find company. Don't be alarmed if you hear them moving about. I'm sorry I can't give you any more light, because all the lights are on. For obvious reasons we keep this place as gloomy as possible.'

The member of the night staff who placed the armchair for Hewson was inclined to be facetious.

'Where will you have it, sir?' he asked, grinning. 'Just 'ere, so as you can 'ave a little talk with Crippen when you're tired of sitting still? Say where, sir.'

Hewson smiled. The man's chaff pleased him if only because, for the moment at least, it lent the proceedings a much-desired air of the commonplace.

'I'll place it myself, thanks,' he said. 'I'll find out where the draughts come from first.'

'You won't find any down here. Well, good night, sir. I'm upstairs if you want me. Don't let 'em sneak up be'ind you and touch your neck with their cold and clammy 'ands.'

Hewson laughed and wished the man good night. It was easier than he had expected. He wheeled the armchair – a heavy one upholstered in plush – a little way down the central gangway, and deliberately turned it so that its back was towards the effigy of Dr Bourdette. For some undefined reason he liked Dr Bourdette a great deal less than his companions. Busying himself with arranging the chair he was almost light-hearted, but when the attendant's footfalls had died away and a deep hush stole over the chamber he realized that he had no slight ordeal before him.

The dim unwavering light fell on the rows of figures which were so uncannily like human beings that the silence and the stillness seemed unnatural and even ghastly. He missed the sound of breathing, the rustling of clothes, the hundred and one minute noises one hears when even the deepest silence has fallen upon a crowd. But the air was as stagnant as water at the bottom of a standing pond. There was not a breath in the chamber to stir a curtain or rustle a hanging drapery or start a shadow. His own shadow, moving in response to a shifted arm or leg, was all that could be coaxed into motion. All was still to the gaze and silent to the ear. 'It must be like this at the bottom of the sea,' he thought, and wondered how to work the phrase into his story on the morrow.

He faced the sinister figures boldly enough. They were only waxworks. So long as he let that thought dominate all others he promised himself that all would be well. It did not, however, save him long from the discomfort occasioned by the waxen stare of Dr Bourdette, which, he knew, was directed upon him from behind. The eyes of the little Frenchman's effigy haunted and tormented him, and he itched with the desire to turn and look.

'Come!' he thought, 'my nerves have started already. If I turn and look at that dressed-up dummy it will be an admission of funk.'

And then another voice in his brain spoke to him.

'It's because you're afraid that you won't turn and look at him.'

The two voices quarrelled silently for a moment or two, and at last Hewson slewed his chair round a little and looked behind him.

Among the many figures standing in stiff, unnatural poses, the effigy of the dreadful little doctor stood out with a queer prominence, perhaps because a steady beam of light beat straight down upon it. Hewson flinched before the parody of mildness which some fiendishly skilled craftsman had managed to convey in wax, met the eyes for one agonized second, and turned again to face the other direction.

'He's only a waxwork like the rest of you,' Hewson muttered defiantly. 'You're all only waxworks.'

They were only waxworks, yes, but waxworks don't move. Not that he had seen the least movement anywhere, but it struck him that, in the moment or two while he had looked behind him, there had been the least subtle change in the grouping of the figures in front. Crippen, for instance, seemed to have turned at least one degree to the left. Or, thought Hewson, perhaps the illusion was due to the fact that he had not slewed his chair back into its exact original position.

Hewson held his breath for a moment, and then drew his courage back to him as a man lifts a weight. He remembered the words of more than one news editor and laughed savagely to himself.

'And they tell me I've got no imagination!' he said beneath his breath.

He took a notebook from his pocket and wrote quickly.

'Mem. – Deathly silence and unearthly stillness of figures. Like being bottom of sea. Hypnotic eyes of Dr Bourdette. Figures seem to move when not being watched.'

He closed the book suddenly over his fingers and looked round quickly and awfully over his right shoulder. He had neither seen nor heard a movement, but it was as if some sixth sense had made him aware of one. He looked straight into the vapid countenance of Lefroy which smiled back as if to say, 'It wasn't I!'

Of course it wasn't he, or any of them; it was his own nerves. Or was it? Hadn't Crippen moved again during that moment when his attention was directed elsewhere? You couldn't trust that little man! Once you took your eyes off him he took advantage of it to shift his position. That was what they were all doing, if he only knew it, he told himself; and half rose out of his chair. This was not quite good enough! He was going. He wasn't going to spend the night with a lot of waxworks which moved while he wasn't looking.

. . . Hewson sat down again. This was very cowardly, and very absurd. They *were* only waxworks and they *couldn't* move; let him hold that thought and all would yet be well. Then why all that silent unrest about him? – a subtle something in the air which did not quite break the silence and happened, whichever way he looked, just beyond the boundaries of his vision.

He swung round quickly to encounter the mild but baleful stare of Dr Bourdette. Then, without warning, he jerked his head back to stare straight at Crippen. Ha! he'd nearly caught Crippen that time! 'You'd better be careful, Crippen – and all the rest of you! If I do see one of you move I'll smash you to pieces! Do you hear?'

He ought to go, he told himself. Already he had experienced enough to write his story, or ten stories, for that matter. Well, then, why not go? The *Morning Echo* would be none the wiser as to how long he had stayed, nor would it care so long as his story was a good one. Yes, but that night watchman upstairs would chaff him. And the manager – one never knew – perhaps the manager would quibble over that five-pound note which he needed so badly. He wondered if Rose were asleep or if she were lying awake and thinking of him. She'd laugh when he told her that he had imagined . . .

This was a little too much! It was bad enough that the waxwork effigies of murderers should move when they weren't being watched, but it was intolerable that they should *breathe*. Somebody was breathing. Or was it his own breath which sounded to him as if it came from a distance? He sat rigid, listening and straining until he exhaled with a long sigh. His own breath after all, or – if not, Something had divined that he was listening and had ceased breathing simultaneously.

Hewson jerked his head swiftly round and looked all about him out of haggard and hunted eyes. Everywhere his gaze encountered the vacant waxen faces, and everywhere he felt that by just some least fraction of a second he had missed seeing a movement of hand or foot, a silent opening or compression of lips, a flicker of eyelids, a look of human intelligence now smoothed out. They were like naughty children in a class, whispering, fidgeting and laughing behind their teacher's back, but blandly innocent when his gaze was turned upon them.

This would not do! This distinctly would not do! He must clutch at something, grip with his mind upon something which belonged essentially to the workaday world, to the daylight London streets. He was Raymond Hewson, an unsuccessful journalist, a living and breathing man, and these figures grouped around him were only dummies, so they could neither move nor whisper. What did it matter if they were supposed to be lifelike effigies of murderers? They were only made of wax and sawdust, and stood there for the entertainment of morbid sightseers and orange-sucking trippers.

That was better! Now what was that funny story which somebody had told him yesterday? . . .

He recalled part of it, but not all, for the gaze of Dr Bourdette urged, challenged, and finally compelled him to turn.

Hewson half-turned, and then swung his chair so as to bring him face to face with the wearer of those dreadful hypnotic eyes. His own eyes were dilated, and his mouth, at first set in a grin of terror, lifted at the corners in a snarl. Then Hewson spoke and woke a hundred sinister echoes.

'You moved, blast you!' he cried. 'Yes, you did, blast you! I saw you!'

Then he sat quite still, staring straight before him, like a man found frozen in the Arctic snows.

Dr Bourdette's movements were leisurely. He stepped off his pedestal with the mincing care of a lady alighting from a bus. The platform stood about two feet from the ground, and above the edge of it a plush-covered rope hung in arc-like curves. Dr Bourdette lifted up the rope until it formed an arch for him to pass under, stepped off the platform and sat down on the edge facing Hewson. Then he nodded and smiled and said, 'Good evening.'

'I need hardly tell you,' he continued, in perfect English in which was traceable only the least foreign accent, 'that not until I overheard the conversation between you and the worthy manager of this establishment did I suspect that I should have the pleasure of a companion here for the night. You cannot move or speak without my bidding, but you can hear me perfectly well. Something tells me that you are – shall I say nervous? My dear sir, have no illusions. I am not one of these contemptible effigies miraculously come to life: I am Dr Bourdette himself.'

He paused, coughed, and shifted his legs.

'Pardon me,' he resumed, 'but I am a little stiff. And let me explain. Circumstances with which I need not fatigue you have made it desirable that I should live in England. I was close to this building this evening when I saw a policeman regarding me a thought too curiously. I guessed that he intended to follow and perhaps ask me embarrassing questions, so I mingled with the crowd and came in here. An extra coin bought my admission to the chamber in which we now meet, and an inspiration showed me a certain means of escape.

'I raised a cry of fire, and when all the fools had rushed to the stairs I stripped my effigy of the caped coat which you behold me wearing, donned it, hid my effigy under the platform at the back and took its place on the pedestal.

'I own that I have since spent a very fatiguing evening, but fortunately I was not always being watched and had opportunities to draw an occasional deep breath and ease the rigidity of my pose. One small boy screamed and exclaimed that he saw me moving. I understand that he was to be whipped and put straight to bed on his return home.

'The manager's description of me, which I had the embarrassment of being compelled to overhear, was biased but not altogether inaccurate. Clearly I am not dead, although it is well that the world thinks otherwise. His account of my hobby, which I have indulged for years, was in the main true although not intelligently expressed. The world is divided between collectors and non-collectors. With the non-collectors we are not concerned. The collectors collect anything, according to their individual tastes, from money to cigarette cards, from moths to match-boxes. I collect throats.'

He paused again and regarded Hewson's throat with interest mingled with disfavour.

'I am obliged to the chance which brought us together tonight,' he continued, 'and perhaps it would seem ungrateful to complain. From motives of personal safety my activities have been somewhat curtailed of late years, and I am glad of this opportunity of gratifying my somewhat unusual whim. But you have a skinny neck, sir, if you will overlook a personal remark. I should never have selected you from choice. I like men with thick necks . . . thick red necks . . .'

He fumbled in an inside pocket and took out something which he tested against a wet forefinger and then proceeded to pass gently to and fro across the palm of his left hand.

'This is a little French razor,' he remarked blandly. 'They are not much used in England, but perhaps you know them? One strops them on wood. The blade, you will observe, is very narrow. They do not cut very deep, but deep enough. In just one little moment you shall see for yourself. I shall ask you the little civil question of all polite barbers: Does the razor suit you, sir?'

He rose up, a diminutive but menacing figure of evil, and approached Hewson with the silent, furtive step of a hunting panther.

'You will have the goodness,' he said, 'to raise your chin a little. Thank you, and a little more. Just a little more. Ah, thank you! . . . *Merci, m'sieur . . . Ah, merci . . . merci . . .*'

Over one end of the chamber was a thick skylight of frosted glass which, by day, let in a few sickly and filtered rays from the floor above. After sunrise these began to mingle with the subdued light from the electric bulbs, and this mingled illumination added a certain ghastliness to a scene which needed no additional touch of horror.

The waxwork figures stood apathetically in their places, waiting to be admired or execrated by the crowds who would presently wander fearfully among them. In their midst, Hewson sat still, leaning far back in his armchair. His chin was uptilted, as if he were waiting to receive attention from a barber, and although there was not a scratch upon his throat, nor anywhere upon his body, he was cold and dead. His previous employers were wrong in having credited him with no imagination.

Dr Bourdette on his pedestal watched the dead man unemotionally. He did not move, nor was he capable of motion. But then, after all, he was only a waxwork.

Mrs Amworth

E. F. Benson

The village of Maxley, where, last summer and autumn, these strange events took place, lies on a heathery and pine-clad upland of Sussex. In all England you could not find a sweeter and saner situation. Should the wind blow from the south, it comes laden with the spices of the sea; to the east high downs protect it from the inclemencies of March; and from the west and north the breezes which reach it travel over miles of aromatic forest and heather. The village itself is insignificant enough in point of population, but rich in amenities and beauty. Half-way down the single street, with its broad road and spacious areas of grass on each side, stands the little Norman church and the antique graveyard long disused: for the rest there are a dozen small, sedate Georgian houses, red-bricked and long-windowed, each with a square of flower-garden in front, and an ampler strip behind; a score of shops, and a couple of score of thatched cottages belonging to labourers on neighbouring estates, complete the entire cluster of its peaceful habitations. The general peace, however, is sadly broken on Saturdays and Sundays, for we lie on one of the main roads between London and Brighton and our quiet street becomes a race-course for flying motor-cars and bicycles. A notice just outside the village begging them to go slowly only seems to encourage them to accelerate their speed, for the road lies open and straight, and there is really no reason why they should do otherwise. By way of protest, therefore, the ladies of Maxley cover their noses and mouths with their handkerchiefs as they see a motor-car approaching, though, as the street is asphalted, they need not really take these precautions against dust. But late on Sunday night the horde of scorchers has passed, and we settle down again to five days of cheerful and leisurely seclusion. Railway strikes which agitate the country so much leave us undisturbed because most of the inhabitants of Maxley never leave it at all.

I am the fortunate possessor of one of these small Georgian houses, and consider myself no less fortunate in having so interesting and stimulating a neighbour as Francis Urcombe, who, the most confirmed of Maxleyites, has not slept away from his house, which stands just opposite to mine in the village street, for nearly two years, at which date, though still in middle life, he resigned his Physiological Professorship at Cambridge University, and devoted himself to the study of those occult and curious phenomena which seem equally to concern the physical and the psychical sides of human nature. Indeed his retirement was not unconnected with his passion for the strange uncharted places that lie on the confines and borders of science, the existence of which is so stoutly denied by the more materialistic minds, for he advocated that all medical students should be obliged to pass some sort of examination in mesmerism, and that one of the tripos papers should be designed to test their knowledge in such subjects as appearances at time of death, haunted houses, vampirism, automatic writing, and possession.

'Of course they wouldn't listen to me,' ran his account of the matter, 'for there is nothing that these seats of learning are so frightened of as knowledge, and the road to knowledge lies in the study of things like these. The functions of the human frame are, broadly speaking, known. They are a country, anyhow, that has been charted and mapped out. But outside that lie huge tracts of undiscovered country, which certainly exist, and the real pioneers of knowledge are those who, at the cost of being derided as credulous and superstitious, want to push on into those misty and probably perilous places. I felt that I could be of more use by setting out without compass or knapsack into the mists than by sitting in a cage like a canary and chirping about what was known. Besides, teaching is very very bad for a man who knows himself only to be a learner: you only need to be a self-conceited ass to teach.'

Here, then, in Francis Urcombe, was a delightful neighbour to one who, like myself, has an uneasy and burning curiosity about what he called the 'misty and perilous places'; and this last spring we had a further and most welcome addition to our pleasant little community, in the person of Mrs Amworth, widow of an Indian civil servant. Her husband had been a judge in the North-West Provinces, and after his death at Peshawar she came back to England, and after a year in London found herself starving for the ampler air and sunshine of the country to take the place of the fogs and griminess of town. She had, too, a special reason for settling in Maxley, since her ancestors up till a hundred years ago had long been native to the place, and in the old churchyard, now disused, are many gravestones bearing her maiden name of Chaston. Big and

energetic, her vigorous and genial personality speedily woke Maxley up
to a higher degree of sociality than it had ever known. Most of us were
bachelors or spinsters or elderly folk not much inclined to exert ourselves
in the expense and effort of hospitality, and hitherto the gaiety of a small
tea-party, with bridge afterwards and goloshes (when it was wet) to trip
home in again for a solitary dinner, was about the climax of our festivities.
But Mrs Amworth showed us a more gregarious way, and set an example
of luncheon-parties and little dinners, which we began to follow. On
other nights when no such hospitality was on foot, a lone man like myself
found it pleasant to know that a call on the telephone to Mrs Amworth's
house not a hundred yards off, and an inquiry as to whether I might come
over after dinner for a game of piquet before bed-time, would probably
evoke a response of welcome. There she would be, with a comrade-like
eagerness for companionship, and there was a glass of port and a cup of
coffee and a cigarette and a game of piquet. She played the piano, too, in
a free and exuberant manner, and had a charming voice and sang to her
own accompaniment; and as the days grew long and the light lingered
late, we played our game in her garden, which in the course of a few
months she had turned from being a nursery for slugs and snails into a
glowing patch of luxuriant blossoming. She was always cheery and jolly;
she was interested in everything, and in music, in gardening, in games of
all sorts was a competent performer. Everybody (with one exception)
liked her, everybody felt her to bring with her the tonic of a sunny day.
That one exception was Francis Urcombe; he, though he confessed he did
not like her, acknowledged that he was vastly interested in her. This
always seemed strange to me, for pleasant and jovial as she was, I could
see nothing in her that could call forth conjecture or intrigued surmise,
so healthy and unmysterious a figure did she present. But of the
genuineness of Urcombe's interest there could be no doubt; one could see
him watching and scrutinizing her. In matter of age, she frankly
volunteered the information that she was forty-five; but her briskness,
her activity, her unravaged skin, her coal-black hair, made it difficult to
believe that she was not adopting an unusual device, and adding ten years
on to her age instead of subtracting them.

Often, also, as our quite unsentimental friendship ripened, Mrs
Amworth would ring me up and propose her advent. If I was busy
writing, I was to give her, so we definitely bargained, a frank negative,
and in answer I could hear her jolly laugh and her wishes for a successful
evening of work. Sometimes, before her proposal arrived, Urcombe
would already have stepped across from his house opposite for a smoke
and a chat, and he, hearing who my intending visitor was, always urged

me to beg her to come. She and I should play our piquet, said he, and he would look on, if we did not object, and learn something of the game. But I doubt whether he paid much attention to it, for nothing could be clearer than that, under that penthouse of forehead and thick eyebrows, his attention was fixed not on the cards, but on one of the players. But he seemed to enjoy an hour spent thus, and often, until one particular evening in July, he would watch her with the air of a man who has some deep problem in front of him. She, enthusiastically keen about our game, seemed not to notice his scrutiny. Then came that evening when, as I see in the light of subsequent events, began the first twitching of the veil that hid the secret horror from my eyes. I did not know it then, though I noticed that thereafter, if she rang up to propose coming round, she always asked not only if I was at leisure, but whether Mr Urcombe was with me. If so, she said, she would not spoil the chat of two old bachelors, and laughingly wished me good night. Urcombe, on this occasion, had been with me for some half-hour before Mrs Amworth's appearance, and had been talking to me about the medieval beliefs concerning vampirism, one of those borderland subjects which he declared had not been sufficiently studied before it had been consigned by the medical profession to the dust-heap of exploded superstitions. There he sat, grim and eager, tracing, with that pellucid clearness which had made him in his Cambridge days so admirable a lecturer, the history of those mysterious visitations. In them all there were the same general features: one of those ghoulish spirits took up its abode in a living man or woman, conferring supernatural powers of bat-like flight and glutting itself with nocturnal blood-feasts. When its host died it continued to dwell in the corpse, which remained undecayed. By day it rested, by night it left the grave and went on its awful errands. No European country in the Middle Ages seemed to have escaped them; earlier yet, parallels were to be found, in Roman and Greek and in Jewish history.

'It's a large order to set all that evidence aside as being moonshine,' he said. 'Hundreds of totally independent witnesses in many ages have testified to the occurrence of these phenomena, and there's no explanation known to me which covers all the facts. And if you feel inclined to say "Why, then, if these are facts, do we not come across them now?" there are two answers I can make you. One is that there were diseases known in the Middle Ages, such as the black death, which were certainly existent then and which have become extinct since, but for that reason we do not assert that such diseases never existed. Just as the black death visited England and decimated the population of Norfolk, so here in this very district about three hundred years ago there was certainly an outbreak of vampirism, and Maxley was the centre of it. My second answer is even more convincing, for I tell you that vampirism is by no means extinct now. An outbreak of it certainly occurred in India a year or two ago.'

At that moment I heard my knocker plied in the cheerful and peremptory manner in which Mrs Amworth is accustomed to announce her arrival, and I went to the door to open it.

'Come in at once,' I said, 'and save me from having my blood curdled. Mr Urcombe has been trying to alarm me.'

Instantly her vital, voluminous presence seemed to fill the room.

'Ah, but how lovely!' she said. 'I delight in having my blood curdled. Go on with your ghost-story, Mr Urcombe. I adore ghost-stories.'

I saw that, as his habit was, he was intently observing her.

'It wasn't a ghost-story exactly,' said he. 'I was only telling our host how vampirism was not extinct yet. I was saying that there was an outbreak of it in India only a few years ago.'

There was a more than perceptible pause, and I saw that, if Urcombe was observing her, she on her side was observing him with fixed eye and parted mouth. Then her jolly laugh invaded that rather tense silence.

'Oh, what a shame!' she said. 'You're not going to curdle my blood at all. Where did you pick up such a tale, Mr Urcombe? I have lived for years in India and never heard a rumour of such a thing. Some story-teller in the bazaars must have invented it: they are famous at that.'

I could see that Urcombe was on the point of saying something further, but checked himself.

'Ah! very likely that was it,' he said.

But something had disturbed our usual peaceful sociability that night, and something had damped Mrs Amworth's usual high spirits. She had no gusto for her piquet, and left after a couple of games. Urcombe had been silent too, indeed he hardly spoke again till she departed.

'That was unfortunate,' he said, 'for the outbreak of – of a very mysterious disease, let us call it, took place at Peshawar where she and her husband were. And –'

'Well?' I asked.

'He was one of the victims of it,' said he. 'Naturally I had quite forgotten that when I spoke.'

The summer was unreasonably hot and rainless, and Maxley suffered much from drought, and also from a plague of big black night-flying gnats, the bite of which was very irritating and virulent. They came sailing in of an evening, settling on one's skin so quietly that one perceived nothing till the sharp stab announced that one had been bitten. They did not bite the hands or face, but chose always the neck and throat

for their feeding-ground, and most of us, as the poison spread, assumed
a temporary goitre. Then about the middle of August appeared the first
of those mysterious cases of illness which our local doctor attributed to
the long-continued heat coupled with the bite of these venomous insects.
The patient was a boy of sixteen or seventeen, the son of Mrs Amworth's
gardener, and the symptoms were an anaemic pallor and a languid
prostration, accompanied by great drowsiness and an abnormal appetite.
He had, too, on his throat two small punctures where, so Dr Ross
conjectured, one of these great gnats had bitten him. But the odd thing
was that there was no swelling or inflammation round the place where he
had been bitten. The heat at this time had begun to abate, but the cooler
weather failed to restore him, and the boy, in spite of the quantity of
good food which he so ravenously swallowed, wasted away to a skin-clad
skeleton.

I met Dr Ross in the street one afternoon about this time, and in answer
to my inquiries about his patient he said that he was afraid the boy was
dying. The case, he confessed, completely puzzled him: some obscure
form of pernicious anaemia was all he could suggest. But he wondered
whether Mr Urcombe would consent to see the boy, on the chance of his
being able to throw some new light on the case, and since Urcombe was
dining with me that night, I proposed to Dr Ross to join us. He could not
do this, but said he would look in later. When he came, Urcombe at once
consented to put his skill at the other's disposal, and together they went
off at once. Being thus shorn of my sociable evening, I telephoned to Mrs
Amworth to know if I might inflict myself on her for an hour. Her answer
was a welcoming affirmative, and between piquet and music the hour
lengthened itself into two. She spoke of the boy who was lying so
desperately and mysteriously ill, and told me that she had often been to
see him, taking him nourishing and delicate food. But today – and her
kind eyes moistened as she spoke – she was afraid she had paid her last
visit. Knowing the antipathy between her and Urcombe, I did not tell her
that he had been called into consultation; and when I returned home she
accompanied me to my door, for the sake of a breath of night air, and in
order to borrow a magazine which contained an article on gardening
which she wished to read.

'Ah, this delicious night air,' she said, luxuriously sniffing in the
coolness. 'Night air and gardening are the great tonics. There is nothing
so stimulating as bare contact with rich mother earth. You are never so
fresh as when you have been grubbing in the soil – black hands, black
nails, and boots covered with mud.' She gave her great jovial laugh.

'I'm a glutton for air and earth,' she said. 'Positively I look forward to death, for then I shall be buried and have the kind earth all round me. No leaden caskets for me – I have given explicit directions. But what shall I do about air? Well, I suppose one can't have everything. The magazine? A thousand thanks, I will faithfully return it. Good night: garden and keep your windows open, and you won't have anaemia.'

'I always sleep with my windows open,' said I.

I went straight up to my bedroom, of which one of the windows looks out over the street, and as I undressed I thought I heard voices talking outside not far away. But I paid no particular attention, put out my lights, and falling asleep plunged into the depths of a most horrible dream, distortedly suggested, no doubt, by my last words with Mrs Amworth. I dreamed that I woke, and found that both my bedroom windows were shut. Half-suffocating I dreamed that I sprang out of bed, and went across to open them. The blind over the first was drawn down, and pulling it up I saw, with the indescribable horror of incipient nightmare, Mrs Amworth's face suspended close to the pane in the darkness outside, nodding and smiling at me. Pulling down the blind again to keep that terror out, I rushed to the second window on the other side of the room, and there again was Mrs Amworth's face. Then the panic came upon me in full blast; here was I suffocating in the airless room, and whichever window I opened Mrs Amworth's face would float in, like those noiseless black gnats that bit before one was awake. The nightmare rose to screaming point, and with strangled yells I awoke to find my room cool and quiet with both windows open and blinds up and a half-moon high in its course, casting an oblong of tranquil light on the floor. But even when I was awake the horror persisted, and I lay tossing and turning. I must have slept long before the nightmare seized me, for now it was nearly day, and soon in the east the drowsy eyelids of morning began to lift.

I was scarcely downstairs next morning – for after the dawn I slept late – when Urcombe rang up to know if he might see me immediately. He came in, grim and preoccupied, and I noticed that he was pulling on a pipe that was not even filled.

'I want your help,' he said, 'and so I must tell you first of all what happened last night. I went round with the little doctor to see his patient, and found him just alive, but scarcely more. I instantly diagnosed in my own mind what this anaemia, unaccountable by any other explanation, meant. The boy is the prey of a vampire.'

He put his empty pipe on the breakfast-table, by which I had just sat down, and folded his arms, looking at me steadily from under his overhanging brows.

'Now about last night,' he said. 'I insisted that he should be moved from his father's cottage into my house. As we were carrying him on a stretcher, whom should we meet but Mrs Amworth? She expressed shocked surprise that we were moving him. Now why do you think she did that?'

With a start of horror, as I remembered my dream that night before, I felt an idea come into my mind so preposterous and unthinkable that I instantly turned it out again.

'I haven't the smallest idea,' I said.

'Then listen, while I tell you about what happened later. I put out all lights in the room where the boy lay, and watched. One window was a little open, for I had forgotten to close it, and about midnight I heard something outside, trying apparently to push it farther open. I guessed who it was – yes, it was full twenty feet from the ground – and I peeped round the corner of the blind. Just outside was the face of Mrs Amworth and her hand was on the frame of the window. Very softly I crept close, and then banged the window down, and I think I just caught the tip of one of her fingers.'

'But it's impossible,' I cried. 'How could she be floating in the air like that? And what had she come for? Don't tell me such –'

Once more, with closer grip, the remembrance of my nightmare seized me.

'I am telling you what I saw,' said he. 'And all night long, until it was nearly day, she was fluttering outside, like some terrible bat, trying to gain admittance. Now put together various things I have told you.'

He began checking them off on his fingers.

'Number one,' he said: 'there was an outbreak of disease similar to that which this boy is suffering from at Peshawar, and her husband died of it. Number two: Mrs Amworth protested against my moving the boy to my house. Number three: she, or the demon that inhabits her body, a creature powerful and deadly, tries to gain admittance. And add this, too: in medieval times there was an epidemic of vampirism here at Maxley. The vampire, so the accounts run, was found to be Elizabeth Chaston . . . I see you remember Mrs Amworth's maiden name. Finally, the boy is stronger this morning. He would certainly not have been alive if he had been visited again. And what do you make of it?'

There was a long silence, during which I found this incredible horror assuming the hues of reality.

'I have something to add,' I said, 'which may or may not bear on it. You say that the – the spectre went away shortly before dawn.'

'Yes.'

I told him of my dream, and he smiled grimly.

'Yes, you did well to awake,' he said. 'That warning came from your subconscious self, which never wholly slumbers, and cried out to you of deadly danger. For two reasons, then, you must help me: one to save others, the second to save yourself.'

'What do you want me to do?' I asked.

'I want you first of all to help me in watching this boy, and ensuring that she does not come near him. Eventually I want you to help me in tracking the thing down, in exposing and destroying it. It is not human: it is an incarnate fiend. What steps we shall have to take I don't yet know.'

It was now eleven of the forenoon, and presently I went across to his house for a twelve-hour vigil while he slept, to come on duty again that night, so that for the next twenty-four hours either Urcombe or myself was always in the room where the boy, now getting stronger every hour, was lying. The day following was Saturday and a morning of brilliant, pellucid weather, and already when I went across to his house to resume my duty the stream of motors down to Brighton had begun. Simultaneously I saw Urcombe with a cheerful face, which boded good news of his patient, coming out of his house, and Mrs Amworth, with a gesture of salutation to me and a basket in her hand, walking up the broad strip of grass which bordered the road. There we all three met. I noticed (and saw that Urcombe noticed it too) that one finger of her left hand was bandaged.

'Good morning to you both,' said she. 'And I hear your patient is doing well, Mr Urcombe. I have come to bring him a bowl of jelly, and to sit with him for an hour. He and I are great friends. I am overjoyed at his recovery.'

Urcombe paused a moment, as if making up his mind, and then shot out a pointing finger at her.

'I forbid that,' he said. 'You shall not sit with him or see him. And you know the reason as well as I do.'

I have never seen so horrible a change pass over a human face as that which now blanched hers to the colour of a grey mist. She put up her hand as if to shield herself from that pointing finger, which drew the sign of the cross in the air, and shrank back cowering on to the road. There was a wild hoot from a horn, a grinding of brakes, a shout – too late – from a passing car, and one long scream suddenly cut short. Her body rebounded from the roadway after the first wheel had gone over it, and the second followed. It lay there, quivering and twitching, and was still.

She was buried three days afterwards in the cemetery outside Maxley, in accordance with the wishes she had told me that she had devised about her interment, and the shock which her sudden and awful death had caused to the little community began by degrees to pass off. To two people only, Urcombe and myself, the horror of it was mitigated from the first by the nature of the relief that her death brought; but, naturally enough, we kept our own counsel, and no hint of what greater horror had been thus averted was ever let slip. But, oddly enough, so it seemed to me, he was still not satisfied about something in connection with her, and would give no answer to my questions on the subject. Then as the days of a tranquil mellow September and the October that followed began to drop away like the leaves of the yellowing trees, his uneasiness relaxed. But before the entry of November the seeming tranquillity broke into hurricane.

I had been dining one night at the far end of the village, and about eleven o'clock was walking home again. The moon was of an unusual brilliance, rendering all that it shone on as distinct as in some etching. I had just come opposite the house which Mrs Amworth had occupied, where there was a board up telling that it was to let, when I heard the click of her front gate, and next moment I saw, with a sudden chill and quaking of my very spirit, that she stood there. Her profile, vividly illuminated, was turned to me, and I could not be mistaken in my identification of her. She appeared not to see me (indeed the shadow of the yew hedge in front of her garden enveloped me in its blackness) and she went swiftly across the road, and entered the gate of the house directly opposite. There I lost sight of her completely.

My breath was coming in short pants as if I had been running – and now indeed I ran, with fearful backward glances, along the hundred yards that separated me from my house and Urcombe's. It was to his that my flying steps took me, and next minute I was within.

'What have you come to tell me?' he asked. 'Or shall I guess?'

'You can't guess,' said I.

'No; it's no guess. She has come back and you have seen her. Tell me about it.'

I gave him my story.

'That's Major Pearsall's house,' he said. 'Come back with me there at once.'

'But what can we do?' I asked.

'I've no idea. That's what we have got to find out.'

A minute later, we were opposite the house. When I had passed it before, it was all dark; now lights gleamed from a couple of windows upstairs. Even as we faced it, the front door opened, and next moment Major Pearsall emerged from the gate. He saw us and stopped.

'I'm on my way to Dr Ross,' he said quickly. 'My wife has been taken suddenly ill. She had been in bed an hour when I came upstairs, and I found her white as a ghost and utterly exhausted. She had been to sleep, it seemed – But you will excuse me.'

'One moment, Major,' said Urcombe. 'Was there any mark on her throat?'

'How did you guess that?' said he. 'There was: one of those beastly gnats must have bitten her twice there. She was streaming with blood.'

'And there's someone with her?' asked Urcombe.

'Yes, I roused her maid.'

He went off, and Urcombe turned to me. 'I know now what we have to do,' he said. 'Change your clothes, and I'll join you at your house.'

'What is it?' I asked.

'I'll tell you on our way. We're going to the cemetery.'

He carried a pick, a shovel, and a screwdriver when he rejoined me, and wore round his shoulders a long coil of rope. As we walked, he gave me the outlines of the ghastly hour that lay before us.

'What I have to tell you,' he said, 'will seem to you now too fantastic for credence, but before dawn we shall see whether it outstrips reality. By a most fortunate happening, you saw the spectre, the astral body, whatever you choose to call it, of Mrs Amworth, going on its grisly business, and therefore, beyond doubt, the vampire spirit which abode in her during life animates her again in death. That is not exceptional – indeed, all these weeks since her death I have been expecting it. If I am right, we shall find her body undecayed and untouched by corruption.'

'But she has been dead nearly two months,' said I.

'If she had been dead two years it would still be so, if the vampire has possession of her. So remember: whatever you see done, it will be done not to her, who in the natural course would now be feeding the grasses above her grave, but to a spirit of untold evil and malignancy, which gives a phantom life to her body.'

'But what shall I see done?' said I.

'I will tell you. We know that now, at this moment, the vampire clad in her mortal semblance is out; dining out. But it must get back before dawn, and it will pass into the material form that lies in her grave. We must wait for that, and then with your help I shall dig up her body. If I am right, you will look on her as she was in life, with the full vigour of the dreadful nutriment she has received pulsing in her veins. And then, when dawn has come, and the vampire cannot leave the lair of her body, I shall strike her with this' – and he pointed to his pick – 'through the

heart, and she, who comes to life again only with the animation the fiend
gives her, she and her hellish partner will be dead indeed. Then we must
bury her again, delivered at last.'

We had come to the cemetery, and in the brightness of the moonshine
there was no difficulty in identifying her grave. It lay some twenty yards
from the small chapel, in the porch of which, obscured by shadow, we
concealed ourselves. From there we had a clear and open sight of the
grave, and now we must wait till its infernal visitor returned home. The
night was warm and windless, yet even if a freezing wind had been raging
I think I should have felt nothing of it, so intense was my preoccupation
as to what the night and dawn would bring. There was a bell in the turret
of the chapel that struck the quarters of the hour, and it amazed me to
find how swiftly the chimes succeeded one another.

The moon had long set, but a twilight of stars shone in a clear sky,
when five o'clock of the morning sounded from the turret. A few minutes
more passed, and then I felt Urcombe's hand softly nudging me; and
looking out in the direction of his pointing finger, I saw that the form of
a woman, tall and large in build, was approaching from the right.
Noiselessly, with a motion more of gliding and floating than walking,
she moved across the cemetery to the grave which was the centre of our
observation. She moved round it as if to be certain of its identity, and for
a moment stood directly facing us. In the greyness to which now my eyes
had grown accustomed, I could easily see her face, and recognize its
features.

She drew her hand across her mouth as if wiping it, and broke into a
chuckle of such laughter as made my hair stir on my head. Then she
leaped on to the grave, holding her hands high above her head, and inch
by inch disappeared into the earth. Urcombe's hand was laid on my arm,
in an injunction to keep still, but now he removed it.

'Come,' he said.

With pick and shovel and rope we went to the grave. The earth was
light and sandy, and soon after six struck we had delved down to the
coffin lid. With his pick he loosened the earth round it, and, adjusting the
rope through the handles by which it had been lowered, we tried to raise
it. This was a long and laborious business, and the light had begun to
herald day in the east before we had it out, and lying by the side of the
grave. With his screwdriver he loosed the fastenings of the lid, and slid it
aside, and standing there we looked on the face of Mrs Amworth. The
eyes, once closed in death, were open, the cheeks were flushed with
colour, the red, full-lipped mouth seemed to smile.

'One blow and it is all over,' he said. 'You need not look.'

Even as he spoke he took up the pick again, and, laying the point of it on her left breast, measured his distance. And though I knew what was coming I could not look away . . .

He grasped the pick in both hands, raised it an inch or two for the taking of his aim, and then with full force brought it down on her breast. A fountain of blood, though she had been dead so long, spouted high in the air, falling with the thud of a heavy splash over the shroud, and simultaneously from those red lips came one long, appalling cry, swelling up like some hooting siren, and dying away again. With that, instantaneous as a lightning flash, came the touch of corruption on her face, the colour of it faded to ash, the plump cheeks fell in, the mouth dropped.

'Thank God, that's over,' said he, and without pause slipped the coffin lid back into its place.

Day was coming fast now, and, working like men possessed, we lowered the coffin into its place again, and shovelled the earth over it . . . The birds were busy with their earliest pipings as we went back to Maxley.

The Reptile

Augustus Muir

'I've got a headache,' said James MacAndrew.

'Better lie down,' said Dr Hardman.

'Aye, sir, I suppose so,' assented MacAndrew, moodily.

'You see,' explained Dr Hardman, 'we're going over the Rauch Museum this afternoon. A museum's the most tiring place in the world, if you aren't fit. Simply make your head worse. With a bad headache nothing can be either pleasant or instructive. Better lie down, Mac-Andrew.'

'I think that, sir,' muttered James MacAndrew, 'I'll just go.' He made his way slowly upstairs to his bedroom while Dr Hardman, Lecturer on German Language and Literature at a Scottish university, hurried off across the lounge of the Berlin hotel to collect the other members of his party. To take a group of students from his Honours Class for a week in Berlin was Dr Hardman's principal joy in the Christmas vacation. For nearly twelve hours a day he expatiated to them – all of them very Scottish and very shy. Dr Hardman, that little, genial, chubby man, was an enthusiast; he packed the days and evenings with pilgrimages and talk, till you would have thought there was nothing more in Berlin to see or to know. He was vaguely irritated with MacAndrew for having a headache.

But MacAndrew, in the secret interstices of his soul, regarded his headache in the light of something Heaven-sent. His eyes were sick of the sight of art galleries; he had almost acquired a crick in the neck from gazing up at pompous statues; and he was weary of those arid journeys to gaze upon a commonplace street, notable only by the fact that it was garnished with the name of some author or soldier who had a column and a half of small type in German dictionaries of biography. With luck, the afternoon in his bed would see the headache gone; and, in any case, the respite would be pleasant. Wincing a little as he stooped, MacAndrew removed his boots, pulled up the tawdry pink quilt, and in ten minutes he was asleep.

MacAndrew was awakened by a firm touch on the shoulder. He sat up in bed. Two men were in the room. Then MacAndrew remembered that he had lain down with a headache, which was now nearly gone. But what in the name of creation, he wondered, were two strangers doing in the bedroom?

'We want you,' said one of the men.

He was a German: MacAndrew guessed by his appearance rather than his accent. The man was squat, with a broad head, hair cut short and standing upright, and thick, uneven features accentuated by a rough and pitted skin. He was smiling down at MacAndrew, but MacAndrew did not like the smile. The other man, at whom MacAndrew cast a quick glance, was a different type: thin and hollow-cheeked, with a nervous mouth behind a tiny, trim, fair moustache and beard, and below the corners of his mouth there were two smooth patches of skin, the size of shillings, on which beard did not grow. He seemed anxious to keep in the background, but his luminous brown eyes did not waver from MacAndrew, sitting up, rather tousled, on the bed.

'What is it ye want?' said MacAndrew as gruffly as politeness would allow: there might be some good excuse for the intrusion. Now that he came to think of it, he had a notion that he had seen the two men before. But where, he could not remember.

'I have made a mistake,' said the squat man. 'It is not we who want you. There is a friend who has sent us. We will take you to him – we have a motor-car waiting downstairs.'

'Who is he?' demanded MacAndrew, puzzled. 'There's nobody hurt, eh? It's not Dr Hardman?'

The squat man shook his head. 'There is no one hurt. It is a friend you do not know, but will you please come quickly – it is urgent!'

MacAndrew pondered for a moment.

'It seems a daft-like affair,' he said cautiously. 'Somebody wants to see me, ye say? Well, what's his name?'

The man with the fair beard approached the bedside eagerly. 'It will be to your advantage,' he exclaimed. 'But you must come now – or it may be too late. We have instructions to make haste.'

'H'm,' muttered MacAndrew doubtfully. 'Is it far?'

'In the motor-car – no,' declared the squat man. 'We will go quick – you will be back very soon. That is so?' He turned to his companion for confirmation.

'Soon, certainly – you will be back before an hour,' he continued hastily. 'It is to your own advantage that we have come. Our friend is waiting. The interview will be short, and you will not be occupied many minutes. And listen! You will be well paid – you will be rewarded highly – for such a small favour.'

'Oh, a favour, is it?' said MacAndrew. 'Well, I want to know more about this favour. What d'ye want with me – I mean, what does this friend of yours want?'

The squat man was about to speak, but his companion waved him back, and again approached the bed. MacAndrew flung aside the quilt, and put his stockinged feet to the floor.

'There is little time to spare, but I will explain!'

It was then that MacAndrew remembered where he had seen the men before; a gesture, a shrug, a glance, an attitude – something suddenly recalled them vividly to his mind. They had been sipping a drink downstairs in the shabby hotel vestibule before lunch. He remembered, too, how they had been watching the passers-by with a certain curiosity, and how he had casually put them down as visitors interested, like himself, in the passing pageant of Berlin life. Why hadn't they tackled him before, if it was so urgent; or had they only noticed him after lunch as he turned to go upstairs to his room? In any case, they were probably mistaking him for somebody else. He was about to put a question on that point when the fair man proceeded:

'It is a very small favour, indeed. And, as I have said, it will not take many minutes. It may seem strange to you, but it would not be so if you knew the explanation. Our friend wishes a photograph of you. That is all.'

MacAndrew glared incredulously. 'A photo? A photo of me? What does he want with a photo of me?'

'I am sorry,' said the squat man. 'I cannot answer your question.'

'And do ye think I'll come a footstep till ye do?' returned MacAndrew tartly.

'But surely, if it is a matter –'

'Ye're wasting your breath, both of ye,' said MacAndrew roughly. 'My own impression is that you're mixing me up with somebody else. My name's MacAndrew. James MacAndrew.'

'Your name is of no consequence,' said the squat man, with a little bow. 'It is your appearance that matters. We are fortunate to have found you. As a matter of fact, you have an amazing resemblance to somebody – so strong that in a photograph it would appear to be the same person.'

'Oh!' said MacAndrew slowly. 'Then I would like to know what this friend of yours is going to do with the photograph! Aye, and I want to know who is the man ye say I resemble!'

'His name does not matter,' said the squat man.

'But how do I know that this isn't some plan to do him harm? Eh?' MacAndrew looked in suspicion from one to the other.

'No one can harm him,' the fair man said quietly. 'He is dead.'

'Dead?' MacAndrew thought for a moment. 'Then why all the fuss about – ?'

'It is a matter of vital importance for our friend,' said the squat man, with warmth. 'He must have a photograph of the dead man today. Today, do you hear? I cannot explain the purpose, but you must believe me – it is of vital importance. And he is willing to pay you for the favour. Look, here is a hundred marks.' As he spoke he drew a note from his pocket and held it out. 'We promise that you will receive another hundred marks from our friend immediately the photograph is taken. And we promise that you will be back here within an hour. Can any offer be fairer?'

The two men eagerly scanned MacAndrew's face. 'You're a couple of queer fish,' was his first thought. And this photo business was queerer still. The story might be true, or it might not. What earthly purpose could there be in having a photograph of him or, rather, of the dead man he so closely resembled? To say the least, it was unusual, this extraordinary offer: it was something quite out of the common rut of MacAndrew's experiences. Of course he wouldn't go; but their amazing request would be something to tell Dr Hardman at dinner – how prolific would be the little professor's gesticulations! And now, to get rid of the men without further fuss: that was the problem before him. The squat man was shoving the hundred-mark note in his direction; the other was tugging the point of his yellow beard nervously. A hundred marks – nearly five pounds. Ten pounds altogether for one hour: not bad going for a fellow so persistently near the rocks as he was. Of course it might be lies, all of it; there might be dirty work; there might be a hard knock or two; well, he would look after himself. Besides, this was broad daylight – a quarter to three on a sunny, winter afternoon. He got to his feet.

'I'll come,' said MacAndrew, suddenly holding out his hand.

'Good! Good!' cried the fair man, excitedly. 'I thank you –'

'If you don't mind,' said MacAndrew, stolidly, 'I'll have the other hundred marks now, before we start. Your friend might forget about it afterwards in his hurry.'

The two men glanced at each other. The fair man nodded, and the other drew a second banknote from his pocket. With care, he laid both notes on MacAndrew's outstretched hand.

'Ah, you English! You English!' he remarked, with a dry laugh.

'I'm no English,' declared MacAndrew, with pride. 'I'm Scottish.'

'Ah!' They nodded and smiled wryly.

'And now,' said MacAndrew, 'I'll see ye both downstairs in a couple of minutes.' He held open his bedroom door.

When MacAndrew reached the vestibule the two men were not in sight. He was about to sit down in one of the spindly wickerwork armchairs and wait, but it occurred to him that he might see them if he strolled out to the front of the hotel. At the door he caught sight of the squat man in the street. With a quick gesture to him, the man hurried off. Thirty yards away, over the heads of the people on the pavement, MacAndrew could see a closed car standing by the kerb.

The squat man held the door open. His companion was already inside, sitting back in the corner. The door slammed; the squat man leapt beside the driver; the car moved off. MacAndrew smiled grimly.

It was a novel sensation, this. To sit here in a motor-car beside a man whom he suspected of having uttered a bundle of lies, in a city with which he was not familiar, and to ride calmly away without the least idea of what he was going to do: that intrigued MacAndrew. It would indeed make a rich tale for Dr Hardman at dinner – aye, richer than he had intended, for at first he had not meant to come. On second thoughts, he did not altogether disbelieve the photograph story; but what was behind it? If it looked like dirty work, if it came to blows – which was possible, though unlikely – well, he would crumple up these two sprats with one big, bony hand. And if it was his money they were after – if they were mean thieves – he had tricked them nicely. For while they awaited him downstairs, he had cleared his pockets and, with proper caution, locked away everything, including the banknotes. He smiled as he recalled his foresight. But he strongly suspected that their game was something quite different.

They had told him the truth about the car, at any rate; it was swiftly threading through the crowded streets like a mouse through a stubble-field. He had no idea of their direction; but he observed that they were coming first to the suburbs, and then into country roads. It seemed a queer place to find a photographer, but MacAndrew made no comment. The car, after many turns, went down a lane and, at a large wooden gate, drew up.

MacAndrew had an impression of a dismal house, with tangled paths.

They hurried in. It seemed to be a side door they entered, for the passage inside was dark and had several bends; and then MacAndrew found himself ushered into a small room. The room was well furnished, but was thick with dust. The man with the fair beard had not accompanied them.

'Look here,' said MacAndrew suddenly, 'where is this you've taken me to?'

The squat man's eyes flickered to him quickly, but the expression on his heavy face did not alter by a line. He pushed a box of cigarettes across the table.

'You must ask no questions. That was agreed. And if it was not agreed, it is agreed now. You have accepted his money. You have been well paid for a simple favour –'

MacAndrew rose. 'But what if I refuse to go on with it? If I tell ye that there's something about this business that's not to my liking?'

'You talk nonsense,' said the squat man. 'Besides, an agreement is an agreement.'

'Take back his dirty money!' shouted MacAndrew, his hand going to his inside pocket. Then he paused awkwardly, remembering that the money was at the hotel. The squat man smiled at his discomfiture.

'Ye can come back with me to my room now,' cried MacAndrew. 'Ye'll have every cent of it –'

'There is no going back,' said the squat man, slowly. 'We hold you to your promise. For one hour your services are – his.'

'We'll see about that,' muttered MacAndrew, grimly, buttoning his jacket.

The squat man glanced out of the window in the twilight, and smiled again. Following his gaze, MacAndrew could see the large wooden gate where they had entered. Beside it stood two men, each of them as big and powerful as MacAndrew himself.

So that was the game! He was a prisoner, a prisoner for one hour. Up to this point, MacAndrew's faculties had been on the rack to try and penetrate to the truth about their motives; but now he flung all speculation to the winds and, with a quick movement, leapt past the squat man, threw open the door, and made into the passage.

The passage was dark, and bent at sharp angles, but he remembered with fair accuracy the way he had come. There had been two doors in the passage, one open, the other closed.

MacAndrew made for the first door and dashed through. Somebody passed him in the darkness. He did not anticipate any real opposition till he reached the wooden gate outside. And even then, if he took these two burly fellows with a rush, he had little doubt he could get clear. Many a time in the Rugby field he had broken through a cordon of such fellows, leaving them splayed out behind him . . . MacAndrew blundered into the second door. It had stood open as they came in; someone had closed it. To his touch it swung back. MacAndrew moved forward. He stumbled against something that felt like a table. MacAndrew stretched out his arms. When he failed to touch the wall on either side, he realized that he was no longer in the passage, but in a room. Behind him he heard the door softly shut.

MacAndrew stood still, breathing quickly. He did not doubt for a moment that this was a trap; the door clicking gently shut behind him told him plainly that he had been meant to enter here. He turned and groped back. As he expected, the door was locked.

Like a thunder-cloud MacAndrew's wrath burst forth. He reviled himself for a fool; for only a fool – and a young fool at that – would have run his head so blindly into such a business. If he had been plausibly and amiably approached in the hotel lounge, he knew he would have refused to come; but his curiosity had been spurred by the blunt and urgent manner of their introduction. Because the whole affair had had the semblance of a challenge to his self-confidence – to his Scottish ability to look after himself – and because of the pure adventure and unusualness of it and the good money in his hand, he had fallen. He had fallen, and here he was, a prisoner, serving their obscure purpose in some obscurer way. MacAndrew drew back and threw his twelve-and-a-half stone of brawn against the door. Gritting his teeth in an access of fury, he hurled his weight again and again at the panels. The door did not budge.

He felt in his pocket for a match, but as he did so he closed his eyes and almost staggered. The room had suddenly been filled with a blinding light. It was like the flash of a photographer's flare. So it *was* a photo they wanted, these swine! As he opened his dazzled eyes he saw the room around him. And he realized that he was wrong about the photograph; their story was lies, after all. They had merely switched on the electric light; but it had happened so unexpectedly that it had given for a moment the fictitious effect of one vivid flash. Slowly he grew accustomed to the light. And MacAndrew's eyes went straight to a couch in the corner.

Motionless on the couch there lay, under a long white sheet, the lineaments of a human form.

The stillness of death was on that figure. In his throat MacAndrew stifled a gasp.

What devilry was this he was involved in? Why had he been brought here? MacAndrew looked quickly around him. A carpet, a chair, a table, and that couch; on the table a man's hat, gloves, stick; heavy shutters padlocked across the window; a curtain masking a second door: that was all the room possessed – that, and the rigid form below the sheet. Like the other, the door behind the curtain was locked; they had forgotten nothing.

Did they mean him to look? Well, he wouldn't. He sat down at the table and waited. A chilling suspicion rose in his mind that it was someone he knew who was below that sheet. That would be why they had meant him to look. Well, he wouldn't; he wouldn't look. If they were watching him from some hidden cranny, they would be disappointed. MacAndrew took out his case and lit a cigarette. It meant a more dreadful effort of will than he had foreseen to keep the lighted match from trembling a little, but he succeeded. At any rate, they would suffer the chagrin of observing his carefree manner. MacAndrew could not explain why he felt he was being watched; but as the moments passed, the impression strengthened.

The moments passed, and to refrain from looking grew more desperately difficult. What if it were someone he knew? Perhaps they would keep him here, just like this, in this locked and shuttered room, till he had whipped up his courage to cross to the couch. But it needed even more courage to sit where he was and quietly smoke. With his determination to be calm, to be casual, the cigarette dropped from his fingers on the bare boards of the table. He was in the act of picking it up when his eye was again attracted by the figure below the sheet. The figure had moved. It was as if the body had drawn in one long, slow, uneasy breath. MacAndrew's cigarette lay unheeded, to burn a brown weal on the table and send in the air its thin waving spear of smoke. With quick strides he was across the room. He threw back the white sheet.

The figure he looked down upon was that of a young woman. The eyes were closed; the lips were parted; her body and limbs were pinioned with tough cord. As he watched, her lips quivered, and a long breath was drawn slowly in, followed by short gasps, as if she were awakening from sleep. Then he saw her eyelids flicker; the whites of her eyes appeared; and he could hear a soft, sickly moan. To MacAndrew the thing was patent. She had undoubtedly been drugged, and they had bound her and carried her here. She was now looking up at him in a dazed way, as if she were not quite certain he was there, and her eyes drooped shut again.

MacAndrew stepped back. It was all incomprehensible. That the figure below the sheet was a girl, and alive, though in a state of stupor, made the tangle of events more puzzling. He could see no purpose, no meaning; nothing to save the perverted designs of pure brutality. The first thing to do was obviously to cut this girl loose; time enough to consider their escape when she had come to her senses. His right hand went into his trousers pocket for his penknife. Get her circulation back, let her breathe more freely, and she could soon recover. His hand, in his pocket, was disentangling the penknife from his bunch of keys, when a rustle across the room made him swing round. Behind the curtain, where a minute or two ago had been a locked door, there was a movement. He heard the sound of the door closing softly. MacAndrew's eyes widened; he found it difficult to credit his senses. Crawling from behind the curtain was a large snake.

The snake looked about five feet long, but might, perhaps, have been less. MacAndrew, in his first high flush of horror, could not judge. In the middle, it was, perhaps, as thick as his wrist. The eyes were like two pinpricks of light; the skin was of a mottled pattern, and on anything but the lithe body of a snake would have been beautiful. It began to move slowly across the carpet; its head, three inches above the floor, was swaying vaguely.

MacAndrew took some time to recover from the paralysing grip of repulsion and surprise. He felt as though the blood pulsing through his veins had flowed in turn through fire and ice; and the raw physical sensations of fear, before it has been tempered by reason, left him momentarily weak. He found himself unconsciously slashing at the girl's bonds with his penknife, but with his mind he was watching the reptile.

MacAndrew stooped quickly and lifted the girl. Her head fell limply back. The snake made its way slowly across the room, passing underneath the table, till it reached the wall. Then it turned towards the couch and paused, its head still swaying from side to side, as if to music. But MacAndrew could hear no music. He could see its insignificant eyes, bright with evil, fixed on him, as he stood beside the couch with the body of the girl drooping and plastic in his arms. It came forward again. It was drawing nearer.

With a sudden movement, MacAndrew made out of the corner where the couch stood. He reached the table, quickly laid the girl upon it, then, exerting all his strength, pushed it into the opposite corner of the room. It was the only temporary place of safety he could devise. MacAndrew picked up the walking stick from the table and, grasping it firmly, turned to face the reptile.

It was still moving inch by inch towards the couch, now and then raising its head higher, and lowering it to continue the rhythmic sway. It came round in a slow circle, as if to explore the confines of the chamber. It seemed to be disregarding their presence. But when it faced them again,

MacAndrew saw the black glitter of its eye. In the horror of these moments as he faced it, the truth emerged mistily in his thick brain. The girl and himself were obviously in the hands of some lunatic: a lunatic whose debased satisfactions were knit up with the idea of death: death, and the more terrible the better. That hollow-eyed creature with the fair beard, probably he had wealth; and the other was his toady, fleecing him while he pandered to him. Death: and better still, the death of a foreigner, and of a foreign girl: let the foreigner fight for both their lives, and let them both perish in horror and in agony.

Behind him, on the table, the girl's breath was coming in quick stresses, interpolated by gentle choking sighs. He glanced round. Her eyelashes were parted, but she saw nothing. She had turned over her head on her flaccid arm. MacAndrew put his hand behind him, and pushed her as far as he could from the edge of the table. The stick, in the fingers of his other hand, quivered.

The snake was near him, now; it was time to act. MacAndrew took a step forward and hit out with all his might. He felt a sudden surge of dread as he realized that he had misjudged the distance by an inch. He staggered and almost fell before he recovered his balance from the abortive blow. The snake came towards him; it seemed to be almost at his feet; and with a gasp MacAndrew swung the stick back, putting his full force into the return stroke. He was just in time. The end of the stick got home behind the reptile's head, and it went writhing across the floor. MacAndrew watched it slide below the couch. Then it crawled back into the open, making the same wide circle as before, but moving more quickly, raising and lowering its head, and all the time coming nearer to him.

This time MacAndrew went out to meet it. He swung his stick, measuring the distance carefully with his eye. He realized that wild lunges were useless. It was vital that he reach the mark with every blow. If he were successful in striking it in the same place behind the head, there was a chance of dazing it. He gave a gasp of satisfaction as the second blow went home. The reptile coiled back in a mass, and the head shot out viciously. MacAndrew hit again; and again he felt the stick jar in his hand as the snake spun over on the carpet. But in a flash it had straightened out, and came round once more in a curve, its head making quick, angry jerks from side to side, its eyes glittering.

In moments of acute emotion, the human brain plays strange tricks; a second seems an hour, and the sizes of things are queerly altered. MacAndrew thought of how birds are lured to sudden doom, impotent in the green fire of an adder's eye. The snake in front of him took on strangely larger proportions, and the weapon in his hand seemed but a wisp of straw. MacAndrew shook himself, conscious that his nerve would give way with the static stress of prolonged inaction, and went forward again, and again hit out, flinging all his power and craft into the stroke. The reptile curled over on the carpet, its tail lashing upwards. Then, with a swift lunge, MacAndrew seized up the chair that lay toppled against the wall.

His chance came the next moment. Exerting every muscle, he crashed down the chair on the ugly head, leaping back to avoid the whipping tail, jumping in to strike at every opportunity. A sense of triumph gave power to his blows. Then he flung the chair down. The tail whirled up: the mottled body curled and writhed round the stout wooden legs; but its head was pinioned by the chair-back, and all his weight was pressing on it. The next moment its head was below his heel, and with joy he heard the crunch.

Dazed, he watched the coils relax; they slipped to the floor with a soft thud. MacAndrew kicked aside the chair. The snake did not move. Still dazed, and by force of habit, MacAndrew suddenly stamped on his cigarette, which smouldered on the carpet. He was vaguely surprised that it was still burning. It seemed an eternity since he had put it into his mouth with bravado, and lit it with that defiant flourish. He leant against the mantelpiece, feeling faint. Putting his hand to his face, he found it wet, and he realized that his body was quivering, and damp with cold sweat.

MacAndrew was dimly conscious of a door opening. In front of him he saw the squat man and the man with the fair beard. He thought the fair man's face was puckering in a horrible smile, but he was not certain. At the moment he was not certain of anything, except that the snake was dead, and he had killed it.

The fair man was talking to him, but he did not listen.

'I've beat ye, ye swine,' said MacAndrew slowly, his strength returning. 'I've beat ye. And now I'm going to kill ye, as I've killed that –'

All his Celtic blood on fire, MacAndrew leapt on the man. Before he realized what he was doing, his fingers had dug into a soft throat, and the two men went to the floor. MacAndrew's eyes were alight, and he cried out with inarticulate wrath, as his fingers bored their way into the puny throat within his hands.

There was a scuffle in the rear. MacAndrew felt a blinding blow on the top of his head, and a chair toppled over him. Then his senses went spinning into a vast white haze . . .

When MacAndrew opened his eyes, he saw people and shops flashing past, and he realized that he was in a motor-car. The squat man sat beside him.

'Feeling better?' said the squat man. 'I must apologize. Perhaps I struck harder than I need have done, but I really thought you had finished him. You should keep your temper better under control, young man. I must remind you that you agreed to our proposals of your own free will. And we kept to our bargain in every particular. In every particular.'

'Liar,' said MacAndrew, wearily; his head felt as if it were bursting, and he was in no fettle to argue.

'Not at all,' said the squat man politely. 'We said we wanted a photograph of you, and we have got it. You have heard of Hugo Richter, who died a month ago? Perhaps not. All the same, he was a great actor. This afternoon you have taken his place. At the time of his death, one scene in his last motion picture remained unphotographed. For weeks we have been searching for a man who resembled him exactly; it is lucky that you came along. In that room three film cameras have captured every expression of your face, every motion in your mind. We are realists, we Germans. Your horror was perfect –'

'Swine! Swine!' said MacAndrew through his teeth. 'The police –'

'Police? They would not listen. There are two witnesses to prove our bargain, and many more to prove that no harm could have come to you.' The squat man laughed harshly. 'It would have spoilt everything, would it not, if we had told you beforehand that it took one of the cleverest men in Berlin three weeks to make that marvellous piece of mechanism which you thought was a serpent? Go to the police, young man – go! It will but advertise the last great Richter film in Central Europe. And now, good-bye. We thank you for your services. Your hotel is round the corner.'

MacAndrew found himself bundled out on the pavement, his head still swimming confusedly. He was sitting in the hotel lounge when Dr Hardman came briskly in with his group of students.

'Ah, MacAndrew!' said the little lecturer cheerfully. 'You have missed a treat! How are you feeling now, MacAndrew?'

'Got an awful headache, sir,' muttered MacAndrew, stifling a groan.

'Headache? Better lie down, MacAndrew. Better go upstairs and lie down!'

MacAndrew's reply to his professor is still spoken of with awe in a certain Scottish University Union.

'Lie down again?' he cried. 'Lie down again in this confounded hotel? Lie down be damned!' And over the small round table, he glowered at the professor.

Mr Meldrum's Mania

John Metcalfe

Elevators (which Mr Meldrum, English, would call 'lifts') are properly considered unromantic and mundane, yet the crowd gathered on the first floor (Meldrum 'ground') of the Forensic Arts Building at six-thirty on a July morning to stare at this particular elevator seemed to imply a possible exception.

It was neither 'accident' nor hold-up. The elevator itself appeared normal – a semi-local stopping at every floor above the twelfth – and it supplied no clue of violence. Indeed, no one affirmed that there *had* been a scene of violence – or otherwise. Three or four hard-bitten newspaper men were now, although reduced to a pathetic state of impotent and dangerous anguish, adopting a transparent pose of sour grapes, protesting that the whole affair was hooey, nothing but a false alarm.

Yet they continued angrily to hang about. The air of the hall held a bleak, mute suggestion of the unsavoury and sinister, as if, some hours ago, it had experienced a large-scale concussion – due to the explosion of an unspeakably tremendous but entirely odourless and silent firework – and was still coldly retrospective, shocked and strained. Yes, something *had* occurred. The elevator had descended from the sixteenth floor around 11.45 last night, and, on that journey, something very curious had taken place. Within the elevator, rumour asserted blandly, had been, besides the operator, a man who had come out of Dr Fazo's office (Dr Fazo himself was not available, had vanished, shortly afterwards, leaving no trace) and one other rather intoxicated individual, wearing a brown Fedora, who had entered at the twelfth. When the elevator reached the bottom, the operator was unstrung, presently raving. He had been packed off (rumour again) to the psychopathic ward at Bellevue, where he had subsequently expired. What had become of his two passengers remained a matter for excited argument.

The crowd increased. Nervous proprietors of a cigar store and an Exchange buffet which opened out into the marble-paved main hall had got wind of the commotion and turned up two hours before their usual time to peer, on tiptoe, at the new operator. Yes, a new operator had already been installed, a huge mulatto, grinning embarrassedly and reaping a week's wages in importunately proffered tips by constantly transporting people to the sixteenth floor. Those temporarily deprived of his society had to content themselves with gazing, in a fixity which later news might prove to have been morbid, at the great gilt-framed, alphabetical director whereon, under the heading 'North', they could pick out the name of Dr Fazo and his room number, sixteen fifty-four.

It was now seven o'clock. The little throng grew noisier. Curious accretions from the outer commerce of Sixth Avenue and Twenty-third Street momently poured in. The hall was packed. Where were the police? Someone – a woman – fainted. Mr Whalen's bluecoats were strangely in abeyance, but – Ah! Talk of angels . . . !

Hubbub declined, then waxed again in a resentful murmuring. 'All out! Get outta here!' Curtly commanding voices cut across conflicting cries of vain expostulation. The police had come at last. Die-hards attempting to engage them in obstructive argument were dealt with summarily. Within three minutes more the place was cleared.

Outside, however, until the tide of early morning traffic gradually effected their disintegration, several excited knots of the ejected lingered for discussion. Some of them clustered on the opposite sidewalk, gazed up at the Forensic Arts Building reprehendingly. What had occurred in there they might not know. Even the newspaper men, whose noses (tuned to supernatural keenness for the scenting of unlikely mysteries from afar) had brought them hurrying to the scene an hour ago – even these sleuths had come up unaccountably against a stubborn series of blank walls. 'Murder will out' – but here apparently was something worse, something which all authorities concerned were ominously bent on hushing up. There were such things as Public Morals and the 'Public Interest' . . . Well, it was useless to attempt to speculate. Doubtless, the only persons really in the secret were the absconding Dr Fazo (who as everybody knew was that same Dr Fazo who was tried for poisoning his sister – elderly, a masseuse – with a home-made lipstick); the Man in the Fedora (who as everybody knew was that identical Fedora-wearing man who, though he lived out somewhere in the Bronx, bought all his underclothes at Stern's and used to run a gambling joint upon East Fifty-third Street); and, finally, the Other Passenger, that Other Guy, called Meldrum. Was that the Meldrum who, after having been a freak at Coney, had ended up by getting fabulously rich, buying estate at Montauk, and marrying the daughter of an English nobleman? Yes, naturally, it was the very same . . . Little by little, as their interest flagged or duties pressed, the chagrined groups of resolute mythologists broke up and scattered. By seven-fifteen at latest none of them remained.

Meldrum! Strangely enough, quite inexplicably, they *had* got that bit straight. That *was* his name. And 'freak' – they were actually getting warm. Meldrum, however, if he had been at hand to overhear, would certainly have laughed at their preposterous conjectures, would have been tickled to observe how their exiguous fund of information had been ingeniously supplemented by invention, how very wide their guesses always were of the real dreadful mark.

Or no – probably, after all, he would not have laughed. The nuclear components of Mr Meldrum's humour had been long ago disastrously dissolved. It was exactly seven months and eighteen days since he had been amused at anything at all.

On that occasion (so ferociously intact was his appreciation of the comic then) he had recalled, while sitting in a dentist's chair, one of the gorgeous inconsequences of Mr Frank R. Sullivan – and chuckled.

Novocaine had been injected. It was the grisly time of waiting for the pull, yet Mr Meldrum chuckled. He had read Mr Sullivan's extravaganza the previous evening, and now, for some reason, its unabashed and flagrant funniness was more than he could bear. The dentist was a little shocked, vaguely offended too. One's victims did not usually laugh. One's manner became cold and threatening. 'Now – wider, please!'

Meldrum's unseasonable merriment was quenched. The tooth ground and cracked numbly in his jaw, and its extraction hurt a trifle more than he had bargained for. He went off chastened.

This was not in New York, but in Toronto. Mr Meldrum, not generally sentimental, had been visiting a town in Ontario where he had spent four years as a boy. Indeed, he had passed several days in his old home, which still belonged to him. Before his new tenants arrived he had rooted pleasantly about in the loft, where books, toys, pictures, other souvenirs of childhood had been stored.

From Toronto he went on to Montreal and Halifax, then sailed for England. The tooth – or rather its now vacant site – still gave him trouble. It did not hurt particularly, yet the disagreeable sensation of numbness persisted. Also – this being the first time he had ever had an adult tooth extracted – the fact that his full complement of thirty-two had been at last reduced to thirty-one rankled absurdly in his mind as quite a serious grievance. Aboard the *Empress of Scotland* he had a birthday – coincidentally enough his thirty-second – and consumed a vast quantity of John Collins, but the liquor only made him more depressed. He would never see thirty-two again and he would never boast thirty-two natural teeth again. All the way over he slept badly, and when the vessel docked at Liverpool he was feeling actually seedy.

At Euston his friend Ronald Spilman met him. London was obscured by a November fog, and, till they reached the flat in St John's Wood, Spilman remained unable to see Mr Meldrum's face distinctly. Then, however, as the electric lights flashed up, Spilman exclaimed: 'Why, you look quite knocked up! Had a bad passage, I suppose? Really, you look quite ill!'

'No,' said Mr Meldrum querulously. 'I'm not ill at all. We did have rather a rough crossing. But it's not that. I think it's this damned tooth that I had pulled when I was staying in Toronto. It still feels sort of swollen.'

For another month this was all that happened. Mr Meldrum – whose given name was Amos – continued peevish, and, notwithstanding several contemptuous London dentists, was still inclined to blame the absent tooth. However, his jaw did gradually get better, and he was forced to cast about for other explanations.

Was it his business that was bothering him again? Mr Meldrum, ungrateful for prosperity, had always felt demeaned and fettered by his business, and when he thought, in contrast, of persons like John Masefield, Hegel, Heliogabalus and Edison and the substantial contributions they had made to human progress his sense of stark inferiority became acute. His own trade seemed altogether too much of a 'racket', consisting in supplying the entire downtown region of Manhattan with 'rare Spanish delicacies'. For some years he had owned a couple of stores near Fourteenth Street and Eighth Avenue and two others by the Battery, and it was with an eye to the replenishing of these emporia with Ibanez, olives, espadrillas and Pio Baroja that he now found himself on European soil. Presently he must journey on to Spain.

Yet it was not his scruples in respect of good old Pio that were worrying him now. He was the prey of a peculiar depression which remained obstinately entrenched within his brain. Mr Spilman, to cheer him, brought a number of his boon-companions to the flat – without avail. Ronald's acquaintance could, roughly, be divided into two partially overlapping sections – the candidates for Bright's disease and the aspirants to cirrhosis – but not even from the impressive individuals who belonged to both could Mr Meldrum now derive a shred of consolation. Once, towards the end of a rather hectic evening, they had pretended that he was a corpse and had fanned at him with hands and handkerchiefs. Mr Meldrum, resuscitated, had bounded angrily from his chair. 'Don't do that!' he cried. 'It hurts. It's not funny!' Ronald gazed at him amazed. ' "Hurts"? Why, we didn't come inside a foot of your old face!'

Mr Meldrum grunted. They were drunk and it was no use arguing. But they *had* hurt his face. He had felt their fingers and their handkerchiefs distinctly.

Next day (about a week before he had to go to Spain) he had, out of pure spite, spent an hour in the British Museum, staring morosely at the mummies. A dark cloud of foreboding was overshadowing him. The skin round and above his nose was 'creepy', and a little itchy. Absently, and without any real interest, he approached his face towards the glass front of a case in order to make out the hieroglyphs upon a cartouche more exactly.

Suddenly he had a shock. He couldn't get nearer to the glass! His face was still a foot or more away from it, yet he 'felt' something – 'felt' the glass! His heart bounded, sickly. Yes, he *was* able to get a bit nearer now – about six inches – but only by defying a sensation of increasing pressure. Not pain, merely resistance and a sort of weird discomfort.

He tried again. Ah, it was better. Trembling, he continued to experiment . . . Not till a footfall sounded close to him did he desist. One of the Museum attendants was regarding him very curiously. Mr Meldrum turned and left the building.

But, on returning to the flat, he remained nervous, and indeed, dismayed. If that sensation came again he must certainly see a doctor.

'Hi!' Ronald called. 'What the hell! What do you think you're doing?'

'Oh – nothing,' said Mr Meldrum. Seated in an armchair, and forgetting Mr Spilman's presence, he had been tentatively making passes with his fingers, round his nose.

The trip to Spain had failed to repair Mr Meldrum's spirits, or his temper. It was, in fact, upon the evening of his home-coming to St John's Wood that he at last felt driven to confide in the shocked Mr Spilman. From this point – his first definite avowal of the symptoms that distressed him – were to date both the growing apprehension and concern of all his friends and the progressive, steadily accelerating march of his own mania.

That it *was* mania Mr Spilman never doubted. His crony, upon arrival, had collapsed on a divan. Ronald, bringing whisky, had noticed a queer, 'hatchy' expression about his eyes. 'Well, Amos, I'm dashed sorry you're not better. Was business bad, or what?'

'Oh, business – business was as good as usual. Madrid was not too bad, and Barcelona; but down south – the flies! You know, even at Christmas, it wasn't cold enough down there to kill them . . .'

'Oh . . .' said Ronald uncomfortably. 'Yes, how annoying. They kept you awake at night?'

'Yes, they did . . . But I didn't mind that till it got light and I could – Ronald!' he broke off, 'I must tell you. I could feel them on my face when I could *see* that they weren't there!'

'Oh, come now! Really . . . !' Mr Spilman essayed a smile, but his hand refilling Mr Meldrum's glass was trembling. Amos's face gave one the creeps. It looked shrivelled, empty like a baby's, and, at the same time, haunted. Ronald, though inwardly repelled, put a hand on his shoulder. 'Of course, it's simply *nerves* – still, go on, get it off your chest.'

Mr Meldrum did. Horror-stricken, he had lain in bed and watched the flies walking, as it were, on nothing – felt them as well, as their perambulations had defined, in space, a contour which did not exist. And in brushing them away at last he had also felt, though less precisely, his own fingers.

'How far away were those flies?' Mr Spilman fearfully inquired.

'About six inches usually. It depended . . . Straight in front of my nose and forehead they were always farther out. It's the same when I try with my fingers. But I haven't got the feeling now – not since I left Spain.'

For a long time they sat talking and drinking. Mr Spilman, though affecting to think lightly of the matter, was perturbed. People with 'delusions' always made his flesh crawl. Upon retiring he was careful to lock his bedroom door.

Mr Meldrum, on the other hand, was relieved at having unloaded his anxieties on his friend. He enjoyed, for a wonder, a fairly good night's rest, and it was only when he got out of bed next morning that his alarm returned.

He was about to go into the bathroom for his customary ablutions when his glance chanced to halt upon the pillow which until very recently had been beneath his head. The impress still remained obscurely, but – was it merely his imagination? – seemed unusual. He had been lying on his right side and now, towards the left of the pillow as one looked at it, in a place corresponding with the then position of his nose, was a long, hook-shaped groove.

He emitted a low, moaning cry. Mr Spilman came running. 'What is it? What's the matter?'

'Oh . . .' Mr Meldrum faltered. This time he had better keep his own counsel. 'Oh, it's – it's nothing . . .'

But his face was ashy and his teeth chattering.

From the nerve-specialist he came away a few days later, discouraged and resentful. True that he had stopped short of telling the neurologist quite *all* his symptoms. For the same reason which restrained him from mentioning the pillow incident to Ronald, he had suppressed the most bizarre. Puzzled, the nerve-specialist had spoken of hyperaesthesia and neuroses, and then, after a pause, proceeded to make ominously casual inquiries concerning Mr Meldrum's family tree and the friends or relatives with whom he might be staying at the moment. Mr Meldrum, shutting up like an oyster, had gone off in something near to panic.

As it happened, however, he was, this very evening, destined to meet Bertram Spoade and in him to discover unexpectedly a friend in need. Mr Spoade was an acquaintance of Ronald's, an eccentric young man who studied geology at the Imperial College of Science and was pretty safely on the cirrhosis list, but for whom Mr Meldrum none the less had always entertained a sneaking tolerance. He was, at any rate, quite easily the least insufferable of Ronald's gang, and when – after the others had uproariously departed with their host to 'make a night of it' – Bertie continued hiccupping on the divan, Amos felt almost glad of his society.

Up to this point the evening had, for Mr Meldrum, not been gay. He had not mentioned his consultation with the neurologist, but sensed a strange constraint in Ronald's manner. Once, with sinister irrelevance, Mr Spilman had asked him, suddenly, about his maiden aunt (Amos's sole surviving relative) and, upon being told that the good lady lived in France, tactlessly grew more evidently anxious than before. To Mr Meldrum's other trials now was added the necessity of seeming more than ordinarily sane, a feat which, when attempted too deliberately, is very difficult.

But now Bertie Spoade and Amos were alone. For a while the hiccups from the divan were the only sounds that broke the silence.

Abruptly, Mr Spoade sat up and spoke. 'Ronald thinks you've gone batty, and I can see – *hic* – you're pretending not to be. I'm – *hic* – interested. I wish – *hic* – you'd tell me all about it.'

Mr Meldrum wondered whether he ought to feel offended, and, on deliberation, decided in the negative. After Ronald and the nerve-specialist he badly needed a sympathetic listener.

'It's my face . . .' he prefaced awkwardly. 'I know it sounds preposterous, but – well, I can feel things in the air in front of it.' He narrated his experiences in the British Museum and with the flies in Spain.

Mr Spoade, intrigued, no longer hiccupped. He plied Mr Meldrum eagerly with questions.

'Can you feel it now, like that?'

Mr Meldrum considered. 'Yes, in a way . . . I mean, it's not necessary now for anything to touch it. I –'

'You mean,' said Bertie, interrupting, 'that you can feel a sort of boundary line in space – a kind of extra surface where the "you" ends and the "not-you" begins. Rather like those chappies who've had their legs amputated and still have pains in their toes, eh?'

'Yes,' agreed Mr Meldrum, whom this analogy had struck as apt, 'it *is* like that, I suppose . . .' In the excitement of discussing his peculiar symptoms he almost forgot, momentarily, to feel afraid.

'Of course,' Mr Spoade continued, 'it's probably the brain. I'm not being rude, but I was doing medicine before I went in for geology. The brain is a rare and curious organ. For instance, pressure on the uncinate gyrus results in the characteristic uncinate group of fits, accompanied by olfactory sensations – odours – which have nothing to account for them outside. Get me? You smell things when there's nothing there to smell . . .'

'Oh . . .' said Mr Meldrum. He somewhat disapproved of this last parallel. His gyrus, he was sure, was quite all right, and certainly he had no fits.

'Or again,' Mr Spoade proceeded, warming, 'it may be a psycho-analyst's job entirely. Pity you aren't in Vienna – or still in U.S.A. Alienists are more in vogue out there. And if I were you I shouldn't bleat too much. People are sure to think that you've gone bugs. Look at old Ronald. He was telling all of us just now that if you went on having queer ideas he'd have to find your relative's address and get you put away. He –'

'WHAT?' exclaimed Mr Meldrum, in alarm. 'He said that?'

'Yes,' replied Mr Spoade composedly. 'He did. He was very pessimistic, talking about Commissioners in Lunacy, and –'

Mr Meldrum had sprung to his feet. 'I won't stay here another hour, not an instant! If he –'

Bertie, too, had risen. 'Well, I don't blame you. Look here, I've got a brain-wave – come along o' me! Just bring a tooth-brush and pyjamas, then in the morning you can fetch your other things. Old Ronald wouldn't mind. In fact . . . Come on!'

But his entreaties were indeed unnecessary. Mr Meldrum was fairly boiling with indignation. He was so angry that all his terror had departed. It was only when, carrying a small suit-case, he was about to follow Bertie from the flat that any qualms returned.

'And then,' Mr Spoade was saying, 'tomorrow I should like to make a little, well, experiment. It struck me that it might be kind of interesting to find what shape your face was now – your other face . . .'

'What *shape* . . .?' Mr Meldrum was staggered.

'Oh, it's all right. I'll explain what I mean tomorrow. Come along!' Dubiously, Mr Meldrum came.

By way of anaesthetic (this was next morning, at about eleven) Mr Meldrum, his neck imprisoned in a vice, found himself confronted by a large geological map of the British Isles hung on the opposite wall.

'Think,' Bertie had instructed, 'of the Llandilo Flags, or the Ordovician System and Trilobites – anything. Brood on 'em while I'm getting ready, and whatever you do, don't jerk your dear old bean about once I begin.'

Built around Mr Meldrum's head was a sort of cardboard scaffolding, like an unfinished box, through two opposite sides of which, when preparations were complete, Bertie had already inserted numerous bonnet-pins. The pins were to be pushed through slowly, perpendicularly, and knob first, and as soon as each knob 'touched' his supernumerary face Mr Meldrum was to exclaim 'Now!' Mr Spoade, at that instant, would stop pushing, and, leaving that pin in position, would pass on to the next. In this way, as he delightedly explained, the pin-knobs would ultimately form a variety of three-dimensional graph, from which the shape of Mr Meldrum's phantom countenance could profitably be deduced.

'Just,' Bertie went on fanatically to point out, 'as if you were a crystal – what? – and I were plotting its indicatrix. Only then it would come out sort of egg-shaped, and I don't expect yours will.' Mr Spoade proceeded to talk of birefringence, of ordinates, and of something to do with light-waves, called 'Mu-mu' in a manner that made Mr Meldrum's brain reel. Mr Meldrum now regretted his position. He felt very undignified and, besides that, began to fear that Mr Spoade was not – not *absolutely* normal. No one, to start with, who was thoroughly, unquestionably sane would have been in possession of so many bonnet-pins.

'Ready!' said Bertie. 'Now, for the Lord's sake, sit still! Don't twitch an eyelid!'

The experiment proceeded without hitch, Mr Meldrum, at intervals, exclaiming 'Now!' or 'Ouch!' and Bertie thereupon desisting instantly from pushing in the pin. Finally Mr Spoade unclamped the vice and set his prisoner free.

'Now we can have a squint. But make it snappy. I've a lecture on at twelve.'

Bertie had taken an oblong of what seemed to be damp blotting-paper or papier mâché, patting and pressing it delicately against the heads of the bonnet-pins, so that the pliant material, following their varying distances from the cardboard wall, formed a sufficiently close 'average' approximation to the ideal surface which the pins had point by point delimited. Having repeated this operation with the other 'wall', Mr Spoade brought the two together, peered into the resulting mould, and burst into hysterical laughter. 'Good Lord . . . he, he! . . . It's – it's a *snout* – or else a bill . . . the Human Tapir, what? . . . If you – Hello!'

Mr Meldrum, too, had looked into the mould, turned pale. Bertie deposited him upon a sofa, brought him whisky. 'Well, I suppose I *oughtn't* to have laughed. Bit of a shock, no doubt. But really . . . ! Just fancy you among the old Proboscidae . . . He, he . . . ! Good Lord . . . !'

Despite perfunctory contrition, Mr Spoade's callous merriment continued. Finally, however, after a startled glance at the clock, he struggled into his coat and swept up a large pile of notebooks. 'I've got to scoot . . . Leave those two moulds to dry. We'll use 'em as a matrix later on . . . So long!'

Mr Meldrum lay inert. Bertie had been gone twenty minutes when at length he rose unsteadily from the sofa. Shivering, he took a long pull at the whisky, staggered into the bedroom, packed his suit-case. Then, returning to the front room, he placed the two moulds on the floor and passionately trod upon them. It was twelve-twenty-five. He still had the key of Ronald's flat, and Ronald, at this hour, would not be home.

Emerging on to the Cromwell Road, Mr Meldrum took a taxi to the Spilman flat – deserted save for a negligible maid – and hastily collected his belongings. In another taxi he drove to Cowcross Street and there handed over all his luggage to the storage department of Messrs Cook. This done, he wandered vaguely down by Ludgate Hill, along the Strand.

Dazed and light-headed, he strolled for half an hour or more indecisively northwards and westwards and then halted. An imposing grey pediment, supported on fat cylindrical grey columns, confronted him. Euston? No, there were pigeons. It was the British Museum again.

Trembling, and after several seconds' hesitation, he turned in.

Once more he was looking at the mummies. Not at the mummies merely. He gazed unseeingly at scarabs, papyri, colossal heads, representations, yet more terrifying, of grotesque, semi-human deities – Horus, Anubis, Set. Perhaps the whisky had made him slightly drunk, keeping his horror at his own condition in abeyance. He was not thinking specifically about the result of Mr Spoade's experiment. Even, after an hour, he began to feel a little hungry. Only when he was about to leave the building for a meal did anything extraordinary occur.

He was turning away from a large case of pottery when someone jostled him. Mr Meldrum, nerves on edge, swung round wrathfully. An ill-favoured individual, smelling of garlic, returned his angry stare. 'Nah then, clumsy . . . !'

Suddenly, Mr Meldrum's pent emotions were canalized, and liberated in the form of rage. He was seething with indignation. 'Clumsy yourself! What do you mean by –'

The garlicky gentleman's features, too, were distorted with passion. 'Look 'ere, you shut it, see? 'Cos if yer don't I'll push yer fice in, see? I'll push yer silly fice in . . . !'

What happened next Mr Meldrum could never recollect distinctly. 'I'll push yer fice in, see?' . . . At these words something snapped in his brain. His face! There was something appallingly wrong with his face. Everyone could see it! He was mad! He heard himself shouting: 'I'm mad, I'm mad!' Then his voice changed. His own voice. With his own ears he could hear it change, dropping, in an instant from a delirious scream to a low, senseless chirr, like a bird's, a kind of twittering. He saw the man in front of him fall back, regarding him in horror. Yes, he was mad. He could feel his jaw working, chattering rapidly up and down, making those curious sounds – knew that his eyes were brailing . . . Attendants were running up, surrounding him. His arms were pinioned. The room swam. He must have fainted.

How had he escaped? He remembered nothing. This was the Strand, and he was walking eastwards, past the Law Courts. His head ached, and his clothes were soiled, his collar torn. Up to a point his memory held good, then stopped. He had had a seizure in the Museum, shouted out that he was mad – but he was not mad now. Not in that way.

By degrees, however, something of his terror returned. How *had* he got away? It was four o'clock and growing dark. There must, he imagined, be some sort of search for him, some sort of hue and cry. He struck northwards, up an alley, avoiding lights.

In a square, a newsboy was running. 'Evenin' Stan*dard* . . . !' Mr Meldrum, signalling, bought a copy.

For some seconds he saw nothing, but presently his glance snapped down, appalled, upon a headline: '*Extraordinary Scene in British Museum. Madman escapes.*' He read on in bewilderment. This was all wrong, ridiculous. No, he could not believe it. *That* was not his name. His name was Meldrum, *Meldrum* . . .

The paper dropped. He leaned against a railing. Meldrum . . . It was clever of him to have given the wrong name, though he had no recollection of having done so. Now it might be easier to evade inquiries and detection. But the name he apparently *had* given was so peculiar; he couldn't make it out. The entire history was incredible. If *he* were mad, the Museum authorities were at least equally insane. He must get off, give all of them the slip, Ronald and Bertie, everyone who knew . . . He must go back at once – back to the States, if he could manage it, on the next boat that sailed.

Retrieving the paper, he glanced round him cautiously. No one was following him. He had been marvellously lucky. He would get something to eat and drink, then think how he might best shake off pursuit. That story in the *Standard* was all bunkum. Also his face was better. It felt almost normal. If he could but return in safety to America he could convince himself that this was nothing but a frightful dream.

On the boat going over, however, an obstinate suspicion clung to him that there was more in it than that. For one thing, his torn collar and soiled clothes proved definitely that he *had* been involved in some quite overt and undignified affray, and, for another, the peculiar sensations round his nose returned. It is necessary to explain that Mr Meldrum had thought it wiser, instead of sailing direct from England, to lose himself for a month upon the Continent, not even risking the removal of his luggage from the warehouse. Drawing funds through Morgan's in the Place Vendôme at Paris, he had gone on to Switzerland and Italy, leaving for New York in a Fabre Line boat from Naples late in February. Now, with his morale somewhat seriously decayed, he spent most of his time in brooding on that mystifying item in the *Evening Standard*.

This account, from which it may be here as well to quote, had run, in part, as follows:

The stately peace of the British Museum was shattered, early this afternoon, by an unusual incident. A man who had been standing before a case of pottery of the period of the Shepherd Kings and whose actions for some time had seemed suspicious, became suddenly involved in a violent fracas with another man stationed close behind him . . . Seized and taken for examination to the Assistant Curator's room he protested that this was the thirty-second occasion on which his opponent, James Buggins, had insulted him, that he was a manufacturer of bonnet-pins, and that his own name was Thote (or Thoash?) . . . What is peculiar about the episode is that the policeman and two attendants in whose custody he was temporarily placed appear unable or unwilling to account for his escape. One of the attendants, in particular, was in such a condition of nervous collapse that he was subsequently removed to a hospital for treatment . . . It is thought, however, that Thote may have been under the influence of liquor . . . The affair is being thoroughly investigated and a search made for him.

Mr Meldrum had refrained from looking at any English papers leaving London. He now refused passionately to believe that he could ever have been able to think of nothing better than such a foolish and unlikely name as 'Thote', or that he had said what he was reported to have said about the thirty-second insult and the bonnet-pins. Still, he wanted to hear no more of it. He was probably very lucky indeed to have escaped, and even now did not feel absolutely safe. Ronald and the curiously imbecile B. Spoade might long ago have 'squealed'. Perhaps at this instant, he was shadowed. Perhaps, upon arrival at New York, he would be summarily arrested . . .

Happily, he was mistaken. It was, for March, a really glorious day, and he was met, outside the Customs shed, by someone who had had advance word of his coming and who, so far from promptly clapping him in irons for the raging maniac he was, laid an affectionate hand of greeting on his shoulder. 'Why, hello, Amos . . . Why, you're looking *swell* . . . !'

Mr Meldrum's eyes filled gratefully. He knew that he was looking like a fly-blown oleograph of last Saturday's leg-of-mutton, but it was tactful of his friend to say the contrary.

'Why, hello – hello – Smith!'

The real name of the man who welcomed Mr Meldrum was not Smith, still, we propose to call him that – just Smith. He had not yet invested in the brown Fedora.

But of this person, for the present, the less said the better.

Spring had arrived. There was a lamb or two in Central Park and a conspicuous goat or two in Greenwich Village. Weary, steel-jawed executives were returning with last season's wives and niblicks from Florida and setting out with fresh ones for Europe. The rent of penthouses had soared.

Despising, however, the vernal excitements of Manhattan, Mr Meldrum had been living morosely in Linoleumville, S.I., in Jeannette, Pa., and in Emporia, Kan. Save for occasional week-end contacts with the person Smith he had been leading the existence of a hermit.

Under the circumstances he cannot be blamed. Although the curious extension of his face was usually no more than 'sentient', so to speak, and only sometimes vaguely 'tangible' to his own finger-tips, he could not but believe that it was visible as well – and that to everyone who passed him in the street. He rarely ventured out except at night and, through the day, sat brooding in his room. Two letters, sent to his business address, had reached him from Ronald, but, having apprehensively perused the first, he threw the second in the fire unopened. Mr Spilman, making no reference to Bertie or the British Museum, had implored his friend to see a good neurologist immediately. If Amos would but realize that his malady possessed no basis in objective fact, all, Ronald vigorously declared, would yet be well. With this opinion Mr Meldrum violently disagreed. To call his trouble 'psychological' was just an insult.

We are now, of course, approaching Dr Fazo and the elevator. Mr Smith – to whom Amos had confided the whole terrible affair – had frequently advised a consultation with an alienist, without success. Ronald's letter, he could see, had had a very bad effect and greatly stiffened Amos's resistance. Still, though discouraged, he was persevering. Upon a sunny Friday morning late in May he donned, for the first time, the brown Fedora, set out from the Grand Central terminal aboard the 10.15, and stubbornly returned to the attack.

Amos (it was now Sunday and lunch-time at Emporia) was expecting him and was standing, with the front-door open, on the veranda. The sun was dazzling in his eyes and the expression on the face of the approaching Mr Smith was indistinct. Mr Meldrum, however, noticed that, when a few yards distant, his friend halted suddenly. Amos moved forward, from the open door, to meet him.

'Well, baby, how's – Why, what the hell . . . !'

Mr Smith, his gaze stony, was trembling, and it was some time before he recovered sufficiently to explain that he was subject to heart-attacks. Even then it was with obvious reluctance that he suffered Mr Meldrum to lead him into the house and to pour him out a glass of fusel oil, slightly impaired by alcohol.

' "Heart-attacks"? You never spoke of *them* before . . .'

Mr Meldrum was in turn alarmed. He by no means credited the 'heart-attack'. To break a painful silence, he inquired presently: 'I suppose you've come to have another go at me about this psycho-analyst of yours, this Dr Fazo? Well, I've been thinking over it again, and p'r'aps . . . p'r'aps I *might* try him after all. It seems the only hope . . .'

Mr Smith's hollow eyes held no consciousness of victory. He was shivering slightly, displaying a tendency to retch. 'I – I don't know that it would do a scrap of good. These alienists . . .'

'What! . . .' Mr Meldrum gazed incredulously. 'Why, you've been trying all along to –'

'No, it'd be no good . . .'

'But I shall go!'

'It's not a scrap of good.'

'I tell you I *shall* go!'

Mr Smith rose. 'I – I'm afraid I've got to hurry. I – I just looked in . . .'

In vain the astonished Amos sought to detain him. Mr Smith was moving forlornly to the door. 'I'll – I'll see you again soon – Sorry I couldn't stop . . . So long!'

'But, Ferdinand . . . !'

It was no use. Mr Ferdinand Smith was now well out of the house and walking rapidly towards the station. Just before turning a corner of the road he was observed by Mr Meldrum to break into a run.

Not until seated in the train and safely on his way back to New York did Mr Smith allow himself to think too concentratedly about what he had seen as, half an hour ago, he had ascended Mr Meldrum's steps, glanced forward, for an instant, past his friend, to the front door.

But then, and in an awful rush, the thing came over him. He understood now, too well, how Mr Meldrum's wonderful 'escape' had been effected. He could guess shrewdly at the reason why that policeman and those two attendants let him go. They, he suspected, must have seen what he himself had seen so recently . . .

What had he seen? With the sun behind him, and casting Mr Meldrum's silhouette upon the lower portion of the open door, he had observed, at first incredulously, a curious shadow. But he could not remain incredulous for long. Mr Meldrum had moved his head slightly, and the shadow had moved too. It was the shadow of something with a strange, beakish prolongation, a little like a crane's head, only the 'bill' had been considerably more curved – and sharper.

Dr Fazo, a bland gentleman of fifty, took at the first encounter an instant fancy to poor Mr Meldrum. Observing a pipe in Mr Meldrum's hand, he had rapped out: 'What mixture do you smoke? . . . Ah, Dunhill's "Royal Yacht". Bit of a sybarite, eh?' Already prepossessed in his new patient's favour, he had immediately resolved to multiply his fees by 1·5.

Of this our hero had suspected nothing. For a month he had been following Dr Fazo's instructions conscientiously, and now his features wore a peculiar expression, at once debauched, propitiatory and coy, like those of a supremely diffident yet amorous bloodhound. Mr Smith, after his inexplicable *volte-face*, had held himself aloof, but became less stand-offish by degrees, and had eventually even formed the habit of accompanying Amos to the alienist's door, frequently meeting him again when he came out. Today – a bright June afternoon – was scheduled to see Mr

Meldrum's nineteenth session. 'Well, so long, baby. I'll be back at quarter to. Good luck!' Mr Smith departed. Amos rang sharply twice, then entered.

The psycho-analyst received him cordially. Dr Fazo had formed his own opinion concerning Mr Meldrum, which was that he was horribly insane, but he did not allow this melancholy conviction to betray itself. Moreover, he had just got hold of an idea, requiring Mr Meldrum's goodwill, money and cooperation. Before, however, proceeding to its discussion, he subjected his patient to the customary examination.

'Good,' he remarked at last. 'Progress *most* satisfactory. Persevere with that tatting exercise – only think of it as drizzling or gallooning, not as tatting. It releases the nodal whorls. And I suggest that the expression "snout" or "pecker" may do harm. Think of it as a "nozzle" instead of a "muzzle" or a "pecker" . . .'

'Yes,' said Mr Meldrum docilely. 'I will. And – could I look at those wax moulds again?'

'Certainly . . . Here they are . . .'

For Amos's greater reassurance Dr Fazo had taken several impressions of his face in wax. The resulting simulacra Mr Meldrum now surveyed with resignation if not actual enthusiasm.

'You see – they're perfectly normal . . . Your notion of a muz – a nozzle, is merely a too-vivid projection and exaggeration of the – ahem – the normal nose-awareness. Like a line divided "externally" in Euclid, don't you see?'

'I see,' said Mr Meldrum, again docilely, though the comparison struck him as inept and puerile. 'Shall I talk now?'

'By all means . . .'

For half an hour Amos 'talked' while Dr Fazo listened, taking notes. Mr Meldrum was exhorted, upon these occasions, to 'let himself go', speaking without apparent rhyme or reason of anything that came into his head – and these requirements he amazingly fulfilled. Dr Fazo had by this time such an acquaintance with the less creditable idiosyncrasies of Amos's subconscious ego as would have caused a weaker man to blench, but from long practice he was blasé and inured. Always, whilst Mr Meldrum raved complacently of kites and cricket bats or prattled evilly of pacifiers and didies, Dr Fazo would be eagerly pawing over these inanities, dredging and delving in the fond expectation of discovering some childhood trauma which might account (too high a plausibility was not essential) for the perverse delusion of a 'snout'. Up to the present he had been disappointed. Amos's subconscious was indeed simply hag-ridden by complexes, but these were seldom of the proper kind. However, Dr

Fazo persevered. If only – as he was tireless in explaining – if only he could light on the deep-buried origin of hidden conflict, expose its overwhelming triviality to the derisive upper storey of his patient's mind, the thing would end. Once Amos could be brought to realize that his entire nozzle mania was the result of, say, his finding seven ears upon his rocking-horse when he intelligently expected three, he was as good as cured. All the energy which his subconscious had been fatuously expending on this banal if rather puzzling incident since he was four years old would be released. His libido, now choked and damned and in a ghastly state of suppuration, would flow on tranquilly again. He would be well.

At the conclusion of the present recital Dr Fazo ran his eye with apparent satisfaction over his notes. To the lay mind these jottings – representing all his worth-while garnerings from Mr Meldrum's mental detritus over a period of five weeks – might have suggested little or have been misleading. They were:

A. NOSE. Nosy P. Nosey Parker. Central Park. Nozzle. Hose-pipe episode at age six.

B. THIRTY-TWO. His age last birthday. Had thirty-two teeth until quite recently. Plays piquet and bezique. Thirty-two cards in pack. (Other instances in support on p. 13.)

C. EGYPT. Wrote articles on scarabs for school magazine. Father was in Egyptian Civil Service. British Museum.

D. SCRIBE. Is peculiarly sensitive to this and to related words.

Dr Fazo snapped his notebook. He would now broach his big idea.

'Listen,' he said. 'I want you to agree to something. Your talking is still too inhibited to be much use and my material is insufficient and conflicting. I want you to let me go up to Canada and look over your toys.'

' "Toys"?' queried Mr Meldrum weakly.

'Toys and other things. Books and games – everything. It needn't really cost you more than, say, six hundred berries. Do you agree?'

Mr Meldrum looked sheepish. 'Oh, I say . . . Do you really mean that – berries?'

'Dollars, dollars. Don't be absurd. Six hundred dollars.'

'Oh, dollars . . .' said Mr Meldrum. 'My nose feels so itchy. Yes, all right. Six hundred dollars.'

During Dr Fazo's absence Mr Meldrum, who had given him the keys to his again untenanted Ontario home, stayed at a little place up the Hudson, anxiously awaiting his return.

Occasionally, however, he forgot to be anxious, and then he was just plainly mad – harmlessly and happily, but still mad. Mr Smith, realizing this, was terribly depressed. Amos had a large framed photograph of Dr Fazo hung in his bedroom, and he would often stand in front of it and bark. His landlady, and her husband, too, thought it was all very sad, and had put up the rent and board money to quite a formidable figure.

Nevertheless, this period was probably the most peaceful that poor Amos had enjoyed from the first onset of his mania. By fits and starts he would begin worrying about his neglected business and about his nose, but in the main his condition was one of pleasurable lunacy. His nozzle now had ceased to trouble him save in a mental sense. He knew its contours so exactly that he avoided automatically those painful contacts and collisions which had annoyed him previously. He no longer, for instance, banged it or stubbed it accidentally or burnt it in the soup. To all intents and purposes it was just as if he had been born that way – with a snout or proboscis fifteen inches long – and as if this proboscis then had suddenly become invisible – really a matter for congratulation. Since the commencement of the alienist's ministrations he had grown plainly madder, yet if he now were happier as a result who could regret the fact? He had talked so incessantly to Dr Fazo of his childhood that a state akin to infantilism had, perhaps mercifully, supervened. He would call horses 'gee-gees' and his watch a 'tick-tick'. Frequently Mr Smith could hardly restrain him, when they were both retiring, from calling out to Mrs Schultzenheimer, his landlady, with a request that she should 'tuck him in' and give the two of them a good-night kiss.

Mr Smith's own feelings towards Amos now were mixed. Although he had managed to persuade himself that the affrighting shadow on the door had been delusion – possibly telepathic – he was far from forgetting that perturbing incident, and his present attitude to Mr Meldrum might be described as one of very gingerly affection. In spite of reason and of common sense he could not always avoid looking at his poor friend's face with something of a horrible expectancy . . .

But, on the whole, these days passed placidly, and it was really surprising how intelligently Amos would often talk about the absent Dr Fazo. Thanks to the alienist's repeated explanations, he had grasped the root ideas of expressive psycho-therapy with thoroughness, and he was never tired of expounding them, in turn, to Mr Smith. 'It's sumsing dat happn when I was little, oo . . . ever so teeny, called a t'auma. An' de t'auma make me nozzly, Ferdy, only I fordet what it was. Good Dr Fazo's finding it in Tanada, an' when he tum back he tell Amos all 'bout naughty t'auma, an' den Amos laugh an' say "Oo . . . Silly . . . !" An' den I give

Dr Fazo six hund'ed be'wies – an' no more t'auma, no more nozzle. Nozzle *all* gone 'way . . . !' It was when, during lucid intervals like these, the mind of Amos would regain, too briefly, all its old familiar power and clarity, that Mr Smith most keenly could appreciate the tragedy of its decay.

Finally, after Dr Fazo had been gone three weeks, the crisis came. Amos and Ferdinand had been strolling after supper by the river, talking little. Exhausted by the heat, they turned in at their lodgings around nine o'clock.

Amos, preceding his companion by a few yards, reappeared at the front door, waving a pale yellow slip of paper, as Mr Smith was entering after him.

The wire from Montreal. They read it together. 'GOOD NEWS GREAT DISCOVERY ARRIVING GRAND CENTRAL EIGHT THIRTY P.M. STANDARD TOMORROW CONGRATULATIONS FAZO.'

A whole chapter of accidents delayed the momentous interview next day. Owing to the derailment of another train near Troy the Montreal express had been held up. It was past ten when Dr Fazo arrived, and then Mr Meldrum missed him at Grand Central. The alienist made it a strict rule to withhold his private address from all his patients, and Mr Smith and Amos spent an hour 'phoning desperately to his office. Finally they got him. Dr Fazo, realizing their anxiety, and himself ignorant of their present whereabouts, had merely dumped his luggage at his home and gone straight on to the Forensic Arts, waiting for them to ring him. Amos was to come to him there at once.

The building was open all night for people known to the night watchman. A certain sedulously bibulous merchant, intimate with Dr Fazo and whose work often necessitated his sitting up very late, had established, on the twelfth floor, a kind of ultra-private and select speakeasy, never closed. Mr Smith, indeed, had made the acquaintance of a rather nice girl in there, and on previous occasions, while he had been escorting Mr Meldrum to the psycho-analyst, he had often filled in an odd moment talking to her about his home town in Ohio which happened also to be hers. He proposed to do this now.

First, however, he saw Amos to Dr Fazo's door. Mr Meldrum, though greatly excited and upon tiptoe with anticipation, had an obscure something in his manner which Mr Smith could not pretend to like. Amos had snapped back, for some reason, from baby language into ordinary speech, and yet his friend was vaguely conscious that this change had not been for the better. Exactly how he realized this or what precisely he was now afraid of in poor Amos Mr Smith could not say, but that he *was* afraid of him was certain – and very glad to have got rid of him if only for a while when, from inside his sanctum, Dr Fazo called on him to enter.

It was arranged that Mr Smith should come back to the office within half an hour's time.

As Amos walked into the dim outer fringe of light thrown by a reading-lamp upon a desk, Dr Fazo experienced an instant faint uneasiness, a twinge as of alarm. It was so slight that he ignored it at the time, but it did strike him that perhaps his patient was not looking quite so well as when he saw him last. Clasping Mr Meldrum's hand, he smiled, however, and motioned him urbanely to a chair.

'Well, I've good news. I think I've run what we were looking for to earth at last. A long chase – but well worth it, for us both.'

Mr Meldrum had sat down. 'Tell me,' he said. 'I –' He stopped. His eyes were glittering. Dr Fazo, searching his face, again had an uncomfortable sensation. Something prompted him, instead of proceeding to an account of his discovery, to veer off, as with an idea of gaining time, upon a trivial topic.

He laughed. 'I was a fool to take that day-train down from Montreal. Properly punished, too. Ninety-five minutes late . . .'

There was a pause. Through a window opening on the airshaft the dull rumble from Sixth Avenue rose faintly. The night was hot. Dr Fazo passed a handkerchief across his forehead, made a humorous gesture as of wringing it out, and emitted a wry 'Whew!' Mr Meldrum's intent silence disconcerted him, but he could no longer put off telling him what he had found. He cleared his throat, shot out his cuffs, altered the position of the light a little, and began:

'I want to impress upon you again that the most obstinate, inveterate neuroses have frequently been traced to something so apparently irrelevant, even ridiculous, that the patient may, at first, experience a certain – ahem – difficulty . . . difficulty in accepting these unrealized traumas as a sufficient explanation of his state. Nevertheless, the trauma *is* the explanation. Once the thing has been disinterred from the subconscious, brought out into the open and, so to speak, projected, the whole trouble goes. I – I've told you all this before, but I want to be sure of your own sympathy, cooperation . . .'

Dr Fazo passed two fingers round the inside of his neck band. It was really very hot, and, he could not deny it, he felt anxious. He had, he considered, put in a very good job of work for Mr Meldrum up in

Canada, but he had some misgivings as to its success. Now came the test. Would the elaborate explanation seem too flimsy and preposterous? Dr Fazo, whilst loyal in the main to his professional ideals, permitted himself a degree of cynicism. He was inclined, on nearing the *experimentum crucis*, to glimpse discouraging resemblances between psycho–analysis and certain allied though less generally established cults. However, he must pull himself together, make the plunge.

'Listen,' he said, then cleared his throat once more. He could not understand his own increasing trepidation. Not only had he an unpleasant consciousness that he had somehow chosen his previous words poorly and (the idea even came to him) *dangerously*, but he was actually at a loss how to proceed. Finally, with Mr Meldrum's dancing eyes upon him, he spoke again.

'Listen – and tell me if you understand – SCRIBE OF THE GODS!'

Had Mr Meldrum moved? Had his face twitched? His expression in the dim lamplight, was peculiar, like that of a somnambulist unwillingly aroused, blindly and pitifully clinging to his sleep. So far, that might be good. Dr Fazo had seen that look before, thought himself, momentarily, on surer ground. He had touched something deep, something significant.

' "Scribe of the Gods," ' he repeated slowly. 'Does that mean anything to you? Yes, I can see it does.'

Amos shuddered slightly. His lips parted. 'Yes . . . it does . . . I –'

'Think back. I want you to think back. You have always been sensitive to that word "scribe", to "Scripture", to the name of the French playwright, Scribe, even to "Scriabin". You never knew why. But I shall tell you. "Scribe of the Gods." Of the Egyptian Gods?'

The silent form confronting Dr Fazo did not stir.

'Think back. And I shall add another word, a name. The name you gave them as your own in the Museum. Because you were thirty-two years old. Not "Thote". They didn't get it right. Not quite, but nearly. It was – THOTH!'

Thoth! It was out at last, and Dr Fazo's bolt was neatly shot. What would he see? But for some reason he did not wish to look too closely at the figure in the chair. Instead, he took up a small parcel which had been lying on his desk. 'I have the proof beside me here. A book. A book you glanced at – when you were a little boy. And, on a certain page, are pencil marks, thumb-stains and childish scribblings. Upon a certain page – the thirty-second . . .'

Again he stopped. What was he going to see? He was aware, and too acutely, of this moment's drama. Yet he refused to glance at Mr Meldrum. Still seated, with his head averted, he busied himself with the untying of the parcel. It was now, as he was pushing back the crackling paper wrappings, that he imagined he could catch a curious noise behind him, a faint sound like a sigh. But even then he did not turn. He opened the book, proceeded, 'Here is the page. The figure 32 is very large. And just below it is the illustration – Thoth. Thoth with moon-disk and crescent, ibis-headed, the amanuensis of the Gods. You thought that, when that number had been reached – when you were thirty-two – you would . . .'

'Yes!' It was Mr Meldrum who had spoken, loudly and electrically. At last the psycho-analyst wheeled round. Mr Meldrum had risen from his chair, was staring – at that beak-faced spectre in the book. Dr Fazo, too, got up. He was more than nervous now. His whole body was bathed in sweat. Something was going wrong. Something was very much amiss. He did not know what it was . . .

'Yes!' Again Mr Meldrum had spoken, more loudly than before. It was the last word Dr Fazo was to hear him utter. And what was he *doing*! He was going – going away, striding immensely towards the door. Dr Fazo wanted to scream. In the next room, which he knew to be untenanted he thought he heard a rustle, then a bump.

'But – but . . .' Gathering his courage, the alienist had spurred himself to those twin syllables of vain remonstrance. The next instant he knew better, no longer wished to detain Mr Meldrum. His blood congealed, his mouth grew square in a tense rictus of extravagant dismay. A waft of cold and as it were aloof, bland and remote horror filled the room.

Mr Meldrum had by this time reached the door and opened it. His passage to it across the office floor had taken only a few seconds, yet those short moments had been long enough for Dr Fazo to feel a chill grue of terror travel up his spine. Mr Meldrum, whose back alone was now visible, was in no separable, individual particular transformed, but from his whole appearance – from his gait, his carriage – had been giving off the threat of a tremendous and an imminent alteration. In his departing presence there had been indicated not indeed the fact, but the incipience, of some appalling change. It was most fortunate that Dr Fazo could not see his face.

The door was closed. The sound of footsteps grew fainter down the corridor. Dr Fazo sank back in his chair. His eyes, wildly staring, did not so much as glance at the six-hundred dollar cheque which had been left upon his desk. Instead, and quite unluckily for him, they fastened upon one of the wax moulds of Mr Meldrum's face.

It was as he stared repelled at this wax mould that Dr Fazo fainted.

What followed has perhaps in part been guessed. In any case a hint or two may indicate a scene best left to the imagination. Mr Smith himself, who was the only person besides the operator to accompany Mr Meldrum in the elevator, was afterwards unable to give any clear account of what he saw. Not that he gave accounts – there were abundant reasons why his lips should remain sealed. Even if he had not got rather tipsy talking to his little twelfth-floor cutie from Ohio he might have hesitated to accept that sight within the lift as actual fact.

As it was, he fancied (mercifully) at the time that he was merely 'seeing things' – as, naturally, he was, though not alone in the strict, technical intention of that phrase. To begin with, he was not then expecting to see Mr Meldrum, and, in a somewhat gruesome sense, it may be doubted that he ever did.

A certain amount of confidence presided over this shortlived encounter. Mr Smith, by 11.30, had become very sozzled and for no reason at all decided to go down to the Western Union and send someone – anyone – a telegram. A few seconds previous to this, Mr Meldrum (if whatever it was that had left Dr Fazo's office can still be narrowly described as 'Mr Meldrum') had got into the elevator on the sixteenth floor. About three seconds later Mr Smith also entered, boisterously, at the twelfth. The thing which for convenience we call 'Mr Meldrum', would not immediately have attracted his attention if it had not continued wearing Mr Meldrum's clothes.

It had taken, at most, three seconds for the elevator to pass downwards from the sixteenth to the twelfth, and it took considerably less than a proportionate time to reach the first – say seven seconds – Mr Meldrum ceased to be, and something hideously different took his place.

Briefly, as soon as Mr Smith had got into the lift his gaze, bent downwards, chanced to fasten on a pair of shoes. He seemed to recognize those shoes, *did* recognize, with qualms, the pants above. Still, there was something strange about them, too. The limbs which they presumably encased had – there was actually no other word – a curious quality of being *neuter*. Although invisible, their character somehow revealed itself. They were each as blankly, as shockingly neuter as an umbrella handle or the turned leg of a sofa. At the same instant that Mr Smith's glance, travelling upwards, fixed itself in a glassy stare of horror on a changing head, came, from the operator, an appalling shriek.

Past the remaining floors (say six or seven) the lift shot swiftly on its downward way. None of the three stirred. At the bottom the cage bumped to a standstill. The grille rattled open, allowing Mr Smith and the now idiot operator to spill themselves upon the marble floor. The third occupant of the elevator got out the last.

Nobody much was about. Mr Smith remained sitting on the floor. The operator had just begun to gibber. Neither of them, however, took his eyes off the back of a retreating figure, moving slowly towards the door on to Sixth Avenue.

Mr Smith, watching it go, felt no remorse, save for his recent ill-advised potations. This kind of thing might be exciting, but it did not pay – brought back, instead, old nightmares, old hallucinations which he had hoped were long ago dismissed as mere delusions. Yes, that was it. What he had seen a moment or two previously was a bad dream made real – or so it seemed. It was that fearful shadow on the doorway in Emporia come to life.

To this point unmolested, unremarked, a beak-faced monster, wearing Mr Meldrum's clothes, stalked out into the night.

To make a long story somewhat longer it is still necessary to tidy up a few loose ends.

Dr Fazo, left fainting in his chair, came to after a minute, regarded the life-mask of Mr Meldrum in imbecile relief. No, there was *nothing* wrong! The extraordinary sympathetic phenomenon which he believed himself to have witnessed (consisting in the gradual emergence from the mould of a peculiar beak-like process over a foot long) had been imagination, a grotesque mistake. Yes, it was a mistake all right, but Dr Fazo wasn't taking any chances. Pausing only to snatch up the cheque, he bolted. The elevator not working, he had to run down fifteen flights of stairs.

In the main hall he came upon the beginnings of a commotion, and the fag-end of Mr Smith, still squatting on the floor. Mr Smith, however, presumed a casual drunk, was not receiving much attention. The gibbering operator held the centre of the stage. Only a short time had elapsed since the elevator had descended, and the Ohio flapper (as well as a man who had noticed someone get into the cage at the sixteenth and had subsequently seen Dr Fazo start off running down the stairs) had yet to offer testimony.

Dr Fazo assisted Mr Smith to his feet. 'Quick! Let's get out of this!'

Get out they did, and only just in time. With one regrettable exception they have not, *in propria persona*, been seen or heard of since.

And what of Mr Meldrum? What of that Thoth incarnate, that grisly hidden fear too aptly disinterred, personified – and stalking, as has been narrated, through the night?

The change of which the onset was foreshadowed dimly in the alienist's office would seem to have been finally accomplished in the lift itself between the twelfth floor and the first. And, after that, the stalking did not last for very long, apparently. At the corner of Seventh Avenue and

Twenty-sixth Street – just a few blocks away – a building had come down, another was beginning to shoot upwards in its place. Into the twelve-foot chasm of an excavation *something* fell – fell down and broke its neck. An hour later the 'corpse' was discovered, and collected trepidantly. The Medical Inspector was available, and summoned, losing his sleep for several nights in consequence. He was a good Elk, a Rotarian, a K. of C. and a Kiwani, and his responsibilities weighed heavily. Finally, with soul-searching, he decided that the matter should be, if possible, hushed up. Those very odd-looking remains, after a deal of discussion *in camera*, were accorded Christian burial. Nobody knew of it except a haunted few.

It is, perhaps, surprising that this should be so. That this extraordinary history did not 'get about' (only by chance, indeed, and after several weeks arriving at the ears of Dr Fazo) is testimony to something – I am not quite sure what. Possibly to the hurrying, hard-headed and neglectful *tempo* of New York. In London such a story would have had the time to seed itself and propagate, have thriven better.

As regards Mr Smith, he never knew quite what to think about it all. Though he had lost a long-loved friend in Mr Meldrum, it appeared foolish to repine. The thing which had walked out of the Forensic Arts Building was not truly Mr Meldrum. It seemed, by the time its transformation was completed, to have been just a sinister emptiness, something without sensations, motives, or affections. When it fell down and broke its neck it had ceased to have a mind – in any sense that 'mind' had ordinarily conveyed to human beings. From that point Mr Smith could hardly have desired the course of fate reversed . . .

How to explain it all? He does not try. '*Omnia exeunt in mysterium*,' as his former landlady, Mrs Schultzenheimer, playfully reminded him one day last fall when he encountered her quite accidentally at Long Beach and, to his chagrin, was immediately recognized.

Yet how could *she* have known? This unexpected meeting was, of course, the 'regrettable exception' alluded to above and brooding upon Mrs Schultzenheimer has made Mr Smith extremely nervous. Although the complete story never became public and that small early-July-morning hubbub round the elevator was soon entirely forgotten, he still has an exaggerated fear of waking echoes. In spite of this, again, he feels a little like the Ancient Mariner, or like the seedy, weedy fellow of the *Nancy Belle*. He must tell somebody. At Dr Fazo's instigation, and to avoid 'repressions', he has himself been psycho'd and has written an account of the whole painful history – but it is most essential that he remain incognito.

It would, I feel, be quite intolerable otherwise. My name, as I have pointed out before, was at the very worst not really Smith, nor is it any name which may be printed over, under, or around this narrative. Nevertheless, I have a morbid dread of something's leaking out, and I have now elaborated and perfected my disguise.

From the date of Mr Meldrum's unfortunate apotheosis I have never worn Ohio flappers or been on nodding terms with brown Fedora hats.

The Beast with Five Fingers

William Fryer Harvey

The story, I suppose, begins with Adrian Borlsover, whom I met when I was a little boy and he an old man. My father had called to appeal for a subscription, and before he left, Mr Borlsover laid his right hand in blessing on my head. I shall never forget the awe in which I gazed up at his face and realized for the first time that eyes might be dark and beautiful and shining, and yet not able to see.

For Adrian Borlsover was blind.

He was an extraordinary man, who came of an eccentric stock. Borlsover sons for some reason always seemed to marry very ordinary women; which perhaps accounted for the fact that no Borlsover had been a genius, and only one Borlsover had been mad. But they were great champions of little causes, generous patrons of odd sciences, founders of querulous sects, trustworthy guides to the bypath meadows of erudition.

Adrian was an authority on the fertilization of orchids. He had held at one time the family living at Borlsover Conyers, until a congenital weakness of the lungs obliged him to seek a less rigorous climate in the sunny south-coast watering-place where I had seen him. Occasionally he would relieve one or other of the local clergy. My father described him as a fine preacher, who gave long and inspiring sermons from what many men would have considered unprofitable texts. 'An excellent proof,' he would add, 'of the truth of the doctrine of direct verbal inspiration.'

Adrian Borlsover was exceedingly clever with his hands. His penmanship was exquisite. He illustrated all his scientific papers, made his own wood-cuts, and carved the reredos that is at present the chief feature of interest in the church at Borlsover Conyers. He had an exceedingly clever knack in cutting silhouettes for young ladies and paper pigs and cows for little children, and made more than one complicated wind-instrument of his own devising.

When he was fifty years old Adrian Borlsover lost his sight. In a wonderfully short time he adapted himself to the new conditions of life. He quickly learnt to read Braille. So marvellous indeed was his sense of touch, that he was still able to maintain his interest in botany. The mere passing of his long supple fingers over a flower was sufficient means for its identification, though occasionally he would use his lips. I have found several letters of his among my father's correspondence; in no case was there anything to show that he was afflicted with blindness, and this in spite of the fact that he exercised undue economy in the spacing of lines. Towards the close of his life Adrian Borlsover was credited with powers of touch that seemed almost uncanny. It has been said that he could tell at once the colour of a ribbon placed between his fingers. My father would neither confirm nor deny the story.

Adrian Borlsover was a bachelor. His elder brother, Charles, had married late in life, leaving one son, Eustace, who lived in the gloomy Georgian mansion at Borlsover Conyers, where he could work undisturbed in collecting material for his great book on heredity.

Like his uncle, he was a remarkable man. The Borlsovers had always been born naturalists, but Eustace possessed in a special degree the power of systematizing his knowledge. He had received his university education in Germany; and then, after post-graduate work in Vienna and Naples, had travelled for four years in South America and the East, getting together a huge store of material for a new study into the processes of variation.

He lived alone at Borlsover Conyers with Saunders, his secretary, a man who bore a somewhat dubious reputation in the district, but whose powers as a mathematician, combined with his business abilities, were invaluable to Eustace.

Uncle and nephew saw little of each other. The visits of Eustace were confined to a week in the summer or autumn – tedious weeks, that dragged almost as slowly as the bath-chair in which the old man was drawn along the sunny sea-front. In their way the two men were fond of each other, though their intimacy would, doubtless, have been greater, had they shared the same religious views. Adrian held to the old-fashioned evangelical dogmas of his early manhood; his nephew for many years had been thinking of embracing Buddhism. Both men possessed, too, the reticence the Borlsovers had always shown, and which their enemies sometimes called hypocrisy. With Adrian it was a reticence as to the things he had left undone; but with Eustace it seemed that the curtain which he was so careful to leave undrawn hid something more than a half-empty chamber.

Two years before his death, Adrian Borlsover developed, unknown to himself, the not uncommon power of automatic writing. Eustace made the discovery by accident. Adrian was sitting reading in bed, the forefinger of his left hand tracing the Braille characters, when his nephew noticed that a pencil the old man held in his right hand was moving slowly along the opposite page. He had left his seat in the window and sat down beside the bed. The right hand continued to move, and now he could see plainly that they were letters and words which it was forming.

'Adrian Borlsover,' wrote the hand, 'Eustace Borlsover, Charles Borlsover, Francis Borlsover, Sigismund Borlsover, Adrian Borlsover, Eustace Borlsover, Saville Borlsover. B for Borlsover. Honesty is the Best Policy. Beautiful Belinda Borlsover.'

'What curious nonsense!' said Eustace to himself.

'King George ascended the throne in 1760,' wrote the hand. 'Crowd, a noun of multitude; a collection of individuals. Adrian Borlsover, Eustace Borlsover.'

'It seems to me,' said his uncle, closing the book, 'that you had much better make the most of the afternoon sunshine and take your walk now.'

'I think perhaps I will,' Eustace answered as he picked up the volume. 'I won't go far, and when I come back, I can read to you those articles in *Nature* about which we were speaking.'

He went along the promenade, but stopped at the first shelter, and, seating himself in the corner best protected from the wind, he examined the book at leisure. Nearly every page was scored with a meaningless jumble of pencil-marks; rows of capital letters, short words, long words, complete sentences, copy-book tags. The whole thing, in fact, had the appearance of a copy-book, and, on a more careful scrutiny, Eustace thought that there was ample evidence to show that the handwriting at the beginning of the book, good though it was, was not nearly so good as the handwriting at the end.

He left his uncle at the end of October with a promise to return early in December. It seemed to him quite clear that the old man's power of automatic writing was developing rapidly, and for the first time he looked forward to a visit that would combine duty with interest.

But on his return he was at first disappointed. His uncle, he thought, looked older. He was listless, too, preferring others to read to him and dictating nearly all his letters. Not until the day before he left had Eustace an opportunity of observing Adrian Borlsover's new-found faculty.

The old man, propped up in bed with pillows, had sunk into a light sleep. His two hands lay on the coverlet, his left hand tightly clasping his right. Eustace took an empty manuscript book and placed a pencil within reach of the fingers of the right hand. They snatched at it eagerly, then dropped the pencil to loose the left hand from its restraining grasp.

'Perhaps to prevent interference I had better hold that hand,' said Eustace to himself, as he watched the pencil. Almost immediately it began to write.

'Blundering Borlsovers, unnecessarily unnatural, extraordinarily eccentric, culpably curious.'

'Who are you?' asked Eustace in a low voice.

'Never you mind,' wrote the hand of Adrian.

'Is it my uncle who is writing?'

'O my prophetic soul, mine uncle!'

'Is it any one I know?'

'Silly Eustace, you'll see me very soon.'

'When shall I see you?'

'When poor old Adrian's dead.'

'Where shall I see you?'

'Where shall you not?'

Instead of speaking his next question, Eustace wrote it. 'What is the time?'

The fingers dropped the pencil and moved three or four times across the paper. Then, picking up the pencil, they wrote: 'Ten minutes before four. Put your book away, Eustace. Adrian mustn't find us working at this sort of thing. He doesn't know what to make of it, and I won't have poor old Adrian disturbed. Au revoir!'

Adrian Borlsover awoke with a start.

'I've been dreaming again,' he said; 'such queer dreams of leaguered cities and forgotten towns. You were mixed up in this one, Eustace, though I can't remember how. Eustace, I want to warn you. Don't walk in doubtful paths. Choose your friends well. Your poor grandfather . . .'

A fit of coughing put an end to what he was saying, but Eustace saw that the hand was still writing. He managed unnoticed to draw the book away. 'I'll light the gas,' he said, 'and ring for tea.' On the other side of the bed-curtain he saw the last sentence that had been written.

'It's too late, Adrian,' he said. 'We're friends already, aren't we, Eustace Borlsover?'

On the following day Eustace left. He thought his uncle looked ill when he said good-bye, and the old man spoke despondently of the failure his life had been.

'Nonsense, uncle,' said his nephew. 'You have got over your difficulties in a way not one in a hundred thousand would have done. Every one marvels at your splendid perseverance in teaching your hand to take the place of your lost sight. To me it's been a revelation of the possibilities of education.'

'Education,' said his uncle dreamily, as if the word had started a new train of thought. 'Education is good so long as you know to whom and for what purpose you give it. But with the lower orders of men, the base and more sordid spirits, I have grave doubts as to its results. Well, good-bye, Eustace; I may not see you again. You are a true Borlsover, with all the Borlsover faults. Marry, Eustace. Marry some good, sensible girl. And if by any chance I don't see you again, my will is at my solicitors. I've not left you any legacy, because I know you're well provided for; but I thought you might like to have my books. Oh, and there's just another thing. You know, before the end, people often lose control over themselves and make absurd requests. Don't pay any attention to them, Eustace. Good-bye!' and he held out his hand. Eustace took it. It remained in his a fraction of a second longer than he had expected and gripped him with a virility that was surprising. There was, too, in its touch a subtle sense of intimacy.

'Why, uncle,' he said, 'I shall see you alive and well for many long years to come.'

Two months later Adrian Borlsover died.

Eustace Borlsover was in Naples at the time. He read the obituary notice in the *Morning Post* on the day announced for the funeral.

'Poor old fellow!' he said. 'I wonder whether I shall find room for all his books.'

The question occurred to him again with greater force when, three days later, he found himself standing in the library at Borlsover Conyers, a huge room built for use and not for beauty in the year of Waterloo by a Borlsover who was an ardent admirer of the great Napoleon. It was arranged on the plan of many college libraries, with tall projecting bookcases forming deep recesses of dusty silence, fit graves for the old hates of forgotten controversy, the dead passions of forgotten lives. At the end of the room, behind the bust of some unknown eighteenth-century divine, an ugly iron corkscrew stair led to a shelf-lined gallery. Nearly every shelf was full.

'I must talk to Saunders about it,' said Eustace. 'I suppose that we shall have to have the billiard-room fitted up with bookcases.'

The two men met for the first time after many weeks in the dining-room that evening.

'Hallo!' said Eustace, standing before the fire with his hands in his pockets. 'How goes the world, Saunders? Why these dress togs?' He himself was wearing an old shooting-jacket. He did not believe in mourning, as he had told his uncle on his last visit; and, though he usually went in for quiet-coloured ties, he wore this evening one of an ugly red, in order to shock Morton the butler, and to make them thrash out the whole question of mourning for themselves in the servants' hall. Eustace was a true Borlsover. 'The world,' said Saunders, 'goes the same as usual, confoundedly slow. The dress togs are accounted for by an invitation from Captain Lockwood to bridge.'

'How are you getting there?'

'There's something the matter with the car, so I've told Jackson to drive me round in the dogcart. Any objection?'

'Oh dear me, no! We've had all things in common for far too many years for me to raise objections at this hour of the day.'

'You'll find your correspondence in the library,' went on Saunders. 'Most of it I've seen to. There are a few private letters I haven't opened. There's also a box with a rat or something inside it that came by the evening post. Very likely it's the six-toed beast Terry was sending us to cross with the four-toed albino. I didn't look because I didn't want to mess up my things; but I should gather from the way it's jumping about that it's pretty hungry.'

'Oh, I'll see to it,' said Eustace, 'while you and the captain earn an honest penny.'

Dinner over and Saunders gone, Eustace went into the library. Though the fire had been lit, the room was by no means cheerful.

'We'll have all the lights on, at any rate,' he said, as he turned the switches. 'And, Morton,' he added, when the butler brought the coffee, 'get me a screwdriver or something to undo this box. Whatever the animal is, he's kicking up the deuce of a row. What is it? Why are you dawdling?'

'If you please, sir, when the postman brought it, he told me that they'd bored the holes in the lid at the post office. There were no breathing holes in the lid, sir, and they didn't want the animal to die. That is all, sir.'

'It's culpably careless of the man, whoever he was,' said Eustace, as he removed the screws, 'packing an animal like this in a wooden box with no means of getting air. Confound it all! I meant to ask Morton to bring me a cage to put it in. Now I suppose I shall have to get one myself.'

He placed a heavy book on the lid from which the screws had been removed, and went into the billiard-room. As he came back into the library with an empty cage in his hand, he heard the sound of something falling, and then of something scuttling along the floor.

'Bother it! The beast's got out. How in the world am I to find it again in this library?'

To search for it did indeed seem hopeless. He tried to follow the sound of the scuttling in one of the recesses, where the animal seemed to be running behind the books in the shelves; but it was impossible to locate it. Eustace resolved to go on quietly reading. Very likely the animal might gain confidence and show itself. Saunders seemed to have dealt in his usual methodical manner with most of the correspondence. There were still the private letters.

What was that? Two sharp clicks and the lights in the hideous candelabras that hung from the ceiling suddenly went out.

'I wonder if something has gone wrong with the fuse,' said Eustace, as he went to the switches by the door. Then he stopped. There was a noise at the other end of the room, as if something was crawling up the iron corkscrew stair. 'If it's gone into the gallery,' he said, 'well and good.' He hastily turned on the lights, crossed the room, and climbed up the stair. But he could see nothing. His grandfather had placed a little gate at the top of the stair, so that children could run and romp in the gallery without fear of accident. This Eustace closed, and, having considerably narrowed the circle of his search, returned to his desk by the fire.

How gloomy the library was! There was no sense of intimacy about the room. The few busts that an eighteenth-century Borlsover had brought back from the grand tour might have been in keeping in the old library. Here they seemed out of place. They made the room feel cold in spite of the heavy red damask curtains and great gilt cornices.

With a crash two heavy books fell from the gallery to the floor; then, as Borlsover looked, another, and yet another.

'Very well. You'll starve for this, my beauty!' he said. 'We'll do some little experiments on the metabolism of rats deprived of water. Go on! Chuck them down! I think I've got the upper hand.' He turned once more to his correspondence. The letter was from the family solicitor. It spoke of his uncle's death, and of the valuable collection of books that had been left to him in the will.

There was one request [he read] which certainly came as a surprise to me. As you know, Mr Adrian Borlsover had left instructions that his body was to be buried in as simple a manner as possible at Eastbourne. He expressed a desire that there should be neither wreaths nor flowers of any kind, and hoped that his friends and relatives would not consider it necessary to wear mourning. The day before his death we received a letter cancelling these instructions. He wished the body to be embalmed (he gave us the address of the man we were to employ – Pennifer,

Ludgate Hill), with orders that his right hand should be sent to you, stating that
it was at your special request. The other arrangements about the funeral remained
unaltered.

'Good Lord,' said Eustace, 'what in the world was the old boy driving
at? And what in the name of all that's holy is that?'

Someone was in the gallery. Someone had pulled the cord attached to
one of the blinds, and it had rolled up with a snap. Someone must be in
the gallery, for a second blind did the same. Someone must be walking
round the gallery, for one after the other the blinds sprang up, letting in
the moonlight.

'I haven't got to the bottom of this yet,' said Eustace, 'But I will do,
before the night is very much older'; and he hurried up the corkscrew
stair. He had just got to the top, when the lights went out a second time,
and he heard again the scuttling along the floor. Quickly he stole on
tiptoe in the dim moonshine in the direction of the noise, feeling, as he
went, for one of the switches. His fingers touched the metal knob at last.
He turned on the electric light.

About ten yards in front of him, crawling along the floor, was a man's
hand. Eustace stared at it in utter amazement. It was moving quickly in
the manner of a geometer caterpillar, the fingers humped up one moment,
flattened out the next; the thumb appeared to give a crablike motion to
the whole. While he was looking, too surprised to stir, the hand
disappeared round the corner. Eustace ran forward. He no longer saw it,
but he could hear it, as it squeezed its way behind the books on one of the
shelves. A heavy volume had been displaced. There was a gap in the row
of books, where it had got in. In his fear lest it should escape him again,
he seized the first book that came to his hand and plugged it into the hole.
Then, emptying two shelves of their contents, he took the wooden boards
and propped them up in front to make his barrier doubly sure.

'I wish Saunders was back,' he said; 'one can't tackle this sort of thing
alone.' It was after eleven, and there seemed little likelihood of Saunders
returning before twelve. He did not dare to leave the shelf unwatched,
even to run downstairs to ring the bell. Morton, the butler, often used to
come round about eleven to see that the windows were fastened, but he
might not come. Eustace was thoroughly unstrung. At last he heard steps
down below.

'Morton!' he shouted. 'Morton!'

'Sir?'

'Has Mr Saunders got back yet?'

'Not yet, sir.'

'Well, bring me some brandy, and hurry up about it. I'm up in the gallery, you duffer.'

'Thanks,' said Eustace, as he emptied the glass. 'Don't go to bed yet, Morton. There are a lot of books that have fallen down by accident. Bring them up and put them back in their shelves.'

Morton had never seen Borlsover in so talkative a mood as on that night. 'Here,' said Eustace, when the books had been put back and dusted, 'you might hold up these boards for me, Morton. That beast in the box got out, and I've been chasing it all over the place.'

'I think I can hear it clawing at the books, sir. They're not valuable, I hope? I think that's the carriage, sir; I'll go and call Mr Saunders.'

It seemed to Eustace that he was away for five minutes but it could hardly have been more than one, when he returned with Saunders. 'All right, Morton, you can go now. I'm up here, Saunders.'

'What's all the row?' asked Saunders, as he lounged forward with his hands in his pockets. The luck had been with him all the evening. He was completely satisfied, both with himself and with Captain Lockwood's taste in wines. 'What's the matter? You look to me to be in an absolutely blue funk.'

'That old devil of an uncle of mine,' began Eustace – 'Oh, I can't explain it all. It's his hand that's been playing Old Harry all the evening. But I've got it cornered behind these books. You've got to help me to catch it.'

'What's up with you, Eustace? What's the game?'

'It's no game, you silly idiot! If you don't believe me, take out one of those books and put your hand in and feel.'

'All right,' said Saunders; 'but wait till I've rolled up my sleeve. The accumulated dust of centuries, eh?' He took off his coat, knelt down, and thrust his arm along the shelf.

'There's something there right enough,' he said. 'It's got a funny, stumpy end to it, whatever it is, and nips like a crab. Ah! no, you don't!' He pulled his hand out in a flash. 'Shove in a book quickly. Now it can't get out.'

'What was it?' asked Eustace.

'Something that wanted very much to get hold of me. I felt what seemed like a thumb and forefinger. Give me some brandy.'

'How are we to get it out of there?'

'What about a landing-net?'

'No good. It would be too smart for us. I tell you, Saunders, it can cover the ground far faster than I can walk. But I think I see how we can manage it. The two books at the end of the shelf are big ones, that go right back against the wall. The others are very thin. I'll take out one at a time, and you slide the rest along, until we have it squashed between the end two.'

It certainly seemed to be the best plan. One by one as they took out the books, the space behind grew smaller and smaller. There was something in it that was certainly very much alive. Once they caught sight of fingers feeling for a way of escape. At last they had it pressed between the two big books.

'There's muscle there, if there isn't warm flesh and blood,' said Saunders, as he held them together. 'It seems to be a hand right enough, too. I suppose this is a sort of infectious hallucination. I've read about such cases before.'

'Infectious fiddlesticks!' said Eustace, his face white with anger; 'bring the thing downstairs. We'll get it back into the box.'

It was not altogether easy, but they were successful at last. 'Drive in the screws,' said Eustace; 'we won't run any risks. Put the box in this old desk of mine. There's nothing in it that I want. Here's the key. Thank goodness there's nothing wrong with the lock.'

'Quite a lively evening,' said Saunders. 'Now let's hear more about your uncle.'

They sat up together until early morning. Saunders had no desire for sleep. Eustace was trying to explain and forget; to conceal from himself a fear that he had never felt before – the fear of walking alone down the long corridor to his bedroom.

'Whatever it was,' said Eustace to Saunders on the following morning, 'I propose that we drop the subject. There's nothing to keep us here for the next ten days. We'll motor up to the Lakes and get some climbing.'

'And see nobody all day, and sit bored to death with each other every night. Not for me, thanks. Why not run up to town? Run's the exact word in this case, isn't it? We're both in such a blessed funk. Pull yourself together, Eustace, and let's have another look at the hand.'

'As you like,' said Eustace; 'there's the key.'

They went into the library and opened the desk. The box was as they had left it on the previous night.

'What are you waiting for?' asked Eustace.

'I am waiting for you to volunteer to open the lid. However, since you seem to funk it, allow me. There doesn't seem to be the likelihood of any rumpus this morning at all events.' He opened the lid and picked out the hand.

'Cold?' asked Eustace.

'Tepid. A bit below blood heat by the feel. Soft and supple too. If it's the embalming, it's a sort of embalming I've never seen before. Is it your uncle's hand?'

'Oh, yes, it's his all right,' said Eustace. 'I should know those long thin fingers anywhere. Put it back in the box, Saunders. Never mind about the screws. I'll lock the desk, so that there'll be no chance of its getting out. We'll compromise by motoring up to town for a week. If we can get off soon after lunch, we ought to be at Grantham or Stamford by night.'

'Right,' said Saunders, 'and tomorrow – oh, well, by tomorrow we shall have forgotten all about this beastly thing.'

If, when the morrow came, they had not forgotten, it was certainly true that at the end of the week they were able to tell a very vivid ghost-story at the little supper Eustace gave on Hallow E'en.

'You don't want us to believe that it's true, Mr Borlsover? How perfectly awful!'

'I'll take my oath on it, and so would Saunders here; wouldn't you, old chap?'

'Any number of oaths,' said Saunders. 'It was a long, thin hand, you know, and it gripped me just like that.'

'Don't, Mr Saunders! Don't! How perfectly horrid! Now tell us another one, do! Only a really creepy one, please.'

'Here's a pretty mess!' said Eustace on the following day, as he threw a letter across the table to Saunders. 'It's your affair, though. Mrs Merritt, if I understand it, gives a month's notice.'

'Oh, that's quite absurd on Mrs Merritt's part,' replied Saunders. 'She doesn't know what she's talking about. Let's see what she says.'

DEAR SIR [he read]. This is to let you know that I must give you a month's notice as from Tuesday, the 13th. For a long time I've felt the place too big for me; but when Jane Parfit and Emma Laidlaw go off with scarcely as much as an 'If you please', after frightening the wits out of the other girls, so that they can't turn out a room by themselves or walk alone down the stairs for fear of treading on half-frozen toads or hearing it run along the passages at night, all I can say is that it's no place for me. So I must ask you, Mr Borlsover, sir, to find a new housekeeper, that has no objection to large and lonely houses, which some people do say, not that I believe them for a minute, my poor mother always having been a Wesleyan, are haunted.

Yours faithfully,

ELIZABETH MERRITT

P.S. – I should be obliged if you would give my respects to Mr Saunders. I hope that he won't run any risks with his cold.

'Saunders,' said Eustace, 'you've always had a wonderful way with you in dealing with servants. You mustn't let poor old Merritt go.'

'Of course she shan't go,' said Saunders. 'She's probably only angling for a rise in salary. I'll write to her this morning.'

'No. There's nothing like a personal interview. We've had enough of town. We'll go back tomorrow, and you must work your cold for all it's worth. Don't forget that it's got on to the chest, and will require weeks of feeding up and nursing.'

'All right; I think I can manage Mrs Merritt.'

But Mrs Merritt was more obstinate than he had thought. She was very sorry to hear of Mr Saunders's cold, and how he lay awake all night in London coughing; very sorry indeed. She'd change his room for him gladly and get the south room aired, and wouldn't he have a hot basin of bread and milk last thing at night? But she was afraid that she would have to leave at the end of the month.

'Try her with an increase of salary,' was the advice of Eustace.

It was no use. Mrs Merritt was obdurate, though she knew of a Mrs Goddard, who had been housekeeper to Lord Gargrave, who might be glad to come at the salary mentioned.

'What's the matter with the servants, Morton?' asked Eustace that evening, when he brought the coffee into the library. 'What's all this about Mrs Merritt wanting to leave?'

'If you please, sir, I was going to mention it myself. I have a confession to make, sir. When I found your note, asking me to open that desk and take out the box with the rat, I broke the lock, as you told me, and was glad to do it, because I could hear the animal in the box making a great noise, and I thought it wanted food. So I took out the box, sir, and got a cage, and was going to transfer it, when the animal got away.'

'What in the world are you talking about? I never wrote any such note.'

'Excuse me, sir; it was the note I picked up here on the floor the day you and Mr Saunders left. I have it in my pocket now.'

It certainly seemed to be in Eustace's handwriting. It was written in pencil, and began somewhat abruptly.

'Get a hammer, Morton,' he read, 'or some tool and break open the lock in the old desk in the library. Take out the box that is inside. You need not do anything else. The lid is already open. Eustace Borlsover.'

'And you opened the desk?'

'Yes, sir; and, as I was getting the cage ready, the animal hopped out.'

'What animal?'

'The animal inside the box, sir.'

'What did it look like?'

'Well, sir, I couldn't tell you,' said Morton, nervously. 'My back was turned, and it was half way down the room when I looked up.'

'What was its colour?' asked Saunders. 'Black?'

'Oh, no, sir; a greyish white. It crept along in a very funny way, sir. I don't think it had a tail.'

'What did you do then?'

'I tried to catch it; but it was no use. So I set the rat-traps and kept the library shut. Then that girl, Emma Laidlaw, left the door open when she was cleaning, and I think it must have escaped.'

'And you think it is the animal that's been frightening the maids?'

'Well, no, sir, not quite. They said it was – you'll excuse me, sir – a hand that they saw. Emma trod on it once at the bottom of the stairs. She thought then it was a half-frozen toad, only white. And then Parfit was washing up the dishes in the scullery. She wasn't thinking about anything in particular. It was close on dusk. She took her hands out of the water and was drying them absentminded like on the roller towel, when she found she was drying someone else's hand as well, only colder than hers.'

'What nonsense!' exclaimed Saunders.

'Exactly, sir; that's what I told her; but we couldn't get her to stop.'

'You don't believe all this?' said Eustace, turning suddenly towards the butler.

'Me, sir? Oh, no, sir! I've not seen anything.'

'Nor heard anything?'

'Well, sir, if you must know, the bells do ring at odd times, and there's nobody there when we go; when we go round to draw the blinds of a night, as often as not somebody's been there before us. But, as I says to Mrs Merritt, a young monkey might do wonderful things, and we all know that Mr Borlsover has had some strange animals about the place.'

'Very well, Morton, that will do.'

'What do you make of it?' asked Saunders, when they were alone. 'I mean of the letter he said you wrote.'

'Oh, that's simple enough,' said Eustace. 'See the paper it's written on? I stopped using that paper years ago, but there were a few odd sheets and envelopes left in the old desk. We never fastened up the lid of the box before locking it in. The hand got out, found a pencil, wrote this note, and shoved it through the crack on to the floor, where Morton found it. That's plain as daylight.'

'But the hand couldn't write!'

'Couldn't it? You've not seen it do the things I've seen.' And he told Saunders more of what had happened at Eastbourne.

'Well,' said Saunders, 'in that case we have at least an explanation of the legacy. It was the hand which wrote, unknown to your uncle, that letter to your solicitor bequeathing itself to you. Your uncle had no more to do with that request than I. In fact, it would seem that he had some idea of this automatic writing and feared it.'

'Then if it's not my uncle, what is it?'

'I suppose some people might say that a disembodied spirit had got your uncle to educate and prepare a little body for it. Now it's got into that little body and is off on its own.'

'Well, what are we to do?'

'We'll keep our eyes open,' said Saunders, 'and try to catch it. If we can't do that, we shall have to wait till the bally clockwork runs down. After all, if it's flesh and blood, it can't live for ever.'

For two days nothing happened. Then Saunders saw it sliding down the banister in the hall. He was taken unawares and lost a full second before he started in pursuit, only to find that the thing had escaped him. Three days later, Eustace, writing alone in the library at night, saw it sitting on an open book at the other end of the room. The fingers crept over the page, as if it were reading; but before he had time to get up from his seat, it had taken the alarm, and was pulling itself up the curtains. Eustace watched it grimly, as it hung on to the cornice with three fingers and flicked thumb and forefinger at him in an expression of scornful derision.

'I know what I'll do,' he said. 'If I only get it into the open, I'll set the dogs on to it.'

He spoke to Saunders of the suggestion.

'It's a jolly good idea,' he said; 'only we won't wait till we find it out of doors. We'll get the dogs. There are the two terriers and the under-keeper's Irish mongrel, that's on to rats like a flash. Your spaniel has not got spirit enough for this sort of game.'

They brought the dogs into the house, and the keeper's Irish mongrel chewed up the slippers, and the terriers tripped up Morton, as he waited at table; but all three were welcome. Even false security is better than no security at all.

For a fortnight nothing happened. Then the hand was caught, not by the dogs, but by Mrs Merritt's grey parrot. The bird was in the habit of periodically removing the pins that kept its seed- and water-tins in place, and of escaping through the holes in the side of his cage. When once at liberty, Peter would show no inclination to return, and would often be about the house for days. Now, after six consecutive weeks of captivity, Peter had again discovered a new way of unloosing his bolts and was at large, exploring the tapestried forests of the curtains and singing songs in praise of liberty from cornice and picture-rail.

'It's no use your trying to catch him,' said Eustace to Mrs Merritt, as she came into the study one afternoon towards dusk with a step-ladder. 'You'd much better leave Peter alone. Starve him into surrender, Mrs Merritt; and don't leave bananas and seed about for him to peck at when he fancies he's hungry. You're far too soft-hearted.'

'Well, sir, I see he's right out of reach now on that picture-rail; so, if you wouldn't mind closing the door, sir, when you leave the room, I'll bring his cage in tonight and put some meat inside it. He's that fond of meat, though it does make him pull out his feathers to suck the quills. They say that if you cook –'

'Never mind, Mrs Merritt,' said Eustace, who was busy writing; 'that will do; I'll keep an eye on the bird.'

For a short time there was silence in the room.

'Scratch poor Peter,' said the bird. 'Scratch poor old Peter!'

'Be quiet, you beastly bird!'

'Poor old Peter! Scratch poor Peter; do!'

'I'm more likely to wring your neck, if I get hold of you.' He looked up at the picture-rail, and there was the hand, holding on to a hook with three fingers, and slowly scratching the head of the parrot with the fourth. Eustace ran to the bell and pressed it hard; then across to the window, which he closed with a bang. Frightened by the noise, the parrot shook its wings preparatory to flight, and, as it did so, the fingers of the hand got hold of it by the throat. There was a shrill scream from Peter, as he fluttered across the room, wheeling round in circles that ever descended, borne down under the weight that clung to him. The bird dropped at last quite suddenly, and Eustace saw fingers and feathers rolled into an inextricable mass on the floor. The struggle abruptly ceased, as finger and thumb squeezed the neck; the bird's eyes rolled up to show the whites, and there was a faint, half-choked gurgle. But, before the fingers had time to loose their hold, Eustace had them in his own.

'Send Mr Saunders here at once,' he said to the maid who came in answer to the bell. 'Tell him I want him immediately.'

Then he went with the hand to the fire. There was a ragged gash across the back, where the bird's beak had torn it, but no blood oozed from the wound. He noted with disgust that the nails had grown long and discoloured.

'I'll burn the beastly thing,' he said. But he could not burn it. He tried to throw it into the flames, but his own hands, as if impelled by some old primitive feeling, would not let him. And so Saunders found him, pale and irresolute, with the hand still clasped tightly in his fingers.

'I've got it at last,' he said, in a tone of triumph.

'Good, let's have a look at it.'

'Not when it's loose. Get me some nails and a hammer and a board of some sort.'

'Can you hold it all right?'

'Yes, the thing's quite limp; tired out with throttling poor old Peter, I should say.'

'And now,' said Saunders, when he returned with the things, 'what are we going to do?'

'Drive a nail through it first, so that it can't get away. Then we can take our time over examining it.'

'Do it yourself,' said Saunders. 'I don't mind helping you with guinea-pigs occasionally, when there's something to be learned, partly because I don't fear a guinea-pig's revenge. This thing's different.'

'Oh, my aunt!' he giggled, hysterically, 'look at it now.' For the hand was writhing in agonized contortions, squirming and wriggling upon the nail like a worm upon the hook.

'Well,' said Saunders, 'you've done it now. I'll leave you to examine it.'

'Don't go, in heaven's name! Cover it up, man; cover it up! Shove a cloth over it! Here!' and he pulled off the antimacassar from the back of a chair and wrapped the board in it. 'Now get the keys from my pocket and open the safe. Chuck the other things out. Oh, Lord, it's getting itself into frightful knots! Open it quick!' He threw the thing in and banged the door.

'We'll keep it there till it dies,' he said. 'May I burn in hell, if I ever open the door of that safe again.'

Mrs Merritt departed at the end of the month. Her successor, Mrs Handyside, certainly was more successful in the management of the servants. Early in her rule she declared that she would stand no nonsense, and gossip soon withered and died.

'I shouldn't be surprised if Eustace married one of these days,' said Saunders. 'Well, I'm in no hurry for such an event. I know him far too well for the future Mrs Borlsover to like me. It will be the same old story again; a long friendship slowly made – marriage – and a long friendship quickly forgotten.'

But Eustace did not follow the advice of his uncle and marry. Old habits crept over and covered his new experience. He was, if anything, less morose, and showed a greater inclination to take his natural part in country society.

Then came the burglary. The men, it was said, broke into the house by way of the conservatory. It was really little more than an attempt, for they only succeeded in carrying away a few pieces of plate from the pantry. The safe in the study was certainly found open and empty, but, as Mr Borlsover informed the police inspector, he had kept nothing of value in it during the last six months.

'Then you're lucky in getting off so easily, sir,' the man replied. 'By the way they have gone about their business, I should say they were experienced cracksmen. They must have caught the alarm when they were just beginning their evening's work.'

'Yes,' said Eustace, 'I suppose I am lucky.'

'I've no doubt,' said the inspector, 'that we shall be able to trace the men. I've said that they must have been old hands at the game. The way they got in and opened the safe shows that. But there's one little thing that puzzles me. One of them was careless enough not to wear gloves, and I'm bothered if I know what he was trying to do. I've traced his finger-marks on the new varnish on the window-sashes in every one of the downstairs rooms. They were very distinctive ones too.'

'Right or left hand, or both?' asked Eustace.

'Oh, right every time. That's the funny thing. He must have been a foolhardy fellow, and I rather think it was him that wrote that.' He took out a slip of paper from his pocket. 'That's what he wrote, sir: "I've got out, Eustace Borlsover, but I'll be back before long." Some jailbird just escaped, I suppose. It will make it all the easier for us to trace him. Do you know the writing, sir?'

'No,' said Eustace. 'It's not the writing of any one I know.'

'I'm not going to stay here any longer,' said Eustace to Saunders at luncheon. 'I've got on far better during the last six months than I expected, but I'm not going to run the risk of seeing that thing again. I shall go up to town this afternoon. Get Morton to put my things together, and join me with the car at Brighton on the day after tomorrow. And bring the proofs of those two papers with you. We'll run over them together.'

'How long are you going to be away?'

'I can't say for certain, but be prepared to stay for some time. We've stuck to work pretty closely through the summer, and I for one need a holiday. I'll engage the rooms at Brighton. You'll find it best to break the journey at Hitchin. I'll wire to you there at the "Crown" to tell you the Brighton address.'

The house he chose at Brighton was in a terrace. He had been there before. It was kept by his old college gyp, a man of discreet silence, who was admirably partnered by an excellent cook. The rooms were on the first floor. The two bedrooms were at the back, and opened out of each other. 'Mr Saunders can have the smaller one, though it is the only one with a fireplace,' he said. 'I'll stick to the larger of the two, since it's got a bathroom adjoining. I wonder what time he'll arrive with the car.'

Saunders came about seven, cold and cross and dirty. 'We'll light the fire in the dining-room,' said Eustace, 'and get Prince to unpack some of the things while we are at dinner. What were the roads like?'

'Rotten. Swimming with mud, and a beastly cold wind against us all day. And this is July. Dear old England!'

'Yes,' said Eustace, 'I think we might do worse than leave old England for a few months.'

They turned in soon after twelve.

'You oughtn't to feel cold, Saunders,' said Eustace, 'when you can afford to sport a great fur-lined coat like this. You do yourself very well, all things considered. Look at those gloves, for instance. Who could possibly feel cold when wearing them?'

'They are far too clumsy, though, for driving. Try them on and see'; and he tossed them through the door on to Eustace's bed and went on with his unpacking. A minute later he heard a shrill cry of terror. 'Oh, Lord,' he heard, 'it's in the glove! Quick, Saunders, quick!' Then came a smacking thud. Eustace had thrown it from him. 'I've chucked it into the bathroom,' he gasped; 'it's hit the wall and fallen into the bath. Come now, if you want to help.' Saunders, with a lighted candle in his hand, looked over the edge of the bath. There it was, old and maimed, dumb and blind, with a ragged hole in the middle, crawling, staggering, trying to creep up the slippery sides, only to fall back helpless.

'Stay there,' said Saunders. 'I'll empty a collar-box or something, and we'll jam it in. It can't get out while I'm away.'

'Yes, it can,' shouted Eustace. 'It's getting out now; it's climbing up the plug-chain. No, you brute, you filthy brute, you don't! Come back, Saunders; it's getting away from me. I can't hold it; it's all slippery. Curse its claws! Shut the window, you idiot! It's got out.' There was the sound of something dropping on to the hard flagstones below, and Eustace fell back fainting.

For a fortnight he was ill.

'I don't know what to make of it,' the doctor said to Saunders. 'I can only suppose that Mr Borlsover has suffered some great emotional shock.

You had better let me send someone to help you nurse him. And by all means indulge that whim of his never to be left alone in the dark. I would keep a light burning all night, if I were you. But he *must* have more fresh air. It's perfectly absurd, this hatred of open windows.'

Eustace would have no one with him but Saunders.

'I don't want the other man,' he said. 'They'd smuggle it in somehow. I know they would.'

'Don't worry about it, old chap. This sort of thing can't go on indefinitely. You know I saw it this time as well as you. It wasn't half so active. It won't go on living much longer, especially after that fall. I heard it hit the flags myself. As soon as you're a bit stronger, we'll leave this place, not bag and baggage, but with only the clothes on our backs, so that it won't be able to hide anywhere. We'll escape it that way. We won't give any address, and we won't have any parcels sent after us. Cheer up, Eustace! You'll be well enough to leave in a day or two. The doctor says I can take you out in a chair tomorrow.'

'What have I done?' asked Eustace. 'Why does it come after me? I'm no worse than other men. I'm no worse than you, Saunders; you know I'm not. It was you who was at the bottom of that dirty business in San Diego, and that was fifteen years ago.'

'It's not that, of course,' said Saunders. 'We are in the twentieth century, and even the parsons have dropped the idea of your old sins finding you out. Before you caught the hand in the library, it was filled with pure malevolence – to you and all mankind. After you spiked it through with that nail, it naturally forgot about other people and concentrated its attention on you. It was shut up in that safe, you know, for nearly six months. That gives plenty of time for thinking of revenge.'

Eustace Borlsover would not leave his room, but he thought there might be something in Saunders's suggestion of a sudden departure from Brighton. He began rapidly to regain his strength.

'We'll go on the first of September,' he said.

The evening of the thirty-first of August was oppressively warm. Though at midday the windows had been wide open, they had been shut an hour or so before dusk. Mrs Prince had long since ceased to wonder at the strange habits of the gentlemen on the first floor. Soon after their arrival she had been told to take down the heavy window curtains in the two bedrooms, and day by day the rooms had seemed to grow more bare. Nothing was left lying about.

'Mr Borlsover doesn't like to have any place where dirt can collect,'

Saunders had said as an excuse. 'He likes to see into all the corners of the room.'

'Couldn't I open the window just a little?' he said to Eustace that evening. 'We're simply roasting in here, you know.'

'No, leave well alone. We're not a couple of boarding-school misses fresh from a course of hygiene lectures. Get the chess-board out.'

They sat down and played. At ten o'clock Mrs Prince came to the door with a note. 'I am sorry I didn't bring it before,' she said, 'but it was left in the letter-box.'

'Open it, Saunders, and see if it wants answering.'

It was very brief. There was neither address nor signature.

'Will eleven o'clock tonight be suitable for our last appointment?'

'Who is it from?' asked Borlsover.

'It was meant for me,' said Saunders. 'There's no answer, Mrs Prince,' and he put the paper into his pocket.

'A dunning letter from a tailor; I suppose he must have got wind of our leaving.'

It was a clever lie, and Eustace asked no more questions. They went on with their game.

On the landing outside Saunders could hear the grandfather's clock whispering the seconds, blurting out the quarter-hours.

'Check,' said Eustace. The clock struck eleven. At the same time there was a gentle knocking on the door; it seemed to come from the bottom panel.

'Who's there?' asked Eustace.

There was no answer.

'Mrs Prince, is that you?'

'She is up above,' said Saunders; 'I can hear her walking about the room.'

'Then lock the door; bolt it too. Your move, Saunders.'

While Saunders sat with his eyes on the chess-board, Eustace walked over to the window and examined the fastenings. He did the same in Saunders's room, and the bathroom. There were no doors between the three rooms, or he would have shut and locked them too.

'Now, Saunders,' he said, 'don't stay all night over your move. I've had time to smoke one cigarette already. It's bad to keep an invalid waiting. There's only one possible thing for you to do. What was that?'

'The ivy blowing against the window. There, it's your move now, Eustace.'

'It wasn't the ivy, you idiot! It was someone tapping at the window';

and he pulled up the blind. On the outer side of the window, clinging to the sash, was the hand.

'What is that it's holding?'

'It's a pocket-knife. It's going to try to open the window by pushing back the fastener with the blade.'

'Well, let it try,' said Eustace. 'Those fasteners screw down; they can't be opened that way. Anyhow, we'll close the shutters. It's your move, Saunders. I've played.'

But Saunders found it impossible to fix his attention on the game. He could not understand Eustace, who seemed all at once to have lost his fear. 'What do you say to some wine?' he asked. 'You seem to be taking things coolly, but I don't mind confessing that I'm in a blessed funk.'

'You've no need to be. There's nothing supernatural about that hand, Saunders. I mean, it seems to be governed by the laws of time and space. It's not the sort of thing that vanishes into thin air or slides through oaken doors. And since that's so, I defy it to get in here. We'll leave the place in the morning. I for one have bottomed the depths of fear. Fill your glass, man! The windows are all shuttered; the door is locked and bolted. Pledge me my Uncle Adrian! Drink, man! What are you waiting for?'

Saunders was standing with his glass half raised. 'It can get in,' he said hoarsely; 'it can get in! We've forgotten. There's the fireplace in my bedroom. It will come down the chimney.'

'Quick!' said Eustace, as he rushed into the other room; 'we haven't a minute to lose. What can we do? Light the fire, Saunders. Give me a match, quick!'

'They must be all in the other room. I'll get them.'

'Hurry, man, for goodness' sake! Look in the bookcase! Look in the bathroom! Here, come and stand here; I'll look.'

'Be quick!' shouted Saunders. 'I can hear something!'

'Then plug a sheet from your bed up the chimney. No, here's a match!' He had found one at last, that had slipped into a crack in the floor.

'Is the fire laid? Good, but it may not burn. I know – the oil from that old reading-lamp and this cotton-wool. Now the match, quick! Pull the sheet away, you fool! We don't want it now.'

There was a great roar from the grate, as the flames shot up. Saunders had been a fraction of a second too late with the sheet. The oil had fallen on to it. It, too, was burning.

'The whole place will be on fire!' cried Eustace, as he tried to beat out the flames with a blanket. 'It's no good! I can't manage it. You must open the door, Saunders, and get help.'

Saunders ran to the door and fumbled with the bolts. The key was stiff in the lock. 'Hurry,' shouted Eustace, 'or the heat will be too much for me.' The key turned in the lock at last. For half a second Saunders stopped to look back. Afterwards he could never be quite sure as to what he had seen, but at the time he thought that something black and charred was creeping slowly, very slowly, from the mass of flames towards Eustace Borlsover. For a moment he thought of returning to his friend; but the noise and the smell of the burning sent him running down the passage, crying: 'Fire! Fire!' He rushed to the telephone to summon help, and then back to the bathroom – he should have thought of that before – for water. As he burst into the bedroom there came a scream of terror which ended suddenly, and then the sound of a heavy fall.

This is the story which I heard on successive Saturday evenings from the senior mathematical master at a second-rate suburban school. For Saunders has had to earn a living in a way which other men might reckon less congenial than his old manner of life. I had mentioned by chance the name of Adrian Borlsover, and wondered at the time why he changed the conversation with such unusual abruptness. A week later Saunders began to tell me something of his own history; sordid enough, though shielded with a reserve I could well understand, for it had to cover not only his failings, but those of a dead friend. Of the final tragedy he was at first especially loath to speak; and it was only gradually that I was able to piece together the narrative of the preceding pages. Saunders was reluctant to draw any conclusions. At one time he thought that the fingered beast had been animated by the spirit of Sigismund Borlsover, a sinister eighteenth-century ancestor, who, according to legend, built and worshipped in the ugly pagan temple that overlooked the lake. At another time Saunders believed the spirit to belong to a man whom Eustace had once employed as a laboratory assistant, 'a black-haired, spiteful little brute,' he said, 'who died cursing his doctor because the fellow couldn't help him to live to settle some paltry score with Borlsover.'

From the point of view of direct contemporary evidence, Saunders's story is practically uncorroborated. All the letters mentioned in the narrative were destroyed, with the exception of the last note which Eustace received, or rather, which he would have received, had not Saunders intercepted it. That I have seen myself. The handwriting was thin and shaky, the handwriting of an old man. I remember the Greek 'e' was used in 'appointment'. A little thing that amused me at the time was that Saunders seemed to keep the note pressed between the pages of his Bible.

I had seen Adrian Borlsover once. Saunders I learnt to know well. It was by chance, however, and not by design, that I met a third person of the story, Morton, the butler. Saunders and I were walking in the Zoological Gardens one Sunday afternoon, when he called my attention to an old man who was standing before the door of the Reptile House.

'Why, Morton,' he said, clapping him on the back, 'how is the world treating you?'

'Poorly, Mr Saunders,' said the old fellow, though his face lighted up at the greeting. 'The winters drag terribly nowadays. There don't seem no summers or springs.'

'You haven't found what you were looking for, I suppose?'

'No, sir, not yet; but I shall some day. I always told them that Mr Borlsover kept some queer animals.'

'And what is he looking for?' I asked, when we had parted from him.

'A beast with five fingers,' said Saunders. 'This afternoon, since he has been in the Reptile House, I suppose it will be a reptile with a hand. Next week it will be a monkey with practically no body. The poor old chap is a born materialist.'

Dry September

William Faulkner

I

Through the bloody September twilight, aftermath of sixty-two rainless days, it had gone like a fire in dry grass – the rumour, the story, whatever it was. Something about Miss Minnie Cooper and a Negro. Attacked, insulted, frightened: none of them, gathered in the barber shop on that Saturday evening where the ceiling fan stirred, without freshening it, the vitiated air, sending back upon them, in recurrent surges of stale pomade and lotion, their own stale breath and odours, knew exactly what had happened.

'Except it wasn't Will Mayes,' a barber said. He was a man of middle age; a thin, sand-coloured man with a mild face, who was shaving a client. 'I know Will Mayes. He's a good nigger. And I know Miss Minnie Cooper, too.'

'What do you know about her?' a second barber said.

'Who is she?' the client said. 'A young girl?'

'No,' the barber said. 'She's about forty, I reckon. She ain't married. That's why I don't believe –'

'Believe, hell!' a hulking youth in a sweat-stained silk shirt said. 'Won't you take a white woman's word before a nigger's?'

'I don't believe Will Mayes did it,' the barber said. 'I know Will Mayes.'

'Maybe you know who did it, then. Maybe you already got him out of town, you damn niggerlover.'

'I don't believe anybody did anything. I don't believe anything happened. I leave it to you fellows if them ladies that get old without getting married don't have notions that a man can't –'

'Then you are a hell of a white man,' the client said. He moved under the cloth. The youth had sprung to his feet.

'You don't?' he said. 'Do you accuse a white woman of lying?'

The barber held the razor poised above the half-risen client. He did not look around.

'It's this durn weather,' another said. 'It's enough to make a man do anything. Even to her.'

Nobody laughed. The barber said in his mild, stubborn tone: 'I ain't accusing nobody of nothing. I just know and you fellows know how a woman that never —'

'You damn niggerlover!' the youth said.

'Shut up, Butch,' another said. 'We'll get the facts in plenty of time to act.'

'Who is? Who's getting them?' the youth said. 'Facts, hell! I —'

'You're a fine white man,' the client said. 'Ain't you?' In his frothy beard he looked like a desert rat in the moving pictures. 'You tell them, Jack,' he said to the youth. 'If there ain't any white men in this town, you can count on me, even if I ain't only a drummer and a stranger.'

'That's right, boys,' the barber said. 'Find out the truth first. I know Will Mayes.'

'Well, by God!' the youth shouted. 'To think that a white man in this town —'

'Shut up, Butch,' the second speaker said. 'We got plenty of time.'

The client sat up. He looked at the speaker. 'Do you claim that anything excuses a nigger attacking a white woman? Do you mean to tell me you are a white man and you'll stand for it? You better go back North where you came from. The South don't want your kind here.'

'North what?' the second said. 'I was born and raised in this town.'

'Well, by God!' the youth said. He looked about with a strained, baffled gaze, as if he was trying to remember what it was he wanted to say or to do. He drew his sleeve across his sweating face. 'Damn if I'm going to let a white woman —'

'You tell them, Jack,' the drummer said. 'By God, if they —'

The screen door crashed open. A man stood in the floor, his feet apart and his heavy-set body poised easily. His white shirt was open at the throat; he wore a felt hat. His hot, bold glance swept the group. His name was McLendon. He had commanded troops at the front in France and had been decorated for valour.

'Well,' he said, 'are you going to sit there and let a black son rape a white woman on the streets of Jefferson?'

Butch sprang up again. The silk of his shirt clung flat to his heavy shoulders. At each armpit was a dark halfmoon. 'That's what I been telling them! That's what I —'

'Did it really happen?' a third said. 'This ain't the first man scare she ever had, like Hawkshaw says. Wasn't there something about a man on the kitchen roof, watching her undress, about a year ago?'

'What?' the client said. 'What's that?' The barber had been slowly forcing him back into the chair; he arrested himself reclining, his head lifted, the barber still pressing him down.

McLendon whirled on the third speaker. 'Happen? What the hell difference does it make? Are you going to let the black sons get away with it until one really does it?'

'That's what I'm telling them!' Butch shouted. He cursed, long and steady, pointless.

'Here, here,' a fourth said. 'Not so loud. Don't talk so loud.'

'Sure,' McLendon said; 'no talking necessary at all. I've done my talking. Who's with me?' He poised on the balls of his feet, roving his gaze.

The barber held the drummer's face down, the razor poised. 'Find out the facts first, boys. I know Willy Mayes. It wasn't him. Let's get the sheriff and do this thing right.'

McLendon whirled upon him his furious, rigid face. The barber did not look away. They looked like men of different races. The other barbers had ceased also above their prone clients. 'You mean to tell me,' McLendon said, 'that you'd take a nigger's word before a white woman's? Why, you damn niggerloving –'

The third speaker rose and grasped McLendon's arm; he too had been a soldier. 'Now, now. Let's figure this thing out. Who knows anything about what really happened?'

'Figure out hell!' McLendon jerked his arm free. 'All that're with me get up from there. The ones that ain't –' He roved his gaze, dragging his sleeve across his face.

Three men rose. The drummer in the chair sat up. 'Here,' he said, jerking at the cloth about his neck; 'get this rag off me. I'm with him. I don't live here, but by God, if our mothers and wives and sisters –' He smeared the cloth over his face and flung it to the floor. McLendon stood in the floor and cursed the others. Another rose and moved towards him. The remainder sat uncomfortable, not looking at one another, then one by one they rose and joined him.

The barber picked the cloth from the floor. He began to fold it neatly. 'Boys, don't do that. Will Mayes never done it. I know.'

'Come on,' McLendon said. He whirled. From his hip pocket protruded the butt of a heavy automatic pistol. They went out. The screen door crashed behind them reverberant in the dead air.

The barber wiped the razor carefully and swiftly, and put it away, and ran to the rear, and took his hat from the wall. 'I'll be back as soon as I can,' he said to the other barbers. 'I can't let –' He went out, running. The two other barbers followed him to the door and caught it on the rebound, leaning out and looking up the street after him. The air was flat and dead. It had a metallic taste at the base of the tongue.

'What can he do?' the first said. The second one was saying 'Jees Christ, Jees Christ' under his breath. 'I'd just as lief be Will Mayes as Hawk, if he gets McLendon riled.'

'Jees Christ, Jees Christ,' the second whispered.

'You reckon he really done it to her?' the first said.

II

She was thirty-eight or thirty-nine. She lived in a small frame house with her invalid mother and a thin, sallow, unflagging aunt, where each morning between ten and eleven she would appear on the porch in a lace-trimmed boudoir cap, to sit swinging in the porch swing until noon. After dinner she lay down for a while, until the afternoon began to cool. Then, in one of the three or four new voile dresses which she had each summer, she would go downtown to spend the afternoon in the stores with the other ladies, where they would handle the goods and haggle over the prices in cold, immediate voices, without any intention of buying.

She was of comfortable people – not the best in Jefferson, but good people enough – and she was still on the slender side of ordinary looking, with a bright, faintly haggard manner and dress. When she was young she had had a slender, nervous body and a sort of hard vivacity which had enabled her for a time to ride upon the crest of the town's social life as exemplified by the high school party and church social period of her contemporaries while still children enough to be unclassconscious.

She was the last to realize that she was losing ground; that those among whom she had been a little brighter and louder flame than any other were beginning to learn the pleasure of snobbery – male – and retaliation – female. That was when her face began to wear that bright, haggard look. She still carried it to parties on shadowy porticoes and summer lawns, like a mask or a flag, with that bafflement of furious repudiation of truth in her eyes. One evening at a party she heard a boy and two girls, all schoolmates, talking. She never accepted another invitation.

She watched the girls with whom she had grown up as they married and got homes and children, but no man ever called on her steadily until the children of the other girls had been calling her 'aunty' for several years, the while their mothers told them in bright voices about how popular Aunt Minnie had been as a girl. Then the town began to see her driving on Sunday afternoons with the cashier in the bank. He was a widower of about forty – a high-coloured man, smelling always faintly of the barber shop or of whisky. He owned the first automobile in town, a red runabout; Minnie had the first motoring bonnet and veil the town ever saw. Then the town began to say: 'Poor Minnie.' 'But she is old enough to take care of herself,' others said. That was when she began to ask her old schoolmates that their children call her 'cousin' instead of 'aunty'.

It was twelve years now since she had been relegated into adultery by public opinion, and eight years since the cashier had gone to a Memphis bank, returning for one day each Christmas, which he spent at an annual bachelors' party at a hunting club on the river. From behind their curtains the neighbours would see the party pass, and during the over-the-way Christmas day visiting they would tell her about him, about how well he looked, and how they heard that he was prospering in the city, watching with bright, secret eyes her haggard, bright face. Usually by that hour there would be the scent of whisky on her breath. It was supplied her by a youth, a clerk at the soda fountain: 'Sure; I buy it for the old gal. I reckon she's entitled to a little fun.'

Her mother kept to her room altogether now; the gaunt aunt ran the house. Against that background Minnie's bright dresses, her idle and empty days, had a quality of furious unreality. She went out in the evenings only with women now, neighbours, to the moving pictures. Each afternoon she dressed in one of the new dresses and went downtown alone, where her young 'cousins' were already strolling in the late afternoons with their delicate, silken heads and thin, awkward arms and conscious hips, clinging to one another or shrieking and giggling with paired boys in the soda fountain when she passed and went on along the serried store fronts, in the doors of which the sitting and lounging men did not even follow her with their eyes any more.

III

The barber went swiftly up the street where the sparse lights, insect-swirled, glared in rigid and violent suspension in the lifeless air. The day had died in a pall of dust; above the darkened square, shrouded by the spent dust, the sky was as clear as the inside of a brass bell. Below the east was a rumour of the twice-waxed moon.

When he overtook them McLendon and three others were getting into a car parked in an alley. McLendon stooped his thick head, peering out beneath the top. 'Changed your mind, did you?' he said 'Damn good thing; by God, tomorrow when this town hears about how you talked tonight –'

'Now, now,' the other ex-soldier said. 'Hawkshaw's all right. Come on, Hawk; jump in.'

'Will Mayes never done it, boys,' the barber said. 'If anybody done it. Why, you all know well as I do there ain't any town when they got better niggers than us. And you know how a lady will kind of think things about men when there ain't any reason to, and Miss Minnie anyway –'

'Sure, sure,' the soldier said. 'We're just going to talk to him a little; that's all.'

'Talk hell!' Butch said. 'When we're through with the –'

'Shut up, for God's sake!' the soldier said. 'Do you want everybody in town –'

'Tell them, by God!' McLendon said. 'Tell every one of the sons that'll let a white woman –'

'Let's go; let's go: here's the other car.' The second car slid squealing out of a cloud of dust at the alley mouth. McLendon started his car and took the lead. Dust lay like fog in the street. The street lights hung nimbused as in water. They drove on out of town.

A rutted lane turned at right angles. Dust hung above it too, and above all the land. The dark bulk of the ice plant, where the Negro Mayes was night watchman, rose against the sky. 'Better stop here, hadn't we?' the soldier said. McLendon did not reply. He hurled the car up and slammed to a stop, the headlights glaring on the blank wall.

'Listen here, boys,' the barber said, 'if he's here, don't that prove he never done it? Don't it? If it was him, he would run. Don't you see he would?' The second car came up and stopped. McLendon got down; Butch sprang down beside him. 'Listen, boys,' the barber said.

'Cut the lights off!' McLendon said. The breathless dark rushed down. There was no sound in it save their lungs as they sought air in the parched dust in which for two months they had lived; then the diminishing crunch of McLendon's and Butch's feet, and a moment later McLendon's voice:

'Will! . . . Will!'

Below the east the wan haemorrhage of the moon increased. It heaved above the ridge, silvering the air, the dust, so that they seemed to breathe, live, in a bowl of molten lead. There was no sound of nightbird nor insect, no sound save their breathing and a faint ticking of contracting metal about the cars. Where their bodies touched one another they seemed to sweat dryly, for no more moisture came. 'Christ!' a voice said. 'Let's get out of here.'

But they didn't move until vague noises began to grow out of the darkness ahead; then they got out and waited tensely in the breathless dark. There was another sound: a blow, a hissing expulsion of breath and McLendon cursing in undertone. They stood a moment longer, then they ran forward. They ran in a stumbling clump, as though they were fleeing something. 'Kill him, kill the son,' a voice whispered. McLendon flung them back.

'Not here,' he said. 'Get him into the car.' 'Kill him, kill the black son!' the voice murmured. They dragged the Negro to the car. The barber had waited beside the car. He could feel himself sweating and he knew he was going to be sick at the stomach.

'What is it, captains?' the Negro said. 'I ain't done nothing. 'Fore God, Mr John.' Someone produced handcuffs. They worked busily about the Negro as though he were a post, quiet, intent, getting in one another's way. He submitted to the handcuffs, looking swiftly and constantly from dim face to dim face. 'Who's here, captains?' he said, leaning to peer into the faces until they could feel his breath and smell his sweaty reek. He spoke a name or two. 'What you all say I done, Mr John?'

McLendon jerked the car door open. 'Get in!' he said.

The Negro did not move. 'What you all going to do with me, Mr John? I ain't done nothing. White folks, captains, I ain't done nothing: I swear 'fore God.' He called another name.

'Get in!' McLendon said. He struck the Negro. The others expelled their breath in a dry hissing and struck him with random blows and he whirled and cursed them, and swept his manacled hands across their faces and slashed the barber upon the mouth, and the barber struck him also. 'Get him in there,' McLendon said. They pushed at him. He ceased struggling and got in and sat quietly as the others took their places. He sat between the barber and the soldier, drawing his limbs in so as not to touch them, his eyes going swiftly and constantly from face to face. Butch clung to the running board. The car moved on. The barber nursed his mouth with his handkerchief.

'What's the matter, Hawk?' the soldier said.

'Nothing,' the barber said. They regained the highroad and turned away from town. The second car dropped back out of the dust. They went on, gaining speed; the final fringe of houses dropped behind.

'Goddamn, he stinks!' the soldier said.

'We'll fix that,' the drummer in front beside McLendon said. On the running board Butch cursed into the hot rush of air. The barber leaned suddenly forward and touched McLendon's arm.

'Let me out, John,' he said.

'Jump out, niggerlover,' McLendon said without turning his head. He drove swiftly. Behind them the sourceless lights of the second car glared in the dust. Presently McLendon turned into a narrow road. It was rutted with disuse. It led back to an abandoned brick kiln – a series of reddish mounds and weed- and vine-choked vats without bottom. It had been used for pasture once, until one day the owner missed one of his mules. Although he prodded carefully in the vats with a long pole, he could not even find the bottom of them.

'John,' the barber said.

'Jump out, then,' McLendon said, hurling the car along the ruts. Beside the barber the Negro spoke:

'Mr Henry.'

The barber sat forward. The narrow tunnel of the road rushed up and past. Their motion was like an extinct furnace blast: cooler, but utterly dead. The car bounded from rut to rut.

'Mr Henry,' the Negro said.

The barber began to tug furiously at the door. 'Look out, there!' the soldier said, but the barber had already kicked the door open and swung on to the running board. The soldier leaned across the Negro and grasped at him, but he had already jumped. The car went on without checking speed.

The impetus hurled him crashing through dust-sheathed weeds, into the ditch. Dust puffed about him, and in a thin, vicious crackling of sapless stems he lay choking and retching until the second car passed and died away. Then he rose and limped on until he reached the highroad and turned towards town, brushing at his clothes with his hands. The moon was higher, riding high and clear of the dust at last, and after a while the town began to glare beneath the dust. He went on, limping. Presently he heard cars and the glow of them grew in the dust behind him and he left the road and crouched again in the weeds until they passed. McLendon's car came last now. There were four people in it and Butch was not on the running board.

They went on; the dust swallowed them; the glare and the sound died away. The dust of them hung for a while, but soon the eternal dust absorbed it again. The barber climbed back on to the road and limped on towards town.

IV

As she dressed for supper on that Saturday evening, her own flesh felt like fever. Her hands trembled among the hooks and eyes, and her eyes had a feverish look, and her hair swirled crisp and crackling under the comb. While she was still dressing the friends called for her and sat while she donned her sheerest underthings and stockings and a new voile dress. 'Do you feel strong enough to go out?' they said, their eyes bright too, with a dark glitter. 'When you have had time to get over the shock, you must tell us what happened. What he said and did; everything.'

In the leafed darkness, as they walked towards the square, she began to breathe deeply, something like a swimmer preparing to dive, until she ceased trembling, the four of them walking slowly because of the terrible heat and out of solicitude for her. But as they neared the square she began to tremble again, walking with her head up, her hands clenched at her sides, their voices about her murmurous, also with that feverish, glittering quality of their eyes.

They entered the square, she in the centre of the group, fragile in her fresh dress. She was trembling worse. She walked slower and slower, as children eat ice cream, her head up and her eyes bright in the haggard banner of her face, passing the hotel and the coatless drummers in chairs along the kerb looking around at her: 'That's the one: see? The one in pink in the middle.' 'Is that her? What did they do with the nigger? Did they –?' 'Sure. He's all right.' 'All right, is he?' 'Sure. He went on a little trip.' Then the drugstore, where even the young men lounging in the doorway tipped their hats and followed with their eyes the motion of her hips and legs when she passed.

They went on, passing the lifted hats of the gentlemen, the suddenly ceased voices, deferent, protective. 'Do you see?' the friends said. Their voices sounded like long, hovering sighs of hissing exultation. 'There's not a Negro on the square. Not one.'

They reached the picture show. It was like a miniature fairyland with its lighted lobby and coloured lithographs of life caught in its terrible and beautiful mutations. Her lips began to tingle. In the dark, when the picture began, it would be all right; she could hold back the laughing so it would not waste away so fast and so soon. So she hurried on before the turning faces, the undertones of low astonishment, and they took their accustomed places where she could see the aisle against the silver glare and the young men and girls coming in two and two against it.

The lights flicked away; the screen glowed silver and soon life began to unfold, beautiful and passionate and sad, while still the young men and girls entered, scented and sibilant in the half dark, their paired backs in silhouette delicate and sleek, their slim, quick bodies awkward, divinely young, while beyond them the silver dream accumulated, inevitably on and on. She began to laugh. In trying to suppress it, it made more noise than ever; heads began to turn. Still laughing, her friends raised her and led her out, and she stood at the kerb, laughing on a high, sustained note, until the taxi came up and they helped her in.

They removed the pink voile and the sheer underthings and the stockings, and put her to bed, and cracked ice for her temples, and sent for the doctor. He was hard to locate, so they ministered to her with hushed ejaculations, renewing the ice and fanning her. While the ice was fresh and cold she stopped laughing and lay still for a time, moaning only a little. But soon the laughing welled again and her voice rose screaming.

'Shhhhhhhhhhh! Shhhhhhhhhhhhhhh!' they said, freshening the ice-pack, smoothing her hair, examining it for grey; 'poor girl!' Then to one another: 'Do you suppose anything really happened?' their eyes darkly aglitter, secret and passionate. 'Shhhhhhhhhh! Poor girl! Poor Minnie!'

V

It was midnight when McLendon drove up to his neat new house. It was trim and fresh as a birdcage and almost as small, with its clean, green-and-white paint. He locked the car and mounted the porch and entered. His wife rose from a chair beside the reading lamp. McLendon stopped in the floor and stared at her until she looked down.

'Look at that clock,' he said, lifting his arm, pointing. She stood before him, her face lowered, a magazine in her hands. Her face was pale, strained and weary-looking. 'Haven't I told you about sitting up like this, waiting to see when I come in?'

'John,' she said. She laid the magazine down. Poised on the balls of his feet, he glared at her with his hot eyes, his sweating face.

'Didn't I tell you?' He went towards her. She looked up then. He caught her shoulder. She stood passive, looking at him.

'Don't John. I couldn't sleep . . . The heat; something. Please, John. You're hurting me.'

'Didn't I tell you?' He released her and half struck, half flung her across the chair, and she lay there and watched him quietly as he left the room.

He went on through the house, ripping off his shirt, and on the dark, screened porch at the rear he stood and mopped his head and shoulders with the shirt and flung it away. He took the pistol from his hip and laid it on the table beside the bed, and sat on the bed and removed his shoes, and rose and slipped his trousers off. He was sweating again already, and he stooped and hunted furiously for the shirt. At last he found it and wiped his body again, and, with his body pressed against the dusty screen, he stood panting. There was no movement, no sound, not even an insect. The dark world seemed to lie stricken beneath the cold moon and the lidless stars.

Couching at the Door

D. K. Broster

The first inkling which Augustine Marchant had of the matter was on one fine summer morning about three weeks after his visit to Prague, that is to say, in June 1898. In his library at Abbot's Medding he was reclining, as his custom was when writing his poetry, on the very comfortable sofa near the french windows, one of which was open to the garden. Pausing for inspiration – he was nearly at the end of his poem, *Salutation to All Unbeliefs* – he let his eyes wander round the beautifully appointed room, with its cloisonné and Satsuma, Buhl and first editions, and then allowed them to stray towards the sunlight outside. And so, between the edge of the costly Herat carpet and the sill of the open window, across the strip of polished oak flooring, he observed what he took to be a small piece of dark fluff blowing in the draught; and instantly made a note to speak to his housekeeper about the parlourmaid. There was slackness somewhere; and in Augustine Marchant's house no one was allowed to slack but himself.

There had been a time when the poet would not for a moment have been received, as he was now, in country and even county society – those days, even before the advent of *The Yellow Book* and *The Savoy*, when he had lived in London, writing the plays and poems which had so startled and shocked all but the 'decadent' and the 'advanced', *Pomegranates of Sin, Queen Theodora and Queen Marozia, The Nights of the Tour de Nesle, Amor Cypriacus* and the rest. But when, as the 'nineties began to wane, he inherited Abbot's Medding from a distant cousin and came to live there, being then at the height of an almost international reputation, Wiltshire society at first tolerated him for his kinship with the late Lord Medding, and then, placated by the excellence of his dinners and further mollified by the patent staidness of his private life, decided that, in his personal conduct at any rate, he must have turned over a new leaf. Perhaps indeed he had never been as bad as he was painted, and if his writings continued to be no less scandalously free-thinking than before, and needed to be just as rigidly kept out of the hands of daughters, well, no country gentleman in the neighbourhood was obliged to read them!

And indeed Augustine Marchant in his fifty-first year was too keenly alive to the value of the good opinion of county society to risk shocking it by any overt doings of his. He kept his licence for his pen. When he went abroad, as he did at least twice a year – but that was another matter altogether. The nose of Mrs Grundy was not sharp enough to smell out his occupations in Warsaw or Berlin or Naples, nor her eyes long-sighted enough to discern what kind of society he frequented even so near home as Paris. At Abbot's Medding his reputation for being 'wicked' was fast declining into just enough of a sensation to titillate a croquet party. He had charming manners, could be witty at moments (though he could not keep it up), still retained his hyacinthine locks (by means of hair restorers), wore his excellently cut velvet coats and flowing ties with just the right air – half poet, half man of the world – and really had, at Abbot's Medding, no dark secret to hide beyond the fact, sedulously concealed by him for five-and-twenty years, that he had never been christened Augustine. Between Augustus and Augustine, what a gulf! But he had crossed it, and his French poems (which had to be smuggled into his native land) were signed *Augustin – Augustin Lemarchant*.

Removing his gaze from the objectionable evidence of domestic carelessness upon the floor, Mr Marchant now fixed it meditatively upon the ruby-set end of the gold pencil which he was using. Rossell & Ward, his publishers, were about to bring out an édition de luxe of *Queen Theodora and Queen Marozia* with illustrations by a hitherto unknown young artist – if they were not too daring. It would be a sumptuous affair in a limited edition. And as he thought of this the remembrance of his recent stay in Prague returned to the poet. He smiled to himself, as a man smiles when he looks at a rare wine, and thought, *Yes, if these blunt-witted Pharisees round Abbot's Medding only knew!* It was a good thing that the upholders of British petty morality were seldom great travellers; a dispensation of – ahem, Providence!

Twiddling his gold pencil between plump fingers, Augustine Marchant returned to his ode, weighing one epithet against another. Except in summer he was no advocate of open windows, and even in summer he considered that to get the most out of that delicate and precious instrument, his brain, his feet must always be kept thoroughly warm; he had therefore cast over them, before settling into his semi-reclining position, a beautiful rose-coloured Indian *sari* of the purest and thickest silk, leaving the ends trailing on the floor. And he became aware, with surprise and annoyance, that the piece of brown fluff or whatever it was down there, travelling in the draught from the window, had reached the nearest end of the *sari* and was now, impelled by the same current, travelling up it.

The master of Abbot's Medding reached out for the silver handbell on the table by his side. There must be more breeze coming in than he had realized, and he might take cold, a catastrophe against which he guarded himself as against the plague. Then he saw that the upward progress of the dark blot – it was about the size of a farthing – could not by any possibility be assigned to any other agency than its own. It was *climbing* up – some horrible insect, plainly, some disgusting kind of almost legless and very hairy spider, round and vague in outline. The poet sat up and shook the *sari* violently. When he looked again the invader was gone. He had obviously shaken it on to the floor, and on the floor somewhere it must still be. The idea perturbed him, and he decided to take his writing out to the summerhouse, and give orders later that the library was to be thoroughly swept out.

Ah! it was good to be out of doors and in a pleasance so delightfully laid out, so exquisitely kept, as his! In the basin of the fountain the sea-nymphs of rosy-veined marble clustered round a Thetis as beautiful as Aphrodite herself; the lightest and featheriest of acacia trees swayed near. And as the owner of all this went past over the weedless turf he repeated snatches of Verlaine to himself about '*sveltes jets d'eau*' and '*sanglots d'extase*'.

Then, turning his head to look back at the fountain, he became aware of a little dark brown object about the size of a halfpenny running towards him over the velvet-smooth sward . . .

He believed afterwards that he must first have had a glimpse of the truth at that instant in the garden, or he would not have acted so instinctively as he did and so promptly. For, a moment later, he was standing at the edge of the basin of Thetis, his face blanched in the sunshine, his hand firmly clenched. Inside that closed hand something feather-soft pulsated . . . Holding back as best he could the disgust and the something more which clutched at him, Augustine Marchant stooped and plunged his whole fist into the bubbling water, and let the stream of the fountain whirl away what he had picked up. Then with uncertain steps he went and sat down on the nearest seat and shut his eyes. After a while he took out his lawn handkerchief and carefully dried his hand with the intaglio ring, dried it, and then looked curiously at the palm. *I did not know I had so much courage*, he was thinking; *so much courage and good sense!* . . . It would doubtless drown very quickly.

Burrows, his butler, was coming over the lawn. 'Mr and Mrs Morrison have arrived, sir.'

'Ah, yes; I had forgotten for the moment.' Augustine Marchant got up and walked towards the house and his guests, throwing back his shoulders and practising his famous enigmatic smile, for Mrs Morrison was a woman worth impressing.

(But what had it been exactly? Why, just what it had looked – a tuft of fur blowing over the grass, a tuft of fur! Sheer imagination that it had moved in his closed hand with a life of its own . . . Then why had he shut his eyes as he stooped and made a grab at it? Thank God, thank God, it was nothing now but a drenched smear swirling round the nymphs of Thetis!)

'Ah, dear lady, you must forgive me! Unpardonable of me not to be in to receive you!' He was in the drawing-room now, fragrant with its banks of hothouse flowers, bending over the hand of the fashionably attired guest on the sofa, in her tight bodice and voluminous sleeves, with a fly-away hat perched at a rakish angle on her gold-brown hair.

'Your man told us that you were writing in the garden,' said her goggle-eyed husband reverentially.

'*Cher maître*, it is we who ought not to be interrupting your rendezvous with the Muse,' returned Mrs Morrison in her sweet, high voice. 'Terrible to bring you from such company into that of mere visitors!'

Running his hand through his carefully tended locks the *cher maître* replied, 'Between a visit from the Muse and one from beauty's self no true poet would hesitate! – Moreover, luncheon awaits us, and I trust it is a good one.'

He liked faintly to shock fair admirers by admitting that he cared for the pleasure of the table; it was quite safe to do so, since none of them had sufficient acumen to see that it was true.

The luncheon was excellent, for Augustine kept an admirable cook. Afterwards he showed his guests over the library – yes, even though it had not received the sweeping which would not be necessary now – and round the garden; and in the summerhouse was prevailed upon to read some of *Amor Cypriacus* aloud. And Mrs Frances (nowadays Francesca) Morrison was thereafter able to recount to envious friends how the Poet himself had read her stanza after stanza from that most *daring* poem of his; and how poor Fred, fanning himself meanwhile with his straw hat – not from the torridity of the verse but because of the afternoon heat – said afterwards that he had not understood a single word. A good thing, perhaps . . .

When they had gone Augustine Marchant reflected rather cynically, *All that was just so much bunkum when I wrote it*. For, ten years ago, in spite of those audacious, glowing verses, he was an ignorant neophyte. Of course, since then . . . He smiled, a private, sly, self-satisfied smile. It was certainly pleasant to know oneself no longer a fraud!

Returning to the summerhouse to fetch his poems, he saw what he took to be Mrs Morrison's fur boa lying on the floor just by the basket chair which she had occupied. Odd of her not to have missed it on departure – a tribute to his verses perhaps. His housekeeper must send it after her by post. But just at that moment his head gardener approached, desiring some instructions, and when the matter was settled, and Augustine Marchant turned once more to enter the summerhouse, he found that he had been mistaken about the dropped boa, for there was nothing on the floor.

Besides, he remembered now that Mrs Morrison's boa had been a rope of grey feathers, not of dark fur. As he took up *Amor Cypriacus* he asked himself lazily what could have led him to imagine a woman's boa there at all, much less a fur one.

Suddenly he knew why. A lattice in the house of memory had opened, and he remained rigid, staring out at the jets of the fountain rising and falling in the afternoon sun. Yes; of that glamorous, wonderful, abominable night in Prague, the part he least wished to recall was connected – incidentally but undeniably – with a fur boa – a long boa of dark fur . . .

He had to go up to town next day to a dinner in his honour. There and then he decided to go up that same night by a late train, a most unusual proceeding, and most disturbing to his valet, who knew that it was doubtful whether he could at such short notice procure him a first-class carriage to himself. However, Augustine Marchant went, and even, to the man's amazement, deliberately chose a compartment with another occupant when he might, after all, have had an empty one.

The dinner was brilliant: Augustine had never spoken better. Next day he went round to the little street not far from the British Museum where he found Lawrence Storey, his new illustrator, working feverishly at his drawings for *Queen Theodora and Queen Marozia*, and quite overwhelmed at the honour of a personal visit. Augustine was very kind to him, and, while offering a few criticisms, highly praised his delineation of those two Messalinas of tenth-century Rome, their long supple hands, their heavy eyes, their full, almost repellent mouths. Storey had followed the same type for mother and daughter, but with a subtle difference.

'They were certainly two most evil women, especially the younger,' he observed ingenuously. 'But I suppose that, from an artistic point of view, that doesn't matter nowadays!'

Augustine, smoking one of his special cigarettes, made a delicate little gesture. 'My dear fellow, Art has nothing whatever to do with what is called "morality"; happily we know that at last! Show me how you thought of depicting the scene where Marozia orders the execution of her mother's papal paramour. Good, very good! Yes, the lines there, even the fall of that loose sleeve from the extended arm, express with clarity what I had in mind. You have great gifts!'

'I have tried to make her look wicked,' said the young man, reddening with pleasure. 'But,' he added deprecatingly, 'it is very hard for a ridiculously inexperienced person like myself to have the right artistic vision. For to you, Mr Marchant, who had penetrated into such wonderful arcana of the forbidden, it would be foolish to pretend to be other than I am.'

'How do you know that I have penetrated into any such arcana?' enquired the poet, half shutting his eyes and looking (though not to the almost worshipping gaze of young Storey) like a great cat being stroked.

'Why, one has only to read you!'

'You must come down and stay with me soon,' were Augustine Marchant's parting words. (He would give the boy a few days' good living, for which he would be none the worse; let him drink some decent wine.) 'How soon do you think you will be able to finish the rough sketches for the rest, and the designs for the *culs de lampe*? A fortnight or three weeks? Good; I shall look to see you then. Good-bye, my dear fellow; I am very, very much pleased with what you have shown me!'

The worst of going up to London from the country was that one was apt to catch a cold in town. When he got back Augustine Marchant was almost sure that this misfortune had befallen him, so he ordered a fire in his bedroom, despite the season, and consumed a *recherché* little supper in seclusion. And, as the cold turned out to have been imaginary, he was very comfortable, sitting there in his silken dressing-gown, toasting his toes and holding up a glass of golden Tokay to the flames. Really *Theodora and Marozia* would make as much sensation when it came out with these illustrations as when it first appeared!

All at once he set down his glass. Not far away on his left stood a big cheval mirror, like a woman's, in which a good portion of the bed behind him was reflected. And, in this mirror, he had just seen the valance of the bed move. There could be no draught to speak of in this warm room, he never allowed a cat in the house, and it was quite impossible that there should be a rat about. If after all some stray cat should have got in it must be ejected at once. Augustine hitched round in his chair to look at the actual bedhanging.

Yes, the topaz-hued silk valance again swung very slightly outward as though it were being pushed. Augustine bent forward to the bellpull to summon his valet. Then the flask of Tokay rolled over on the table as he leaped from his chair instead. Something like a huge, dark caterpillar was emerging very slowly from under his bed, moving as a caterpillar moves, with undulations running over it. Where its head should have been was merely a tapering end smaller than the rest of it, but of like substance. It was a dark fur boa.

Augustine Marchant felt that he screamed, but he could not have done so, for his tongue clave to the roof of his mouth. He merely stood staring, staring, all the blood gone from his heart. Still very slowly, the thing continued to creep out from under the valance, waving that eyeless, tapering end to and fro, as though uncertain where to proceed. *I am going mad, mad, mad!* thought Augustine, and then, with a revulsion, *No, it can't be! It's a real snake of some kind!*

That could be dealt with. He snatched up the poker as the boa-thing, still swaying the head which was no head, kept pouring steadily out from under the lifted yellow frill, until quite three feet were clear of the bed. Then he fell upon it furiously with blow after blow.

But they had no effect on the furry, spineless thing; it merely gave under them and rippled up in another place. Augustine hit the bed, the floor; at last, really screaming, he threw down his weapon and fell upon the thick, hairy rope with both hands, crushing it together into a mass – there was little if any resistance in it – and hurled it into the fire and, panting, kept it down with shovel and tongs. The flames licked up instantly and, with a roar, made short work of it, though there seemed to be some slight effort to escape, which was perhaps only the effect of the heat. A moment later there was a very strong smell of burned hair, and that was all.

Augustine Marchant seized the fallen flask of Tokay and drained from its mouth what little was left in the bottom ere, staggering to the bed, he flung himself upon it and buried his face in the pillows, even heaping them over his head as if he could thus stifle the memory of what he had seen.

He kept his bed next morning; the supposed cold afforded a good pretext. Long before the maid came in to re-lay the fire he had crawled out to make sure that there were no traces left of – what he had burned there. There were none. A nightmare could not have left a trace, he told himself. But well he knew that it was not a nightmare.

And now he could think of nothing but that room in Prague and the long fur boa of the woman. Some department of his mind (he supposed) must have projected that thing, scarcely noticed at the time, scarcely remembered, into the present and the here. It was terrible to think that one's mind possessed such dark, unknown powers. But not so terrible as if the – apparition – had been endowed with an entirely separate objective existence. In a day or two he would consult his doctor and ask him to give him a tonic.

But, expostulated an uncomfortably lucid part of his brain, you are trying to run with the hare and hunt with the hounds. Is it not better to believe that the thing *had* an objective existence, for you have burned it to nothing? Well and good! But if it is merely a projection from your own mind, what is to prevent it from reappearing, like the phoenix, from the ashes?

There seemed no answer to that, save in an attempt to persuade himself that he had been feverish last night. Work was the best antidote. So Augustine Marchant rose, and was surprised and delighted to find the atmosphere of his study unusually soothing and inspiring, and that day, against all expectation, *Salutation to All Unbeliefs* was completed by some stanzas with which he was not too ill-pleased. Realizing nevertheless that he should be glad of company that evening, he had earlier sent round a note to the local solicitor, a good fellow, to come and dine with him; played a game of billiards with the lawyer afterwards and retired to bed after some vintage port and a good stiff whisky and soda with scarcely a thought of the visitant of the previous night.

He woke at that hour when the thrushes in early summer punctually greet the new day – three o'clock. They were greeting it even vociferously, and Augustine Marchant was annoyed with their enthusiasm. His golden damask window-curtains kept out all but a glimmer of the new day, yet as, lying upon his back, the poet opened his eyes for a moment, his only half-awakened sense of vision reported something swinging to and fro in the dimness like a pendulum of rope. It was indistinct but seemed to be hanging from the tester of the bed. And, wide awake in an instant, with an unspeakable anguish of premonition tearing through him, he felt, next moment, a light thud on the coverlet about the level of his knees. Something had arrived on the bed . . .

And Augustine Marchant neither shrieked nor leaped from his bed; he could not. Yet, now that his eyes were grown used to the twilight of the room, he saw it clearly, the fur rope which he had burned to extinction two nights ago, dark and shining as before, rippling with a gentle movement as it coiled itself neatly together in the place where it had struck the bed, and subsided there in a symmetrical round, with only that tapering end a little raised and, as it were, looking at him – only, eyeless and featureless, it could not look. One thought of disgusted relief, that it was not at any rate going to attack him, and Augustine Marchant fainted.

Yet his swoon must have merged into sleep, for he woke in a more or less ordinary fashion to find his man placing his early tea-tray beside him and enquiring when he should draw his bath. There was nothing on the bed.

I shall change my bedroom, thought Augustine to himself, looking at the haggard, fallen-eyed man who faced him in the mirror as he shaved. *No, better still, I will go away for a change. Then I shall not have these dreams. I'll go to old Edgar Fortescue for a few days; he begged me again not long ago to come any time.*

So to the house of that old Maecenas he went. He was much too great a man now to be in need of Sir Edgar's patronage. It was homage which he received there, both from host and guests. The stay did much to soothe his scarified nerves. Unfortunately the last day undid the good of all the foregoing ones.

Sir Edgar possessed a pretty young wife – his third – and, among other charms of his place in Somerset, an apple orchard underplanted with flowers. And in the cool of the evening Augustine walked there with his host and hostess almost as if he were the Almighty with the dwellers in Eden. Presently they sat down upon a rustic seat (but a very comfortable one) under the shade of the apple boughs, amid the incongruous but pleasant parterres.

'You have come at the wrong season for these apple trees, Marchant,' observed Sir Edgar after a while, taking out his cigar. 'Blossom-time or apple-time – they are showy at either, in spite of the underplanting. What is attracting you on that tree – a titmouse? We have all kinds here, pretty, destructive little beggars!'

'I did not know that I was looking – it's nothing – thinking of something else,' stammered the poet. Surely, surely he had been mistaken in thinking that he had seen a sinuous, dark furry thing undulating like a caterpillar down the stem of that particular apple tree at a few yards' distance?

Talk went on, even his; there was safety in it. It was only the breeze which faintly rustled that bed of heliotrope behind the seat. Augustine wanted desperately to get up and leave the orchard, but neither Sir Edgar nor his wife seemed disposed to move, and so the poet remained at his end of the seat, his left hand playing nervously with a long bent of grass which had escaped the scythe.

All at once he felt a tickling sensation on the back of his hand, looked down and saw that featureless snout of fur protruding upward from underneath the rustic bench and sweeping itself backward and forward against his hand with a movement which was almost caressing. He was on his feet in a flash.

'Do you mind if I go in?' he asked abruptly. 'I'm not – feeling very well.'

★

If the thing could follow him it was of no use to go away. He returned to Abbot's Medding looking so much the worse for his change of air that Burrows expressed respectful hope that he was not indisposed. And almost the first thing that occurred, when Augustine sat down at his writing-table to attend to his correspondence, was the unwinding of itself from one of its curved legs, of a soft, brown, oscillating serpent which slowly waved an end at him as if in welcome . . .

In welcome, yes, that was it! The creature, incredible though it was, the creature seemed glad to see him! Standing at the other end of the room, his hands pressed over his eyes – for what was the use of attempting to hurt or destroy it – Augustine Marchant thought shudderingly that, like a witch's cat, a 'familiar' would not, presumably, be ill-disposed towards its master. Its master! Oh, God!

The hysteria which he had been trying to keep down began to mount uncontrollably when, removing his hand, Augustine glanced again towards his writing-table and saw that the boa had coiled itself in his chair and was sweeping its end to and fro over the back, somewhat in the way that a cat, purring meanwhile, rubs itself against furniture or a human leg in real or simulated affection.

'Oh, go away from there!' he suddenly screamed at it, advancing with outstretched hand. 'In the devil's name, get out.'

To his utter amazement, he was obeyed. The rhythmic movements ceased, the fur snake poured itself down out of the chair and writhed towards the door. Venturing back to his writing-table after a moment Augustine saw it coiled on the threshold, the blind end turned towards him as usual, as though watching. And he began to laugh. What would happen if he rang and someone came; would the opening door scrape it aside – would it vanish? Had it, in short, an existence for anyone else but himself?

But he dared not make the experiment. He left the room by the french window, feeling that he could never enter the house again. And perhaps, had it not been for the horrible knowledge just acquired that it could follow him, he might easily have gone away for good from Abbot's Medding and all his treasures and comforts. But of what use would that be – and how should he account for so extraordinary an action? No, he must think and plan while he yet remained sane.

To what, then, could he have recourse? The black magic in which he had dabbled with such disastrous consequences might possibly help him. Left to himself he was but an amateur, but he had a number of books . . . There was also that other realm whose boundaries sometimes marched side by side with magic – religion. But how could he pray to a Deity in whom he did not believe? Rather pray to the Evil which had sent this curse upon him, to show him how to banish it. Yet since he had deliberately followed what religion stigmatized as sin, what even the world would label as lust and necromancy, supplication to the dark powers was not likely to deliver him from them. They must somehow be outwitted.

He kept his *grimoires* and books of the kind in a locked bookcase in another room, not in his study; in that room he sat up till midnight. But the spells which he read were useless; moreover, he did not really believe in them. The irony of the situation was that, in a sense, he had only played at sorcery; it had but lent a spice to sensuality. He wandered wretchedly about the room dreading at any moment to see his 'familiar' wreathed round some object in it. At last he stopped at a small bookcase which held some old forgotten books of his mother's – Longfellow and Mrs Hemans, *John Halifax, Gentleman*, and a good many volumes of sermons and mild essays. And when he looked at that blameless assembly a cloud seemed to pass over Augustine Marchant's vision, and he saw his mother, gentle and lace-capped as years and years ago she used to sit, hearing his lessons, in an antimacassared chair. She had been everything to him then, the little boy whose soul was not smirched. He called silently to her now, 'Mamma, Mamma, can't you help me? Can't you send this thing away?'

When the cloud had passed he found that he had stretched out his hand and removed a big book. Looking at it he saw that it was her Bible, with *Sarah Amelia Marchant* on the faded yellow flyleaf. Her spirit *was* going to help him! He turned over a page or two, and out of the largish print there sprang instantly at him: *Now the serpent was more subtle than any beast in the field*. Augustine shuddered and almost put the Bible back, but the conviction that there was help there urged him to go on. He turned a few more pages of Genesis and his eyes were caught by this verse, which he had never seen before in his life:

And if thou doest well, shalt thou not be accepted? And if thou doest not well, sin lieth at the door. And unto thee shall be his desire, and thou shalt rule over him.

What strange words! What could they possibly mean? Was there light for him in them? *Unto thee shall be his desire*. That Thing, the loathsome semblance of affection which hung about it . . . *Thou shalt rule over him*. It *had* obeyed him, up to a point . . . Was this Book, of all others, showing him the way to be free? But the meaning of the verse was so obscure! He had not, naturally, such a thing as a commentary in the house. Yet, when he came to think of it, he remembered that some pious and anonymous person, soon after the publication of *Pomegranates of Sin*, had sent him a Bible in the Revised Version, with an inscription recommending him to read it. He had it somewhere, though he had always meant to get rid of it.

After twenty minutes' search through the sleeping house he found it in one of the spare bedrooms. But it gave him little enlightenment, for there was scant difference in the rendering, save that for *lieth at the door*, this version had *coucheth*, and that the margin held an alternative translation for the end of the verse: *And unto thee is its desire, but thou shouldst rule over it.*

Nevertheless, Augustine Marchant stood after midnight in this silent, sheeted guest-chamber repeating, '*But thou shouldst rule over it.*'

And all at once he thought of a way of escape.

It was going to be a marvellous experience, staying with Augustine Marchant. Sometimes Lawrence Storey hoped there would be no other guests at Abbot's Medding; at other times he hoped there would be. A *tête-à-tête* of four days with the great poet – could he sustain his share worthily? For Lawrence, despite the remarkable artistic gifts which were finding their first real flowering in these illustrations to Augustine's poem, was still unspoiled, still capable of wonder and admiration, still humble and almost naïve. It was still astonishing to him that he, an architect's assistant, should have been snatched away, as Ganymede by the eagle, from the lower world of elevations and drains to serve on Olympus. It was not, indeed, Augustine Marchant who had first discovered him, but it was Augustine Marchant who was going to make him famous.

The telegraph poles flitted past the second-class carriage window, and more than one traveller glanced with a certain envy and admiration at the fair, good-looking young man who diffused such an impression of happiness and candour, and had such a charming smile on his boyish lips. He carried with him a portfolio which he never let out of reach of his hand; the oldish couple opposite, speculating upon its contents, might have changed their opinion of him had they seen them.

But no shadow of the dark weariness of things unlawful rested on Lawrence Storey; to know Augustine Marchant, to be illustrating his great poem, to have learned from him that art and morality had no kinship, this was to plunge into a new realm of freedom and enlarging experience. Augustine Marchant's poetry, he felt, had already taught his hand what his brain and heart knew nothing of.

There was a dogcart to meet him at the station, and in the scented June evening he was driven with a beating heart past meadows and hayfields to his destination.

Mr Marchant, awaiting him in the hall, was at his most charming. 'My dear fellow, are those the drawings? Come, let us lock them away at once in my safe! If you had brought me diamonds I should not be one quarter so concerned about thieves. And did you have a comfortable journey? I have had you put in the orange room; it is next to mine. There is no one else staying here, but there are a few people coming to dinner to meet you.'

There was only just time to dress for dinner, so that Lawrence did not get an opportunity to study his host until he saw him seated at the head of the table. Then he was immediately struck by the fact that he looked curiously ill. His face – ordinarily by no means attenuated – seemed to have fallen in, there were dark circles under his eyes, and the perturbed Lawrence, observing him as the meal progressed, thought that his manner too seemed strange and once or twice quite absent-minded. And there was one moment when, though the lady on his right was addressing him, he sharply turned his head away and looked down at the side of his chair just as if he saw something on the floor. Then he apologized, saying that he had a horror of cats, and that sometimes the tiresome animal from the stables . . . But after that he continued to entertain his guests in his own inimitable way, and, even to the shy Lawrence, the evening proved very pleasant.

The ensuing three days were wonderful and exciting to the young artist – days of uninterrupted contact with a master mind which acknowledged, as the poet himself admitted, none of the petty barriers which man, for his own convenience, had set up between alleged right and wrong. Lawrence had learned why his host did not look well; it was loss of sleep, the price exacted by inspiration. He had a new poetic drama shaping in his mind which would scale heights that he had not yet attempted.

There was almost a touch of fever in the young man's dreams tonight – his last night but one. He had several. First he was standing by the edge of a sort of mere, inexpressibly desolate and unfriendly, a place he had never seen in his life, which yet seemed in some way familiar; and something said to him, 'You will never go away from here!' He was alarmed, and woke, but went to sleep again almost immediately, and this time was back, oddly enough, in the church where in his earliest years he had been taken to service by the aunt who had brought him up – a large church full of pitch-pine pews with narrow ledges for hymn-books, which ledges he used surreptitiously to lick during the long dull periods of occultation upon his knees. But most of all he remembered the window with Adam and Eve in the Garden of Eden, on either side of an apple tree round whose trunk was coiled a monstrous snake with a semi-human head. Lawrence had hated and dreaded that window, and because of it he would never go near an orchard and had no temptation to steal apples . . . Now he was back in that church again, staring at the window, lit up with some infernal glow from behind. He woke again, little short of terrified – he, a grown man! But again he went to sleep quite quickly.

This third dream had for background, as sometimes happens in nightmares, the very room in which he lay. He dreamed that a door opened in the wall, and in the doorway, quite plain against the light from another room behind him, stood Augustine Marchant in his dressing-gown. He was looking down at something on the ground which Lawrence did not see, but his hand was pointing at Lawrence in the bed, and he was saying in a voice of command, 'Go to him, do you hear? Go to him! Go to *him*! Am I not your master?'

And Lawrence, who could neither move nor utter a syllable, wondered uneasily what this could be which was thus commanded, but his attention was chiefly focused on Augustine Marchant's face. After he had said these words several times, and apparently without result, a dreadful change came upon it, a look of the most unutterable despair. It seemed visibly to age and wither; he said, in a loud, penetrating whisper, 'Is there no escape then?' covered his ravaged face a moment with his hands, and then went back and softly closed the door. At that Lawrence woke; but in the morning he had forgotten all three dreams.

The *tête-à-tête* dinner on the last night of his stay would have lingered in a gourmet's memory, so that it was a pity the young man did not know in the least what he was eating. At last there was happening what he had scarcely dared hope for; the great poet of the sensuous was revealing to him some of the unimaginably strange and secret sources of his inspiration. In the shaded rosy candlelight, his elbows on the table among trails of flowers he, who was not even a neophyte, listened like a man learning for the first time of some spell or spring which will make him more than mortal.

'Yes,' said Augustine Marchant, after a long pause, 'yes, it was a marvellous, an undying experience – one that is not given to many. It opened doors, it – but I despair of doing it justice in mere words.' His look was transfigured, almost dreamy.

'But she – the woman – how did you –?' asked Lawrence Storey in a hushed voice.

'Oh, the woman?' said Augustine, suddenly finishing off his wine. 'The woman was only a common streetwalker.'

A moment or two later Lawrence was looking at his host wonderingly and wistfully. 'But this was in Prague. Prague is a long way off.'

'One does not need to go so far, in reality. Even in Paris –'

'One could – have that experience in Paris?'

'If you knew where to go. And, of course, it is necessary to have credentials. I mean that – like all such enlightenments – it has to be kept secret, most secret, from the vulgar minds who lay their restrictions on the finer. That is self-evident.'

'Of course,' said the young man, and sighed deeply.

His host looked at him affectionately. 'You, my dear Lawrence – I may call you Lawrence? – want just that touch of – what shall I call them – *les choses cachées* – to liberate your immense artistic gifts from the shackles which still bind them. Through that gateway you would find the possibility of their full fruition! It would fertilize your genius to a still finer blossoming . . . But you would have scruples – and you are very young.'

'You know,' said Lawrence in a low and trembling tone, 'what I feel about your poetry. You know how I ache to lay the best that is in me at your feet. If only I could make my drawings for the Two Queens more worthy – already it is an honour which overwhelms me that you should have selected me to do them – but they are not what they should be. I am *not* sufficiently liberated . . .'

Augustine leaned forward on the flower-decked table. His eyes were glowing. 'Do you truly desire to be?'

The young man nodded, too full of emotion to find his voice.

The poet got up, went over to a cabinet in a corner and unlocked it. Lawrence watched his fine figure in a sort of trance. Then he half rose with an exclamation.

'What is it?' asked Augustine very sharply, facing round.

'Oh, nothing, sir – only I believe you hate cats, and I thought I saw one, or rather its tail, disappearing into that corner.'

'There's no cat here,' said Augustine quickly. His face had become all shiny and mottled, but Lawrence did not notice it. The poet stood a moment looking at the carpet; one might almost have thought that he was gathering resolution to cross it; then he came swiftly back to the table.

'Sit down again,' he commanded. 'Have you a pocket-book with you, a pocket-book which you never leave about? Good! Then write *this* in one place; and *this* on another page – write it small – among other entries is best – not on a blank page – write it in Greek characters if you know them . . .'

'What – what is it?' asked Lawrence, all at once intolerably excited, his eyes fixed on the piece of paper in Augustine's hand.

'The two halves of the address in Paris.'

Augustine Marchant kept a diary in those days, a locked diary, written in cipher. And for more than a month after Lawrence Storey's visit the tenor of the entries there was almost identical:

No change . . . always with me . . . How much longer can I endure it? The alteration in my looks is being remarked upon to my face. I shall have to get rid of Thornton [*his man*] on some pretext or other, for I begin to think that he has seen

It. No wonder, since It follows me about like a dog. When It is visible to everyone it will be the end . . . I found It in bed with me this morning, pressed up against me as if for warmth . . .

But there was a different class of entry also, appearing at intervals with an ever-increasing note of impatience:

Will L.S. go there? . . . When shall I hear from L.S.? . . . Will the experiment do what I think? It is my last hope.

Then, suddenly, after five weeks had elapsed, an entry in a trembling hand:

For twenty-four hours I have seen no sign of It! Can it be possible?

And next day:

Still nothing. I begin to live again. – This evening has just come an ecstatic letter from L.S., from Paris, telling me that he had 'presented his credentials' and was to have the experience next day. He has had it by now – by yesterday, in fact. Have I really freed myself? It looks like it!

In one week from the date of that last entry it was remarked in Abbot's Medding how much better Mr Marchant was looking again. Of late he had not seemed at all himself; his cheeks had fallen in, his clothes seemed to hang loosely upon him, who had generally filled them so well, and he appeared nervous. Now he was as before, cheery, courtly, debonair. And last Sunday, will you believe it, he went to church! The rector was so astonished when he first became aware of him from the pulpit that he nearly forgot to give out his text. And the poet joined in the hymns, too! Several observed this amazing phenomenon.

It was the day after this unwonted appearance at St Peter's. Augustine was strolling in his garden. The air had a new savour, the sun a new light; he could look again with pleasure at Thetis and her nymphs of the fountain, could work undisturbed in the summerhouse. Free, free! All the world was good to the senses once again, and the hues and scents of early autumn better, in truth, than the brilliance of that summer month which had seen this curse descend upon him.

The butler brought him out a letter with a French stamp. From Lawrence Storey, of course; to tell him – what? Where had he caught his first glimpse of it? In one of those oppressively furnished French bedrooms? And how had he taken it?

At first, however, Augustine was not sure that the letter was from Storey. The writing was very different, cramped instead of flowing, and, in places, spluttering, the pen having dug into the paper as if the hand

which held it had not been entirely under control – almost, thought
Augustine, his eyes shining with excitement, almost as though something
had been twined, liana-like, round the wrist. (He had a sudden sick
recollection of a day when that had happened to him, quickly submerged
in a gush of eager anticipation.) Sitting down upon the edge of the
fountain he read – not quite what he had looked for:

I don't know what is happening to me [*began the letter without other opening*].
Yesterday I was in a café by myself, and had just ordered some absinthe – though
I do not like it. And quite suddenly, although I knew that I was in the café, I
realized that I was also back in that room. I could see every feature of it, but I
could see the café too, with all the people in it; the one was, as it were,
superimposed upon the other, the room, which was a good deal smaller than the
café, being inside the latter, as a box may be within a larger box. And all the
while the room was growing clearer, the café fading. I saw the glass of absinthe
suddenly standing on nothing, as it were. All the furniture of the room, all the
accessories you know of, were mixed up with the chairs and tables of the café. I
do not know how I managed to find my way back to the *comptoir*, pay and get out.
I took a fiacre back to my hotel. By the time I arrived there I was all right. I
suppose that it was only the after-effects of a very strange and violent emotional
experience. But I hope to God that it will not recur!

'How interesting!' said Augustine Marchant, dabbling his hand in the
swirling water where he had once drowned a piece of dark fluff. 'And
why indeed should I have expected that It would couch at his door in the
same form as at mine?'
Four days more of new-found peace and he was reading this:

In God's name – or the Devil's – come over and help me! I have hardly an hour
now by night or day when I am sure of my whereabouts. I could not risk the
journey back to England alone. It is like being imprisoned in some kind of infernal
half-transparent box, always growing a little smaller. Wherever I go now I carry
it about with me; when I am in the street I hardly know which is the pavement
and which is the roadway, because I am always treading on that black carpet with
the cabalistic designs; if I speak to anyone they may suddenly disappear from
sight. To attempt to work is naturally useless. I would consult a doctor, but that
would mean telling him everything . . .

'I hope to God he won't do that!' muttered Augustine uneasily. 'He can't
– he swore to absolute secrecy. I hadn't bargained, however, for his ceasing
work. Suppose he finds himself unable to complete the designs for *Theodora
and Marozia!* That would be serious . . . However, to have freed myself is
worth *any* sacrifice . . . But Storey cannot, obviously, go on living indefi-

nitely on two planes at once . . . Artistically, though, it might inspire him to something quite unprecedented. I'll write to him and point that out; it might encourage him. But go near him in person – is it likely!'

The next day was one of great literary activity. Augustine was so deeply immersed in his new poetical drama that he neglected his correspondence and almost his meals – except his dinner, which seemed that evening to be shared most agreeably and excitingly by these new creations of his brain. Such, in fact, was his preoccupation with them that it was not until he had finished the savoury and poured out a glass of his superlative port that he remembered a telegram which had been handed to him as he came in to dinner. It still lay unopened by his plate. Now, tearing apart the envelope, he read with growing bewilderment these words above his publishers' names:

Please inform us immediately what steps to take are prepared send to France recover drawings if possible what suggestions can you make as to successor Rossell and Ward.

Augustine was more than bewildered; he was stupefied. Had some accident befallen Lawrence Storey of which he knew nothing? But he had opened all his letters this morning though he had not answered any. A prey to a sudden very nasty anxiety he got up and rang the bell.

'Burrows, bring me *The Times* from the library.'

The newspaper came, unopened. Augustine, now in a frenzy of uneasiness, scanned the pages rapidly. But it was some seconds before he came upon the headline: TRAGIC DEATH OF A YOUNG ENGLISH ARTIST and read the following, furnished by the Paris correspondent:

Connoisseurs who were looking forward to the appearance of the superb illustrated edition of Mr Augustine Marchant's *Queen Theodora and Queen Marozia* will learn with great regret of the death by drowning of the gifted young artist, Mr Lawrence Storey, who was engaged upon the designs for it. Mr Storey had recently been staying in Paris, but left one day last week for a remote spot in Brittany, it was supposed in pursuance of his work. On Friday last his body was discovered floating in a lonely pool near Carhaix. It is hard to see how Mr Storey could have fallen in, since this piece of water – the Mare de Plougouven – has a completely level shore surrounded by reeds, and is not in itself very deep, nor is there any boat upon it. It is said the unfortunate young Englishman had been somewhat strange in his manner recently and complained of hallucinations; it is therefore possible that under their influence he deliberately waded out into the Mare de Plougouven. A strange feature of the case is that he had fastened round him under his coat the finished drawings for Mr Marchant's book, which were of course completely spoiled by the water before the body was found. It is to be hoped that they were not the only --

Augustine threw *The Times* furiously from him and struck the dinner table with his clenched fist.

'Upon my soul, that is too much! It is criminal! My property – and I who had done so much for him! Fastened them round himself – he must have been crazy!'

But had he been so crazy? When his wrath had subsided a little Augustine could not but ask himself whether the young artist had not in some awful moment of insight guessed the truth, or part of it – that his patron had deliberately corrupted him? It looked almost like it. But, if he had really taken all the finished drawings with him to this place in Brittany, what an unspeakably mean trick of revenge thus to destroy them! . . . yet, even if it were so, he must regard their loss as the price of his own deliverance, since, from his point of view, the desperate expedient of passing on his 'familiar' had been a complete success. By getting someone else to plunge even deeper than he had done into the unlawful (for he had seen to it that Lawrence Storey should do that) he had proved, as that verse in Genesis said, that he *had* ruled over – what had pursued him in tangible form as a consequence of his own night in Prague. He could not be too thankful. The literary world might well be thankful too. For his own art was of infinitely more import-ance than the subservient, the parasitic art of an illustrator. He could with a little search find half a dozen just as gifted as that poor hallucination-ridden Storey to finish *Theodora and Marozia* – even, if necessary, to begin an entirely fresh set of drawings. And meanwhile, in the new lease of creative energy which this unfortunate but necessary sacrifice had made possible for him, he would begin to put on paper the masterpiece which was now taking brilliant shape in his liberated mind. A final glass, and then an evening in the workshop!

Augustine poured out some port, and was raising the glass, prepared to drink to his own success, when he thought he heard a sound near the door. He looked over his shoulder. Next instant the stem of the wine-glass had snapped in his hand and he had sprung back to the farthest limit of the room.

Reared up for quite five feet against the door, huge, dark, sleeked with wet and flecked with bits of green waterweed, was something half python, half gigantic cobra, its head drawn back as if to strike – its head, for in its former featureless tapering end were now two reddish eyes, such as furriers put into the heads of stuffed creatures. And they were fixed in an unwaver-ing and malevolent glare upon him, as he cowered there clutching the bowl of the broken wine-glass, the crumpled copy of *The Times* lying at his feet.

The Two Bottles of Relish

Lord Dunsany

Smithers is my name. I'm what you might call a small man and in a small way of business.

I travel for Num-numo, a relish for meats and savouries – the world-famous relish I ought to say. It's really quite good, no deleterious acids in it, and does not affect the heart; so it is quite easy to push. I wouldn't have got the job if it weren't. But I hope some day to get something that's harder to push, as of course the harder they are to push, the better the pay. At present I can just make my way, with nothing at all over; but then I live in a very expensive flat. It happened like this, and that brings me to my story. And it isn't the story you'd expect from a small man like me, yet there's nobody else to tell it. Those that know anything of it besides me are all for hushing it up. Well, I was looking for a room to live in in London when first I got my job. It had to be in London, to be central; and I went to a block of buildings, very gloomy they looked, and saw the man that ran them and asked him for what I wanted. Flats they called them; just a bedroom and a sort of a cupboard. Well, he was showing a man round at the time who was a gent, in fact more than that, so he didn't take much notice of me – the man that ran all those flats didn't, I mean. So I just ran behind for a bit, seeing all sorts of rooms and waiting till I could be shown my class of thing. We came to a very nice flat, a sitting-room, bedroom and bathroom, and a sort of little place that they called a hall. And that's how I came to know Linley. He was the bloke that was being shown round.

'Bit expensive,' he said.

And the man that ran the flats turned away to the window and picked his teeth. It's funny how much you can show by a simple thing like. What he meant to say was that he'd hundreds of flats like that, and thousands of people looking for them, and he didn't care who had them or whether they all went on looking. There was no mistaking him, somehow. And yet he never said a word, only looked away out of the window and picked his teeth. And I ventured to speak to Mr Linley then; and I said, 'How about it, sir, if I paid half, and shared it? I wouldn't be in the way, and I'm out all day, and whatever you said would go, and really I wouldn't be no more in your way than a cat.'

You may be surprised at my doing it; and you'll be much more surprised at him accepting it – at least, you would if you knew me, just a small man in a small way of business. And yet I could see at once that he was taking to me more than he was taking to the man at the window.

'But there's only one bedroom,' he said.

'I could make up my bed easy in that little room there,' I said.

'The Hall,' said the man, looking round from the window, without taking his toothpick out.

'And I'd have the bed out of the way and hid in the cupboard by any hour you like,' I said.

He looked thoughtful, and the other man looked out over London; and in the end, do you know, he accepted.

'Friend of yours?' said the flat man.

'Yes,' answered Mr Linley.

It was really very nice of him.

I'll tell you why I did it. Able to afford it? Of course not. But I heard him tell the flat man that he had just come down from Oxford and wanted to live for a few months in London. It turned out he wanted just to be comfortable and do nothing for a bit while he looked things over and chose a job, or probably just as long as he could afford it. Well, I said to myself, what's the Oxford manner worth in business, especially a business like mine? Why, simply everything you've got. If I picked up only a quarter of it from this Mr Linley I'd be able to double my sales, and that would soon mean I'd be given something a lot harder to push, with perhaps treble the pay. Worth it every time. And you can make a quarter of an education go twice as far again if you're careful with it. I mean you don't have to quote the whole of *The Inferno* to show that you've read Milton; half a line may do it.

Well, about that story I have to tell. And you mightn't think that a little man like me could make you shudder. Well, I soon forgot about the Oxford manner when we settled down in our flat. I forgot it in the sheer wonder of the man himself. He had a mind like an acrobat's body, like a bird's body. It didn't want education. You didn't notice whether he was educated or not. Ideas were always leaping up in him, things you'd never have thought of. And not only that, but if any ideas were about, he'd sort of catch them. Time and again I've found him knowing just what I was going to say. Not thought-reading, but what they call intuition. I used to try to learn a bit about chess, just to take my thoughts off Num-numo in the evening, when I'd done with it. But problems I never could do. Yet he'd come along and glance at my problem and say, 'You probably move that piece first,' and I'd say, 'But where?' and he'd say, 'Oh, one of those three squares.' And I'd say, 'But it will be taken on all of them.' And the piece a queen all the time, mind you. And he'd say, 'Yes, it's doing no good there: you're probably meant to lose it.'

And, do you know, he'd be right.

You see, he'd been following out what the other man had been thinking. That's what he'd been doing.

Well, one day there was that ghastly murder at Unge. I don't know if you remember it. But Steeger had gone down to live with a girl in a bungalow on the North Downs, and that was the first we had heard of him.

The girl had £200, and he got every penny of it, and she utterly disappeared. And Scotland Yard couldn't find her.

Well, I'd happened to read that Steeger had bought two bottles of Num-numo; for the Otherthorpe police had found out everything about him, except what he did with the girl; and that of course attracted my attention, or I should have never thought again about the case or said a word of it to Linley. Num-numo was always on my mind, as I always spent every day pushing it, and that kept me from forgetting the other thing. And so one day I said to Linley, 'I wonder with all that knack you have for seeing through a chess problem, and thinking of one thing and another, that you don't have a go at that Otherthorpe mystery. It's a problem as much as chess,' I said.

'There's not the mystery in ten murders that there is in one game of chess,' he answered.

'It's beaten Scotland Yard,' I said.

'Has it?' he asked.

'Knocked them end-wise,' I said.

'It shouldn't have done that,' he said. And almost immediately after he said, 'What are the facts?'

We were both sitting at supper, and I told him the facts, as I had them straight from the papers. She was a pretty blonde, she was small, she was called Nancy Elth, she had £200, they lived at the bungalow for five days. After that he stayed there for another fortnight, but nobody ever saw her alive again. Steeger said she had gone to South America, but later said he had never said South America, but South Africa. None of her money remained in the Bank where she had kept it, and Steeger was shown to have come by at least £150 just at that time. Then Steeger turned out to be a vegetarian, getting all his food from the greengrocer, and that made the constable in the village of Unge suspicious of him, for a vegetarian was something new to the constable. He watched Steeger after that, and it's well he did, for there was nothing that Scotland Yard asked him that he couldn't tell them about him, except of course the one thing. And he told the police at Otherthorpe five or six miles away, and they came and took a hand at it too. They were able to say for one thing that he never went outside the bungalow and its tidy garden ever since she disappeared. You see, the more they watched him the more suspicious they got, as you naturally do if you're watching a man; so that very soon they were watching every move he made, but if it hadn't been for his being a vegetarian they'd never have started to suspect him, and there wouldn't have been enough evidence even for Linley. Not that they found out anything much against him, except that £150 dropping in from nowhere, and it was Scotland Yard that found that, not the police of Otherthorpe. No, what the constable of Unge found out was about the larch-trees, and that beat Scotland Yard utterly, and beat Linley up to the very last, and of course it beat me. There were ten larch-trees in the bit of a garden, and he'd made some sort of an arrangement with the landlord, Steeger had, before he took the bungalow, by which he could do what he liked with the larch-trees. And then from about the time that little Nancy Elth must have died he cut every one of them down. Three times a day he went at it for nearly a week, and when they were all down he cut them all up into logs no more than two foot long and laid them all in neat heaps. You never saw such work. And what for? To give an excuse for the axe was one theory. But the excuse was bigger than the axe; it took him a fortnight, hard work every day. And he could have killed a little thing like Nancy Elth without an axe, and cut her up too. Another theory was that he wanted firewood, to make away with the body. But he never used it. He left it all standing there in those neat stacks. It fairly beat everybody.

Well, those are the facts I told Linley. Oh yes, and he bought a big butcher's knife. Funny thing, they all do. And yet it isn't so funny after all; if you've got to cut a woman up, you've got to cut her up; and you can't do that without a knife. Then, there were some negative facts. He hadn't burned her. Only had a fire in the small stove now and then, and only used it for cooking. They got on to that pretty smartly, the Unge constable did, and the men that were lending him a hand from Otherthorpe. There were some little woody places lying round, shaws they call them in that part of the country, the country people do, and they could climb a tree handy and unobserved and get a sniff at the smoke in almost any direction it might be blowing. They did that now and then, and there was no smell of flesh burning, just ordinary cooking. Pretty smart of the Otherthorpe police that was, though of course it didn't help to hang Steeger. Then later on the Scotland Yard men went down and got another fact – negative, but narrowing things down all the while. And that was that the chalk under the bungalow and under the little garden had none of it been disturbed. And he'd never been outside it since Nancy disappeared. Oh yes, and he had a big file besides the knife. But there was no sign of any ground bones found on the file, or any blood on the knife. He'd washed them of course. I told all that to Linley.

Now I ought to warn you before I go any further. I am a small man myself and you probably don't expect anything horrible from me. But I ought to warn you this man was a murderer, or at any rate somebody was; the woman had been made away with, a nice pretty little girl too, and the man that had done that wasn't necessarily going to stop at things you might think he'd stop at. With the mind to do a thing like that, and with the long thin shadow of the rope to drive him further, you can't say what he'll stop at. Murder tales seem nice things sometimes for a lady to sit and read by herself by the fire. But murder isn't a nice thing, and when a murderer's desperate and trying to hide his tracks he isn't even as nice as he was before. I'll ask you to bear that in mind. Well, I've warned you.

So I says to Linley, 'And what do you make of it?'

'Drains?' said Linley.

'No,' I says, 'you're wrong there. Scotland Yard has been into that. And the Otherthorpe people before them. They've had a look in the drains, such as they are, a little thing running into a cesspool beyond the garden; and nothing has gone down it – nothing that oughtn't to have, I mean.'

He made one or two other suggestions, but Scotland Yard had been before him in every case. That's really the crab of my story, if you'll excuse the expression. You want a man who sets out to be a detective to take his magnifying glass and go down to the spot; to go to the spot before everything; and then to measure the footmarks and pick up the clues and find the knife that the police have overlooked. But Linley never even went near the place, and he hadn't got a magnifying glass, not as I ever saw, and Scotland Yard were before him every time.

In fact they had more clues than anybody could make head or tail of. Every kind of clue to show that he'd murdered the poor little girl; every kind of clue to show that he hadn't disposed of the body; and yet the body wasn't there. It wasn't in South America either, and not much more likely in South Africa. And all the time, mind you, that enormous bunch of chopped larch-wood, a clue that was staring everyone in the face and leading nowhere. No, we didn't seem to want any more clues, and Linley never went near the place. The trouble was to deal with the clues we'd got. I was completely mystified; so was Scotland Yard; and Linley seemed to be getting no forwarder; and all the while the mystery was hanging on me. I mean if it were not for the trifle I'd chanced to remember, and if it were not for one chance word I said to Linley, that mystery would have gone the way of all the other mysteries that men have made nothing of, a darkness, a little patch of night in history.

Well, the fact was Linley didn't take much interest in it at first, but I was so absolutely sure that he could do it, that I kept him to the idea. 'You can do chess problems,' I said.

'That's ten times harder,' he said, sticking to his point.

'Then why don't you do this?' I said.

'Then go and take a look at the board for me,' said Linley.

That was his way of talking. We'd been a fortnight together, and I knew it by now. He meant to go down to the bungalow at Unge. I know you'll say why didn't he go himself; but the plain truth of it is, that if he'd been tearing about the countryside he'd never have been thinking, whereas sitting there in his chair by the fire in our flat there was no limit to the ground he could cover, if you follow my meaning. So down I went by train next day, and got out at Unge station. And there were the North Downs rising up before me, somehow like music.

'It's up there, isn't it?' I said to the porter.

'That's right,' he said. 'Up there by the lane; and mind to turn to your right when you get to the old yew-tree, a very big tree, you can't mistake it, and then . . .' and he told me the way so that I couldn't go wrong. I found them all like that, very nice and helpful. You see, it was Unge's day at last. Everyone had heard of Unge now; you could have got a letter there any time just then without putting the county or post town; and this was what Unge had to show. I dare say if you tried to find Unge now . . . well, anyway, they were making the hay while the sun shone.

Well, there the hill was, going up into sunlight, going up like a song. You don't want to hear about the spring, and all the may rioting, and the colour that came down over everything later on in the day, and all those birds; but I thought, 'What a nice place to bring a girl to.' And then when I thought that he'd killed her there, well I'm only a small man, as I said, but when I thought of her on that hill with all the birds singing, I said to myself, 'Wouldn't it be odd if it turned out to be me after all that got that man killed, if he did murder her.' So I soon found my way up to the bungalow and began prying about, looking over the hedge into the garden. And I didn't find much, and I found nothing at all that the police hadn't found already, but there were those heaps of larch logs staring me in the face and looking very queer.

I did a lot of thinking, leaning against the hedge, breathing the smell of the may, and looking over the top of it at the larch logs, and the neat little bungalow the other side of the garden. Lots of theories I thought of, till I came to the best thought of all; and that was that if I left the thinking to Linley, with his Oxford-and-Cambridge education, and only brought him the facts, as he had told me, I should be doing more good in my way than if I tried to do any big thinking. I forgot to tell you that I had gone to Scotland Yard in the morning. Well, there wasn't really much to tell. What they asked me was, what I wanted. And, not having an answer exactly ready, I didn't find out very much from them. But it was quite different at Unge; everyone was most obliging; it was their day there, as I said. The constable let me go indoors, so long as I didn't touch anything, and he gave me a look at the garden from the inside. And I saw the stumps of the ten larch-trees, and I noticed one thing that Linley said was very observant of me, not that it turned out to be any use, but any way I was doing my best; I noticed that the stumps had been all chopped anyhow. And from that I thought that the man that did it didn't know much about chopping. The constable said that was a deduction. So then I said that the axe was blunt when he used it; and that certainly made the constable think, though he didn't actually say I was right this time. Did I tell you that Steeger never went outdoors, except to the little garden to chop wood, ever since Nancy disappeared? I think I did. Well, it was perfectly true. They'd watched him night and day, one or another of them, and the Unge constable told me that himself. That limited things a good deal. The only thing I didn't like about it was that I felt Linley ought to have found all that out instead of ordinary policemen, and I felt that he could have too. There'd have been romance in a story like that. And they'd never have done it if the news hadn't gone round that the man was a vegetarian and only dealt at the greengrocers. Likely as not even that was only started out of pique by the butcher. It's queer what little things may trip a man up. Best to keep straight is my motto. But perhaps I'm straying a bit away from my story. I should like to do that for ever – forget that it ever was; but I can't.

Well, I picked up all sorts of information; clues I suppose I should call it in a story like this, though they none of them seemed to lead anywhere. For instance, I found out everything he ever bought at the village, I could even tell you the kind of salt he bought, quite plain with no phosphates in it, that they sometimes put in to make it tidy. And then he got ice from the fishmongers, and plenty of vegetables, as I said, from the greengrocer,

Mergin & Sons. And I had a bit of a talk over it all with the constable. Slugger he said his name was. I wondered why he hadn't come in and searched the place as soon as the girl was missing. 'Well, you can't do that,' he said. 'And besides, we didn't suspect at once, not about the girl, that is. We only suspected there was something wrong about him on account of him being a vegetarian. He stayed a good fortnight after the last that was seen of her. And then we slipped in like a knife. But, you see, no one had been inquiring about her, there was no warrant out.'

'And what did you find?' I asked Slugger, 'when you went in?'

'Just a big file,' he said, 'and the knife and the axe that he must have got to chop her up with.'

'But he got the axe to chop trees with,' I said.

'Well, yes,' he said, but rather grudgingly.

'And what did he chop them for?' I asked.

'Well, of course my superiors has theories about that,' he said, 'that they mightn't tell to everybody.'

You see, it was those logs that were beating them.

'But did he cut her up at all?' I asked.

'Well, he said that she was going to South America,' he answered. Which was really very fair-minded of him.

I don't remember now much else that he told me. Steeger left the plates and dishes all washed up and very neat, he said.

Well, I brought all this back to Linley, going up by the train that started just about sunset. I'd like to tell you about the late spring evening, so calm over that grim bungalow, closing in with a glory all round it as though it were blessing it; but you'll want to hear of the murder. Well, I told Linley everything, though much of it didn't seem to me to be worth the telling. The trouble was that the moment I began to leave anything out, he'd know it, and make me drag it in. 'You can't tell what may be vital,' he'd say. 'A tin-tack swept away by a housemaid might hang a man.'

All very well, but be consistent, even if you are educated at Eton and Harrow, and whenever I mentioned Num-numo, which after all was the beginning of the whole story, because he wouldn't have heard of it if it hadn't been for me, and my noticing that Steeger had bought two bottles of it, why then he said that things like that were trivial and we should keep to the main issues. I naturally talked a bit about Num-numo, because only that day I had pushed close on fifty bottles of it in Unge. A murder certainly stimulates people's minds, and Steeger's two bottles gave me an opportunity that only a fool could have failed to make something of. But of course all that was nothing at all to Linley.

You can't see a man's thoughts, and you can't look into his mind, so that all the most exciting things in the world can never be told of. But what I think happened all that evening with Linley, while I talked to him before supper, and all through supper, and sitting smoking afterwards in front of our fire, was that his thoughts were stuck at a barrier there was no getting over. And the barrier wasn't the difficulty of finding ways and means by which Steeger might have made away with the body, but the impossibility of finding why he chopped those masses of wood every day for a fortnight, and paid, as I'd just found out, £25 to his landlord to be allowed to do it. That's what was beating Linley. As for the ways by which Steeger might have hidden the body, it seemed to me that every way was blocked by the police. If you said he buried it, they said the chalk was undisturbed; if you said he carried it away, they said he never left the place; if you said he burned it, they say no smell of burning was ever noticed when the smoke blew low, and when it didn't they climbed trees after it. I'd taken to Linley wonderfully, and I didn't have to be educated to see there was something big in a mind like his, and I thought that he could have done it. When I saw the police getting in before him like that, and no way that I could see of getting past them, I felt real sorry.

Did anyone come to the house, he asked me once or twice. Did anyone take anything away from it? But we couldn't account for it that way. Then perhaps I made some suggestion that was no good, or perhaps I started talking of Num-numo again, and he interrupted me rather sharply.

'But what would you do, Smithers?' he said. 'What would you do yourself?'

'If I'd murdered poor Nancy Elth?' I asked.

'Yes,' he said.

'I can't ever imagine doing such a thing,' I told him.

He sighed at that, as though it were something against me.

'I suppose I should never be a detective,' I said. And he just shook his head.

Then he looked broodingly into the fire for what seemed an hour. And then he shook his head again. We both went to bed after that.

I shall remember the next day all my life. I was till evening, as usual, pushing Num-numo. And we sat down to supper about nine. You couldn't get things cooked at those flats, so of course we had it cold. And Linley began with a salad. I can see it now, every bit of it. Well, I was still a bit full of what I'd done in Unge, pushing Num-numo. Only a fool, I know, would have been unable to push it there; but still, I *had* pushed it; and about fifty bottles, forty-eight to be exact, are something in a small village, whatever the circumstances. So I was talking about it a bit; and then all of a sudden I realized that Num-numo was nothing to Linley, and I pulled myself up with a jerk. It was really very kind of him; do you know what he did? He must have known at once why I stopped talking, and he just stretched out a hand and said, 'Would you give me a little of your Num–numo for my salad.'

I was so touched I nearly gave it him. But of course you don't take Num-numo with salad. Only for meats and savouries. That's on the bottle.

So I just said to him, 'Only for meats and savouries.' Though I don't know what savouries are. Never had any.

I never saw a man's face go like that before.

He seemed still for a whole minute. And nothing speaking about him but that expression. Like a man that's seen a ghost, one is tempted to write. But it wasn't really at all. I'll tell you what he looked like. Like a man that's seen something that no one has ever looked at before, something he thought couldn't be.

And then he said in a voice that was all quite changed, more low and gentle and quiet it seemed, 'No good for vegetables, eh?'

'Not a bit,' I said.

And at that he gave a kind of sob in his throat. I hadn't thought he could feel things like that. Of course I didn't know what it was all about; but, whatever it was, I thought all that sort of thing would have been knocked out of him at Eton and Harrow, an educated man like that. There were no tears in his eyes, but he was feeling something horribly.

And then he began to speak with big spaces between his words, saying, 'A man might make a mistake perhaps, and use Num–numo with vegetables.'

'Not twice,' I said. What else could I say?

And he repeated that after me as though I had told of the end of the world, and adding an awful emphasis to my words, till they seemed all clammy with some frightful significance, and shaking his head as he said it.

Then he was quite silent.

'What is it?' I asked.

'Smithers,' he said.

'Yes,' I said.

'Smithers,' said he.

And I said, 'Well?'

'Look here, Smithers,' he said, 'you must phone down to the grocer at Unge and find out from him this.'

'Yes?' I said.

'Whether Steeger bought those two bottles, as I expect he did, on the same day, and not a few days apart. He couldn't have done that.'

I waited to see if any more was coming, and then I ran out and did what

I was told. It took me some time, being after nine o'clock, and only then with the help of the police. About six days apart they said; and so I came back and told Linley. He looked up at me so hopefully when I came in, but I saw that it was the wrong answer by his eyes.

You can't take things to heart like that without being ill, and when he didn't speak I said, 'What you want is a good brandy, and go to bed early.'

And he said, 'No. I must see someone from Scotland Yard. Phone round to them. Say here at once.'

But I said, 'I can't get an inspector from Scotland Yard to call on us at this hour.'

His eyes were all lit up. He was all there all right.

'Then tell them,' he said, 'they'll never find Nancy Elth. Tell one of them to come here, and I'll tell him why.' And he added, I think only for me, 'They must watch Steeger, till one day they get him over something else.'

And, do you know, he came. Inspector Ulton; he came himself.

While we were waiting I tried to talk to Linley. Partly curiosity, I admit. But I didn't want to leave him to those thoughts of his, brooding away by the fire. I tried to ask him what it was all about. But he wouldn't tell me. 'Murder is horrible,' is all he would say. 'And as a man covers his tracks up it only gets worse.'

He wouldn't tell me. 'There are tales,' he said, 'that one never wants to hear.'

That's true enough. I wish I'd never heard this one. I never did actually. But I guessed it from Linley's last words to Inspector Ulton, the only ones that I overheard. And perhaps this is the point at which to stop reading my story, so that you don't guess it too; even if you think you want murder stories. For don't you rather want a murder story with a bit of a romantic twist, and not a story about real foul murder? Well, just as you like.

In came Inspector Ulton, and Linley shook hands in silence, and pointed the way to his bedroom; and they went in there and talked in low voices, and I never heard a word.

A fairly hearty-looking man was the Inspector when they went into that room.

They walked through our sitting-room in silence when they came out, and together they went into the hall, and there I heard the only words they said to each other. It was the Inspector that first broke that silence.

'But why,' he said, 'did he cut down the trees?'

'Solely,' said Linley, 'in order to get an appetite.'

The Man Who Liked Dickens

Evelyn Waugh

Although Mr McMaster had lived in Amazonas for nearly sixty years, no one except a few families of Shiriana Indians was aware of his existence. His house stood in a small savannah, one of those little patches of sand and grass that crop up occasionally in that neighbourhood, three miles or so across, bounded on all sides by forest.

The stream which watered it was not marked on any map; it ran through rapids, always dangerous and at most seasons of the year impassable, to join the upper waters of the River Uraricuera, whose course, though boldly delineated in every school atlas, is still largely conjectural. None of the inhabitants of the district, except Mr McMaster, had ever heard of the republic of Colombia, Venezuela, Brazil or Bolivia, each of whom had at one time or another claimed its possession.

Mr McMaster's house was larger than those of his neighbours, but similar in character – a palm-thatch roof, breast-high walls of mud and wattle, and a mud floor. He owned a dozen or so head of puny cattle which grazed in the savannah, a plantation of cassava, some banana and mango trees, a dog, and, unique in the neighbourhood, a single-barrelled, breech-loading shotgun. The few commodities which he employed from the outside world came to him through a long succession of traders, passed from hand to hand, bartered for in a dozen languages at the extreme end of one of the longest threads in the web of commerce that spreads from Manáos into the remote fastness of the forest.

One day, while Mr McMaster was engaged in filling some cartridges, a Shiriana came to him with the news that a white man was approaching through the forest, alone and very sick. He closed the cartridge and loaded his gun with it, put those that were finished into his pocket and set out in the direction indicated.

The man was already clear of the bush when Mr McMaster reached him, sitting on the ground, clearly in a bad way. He was without hat or boots, and his clothes were so torn that it was only by the dampness of his body that they adhered to it; his feet were cut and grossly swollen, every exposed surface of skin was scarred by insect and bat bites; his eyes were wild with fever. He was talking to himself in delirium, but stopped when Mr McMaster approached and addressed him in English.

'I'm tired,' the man said; then: 'Can't go on any farther. My name is Henty and I'm tired. Anderson died. That was a long time ago. I expect you think I'm very odd.'

'I think you are ill, my friend.'

'Just tired. It must be several months since I had anything to eat.'

Mr McMaster hoisted him to his feet and, supporting him by the arm, led him across the hummocks of grass towards the farm.

'It is a very short way. When we get there I will give you something to make you better.'

'Jolly kind of you.' Presently he said: 'I say, you speak English. I'm English, too. My name is Henty.'

'Well, Mr Henty, you aren't to bother about anything more. You're ill and you've had a rough journey. I'll take care of you.'

They went very slowly, but at length reached the house.

'Lie there in the hammock. I will fetch something for you.'

Mr McMaster went into the back room of the house and dragged a tin canister from under a heap of skins. It was full of a mixture of dried leaf and bark. He took a handful and went outside to the fire. When he returned he put one hand behind Henty's head and held up the concoction of herbs in a calabash for him to drink. He sipped, shuddering slightly at the bitterness. At last he finished it. Mr McMaster threw out the dregs on the floor. Henty lay back in the hammock sobbing quietly. Soon he fell into a deep sleep.

'Ill-fated' was the epithet applied by the Press to the Anderson expedition to the Parima and upper Uraricuera region of Brazil. Every stage of the enterprise from the preliminary arrangements in London to its tragic dissolution in Amazonas was attacked by misfortune. It was due to one of the early setbacks that Paul Henty became connected with it.

He was not by nature an explorer; an even-tempered, good-looking young man of fastidious tastes and enviable possessions, unintellectual, but appreciative of fine architecture and the ballet, well travelled in the more accessible parts of the world, a collector though not a connoisseur, popular among hostesses, revered by his aunts. He was married to a lady of exceptional charm and beauty, and it was she who upset the good order of his life by confessing her affection for another man for the second time in the eight years of their marriage. The first occasion had been a short-lived infatuation with a tennis professional, the second was a captain in the Coldstream Guards, and more serious.

Henty's first thought under the shock of this revelation was to go out and dine alone. He was a member of four clubs, but at three of them he was liable to meet his wife's lover. Accordingly, he chose one which he rarely frequented, a semi-intellectual company composed of publishers, barristers, and men of scholarship awaiting election to the Athenaeum.

Here, after dinner, he fell into conversation with Professor Anderson and first heard of the proposed expedition to Brazil. The particular misfortune that was retarding arrangements at the moment was defalcation of the secretary with two-thirds of the expedition's capital. The principals were ready – Professor Anderson, Dr Simmons the anthropologist, Mr Necher the biologist, Mr Brough the surveyor, wireless operator and mechanic – the scientific and sporting apparatus was packed up in crates ready to be embarked, the necessary facilities had been stamped and signed by the proper authorities, but unless twelve hundred pounds was forthcoming the whole thing would have to be abandoned.

Henty, as has been suggested, was a man of comfortable means; the expedition would last from nine months to a year; he could shut his country house – his wife, he reflected, would want to remain in London near her young man – and cover more than the sum required. There was a glamour about the whole journey which might, he felt, move even his wife's sympathies. There and then, over the club fire he decided to accompany Professor Anderson.

When he went home that evening he announced to his wife: 'I have decided what I shall do.'

'Yes, darling?'

'You are certain that you no longer love me?'

'*Darling*, you *know*, I *adore* you.'

'But you are certain you love this guardsman, Tony whatever-his-name-is, more?'

'Oh, yes, *ever* so much more. Quite a different thing altogether.'

'Very well, then. I do not propose to do anything about a divorce for a year. You shall have time to think it over. I am leaving next week for the Uraricuera.'

'Golly, where's that?'

'I am not perfectly sure. Somewhere in Brazil, I think. It is unexplored. I shall be away a year.'

'But, darling, how ordinary! Like people in books – big game, I mean, and all that.'

'You have obviously already discovered that I am a very ordinary person.'

'Now, Paul, don't be disagreeable – oh, there's the telephone. It's probably Tony. If it is, d'you mind terribly if I talk to him alone for a bit?'

But in the ten days of preparation that followed she showed greater tenderness, putting off her soldier twice in order to accompany Henty to the shops where he was choosing his equipment and insisting on his purchasing a worsted cummerbund. On his last evening she gave a supper-party for him at the Embassy to which she allowed him to ask any of his friends he liked; he could think of no one except Professor Anderson, who looked oddly dressed, danced tirelessly and was something of a failure with everyone. Next day Mrs Henty came with her husband to the boat train and presented him with a pale blue, extravagantly soft blanket, in a suède case of the same colour furnished with a zip fastener and monogram. She kissed him good-bye and said, 'Take care of yourself in wherever it is.'

Had she gone as far as Southampton she might have witnessed two dramatic passages. Mr Brough got no farther than the gangway before he was arrested for debt – a matter of £32; the publicity given to the dangers of the expedition was responsible for the action. Henty settled the account.

The second difficulty was not to be overcome so easily. Mr Necher's mother was on the ship before them; she carried a missionary journal in which she had just read an account of the Brazilian forests. Nothing would induce her to permit her son's departure; she would remain on board until he came ashore with her. If necessary, she would sail with him, but go into those forests alone he should not. All argument was unavailing with the resolute old lady who eventually, five minutes before the time of embarkation, bore her son off in triumph, leaving the company without a biologist.

Nor was Mr Brough's adherence long maintained. The ship in which they were travelling was a cruising liner taking passengers on a round voyage. Mr Brough had not been on board a week and had scarcely accustomed himself to the motion of the ship before he was engaged to be married; he was still engaged, although to a different lady, when they reached Manáos and refused all inducements to proceed farther, borrowing his return fare from Henty and arriving back in Southampton engaged to the lady of his first choice, whom he immediately married.

In Brazil the officials to whom their credentials were addressed were all out of power. While Henty and Professor Anderson negotiated with the new administrators, Dr Simmons proceeded up river to Boa Vista where he established a base camp with the greater part of the stores. These were instantly commandeered by the revolutionary garrison, and he himself imprisoned for some days and subjected to various humiliations which so enraged him that, when released, he made promptly for the coast, stopping at Manáos only long enough to inform his colleagues that he insisted on laying his case personally before the central authorities at Rio.

Thus, while they were still a month's journey from the start of their labours, Henty and Professor Anderson found themselves alone and deprived of the greater part of their supplies. The ignominy of immediate return was not to be borne. For a short time they considered the advisability of going into hiding for six months in Madeira or Teneriffe, but even there detection seemed probable, there had been too many photographs in the illustrated papers before they left London. Accordingly, in low spirits, the two explorers at last set out alone for the Uraricuera with little hope of accomplishing anything of any value to anyone.

For seven weeks they paddled through green, humid tunnels of forest. They took a few snapshots of naked, misanthropic Indians, bottled some snakes and later lost them when their canoe capsized in the rapids; they overtaxed their digestions, imbibing nauseous intoxicants at native galas, they were robbed of the last of their sugar by a Guianese prospector. Finally, Professor Anderson fell ill with malignant malaria, chattered feebly for some days in his hammock, lapsed into a coma and died, leaving Henty alone with a dozen Maku oarsmen, none of whom spoke a word of any language known to him. They reversed their course and drifted down stream with a minimum of provisions and no mutual confidence.

One day, a week or so after Professor Anderson's death, Henty awoke to find that his boys and his canoe had disappeared during the night, leaving him with only his hammock and pyjamas some two or three hundred miles from the nearest Brazilian habitation. Nature forbade him to remain where he was although there seemed little purpose in moving. He set himself to follow the course of the stream, at first in the hope of meeting a canoe. But presently the whole forest became peopled for him with frantic apparitions, for no conscious reason at all. He plodded on, now wading in the water, now scrambling through the bush.

Vaguely at the back of his mind he had always believed that the jungle was a place full of food, that there was danger of snakes and savages and wild beasts, but not of starvation. But now he observed that this was far from being the case. The jungle consisted solely of immense tree trunks, embedded in a tangle of thorn and vine rope, all far from nutritious. On the first day he suffered hideously. Later he seemed anaesthetized and was chiefly embarrassed by the behaviour of the inhabitants who came out to meet him in footmen's livery, carrying his dinner, and then irresponsibly disappeared or raised the covers of their dishes and revealed live tortoises. Many people who knew him in London appeared and ran round him with derisive cries, asking him questions to which he could not possibly know the answer. His wife came, too, and he was pleased to see her, assuming that she had got tired of her guardsman and was there to fetch him back, but she soon disappeared, like all the others.

It was then that he remembered that it was imperative for him to reach Manáos; he redoubled his energy, stumbling against boulders in the stream and getting caught up among the vines. 'But I mustn't waste my breath,' he reflected. Then he forgot that, too, and was conscious of nothing more until he found himself lying in a hammock in Mr McMaster's house.

His recovery was slow. At first, days of lucidity alternated with delirium, then his temperature dropped and he was conscious even when most ill. The days of fever grew less frequent, finally occurring in the normal system of the tropics between long periods of comparative health. Mr McMaster dosed him regularly with herbal remedies.

'It's very nasty,' said Henty, 'but it does do good.'

'There is medicine for everything in the forest,' said Mr McMaster, 'to make you well and to make you ill. My mother was an Indian and she taught me many of them. I have learned others from time to time from my wives. There are plants to cure you and give you fever, to kill you and send you mad, to keep away snakes, to intoxicate fish so that you can pick them out of the water with your hands like fruit from a tree. There are medicines even I do not know. They say that it is possible to bring dead people to life after they have begun to stink, but I have not seen it done.'

'But surely you are English?'

'My father was – at least a Barbadian. He came to British Guiana as a missionary. He was married to a white woman but he left her in Guiana to look for gold. Then he took my mother. The Shiriana women are ugly but very devoted. I have had many. Most of the men and women living in this savannah are my children. That is why they obey – for that reason and because I have the gun. My father lived to a great age. It is not twenty years since he died. He was a man of education. Can you read?'

'Yes, of course.'

'It is not everyone who is so fortunate. I cannot.'

Henty laughed apologetically. 'But I suppose you haven't much opportunity here.'

'Oh, yes, that is just it. I have a great many books. I will show you when you are better. Until five years ago there was an Englishman – at least a black man, but he was well educated in Georgetown. He died. He used to read to me every day until he died. You shall read to me when you are better.'

'I shall be delighted to.'

'Yes, you shall read to me,' Mr McMaster repeated, nodding over the calabash.

During the early days of his convalescence Henty had little conversation with his host; he lay in the hammock staring up at the thatched roof and thinking about his wife, rehearsing over and over again different incidents of their life together, including her affairs with the tennis professional and the soldier. The days, exactly twelve hours each, passed without distinction. Mr McMaster retired to sleep at sundown, leaving a little lamp burning – a hand-wove wick drooping from a pot of beef fat – to keep away vampire bats.

The first time that Henty left the house Mr McMaster took him for a little stroll around the farm.

'I will show you the black man's grave,' he said, leading him to a mound between the mango trees. 'He was very kind to me. Every afternoon until he died, for two hours, he used to read to me. I think I will put up a cross – to commemorate his death and your arrival – a pretty idea. Do you believe in God?'

'I've never really thought about it much.'

'You are perfectly right. I have thought about it a *great* deal and I still do not know . . . Dickens did.'

'I suppose so.'

'Oh yes, it is apparent in all his books. You will see.'

That afternoon Mr McMaster began the construction of a headpiece for the Negro's grave. He worked with a large spokeshave in a wood so hard that it grated and rang like metal.

At last when Henty had passed six or seven consecutive days without fever, Mr McMaster said, 'Now I think you are well enough to see the books.'

At one end of the hut there was a kind of loft formed by a rough platform erected up in the eaves of the roof. Mr McMaster propped a ladder against it and mounted. Henty followed, still unsteady after his illness. Mr McMaster sat on the platform and Henty stood at the top of the ladder looking over. There was a heap of small bundles there, tied up with rag, palm leaf and raw hide.

'It has been hard to keep out the worms and ants. Two are practically destroyed. But there is an oil the Indians know how to make that is useful.'

He unwrapped the nearest parcel and handed down a calf-bound book. It was an early American edition of *Bleak House*.

'It does not matter which we take first.'

'You are fond of Dickens?'

'Why, yes, of course. More than fond, far more. You see, they are the only books I have ever heard. My father used to read them and then later the black man . . . and now you. I have heard them all several times by now but I never get tired; there is always more to be learned and noticed, so many characters, so many changes of scene, so many words . . . I have all Dickens's books except those that the ants devoured. It takes a long time to read them all – more than two years.'

'Well,' said Henty lightly, 'they will well last out my visit.'

'Oh, I hope not. It is delightful to start again. Each time I think I find more to enjoy and admire.'

They took down the first volume of *Bleak House* and that afternoon Henty had his first reading.

He had always rather enjoyed reading aloud and in the first year of marriage had shared several books in this way with his wife, until one day, in one of her rare moments of confidence, she remarked that it was torture to her. Sometimes after that he had thought it might be agreeable to have children to read to. But Mr McMaster was a unique audience.

The old man sat astride his hammock opposite Henty, fixing him throughout with his eyes, and following the words, soundlessly, with his lips. Often when a new character was introduced he would say, 'Repeat the name, I have forgotten him,' or, 'Yes, yes, I remember her well. She dies, poor woman.' He would frequently interrupt with questions not as Henty would have imagined about the circumstances of the story – such things as the procedure of the Lord Chancellor's Court or the social conventions of the time, though they must have been unintelligible, did not concern him – but always about the characters. 'Now, why does she say that? Does she really mean it? Did she feel faint because of the heat of the fire or of something in that paper?' He laughed loudly at all the jokes and at some passages which did not seem humorous to Henty, asking him to repeat them two or three times; and later at the descriptions of the sufferings of the outcasts in 'Tom-all-alone' tears ran down his cheeks into his beard. His comments on the story were usually simple. 'I think that Dedlock is a very proud man,' or 'Mrs Jellyby does not take enough care of her children.' Henty enjoyed the readings almost as much as he did.

At the end of the first day the old man said, 'You read beautifully, with a far better accent than the black man. And you explain better. It is almost as though my father were here again.' And always at the end of a session he thanked his guest courteously. 'I enjoyed that very much. It was an extremely distressing chapter. But, if I remember rightly, it will all turn out well.'

By the time that they were well into the second volume, however, the novelty of the old man's delight had begun to wane, and Henty was feeling strong enough to be restless. He touched more than once on the subject of his departure, asking about canoes and rains and the possibility of finding guides. But Mr McMaster seemed obtuse and paid no attention to these hints.

One day, running his thumb through the pages of *Bleak House* that remained to be read, Henty said, 'We still have a lot to get through. I hope I shall be able to finish it before I go.'

'Oh, yes,' said Mr McMaster. 'Do not disturb yourself about that. You will have time to finish it, my friend.'

For the first time Henty noticed something slightly menacing in his host's manner. That evening at supper, a brief meal of farine and dried beef eaten just before sundown, Henty renewed the subject.

'You know, Mr McMaster, the time has come when I must be thinking about getting back to civilization. I have already imposed myself on your hospitality for too long.'

Mr McMaster bent over his plate, crunching mouthfuls of farine, but made no reply.

'How soon do you think I shall be able to get a boat? . . . I said how soon do you think I shall be able to get a boat? I appreciate all your kindness to me more than I can say, but . . .'

'My friend, any kindness I may have shown is amply repaid by your reading of Dickens. Do not let us mention the subject again.'

'Well, I'm very glad you have enjoyed it. I have, too. But I really must be thinking of getting back . . .'

'Yes,' said Mr McMaster. 'The black man was like that. He thought of it all the time. But he died here . . .'

Twice during the next day Henty opened the subject but his host was evasive. Finally he said, 'Forgive me, Mr McMaster, but I really must press the point. When can I get a boat?'

'There is no boat.'

'Well, the Indians can build one.'

'You must wait for the rains. There is not enough water in the river now.'

'How long will that be?'

'A month . . . two months . . .'

They had finished *Bleak House* and were nearing the end of *Dombey and Son* when the rains came.

'Now it is time to make preparations to go.'

'Oh, that is impossible. The Indians will not make a boat during the rainy season – it is one of their superstitions.'

'You might have told me.'

'Did I not mention it? I forgot.'

Next morning Henty went out alone while his host was busy, and, looking as aimless as he could, strolled across the savannah to the group of Indian houses. There were four or five Shirianas sitting in one of the doorways. They did not look up as he approached them. He addressed them in the few words of Maku he had acquired during the journey but they made no sign whether they understood him or not. Then he drew a sketch of a canoe in the sand, he went through some vague motions of carpentry, pointed from them to him, then made motions of giving something to them and scratched out the outlines of a gun and a hat and a few other recognizable articles of trade. One of the women giggled, but no one gave any sign of comprehension, and he went away unsatisfied.

At their midday meal Mr McMaster said: 'Mr Henty, the Indians tell me that you have been trying to speak with them. It is easier that you say anything you wish through me. You realize, do you not, that they would do nothing without my authority. They regard themselves, quite rightly in most cases, as my children.'

'Well, as a matter of fact, I was asking them about a canoe.'

'So they gave me to understand . . . and now if you have finished your meal perhaps we might have another chapter. I am quite absorbed in the book.'

They finished *Dombey and Son*; nearly a year had passed since Henty had left England, and his gloomy foreboding of permanent exile became suddenly acute when, between the pages of *Martin Chuzzlewit*, he found a document written in pencil in irregular characters.

Year 1919.

I James McMaster of Brazil, do swear to Barnabas Washington of Georgetown that if he finish this book in fact Martin Chuzzlewit I will let him go away back as soon as finished.

There followed a heavy pencil X, and after it: *Mr McMaster made this mark signed Barnabas Washington.*

'Mr McMaster,' said Henty, 'I must speak frankly. You saved my life, and when I get back to civilization I will reward you to the best of my ability. I will give you anything within reason. But at present you are keeping me here against my will. I demand to be released.'

'But, my friend, what is keeping you? You are under no restraint. Go when you like.'

'You know very well that I can't get away without your help.'

'In that case you must humour an old man. Read me another chapter.'

'Mr McMaster, I swear by anything you like that when I get to Manáos I will find someone to take my place. I will pay a man to read to you all day.'

'But I have no need of another man. You read so well.'

'I have read for the last time.'

'I hope not,' said Mr McMaster politely.

That evening at supper only one plate of dried meat and farine was brought in and Mr McMaster ate alone. Henty lay without speaking, staring at the thatch.

Next day at noon a single plate was put before Mr McMaster, but with it lay his gun, cocked, on his knee, as he ate. Henty resumed the reading of *Martin Chuzzlewit* where it had been interrupted.

Weeks passed hopelessly. They read *Nicholas Nickleby* and *Little Dorrit* and *Oliver Twist*. Then a stranger arrived in the savannah, a half-caste prospector, one of that lonely order of men who wander for a lifetime through the forests, tracing the little streams, sifting the gravel and, ounce by ounce, filling the little leather sack of gold dust, more often than not dying of exposure and starvation with five hundred dollars' worth of gold hung round their necks. Mr McMaster was vexed at his arrival, gave him farine and *passo* and sent him on his journey within an hour of his arrival, but in that hour Henty had time to scribble his name on a slip of paper and put it into the man's hand.

From now on there was hope. The days followed their unvarying routine: coffee at sunrise, a morning of inaction while Mr McMaster pottered about on the business of the farm, farine and *passo* at noon, Dickens in the afternoon, farine and *passo* and sometimes some fruit for supper, silence from sunset to dawn with the small wick glowing in the beef fat and the palm thatch overhead dimly discernible; but Henty lived in quiet confidence and expectation.

Some time, this year or the next, the prospector would arrive at a Brazilian village with news of his discovery. The disasters to the Anderson expedition would not have passed unnoticed. Henty could imagine the headlines that must have appeared in the popular Press; even now probably there were search parties working over the country he had crossed; any day English voices might sound over the savannah and a dozen friendly adventurers come crashing through the bush. Even as he was reading, while his lips mechanically followed the printed pages, his mind wandered away from his eager, crazy host opposite, and he began to narrate to himself incidents of his home-coming – the gradual re-encounters with civilization; he shaved and bought new clothes at Manáos, telegraphed for money, received wires of congratulation; he enjoyed the leisurely river journey to Belem, the big liner to Europe; savoured good claret and fresh meat and spring vegetables; he was shy at meeting his wife and uncertain how to address . . . 'Darling, you've been much longer than you said. I quite thought you were lost . . .'

And then Mr McMaster interrupted. 'May I trouble you to read that passage again? It is one I particularly enjoy.'

The weeks passed; there was no sign of rescue, but Henty endured the day for hope of what might happen on the morrow; he even felt a slight stirring of cordiality towards his gaoler and was therefore quite willing to join him when, one evening after a long conference with an Indian neighbour, he proposed a celebration.

'It is one of the local feast days,' he explained, 'and they have been making piwari. You may not like it, but you should try some. We will go across to this man's home tonight.'

Accordingly after supper they joined a party of Indians that were assembled round the fire in one of the huts at the other side of the savannah. They were singing in an apathetic, monotonous manner and passing a large calabash of liquid from mouth to mouth. Separate bowls were brought for Henty and Mr McMaster, and they were given hammocks to sit in.

'You must drink it all without lowering the cup. That is the etiquette.'

Henty gulped the dark liquid, trying not to taste it. But it was not unpleasant, hard and muddy on the palate like most of the beverages he had been offered in Brazil, but with a flavour of honey and brown bread. He leant back in the hammock feeling unusually contented. Perhaps at that very moment the search party was in camp a few hours' journey from them. Meanwhile he was warm and drowsy. The cadence of song rose and fell interminably, liturgically. Another calabash of piwari was offered him and he handed it back empty. He lay full length watching the play of shadows on the thatch as the Shirianas began to dance. Then he shut his eyes and thought of England and his wife and fell asleep.

★

He awoke, still in the Indian hut, with the impression that he had outslept his usual hour. By the position of the sun he knew it was late afternoon. No one else was about. He looked for his watch and found to his surprise that it was not on his wrist. He had left it in the house, he supposed, before coming to the party.

'I must have been tight last night,' he reflected. 'Treacherous drink, that.' He had a headache and feared a recurrence of fever. He found when he set his feet to the ground that he stood with difficulty; his walk was unsteady and his mind confused as it had been during the first weeks of his convalescence. On the way across the savannah he was obliged to stop more than once, shutting his eyes and breathing deeply. When he reached the house he found Mr McMaster sitting there.

'Ah, my friend, you are late for the reading this afternoon. There is scarcely another half-hour of light. How do you feel?'

'Rotten. That drink doesn't seem to agree with me.'

'I will give you something to make you better. The forest has remedies for everything; to make you awake and to make you sleep.'

'You haven't seen my watch anywhere?'

'You have missed it.'

'Yes. I thought I was wearing it. I say, I've never slept so long.'

'Not since you were a baby. Do you know how long? Two days.'

'Nonsense. I can't have.'

'Yes, indeed. It is a long time. It is a pity because you missed our guests.'

'Guests?'

'Why, yes. I have been quite gay while you were asleep. Three men from outside. Englishmen. It is a pity you missed them. A pity for them, too, as they particularly wished to see you. But what could I do? You were so sound asleep. They had come all the way to find you so – I thought you would not mind – as you could not greet them yourself I gave them a little souvenir, your watch. They wanted something to take home to your wife who is offering a great reward for news of you. They were very pleased with it. And they took some photographs of the little cross I put up to commemorate your coming. They were pleased with that, too. They were very easily pleased. But I do not suppose they will visit us again, our life here is so retired . . . no pleasures except reading . . . I do not suppose we shall ever have visitors again . . . Well, well, I will get you some medicine to make you feel better. Your head aches; does it not . . . ? We will not have any Dickens today . . . but tomorrow, and the day after that, and the day after that. Let us read *Little Dorrit* again. There are passages in that book I can never hear without the temptation to weep.'

Taboo

Geoffrey Household

I had this story from Lewis Banning, the American; but as I also know Shiravieff pretty well and have heard some parts of it from him since, I think I can honestly reconstruct his own words.

Shiravieff had asked Banning to meet Colonel Romero, and after lunch took them, as his habit is, into his consulting room; his study, I should call it, for there are no instruments or white enamel to make a man unpleasantly conscious of the workings of his own body, nor has Shiravieff, among the obscure groups of letters that he is entitled to write after his name, any one which implies a medical degree. It is a long, restful room, its harmony only broken by sporting trophies. The muzzle of an enormous wolf grins over the mantelpiece, and there are fine heads of ibex and aurochs on the opposite wall. No doubt Shiravieff put them there deliberately. His patients from the counties came in expecting a quack doctor but at once gained confidence when they saw he had killed wild animals in a gentlemanly manner.

The trophies suit him. With his peaked beard and broad smile, he looks more the explorer than the psychologist. His unvarying calm is not the priestlike quality of the doctor; it is the disillusionment of the traveller and exile, of one who has studied the best and the worst in human nature and discovered that there is no definable difference between them.

Romero took a dislike to the room. He was very sensitive to atmosphere, though he would have denied it indignantly.

'A lot of silly women,' he grumbled obscurely, 'pouring out emotions.'

They had, of course, poured out plenty of emotions from the same chair that he was occupying; but, since Shiravieff made his reputation on cases of shell shock, there must have been a lot of silly men too. Romero naturally would not mention that. He preferred to think that hysteria was confined to the opposite sex. Being a Latin in love with England, he worshipped and cultivated our detachment.

'I assure you that emotions are quite harmless once they are out of the system,' answered Shiravieff, smiling. 'It's when they stay inside that they give trouble.'

'*Ça!* I like people who keep their emotions inside,' said Romero. 'It is why I live in London. The English are not cold – it is nonsense to say they are cold – but they are well bred. They never show a sign of what hurts them most. I like that.'

Shiravieff tapped his long forefinger on the table in a fast, nervous rhythm.

'And what if they *must* display emotion?' he asked irritably. 'Shock them – shock them, you understand, so that they must! They can't do it, and they are hurt for life.'

They had never before seen him impatient. Nobody had. It was an unimaginable activity, as if your family doctor were to come and visit you without his trousers. Romero had evidently stirred up the depths.

'I've shocked them, and they displayed plenty of emotion,' remarked Banning.

'Oh, I do not mean their little conventions,' said Shiravieff slowly and severely. 'Shock them with some horrid fact that they can't blink away, something that would outrage the souls of any of us. Do you remember de Maupassant's story of the man whose daughter was buried alive – how she returned from the grave and how all her life he kept the twitching gesture with which he tried to push her away? Well, if that man had shrieked or thrown a fit or wept all night he mightn't have suffered from the twitch.'

'Courage would have saved him,' announced the colonel superbly.

'No!' shouted Shiravieff. 'We're all cowards, and the healthiest thing we can do is to express fear when we feel it.'

'The fear of death –' began Romero.

'I am not talking about the fear of death. It is not that. It is our horror of breaking a taboo that causes shock. Listen to me. Do either of you remember the Zweibergen case in 1926?'

'The name's familiar,' said Banning. 'But I can't just recall . . . was it a haunted village?'

'I congratulate you on your healthy mind,' said Shiravieff ironically. 'You can forget what you don't want to remember.'

He offered them cigars and lit one himself. Since he hardly ever smoked it calmed him immediately. His grey eyes twinkled as if to assure them that he shared their surprise at his irritation. Banning had never before realized, so he said, that the anti-smoke societies were right, that tobacco was a drug.

'I was at Zweibergen that summer. I chose it because I wanted to be alone. I can only rest when I am alone,' began Shiravieff abruptly. 'The eastern Carpathians were remote ten years ago – cut off from the tourists by too many frontiers. The Hungarian magnates who used to shoot the forests before the war had vanished, and their estates were sparsely settled. I didn't expect any civilized company.

'I was disappointed to find that a married couple had rented the old shooting box. They were obviously interesting, but I made no advances to them beyond passing the time of day whenever we met on the village street. He was English and she American – one of those delightful women who are wholly and typically American. No other country can fuse enough races to produce them. Her blood, I should guess, was mostly Slav. They thought me a surly fellow, but respected my evident desire for privacy – until the time when all of us in Zweibergen wanted listeners. Then the Vaughans asked me to dinner.

'We talked nothing but commonplaces during the meal, which was, by the way, excellent. There were a joint of venison and some wild strawberries, I remember. We took our coffee on the lawn in front of the house, and sat for a moment in silence – the mountain silence – staring out across the valley. The pine forest, rising tier upon tier, was very black in the late twilight. White, isolated rocks were scattered through it. They looked as if they might move on at any minute – like the ghosts of great beasts pasturing upon the treetops. Then a dog howled on the alp above us. We all began talking at once. About the mystery, of course.

'Two men had been missing in that forest for nearly a week. The first of them belonged to a little town about ten miles down the valley; he was returning after nightfall from a short climb in the mountains. He might have vanished into a snowdrift or ravine, for the paths were none too safe. There were no climbing clubs in that district to keep them up. But it seemed to be some less common accident that had overtaken him. He was out of the high peaks. A shepherd camping on one of the lower alps had exchanged a good night with him, and watched him disappear among the trees on his way downwards. That was the last that had been seen or heard of him.

'The other was one of the search party that had gone out on the following day. The man had been posted as a stop, while the rest beat the woods towards him. It was the last drive, and already dark. When the line came up to his stand he was not there.

'Everybody suspected wolves. Since 1914 there had been no shooting over the game preserves, and animal life of all sorts was plentiful. But the wolves were not in pack, and the search parties did not find a trace of blood. There were no tracks to help. There was no sign of a struggle. Vaughan suggested that we were making a mystery out of nothing – probably the two men had become tired of domestic routine, and taken the opportunity to disappear. By now, he expected, they were on their way to the Argentine.

'His cool dismissal of tragedy was inhuman. He sat there, tall, distant, and casually strong. His face was stamped ready-made out of that pleasant upper-class mould. Only his firm mouth and thin sensitive nostrils showed that he had any personality of his own. Kyra Vaughan looked at him scornfully.

' "Is that what you really think?" she asked.

' "Why not?" he answered. "If those men had been killed it must have been by something prowling about and waiting for its chance. And there isn't such a thing."

' "If you want to believe the men aren't dead, believe it!" Kyra said.

'Vaughan's theory that the men had disappeared of their own free will was, of course, absurd; but his wife's sudden coldness to him seemed to me to be needlessly impatient. I understood when I knew him better. Vaughan – your reserved Englishman, Romero! – was covering up his thoughts and fears, and chose, quite unconsciously, to appear stupid rather than to show his anxiety. She recognized the insincerity without understanding its cause, and it made her angry.

'They were a queer pair, those two; intelligent, cultured, and so interested in themselves and each other that they needed more than one life to satisfy their curiosity. She was a highly strung creature, with swift brown eyes and a slender, eager body that seemed to grow like a flower from the ground under her feet. And natural! I don't mean she couldn't act. She could – but when she did, it was deliberate. She was defenceless before others' suffering and joy, and she didn't try to hide it.

'Lord! She used to live through enough emotions in one day to last her husband for a year!

'Not that he was unemotional. Those two were very much alike, though you'd never have guessed it. But he was shy of tears and laughter, and he had armed his whole soul against them. To a casual observer he seemed the calmer of the two, but at bottom he was an extremist. He might have been a poet, a Saint Francis, a revolutionary. But was he? No! He was an Englishman. He knew he was in danger of being swayed by emotional ideas, of giving his life to them. And so? And so he balanced every idea with another, and secured peace for himself between the scales.

She, of course, would always jump into one scale or the other. And he loved her for it. But his non-committal attitudes got on her nerves.'

'She could do no wrong in your eyes,' said Romero indignantly. His sympathies had been aroused on behalf of the unknown Englishman. He admired him.

'I adored her,' said Shiravieff frankly. 'Everybody did. She made one live more intensely. Don't think I undervalued him, however. I couldn't help seeing how his wheels went round, but I liked him thoroughly. He was a man you could trust, and good company as well. A man of action. What he did had little relation to the opinions he expressed.

'Well, after that dinner with the Vaughans I had no more desire for a lonely holiday; so I did the next best thing, and took an active interest in everything that was going on. I heard all the gossip, for I was staying in the general clearing house, the village inn. In the evenings I often joined the district magistrate as he sat in the garden with a stein of beer in front of him and looked over the notes of the depositions which he had taken that day.

'He was a very solid functionary – a good type of man for a case like that. A more imaginative person would have formed theories, found evidence to fit them, and only added to the mystery. He did not want to discuss the case. No, he had no fear of an indiscretion. It was simply that he had nothing to say, and was clear headed enough to realize it. He admitted that he knew no more than the villagers whose depositions filled his portfolio. But he was ready to talk on any other subject – especially politics – and our long conversations gave me a reputation for profound wisdom among the villagers. Almost I had the standing of a public official.

'So, when a third man disappeared, this time from Zweibergen itself, the mayor and the village constable came to me for instructions. It was the local grocer who was missing. He had climbed up through the forest in the hope of bagging a blackcock at dusk. In the morning the shop did not open. Only then was it known that he had never returned. A solitary shot had been heard about 10.30 p.m., when the grocer was presumably trudging homewards.

'All I could do, pending the arrival of the magistrate, was to send out search parties. We quartered the forest, and examined every path. Vaughan and I, with one of the peasants, went up to my favourite place for blackcock. It was there, I thought, that the grocer would have gone. Then we inspected every foot of the route which he must have taken back to the village. Vaughan knew something about tracking. He was one of those surprising Englishmen whom you may know for years without realizing that once there were coloured men in Africa or Burma or Borneo who knew him still better, and drove game for him, and acknowledged him as someone juster than their gods, but no more comprehensible.

'We had covered some four miles when he surprised me by suddenly showing interest in the undergrowth. Up to then I had been fool enough to think that he was doing precisely nothing.

' "Someone has turned aside from the path here," he said. "He was in a hurry. I wonder why."

'A few yards from the path there was a white rock about thirty feet high. It was steep, but projecting ledges gave an easy way up. A hot spring at the foot of it bubbled out of a cavity hardly bigger than a fox's earth. When Vaughan showed me the signs, I could see that the scrub which grew between the rocks and the path had been roughly pushed aside. But I pointed out that no one was likely to dash off the path through that thicket.

' "When you know you're being followed, you like to have a clear space around you," Vaughan answered. "It would be comforting to be on top of that rock with a gun in your hands – if you got there in time. Let's go up."

'The top was bare stone, with clumps of creeper and ivy growing from the crannies. Set back some three yards from the edge was a little tree, growing in a pocket of soil. One side of its base was shattered into slivers. It had received a full charge of shot at close quarters. The peasant crossed himself. He murmured:

' "They say there's always a tree between you and it."

'I asked him what "it" was. He didn't answer immediately, but played with his stick casually, and as if ashamed, until the naked steel point was in his hand. Then he muttered:

' "The werewolf."

'Vaughan laughed and pointed to the shot marks six inches from the ground.

' "The werewolf must be a baby one, if it's only as tall as that," he said. "No, the man's gun went off as he fell. Perhaps he was followed too close as he scrambled up. About there is where his body would have fallen."

'He knelt down to examine the ground.

' "What's that?" he asked me. "If it's blood, it has something else with it."

'There was only a tiny spot on the bare rock. I looked at it. It was undoubtedly brain tissue. I was surprised that there was no more of it. It must, I suppose, have come from a deep wound in the skull. Might have been made by an arrow, or a bird's beak, or perhaps a tooth.

'Vaughan slid down the rock, and prodded his stick into the sulphurous mud of the stream bed. Then he hunted about in the bushes like a dog.

' "There was no body dragged away in that direction," he said.

'We examined the farther side of the rock. It fell sheer, and seemed an impossible climb for man or beast. The edge was matted with growing things. I was ready to believe that Vaughan's eyes could tell if anything had passed that way.

' "Not a sign!" he said. "Where the devil has his body gone to?"

'The three of us sat on the edge of the rock in silence. The spring bubbled and wept beneath, and the pines murmured above us. There was no need of a little particle of human substance, recognizable only to a physiologist's eye, to tell us that we were on the scene of a kill. Imagination? Imagination is so often only a forgotten instinct. The man who ran up that rock wondered in his panic why he gave way to his imagination.

'We found the magistrate in the village when we returned and reported our find to him.

' "Interesting! But what does it tell us?" he said.

'I pointed out that at least we knew the man was dead or dying.

' "There's no certain proof. Show me his body. Show me any motive for killing him."

'Vaughan insisted that it was the work of an animal. The magistrate disagreed. If it were wolf, he said, we might have some difficulty in collecting the body, but none in finding it. And as for bear – well, they were so harmless that the idea was ridiculous.

'Nobody believed in any material beast, for the whole countryside had been beaten. But tales were told in the village – the old tales. I should never have dreamed that those peasants accepted so many horrors as fact if I hadn't heard those tales in the village inn. The odd thing is that I couldn't say then, and I can't say now, that they were altogether wrong. You should have seen the look in those men's eyes as old Weiss, the game warden, told how time after time his grandfather had fired point-blank at a grey wolf whom he met in the woods at twilight. He had never killed it until he loaded his gun with silver. Then the wolf vanished after the shot, but Heinrich the cobbler was found dying in his house with a beaten silver dollar in his belly.

'Josef Weiss, his son, who did most of the work on the preserves and was seldom seen in the village unless he came down to sell a joint or two of venison, was indignant with his father. He was a heavily built, sullen fellow, who had read a little. There's nobody so intolerant of superstition as your half-educated man. Vaughan, of course, agreed with him – but then capped the villagers' stories with such ghastly tales from native folklore and medieval literature that I couldn't help seeing he had been brooding on the subject. The peasants took him seriously. They came and went in pairs. No one would step out into the night without a companion. Only the shepherd was unaffected. He didn't disbelieve, but he was a mystic. He was used to passing to and fro under the trees at night.

' "You've got to be a part of those things, sir," he said to me, "then you'll not be afraid of them. I don't say a man can turn himself into a wolf – the Blessed Virgin protect us! – but I know why he'd want to."

'That was most interesting.

' "I think I know too," I answered. "But what does it feel like?"

' "It feels as if the woods had got under your skin, and you want to walk wild and crouch at the knees."

' "He's perfectly right," said Vaughan convincingly.

'That was the last straw for those peasants. They drew away from Vaughan, and two of them spat into the fire to avert his evil eye. He seemed to them much too familiar with the black arts.

' "How do you explain it?" asked Vaughan, turning to me.

'I told him it might have a dozen different causes, just as fear of the dark has. And physical hunger might also have something to do with it.

'I think our modern psychology is inclined to give too much importance to sex. We forget that man is, or was, a fleet-footed hunting animal equipped with all the necessary instincts.

'As soon as I mentioned hunger, there was a chorus of assent – though they really didn't know what I or the shepherd or Vaughan was talking about. Most of those men had experienced extreme hunger. The innkeeper was reminded of a temporary famine during the war. The shepherd told us how he had once spent a week stuck on the face of a cliff before he was found. Josef Weiss, eager to get away from the supernatural, told his experiences as a prisoner of war in Russia. With his companions he had been forgotten behind the blank walls of a fortress while their guards engaged in revolution. Those poor devils had been reduced to very desperate straits indeed.

'For a whole week Vaughan and I were out with the search parties day and night. Meanwhile Kyra wore herself out trying to comfort the womenfolk. They couldn't help loving her – yet half suspected that she herself was at the bottom of the mystery. I don't blame them. They couldn't be expected to understand her intense spirituality. To them she was like a creature from another planet, fascinating and terrifying.

Without claiming any supernatural powers for her, I've no doubt that
Kyra could have told the past, present and future of any of those villagers
much more accurately than the travelling gipsies.

'On our first day of rest I spent the afternoon with the Vaughans. He
and I were refreshed by twelve hours' sleep, and certain that we could hit
on some new solution to the mystery that might be the right one. Kyra
joined in the discussion. We went over the old theories again and again,
but could make no progress.

' "We shall be forced to believe the tales they tell in the village," I said
at last.

' "Why don't you?" asked Kyra Vaughan.

'We both protested. Did she believe them, we asked.

' "I'm not sure," she answered. "What does it matter? But I know that
evil has come to those men. Evil . . ." she repeated.

'We were startled. You smile, Romero, but you don't realize how that
atmosphere of the uncanny affected us.

'Looking back on it, I see how right she was. Women – good Lord,
they get hold of the spiritual significance of something, and we take them
literally!

'When she left us I asked Vaughan whether she really believed in the
werewolf.

' "Not exactly," he explained. "What she means is that our logic isn't
getting us anywhere – that we ought to begin looking for something
which, if it isn't a werewolf, has the spirit of the werewolf. You see, even
if she saw one, she would be no more worried than she is. The outward
form of things impresses her so little."

'Vaughan appreciated his wife. He didn't know what in the world she
meant, but he knew that there was always sense in her parables, even if it
took one a long time to make the connection between what she actually
said and the way in which one would have expressed the same thing
oneself. That, after all, is what understanding means.

'I asked what he supposed she meant by evil.

' "Evil?" he replied. "Evil forces – something that behaves as it has no
right to behave. She means almost – possession. Look here! Let's find out
in our own way what she means. Assuming it's visible, let's see this
thing."

'It was, he still thought, an animal. Its hunting had been successful, and
now that the woods were quiet it would start again. He didn't think it had
been driven away for good.

' "It wasn't driven away by the first search parties," he pointed out.
"They frightened all the game for miles around, but this thing simply

took one of them. It will come back, just as surely as a man-eating lion comes back. And there's only one way to catch it – bait!"

' "Who's going to be the bait?" I asked.

' "You and I."

'I suppose I looked startled. Vaughan laughed. He said that I was getting fat, that I would make most tempting bait. Whenever he made jokes in poor taste, I knew that he was perfectly serious.

' "What are you going to do?" I asked. "Tie me to a tree and watch out with a gun?"

' "That's about right, except that you needn't be tied up – and as the idea is mine you can have first turn with the gun. Are you a good shot?"

'I am and so was he. To prove it, we practised on a target after dinner, and found that we could trust each other up to fifty yards in clear moonlight. Kyra disliked shooting. She had a horror of death. Vaughan's excuse didn't improve matters. He said that we were going deer stalking the next night and needed some practice.

' "Are you going to shoot them while they are asleep?" she asked disgustedly.

' "While they are having their supper, dear."

' "Before, if possible," I added.

'I disliked hurting her by jokes that to her were pointless, but we chose that method deliberately. She couldn't be told the truth, and now she would be too proud to ask questions.

'Vaughan came down to the inn the following afternoon, and we worked out a plan of campaign. The rock was the starting point of all our theories, and on it we decided to place the watcher. From the top there was a clear view of the path for fifty yards on either side. The watcher was to take up his stand, while covered by the ivy, before sunset, and at a little before ten the bait was to be on the path and within shot. He should walk up and down, taking care never to step out of sight of the rock, until midnight, when the party would break up. We reckoned that our quarry, if it reasoned, would take the bait to be a picket posted in that part of the forest.

'The difficulty was getting home. We had to go separately in case we were observed, and hope for the best. Eventually we decided that the man on the path, who might be followed, should go straight down to the road as fast as he could. There was a timber slide quite close, by which he could cut down in ten minutes. The man on the rock should wait awhile and then go home by the path.

' "Well, I shall not see you again until tomorrow morning," said Vaughan as he got up to go. "You'll see me but I shan't see you. Just whistle once; very softly, as I come up the path, so that I know you're there."

'He remarked that he had left a letter for Kyra with the notary in case of accidents, and added, with an embarrassed laugh, that he supposed it was silly.

'I thought it was anything but silly, and said so.

'I was on the rock by sunset. I wormed my legs and body back into the ivy, leaving head and shoulders free to pivot with the rifle. It was a little .300 with a longish barrel. I felt certain that Vaughan was as safe as human science and a steady hand could make him.

'The moon came up, and the path was a ribbon of silver in front of me. There's something silent about moonlight. It's not light. It's a state of things. When there was sound it was unexpected, like the sudden shiver on the flank of a sleeping beast. A twig cracked now and then. An owl hooted. A fox slunk across the pathway, looking back over his shoulder. I wished that Vaughan would come. Then the ivy rustled behind me. I couldn't turn round. My spine became very sensitive, and a point at the back of my skull tingled as if expecting a blow. It was no good my telling myself that nothing but a bird could possibly be behind me – but of course it was a bird. A nightjar whooshed out of the ivy, and my body became suddenly cold with sweat. That infernal fright cleared all vague fears right out of me. I continued to be uneasy, but I was calm.

'After a while I heard Vaughan striding up the path. Then he stepped within range, a bold, clear figure in the moonlight. I whistled softly, and he waved his hand from the wrist in acknowledgement. He walked up and down, smoking a cigar. The point of light marked his head in the shadows. Wherever he went, my sights were lined a yard or two behind him. At midnight he nodded his head towards my hiding place and trotted rapidly away to the timber slide. A little later I took the path home.

'The next night our roles were reversed. It was my turn to walk the path. I found that I preferred to be the bait. On the rock I had longed for another pair of eyes, but after an hour on the ground I did not even want to turn my head. I was quite content to trust Vaughan to take care of anything going on behind me. Only once was I uneasy. I heard, as I thought, a bird calling far down in the woods. It was a strange call, almost a whimper. It was like the little frightened exclamation of a woman. Birds weren't popular with me just then. I had a crazy memory of some Brazilian bird which drives a hole in the back of your head and lives on brains. I peered down through the trees, and caught a flicker of white in a moonlit clearing below. It showed only for a split second, and

I came to the conclusion that it must have been a ripple of wind in the silver grass. When the time was up I went down the timber slide and took the road home to the inn. I fell asleep wondering whether we hadn't let our nerves run away with us.

'I went up to see the Vaughans in the morning. Kyra looked pale and worried. I told her at once that she must take more rest.

' "She won't," said Vaughan. "She can't resist other people's troubles."

' "You see, I can't put them out of my mind as easily as you," she answered provocatively.

' "Oh Lord!" Vaughan exclaimed. "I'm not going to start an argument."

' "No – because you know you're in the wrong. Have you quite forgotten this horrible affair?"

'I gathered up the reins of the conversation, and gentled it into easier topics. As I did so, I was conscious of resistance from Kyra; she evidently wanted to go on scrapping. I wondered why. Her nerves, no doubt, were overstrained, but she was too tired to wish to relieve them by a quarrel. I decided that she was deliberately worrying her husband to make him admit how he was spending his evenings.

'That was it. Before I left, she took me apart on the pretext of showing me the garden and pinned the conversation to our shooting expeditions. Please God I'm never in the dock if the prosecuting counsel is a woman! As it was, I had the right to ask questions in my turn, and managed to slip from under her cross-examination without allowing her to feel it. It hurt. I couldn't let her know the truth, but I hated to leave her in that torment of uncertainty. She hesitated an instant before she said good-bye to me. Then she caught my arm, and cried:

' "Take care of him!"

'I smiled and told her that she was overwrought, that we were doing nothing dangerous. What else could I say?

'That night, the third of the watching, the woods were alive. The world which lives just below the fallen leaves – mice and moles and big beetles – were making its surprising stir. The night birds were crying. A deer coughed far up in the forest. There was a slight breeze blowing, and from my lair on top of the rock I watched Vaughan trying to catch the scents it bore. He crouched down in the shadows. A bear ambled across the path up wind, and began to grub for some succulent morsel at the roots of a tree. It looked as woolly and harmless as a big dog. Clearly neither it nor its kind were the cause of our vigil. I saw Vaughan smile, and knew that he was thinking the same thought.

'A little after eleven the bear looked up, sniffed the air, and disappeared into the black bulk of the undergrowth as effortlessly and completely as if a spotlight had been switched off him. One by one the sounds of the night ceased. Vaughan eased the revolver in his pocket. The silence told its own tale. The forest had laid aside its business, and was watching like ourselves.

'Vaughan walked up the path to the far end of his beat. I looked away from him an instant, and down the path through the trees my eyes caught that same flicker of white. He turned to come back, and by the time that he was abreast of the rock I had seen it again. A bulky object it seemed to be, soft white, moving fast. He passed me, going towards it, and I lined my sights on the path ahead of him. Bounding up through the woods it came, then into the moonlight, and on to him. I was saved only by the extreme difficulty of the shot. I took just a fraction of a second longer than I needed, to make very sure of not hitting Vaughan. In that fraction of a second, thank God, she called to him! It was Kyra. A white ermine coat and her terrified running up the path had made her a strange figure.

'She clung to him while she got her breath back. I heard her say:

' "I was frightened. There was something after me. I know it."

'Vaughan did not answer, but held her very close and stroked her hair. His upper lip curled back a little from his teeth. For once his whole being was surrendered to a single emotion: the desire to kill whatever had frightened her.

' "How did you know I was here?" he asked.

' "I didn't. I was looking for you. I looked for you last night, too."

' "You mad, brave girl!" he said.

' "But you mustn't, mustn't be alone. Where's Shiravieff?"

' "Right there." He pointed to the rock.

' "Why don't you hide yourself, too?"

' "One of us must show himself," he answered.

'She understood instantly the full meaning of his reply.

' "Come back with me!" she cried. "Promise me to stop it!"

' "I'm very safe, dear," he answered. "Look!"

'I can hear his tense voice right now, and remember their exact words. Those things eat into the memory. He led her just below the rock. His left arm was round her. At the full stretch of his right arm he held out his handkerchief by two corners. He did not look at me, nor alter his tone.

' "Shiravieff," he said, "make a hole in that!"

'It was just a theatrical bit of nonsense, for the handkerchief was the easiest of easy marks. At any other time I would have been as sure as he of the result of the shot. But what he didn't know was that I had so nearly fired at another white and much larger mark – I was trembling so that I could hardly hold the rifle. I pressed the trigger. The hole in the handkerchief was dangerously near his hand. He put it down to bravado rather than bad shooting.

'Vaughan's trick had its effect. Kyra was surprised. She did not realize how easy it was, any more than she knew how much harder to hit is a moving mark seen in a moment of excitement.

' "But let me stay with you," she appealed.

' "Sweetheart, we're going back right now. Do you think I'm going to allow my most precious possession to run wild in the woods?"

' "What about mine?" she said, and kissed him.

'They went away down the short cut. He made her walk a yard in front of him, and I caught the glint of the moonlight on the barrel of his revolver. He was taking no risks.

'I myself went back by the path – carelessly, for I was sure that every living thing had been scared away by the voices and the shot. I was nearly down when I knew I was being followed. You've both lived in strange places – do you want me to explain the sensation? No? Well then, I knew I was being followed. I stopped and faced back up the path. Instantly something moved past me in the bushes, as if to cut off my retreat. I'm not superstitious. Once I heard it, I felt safe, for I knew where it was. I was sure I could move faster down that path than anything in the undergrowth – and if it came out into the open, it would have to absorb five steel explosive bullets. I ran. So far as I could hear, it didn't follow.

'I told Vaughan the next morning what had happened.

' "I'm sorry," he said, "I had to take her back. You understand, don't you?"

' "Of course," I answered in surprise. "What else could you do?"

' "Well, I didn't like leaving you alone. We had advertised our presence pretty widely. True, we should have frightened away any animal – but all we know about this animal is that it doesn't behave like one. There was a chance of our attracting instead of frightening it. We're going to get it tonight," he added savagely.

'I asked if Kyra would promise to stay at home.

' "Yes. She says we're doing our duty, and that she won't interfere. Do you think this is our duty?'

' "No!" I said.

' "Nor do I. I never feel that anything which I enjoy can possibly be my duty. And, by God, I enjoy this now!"

'I think he did enjoy it as he waited on the rock that night. He wanted revenge. There was no reason to believe that Kyra had been frightened by anything more than night and loneliness, but he was out against the whole set of circumstances that had dared to affect her. He wanted to be the bait instead of the watcher – I believe, with some mad hope of getting his hands on his enemy. But I wouldn't let him. After all, it was my turn.

'Bait! As I walked up and down the path, the word kept running through my mind. There wasn't a sound. The only moving thing was the moon which passed from tree top to tree top as the night wore on. I pictured Vaughan on the rock, the foresight of his rifle creeping backwards and forwards in a quarter circle as it followed my movements. I visualized the line of his aim as a thread of light passing down and across in front of my eyes. Once I heard Vaughan cough. I knew that he had seen my nervousness and was reassuring me. I stood by a clump of bushes some twenty yards away, watching a silver leaf that shook as some tiny beast crawled up it.

'Hot breath on the back of my neck – crushing weight on my shoulders – hardness against the back of my skull – the crack of Vaughan's rifle – they were instantaneous, but not too swift for me to know all the terror of death. Something leapt away from me, and squirmed into the springhead beneath the rock.

' "Are you all right?" shouted Vaughan, crashing down through the ivy.

' "What was it?"

' "A man. I've winged him. Come on! I'm going in after him!"

'Vaughan was berserk mad. I've never seen such flaming disregard of danger. He drew a deep breath, and tackled the hole as if it were a man's ankles. Head and shoulders, he sloshed into the mud of the cavity, emptying his Winchester in front of him. If he couldn't wriggle forward swiftly without drawing breath he would be choked by the sulphur fumes or drowned. If his enemy were waiting for him, he was a dead man. He disappeared and I followed. No, I didn't need any courage. I was covered by the whole length of Vaughan's body. But it was a vile moment. We'd never dreamed that anything could get in and out through that spring. Imagine holding your breath, and trying to squirm through hot water, using your hips and shoulders like a snake, not knowing how you would return if the way forward was barred. At last I was able to raise myself on my hands and draw a breath. Vaughan had dragged himself clear and was on his feet, holding a flashlight in front of him.

' "Got him!" he said.

'We were in a low cave under the rock. There was air from the cracks above us. The floor was of dry sand, for the hot stream flowed into the cave close to the hole by which it left. A man lay crumpled up at the far end of the hollow. We crossed over to him. He held a sort of long pistol in his hand. It was a spring humane-killer. The touch of that wide muzzle against my skull is not a pleasant memory. The muzzle is jagged, you see, so that it grips the scalp while the spike is released.

'We turned the body over – it was Josef Weiss. Werewolf? Possession? I don't know. I would call it an atavistic neurosis. But that's a name, not an explanation.

'Beyond the body there was a hole some six feet in diameter, as round as if it had been bored by a rotary drill. The springs which had forced that passage had dried up, but the mottled-yellow walls were smooth as marble with the deposit left by the water. Evidently Weiss had been trying to reach that opening when Vaughan dropped him. We climbed that natural sewer pipe. For half an hour the flashlight revealed nothing but the sweating walls of the hole. Then we were stopped by a roughly hewn ladder which sprawled across the passage. The rungs were covered with mud, and here and there were dark stains on the wood. We went up. It led to a hollow evidently dug out with spade and chisel. The roof was of planks, with a trapdoor at one end. We lifted it with our shoulders, and stood up within the four walls of a cottage. A fire was smouldering on the open hearth, and as we let in the draught of air, a log burst into flame. A gun stood in the ingle. On a rack were some iron traps and a belt of cartridges. There was a table in the centre of the room with a long knife on it. That was all we saw with our first glance. With our second we saw a lot more. Weiss had certainly carried his homicidal mania to extremes. I imagine his beastly experiences as a prisoner of war had left a kink in the poor devil's mind. Then, digging out a cellar or repairing the floor, he had accidentally discovered the dry channel beneath the cottage, and followed it to its hidden outlet. That turned his secret desires into action. He could kill and remove his victim without any trace. And so he let himself go.

'At dawn we were back at the cottage with the magistrate. When he came out, he was violently, terribly sick. I have never seen a man be so sick. It cleared him. No, I'm not being humorous. It cleared him mentally. He needed none of those emotional upheavals which we have to employ to drive shock out of our system. Didn't I tell you he was unimaginative? He handled the subsequent inquiry in a masterly fashion. He accepted as an unavoidable fact the horror of the thing, but he wouldn't listen to tales which could not be proved. There was never any definite proof of the extra horror in which the villagers believed.'

There was an exclamation from Lewis Banning.

'Ah – you remember now. I thought you would. The Press reported that rumour as a fact, but there was no definite proof, I tell you.

'Vaughan begged me to keep it from his wife. I was to persuade her to go away at once before a breath of it could reach her. I was to tell her that he might have received internal injuries, and should be examined without delay. He himself believed the tale that was going round, but he was very conscious of his poise. I suspect that he was feeling a little proud of himself – proud that he was unaffected. But he dreaded the effect of the shock on his wife.

'We were too late. The cook had caught the prevailing fever, and told that unpleasant rumour to Kyra. She ran to her husband, deadly pale, desperate, instinctively seeking protection against the blow. He could protect himself, and would have given his life to be able to protect her. He tried, but only gave her words and more words. He explained that, looking at the affair calmly, it didn't matter; that no one could have known; that the best thing was to forget it; and so on. It was absurd. As if anyone who believed what was being said could look at the affair calmly!

'Sentiments of that kind were no comfort to his wife. She expected him to show his horror, not to isolate himself as if he had shut down a lid, not to leave her spiritually alone. She cried out at him that he had no feeling and rushed to her room. Perhaps I should have given her a sedative, but I didn't. I knew that the sooner she had it out with herself, the better, and that her mind was healthy enough to stand it.

'I said so to Vaughan, but he did not understand. Emotion, he thought, was dangerous. It mustn't be let loose. He wanted to tell her again not to "worry". He didn't see that he was the only person within ten miles who wasn't "worried".

'She came down later. She spoke to Vaughan scornfully, coldly, as if she had found him unfaithful to her. She said to him:

' "I can't see the woman again. Tell her to go, will you?"

'She meant the cook. Vaughan challenged her. He was just obstinately logical and fair.

' "It's not her fault," he said. "She's an ignorant woman, not an anatomist. We'll call her in, and you'll see how unjust you are."

' "Oh no!" she cried – and then checked herself.

' "Send for her then!" she said.

'The cook came in. How could she know, she sobbed – she had noticed nothing – she was sure that what she had bought from Josef Weiss was really venison – she didn't think for a moment . . . Well, blessed are the simple!

' "My God! Be quiet!" Kyra burst out. "You all of you think what you want to think. You all lie to yourselves and pretend and have no feelings!"

'I couldn't stand any more. I begged her not to torture herself and not to torture me. It was the right note. She took my hands and asked me to forgive her. Then the tears came. She cried, I think, till morning. At breakfast she had a wan smile for both of us, and I knew that she was out of danger – clear of the shock for good. They left for England the same day.

'I met them in Vienna two years ago, and they dined with me. We never mentioned Zweibergen. They still adored one another, and still quarrelled. It was good to hear them talk and watch them feeling for each other's sympathy.

'Vaughan refused his meat at dinner, and said that he had become a vegetarian.

' "Why?" I asked deliberately.

'He answered that he had recently had a nervous breakdown – could eat nothing, and had nearly died. He was all right now, he said; no trace of the illness remained but his distaste for meat . . . it had come over him quite suddenly . . . he could not think why.

'I tell you the man was absolutely serious. He could *not* think why. Shock had lain hidden in him for ten years, and then had claimed its penalty.'

'And you?' asked Banning. 'How did you get clear of shock? You had to control your emotions at the time.'

'A fair question,' said Shiravieff. 'I've been living under a suspended sentence. There have been days when I thought I should visit one of my colleagues and ask him to clean up the mess. If I could only have got the story out of my system, it would have helped a lot – but I couldn't bring myself to tell it.'

'You have just told it,' said Colonel Romero solemnly.

The Thought

L. P. Hartley

Henry Greenstream had always looked forward to his afternoon walk. It divided the day for him. In ideal circumstances a siesta preceded it and he awoke to a new morning, a false dawn, it is true, but as pregnant with unexpressed promise as the real one. For some weeks now, however, sleep had deserted his after-luncheon cushion; he could get to the brink of unconsciousness, when thoughts and pictures drifted into his mind independently of his will, but not over.

Still, the walk was the main thing even if he started on it a little tired. It calmed, it satisfied, it released. For an hour and twenty-five minutes he enjoyed the freedom of the birds of the air. Impressions and sensations offered themselves to him in an unending flow, never outstaying their welcome, never demanding more from his attention than a moment's recognition. Lovely and pleasant voices that tonelessly proclaimed the harmony between him, Henry Greenstream, and the spirit of all created things.

Or they had proclaimed it till lately. Lately the rhythm of his thoughts had been disturbed by an interloper, yes, an interloper, but an interloper from within. Like a cuckoo that soon ceased to be a visitor, the stranger had entered his mind and now dwelt there, snatching at the nourishment meant for its legitimate neighbours. They pined, they grew sickly while Henry Greenstream suckled the parasite.

He knew what it was and whence it came. It was an infection from his conscience which had taken offence at an act so trivial that surely no other conscience would have noticed it. Indeed, he had himself almost forgotten what it originated in – something about a breach of confidence that (reason assured him a thousand times) could have harmed nobody. And when it stirred inside him it was not to remind him of his fault and recall the circumstances of his lapse, but simply to hurt him; to prick the tender tegument which, unpierced, assures comfort to the mind.

If it did not spoil his life it fretted him, reducing his capacity for enjoyment; and most of all did it make its presence felt when he took his afternoon exercise. The aery shapes that then haunted his imagination could not suppress it, nor was the scenery through which he passed such as to distract him from himself. Town gave way to suburb; suburb to ribbon development; only when it was time to turn back did he emerge into the unspoilt countryside. Motors rushed by; an occasional tramp asked for a match; dogs idled on the pavement. All this was uninspiring, but at the same time it fostered his mood; even the ugly little houses, with their curtains drawn aside to reveal a plant or a pretentious piece of china, invited pleasing speculations. Confidently he looked forward to his reunion with these humble landmarks. But they had lost their power to draw him out, and lately he had invented a new and less satisfying form of mental pastime. Much less satisfying; for it consisted in counting the minutes that elapsed between one visitation of the Thought and the next. Even so might a Chinese malefactor seek to beguile himself while under the water-torture by calculating the incidence of the drops.

Where the signpost pointed to Aston Highchurch Mr Greenstream paused. He had been walking half an hour and the Thought had recurred twenty-two times; that was an average of nearly once a minute, a higher average than yesterday, when he had got off with fourteen repetitions. It was in fact a record: a bad record. What could he do to banish this tedious symptom? Stop counting, perhaps? Make his mind a blank? He wandered on with uncertain footsteps unlike his ordinary purposeful stride. Ahead of him the October sun was turning down the sky, behind, the grass (for the fields now began to outnumber the houses) took on a golden hue; above, the clouds seemed too lazy to obey what little wind there was. It was a lovely moment that gathered to itself all the harmony of which the restless earth was capable. Mr Greenstream opened his heart to the solace of the hour and was already feeling refreshed when ping! the Thought stung him again.

'I must do something about this,' thought Mr Greenstream, 'or I shall go mad.'

He looked round. To his left, in the hedge beyond the grass verge, was a wicket-gate, and from it a path ran diagonally over the shoulder of a little hill, a shabby asphalt path that gleamed in the sunlight and disappeared, tantalizingly, into the horizon. Mr Greenstream knew where it led, to Aston Highchurch; but so conservative was he that in all these years of tramping down the main road he had never taken it. He did so now. In a few minutes he was on the high land in what seemed a different world, incredibly nearer the sky. Turning left along a country lane bordered by trees and less agreeably by chicken runs, he kept catching sight of a church; and at length he came to a path that led straight to it across a stubble field. It lay with its back to him, long and low, with a square tower at the farther end that gave it the look of a cat resting on tucked-in legs, perhaps beginning to purr.

Mr Greenstream stopped at the churchyard gate and stared up at the tower to make out what the objects were which, hanging rather crazily at the corners below the parapet, had looked in the distance like whiskers, and completed the feline impression made by the church. A whiskered church! The idea amused Mr Greenstream until his watchful tormentor, ever jealous of his carefree moments, prodded him again. With a sigh he entered the porch and listened. No sound. The door opened stiffly to confront him with a pair of doors, green baize this time. He went back and shut the outer door, then the inner ones, and felt he had shut out the world. The church was empty; he had it to himself.

It was years since Mr Greenstream had been inside a church except on ceremonial occasions or as a sightseer, and he did not quite know what to do. This was a Perpendicular church, light, airy and spacious, under rather than over furnished. The seats were chairs made of wood so pale as to be almost white: they were lashed together with spars, and the whole group, with its criss-cross of vertical and horizontal lines, made an effect that was gay and pretty and in so far as it suggested rigging, faintly nautical.

Mr Greenstream wandered up the nave but felt a reluctance, for which he could not quite account, to mount the chancel steps: in any case there was little of note there and the east window was evidently modern. Straying back along the north aisle wall he read the monumental inscriptions, black lettering on white marble or white lettering on black marble. Then he came face to face with the stove, an impressive cylinder from which issued a faint crackling. His tour seemed to be over; but he was aware of a feeling of expectancy, as if the church were waiting for him to do something.

'After all, why not?' he thought, sinking to his knees. But he could not pray at once – he had lost the habit, he did not know how to begin. Moreover he felt ashamed of coming to claim the benefits of religion when for many years he had ignored its obligations. Such a prayer would be worse than useless; it was an insult; it would put God against him. Then the Thought came with its needle-jab and he waited no longer but prayed vehemently and incoherently for deliverance. But a morbid fear assailed him that it was not enough to think the words, for some of them, perhaps the most operative, might be left out, telescoped or elided by the uncontrollable hurry of his mind, so he repeated his petition out loud. Until he had ceased to speak he did not notice how strange his voice sounded in the empty church, almost as if it did not belong to him. Rising shakily to his feet he blinked, dazzled by the daylight, and stumbled out of the church, without a backward look.

Not once on the homeward journey to his narrow house in Midgate was Mr Greenstream troubled by the Thought. His relief and gratitude were inexpressible; but it was not till the next day that he realized that the visit to Aston Highchurch had been a turning-point in his life. Doctors had told him that his great enemy was his morbid sense of guilt. Now, so long as St Cuthbert's, Aston Highchurch, stood, he need not fear it.

Fearful yet eager he began to peer down a future in which, thanks to the efficacy of prayer, the desires of his heart would meet with no lasting opposition from the voice of his conscience. He could indulge them to the full. Whatever they were, however bad they were, he need not be afraid that they would haunt him afterwards. The Power whose presence he had felt in church would see to that.

It was a summer evening and the youth of Aston Highchurch would normally have been playing cricket on the village green, but the game fell through because a handful of the regulars had failed to turn up. There was murmuring among the disappointed remnant, and inquiry as to what superior attraction had lured away the defaulters.

'I know,' said a snub-nosed urchin, 'because I heard them talking about it.'

'Well, tell us, Tom Wignall.'

'They said I wasn't to.'

'Come on, you tell us or . . .'

According to their code a small but appreciable amount of physical torture released the sufferer from further loyalty to his plighted word. After a brief but strident martyrdom the lad, nothing loth, yielded to the importunity of his fellows.

'It's about that praying chap.'

'What, old Greenpants?'

'Yes. They've gone to watch him at it.'

'Where?'

'In the tower gallery. Fred Buckland pinched the key when the old man wasn't looking.'

'Coo, they'll cop it if they're caught.'

'Why, they aren't doing no harm. You can't trespass in a church.'

'That's all you know. They haven't gone there just to watch neither.'

'Why, what are they going to do?'

'Well,' said Tom Wignall importantly, 'they're going to give him a fright. Do you know what he does?'

'He prays, doesn't he?'

'Yes, but he don't pray to himself. He prays out loud, and he shouts sometimes, and rocks himself about. And he doesn't pray for his father and mother . . .'

'He hasn't got any, so I've heard,' said an older boy, who, to judge from his caustic tone, seemed to be listening with some impatience to Tom Wignall's revelations. 'He's an orphan.'

'Anyhow,' the speaker resumed unabashed, 'he doesn't pray for his king or his country, or to be made good or anything like that. He confesses his sins.'

'Do you mean he's done a murder?'

'Fred Buckland couldn't hear what it was, but it must have been something bad or he wouldn't have come all this way to confess it.'

This reasoning impressed the audience.

'Must have been murder,' they assured each other, 'or forgery, anyhow.'

'But that isn't all,' continued the speaker, intoxicated by the attention he was receiving. 'He prays for what he didn't ought.'

'Why, you can pray for anything you like,' opined one of the listeners.

'That you can't. There's heaps of things you mustn't pray for. You mustn't pray to get rich, for one thing, and,' he lowered his voice, 'you mustn't pray for anyone to die.'

'Did he do that?'

'Fred Buckland said that's what it sounded like.'

There was a pause.

'I think the poor chap's barmy if you ask me,' said the older boy. 'I bet his prayers don't do no one any harm nor him any good either.'

'That's where you make a mistake,' said the spokesman of the party. 'That's where you're wrong. Fred Buckland says he's got much, much richer these last six months. Why, he's got a car and a chauffeur and all. Fred Buckland says he wouldn't be surprised if he's a millionaire.'

'You bet he is,' scoffed the older boy. 'You bet that when he prayed somebody dropped down dead and left him a million. Sounds likely, doesn't it?'

The circle of listeners stirred. All the faces broadened with scepticism and one boy took up his bat and played an imaginary forward stroke. Tom Wignall felt that he was losing ground. He was like a bridge-player who has held up his ace too long.

'Anyhow,' he said defiantly, 'Fred Buckland says that church is no place for the likes of him who've got rich by praying in a way they ought to be ashamed of. And I tell you, he's going to give old Greenpants a fright. He's going to holler down at him from the tower in a terrible deep voice, and Greenpants'll think it's God answering him from heaven, or perhaps the Devil, and he'll get such a fright he'll never set foot in Aston again. And good riddance, I say.'

Tom's own voice rose as he forced into it all the dramatic intensity he could muster. But he had missed his moment. One or two of his companions looked serious and nodded, but the rest, with the unerring instinct of boys for a change of leadership, a shifting of moral ascendancy, threw doubtful glances towards their senior. They were wavering. They would take their cue from him.

'Lousy young bastards,' he said, 'leaving us all standing about like fools on a fine evening like this. I should like to tan their hides.'

There was a murmur of sympathetic indignation, and he added, 'What makes them think the chap's coming today to pray, anyhow?'

Tom Wignall answered sullenly: 'He comes most days now . . . And, if you want to know, Jim Chantry passed him on his motor-bike the other side of Friar's Bridge. He didn't half jump when Jim honked in his ear,' Tom concluded with unrepentant relish. 'He'll be here any time now.'

'Well,' said the older boy stretching himself luxuriously, 'you chaps can go and blank yourselves. There's nothing else for you to do. I'm off.' He sauntered away, grandly, alone, towards the main road. Those silly mutts need a lesson. I'll spoil their little game for them, he thought.

The tower gallery at St Cuthbert's, Aston Highchurch, was a feature most unusual in parish churches. But the tower was rather unusual, too. Its lower storey, which rose fifty or more feet to the belfry floor, was open to the main body of the building; only an arch divided it from the nave. The gallery, a stone passage running along the tower wall just above the west window, was considerably higher than the apex of the arch. It was only visible from the western end of the church, and itself commanded a correspondingly restricted view – a view that was further impeded by the lightly swaying bell-ropes. But Fred Buckland and his four conspirators could see, through the flattened arc of the arch, a portion of the last six rows of chairs. The sunlight coming through the window below them fell on the chairs, picking them out in gold and making a bright patch like the stage of a theatre.

'He ought to be here by now, didn't he?' one urchin whispered.

'Shut up!' hissed the ringleader. 'It'll spoil everything if he hears us.'

They waited, three of them with their backs pressed against the wall, their faces turned this way and that as in a frieze, looking very innocent and naughty. Fred, who had more than once sung carols from this lofty perch, embraced a baluster and let his feet dangle over the edge.

Five minutes passed, ten, a quarter of an hour. The sinking sun no longer lay so brightly on the foreground; shadows began to creep in from the sides. The boys even began to see each other less plainly.

'I'm frightened,' whispered a voice. 'I wish we hadn't come. I want to go home.'

'Shut up, can't you?'

More minutes passed and the church grew darker.

'I say, Fred,' a second voice whispered, 'what time does your old man come to shut the church up?'

'Seven o'clock these evenings. It still wants a quarter to.'

They waited; then one whispered in a tense voice, 'I believe that's him.'

'Who?'

'Old Greenpants, of course.'

'Did you hear anything?'

'No, but I thought I saw something move.'

'You're barmy. That's the shadow of the bell-rope.'

They strained their eyes.

'I don't think it was, Fred. It moves when the bell-rope doesn't.'

'Funny if somebody else should be spying on old Greenpants.'

'Maybe it's him who's spying on us.'

'What, old Greenpants?'

'Of course. Who else could it be?'

'I wish I could see what that was moving,' the boy said again. 'There, close by the stove.'

'I suppose it couldn't get up to us?'

'Not unless it came by the bell-rope,' said Fred decisively. 'I've locked the door of the stairs and the only other key my dad has. You're in a funk, that's your trouble. Only the Devil could shin up one of them ropes.'

'They wouldn't let him come into church, would they?'

'He might slip in if the north door was open.'

Almost as he spoke a puff of wind blew up in their faces and the six bell-ropes swayed in all directions, lashing each other and casting fantastic shadows.

'That's him,' Fred hissed. 'Don't you hear his footsteps? I bet that's him. Just wait till he gets settled down. Now, all together: "God is going to punish thee, Henry Greenstream, thou wicked man".'

In creditable unison, their voices quavered through the church. What result they expected they hardly knew themselves, nor did they have time to find out; for the sacristan, appearing with a clatter of boots at the gallery door, had them all like rats in a trap. Fear of committing sacrilege by blasphemy for a moment took away his powers of speech; then he burst out, 'Come on, you little blackguards! Get down out of here! Oh, you'll be sore before I've finished with you!'

A spectator, had there been one, would have noticed that the sounds of snivelling and scuffling were momentarily stilled as the staircase swallowed them up. A minute later they broke out again, with louder clamour; for though Fred got most of the blows the others quickly lost their morale, seeing how completely their leader had lost his.

'I'll take a strap to you when I get you home,' thundered the sacristan, 'trying to disturb a poor gentleman at his devotions.'

'But, Dad, he wasn't in the church!' protested Fred between his sobs.

'It wasn't your fault if he wasn't,' returned his father grimly.

For some months after being warned Henry Greenstream came no more to St Cuthbert's, Aston Highchurch. Perhaps he found another sanctuary, for certainly there was no lack of them in the district. Perhaps, since he had a motor, he found it more convenient to drive out into the country where (supposing he needed them) were churches in sparsely populated areas, untenanted by rude little boys. He had never been a man to advertise his movements, and latterly his face had worn a closed look, as if he had been concealing them from himself. But he had to tell the chauffeur where to go, and the man was immensely surprised when, one December afternoon, he received an order to drive to Aston Highchurch. 'We hadn't taken that road for an age,' he afterwards explained.

'Stop when I tap the window,' Mr Greenstream said, 'and then I shall want you to do something for me.'

At the point where the footpath leads across the fields Mr Greenstream tapped and got out of the car.

'I'm going on to the church now,' he said, 'but I want you to call at the Rectory, and ask the Reverend Mr Ripley if he would step across to the church and . . . and hear my confession. Say it's rather urgent. I don't know how long I shall be gone.'

The chauffeur, for various reasons, had not found Mr Greenstream's service congenial; he had in fact handed his notice in that morning. But something in his employer's tremulous manner touched him and, surprising himself, he said:

'You wouldn't like me to go with you as far as the church, sir?'

'Oh, no, thank you, Williams, I think I can get that far.'

'I only thought you didn't look very fit, sir.'

'Is that why you decided to leave me?' asked Mr Greenstream, and the man bit his lip and was silent.

Mr Greenstream walked slowly towards the church, absently and unsuccessfully trying to avoid the many puddles left by last night's storm. It had been a violent storm, and now though the wind was gone, the sky, still burning streakily as with the embers of its own ill-temper, had a wild, sullen look.

Mr Greenstream reached the porch but didn't go in. Instead he walked round the church, stumbling among the graves, for some were unmarked by headstones; and on the north side, where no one ever went, the ground was untended and uneven.

It took him some minutes to make the circuit, but when he had completed it he started again. It was on his second tour that he discovered – literally stumbled against – the gargoyle, which, of course, has been replaced now. The storm had split it but the odd thing was that the two halves, instead of being splintered and separated by their fall, lay intact on the sodden grass within a few inches of each other. Mr Greenstream could not have believed the grinning mask was so big. It had split where the spout passed through it: one half retained the chin, the other was mostly eye and cheek and ear. Mr Greenstream could see the naked spout hanging out far above him, long and bent and shining like a black snake. The comfortless sight may have added to the burden of his thoughts, for he walked on more slowly. This time, however, he did not turn aside at the porch, but went straight in, carefully shutting the inner and outer doors behind him.

It was past four o'clock and the church was nearly dark, the windows being only visible as patches of semi-opaque brightness. But there *was* a light which shone with a dull red glow, a burning circle hanging in the air a foot or two from the ground. It looked like a drum that had caught fire within, but it was not truly luminous; it seemed to attract the darkness rather than repel it. For a moment Mr Greenstream could not make out what the strange light was. But when he took a step or two towards it and felt the heat on his face and hands he knew at once. It was the stove. The zealous sacristan, mindful of the chilly day, had stoked it up until it was red hot.

Mr Greenstream was grateful for the warmth, for his hands were cold and his teeth chattering. He would have liked to approach the stove and bend over it. But the heat was too fierce for that, it beat him back. So he withdrew to the outer radius of its influence. Soon he was kneeling, and soon – the effect of the warmth on a tired mind and a tired body, asleep.

It must have been the cold that woke him, cold, piercing cold, that seemed solid, like a slab of ice pressing against his back. The stove still glared red in front of him, but it had no more power to warm him physically than has a friendly look or a smiling face. Whence did it come, this deadly chill? Ah! He looked over his left shoulder and saw that the doors, which he remembered shutting, were now open to the sky and the north wind. To shut them again was the work of a moment. But why were they open? he wondered, turning back into the church. Why, of course, of course, the clergyman had opened them, the Rector of Aston Highchurch, who was coming at his request to hear his confession. But where was he, and why did he not speak? And what was the reddish outline that moved towards him in the darkness? For a moment his fancy confused it with the stove, or it might be the stove's reflection, thrown on one of the pillars. But on it came, bearing before it that icy breath he now knew had nothing to do with the north wind.

'Mr Ripley, Mr Ripley,' he murmured, falling back into the warmth of the stove, feeling upon his neck its fierce assault. Then he heard a voice like no voice he had ever heard, as if the darkness spoke with the volume of a thousand tongues.

'I am your confessor. What have you to say?'

'My death must be my answer,' he replied, the consciousness of annihilation on him.

When Mr Greenstream's chauffeur learned that the Rector was not at home he left a message and then returned to the car, for he knew from experience that his master's unaccountable church-going often kept him a long time. But when an hour had gone by he felt vaguely anxious and decided to see if anything was the matter. To his surprise he found the church door open, and noticed a smell coming from it which he had never associated with a church. Moving gingerly in the dark, he advanced towards where a sound of hissing made itself heard. Then he struck a match, and what he saw caused him to turn and run in terror for the door. On the threshold he almost collided with Mr Ripley, hastening from the Rectory on his errand of mercy. Together they overcame the repugnance which either of them would have felt singly, lifted Mr Greenstream's body from the stove across which it hung and laid it reverently on the pavement.

The newspapers at first gave out that Mr Greenstream had been burned to death, but the medical authorities took a different view.

'In my opinion,' one doctor said, 'he was dead before he even touched the stove and, paradoxical as it may seem, the physical signs indicate that he was frozen, not burned to death.

'He was perhaps trying to warm himself – why, we shall never know.'

Comrade Death

Gerald Kersh

Sarek was a master-eavesdropper, but in order to hear the conversation of the two men at the adjoining table, he had to concentrate. The street was full of noise – clattering hoofs and heels, and the rumbling wheels of innumerable cabs.

Sarek forgot to puff at his cigar; the smoke stung his eyes. He even forgot to blink: his eyes became inflamed; they stared through a blue cloud, preoccupied and expressionless – eyes of blood and iron. He sat still. Only once, when he caught the words: *We can achieve power only through propaganda*, did Sarek show some sign of life – he grinned. And at last, when the conversation ended and one of the men went away, Sarek turned his head and addressed the other:

'Pardon me; but you are Joseph Pashenka, aren't you?'

'Yes.'

'The leader of the Workers' Party?'

'Yes. What can I do for you?'

'My name is Sarek, Hector Sarek, representative of the Skyrocket Ironmongery Company. You will think me very rude, but you spoke so loudly that I couldn't help overhearing what you said just now.'

'Well, all right. What about it?'

'My dear Mr Pashenka,' said Sarek, 'how you jump at a man! . . . So you're the workers' leader! The gentleman who wants to start a revolution, just by talking. Achieve power only through propaganda. Well, well. I read some of your pamphlets, once, I think. Very enlightening, very instructive; but when all is said and done, nothing but *words*. Well, words aren't enough. One bullet, my dear sir –' Sarek flicked out his fingers in a gesture which symbolized scattered brains.

'Well what do you want?'

'I just want to put it to you that words aren't enough. Bullets speak louder. What you need is bullets.'

Pashenka laughed. 'If you're an *agent-provocateur*, you're very clumsy at the job!' he said.

'No, no, no! I have no politics. I'm just a plain business man. There's my card: *Sarek, Skyrocket Ironmongery*. No politics; I haven't the talent. But for political purposes, bullets are better. Now, why don't you do something in the Russian style – just one or two little acts of terrorism. You'd be surprised at the money and support it would bring in. Assassinate one or two unpopular Ministers –'

'You're just a common *agent-provocateur*!'

'– bombs are spectacular, but clumsy. A bomb is not infallible; it may kill the wrong person. But a revolver, in the hands of a practical man – now that's what I call a reliable weapon!'

'And what should I want with bombs and revolvers?'

'Not bombs; only revolvers. I merely offered a suggestion. Arm your supporters with good, reliable small-arms. Then you're ready for absolutely any emergency. The political situation is unstable – unlike Krieger revolvers. It is to them that I should like to call your attention. I may mention, in passing, that President Sadko was shot with a Krieger revolver. They're made in three calibres: ·32, ·38, and ·44. There is a small model, firing a ·22 bullet; an elegant little weapon, with a mother-o'-pearl handle; suitable for ladies. There are two varieties of bullet – soft lead, or nickel-coated. The nickel-coated bullets have a superior power of penetration, but the soft lead bullets expand, and inflict a wound which makes up for any slight inaccuracy of aim. You may always trust a Krieger bullet to reach a vital part. Poor President Sadko was killed with a Krieger nickel-coated – it passed through his body, and injured a gendarme standing twenty feet behind him. That speaks for itself. There are special rates for large quantities, and a solid cowhide holster is included, free of charge. Just think! With each pistol, a solid cowhide –'

'I don't know whether you're mad, or what!' exclaimed Pashenka.

'Not at all,' said Sarek. 'I'm just a practical man. You can't overthrow your enemies with words alone. You've got to have arms. And the advantage of arming with Krieger –'

'You don't mean to tell me –'

'Let me quote you –'

Pashenka's solemn face suddenly broke into a network of humorous wrinkles. He began to laugh.

'Ha-ha-ha-ha-ha! No! You don't really mean to say that you're a traveller in fire-arms?'

'Why not?' said Sarek. 'They're a commodity, aren't they?'

'A traveller in fire-arms!' cried Pashenka, who seemed to find something humorous in it. 'Oh Lord! Pistols! Bullets! A traveller in pistols! I never heard of anything so ridiculous in all my life! Ha-ha-ha-ha-ha!'

'Not so ridiculous,' said Sarek, without emotion. 'You'd better pick up my card; you may need it yet; you never know.'

'Thanks.' Pashenka rose, buttoning his frock-coat. He looked closely at Sarek, but in the flat and nondescript Slavonic face, the pursed lips, and the lifeless grey eyes, he could read nothing. Pashenka paused; the inclination to laugh gave place to a vague uneasiness.

'If you are an arms salesman,' he said at length, 'I can tell you one thing – you'll end up in the workhouse or the asylum.'

'Perhaps,' said Sarek, calmly.

Just then a girl approached the café, and Sarek, taking off his hat, went to greet her.

They sat down.

'You look tired,' said Sarek; 'have you just come from the workshop?'

'Yes,' said the girl, 'I had a hard day.'

'Well, listen, Cosima; you must have an egg, beaten up in sherry; that takes away the tiredness. Yes? Then you'll come with me to Grigorieff's and have dinner. Yes?' Sarek's voice had become less impersonal; he looked more alive. But Cosima shook her head.

'I'm sorry, but I came here to meet Janos,' she said.

Sarek's scanty eyebrows contracted.

'I shouldn't persist,' he said, 'it's a waste of energy. You told me once you don't love me at all. Is that so?'

Cosima nodded.

'All right. You don't love me. Good. You love Janos?'

Cosima nodded.

'You like herbs?' asked Sarek.

'What d'you mean?'

'Well, you'll have a meal of herbs where love is,' said Sarek, with an undertone of mockery.

'You shouldn't speak like that. One day Janos will be a great artist, Hector.'

'Hm! One day I shall be even greater.' He stared at her through the smoke of his cigar.

Janos appeared, and flung himself into a chair.

'What was that I heard about "greatness"?' he asked.

'Cosima said you were going to be a great artist,' said Sarek, 'and I said that I should be even greater.'

'As an artist?' asked Janos, with a smile.

'No. I haven't the talent.'

'And how goes the ironmongery business?'

'Very well, thank you. Kriegers have bought up Skyrocket Ironmongery. Now, I travel for Kriegers.'

'Kriegers?' said Janos. 'They make all the guns, don't they?'

'That's right.'

'And you will still be selling ploughs and tools?'

'No. I'm on something much more progressive, now – arms.'

'Progressive!' cried Janos, with some irritation, 'I can't see that. Ploughs and tools give you comfort, and life. Guns give you nothing but pain and death.'

'You're an idealist,' said Sarek, 'and that's all very nice. But there are things you don't realize. The world moves: movement is life. Nations go to war – that's bad for some and good for others, like everything else. Nations have got to arm, so as to keep their power. Guns are power. I like guns. You always talk about the triumph of mind over matter; well, you see that expressed in a gun. You have your finger on the trigger, and an enemy over the sights – that's the triumph of mind over matter. Not long ago they only had the old muzzle-loading guns. Now, they've got Krieger machine-guns –'

'And what's a Krieger machine-gun?'

'Oh, something quite new. It fires bullets at the rate of hundreds a minute, all in a stream – *rat-at-at-at-at-at-at*! – like that. You could mow down men like corn with one.'

'Is that the gun that's going to be demonstrated in the Park on Wednesday?'

'Well, not quite. A French manufacturer got in first; he's demonstrating the Circonflex gun. All the officials of the War Office will be there. He'll make a fortune out of it. What an advertisement! How the newspapers' will talk! What –'

'Beastly weapon, I think,' said Janos. 'Who wants to mow down men like corn, anyway?'

'I don't know,' said Sarek, 'but if you want to mow down an army why not do it efficiently, in the modern style?'

'And don't you *care*?' asked Cosima.

'No,' said Sarek; and Janos uttered an exclamation of disgust.

'Say "Ugh!" as much as you like, but it's the coming thing,' said Sarek.

'There's big money in machine-guns. Why not come and see the demonstration? There's to be a big military band –'

'I'm not interested,' said Janos; 'I like creation, not destruction.'

'And you, Cosima?' asked Sarek.

'Me, too.'

Sarek spat venom: 'Ha! A machine-gun hasn't got to be created, I suppose? Good God, Hiram Maxim had more creation in his little finger than you've got in your whole body – you painters! Copying a naked woman in paint on a bit of canvas – that's what you call creation!'

'Come on, Cosima,' said Janos.

They went away. Sarek sat perfectly still; again the smoke of his cigar curled up into his eyes and made them bloodshot.

On the following Wednesday, Sarek stood in the Constantine Park and watched the activities of the salesmen of the Circonflex gun. An immense white target had been erected. Now they were fitting the barrel to the tripod.

The pressmen and the Government officials were assembling. Sarek stood near Kovas, the War Minister, and listened to his conversations. Kovas, the centre of a ring of generals, protested, with some petulance:

'Seeing is believing. This gun is too good to be true. It will revolutionize war if it works.'

'*If* it works,' said an aged officer, '*if*. Did this man invent the gun?'

'Heaven knows,' said Kovas. 'It's quite impossible to understand him. He gabbles on and on in his infernal French. He goes too fast for me. Whether he invented it, or sells it, or what, the devil only knows. One says, "*Oui monsieur*," out of politeness. If it works, I buy it; if the devil himself invented it that's all I know.'

Sarek glanced about him. The demonstrator's hired brass band was forming a semicircle. One of the players, with a mighty brazen tuba, blew a deep, tentative note, and tinkered with the mouthpiece of his instrument . . .

In that moment Sarek was struck by an inspiration. It paralysed him, for a moment, as if he had been struck by lightning. He spat out his cigar, darted through the crowd, and tugged at the arm of the band conductor.

'When are you going to start playing?' he asked.

'The minute the gentleman finishes his speech.'

'And when is the speech?'

'As soon as the demonstration is over.'

'Listen,' whispered Sarek, 'do you want to earn five hundred *kronen*?'

'Well . . . how?'

'You have instructions to start playing just *after* the speech? Well, listen. Start playing *just as the man starts to talk*. A loud military march. Keep it up for five minutes, and I'll give you five hundred *kronen!*'

The conductor hesitated.

'Six hundred,' said Sarek.

'Make it eight.'

'All right.' Sarek took out a banknote. 'Five hundred now; the rest afterwards.'

'Very good, sir.' The conductor furtively pocketed the note.

'You won't fail me? Play the *Skobeleff March* – as loud as the devil! – *crescendo*, all the time! – blow your trombones out straight! blow their hats off! Keep it up for five minutes. Do it well, and I'll make it a thousand *kronen*.'

'You leave it to me.'

'As he utters the first words.'

'Trust me!'

Sarek went back to his place. He wriggled into a strategic position, between the newspaper reporters and the War Minister. His heart was thumping; he felt that his collar was decapitating him.

Suddenly the crowd became silent.

Sweat poured down into Sarek's eyes.

The demonstrator knelt, aimed his gun, and squeezed the trigger.

With shocking abruptness, and a noise reminiscent of an iron bar drawn over corrugated iron, the gun began to fire. The cartridge belt ran through. A cloud of smoke drifted back into the faces of the spectators, and the white target quivered under the impact of the bullets. A line of bullet holes appeared; then another, and a third.

The demonstrator was, in fact, drawing an enormous letter K – the initial letter of the name of Kovas. He gave point to his delicate compliment of bowing in the direction of the War Minister.

'Amazing!' said Kovas, smiling with pleasure.

Sarek caught his breath. The demonstrator shouted:

'Now, my lords, ladies and gentlemen, it is my honour to write – in one thousand bullets – the Sign of the Cross!'

The gun roared again: the barrel crept upwards, paused, descended, and then swept from left to right. A crude, perforated cross became plainly visible on the blank white boards. Men began to take off their hats.

The demonstrator rose, waving his grease-blackened hands. There was a bellow of applause. He cleared his throat.

'My lords, ladies and gentlemen, I have had the honour of demonstrating –'

(Sarek flung an agonized glance towards the band – the conductor was raising his baton –)

'– what I may term, with all the modesty, the greatest military invention since the days of Schwartz –'

(Sarek ground on his teeth – a fat horn-player filled his lungs with air; his chest bulged –)

'A weapon which will revolutionize warfare! The –'

Down came the conductor's baton, and instantly the band began to force out the ear-splitting bars of the *Skobeleff March*:

> Mighty, mighty are our mountains,
> Mighty is the rushing river –

Sarek stook on tip-toe and shouted, in a tremendous voice:

'The Krieger Machine-gun!' He turned to Kovas: 'Your Highness has seen the letter K written in lead. That stands for Krieger! The Krieger Machine-gun, which gives one man the strength of a company. The Krieger Machine-gun, which fires at the rate of three hundred bullets a minute! Long may it stand between you and your enemies!'

Through packed masses of people the reporters bored their way to the offices of their papers. The band blared. Twenty yards away the demonstrator screamed at the conductor, but his voice was drowned in the uproar.

'Krieger? I thought Circonflex,' said Kovas.

'An error,' said Sarek.

'Krieger or Circonflex – I buy,' said Kovas.

In the career of any successful man that first skilful stroke – always in conjunction with good fortune – is half the battle. Since the day when Kovas had placed the first great order for Krieger machine-guns, Sarek had never looked back. And now, ten years after, walking with the firm and confident step of the conqueror, Sarek came into the presence of Pancho Pablo, President of Gaudeama in South America.

In a little while they came down to business.

'The position is grave,' said Pancho Pablo, 'soon it will be war. *Guerra al cuchillo*! War to the knife – them or us – Gaudeama or Contrabono. The world is too small for both.'

'You are the weaker,' said Sarek.

'That is so – much weaker. We are badly armed. They have good rifles.

We have only eight field-guns. They have seventeen. They will eat us alive.'

'It is an elementary rule, in strategy, that the weaker should strike first,' said Sarek. 'The longer you wait the weaker you get. In the end, they simply take you, without a battle. Declare war.'

'I daren't. Say I increase my army, mobilize a few thousand peons? Shall I arm them with machetes and reaping-hooks? I have no money to buy arms.'

'And say I arm you with Krieger rifles, Krieger machine-guns, and Krieger cannons? Say I supply unlimited ammunition? Say, in short, that I win you this war?'

'Oh, Señor! if you would!'

'Let us come to a friendly arrangement,' said Sarek, smoothly. 'I need one or two commodities. I need nitrates; give me the Perro Nitrate Beds for ten years. I need rubber; give me the Aguilar Rubber Forest for five years or so, plus a concession on the Contrabono Copper Mines, after you have won the war. Then I'll arm you to the teeth. I'll give you guns and ammunition enough to blow Contrabono off the map. I'll even send you skilled technicians and officers. Yes?'

'You are asking a great deal,' said the President.

'I never haggle,' said Sarek. 'If you accept my offer you will be sure to beat Contrabono within three months; if you refuse, Contrabono will be certain to beat you within three weeks. Take it or leave it; it is merely a friendly offer. Don't let me persuade you one way or the other.'

'Hm . . .'

'A hundred thousand rifles; two hundred machine-guns; twenty field-guns of the latest model; ammunition unlimited – enough to kill a continent!'

'You guarantee me the war, in effect?'

'Oh, absolutely,' said Sarek. 'I will definitely guarantee that no war will start until you are fully equipped.'

'And then I will march on Contrabono,' said Pancho Pablo, with relief. 'Ah, Señor Sarek. I was on the verge of despair; but you come to me like an angel from heaven. God bless you! You are an angel of mercy. Now I shall be able to blow Contrabono into the Pacific.'

Three days later, Sarek sat in the office of Juan Amarillo, President of Contrabono.

Sarek said: 'Let me be quite frank with you. I am in South America for my health, but, seeing the state of affairs between Gaudeama and Contrabono, I felt that some business might be done. I intended to call on Pancho Pablo, but I have received information that he is already arming with Circonflex –'

'*What?*'

'Oh yes. He has ordered about 50,000 rifles, a few machine-guns, and some cannons, I think.'

'How do you know?'

'What I tell you is fact. You will need to strengthen yourself.'

'I shall march on him immediately.'

'You should have thought of that six months ago. You are too late now; he is already well enough equipped to stand against you until the remainder of his equipment arrives. He has, in fact, arranged to hand Circonflex concessions on your copper mines.'

'Good God!'

'Yes, it is rather bad. Some firms do business that way – arms in exchange for commodities. Kriegers, however, keep clear of such dirty transactions.'

'But this is outrageous! What do you advise me to do? As the active partner in one of the greatest armaments firms in Europe?'

'Well . . . You might import a dozen field-guns or so, and a few thousand rifles. Krieger guns are superior to Circonflex. Try some machine-guns; they are the modern weapons. Wars are won on equipment nowadays. Get good, reliable machine-guns and cannons. I will arrange quick delivery. For a few million dollars you make yourself secure. Arms are a kind of insurance policy against war, or against defeat. Guns are power. Buy Krieger guns.'

'We have very little ready money.'

'That should be a simple matter. Impose an additional tax on the land; a few cents here and there on various necessities. Get about a dollar and a half from every peasant and the trick is done. Then, again, Kuhnberg will pay you half a million for the match monopoly. It is simple.'

'Wait. As a matter of fact I have been considering buying more arms. Say I buy about enough rifles to bring my infantry up to 175,000; a few of these machine-guns . . .'

'Then bring a few thousand of your best able-bodied peons off the land, drill them, and arm them with the old rifles –'

'Requisition a few hundred horses for cavalry; call up my *vaqueros*, and put them into uniform . . .'

'Then you would be sure of beating Gaudeama, Señor Amarillo.'

Just then there came the sound of angry voices in the square below.

A fat little secretary popped his head in at the door, and said:

'Your Excellency, they have caught a spy.'

Amarillo became blue with rage.

'A spy! Again a spy? From Gaudeama? A dirty Gaudeama spy! Where did they catch him?'

'In the Guayacum Pass, Excellency. He was drawing plans.'

'Bring him in here!' shouted Amarillo. 'Bring him before me. Damn him, I'll shoot him like a dog – I'll shoot him down like a mad dog, I say. Bring him in.'

'Yes, Excellency.'

There was a pause. Then footsteps in the passage.

'That will make eight spies in three months,' said Amarillo.

The door opened.

Dirty, dishevelled, bleeding at the nose, his wrists cut by a chain handcuff, Janos the artist was prodded into the room at the point of a bayonet.

'What the devil is all this?' demanded Janos. 'I was sketching peacefully in the Pass over there, when half a dozen of these infernal louts grabbed hold of me and brought me here. I demand an explanation.'

'Oh, you demand an explanation!' screamed Amarillo. 'Oh, you were sketching peacefully! Spying peacefully, you mean, you dirty spy. What were you after?'

'I –'

'Silence, dog! Juan, show me that sketching-block. Aah! Sketching peacefully! Peacefully sketching an important strategic point! Pancho Pablo sent you, did he? I'll show you! I'll have you shot in the back, like a dog.'

'Nobody sent me,' said Janos. 'I'm an artist.'

'What an excuse! Artist! You liar. You don't even look like one. I've never seen such a clumsy disguise. That coat! That beard! Bah! Do you want a priest?'

Janos turned pale. He glanced wildly round the room. Then he caught sight of Sarek, smiled with relief, and uttered a cry of joy:

'Why, Sarek! Sarek, you recognize me? You remember me, Janos? Hector Sarek! You remember me – me and Cosima? We're married. We have a boy, nine years old. You wouldn't let them shoot me, would you, Sarek?'

Everybody looked at Sarek.

'Do you know this man?' asked Amarillo.

'Of course he does,' said Janos.

Sarek puffed out smoke and said with a shrug: 'I pay the penalty of being fairly well known. So many people have my name pat. I don't know him from Adam.'

'Sarek!' shouted Janos. 'You do! You remember Cosima – you used to be in love with her – we're married – we have a son –'

'Spare me these ravings,' said Sarek.

'Take him away. Send him a priest if he fancies one. Then a firing-squad,' said Amarillo. And when the echoes of Janos's last cry of despair had died away in the passage he turned to Sarek, and added: 'Even if the fellow isn't a spy we daren't take chances in times like these . . . Now, let us discuss the delivery of these guns . . .'

When he returned to Europe Sarek called on Cosima.

When he saw her something inside his heart seemed to swell. In maturing her the years had made her more beautiful. The black dress of widowhood accentuated the slimness of her waist. Above the high black collar, like some exotic firework, burst the superb golden cascade of her hair, fastened in a large loose knot.

'I have never been able to forget you,' said Sarek, in his dry, toneless voice.

'You've heard about poor Janos?'

'I was in Contrabono when they shot him. I did my best to save him. I spent ten thousand dollars in bribes, but I didn't begrudge anything, I was thinking of you.'

'It was awfully kind of you, Hector. It was like you. You always did have a good heart.'

Sarek stuck to his point: 'I thought of you. I've been thinking of you for years.' The vague swelling in his heart became oppressive: it was the repressed passion of a lifetime, struggling to find expression.

'Tell me, how do you live now?'

'I've gone back to the millinery business. It's quite nice.'

'Hard.'

'I don't mind it. I earn enough for little Otto and myself.'

'Listen to me, Cosima. I've got a lot of money, now – hundreds of thousands. But I don't care. Two meals a day, a bed, and a handful of "Virginia" cigars, and I'm satisfied. I've got power; influence. I only use it to make more money. And I don't care about money, actually. I'm alone. I'm a lonely man. Listen; why not marry me?'

'Marry . . . But you're joking!'

'No, I never joke – I haven't the talent.'

'But, Hector – surely there are plenty of other nice girls –'

'I want to make you understand, Cosima, that I love you very much. I don't know how to put these things nicely; I haven't the knack. You say "plenty of other nice girls". Listen. I'm a narrow-minded man. I have only single purposes. I want a thing: I try to get it. I have wanted you for over ten years. I haven't been able to get you out of my mind. When I wanted to sell guns, then ploughs didn't exist any more for me; when I fell in love with you, other women didn't exist any more. I want you to marry me.'

'Hector, I can't take you seriously.'

'Cosima!' cried Sarek, with a desperate gesture. 'I'm not joking. I want you to marry me.'

'But I can't. I don't love you.'

'Why not?'

'I love Janos.'

'But he's dead. He doesn't exist any more. You can't love somebody that doesn't exist.'

'You don't understand. I still love him, even though . . . I shan't see him any more . . .'

Sarek felt a murderous rage surge up inside him. He controlled himself, however, and said:

'Don't cry. No use crying. Listen, Cosima. You've got a son. Think of all the things I could do for him. Even if you don't love me much, you can still marry me. People marry like that every day. You want to be faithful to Janos's memory? All right. Don't love me. But why not marry me, just the same?'

'No.'

Sarek paused. He stared at the floor, and when he looked up again there was something in his eyes that made Cosima shudder.

'Very well,' he said, 'now listen. With me, it's one thing, or the other. You don't love me. Very well. Then you'll hate me. I'll tell you something. I told you that I tried to save Janos? Well, it was a lie. I didn't – I sent him to his death. He was arrested while I was with the President; a word from me might have saved him. But no. I knew that my time was coming. He insulted me once . . . besides, he had you, and I was determined to get you. Are you listening? Well, they said: "Do you know him?" and I said "No". Do you hear? Janos went on his bended knees and begged for mercy. I just went on smoking my cigar. And I'm glad I did it! . . . Well? Well? What are you shaking your head like that for? Now do you hate me?'

'No,' said Cosima. 'Because I don't believe you.'

'But it's true.'

'No, it isn't, Hector. It can't possibly be. You'd never do a terrible thing like that. No, no, no! Say what you like, you'd never get me to believe it. I believe that you tried to save him – yes. But kill him? No. You always did have a good, kind heart, Hector, so I don't believe you.'

For the first time in his life Sarek tore his hair. Tears of exasperation appeared in his eyes. He stamped on the floor in a frenzy of impotent rage. And then Cosima said something which took his breath away like ice-cold water:

'Poor Hector! Poor man, how you must be suffering, to say such awful things.'

Sarek was suffering the hellish agonies of the strong man who sees himself overcome by the weak: the clever man who experiences defeat at the hands of the stupid: the wicked man vanquished by simplicity – an exquisite mental torture. A Krieger soft-lead bullet could not have hurt him more. He felt that he was going mad.

He finally managed to say:

'How . . . how *dare* you pity me? How dare *you* pity *me*? How dare you?'

'You see,' said Cosima, sweetly, 'I understand you so well, Hector. You have a sweet nature and a heart of gold, only you try not to show it –'

Defeated and utterly humiliated, Sarek pressed his hands over his ears and rushed out.

He rarely drank alcohol, but now he went to the nearest café and hastily swallowed a double cognac. Then he lit a cigar and sat thinking, with the smoke lapping at his face . . .

He smiled slightly and blinked his smoke-stung eyes.

'Sarek, representing Comrade Death.'

He ordered another cognac.

Forty red years have passed, with the drone of flying lead. Sarek has aged, in a horrible kind of way. He seems to have introverted, physically. His external parts seem to be trying to creep inwards and hide themselves: his stomach yearns towards his spine, and his cheeks endeavour to meet in his mouth. His head is a death's-head, with prominent ears. He is covered with honours. European Powers have made a nobleman of him. On special occasions, when he wears all his orders and medals, he looks like some little Chinese God of Fear hung with offerings, and moves with a golden jingling sound. He is unspeakably rich; he has far more money than he knows what to do with. He has become a universal provider in the realms of the macabre. He endows hospitals and asylums, and fills them up. Not only does he build orphanages: he even provides the orphans. He lives in palaces of incredible splendour; Rolls-Royces are not good enough for him. He owns half of Europe. He is still alone. He goes to his offices at eight every morning; he lives on boiled fish and bismuth, with an occasional purgative; and still smokes twopenny cigars. Sarek sits at the head of a long table, presiding over a meeting of six directors of different nationalities. Half buried in his deep chair, without bothering to take his cigar out of his mouth, he addresses them in a squeaky voice:

'Yes, gentlemen. Half a century has passed since I took the first big order for Krieger machine-guns. Since then how civilization has progressed! Weapons which were highly modern ten years ago are now as obsolete as if they had existed in the Middle Ages. Rifles begin to fall into disuse. Soon the most efficient modern machine-gun will be placed in a glass case and ticketed: "Ancient History". For civilization progresses inexorably. Let us consider: The Franco-Prussian War was considered quite a war in 1870 –'

'Ha-ha-ha-ha!'

'But it was mere milk and water. The Boer War was a mere interchange of bullets. Bang! – a man falls over. Skittles – coconut-shies – child's play! The Russo-Japanese affair was better, but not very much; it was relatively unproductive. Those wars were barbaric. Only between 1914 and 1918 did modern civilization begin to justify itself.'

'Hear, hear!'

'Then,' Sarek went on, 'nations fought in quite commendable manner: guns burnt ammunition day and night – thousands of tons an hour – for quite a while.

'But the first real stride towards ideal conditions was – if I may say so – brought about by myself, forty years ago. The Gaudeama-Contrabono affair, in which they reduced each other to pulp in a two-years' war. Krieger guns were used on both sides. It was a vigorous little war; it taught us a lesson.' Sarek cleared his throat, and slipped a bismuth tablet into his mouth. 'It was the first step towards the abolition of the cruel and merciless warfare of the rival armament firms. We came to our senses. We asked ourselves: "Why should we manufacturers cut one another's throats in rivalry? Let us strive towards a world peace between the makers of guns." We became united, controlled, international. By 1914 we were at peace.'

There was a respectful murmur.

'Yes, we were at peace. The air was black with our projectiles. Krieger shells flew both ways. There was nothing one-sided about us; we were free from the follies of morbid nationalism. Krieger cannons fired Krieger shells into Krieger batteries; Krieger hand-grenades silenced sectors armed with Krieger machine-guns. Krieger tanks squashed Krieger riflemen. Krieger star-shells threw light on Krieger-armed combatants; Krieger bullets mowed them down, the Krieger shrapnel disembowelled them. Krieger torpedoes blew up Krieger battleships. Krieger submarines were blown to atoms by Krieger mines. Krieger searchlights picked out Krieger 'planes: *pom-pom*! went the Krieger anti-aircraft guns; and more orders poured into the factories. Then I breathed a sigh of satisfaction. It was no longer a case of dog eat dog. We were united.'

'Hear, hear!'

'Then, at the end of the War, the late Baron Krieger said to me: "Sarek, this is the end. There will be no more war. The nations have had a frightful lesson. They are tired of slaughter." But I told him: "Wait, my friend. There is still a great deal to hope for. Things are not half as bad as you say." Events are proving me right.'

'So they are.'

'There is one important thing which I have not yet mentioned.'

The Japanese representative raised his head and uttered one sibilant word:

'Gas!'

'Exactly,' said Sarek, 'gas. After the War, people became air-minded. That could have only one outcome, since it is obvious that the primary function of an aeroplane is bombardment. An aeroplane is mainly something to drop things out of. Thus, I concentrated on gas.'

There was a grating of chairs; the directors drew closer.

'From air-mindedness it is only a short stop to gas-consciousness,' said Sarek. 'Now the public is gas-conscious. They are terrified of the War in the Air which they know is coming. Hence the colossal sales of our gas mask, the Krieger Impenetrable. Orders are pouring in from all parts of Europe. I leave it to you, gentlemen, to fix retail prices for your respective countries. Soon the Krieger Impenetrable Mask will be on sale in every hardware store. We are introducing three new sizes – the O2, for babies up to two years old; the O3, for children up to five; and the X13, outsize, for obese people. Gas-mask clubs are being organized in every town.'

'Have you considered making the Omega gas in the form of pocket-grenades?' asked the Italian representative.

'They will be ready soon,' said Sarek.

'The Omega gas is a good gas,' said the German representative. 'The Krieger Mask is the only mask that can keep it out.'

'Hence the popularity of the Krieger Mask,' said the American representative.

Sarek cut him short:

'Well. You have your instructions. There is no more, for today. Now you must excuse me . . .'

Sarek rested for a while. His personal attendant, a lean Croat, brought him a glass of milk, which he handed to him without a word.

'Marko,' said Sarek wearily, 'I'm tired out. I'm old. I'm tired. Why do I go on? What the devil do I do it for? I don't get any pleasure out of it. Why?'

Marko said nothing.

'I'm big!' shouted Sarek. 'I'm boss of the whole world! I'm guns. Guns are power. I'm power. Kings and Presidents crawl on their bellies at my feet. I speak to Governments as I speak to a dog. But what do I want with it? I don't *feel* big. I feel small. I was beaten by a woman. Marko; a damned blonde woman. I schemed. I plotted. I swore I'd get her. And in the end she wouldn't have me – after I'd prostrated myself in front of her. I was beaten. I was ashamed. I waited. Years after she came to me. See? She came to me. She said: "My dear friend Hector, they're taking my grandson Janos to the front. Stop them. He's all I have in the world." I said: "No. I'll not lift a finger. Let him die, then you'll stop pitying me, perhaps, and start to hate me a little." The boy was killed. She said: "You would have helped me if you could, Hector; you always did have a kind heart." And she went away still pitying me. And to this day she pities me. So, you see, I'm not big; I'm small. It eats my heart up, I feel so small. I'm alone. I'm old. I'm tired. I wish to God I could die.'

Marko said nothing. He was a deaf-mute. He had never heard nor spoken. And to his ear alone Sarek confided all the agonies of his soul, as a child talks to a doll.

Sarek rang a bell, and told his secretary:

'As soon as President Rozma comes, show him in.'

President Rozma turned a haggard gaze to Sarek and complained:

'I tell you, war looms. Incidents are occurring on the frontiers . . . there have been revolver shots . . . Our flag was insulted . . . We are in danger.'

'You have a belligerent neighbour,' said Sarek.

'Feuerbauch? He is not a man – he is a Mills-bomb with the pin removed,' said Rozma.

'Feuerbauch is an ambitious man.'

'Not only has he made himself Dictator of his own country, he wants to be Dictator of the Earth. See the result of making a man of the people a Dictator! He started with nothing. He does not consider the consequences of what he does. He has nothing to lose –'

'Well?' said Sarek.

'I am concerned mainly with defence,' said Rozma. 'I understand that Feuerbauch has been accumulating enormous supplies of the Omega gas.'

'Yes. You are afraid of a gas attack?'

'I am.' Rozma shuddered. 'Consider. Clouds of the Omega gas in my congested industrial districts! My God!'

'Put your trust in Providence, and keep your gas-masks air-tight. How are you off for masks?'

'We are fully equipped with your Number Three Masks.'

'Against the Omega gas the Number Three Mask is useless. It is obsolete. The only mask worth having, now, is the Krieger Impenetrable, which is proof against every gas known to science.'

'It is rather hard. Two years ago I spent millions on masks. Now I must throw that money into the sea.'

'You needn't, if you don't want to,' said Sarek. 'Just retain your old masks, and when the Omega gas comes over sniff deeply, and all your troubles will be over.'

'That is no argument,' said Rozma. 'I must buy. A million of your Impenetrable Masks. They are proof against the Omega gas?'

'They are.'

'I, also, shall buy Omega gas.'

'Why not buy Moribot?'

'What is Moribot?'

'It is a new chemical – a powder. A little on a cornfield, and the crop is destroyed; a little on a meadow, and the cattle die. It is a good thing for paralysing a food supply. It's dear.'

'I'll make a test. If it is good, I will buy that also. I am a man of peace; but this Feuerbauch is a madman, a devil.'

'Well, we will find you some holy water to sprinkle on his tail . . .'

After Rozma was gone the secretary informed Sarek:

'Herr Feuerbauch is here.'

A spark of excitement kindled in Sarek's eyes. He sat upright, and lit another cigar.

'Show him in,' he said.

The colossal figure of Feuerbauch, the Dictator, loomed in the doorway.

Helmuth von Feuerbauch was a man of might. He had the physique and the mentality of a rogue elephant. There was ferocity in his little blue eyes, and a tigerish curve to his mouth. Absolute force was expressed in the set of his shoulders. He had a back like a door. His blond head was made more for butting than thinking, like the head of an ox. He extended to Sarek a fist that might have strangled a bullock.

'Sit down,' said Sarek, 'there are important things I want to tell you.'

'Well, what?' said Feuerbauch. 'If it's about that poor fool of a Rozma, don't bother. I know already. He's frightened.'

'Oh, Rozma's afraid, all right,' said Sarek. 'He wants gas-masks – Krieger Impenetrables.'

'And you're selling them to him?'

'Yes, why not?'

'But, damn it, what about all my Omega gas? What am I going to do with all my lovely Omega gas? Your masks resist it.'

'That wasn't what I wanted to tell you about,' said Sarek.

'Then what?'

'Listen,' said Sarek. 'I'm a man who has interested himself in chemical warfare. I've got money unlimited. I've bought the finest brains on earth. Do you know what there is in the cellar under this building? A laboratory.'

'A laboratory!'

'Yes. A secret place. Some of the greatest scientists in the world are at work down there at this moment. They work day and night. They've been discovering things – frightful things. You couldn't imagine what things! My finest official products are rubbish compared with two or three that I have up my sleeve –'

'What are they?'

'Wait a minute. What do you think is the deadliest gas known to man?'

'The Omega gas.'

'Wrong. Necrogene. Compared with the gas Necrogene Omega is fresh air. No mask can keep it out. There is no anti-gas.'

'Good Lord!'

'The Krieger Impenetrable is useless against it. One sniff and you're dead. Nothing on earth can save you. Nausea, vomiting, coma; and death within five minutes.'

'Great God! With a gas like that I could hold the world in my hand!'

'So you could. It's going to the highest bidder –'

'I'll be the highest bidder. Name the price – anything you like, reasonable or otherwise – but give me that gas.'

'Well, I might. I like your methods, Feuerbauch; there's no sentiment about self-defence about you. Yes, I think I will –'

'Then –'

'One moment, please. If you insist on banging the table with your fist like that I shall ask you to leave. My nerves are not good . . . Now tell me, what is the most powerful explosive you know of?'

'There is nothing more violent than Ultimon,' said Feuerbauch.

Sarek laughed. 'Ultimon! *Pfui!* And what if I tell you that I have an explosive beside which Ultimon looks like a penny squib?'

'What? *What?* What is it?'

'Disintegrol.'

'What's that?'

'What the name implies – Oil of Disintegration. It is more than an explosive: it is a kind of explosive principle. The way it works is a mystery. We know how to use it and how to control it; but how it works we don't know.'

'What happens?'

'It combines with most substances to form an extremely unstable high explosive. That's Disintegrol. We've made tests. One milligramme dropped on a common brick turned the brick into something equal to about seven kilos of Ammonal.'

'God!'

'We made some amusing tests. We put a milligramme on a hairbrush, and waited. The hairbrush exploded and blew a hole eight feet deep and twenty feet in diameter. We put half a milligramme on a ballistite cartridge and buried it in a field. There was nearly an earthquake! And as for the field – it no longer exists. There is only a huge pit.'

'What an explosive!'

'You know that little island in Lake Kraken? We sprayed it with Disintegrol, in a fine vapour. Ten minutes later the island ceased to be. Showers of powdered earth fell ten miles away.'

'No!'

'Unhappily, one of our technicians had a pin-prick in his insulated glove. His hand exploded like a bomb and blew him to pieces.'

Feuerbauch actually shuddered.

'If,' said Sarek, 'if you sprayed a city with Disintegrol from an aeroplane you would turn that city into a gigantic bomb. Nothing could be done. Bang! – no more city! Stone and brick are excellent mediums for it. Organic matter also. If you swallowed a capsule of Disintegrol, my friend, I can guarantee that you'd never again be troubled with internal irregularities. What a magnificent bomb you'd make!'

Feuerbauch trembled. His little blue eyes, staring past Sarek, seemed to contemplate some terrible triumphs.

'Disintegrol!' he said. 'Why talk of gases when there is Disintegrol? By God and the devil, I could blow the world out of the solar system.'

'We have special insulating material for aeroplanes and a spraying apparatus by means of which Disintegrol can be sent on the wind in the form of a vapour. That simply means that all of a sudden a city blows up.'

'Give it to me,' said Feuerbauch, with dilated eyes.

'I should be a fool to do that,' said Sarek.

'Then what are you going to do with it?'

'Keep it up my sleeve,' said Sarek. 'In the meantime, I am going to let you have the gas Necrogene. Later on, I may let you blow up the world. You must look after my interests. Meanwhile, I prefer to hold one or two of the trump cards. You understand my attitude?'

'I think I understand. But you will give me Necrogene?'

'I'll sell you Necrogene.' Sarek paused. From a case of gold studded with jewels he took another of his twopenny cigars, and lit it. He went on, in a faint, dreamy voice: 'I'm an old man. I'm very, very old; and very, very tired; and very, very bored. Yes. One day I'll let you have Disintegrol, and then . . . then, my friend, there will be such a bang! Yes, one day . . .'

'Why not now?' demanded Feuerbauch.

'Well . . . I don't know,' murmured Sarek. 'Why not? Why not now? . . . I have so many things, downstairs. I have brought destruction to a fine art. Why not let you have it now? Why not . . .'

'Now!' shouted Feuerbauch.

'Perhaps now,' said Sarek.

'Let me, at least, see it,' said Feuerbauch.

Sarek pressed a button. A minute or two passed. Sarek sat still, limp as a man in a faint. Feuerbauch took out a bent black pipe, filled it, and sucked out big blue clouds. He watched the smoke curling vividly across the sunbeams, and there came into his mind a vision of great open plains . . . Men advanced, dressed in gas-proof suits, grotesquely masked in Krieger Impenetrables, which resembled the distorted bones of a face. Suddenly a cloud crept across the plain – a sneaking, curling cloud, which writhed and darted with the wind; and, like toy soldiers stricken by a wind, the men fell, in lines, writhing. Then, from the west, behind a blinding barrage of Necrogene, Disintegrol, and liquid fire, a padded army swept forward, dumbly, to a bloody victory . . . and, through the shattered streets of blood-besprinkled cities he, Feuerbauch, rode like a god in his huge black armoured limousine, while multitudes under the truncheons of his Guards forced their mournful faces into wry smiles, and uttered feeble cheers . . .

'Ah!' said Feuerbauch.

A man in a white coat came in. Sarek said: 'Is all clear?'

'Yes, Excellency.'

'Then conduct us to the laboratory.'

The white-coated man bowed and conducted them out. In another room he helped them to put on great, flapping white suits, triple-sealed at the seams; and curious gas-masks with double respirators and immense, goggling eyes which made them look like unheard-of fishes from some unattainable dark depths of a tropic sea. Feuerbauch was instantly enclosed by a horrible silence. He began to sweat. To him, silence was death. But as he opened his mouth to speak the man in the white coat attached a little black disc to the side of his head, and into the Dictator's ear broke the voice of Sarek, enormously amplified:

'This is necessary. Our laboratories are dangerous, terribly dangerous. Even with all our precautions we lose five men every week. We are playing with the destructive forces of Nature.'

'I fear nothing!' said Feuerbauch, shouting to break down the trembling of his voice.

The doors of a lift clicked behind them. They sank down quickly, down and down: the well of the lift seemed to have no bottom.

'We have tunnelled down right below the city,' said Sarek, 'the whole world knows the city above – that is my city, the Arms City; what the stupid newspapers call Death City. But down here, I have my own secrets. This is the Under World . . .'

'Perhaps I had better go back,' said Feuerbauch.

'As you wish,' said Sarek, 'but I hate a coward.'

'I fear nothing,' said Feuerbauch. 'In any case, I have taken the usual precautions. If I do not return within three hours you will be asked why I have not communicated. If, then, I do not communicate, three hundred aeroplanes will ask further questions.'

The lift stopped.

Sarek's Under World was a place of utter silence over which there brooded an atmosphere of horror. 'I don't see why you can't work above ground,' said Feuerbauch. Then he stopped abruptly with a gasp. Staring at him through the lenses of his goggles stood something that resembled a hippopotamus.

Was it a man? His jaws were blackened and swollen beyond the bounds of fantasy. His nose was gone: the horrible enlargement of his face had swallowed it. His eyes bulged, bright red, under hideously distorted brow-ridges. As he opened his mouth to speak, Feuerbauch could see that he had no teeth.

'Our Doctor Krok,' said Sarek. 'Don't be alarmed. He is the result of a slight accident. He can claim the honour of discovering the Krok Poison. But, unhappily, the good doctor was so careless as to permit one imperceptible drop to touch his skin. Observe the result.'

'One imperceptible drop!' said Feuerbauch. 'And what, in God's name, if the drop had been larger?'

'The unfortunate Doctor Krok would have disintegrated, within twenty-four hours, into a sort of liquid,' said Sarek.

Sweat misted the insides of the Dictator's goggles. Sarek added, in a low voice: 'But you ought to see him without any clothes on!'

Feuerbauch followed him, blindly. Soon, Sarek's voice said: 'In this room, you are in the presence of eternal death.'

'Death?'

'Most certain death. Here we store Necrogene.' Sarek pointed. Feuerbauch could see innumerable black containers, lying in nests of wood-shavings – smooth, shining, fat, oval, like eggs. 'Necrogene. There lies, on this floor, enough poison to kill the whole of this city within fifteen minutes.'

'God!'

'But wait. All this is nothing.'

'Nothing, you say? Nothing?'

'Well, next to nothing. To look at, those cylinders might be harmless. Would you like to see my museum? I have some curious specimens.'

'Of what?'

'Human remains. They are rather entertaining. There is, for example, all that was left of three men after an accident with the Krok Poison – one coffee-spoonful in a small test tube; a sort of liquid carbon . . . And then, again, gas; I can show you some quite amazing things the Necrogene has done to men. They have twisted themselves into positions – well, I tell you, if they had studied acrobatics all their lives they could never have achieved such contortions! Amazing! One poor fellow bit himself in the small of the back. But you'd never believe. Come, let me show you –'

'No. No. I take your word. No. I don't want to see.'

'You may as well see the effects of the gas you are going to employ.'

'My experts will attend to that. I . . .'

'You prefer to come in afterwards as the conqueror?' Sarek laughed. 'Good. Now I will show you Disintegrol.'

They passed through a long, white room, padded with felt. Sarek pointed to rows of small brown bottles. 'Disintegrol. We have even invented a special insulating substance, Sekurite. That is the material of which those bottles is made.' He picked one up. The Dictator leapt away. 'Oh, don't be alarmed, Feuerbauch; look –' Sarek dropped a bottle, which bounced a little and then lay still; he kicked it aside. 'As long as it is not exposed to air you can give it to the baby to cut his teeth on . . . Come . . .'

'I want to go,' said Feuerbauch.

'And I say come!' said Sarek.

Feuerbauch looked behind him. The immense sliding doors had automatically closed. He wanted to be sick. Sarek beckoned again; he followed. Another door slid back. 'Gas Department,' said Sarek.

The room was lit by hidden blue lamps. It was high and long, and cut by the gleaming white lengths of glass benches at which masked men, quite still and silent, stood staring into bottles. Above hung glass tubes in terrifying coils. 'You would not think so, but these men have all the technique of hidden death at their fingertips,' said Sarek. 'Look.' He beckoned. A little man came forward under the blue lights – a minutely-proportioned man, with the figure of a schoolboy. Through the clear glass of his goggles gleamed a pair of large, blue, childish eyes. 'Necros,' said Sarek, 'inventor of Necrogene, and my greatest research-worker.'

Necros bowed. 'Thank you, Excellency,' he said in a high, penetrating voice which, in Feuerbauch's microphone sounded like the crowing of a young cock.

'And how goes the new gas, Necros?'

'Very well, Excellency.'

'Near completion?'

'Complete, Excellency. I suggest that we call it Sarek's Last Word.'

'But why haven't you told me before?'

'Excellency, I finished work today. Besides –'

'Is it good?'

'Good? Excellency, it is frightful!'

'Excellent.'

'Compared with this, Excellency, Necrogene is no more poisonous than a night mist.'

'Indeed!' Sarek laughed. 'There is no end. What are its effects?'

'Excellency, I tried it on a mouse, a guinea-pig, a chimpanzee, and – by accident – on a man.'

'What man?'

'Mischa, your Excellency. Poor Mischa.'

'What happened?'

'Excellency, the effects of the gas are like this: it attacks the higher centres. Thus, the mouse, on inhaling it, walked in circles for five minutes, and then began to eat itself.'

'Ah! And the other animals?'

'The guinea-pig also walked in circles, and scratched itself to death. The chimpanzee walked also in circles and then destroyed itself by beating its head against the bars of its cage.'

'And Mischa?'

'He walked in circles for an hour and then began to tear himself to pieces with his hands.'

'Quite spectacular! What did you do?'

'Mischa was my good friend, Excellency, so I put him out of his misery. The reason why I did not tell you before is that I am not quite sure of it.'

'How, not sure?'

'Excellency, I can't hold it.'

'What do you mean?'

'It penetrates everything, even glass.'

'Then how do you keep it?'

'Excellency,' said Necros, bursting into tears, 'that is the trouble – I can't keep it. It is all gone!'

There was silence. Then, suddenly, Feuerbauch – about whose head the laboratory was spinning like a wheel – heard Sarek's voice saying: 'Feuerbauch . . . you are walking in circles!'

Feuerbauch blinked. Sarek was before him. Then Sarek was gone; then Sarek was there again. He turned his head. Carefully picking his footsteps, Sarek was walking round and round, followed by Necros and the hideous Doctor Krok. A door opened. Sarek began to laugh uproariously – a piercing, shrieking laugh. Then the others laughed too . . . Feuerbauch was becoming giddy, and inside his head there was a sensation of prickling, like soda-water bubbles on a sore tongue . . . He began to laugh, too; and when he looked again, Sarek had an armful of brown bottles, Disintegrol bottles, which he was hastening to uncork.

Feuerbauch had a sudden impulse to tear off his clothes and dance. His mask fell away; then his gas-proof suit. He snatched a bottle from Sarek, shouting: 'Give me some, too!'

Disintegrol tasted bitter. He drank a little, and spat it out; then poured it on his hair.

The last thing he ever heard was the voice of Sarek:

'Look! look! look! look! look! look! look! Now they're all walking in circles! Ha-ha-ha-ha-ha-ha-hahahahahahaaah! Oh, what a bang we shall make!'

Then he was seized by an overwhelming desire to pull out his fingers and throw them away . . .

At three o'clock that afternoon, Seismographs in distant cities recorded a terrible earthquake. At three-thirty, news came through that, where there had been a city, there was now a pit a mile deep. For three months afterwards, there were beautiful vivid red sunsets, due to the action of the sunlight passing through the high-floating clouds of infinitesimally fine dust.

Among this dust, presumably, there floated all that was left of Sarek.

Leiningen Versus the Ants

Carl Stephenson

'Unless they alter their course, and there's no reason why they should, they'll reach your plantation in two days at the latest.'

Leiningen sucked placidly at a cigar about the size of a corn cob and for a few seconds gazed without answering at the agitated District Commissioner. Then he took the cigar from his lips and leaned slightly forward. With his bristling grey hair, bulky nose, and lucid eyes, he had the look of an ageing and shabby eagle.

'Decent of you,' he murmured, 'paddling all this way just to give me the tip. But you're pulling my leg, of course, when you say I must do a bunk. Why, even a herd of saurians couldn't drive me from this plantation of mine.'

The Brazilian official threw up lean and lanky arms and clawed the air with wildly distended fingers. 'Leiningen!' he shouted, 'you're insane! They're not creatures you can fight – they're an elemental – an "act of God"! Ten miles long, two miles wide – ants, nothing but ants! And every single one of them a fiend from hell; before you can spit three times they'll eat a full-grown buffalo to the bones. I tell you if you don't clear out at once there'll be nothing left of you but a skeleton picked as clean as your own plantation.'

Leiningen grinned. 'Act of God, my eye! Anyway, I'm not an old woman; I'm not going to run for it just because an elemental's on the way. And don't think I'm the kind of fathead who tries to fend off lightning with his fists, either. I use my intelligence, old man. With me, the brain isn't a second blindgut; I know what it's there for. When I began this model farm and plantation three years ago, I took into account all that could conceivably happen to it. And now I'm ready for anything and everything – including your ants.'

The Brazilian rose heavily to his feet. 'I've done my best,' he gasped.

'Your obstinacy endangers not only yourself, but the lives of your four hundred workers. You don't know these ants!'

Leiningen accompanied him down to the river, where the Government launch was moored. The vessel cast off. As it moved downstream, the exclamation mark neared the rail and began waving its arms frantically. Long after the launch had disappeared round the bend, Leiningen thought he could still hear that dimming, imploring voice. 'You don't know them, I tell you! *You don't know them!*'

But the reported enemy was by no means unfamiliar to the planter. Before he started work on his settlement, he had lived long enough in the country to see for himself the fearful devastations sometimes wrought by these ravenous insects in their campaigns for food. But since then he had planned measures of defence accordingly, and these, he was convinced, were in every way adequate to withstand the approaching peril.

Moreover, during his three years as planter, Leiningen had met and defeated drought, flood, plague, and all other 'acts of God' which had come against him – unlike his fellow settlers in the district, who had made little or no resistance. This unbroken success he attributed solely to the observance of his lifelong motto: *The human brain needs only to become fully aware of its powers to conquer even the elements.* Dullards reeled senselessly and aimlessly into the abyss; cranks, however brilliant, lost their heads when circumstances suddenly altered or accelerated and ran into stone walls; sluggards drifted with the current until they were caught in whirlpools and dragged under. But such disasters, Leiningen contended, merely strengthened his argument that intelligence, directed aright, invariably makes man the master of his fate.

Yes, Leiningen had always known how to grapple with life. Even here, in this Brazilian wilderness, his brain had triumphed over every difficulty and danger it had so far encountered. First he had vanquished primal forces by cunning and organization, then he had enlisted the resources of modern science to increase miraculously the yield of his plantation. And now he was sure he would prove more than a match for the 'irresistible' ants.

That same evening, however, Leiningen assembled his workers. He had no intention of waiting till the news reached their ears from other sources. Most of them had been born in the district; the cry, 'The ants are coming!' was to them an imperative signal for instant, panic-stricken flight, a spring for life itself. But so great was the Indians' trust in Leiningen, in Leiningen's word, and in Leiningen's wisdom, that they received his curt tidings, and his orders for the imminent struggle, with the calmness with which they were given. They waited, unafraid, alert, as if for the beginning of a new game or hunt which he had just described to them. The ants were indeed mighty, but not so mighty as the boss. Let them come!

They came at noon the second day. Their approach was announced by the wild unrest of the horses, scarcely controllable now either in stall or under rider, scenting from afar a vapour instinct with horror.

It was announced by a stampede of animals, timid and savage, hurtling past each other; jaguars and pumas flashing by nimble stags of the pampas; bulky tapirs, no longer hunters, themselves hunted, outpacing fleet kinkajous; maddened herds of cattle, heads lowered, nostrils snorting, rushing through tribes of loping monkeys, chattering in a dementia of terror; then followed the creeping and springing denizens of bush and steppe, big and little rodents, snakes, and lizards.

Pell-mell the rabble swarmed down the hill to the plantation, scattered right and left before the barrier of the water-filled ditch, then sped onwards to the river, where, again hindered, they fled along its banks out of sight.

This water-filled ditch was one of the defence measures which Leiningen had long since prepared against the advent of the ants. It encompassed three sides of the plantation like a huge horseshoe. Twelve feet across, but not very deep, when dry it could hardly be described as an obstacle to either man or beast. But the ends of the 'horseshoe' ran into the river which formed the northern boundary, and fourth side, of the plantation. And at the end nearer the house and outbuildings in the middle of the plantation, Leiningen had constructed a dam by means of which water from the river could be diverted into the ditch.

So now, by opening the dam, he was able to fling an imposing girdle of water, a huge quadrilateral with the river as its base, completely around the plantation, like the moat encircling a medieval city. Unless the ants were clever enough to build rafts, they had no hope of reaching the plantation, Leiningen concluded.

The twelve-foot water ditch seemed to afford in itself all the security needed. But while awaiting the arrival of the ants, Leiningen made a further improvement. The western section of the ditch ran along the edge of the tamarind wood, and the branches of some great trees reached over the water. Leiningen now had them lopped so that ants could not descend from them within the 'moat'.

The women and children, then the herds of cattle, were escorted by peons on rafts over the river, to remain on the other side in absolute safety until the plunderers had departed. Leiningen gave this instruction, not because he believed the non-combatants were in any danger, but in order to avoid hampering the efficiency of the defenders. 'Critical situations first become crises,' he explained to his men, 'when oxen or women get excited.'

Finally, he made a careful inspection of the 'inner moat' – a smaller ditch lined with concrete, which extended around the hill on which stood the ranch house, barns, stables, and other buildings. Into this concrete ditch emptied the inflow pipes from three great petrol tanks. If by some miracle the ants managed to cross the water and reach the plantation, this 'rampart of petrol' would be an absolutely impassable protection for the besieged and their dwellings and stock. Such, at least, was Leiningen's opinion.

He stationed his men at irregular distances along the water ditch, the first line of defence. Then he lay down in his hammock and puffed drowsily away at his pipe until a peon came with the report that the ants had been observed far away in the south.

Leiningen mounted his horse, which at the feel of its master seemed to forget its uneasiness, and rode leisurely in the direction of the threatening offensive. The southern stretch of ditch – the upper side of the quadrilateral – was nearly three miles long; from its centre one could survey the entire countryside. This was destined to be the scene of the outbreak of war between Leiningen's brain and twenty square miles of life-destroying ants.

It was a sight one could never forget. Over the range of hills, as far as the eye could see, crept a darkening hem, ever longer and broader, until the shadow spread across the slope from east to west, then downwards, downwards, uncannily swift, and all the green herbage of that wide vista was being mown as by a giant sickle, leaving only the vast moving shadow, extending, deepening, and moving rapidly nearer.

When Leiningen's men, behind their barrier of water, perceived the approach of the long-expected foe, they gave vent to their suspense in screams and imprecations. But as the distance began to lessen between the 'sons of hell' and the water ditch, they relapsed into silence. Before the advance of that awe-inspiring throng, their belief in the powers of the boss began to steadily dwindle.

Even Leiningen himself, who had ridden up just in time to restore their loss of heart by a display of unshakable calm, even he could not free himself from a qualm of malaise. Yonder were thousands of millions of voracious jaws bearing down upon him, and only a suddenly insignificant, narrow ditch lay between him and his men and being gnawed to the bones 'before you can spit three times'.

Hadn't his brain for once taken on more than it could manage? If the blighters decided to rush the ditch, fill it to the brim with their corpses, there'd still be more than enough to destroy every trace of that cranium of his. The planter's chin jutted; they hadn't got him yet, and he'd see to it they never would. While he could think at all, he'd flout both death and the devil.

The hostile army was approaching in perfect formation; no human battalions, however well drilled, could ever hope to rival the precision of that advance. Along a front that moved forward as uniformly as a straight line, the ants drew nearer and nearer to the water ditch. Then, when they learned through their scouts the nature of the obstacle, the two outlying wings of the army detached themselves from the main body and marched down the western and eastern sides of the ditch.

This surrounding manoeuvre took rather more than an hour to accomplish; no doubt the ants expected that at some point they would find a crossing.

During this outflanking movement by the wings, the army on the centre and southern front remained still. The besieged were therefore able to contemplate at their leisure the thumb-long, reddish-black, long-legged insects; some of the Indians believed they could see, too, intent on them, the brilliant, cold eyes, and the razor-edged mandibles, of this host of infinity.

It is not easy for the average person to imagine that an animal, not to mention an insect, can *think*. But now both the European brain of Leiningen and the primitive brains of the Indians began to stir with the unpleasant foreboding that inside every single one of that deluge of insects dwelt a thought. And that thought was: Ditch or no ditch, we'll get to your flesh!

Not until four o'clock did the wings reach the 'horseshoe' ends of the ditch, only to find these ran into the great river. Through some kind of secret telegraphy, the report must then have flashed very swiftly indeed along the entire enemy line. And Leiningen, riding – no longer casually – along his side of the ditch, noticed by energetic and widespread movements of troops that for some unknown reason the news of the check had its greatest effect on the southern front, where the main army was massed. Perhaps the failure to find a way over the ditch was persuading the ants to withdraw from the plantation in search of spoils more easily attainable.

An immense flood of ants, about a hundred yards in width, was pouring in a glimmering-black cataract down the far slope of the ditch. Many thousands were already drowning in the sluggish, creeping flow, but they were followed by troop after troop, who clambered over their sinking comrades, and then themselves served as dying bridges to the reserves hurrying on in their rear.

Shoals of ants were being carried away by the current into the middle of the ditch, where gradually they broke asunder and then, exhausted by their struggles, vanished below the surface. Nevertheless, the wavering, floundering, hundred-yard front was remorselessly if slowly advancing towards the besieged on the other bank. Leiningen had been wrong when he supposed the enemy would first have to fill the ditch with their bodies before they could cross; instead, they merely needed to act as stepping stones, as they swam and sank, to the hordes ever pressing onwards from behind.

Near Leiningen a few mounted herdsmen awaited his orders. He sent one to the weir – the river must be dammed more strongly to increase the speed and power of the water coursing through the ditch.

A second peon was despatched to the outhouses to bring spades and petrol sprinklers. A third rode away to summon to the zone of the offensive all the men, except the observation posts, on the nearby sections of the ditch, which were not yet actively threatened.

The ants were getting across far more quickly then Leiningen would have deemed possible. Impelled by the mighty cascade behind them, they struggled nearer and nearer to the inner bank. The momentum of the attack was so great that neither the tardy flow of the stream nor its downward pull could exert its proper force; and into the gap left by every submerging insect, hastened forward a dozen more.

When reinforcements reached Leiningen, the invaders were half way over. The planter had to admit to himself that it was only by a stroke of luck for him that the ants were attempting the crossing on a relatively short front: had they assaulted simultaneously along the entire length of the ditch, the outlook for the defenders would have been black indeed.

Even as it was, it could hardly be described as rosy, though the planter seemed quite unaware that death in a gruesome form was drawing closer and closer. As the war between his brain and the 'act of God' reached its climax, the very shadow of annihilation began to pale to Leiningen, who now felt like a champion in a new Olympic game, a gigantic and thrilling contest, from which he was determined to emerge victor. Such, indeed, was his aura of confidence that the Indians forgot their stupefied fear of the peril only a yard or two away; under the planter's supervision, they began fervidly digging up to the edge of the bank and throwing clods of earth and spadefuls of sand into the midst of the hostile fleet.

The petrol sprinklers, hitherto used to destroy pests and blights on the plantation, were also brought into action. Streams of evil-reeking oil now

soared and fell over an enemy already in disorder through the bombardment of earth and sand.

The ants responded to these vigorous and successful measures of
defence by further developments of their offensive. Entire clumps of
huddling insects began to roll down the opposite bank into the water. At
the same time, Leiningen noticed that the ants were now attacking along
an ever-widening front. As the numbers both of his men and his petrol
sprinklers were severely limited, this rapid extension of the line of battle
was becoming an overwhelming danger.

To add to his difficulties, the very clods of earth they flung into that
black floating carpet often whirled fragments towards the defenders' side,
and here and there dark ribbons were already mounting the inner bank.
True, wherever a man saw these they could still be driven back into the
water by spadefuls of earth or jets of petrol. But the file of defenders was
too sparse and scattered to hold off at all points these landing parties, and
though the peons toiled like madmen, their plight became momently
more perilous.

One man struck with his spade at an enemy clump, did not draw it
back quickly enough from the water; in a trice the wooden haft swarmed
with upward scurrying insects. With a curse, he dropped the spade into
the ditch; too late, they were already on his body. They lost no time;
wherever they encountered bare flesh they bit deeply; a few, bigger than
the rest, carried in their hindquarters a sting which injected a burning and
paralysing venom. Screaming, frantic with pain, the peon danced and
twirled like a dervish.

Realizing that another such casualty, yes, perhaps this alone, might
plunge his men into confusion and destroy their morale, Leiningen roared
in a bellow louder than the yells of the victim: 'Into the petrol, idiot!
Douse your paws in the petrol!' The dervish ceased his pirouette as if
transfixed, then tore off his shirt and plunged his arm and the ants
hanging to it up to the shoulder in one of the large open tins of petrol.
But even then the fierce mandibles did not slacken; another peon had to
help him squash and detach each separate insect.

Distracted by the episode, some defenders had turned away from the
ditch. And now cries of fury, a thudding of spades, and a wild trampling
to and fro, showed that the ants had made full use of the interval, though
luckily only a few had managed to get across. The men set to work again
desperately with the barrage of earth and sand. Meanwhile an old Indian,
who acted as medicine man to the plantation workers, gave the bitten
peon a drink he had prepared some hours before, which, he claimed,
possessed the virtue of dissolving and weakening ants' venom.

Leiningen surveyed his position. A dispassionate observer would have estimated the odds against him at a thousand to one. But then such an onlooker would have reckoned only by what he saw – the advance of myriad battalions of ants against the futile efforts of a few defenders – and not by the unseen activity that can go on in a man's brain.

For Leiningen had not erred when he decided he would fight elemental with elemental. The water in the ditch was beginning to rise; the stronger damming of the river was making itself apparent.

Visibly the swiftness and power of the masses of water increased, swirling into quicker and quicker movement its living black surface, dispersing its pattern, carrying away more and more of it on the hastening current.

Victory had been snatched from the very jaws of defeat. With a hysterical shout of joy, the peons feverishly intensified their bombardment of earth clods and sand.

And now the wide cataract down the opposite bank was thinning and ceasing, as if the ants were becoming aware that they could not attain their aim. They were scurrying back up the slope to safety.

All the troops so far hurled into the ditch had been sacrificed in vain. Drowned and floundering insects eddied in thousands along the flow, while Indians running on the bank destroyed every swimmer that reached the side.

Not until the ditch curved towards the east did the scattered ranks assemble again in a coherent mass. And now, exhausted and half numbed, they were in no condition to ascend the bank. Fusillades of clods drove them round the bend towards the mouth of the ditch and then into the river, wherein they vanished without leaving a trace.

The news ran swiftly along the entire chain of outposts, and soon a long scattered line of laughing men could be seen hastening along the ditch towards the scene of victory.

For once they seemed to have lost all their native reserve, for it was in wild abandon now they celebrated the triumph – as if there were no longer thousands of millions of merciless, cold, and hungry eyes watching them from the opposite bank, watching and waiting.

The sun sank behind the rim of the tamarind wood and twilight deepened into the night. It was not only hoped but expected that the ants would remain quiet until dawn. But to defeat any forlorn attempt at a crossing, the flow of water through the ditch was powerfully increased by opening the dam still further.

In spite of this impregnable barrier, Leiningen was not yet altogether convinced that the ants would not venture another surprise attack. He ordered his men to camp along the bank overnight. He also detailed parties of them to patrol the ditch in two of his motor-cars and ceaselessly to illuminate the surface of the water with headlights and electric torches.

After having taken all the precautions he deemed necessary, the farmer ate his supper with considerable appetite and went to bed. His slumbers were in no wise disturbed by the memory of the waiting, live, twenty square miles.

Dawn found a thoroughly refreshed and active Leiningen riding along the edge of the ditch. The planter saw before him a motionless and unaltered throng of besiegers. He studied the wide belt of water between them and the plantation, and for a moment almost regretted that the fight had ended so soon and so simply. In the comforting, matter-of-fact light of morning, it seemed to him now that the ants hadn't the ghost of a chance to cross the ditch. Even if they plunged headlong into it on all three fronts at once, the force of the now powerful current would inevitably sweep them away. He had got quite a thrill out of the fight – a pity it was already over.

He rode along the eastern and southern sections of the ditch and found everything in order. He reached the eastern section, opposite the tamarind wood, and here, contrary to the other battle fronts, he found the enemy very busy indeed. The trunks and branches of the trees and the creepers of the lianas, on the far bank of the ditch, fairly swarmed with industrious insects. But instead of eating the leaves there and then, they were merely gnawing through the stalks, so that a thick green shower fell steadily to the ground.

No doubt they were victualling columns sent out to obtain provender for the rest of the army. The discovery did not surprise Leiningen. He did not need to be told that ants are intelligent, that certain species even use others as milch cows, watchdogs, and slaves. He was well aware of their power of adaptation, their sense of discipline, their marvellous talent for organization.

His belief that a foray to supply the army was in progress was strengthened when he saw the leaves that fell to the ground being dragged to the troops waiting outside the wood. Then all at once he realized the aim that rain of green was intended to serve.

Each single leaf, pulled or pushed by dozens of toiling insects, was borne straight to the edge of the ditch. Even as Macbeth watched the approach of Birnam Wood in the hands of his enemies, Leiningen saw the tamarind wood move nearer and nearer in the mandibles of the ants. Unlike the fey Scot, however, he did not lose his nerve; no witches had prophesied his doom, and if they had he would have slept just as soundly.

All the same, he was forced to admit to himself that the situation was now far more ominous than that of the day before.

He had thought it impossible for the ants to build rafts for themselves – well, here they were, coming in thousands, more than enough to bridge the ditch. Leaves after leaves rustled down the slope into the water, where the current drew them away from the bank and carried them into midstream. And every single leaf carried several ants. This time the farmer did not trust to the alacrity of his messengers. He galloped away, leaning from his saddle and yelling orders as he rushed past outpost after outpost: 'Bring petrol pumps to the south-west front! Issue spades to every man along the line facing the wood!' And arrived at the eastern and southern sections, he dispatched every man except the observation posts to the menaced west.

Then, as he rode past the stretch where the ants had failed to cross the day before, he witnessed a brief but impressive scene. Down the slope of the distant hill there came towards him a singular being, writhing rather than running, an animal-like blackened statue with a shapeless head and four quivering feet that knuckled under almost ceaselessly. When the creature reached the far bank of the ditch and collapsed opposite Leiningen, he recognized it as a pampas stag, covered over and over with ants.

It had strayed near the zone of the army. As usual, they had attacked its eyes first. Blinded, it had reeled in the madness of hideous torment straight into the ranks of its persecutors, and now the beast swayed to and fro in its death agony.

With a shot from his rifle Leiningen put it out of its misery. Then he pulled out his watch. He hadn't a second to lose, but for life itself he could not have denied his curiosity the satisfaction of knowing how long the ants would take – for personal reasons, so to speak. After six minutes the white polished bones alone remained. That's how he himself would look before you can – Leiningen spat once, and put spurs to his horse.

The sporting zest with which the excitement of the novel contest had inspired him the day before had now vanished; in its place was a cold and violent purpose. He would send these vermin back to the hell where they belonged, somehow, anyhow. Yes, but how, was indeed the question; as things stood at present it looked as if the devils would raze him and his men from the earth instead. He had underestimated the might of the enemy; he really would have to bestir himself if he hoped to outwit them.

The biggest danger now, he decided, was the point where the western section of the ditch curved southwards. And, arrived there, he found his worst expectations justified. The very power of the current had huddled the leaves and their crews of ants so close together at the bend that the bridge was almost ready.

True, streams of petrol and clumps of earth still prevented a landing. But the number of floating leaves was increasing ever more swiftly. It could not be long now before a stretch of water a mile in length was decked by a green pontoon over which the ants could rush in millions.

Leiningen galloped to the weir. The damming of the river was controlled by a wheel on its bank. The planter ordered the man at the wheel first to lower the water in the ditch almost to vanishing point, next to wait a moment, then suddenly to let the river in again. This manoeuvre of lowering and raising the surface, of decreasing then increasing the flow of water through the ditch, was to be repeated over and over again until further notice.

This tactic was at first successful. The water in the ditch sank, and with it the film of leaves. The green fleet nearly reached the bed and the troops on the far bank swarmed down the slope to it. Then a violent flow of water at the original depth raced through the ditch, overwhelming leaves and ants, sweeping them along.

This intermittent rapid flushing prevented just in time the almost completed fording of the ditch. But it also flung here and there squads of the enemy vanguard simultaneously up the inner bank. These seemed to know their duty only too well, and lost no time accomplishing it. The air rang with the curses of bitten Indians. They had removed their shirts and pants to detect the quicker the upwards-hastening insects; when they saw one, they crushed it; and fortunately the onslaught as yet was only by skirmishers.

Again and again, the water sank and rose, carrying leaves and drowned ants away with it. It lowered once more nearly to its bed; but this time the exhausted defenders waited in vain for the flush of destruction. Leiningen sensed disaster; something must have gone wrong with the machinery of the dam. Then a sweating peon tore up to him:

'They're over!'

While the besieged were concentrating upon the defence of the stretch opposite the wood, the seemingly unaffected line beyond the wood had become the theatre of decisive action. Here the defenders' front was sparse and scattered; everyone who could be spared had hurried away to the south.

Just as the man at the weir had lowered the water almost to the bed of the ditch, the ants on a wide front began another attempt at a direct crossing like that of the preceding day. Into the emptied bed poured an irresistible throng. Rushing across the ditch, they attained the inner bank before the slow-witted Indians fully grasped the situation. Their frantic screams dumbfounded the man at the weir. Before he could direct the river anew into the safeguarding bed he saw himself surrounded by raging ants. He ran like the others, ran for his life.

When Leiningen heard this, he knew the plantation was doomed. He wasted no time bemoaning the inevitable. For as long as there was the slightest chance of success, he had stood his ground, and now any further resistance was both useless and dangerous. He fired three revolver shots into the air – the prearranged signal for his men to retreat instantly within the 'inner moat'. Then he rode towards the ranch house.

This was two miles from the point of invasion. There was therefore time enough to prepare the second line of defence against the advent of the ants. Of the three great petrol cisterns near the house, one had already been half emptied by the constant withdrawals needed for the pumps during the fight at the water ditch. The remaining petrol in it was now drawn off through underground pipes into the concrete trench which encircled the ranch house and its outbuildings.

And there, drifting in twos and threes, Leiningen's men reached him. Most of them were obviously trying to preserve an air of calm and indifference, belied, however by their restless glances and knitted brows. One could see their belief in a favourable outcome of the struggle was already considerably shaken.

The planter called his peons around him.

'Well, lads,' he began, 'we've lost the first round. But we'll smash the beggars yet, don't you worry. Anyone who thinks otherwise can draw his pay here and now and push off. There are rafts enough and to spare on the river and plenty of time still to reach 'em.'

Not a man stirred.

Leiningen acknowledged his silent vote of confidence with a laugh that was half a grunt. 'That's the stuff, lads. Too bad if you'd missed the rest of the show, eh? Well, the fun won't start till morning. Once these blighters turn tail, there'll be plenty of work for everyone and higher wages all round. And now run along and get something to eat; you've earned it all right.'

In the excitement of the fight the greater part of the day had passed without men once pausing to snatch a bite. Now that the ants were for the time being out of sight, and the 'wall of petrol' gave a stronger feeling of security, hungry stomachs began to assert their claims.

The bridges over the concrete ditch were removed. Here and there solitary ants had reached the ditch; they gazed at the petrol meditatively, then scurried back again. Apparently they had little interest at the moment for what lay beyond the evil-reeking barrier; the abundant spoils of the plantation were the main attraction. Soon the trees, shrubs, and beds for miles around were hulled with ants zealously gobbling the yield of long weary months of strenuous toil.

As twilight began to fall, a cordon of ants marched around the petrol trench, but as yet made no move towards its brink. Leiningen posted sentries with headlights and electric torches, then withdrew to his office, and began to reckon up his losses. He estimated these as large, but, in comparison with his bank balance, by no means unbearable. He worked out in some detail a scheme of intensive cultivation which would enable him, before very long, to more than compensate himself for the damage now being wrought to his crops. It was with a contented mind that he finally betook himself to bed where he slept deeply until dawn, undisturbed by any thought that next day little more might be left of him than a glistening skeleton.

He rose with the sun and went out on the flat roof of his house. And a scene like one from Dante lay around him; for miles in every direction there was nothing but a black, glittering multitude, a multitude of rested, sated, but none the less voracious ants: yes, look as far as one might, one could see nothing but that rustling black throng, except in the north, where the great river drew a boundary they could not hope to pass. But even the high stone breakwater, along the bank of the river, which Leiningen had built as a defence against inundations, was, like the paths, the shorn trees and shrubs, the ground itself, black with ants.

So their greed was not glutted in razing that vast plantation? Not by a long chalk; they were all the more eager now on a rich and certain booty – four hundred men, numerous horses, and bursting granaries.

At first it seemed that the petrol trench would serve its purpose. The besiegers sensed the peril of swimming it, and made no move to plunge blindly over its brink. Instead they devised a better manoeuvre; they began to collect shreds of bark, twigs, and dried leaves and dropped these into the petrol. Everything green, which could have been similarly used, had long since been eaten. After a time, though, a long procession could be seen bringing from the west the tamarind leaves used as rafts the day before.

Since the petrol, unlike the water in the outer ditch, was perfectly still, the refuse stayed where it was thrown. It was several hours before the ants succeeded in covering an appreciable part of the surface. At length, however, they were ready to proceed to a direct attack.

Their storm troops swarmed down the concrete side, scrambled over the supporting surface of twigs and leaves, and impelled these over the few remaining streaks of open petrol until they reached the other side. Then they began to climb up this to make straight for the helpless garrison.

During the entire offensive, the planter sat peacefully, watching them with interest, but not stirring a muscle. Moreover, he had ordered his men not to disturb in any way whatever the advancing horde. So they squatted listlessly along the bank of the ditch and waited for a sign from the boss.

The petrol was now covered with ants. A few had climbed the inner concrete wall and were scurrying towards the defenders.

'Everyone back from the ditch!' roared Leiningen. The men rushed away, without the slightest idea of his plan. He stooped forward and cautiously dropped into the ditch a stone which split the floating carpet and its living freight, to reveal a gleaming patch of petrol. A match spurted, sank down to the oily surface – Leiningen sprang back; in a flash a towering rampart of fire encompassed the garrison.

This spectacular and instant repulse threw the Indians into ecstasy. They applauded, yelled, and stamped, like children at a pantomime. Had it not been for the awe in which they held the boss, they would infallibly have carried him shoulder high.

It was some time before the petrol burned down to the bed of the ditch, and the wall of smoke and flame began to lower. The ants had retreated in a wide circle from the devastation, and innumerable charred fragments along the outer bank showed that the flames had spread from the holocaust in the ditch well into the ranks beyond, where they had wrought havoc far and wide.

Yet the perseverance of the ants was by no means broken; indeed, each set-back seemed only to whet it. The concrete cooled, the flicker of the dying flames wavered and vanished, petrol from the second tank poured into the trench – and the ants marched forward anew to the attack.

The foregoing scene repeated itself in every detail, except that on this occasion less time was needed to bridge the ditch, for the petrol was now already filmed by a layer of ash. Once again they withdrew; once again petrol flowed into the ditch. Would the creatures never learn that their self-sacrifice was utterly senseless? It really was senseless, wasn't it? Yes, of course it was senseless – provided the defenders had an *unlimited* supply of petrol.

When Leiningen reached this stage of reasoning, he felt for the first time since the arrival of the ants that his confidence was deserting him. His skin began to creep; he loosened his collar. Once the devils were over the trench there wasn't a chance in hell for him and his men. God, what a prospect, to be eaten alive like that!

For the third time the flames immolated the attacking troops, and burned down to extinction. Yet the ants were coming on again as if nothing had happened. And meanwhile Leiningen had made a discovery that chilled him to the bone – petrol was no longer flowing into the ditch. Something must be blocking the outflow pipe of the third and last cistern – a snake or a dead rat? Whatever it was, the ants could be held off no longer, unless petrol could by some method be led from the cistern into the ditch.

Then Leiningen remembered that in the outhouse near by were two old disused fire engines. Spry as never before in their lives, the peons dragged them out of the shed, connected their pumps to the cistern, uncoiled and laid the hose. They were just in time to aim a stream of petrol at a column of ants that had already crossed and drive them back down the incline into the ditch. Once more an oily girdle surrounded the garrison, once more it was possible to hold the position – for the moment.

It was obvious, however, that this last resource meant only the postponement of defeat and death. A few of the peons fell on their knees and began to pray; others, shrieking insanely, fired their revolvers at the black, advancing masses, as if they felt their despair was pitiful enough to sway fate itself to mercy.

At length, two of the men's nerves broke: Leiningen saw a naked Indian leap over the north side of the petrol trench, quickly followed by a second. They sprinted with incredible speed towards the river. But their fleetness did not save them; long before they could attain the rafts, the enemy covered their bodies from head to foot.

In the agony of their torment, both sprang blindly into the wide river, where enemies no less sinister awaited them. Wild screams of mortal anguish informed the breathless onlookers that crocodiles and sword-toothed piranhas were no less ravenous than ants, and even nimbler in reaching their prey.

In spite of this bloody warning, more and more men showed they were making up their minds to run the blockade. Anything, even a fight midstream against alligators, seemed better than powerlessly waiting for death to come and slowly consume their living bodies.

Leiningen flogged his brain till it reeled. Was there nothing on earth could sweep this devils' spawn back into the hell from which it came?

Then out of the inferno of his bewilderment rose a terrifying inspiration. Yes, one hope remained, and one alone. It might be possible to dam the great river completely so that its waters would fill not only the water ditch but overflow into the entire gigantic 'saucer' of land in which lay the plantation.

The far bank of the river was too high for the waters to escape that way. The stone breakwater ran between the river and the plantation; its only gaps occurred where the 'horseshoe' ends of the water ditch passed into the river. So its waters would not only be forced to inundate into the plantation, they would also be held there by the breakwater until they rose to its own level. In half an hour, perhaps even earlier, the plantation and its hostile army of occupation would be flooded.

The ranch house and outbuildings stood upon rising ground. Their foundations were higher than the breakwater, so the flood would not reach them. And any remaining ants trying to ascend the slope could be repulsed by petrol.

It was possible – yes, if one could only get to the dam! A distance of nearly two miles lay between the ranch house and the weir – two miles of ants. Those two peons had managed only a fifth of that distance at the cost of their lives. Was there an Indian daring enough after that to run the gauntlet five times as far? Hardly likely; and if there were, his prospect of getting back was almost nil.

No, there was only one thing for it, he'd have to make the attempt himself; he might just as well be running as sitting still, anyway, when the ants finally got him. Besides, there *was* a bit of a chance. Perhaps the ants weren't so almighty, after all; perhaps he had allowed the mass suggestion of that evil black throng to hypnotize him, just as a snake fascinates and overpowers.

The ants were building their bridges. Leiningen got up on a chair. 'Hey, lads, listen to me!' he cried. Slowly and listlessly, from all sides of the trench, the men began to shuffle towards him, the apathy of death already stamped on their faces.

'Listen, lads!' he shouted. 'You're frightened of those beggars, but you're a damn sight more frightened of me, and I'm proud of you. There's still a chance to save our lives – by flooding the plantation from the river. Now one of you might manage to get as far as the weir – but he'd never come back. Well, I'm not going to let you try it; if I did I'd be worse than one of those ants. No, I called the tune, and now I'm going to pay the piper.

'The moment I'm over the ditch, set fire to the petrol. That'll allow time for the flood to do the trick. Then all you have to do is to wait here all snug and quiet till I'm back. Yes, I'm coming back, trust me' – he grinned – 'when I've finished my slimming-cure.'

He pulled on high leather boots, drew heavy gauntlets over his hands, and stuffed the spaces between breeches and boots, gauntlets and arms, shirt and neck, with rags soaked in petrol. With close-fitting mosquito goggles he shielded his eyes, knowing too well the ants' dodge of first robbing their victim of sight. Finally, he plugged his nostrils and ears with cotton wool, and let the peons drench his clothes with petrol.

He was about to set off when the old Indian medicine man came up to him; he had a wondrous salve, he said, prepared from a species of chafer whose odour was intolerable to ants. Yes, this odour protected these chafers from the attacks of even the most murderous ants. The Indian smeared the boss's boots, his gauntlets, and his face over and over with the extract.

Leiningen then remembered the paralysing effect of ants' venom, and the Indian gave him a gourd full of the medicine he had administered to the bitten peon at the water ditch. The planter drank it down without noticing its bitter taste; his mind was already at the weir.

He started off towards the north-west corner of the trench. With a bound he was over – and among the ants.

The beleagured garrison had no opportunity to watch Leiningen's race against death. The ants were climbing the inner bank again – the lurid ring of petrol blazed aloft. For the fourth time that day the reflection from the fire shone on the sweating faces of the imprisoned men, and on the reddish-black cuirasses of their oppressors. The red and blue, dark-edged flames leaped vividly now, celebrating what? The funeral pyre of the four hundred, or of the hosts of destruction?

Leiningen ran. He ran in long, equal strides, with only one thought, one sensation, in his being – he *must* get through. He dodged all trees and shrubs; except for the split seconds his soles touched the ground the ants should have no opportunity to alight on him. That they would get to him soon, despite the salve on his boots, the petrol on his clothes, he realized only too well, but he knew even more surely that he must, and that he would, get to the weir.

Apparently the salve was some use after all; not until he had reached half way did he feel ants under his clothes, and a few on his face. Mechanically, in his stride, he struck at them, scarcely conscious of their bites. He saw he was drawing appreciably nearer the weir – the distance grew less and less – sank to five hundred – three – two – one hundred yards.

Then he was at the weir and gripping the ant-hulled wheel. Hardly had he seized it when a horde of infuriated ants flowed over his hands, arms, and shoulders. He started the wheel – before it turned once on its axis the swarm covered his face. Leiningen strained like a madman, his lips pressed tight; if he opened them to draw breath . . .

He turned and turned; slowly the dam lowered until it reached the bed of the river. Already the water was overflowing the ditch. Another minute, and the river was pouring through the nearby gap in the breakwater. The flooding of the plantation had begun.

Leiningen let go the wheel. Now, for the first time, he realized he was coated from head to foot with a layer of ants. In spite of the petrol, his clothes were full of them, several had got to his body or were clinging to his face. Now that he had completed his task, he felt the smart raging over his flesh from the bites of sawing and piercing insects.

Frantic with pain, he almost plunged into the river. To be ripped and slashed to shreds by piranhas? Already he was running the return journey, knocking ants from his gloves and jacket, brushing them from his bloodied face, squashing them to death under his clothes.

One of the creatures bit him just below the rim of his goggles; he managed to tear it away, but the agony of the bite and its etching acid drilled into the eye nerves; he saw now through circles of fire into a milky mist, then he ran for a time almost blinded, knowing that if he once tripped and fell . . . The old Indian's brew didn't seem much good; it weakened the poison a bit, but didn't get rid of it. His heart pounded as if it would burst; blood roared in his ears; a giant's fist battered his lungs.

Then he could see again, but the burning girdle of petrol appeared infinitely far away; he could not last half the distance. Swift-changing pictures flashed through his head, episodes in his life, while in another part of his brain a cool and impartial onlooker informed this ant-blurred, gasping, exhausted bundle named Leiningen that such a rushing panorama of scenes from one's past is seen only in the moment before death.

A stone in the path . . . too weak to avoid it . . . the planter stumbled and collapsed. He tried to rise . . . He must be pinned under a rock . . . it was impossible . . . the slightest movement was impossible . . .

Then all at once he saw, starkly clear and huge, and, right before his eyes, furred with ants, towering and swaying in its death agony, the pampas stag. In six minutes – gnawed to the bones. God, he *couldn't* die like that! And something outside him seemed to drag him to his feet. He tottered. He began to stagger forward again.

Through the blazing ring hurtled an apparition which, as soon as it reached the ground on the inner side, fell full length and did not move. Leiningen, at the moment he made that leap through the flames, lost consciousness for the first time in his life. As he lay there, with glazing eyes and lacerated face, he appeared a man returned from the grave. The peons rushed to him, stripped off his clothes, tore away the ants from a body that seemed almost one open wound; in some places the bones were showing. They carried him into the ranch house.

As the curtain of flames lowered, one could see, in place of the illimitable host of ants, an extensive vista of water. The thwarted river had swept over the plantation, carrying with it the entire army. The water had collected and mounted in the great 'saucer', while the ants had in vain attempted to reach the hill on which stood the ranch house. The girdle of flames held them back.

And so, imprisoned between water and fire, they had been delivered into the annihilation that was their god. And near the farther mouth of the water ditch, where the stone mole had its second gap, the ocean swept the lost battalions into the river, to vanish for ever.

The ring of fire dwindled as the water mounted to the petrol trench, and quenched the dimming flames. The inundation rose higher and higher: because its outflow was impeded by the timber and underbrush it had carried along with it, its surface required some time to reach the top of the high stone breakwater and discharge over it the rest of the shattered army.

It swelled over ant-stippled shrubs and bushes, until it washed against the foot of the knoll whereon the besieged had taken refuge. For a while an alluvium of ants tried again and again to attain this dry land, only to be repulsed by streams of petrol back into the merciless flood.

Leiningen lay on his bed, his body swathed from head to foot in bandages. With fomentations and salves, they had managed to stop the bleeding, and had dressed his many wounds. Now they thronged around him, one question in every face. Would he recover? 'He won't die,' said the old man who had bandaged him, 'if he doesn't want to.'

The planter opened his eyes. 'Everything in order?' he asked.

'They're gone,' said his nurse. 'To hell.' He held out to his master a gourd full of a powerful sleeping-draught. Leiningen gulped it down.

'I told you I'd come back,' he murmured, 'even if I am a bit streamlined.' He grinned and shut his eyes. He slept.

The Brink of Darkness

Yvor Winters

Late in October the first snow had come, large heavy flakes with shaggy edges, far apart, moving down in vast circles from a soft sky. The trees in the orchard outside the window of the dining-room were hard and cold, and shone like smooth rock against the earth and the colourless air. And the big rough flakes moved cautiously among them, here and there, as if exploring the terrain. There was a slight flurry, and the flakes gathered faster; then followed flurry upon flurry, a few moments apart, a steady slow pulsation, and with each the air was whiter and darker; till at last, the flurries coming imperceptibly closer and closer together, the air was an unbroken sheet of snow through which one could hardly move, the flakes were small and quick, and darkness, amid the confusion, had superseded twilight.

During the winter months the snow had lain deep over the rounded hills, and I had gone out on skis with my two Airedales. The clouds were of a soft even grey, and they seemed to have no lower edges, so that the sky had no identity – there was merely the soft air. The snow merged into the air from below with no visible dividing line. Often I should not have known whether I was going uphill or down, had it not been for the pull of gravity and the visible inclination of the skis. Often I came to the top of a rise and started down with no warning save the change in speed, or arrived at the bottom of a hill with no warning save the sudden slowing. I could travel for miles and see only one or two houses. Sometimes a mouse appeared, floundering as if in heavy air, and the dogs would lunge clumsily after it, snap it up, and drop it dead, leaving a small spot of blood suspended in greyness; but the few rabbits were better equipped and evaded them.

Once I passed a small pen made of chicken-wire, behind a barn, a pen in which there were fifteen or eighteen yearling coyotes. The farmers often captured the cubs during the spring ploughing, and kept them into the next winter in order to slaughter them for the fur. These were about ready for killing. They swung in a group to the fence as I passed, lifting the foreparts of their bodies swiftly and gently, to drop them precisely facing, their shoulders flat, the front legs straight and close together, the wide sharp ears erect, the narrow little noses examining the air detail by detail. It was strange that they never broke through so slight a fence, yet there they were; young dogs would have torn through it with scarcely a pause, scarcely the sense of an obstacle. But these creatures were innocent and delicate, spirits impeded by a spell, puffs of smoke precise at the tips. As I passed, they turned their heads, watching me, then moved away and apart, to lie down in the snow or crawl under their small shelter. They had been the only sign of life amid four hours of snow, and they had made no sound. They had focused upon me for a moment their changing, shadowy curiosity, and then had been dissipated as if by the quiet of the hills.

I remembered the preceding fall. The three of us, myself and the Stones, had been puzzled by the luminosity of the stubble at night. On the slope south of the house, even on moonless nights, it had a curious glow, a kind of phosphorescence, that appeared to light the air for a few inches above the ground and then to stop suddenly. When the moon was full, the glow for several feet above the fields was so dense that the eye could scarcely penetrate to the ground. At a definite level above the field the glow stopped suddenly, and one could look for miles through watery moonlight over hills that seemed smothered in soft fire. The dogs, running through the fire, below the height of visibility, were dark vortices, blurred and shapeless, stirring rapidly in the motionless flame. Above the roof of the house, in the cold nights of late autumn, Orion, the Pleiades, and all the bright powder of the northern heaven, moved steadily from east to west; and the Great Dipper, low to the north, with few stars near it, its large stars plain and heavy, moved with an equal and compensatory pace from west to east and slipped in behind one of the hills.

In spite of the bright autumn and the shadowy winter, the village had been an unbearable blaze of heat in June. The winter wheat, which had germinated and grown eight or ten inches high under the snow, had shot up prodigiously in the spring warmth. The round hills were green, for even the spring crop was well along. The tall elms were in leaf; the apricot orchard about the house was heavy and dark; each tree was a black void growing shadowy and visible at the edges. The summer beat on the ground with no motion. The two white goats across the road lay panting in the shade, trembling watery blotches, barely discernible.

Once the Stones went up into the mountains for the afternoon, taking me with them. The mountains were only ten miles back of the village, and on the way we stopped at a farm owned by Mr Stone and leased to a family of Seventh Day Adventists. The Stones wanted to get the girl of the family to come and help with the housework. She came to the gate with a shovel and a bucket as we drove up, a tall coarse-boned person, somewhere between twenty-five and thirty-five, with sharply drooping and very long shoulders and a small face, snub-nosed and almost featureless, her mouth open. She looked like one who had been intensely preoccupied, and who had discovered us suddenly. She was sweaty and had dust on her clothes and was visibly panting. She promised to come.

During January and the first week in February, the weather was extremely cold. The kitchen range was red hot, and so was the stove in the dining-room, but the corners of the rooms were never warm enough, and in the halls you could always see your breath. I kept my stove on the second floor as hot as I dared, and I usually sat up till one and two in the morning to keep the fire from dying down, for no bed-clothes were adequate. One night the mercury fell to sixty below zero. During this cold spell Mrs Stone took to her bed, become suddenly very weak. She had always been frail; it appeared now that out of humility and consideration for others she had been concealing her weakness till she had arrived at the point where concealment was impossible. Her strength ebbed very rapidly, and as the cold began to grow less savage, she suddenly died.

The undertakers were not allowed to remove her body from the house, for she had not wished it. They came and went. The nurse, a tall, grey-haired woman, asked me to bed the dogs in the barn for a few nights, for the body was to be placed in the hall at the foot of the stairs. The casket was wheeled in, when the undertakers had gone, a soft grey affair, with some sort of lacy material supported above it and dropping away on either side in the form of a tent. From within came the heavy odour of hot-house flowers; as the casket moved, the slight stiff shifting of the body was just visible through the curtain.

Asa Stone, who lived on a neighbouring farm, took his father away for the night. The old man, in spite of his bulk, seemed shrunken; his face, pale and lifeless, fell away in heavy lines, and he seldom looked up. Asa led him by the arm to keep him from stumbling.

A neighbour woman came in to sit up with the nurse and myself. The three of us went into the hall and drew back the curtain from the casket. She was dressed in white, her head surrounded by lilies of the valley, her hair, in spite of her sixty years, pure black against the flowers. As we moved the casket a little, there was again the slight stiff shifting of the body. The face was very firm. The jaw was strong, almost too strong for a woman, had it not seemed a strength employed to achieve gentleness. The mouth, wide in proportion to the jaw, suggested her slight smile, but it was not smiling. It was finished. It seemed to have come to an ultimate balance, to have found itself. We dropped the curtain and returned to the dining-room.

Towards morning I went upstairs to lie down for a few hours, for I had to teach during the day. I came down about seven, passed the coffin in the first grey of the dawn, moved through the motionless cold, which seemed to be gathering heavier about it and which was somehow identified with the thin sweet odour, perhaps the odour of death, perhaps of the flowers, of which the casket itself, with its frosty tent, might have been the visible core.

At noon I returned. As I opened the door into the darkened hall, the casket awaited me, the sweet odour deepening on the still air. I was a trifle sickened; it affected me like the smell of ether. I had lunch and returned to my teaching. The casket awaited me in the darkness at five o'clock. In the dining-room the two women were talking and sometimes laughing as they got supper ready. I went up to my room and lay down but could not sleep. I was beginning to shudder a little as I passed the body, yet it was not from fear of the dead. The ghost, if she stood there waiting beside the body, fixing in memory the house in which she had lived for so many years and which she must now leave forever, was too patient, too gentle, to be feared. The thought of her inexpressible solitude filled me with pity.

On the morning after the third night the family began to gather for the funeral. Alvin, the younger son, and his wife, were the first to come, their features obscured with sorrow. Asa and Clara came with Mr Stone between them; the children would be brought over later. Asa's features were those of his mother, but somehow smaller and harder, and with none of her serenity. He was a man who was seldom still for long, who seemed to know little of peace, whether of body or of spirit.

Asa and Clara moved the casket into the parlour and took away the veil. Soon the florist arrived, and I helped him bank the flowers.

In the kitchen there were coffee and a light breakfast for those who needed them. I went out for a cup of coffee. As I entered the kitchen, the Adventist girl from the country came in, her great awkward shoulders drooping and swinging as she moved, her eyes red. Her brother came behind her. He had been deformed from birth. He was over six feet tall, a man of great power and agility, but without forearms; where his elbows should have been, there were thick, red, wrinkled wrists, and on each wrist there were two long red fingers without nails. His nose was long and coarse, and his voice was nasal. To make up for the shortness of his arms, he had developed violent but agile motions of the upper body; doing even the simplest things, he seemed the victim of some unhappy and uncontrollable agitation. He was a teamster by trade, when he had time from his farm, and he often worked for Asa. His abnormality had made him an exile from human society, and as a result he had acquired an unusual sympathy for horses and mules, with whom he could accomplish extraordinary things, and that part of his nature which was not satisfied by this companionship had turned to religion. When driving a team, he sang in a loud nasal drone, almost devoid of variation, hymns which he intended merely to quiet his own spirit, but which, on a still day, could be heard among the hills for a mile or more. He sat at the kitchen table now, as I drank my coffee, his large bony trunk darting suddenly this way and that, his wrinkled fingers squirming about a piece of bread or a knife, his sharp mouth dropping pious ejaculations between swallows. 'Eli can sure talk religion,' Asa had once said of him with admiration.

At the church I sat with the family, in a private room to the side of the pulpit. After the sermon I looked once more into the casket. The black hair seemed not to have stirred. The face was not heavily wrinkled, but there were a few small wrinkles about the mouth and eyes. The skin was preternaturally and evenly white, and in the wrinkles there seemed a trace as of an underlying darkness, even and impenetrable. At the grave, a mile and a half outside of town, the ceremonies were brief, for a vile sleet had set in. The coffin was lowered; the last prayer was read; and the grave was filled with stones and mud. As we drove away, I looked back to see a huge mound of hot-house flowers, dark heavy green, and clear hard white and yellow, lying as if murdered in the colourless air, beneath driving sleet.

That afternoon Alvin and Asa began moving the furniture from the lower part of the house. Two days later they had finished. I was to keep my rooms in the upper part till the house should be sold, since there were only a few months left till the summer vacation. The old man would stay with Alvin. That was late in February. A few days later another heavy freeze set in.

I made no attempt to keep the lower part of the house warm, although I had to use it occasionally. It was absolutely bare. Even the curtains and window-blinds were gone, and when I went down to the kitchen at night for a glass of water, or crossed the parlour and kitchen to reach the basement for coal, I moved through a naked glare of electric light, with wide bare windows on two sides of me, my feet echoing, my hands stiff with the cold. I came to see myself moving in this room, as if from the outside, and I sometimes wondered who I was. When I came home at dusk from teaching and entered the lower hall, I thought I could still feel the earthly cloud at its centre. Sometimes my flesh went chill. i came gradually to carry more and more coal upstairs every morning, and soon I was getting enough to last me through the night. Upstairs were the dogs and the stove; below was the echoing desolation.

During the three nights that Mrs Stone had lain below me in the hall, my sensitivity to death, to the obscure and the irrelevant, had been augmented. I felt that I saw farther and farther into the events about me, that I perceived a new region of significance, even of sensation, extending a short distance behind that of which I had always been aware, suggesting the existence of far more than was even now perceptible. This might have unnerved me had it not been for the firmness of the woman in the coffin. In her were united the familiar and the inchoate. The certainty of her expression gave me pause. She was like a friend bidding me be quiet with raised hand, a friend whose bidding I could trust to be authoritative. But with her departure there remained only the demonic silence which she had introduced, and to which for three nights she had given coherence and a meaning.

The dogs, large and unkempt, a mother and her son, were old enough to enjoy spending most of their time on my bed in the cold weather. When I came up the stairs, they would be waiting, their heads on their paws, their faces expressing an identical gentle question. I had kept their bed in another room at first, but the cold had forced me to close the room, and I was glad enough to have the two sleep with me. The field mice from round about were invading the empty building in greater and greater numbers. They were too quick for the dogs at close quarters, especially on the second floor, where there was still a good deal of furniture. The mice lost all fear, and the dogs no longer disturbed them, but would lie still for half an hour, regarding the scratching, shadowy little creatures with indifferent curiosity or remote amusement. During the first week in March, while the cold spell still endured, the dogs did not come one morning when I called them as I was about to leave the house. Nor did they come the next day nor the next. I knew well enough what had happened, and I would not have been greatly troubled had it not been for the weather and a few porcupines in a small wood lot several miles away. Every afternoon I walked over the hills, trying to get a sight of them on the snow. A light snow had fallen after their going, and their tracks had been covered. I did not know how long it might take them to find their way in from among the hills. Here and there a farmer had seen them. They had been living for several days on the offal of a slaughtered calf and had been sleeping in haystacks. Several farmers had tried to catch them for me, but the dogs were powerful, and, when in trouble, as suspicious and nearly as dangerous as wolves. They seemed to be moving in a wide circle, which I gradually mapped, but on which I never intercepted them. If I didn't meet them, at least it was only a question of time till they would pick up my trail and follow me in. The hills were a cold thin blue, darker where the wind had riffled the snow and the earth showed through, their edges definite against the sky with a cold hair-line precision. There were no clouds, and as I returned home at dusk, a few small white stars appearing, the sky stood above me unvaulted, a steely grey, without distance or dimension.

While the dogs were gone, I spent as much of my nights as I could in reading, and when I could no longer read, I took to watching the mice. At first they had seemed to me uncanny, but gradually I came to be fond of them. I put out food for them, and sometimes a dish of milk. With their food they were likely to be boisterous, snatching it and running off, or throwing it about in play if they were not hungry; with their drink they were delicate and gentle, advancing to the rim of the saucer like far-away gazelles, the natives of this dissolving wilderness, their feet as sensitive as ants, their round eyes rolling quickly this way and that.

One night after I had been watching the mice without moving for nearly an hour, I got up suddenly and went downstairs for a glass of water. The sound of my feet rang out with tremendous volume as I descended the stair; as I crossed the glare of the front room, the echo seemed to resound from the room above, as if I were walking up there. I stood still to quiet the noise. I was alone and erect, a few feet from the broad window, bright emptiness behind me. The light from the window fell on the snow outside. It had been warm enough at noon for a slight glaze to form. The shape of the light on the glaze was sharp-edged and clear. Only, at the upper left-hand corner of the window there was darkness, a tangle of withered vines outside. I stared at the smooth surface of the snow thus suddenly revealed to me, like a new meaning not divisible into any terms I knew. Again I had the illusion of seeing myself in the empty room, in the same light, frozen to my last footprints, cold and unmeaning. A slight motion caught my eye, and I glanced up at the darkened corner of the window to be fixed with horror. There, standing on the air outside the window, translucent, a few lines merely, and scarcely visible, was a face, my face, the eyes fixed upon my own. I moved on quickly to the kitchen; the reflection started and vanished.

The next morning, upon reaching my office, I heard of the catastrophe of the night before. One of my students, the son of one of my colleagues, a boy who was to have graduated this spring but who had been confined to the pest-house with meningitis, had, in the night, while no nurse was present, been seized with delirium, had leapt from his bed and escaped from the door of the hospital in his night-clothes. He had run the four blocks separating the hospital and his home, had broken a window and climbed in. An hour later, at midnight, his parents had returned, to find him sitting before a smouldering fireplace in an icy house, moaning to be taken to his room. He had never regained consciousness; before morning he was dead.

There was another funeral in the Presbyterian church. This time the coffin was kept closed, from respect for the disease. The coffin was banked high behind and on either end with yellow chrysanthemums. The boy's fraternity came in a body, twenty and some boys, seated in two front rows at one side, looking curiously young and helpless before the coffin. The waxen petals of the chrysanthemums glowed in the dusk of the church; they seemed almost to move, curling and uncurling ever so little. There was something innocent and pathetic about the flowers, these earthy blossoms, cut clean from the ground from which they had struggled, foaming dimly, still dimly alive in the gloom, struggling imperceptibly, curling imperceptibly inward, as if they were the sluggish dead incarnate, dying slowly again in pity, returning numbly to the earth.

At the end of four days, towards nightfall, the bitch returned, emaciated and limping, her head and throat, inside and out, completely covered with quills, her mouth forced open with the mass of them, her tongue hanging out, swollen, and white with quills as far back as I could see. I was prepared for this kind of return. I held her and poured vinegar over the entire wounded area, to soften the quills. She screamed, but lay still. Had it been the other dog, I would have sent for help and for morphine; I knew that morphine would only make the bitch stupidly savage without calming her, even in doses so large as to be dangerous. I sat astride her body, letting my entire weight fall on her ribs to hold her down. She tossed this way and that, screaming, her mouth foaming with blood. It was strange how the things wedged themselves into the cartilage: sometimes I had to pull several times before I could loosen one, and it would come out followed by a gush of blood. The light on the floor was poor and the work was hard; at the end of two hours I was exhausted almost to numbness.

The bitch was panting and weak; sometimes she moaned feebly; the floor was spattered with blood for three or four feet around; but she was clean of visible quills, and few seemed to have buried themselves. I washed her with disinfectant, poured a drink of warmish water into her mouth, and turned her loose. She staggered feebly to her feet and walked over and lay down on the rug behind the stove. The inner surface of her mouth was devoid of membrane, was a bloody pulp, and her head was a clotting spongy mass. It had happened before, and she would survive it; we both of us knew it; she moved her tail feebly, and then cautiously laid her head on her paws. In the morning some boys led the other dog in staggering; they had found him late the night before in the same condition as the bitch, and had taken him to a veterinary before bringing him home.

For the next week most of my free time was spent in nursing the dogs; my bed cover and my rugs were stained with blood; the corners of the room accumulated deeper and deeper dust; the dust lay under the bed in soft whorls; I was busy and very tired and slowly lost the habit of noticing. Once near the end of March, some friends of the Stones from the next town stopped by to see the old man. I explained his absence, and asked them in for a cup of coffee. They came in dubiously, a tall silent old farmer and his grey small wife, the two of them troubled by the combination of my books, of my general affability, and of the dire squalor in which I lived. The dogs sniffed them curiously, extending their raw and scabious heads, and I sent them back to the bed. The old people finally took their leave with great formality.

During the first week in April, Alvin appeared at the door to say that the house had been sold and that the new owner wished to take possession as soon as possible. I arranged for the room across the street and began to move at once. A Chinook had begun the day before Alvin's appearance and continued for three days; it was the last thaw of the season. On most of the hills the winter wheat was already high, and the hills lay green as the snow vanished. Far across the valley I could hear the puffing of a tractor, and now and then I could see the tiny iron thing crawling rapidly in straight lines across the hills, appearing and disappearing suddenly and in unlikely ways, leaving black earth behind.

Now my belongings were moved, and I would stay in the new house until early June. My new landlord was a teamster with seven children and a tired wife. I should not be with them long enough to become acquainted. The children swarming about the little house bothered me, but I liked them well enough in a way; they were a part of the season. Just outside my door was an old phonograph, which one of the older girls played incessantly. The grass was already green under my new window; the trees were in bud; the two white goats would kid in a week, and the kids, bloody and tottering at first, would be within a few days leaping here and there in the cold shadows, balancing and spinning on a single foot, front or rear, it mattered little, nipping buds they would not care to eat, trying to make friends with the dogs, to the patient embarrassment of the dogs and the consternation of their mothers.

I thought back over the past months, of the manner in which I had been disturbed, uncentred, and finally obsessed as by an insidious power. I remembered that I had read somewhere of a kind of Eastern demon who gains power over one only in proportion as one recognizes and fears him. I felt that I had been the victim of a deliberate and malevolent invasion, an invasion utilizing and augmenting to appalling and shadowy proportions all of the most elusive accidents of my life, my new penumbra of perception thus rendering to what would otherwise have appeared the contingent the effect of coherent and cumulative meaning. Finally, through some miscalculation on the part of the invader, or through some other accident, I had begun to recover the limits of my old identity. I had begun this recovery at the time of the immersion in the brute blood of the bitch. The invading power I could not identify. I felt it near me still, but slowly receding.

I got up from where I sat and stretched myself out in the sun. I was minutely aware of my movements, my inclinations, my bodily functions. I could not blink my eyes without being conscious of the darkness; I knew I was tired. It was as if there were darkness evenly underlying the brightness of the air, underlying everything, as if I might slip suddenly into it at any instant, and as if I held myself where I was by an act of the will from moment to moment. From far over the hills I heard a low snoring drone, rising and falling, as if it came from a lonely bull in a far pasture. A quick and powerful team, four abreast, and drawing a wheel plough, came over the rise at the distance of a quarter of a mile. The plough came down the slope swiftly and started around the base of the hill to circle slowly upwards again, the horses arching and rippling, the driver bending forwards and moving rapidly here and there to urge them on. From the sound and from the strange movements of the driver, I recognized Eli. I lay back and closed my eyes. The sun poured steadily into me. In a month I should be leaving for Colorado. I would never return.

Activity Time

Monica Dickens

There it was again. Thump! on the end of the trailer, followed by a giggle and another thump right by the head of his bed. That crude young couple in Number 23 South coming home from the bar and trying to scare him as he lay hoping for sleep in Number 21.

Neighbours. When he sold the house after his wife died, and moved upstate into a rented trailer in Canalside Mobilehome Park, Dick had thought that he was finished with the aggravation of them. No lawn for their dogs to run over; no hedge for their children to trample down, taking a short cut to school; no windows to be splattered with eggs or marked with soap on Hallowe'en night.

Canalside Park, which nestled by one of the huge stone abutments under the soaring span of the bridge, should be more secure. He had spoken to his landlord about the crude couple, and the landlord, who laughed at everything, had laughed and said, 'Open the window and pour boiling water on them.' But all the trailer windows were fastened shut for the winter.

Since the angina attack, Dick had hardly been out in this terrible winter when snow had fallen for three days and now lay about the trailer park in dirty lumps. He had sold his car when his eyes got bad, and he could not ride his bicycle. His doctor had arranged, just for this winter – he was no deadbeat Welfare customer – for him to have Meals on Wheels. Every weekday, a dirty white Volkswagen crunched on the icy cinders, and Dick quickly let down the curtain, so Rosemary would not know he had been watching for her.

Rosemary was a Scottish girl with bright cheeks and raspberry lipstick, and a way of laying the containers of food on the flap table in his tiny kitchen as if she were setting out a banquet.

'What have you brought me today?' He knew what it was, because she brought him a menu at the beginning of the month. The fish was dreadful. The chicken had often seen better days. She would wait while he turned back the cover of the foil dish, so that he could say, 'Swiss steak! I thought that kind of stuff only went into dog food.'

'Hoo, come on now, Dick,' she would say in her soft Scottish voice.

'Why do they always think old people want to eat carrots?'

'Hoo, come on, Dick. I'll pop it in the wee toaster oven, so it'll be ready when you want it.'

'While you're here, will you look at my ankle?' He tried to make Rosemary stay, and although she had a dozen customers to visit in the dirty little car, she would refasten his elastic bandage, or turn the mattress, or sew on a button before she hurried away with, 'See you tomorrow.'

She was usually the only person he did see. He showed her the knick-knacks he and Alice had collected on vacations, and could not resist giving her a little mug from Aberdeen, South Dakota, to remind her of her homeland.

Rosemary was going to have a baby, but not yet. She would last him out the winter. One Friday, however, when she brought him his sliced beef and noodles, with the salad and jelly in styrofoam bowls and a piece of cornbread so neatly wrapped, she said, 'I won't be coming any more. The doctor says no more driving.'

'The baby? But surely –'

'It's twins.' She pulled a funny face. 'I've to be careful they're not born too soon.'

'Who will bring the meals to me?' As he said it, he heard the selfishness of not first asking, 'Are you all right?', but it was too late, because she was answering, 'There's a nice new volunteer, and not in any danger of having a baby, ha ha.'

She bent to stroke the old white cat, pulled her hand away when she saw the sores it had scratched on itself, and patted Dick on the shoulder. 'I'll bring the twins to see you,' she said as she went out with her raspberry coloured smile, and he said, 'You do that, dear,' although he knew she never would.

She had brought him an extra can of stew and an orange, which his stiff fingers could not peel. At weekends, Annette from 16 West brought in his few groceries, and came across the snow and mud with a plate of Sunday dinner and a piece of pie. Her food was not good – even worse than Meals on Wheels – but it pleased her to do this, so he put up with it.

'Another poor creature gone off the bridge,' she told him this Sunday when she brought the pot roast.

'That's three jumpers since October.' Dick kept a tally of the feckless, cowardly people who launched themselves into eternity from the arching span of the canal bridge, high above him. 'As long as they don't fall on my roof.'

The new volunteer was never quite on time. Rosemary was like a clock, but now Dick waited longer at the window for Florence's wide old blue car with the rust patches.

When he complained, she said, 'There's folks worse off than you that need my time.'

Florence was wide, like her car, a comfortably shaped woman smelling of cheap lavender, her short black hair turning white in patches. Alice's thick hair had been snow white, like the cat. The thing she minded most about the brain tumour operation was having a large chunk of hair shaved. If she had known she was going to die on the table, she need not have fussed.

Florence had been a nurse. 'I know how to make an old gentleman comfortable.' If he was not well enough to get up, she would go at him with her strong rounded arms, and plump up his pillows, and from his bed in the space across the end of the trailer, he could see her fluffing up the settee cushions and dusting things off with a wad of paper towel.

He wanted to show her Alice's picture, but the little photograph in the silver frame was not in its place on the bureau.

'More years you gain, more things you lose,' Florence said. But there began to be other things missing – a carved salt spoon from Vermont, the spotted china dog from Gettysburg. Dick did not feel well. His appetite had gone off, and he began to think there was something wrong with the food. He gave most of it to the old cat.

On Monday, instead of giving Florence the seventy-five cents in an envelope, as he had with Rosemary, he mumbled that he could not manage it this week.

'Think nothing of it,' she said, but he had nothing to do but think, and the thoughts grew more confused.

He stayed long in bed, and went in and out of dreams. One afternoon, with a lowering sun gilding the stone bridgework, he awoke in fright and pain and vomited. So. She was not only a thief, but a poisoner as well.

When he had collected enough breath, he rolled out of the low bed, staggered into the kitchen and picked up the cat's dish. Thank God it had not eaten any of this morning's meat loaf. Elder Services still had not put in his phone, so he put a sweater and overcoat over his pyjama jacket, and boots over the trousers, and shambled through the fading light to the pay phone in the laundry.

There were a couple of women in there. There were always women in there, eternally feeding or emptying the rotating drums. They looked at him without recognition and went on with their talking and folding.

When a woman answered at Elder Services, he told her right away, no beating about the bush: 'Complaint against the new Wheels on Meals woman . . . Things missing in my home. I strongly suspect . . . And the food's gone off. I'm scared.' He heard his voice grow shrill. 'She'll steal the money, you know. It's not right to put elderly people –'

'Excuse me.' The woman cut into his rising voice. 'I think you have the wrong number. This is Bayside Auto Parts.'

'Oh, damn.' He was looking in his pocket for another dime to try and dial the right number, but he heard the women giggling and whispering, so he let it go.

He was in the kitchen next morning when Florence stumped up the steps, put her basket on the table, thrust her fists into the pockets of the tomato red coat which flared over her wide hips and said, 'It's turkey with all the fixings. Now complain about *that*!'

But he had not complained. Or had he? He never got through. Or did he? She was not only a thief and a poisoner, but a mind-bedeviller as well.

When she left, the cat was by the door, and she shooed it out into the icy rain.

'No, don't.' Dick was letting the old cat use a litter box.

'Nonsense,' Florence said briskly. 'Good for him to run.'

By nightfall, the cat had not come back. Dick had managed to fall asleep when – thump! He started awake, got himself out of bed and somehow through the trailer, hanging on to furniture, dragged open the door and shouted into the night, 'God damn you!'

A faraway laugh. The woman's voice. Slam of a metal trailer door. Very faint, the woman's voice again. Or was it a cat mewing?

'Kippy! Kippy!' He stood on the top step in the rain. Nothing. The trailers slept in rows. The bridge stood sentinel.

When the car stopped outside next morning, he was upright on the settee, fully dressed in jacket and trousers, alert, though his heart was twanging.

As the door opened, he began, 'Now look here –'

A tall young man in a yellow oilskin stepped in, filling the trailer with his loose-jointed presence. 'Sorry I'm late. It took me a while to –'

'Where's Florence?'

'Who?'

'Brought me my meals.'

'Rosemary? Well . . .' He sketched a mound in front of him.

'No, no.' The boy was daft. 'The woman since her.'

'Dunno. I took over Rosemary's route. Gotta go.'

He dumped down the foil dish and bowls. Clumsy in the small kitchen, he stumbled on his way to the door. 'Oops – sorry.' He bent to pick up something. 'Clean break. I'll bring glue tomorrow.' Dick was left staring at the two halves of the missing china dog from Gettysburg.

A long while later, he was able to stand up. After some difficulty with the sleeves, he put on his coat and went out. Amid all the confusion and lies and wavery thoughts he could not pin down, one fact came clear to the front of his mind. He had heard the cat mewing last night.

The rain had lashed itself into a full-blown storm. Walking about between the trailers, he strained to hear the mewing again, but the wind made too much noise in the trees. Soaking wet, his thin hair plastered against his chilled face, he walked out to the road where the cars swished past, expecting to see a flattened body, its insides already washed away. Distraught, he wandered to the bank of the canal, where small ice floes bumped about in the tide that swirled out under the bridge to the open bay – carrying the cat's body with it? High above him on the lighted bridge, a tiny figure walked by the rail. *Go on then, damn you – jump!*

Wet through, shivering, he somehow got himself back to the laundry room, and found the number of the local vet.

'. . . to ask if anyone reported a dead or injured cat. What? Yes. Pure white.'

'A white cat.' The vet's voice was young and confident. 'Someone did bring in an old one yesterday to be put down. None too soon.'

'Who? Who brought it?'

'The owner, I suppose.'

'What she –' Dick's voice was a hoarse whisper. 'What she look –'

'I don't remember. Woman in a red coat.'

Whether he hung up the phone or let it drop, he never afterwards knew. Whether he ever made the call to the vet, he was not sure. He was not sure of anything. Times were out of joint. Things that hadn't yet happened had already happened. While he was in the Intensive Care Unit, wired up fore and aft, he need not struggle to make sense of the confusion. When Annette from 16 West came with a harried face, she brought him Alice's photograph.

'I thought she stole it.'

'Who? I found it behind the bureau when I was cleaning up a bit. Give me a fright, you taking a heart attack.'

'It was the cat. When the cat died –'

'What do you mean, cat died?' Thinking she spoke too loud, Annette glanced round the unit, where wired and tubed bodies lay sacrificially on high beds, and the nurses moved like silent priestesses in the central glass booth where they received the messages of the bodies. 'He's hale and hearty. I found him outside your door, and I'm in to feed him every day and clean his litter box.'

Dick struggled to sit up, eyes staring, breath rasping. One of the priestesses put a hand on his chest, and he fell back through the pillows into a wide black hole which welcomed him as the black waters of the canal welcomed the jumpers.

The hospital was a limbo, not needing organized thought, which was becoming difficult. They kept congratulating him on doing well enough to be discharged.

'I'd rather –'

But the social worker had it all arranged. Jokey, considerate ambulance men, extensions of the reassuring hospital staff, took him across the bridge to Fairview Nursing Home and wheeled him into a small room with a fair view of a high slatted fence with dead Christmas wreaths hanging on its pointed tops like severed heads.

The private room was expensive, but it was only a few weeks, and he had money in the bank from the sale of the house. Across the corridor, an old man shrieked and hooted, and another old man cursed him with a foul tongue. The cusser was called John, and when their doors were left open at night Dick could see him struggling in his sleep, as if in continual conflict with some nightmare opponent.

The food was even worse than in the hospital. When Annette came, he asked her to bring him a Sunday dinner. She brought tough chicken and buttered corn, which he spilled on his lap rug, and the Administrator marched in with the dictum: Against State Law to bring in food.

'Get me out of here.' Dick tried his feet on the floor, found they would not take weight, and returned them to the foot rests before Annette noticed.

'I don't know.' She wore her harried face. 'They stopped me on the way in and told me to try to explain to you what the doctor said. Remember the letter to the lawyer I helped you to sign, dear? He's cancelling the trailer rental, as you agreed.'

'Who agreed? They forged my signature. You did it. I must go back. What about the cat?'

'Remember, dear, I told you. I had to have him put to sleep, his sores were so bad, and that nice young vet said, "None too soon." '

'Murderess.' He spat at her.

'That's it.' Annette stood up. 'I've tried to help, but I'll not come here to be insulted.'

'Don't.' Dick was so angry that he almost managed to stand up. He pushed against the arms of the wheelchair; it shot backwards, and when he collapsed he would have fallen, if Annette had not caught him in her treacherous arms. Hanging limply, he stared at the arm across his chest in the cranberry red coat sleeve.

Spring came, and summer, and in the fall, when the brown leaves blew in drifts against the fence where the wreaths still hung, the Administrator told him that since his money had run out and he was now on a lower fee as a Medicaid patient, he would go into a threesome room as soon as a bed was available.

'I won't.'

'Come along, old feller. Activity time.' A new nurse wheeled him to the dining room, where the bodies were ranged around the walls. Had she heard him? Speaking was getting more difficult all the time. Trying to say, 'I won't,' he twisted round and smelled lavender, and saw that the new nurse was Meals on Wheels Florence, with a straining white uniform and magpie hair.

After she settled him by the wall and tied him to the chair with the soft straitjacket, he grabbed her plump hand. 'I know you.'

'This is my first day.'

'Florence.'

'Mrs Macky.'

She was different. Not so mean and crafty. He was getting things mixed up again. It was not really Florence, but he put Alice's photograph and his bits and pieces into his bedside drawer, with the candy the night staff would steal if you left it out.

State Law insisted on Activities every day. Each morning Mrs Activities, a wiry, manic woman with bolting eyes, read bits out of the newspaper, while the heads nodded all around her and bodies flopped against restrainers. When Mrs Activities did flower arranging, you knew someone had died. The wreaths were sent to Fairview after the funeral. Once when Dick was in his chair near the entrance, waiting for Annette who never came, the trolley of flowers was trundled in from the car park, and the woman in the next chair remarked, 'Anyone seen Mabel lately?'

Dick was losing his grip. He hung on desperately, but his mind was slipping away, like his body. Maybe he should be in the funny farm. Maybe he already was. For the Hallowe'en party, the bodies wore masks.

Some of them looked better than usual. Mrs Macky wore a witch's costume. At least that made sense.

'You want me dead, don't you?' he asked her when she put him back to bed.

'Hup she goes.' None of the nurses answered you. They said sayings, or just laughed, or scolded. Dick had tried to write a list of complaints, a letter to Annette, to Elder Services who sold auto parts, but the pad and pencil fell to the floor.

'Everything all right?' The Administrator came into the room dressed as a ghost, watching him through holes in the sheet.

Dick shook his head. It kept on shaking.

'He likes to complain,' Mrs Macky said comfortably, a witch in a pointed hat.

'You're lucky to be here,' the Administrator said. 'We've a long waiting list.'

Of private paying patients. 'You want my bed.' He could not be sure if he had said that, or, 'You want me dead', or if he had spoken at all.

He saw them exchange a look, the holes in the sheet, the eyes under the witch's hat. So that was it. All was lost.

Even if Mrs Macky was not actively trying to kill him, she was not trying to keep him alive. She lied, pretending he had had a bath, or not had pills, to overdose him. She lied about the time of day, the day of the week, to confuse him. She put his meal on the tray table, and if he could not feed himself she came in hours later with, 'Not hungry?' and took away the cold food. He wore diapers and rubber pants, and wept to think what Alice would say. His bell was on a string, but the string had been disconnected. It led nowhere. When Mrs Macky came in red and flustered after he had lain soaking for hours, she said, 'On a day like this, wet diapers is pretty low on my list of priorities.' The hooter hooted like an owl. Why didn't old John cuss him out?

That night he dreamt of jumping from the bridge, falling, falling . . . His heart dropped, and he awoke in sweat and sat up to see through the open door a naked, bony corpse on the bed across the corridor where cussing John slept. But was it a corpse? Suddenly, the eyes popped open and stared at him, round and bulging, like balls of pale pink bubble gum.

He raised an arm in limp salute, but John could no longer see him. A nurse had placed two fingers on his eyelids and was holding them down. Dick wanted to shout, *Stop it! Leave him alone!* but his mouth was too dry. Another nurse, blonde, with hair cut square to match her figure, had arranged John's arms straight down by his sides, so that he lay at attention, and turned away to wring out a cloth in a bowl of water. One of John's arms flopped off the edge of the bed and swung to and fro. Dick saw it as a sign of life, a call for help, but he was powerless, as useless as a cabbage. The nurse with the cloth turned round, casually replaced the arm and began to wash John's narrow, hairless chest, whistling tunelessly through her teeth as she casually wiped and rinsed. The skin looked clammy, shiny, reptilian.

The other nurse was doing something to the old man's slack mouth, stretching the lips with her fingers while she savagely rammed in his false teeth. He looked worse, now. She had propped him up against his pillows, and his head was lolling on one side while his jaw gaped in toothy imbecility. Deftly, she wound a bandage around his head and under his jaw, giving his face a firm expression that wasn't the dribbling old man Dick knew.

He looked like a corpse now, like pictures in old books of ghosts in their grave-clothes. But he wasn't dead. Dick knew that, because his eyes had popped open again and were staring across at him in a kind of blank despair, as if he were resigned to his fate. One of the nurses tutted in disgust and playfully slapped John's side. 'Come on now, you stubborn old bag o' bones,' she said, sighing and holding his eyelids down again.

Something dreadful was happening further down. The blonde nurse seemed to be pressing on John's stomach – where his bladder must be. Dick turned his head away. It wasn't right to watch such indignities. Oh, why couldn't they leave him to die in peace?

They were plugging him now, rolling him over on to his face, rolling him back, throwing remarks to each other across his defenceless body. 'Seen that crummy movie at the Bridge cinema?' 'Nah, Gary's doing nights up the gas station this week.' They filled his nostrils with little pellets of cotton, so that he couldn't breathe. It was murder, but who could Dick tell? The eyes stayed closed now, and the nurses pushed John's arms into the sleeves of a paper shroud and tied tapes in bows down his back. They took away the pillows and rocked the body to and fro like a rolling pin as they inserted a clean sheet underneath it. One of them tied a label to John's big toe, and the other taped a card to his chest, then they wrapped him up in the sheet like a Christmas parcel and left the room. Dick heard them chatting and laughing as the rubber soles of their white lace-up shoes squeaked away down the corridor.

In the morning light, they would not say that John was dead, but the bed was empty, made up clean like a mortuary slab. The hooter hooted last trumps for him, and a new man was wheeled in. *Watch out*, Dick wanted to say to him. *All is lost*. Later that day – next day, next week? –

the new man was wheeled out. 'Come along, old feller. Activity time. We're going to do flower arranging.'

They want me dead. If I don't die soon, they won't wait, they'll lay me out while I'm still alive, still breathing. They had done it before, they would do it again, given half a chance. This was not something he had imagined, or remembered all wrong. This nightmare was real. This was murder. For the first time, he understood the cowards who jumped off the canal bridge. Was it horror like this they were so desperate to escape?

Dick tried to speak to the room cleaners, but State Law forbade them to talk to patients. He tried to call for help to anyone who passed the door – the hurrying young nurses, glum visitors, the man who came to restock the Coca-Cola machine – but his voice was a croak and his blotched, stranger's claw could only pluck at the sheets.

He remembered the safety of the hospital. Had he been there yet, or was he going? A heart attack. He'd make one, and the ambulance men would come with jokes and take him away to intensive care. Next time the cramping pains came in his chest, instead of pulling on the broken bell string, he forced himself somehow to move his racked body forward. Inch by inch, he got a leg over the edge, then another, feet dangling, sore bottom on the edge of the bed, shoulders on the mattress. He had a leg over the rail in the teeth of the wind, straining in an agony that almost burst his heart. Mrs Macky tried to pull him back, but he pitched over the rail and was a long time falling without breath before he hit the black waters of the shining linoleum, and the trolley of lavender flowers trundled past.

Earth to Earth

Robert Graves

Elsie and Roland Hedge – she a book illustrator, he an architect with suspect lungs – had been warned against Dr Eugene Steinpilz. 'He'll bring you no luck,' I told them. 'My little finger says so decisively.'

'You too?' asked Elsie indignantly. (This was at Brixham, South Devon, in March, 1940.) 'I suppose you think that because of his foreign accent and his beard he must be a spy?'

'No,' I said coldly, 'that point hadn't occurred to me. But I won't contradict you.' I was annoyed.

The very next day Elsie deliberately picked a friendship – I don't like that phrase, but that's what she did – with the Doctor, an Alsatian with an American passport, who described himself as a *Naturphilosoph*; and both she and Roland were soon immersed in Steinpilzeri up to the nostrils. It began when he invited them to lunch and gave them cold meat and two rival sets of vegetable dishes – potatoes (baked), carrots (creamed), bought from the local fruiterer; and potatoes (baked) and carrots (creamed), grown on compost in his own garden.

The superiority of the latter over the former in appearance, size, and especially flavour came as an eye-opener to Elsie and Roland; and so Dr Steinpilz soon converted the childless and devoted couple to the Steinpilz method of composting. It did not, as a matter of fact, vary greatly from the methods you read about in the *Gardening Notes* of your favourite national newspaper, except that it was far more violent. Dr Steinpilz had invented a formula for producing extremely fierce bacteria, capable (Roland claimed) of breaking down an old boot or the family Bible or a torn woollen vest into beautiful black humus almost as you watched.

The formula could not be bought, however, and might be communicated under oath of secrecy only to members of the Eugene Steinpilz Fellowship – which I refused to join. I won't pretend therefore to know the formula myself, but one night I overheard Elsie and Roland arguing as to whether the planetary influences were favourable; and they also mentioned a ram's horn in which, it seems, a complicated mixture of triturated animal and vegetable products – technically called 'the Mother' – was to be cooked up. I gather also that a bull's foot and goat's pancreas were part of the works, because Mr Pook, the butcher, afterwards told me that he had been puzzled by Roland's request for these unusual cuts. Milkwort and pennyroyal and bee-orchid and vetch certainly figured among 'the Mother's' herbal ingredients; I recognized these one day in a gardening basket Elsie had left in the post office.

The Hedges soon had their first compost heap cooking away in the garden, which was about the size of a tennis court and consisted mostly of well-kept lawn. Dr Steinpilz, who supervised, now began to haunt the cottage like the smell of drains; I had to give up calling on them. Then, after the Fall of France, Brixham became a war zone whence everyone but we British and our Free French or Free Belgian allies was extruded. Consequently Dr Steinpilz had to leave; which he did with very bad grace, and was killed in a Liverpool air raid the day before he should have sailed back to New York.

I think Elsie must have been in love with the Doctor, and certainly Roland had a hero worship for him. They treasured a signed collection of all his esoteric books, each titled after a different semi-precious stone; and used to read them out loud to each other at meals, in turns. And to show that this was a practical philosophy, not just a random assembly of beautiful thoughts about Nature, they began composting in a deeper and even more religious way than before. The lawn had come up, of course; but they used the sods to sandwich layers of kitchen waste, which they mixed with the scrapings of an abandoned pigsty, two barrowfuls of sodden poplar leaves from the recreation ground, and a sack of rotten turnips. Once I caught the fanatic gleam in Elsie's eye as she turned the hungry bacteria loose on the heap, and could not repress a premonitory shudder.

So far, not too bad, perhaps. But when serious bombing started and food became so scarce that housewives were fined for not making over their swill to the national pigs, Elsie and Roland grew worried. Having already abandoned their ordinary sanitary system and built an earth-closet in the garden, they now tried to convince neighbours of their duty to do the same, even at the risk of catching cold and getting spiders down the neck. Elsie also sent Roland after the slow-moving Red Devon cows as they lurched home along the lane at dusk, to rescue the precious droppings with a kitchen shovel; while she visited the local ash dump with a packing case mounted on wheels, and collected whatever she found there of an organic nature – dead cats, old rags, withered flowers, cabbage stalks, and such household waste as even a national wartime pig would have coughed at. She also saved every drop of their bath water for sprinkling the heaps; because it contained, she said, valuable animal salts.

The test of a good compost heap, as every illuminate knows, is whether a certain revolting-looking, if beneficial, fungus sprouts from it. Elsie's heaps were grey with this crop, and so hot inside they could be used for haybox cookery; which must have saved her a deal of fuel. I called them 'Elsie's heaps', because she now considered herself Dr Steinpilz's earthly delegate; and loyal Roland did not dispute this claim.

A critical stage in the story came during the Blitz. It will be remembered that trainloads of Londoners, who had been evacuated to South Devon when War broke out, thereafter de-evacuated and re-evacuated and re-de-evacuated themselves, from time to time, in a most disorganized fashion. Elsie and Roland, as it happened, escaped having evacuees billeted on them, because they had no spare bedroom; but one night an old naval pensioner came knocking at their door and demanded lodging for the night. Having been burned out of Plymouth, where everything was chaos, he had found himself walking away and blundering along in a daze until he fetched up here, hungry and dead-beat. They gave him a meal and bedded him on the sofa; but when Elsie came down in the morning to fork over the heaps, she found him dead of heart failure.

Roland broke a long silence by coming, in some embarrassment, to ask my advice. Elsie, he said, had decided that it would be wrong to trouble the police about the case; because the police were so busy these days, and the poor old fellow had claimed to possess neither kith nor kin. So they'd read the burial service over him and, after removing his belt buckle, trouser buttons, metal spectacle case, and a bunch of keys, which were irreducible, had laid him reverently in the new compost heap. Its other contents, Roland added, were a cartload of waste from the cider factory and salvaged cow dung.

'If you mean "Will I report you to Civil Authorities?" the answer is no,' I assured him. 'I wasn't looking at the relevant hour, and, after all, what you tell me is only hearsay.'

The War went on. Not only did the Hedges convert the whole garden into serried rows of Eugene Steinpilz memorial heaps, leaving no room for planting the potatoes or carrots to which the compost had been prospectively devoted, but they regularly scavenged offal from the fish-market. Every Spring, Elsie used to pick big bunches of primroses and put them straight on the compost, without even a last wistful sniff; virgin primroses were supposed to be particularly relished by the fierce bacteria.

Here the story becomes a little painful for readers of a family journal like this; I will soften it as much as possible. One morning a policeman called on the Hedges with a summons, and I happened to see Roland peep anxiously out of the bedroom window, but quickly pull his head in again.

The policeman rang and knocked and waited, then tried the back door; and presently went away. The summons was for a blackout offence, but apparently the Hedges did not know this.

Next morning the policeman called again, and when nobody answered, forced the lock of the back door. They were found dead in bed together, having taken an overdose of sleeping tablets. A note on the coverlet ran simply:

Please lay our bodies on the heap nearest the pigsty. Flowers by request. Strew some on the bodies, mixed with a little kitchen waste, and then fork the earth lightly over.

E.H., R.H.

George Irks, the new tenant, proposed to grow potatoes and dig for victory. He hired a cart and began throwing the compost into the River Dart, 'not liking the look of them toadstools'. The five beautifully clean human skeletons which George unearthed in the process were still awaiting identification when the War ended.

The Dwarf

Ray Bradbury

Aimee watched the sky, quietly.

Tonight was one of those motionless hot summer nights. The concrete pier empty, the strung red, white, yellow bulbs burning like insects in the air above the wooden emptiness. The managers of the various carnival pitches stood, like melting wax dummies, eyes staring blindly, not talking, all down the line.

Two customers had passed through an hour before. Those two lonely people were now in the roller coaster, screaming murderously as it plummeted down the blazing night, around one emptiness after another.

Aimee moved slowly across the strand, a few worn wooden hoopla rings sticking to her wet hands. She stopped behind the ticket booth that fronted the MIRROR MAZE. She saw herself grossly misrepresented in three rippled mirrors outside the Maze. A thousand tired replicas of herself dissolved in the corridor beyond, hot images among so much clear coolness.

She stepped inside the ticket booth and stood looking a long while at Ralph Banghart's thin neck. He clenched an unlit cigar between his long uneven yellow teeth as he laid out a battered game of solitaire on the ticket shelf.

When the roller coaster wailed and fell in its terrible avalanche again, she was reminded to speak.

'What kind of people go up in roller coasters?'

Ralph Banghart worked his cigar a full thirty seconds. 'People wanna die. That rollie coaster's the handiest thing to dying there is.' He sat listening to the faint sound of rifle shots from the shooting gallery. 'This whole damn carny business's crazy. For instance, that dwarf. You seen him? Every night, pays his dime, runs in the Mirror Maze all the way back through to Screwy Louie's Room. You should see this little runt head back there. My God!'

'Oh, yes,' said Aimee, remembering. 'I always wonder what it's like to be a dwarf. I always feel sorry when I see him.'

'I could play him like an accordion.'

'Don't say that!'

'My Lord.' Ralph patted her thigh with a free hand. 'The way you carry on about guys you never even met.' He shook his head and chuckled. 'Him and his secret. Only he don't know I know, see? Boy howdy!'

'It's a hot night.' She twitched the large wooden hoops nervously on her damp fingers.

'Don't change the subject. He'll be here, rain or shine.'

Aimee shifted her weight.

Ralph seized her elbow. 'Hey! You ain't mad? You wanna see that dwarf, don't you? Sh!' Ralph turned. 'Here he comes now!'

The Dwarf's hand, hairy and dark, appeared all by itself reaching up into the booth window with a silver dime. An invisible person called, 'One!' in a high, child's voice.

Involuntarily, Aimee bent forward.

The Dwarf looked up at her, resembling nothing more than a dark-eyed, dark-haired, ugly man who has been locked in a winepress, squeezed and wadded down and down, fold on fold, agony on agony, until a bleached, outraged mass is left, the face bloated shapelessly, a face you know must stare wide-eyed and awake at two and three and four o'clock in the morning, lying flat in bed, only the body asleep.

Ralph tore a yellow ticket in half. 'One!'

The Dwarf, as if frightened by an approaching storm, pulled his black coat-lapels tightly about his throat and waddled swiftly. A moment later, ten thousand lost and wandering dwarfs wriggled between the mirror flats, like frantic dark beetles, and vanished.

'Quick!'

Ralph squeezed Aimee along a dark passage behind the mirrors. She felt him pat her all the way back through the tunnel to a thin partition with a peekhole.

'This is rich,' he chuckled. 'Go on – look.'

Aimee hesitated, then put her face to the partition.

'You *see* him?' Ralph whispered.

Aimee felt her heart beating. A full minute passed.

There stood the Dwarf in the middle of the small blue room. His eyes were shut. He wasn't ready to open them yet. Now, now he opened his eyelids and looked at a large mirror set before him. And what he saw in the mirror made him smile. He winked, he pirouetted, he stood sidewise, he waved, he bowed, he did a little clumsy dance.

And the mirror repeated each motion with long, thin arms, with a tall, tall body, with a huge wink and an enormous repetition of the dance, ending in a gigantic bow!

'Every night the same thing,' whispered Ralph in Aimee's ear. 'Ain't that rich?'

Aimee turned her head and looked at Ralph steadily out of her motionless face, for a long time, and she said nothing. Then, as if she could not help herself, she moved her head slowly and very slowly back to stare once more through the opening. She held her breath. She felt her eyes begin to water.

Ralph nudged her, whispering.

'Hey, what's the little gink doin' now?'

They were drinking coffee and not looking at each other in the ticket booth half an hour later, when the Dwarf came out of the mirrors. He took his hat off and started to approach the booth, when he saw Aimee and hurried away.

'He wanted something,' said Aimee.

'Yeah.' Ralph squashed out his cigarette, idly. 'I know what, too. But he hasn't got the nerve to ask. One night in this squeaky little voice he says, "I bet those mirrors are expensive." Well, I played dumb. I said yeah they were. He sort of looked at me, waiting, and when I didn't say any more, he went home, but next night he said, "I bet those mirrors cost fifty, a hundred bucks." I bet they do, I said. I laid me out a hand of solitaire.'

'Ralph,' she said.

He glanced up. 'Why you look at me that way?'

'Ralph,' she said, 'why don't you sell him one of your extra ones?'

'Look, Aimee, do I tell you how to run your hoop circus?'

'How much do those mirrors cost?'

'I can get 'em secondhand for thirty-five bucks.'

'Why don't you tell him where he can buy one, then?'

'Aimee, you're not smart.' He laid his hand on her knee. She moved her knee away. 'Even if I told him where to go, you think he'd buy one? Not on your life. And why? He's self-conscious. Why, if he even knew I knew he was flirtin' around in front of that mirror in Screwy Louie's Room, he'd never come back. He plays like he's goin' through the Maze to get lost, like everybody else. Pretends like he don't care about that special room. Always waits for business to turn bad, late nights, so he has that room to himself. What he does for entertainment on nights when business is good, God knows. No, sir, he wouldn't dare go buy a mirror anywhere. He ain't got no friends, and even if he did he couldn't ask them to buy him a thing like that. Pride, by God, pride. Only reason he even mentioned it to me is I'm practically the only guy he knows. Besides, look at him – he ain't got enough to buy a mirror like those. He might be savin' up, but where in hell in the world today can a dwarf work? Dime a dozen, drag on the market, outside of circuses.'

'I feel awful. I feel sad.' Aimee sat staring at the empty boardwalk. 'Where does he live?'

'Flytrap down on the waterfront. The Ganghes Arms. Why?'

'I'm madly in love with him, if you must know.'

He grinned around his cigar. 'Aimee,' he said. 'You and your very funny jokes.'

A warm night, a hot morning, and a blazing noon. The sea was a sheet of burning tinsel and glass.

Aimee came walking, in the locked-up carnival alleys out over the warm sea, keeping in the shade, half a dozen sun-bleached magazines under her arm. She opened a flaking door and called into hot darkness. 'Ralph?' She picked her way through the black hall behind the mirrors, her heels tacking the wooden floor. 'Ralph?'

Someone stirred sluggishly on the canvas cot. 'Aimee?'

He sat up and screwed a dim light bulb into the dressing table socket. He squinted at her, half blinded. 'Hey, you look like the cat swallowed a canary.'

'Ralph, I came about the midget!'

'Dwarf, Aimee honey, dwarf. A midget is in the cells, born that way. A dwarf is in the glands . . .'

'Ralph! I just found out the most wonderful thing about him!'

'Honest to God,' he said to his hands, holding them out as witnesses to his disbelief. 'This woman! Who in hell gives two cents for some ugly little –'

'Ralph!' She held out the magazines, her eyes shining. 'He's a writer! Think of that!'

'It's a pretty hot day for thinking.' He lay back and examined her, smiling faintly.

'I just happened to pass the Ganghes Arms, and saw Mr Greeley, the manager. He says the typewriter runs all night in Mr Big's room!'

'Is *that* his name?' Ralph began to roar with laughter.

'Writes just enough pulp detective stories to live. I found one of his stories in the secondhand magazine place, and, Ralph, guess what?'

'I'm tired, Aimee.'

'This little guy's got a soul as big as all outdoors; he's got *everything* in his head!'

'Why ain't he writin' for the big magazines, then, I ask you?'

'Because maybe he's afraid – maybe he doesn't know he can do it. That happens. People don't believe in themselves. But if he only tried, I bet he could sell stories anywhere in the world.'

'Why ain't he rich, I wonder?'

'Maybe because ideas come slow because he's down in the dumps. Who wouldn't be? So small that way? I bet it's hard to think of anything except being so small and living in a one-room cheap apartment.'

'Hell!' snorted Ralph. 'You talk like Florence Nightingale's grandma.'

She held up the magazine. 'I'll read you part of his crime story. It's got all the guns and tough people, but it's told by a dwarf. I bet the editors never guessed the author knew what he was writing about. Oh, please don't sit there like that, Ralph! Listen.'

And she began to read aloud.

'I am a dwarf and I am a murderer. The two things cannot be separated. One is the cause of the other.

'The man I murdered used to stop me on the street when I was twenty-one, pick me up in his arms, kiss my brow, croon wildly to me, sing Rock-a-bye Baby, haul me into meat markets, toss me on the scales and cry, "Watch it. Don't weigh your thumb, there, butcher!"

'Do you *see* how our lives moved towards murder? This fool, this persecutor of my flesh and soul!

'As for my childhood: my parents were small people, not quite dwarfs, not quite. My father's inheritance kept us in a doll's house, an amazing thing like a white-scrolled wedding cake – little rooms, little chairs, miniature paintings, cameos, ambers with insects caught inside, everything tiny, tiny, tiny! The world of Giants far away, an ugly rumour beyond the garden wall. Poor mama, papa! They meant only the best for me. They kept me, like a porcelain vase, small and treasured, to themselves, in our ant world, our beehive rooms, our microscopic library, our land of beetle-sized doors and moth windows. Only now do I see the magnificent size of my parents' psychosis! They must have dreamed they would live forever, keeping me like a butterfly under glass. But first father died, and then fire ate up the little house, the wasp's nest, and every postage-stamp mirror and saltcellar closet within. Mama, too, gone! And myself alone, watching the fallen embers, tossed out into a world of

Monsters and Titans, caught in a landslide of reality, rushed, rolled, and smashed to the bottom of the cliff!

'It took me a year to adjust. A job with a sideshow was unthinkable. There seemed no place for me in the world. And then, a month ago, the Persecutor came into my life, clapped a bonnet on my unsuspecting head, and cried to friends, "I want you to meet the little woman!" '

Aimee stopped reading. Her eyes were unsteady and the magazine shook as she handed it to Ralph. 'You finish it. The rest is a murder story. It's all right. But don't you see? That little man. That little man.'

Ralph tossed the magazine aside and lit a cigarette lazily. 'I like Westerns better.'

'Ralph, you got to read it. He needs someone to tell him how good he is and keep him writing.'

Ralph looked at her, his head to one side. 'And guess who's going to do it? Well, well, ain't we just the Saviour's right hand?'

'I won't listen!'

'Use your head, damn it! You go busting in on him he'll think you're handing him pity. He'll chase you screamin' outa his room.'

She sat down, thinking about it slowly, trying to turn it over and see it from every side. 'I don't know. Maybe you're right. Oh, it's not just pity, Ralph, honest. But maybe it'd look like it to him. I've got to be awful careful.'

He shook her shoulder back and forth, pinching softly, with his fingers. 'Hell, hell, lay off him, is all I ask; you'll get nothing but trouble for your dough. God, Aimee, I never *seen* you so hepped on anything. Look, you and me, let's make it a day, take a lunch, get us some gas, and just drive on down the coast as far as we can drive; swim, have supper, see a good show in some little town – to hell with the carnival, how about it? A damn nice day and no worries. I been savin' a coupla bucks.'

'It's because I know he's different,' she said, looking off into darkness. 'It's because he's something we can never be – you and me and all the rest of us here on the pier. It's so funny, so funny. Life fixed him so he's good for nothing but carny shows, yet there he is on the land. And life made us so we wouldn't have to work in the carny shows, but here we are, anyway, way out here at sea on the pier. Sometimes it seems a million miles to shore. How come, Ralph, that we got the bodies, but he's got the brains and can think things we'll never even guess?'

'You haven't even been listening to me!' said Ralph.

She sat with him standing over her, his voice far away. Her eyes were half shut and her hands were in her lap, twitching.

'I don't like that shrewd look you're getting on,' he said, finally.

She opened her purse slowly and took out a small roll of bills and started counting. 'Thirty-five, forty dollars. There. I'm going to phone Billie Fine and have him send out one of those tall-type mirrors to Mr Bigelow at the Ganghes Arms. Yes, I am!'

'What!'

'Think how wonderful for him, Ralph, having one in his own room any time he wants it. Can I use your phone?'

'Go ahead, *be* nutty.'

Ralph turned quickly and walked off down the tunnel. A door slammed.

Aimee waited, then after a while put her hands to the phone and began to dial, with painful slowness. She paused between numbers, holding her breath, shutting her eyes, thinking how it might seem to be small in the world, and then one day someone sends a special mirror by. A mirror for your room where you can hide away with the big reflection of yourself, shining, and write stories and stories, never going out into the world unless you had to. How might it be then, alone, with the wonderful illusion all in one piece in the room. Would it make you happy or sad, would it help your writing or hurt it? She shook her head back and forth, back and forth. At least this way there would be no one to look down at you. Night after night, perhaps rising secretly at three in the cold morning, you could wink and dance around and smile and wave at yourself, so tall, so tall, so very fine and tall in the bright looking-glass.

A telephone voice said, 'Billie Fine's.'

'Oh, *Billie!*' she cried.

Night came in over the pier. The ocean lay dark and loud under the planks. Ralph sat cold and waxen in his glass coffin, laying out the cards, his eyes fixed, his mouth stiff. At his elbow, a growing pyramid of burnt cigarette butts grew larger. When Aimee walked along under the hot red and blue bulbs, smiling, waving, he did not stop setting the cards down slow and very slow. 'Hi, Ralph!' she said.

'How's the love affair?' he asked, drinking from a dirty glass of iced water. 'How's Charlie Boyer, or is it Cary Grant?'

'I just went and bought me a new hat,' she said, smiling. 'Gosh, I feel *good*! You know why? Billie Fine's sending a mirror out tomorrow! Can't you just see the nice little guy's face?'

'I'm not so hot at imagining.'

'Oh, Lord, you'd think I was going to marry him or something.'

'Why not? Carry him around in a suitcase. People say, Where's your husband? all you do is open your bag, yell, Here he is! Like a silver cornet. Take him outa his case any old hour, play a tune, stash him away. Keep a little sandbox for him on the back porch.'

'I was feeling so good,' she said.

'Benevolent is the word.' Ralph did not look at her, his mouth tight. 'Ben-ev-o-*lent*. I suppose this all comes from me watching him through that knothole, getting my kicks? That why you sent the mirror? People like you run around with tambourines, taking the joy out of my life.'

'Remind me not to come to your place for drinks any more. I'd rather go with no people at all than mean people.'

Ralph exhaled a deep breath. 'Aimee, Aimee. Don't you know you can't help that guy? He's bats. And this crazy thing of yours is like saying, Go ahead, *be* batty, I'll help you, pal.'

'Once in a lifetime anyway, it's nice to make a mistake if you think it'll do somebody some good,' she said.

'God deliver me from do-gooders, Aimee.'

'Shut up, shut up!' she cried, and then said nothing more.

He let the silence lie awhile, and then got up, putting his finger-printed glass aside. 'Mind the booth for me?'

'Sure. Why?'

She saw ten thousand cold white images of him stalking down the glassy corridors, between mirrors, his mouth straight and his fingers working themselves.

She sat in the booth for a full minute and then suddenly shivered. A small clock ticked in the booth and she turned the deck of cards over, one by one, waiting. She heard a hammer pounding and knocking and pounding again, far away inside the Maze; a silence, more waiting, and then ten thousand images folding and refolding and dissolving, Ralph striding, looking out at ten thousand images of her in the booth. She heard his quiet laughter as he came down the ramp.

'Well, what's put you in such a good mood?' she asked, suspiciously.

'Aimee,' he said, carelessly, 'we shouldn't quarrel. You say tomorrow Billie's sending that mirror to Mr Big's?'

'You're not going to try anything funny?'

'Me?' He moved her out of the booth and took over the cards, humming, his eyes bright. 'Not me, oh no, not me.' He did not look at her, but started quickly to slap out the cards. She stood behind him. Her right eye began to twitch a little. She folded and unfolded her arms. A minute ticked by. The only sound was the ocean under the night pier, Ralph breathing in the heat, the soft ruffle of the cards. The sky over the pier was hot and thick with clouds. Out at sea, faint glows of lightning were beginning to show.

'Ralph,' she said at last.

'Relax, Aimee,' he said.

'About that trip you wanted to take down the coast –'

'Tomorrow,' he said. 'Maybe next month. Maybe next year. Old Ralph Banghart's a patient guy. I'm not worried, Aimee. Look.' He held up a hand. 'I'm calm.'

She waited for a roll of thunder at sea to fade away.

'I just don't want you mad, is all. I just don't want anything bad to happen, promise me.'

The wind, now warm, now cool, blew along the pier. There was a smell of rain in the wind. The clock ticked. Aimee began to perspire heavily, watching the cards move and move. Distantly, you could hear targets being hit and the sound of the pistols at the shooting gallery.

And then, there he was.

Waddling along the lonely concourse, under the insect bulbs, his face twisted and dark, every movement an effort. From a long way down the pier he came, with Aimee watching. She wanted to say to him, This is your last night, the last time you'll have to embarrass yourself by coming here, the last time you'll have to put up with being watched by Ralph, even in secret. She wished she could cry out and laugh and say it right in front of Ralph. But she said nothing.

'Hello, hello!' shouted Ralph. 'It's free, on the house, tonight! Special for old customers!'

The Dwarf looked up, startled, his little black eyes darting and swimming in confusion. His mouth formed the word thanks and he turned, one hand to his neck, pulling his tiny lapels tight up about his convulsing throat, the other hand clenching the silver dime secretly. Looking back he gave a little nod, and then scores of dozens of compressed and tortured faces, burnt a strange dark colour by the lights, wandered in the glass corridors.

'Ralph,' Aimee took his elbow. 'What's going on?'

He grinned. 'I'm being benevolent, Aimee, benevolent.'

'Ralph,' she said.

'Sh,' he said. '*Listen*.'

They waited in the booth in the long warm silence.

Then, a long way off, muffled, there was a scream.

'Ralph!' said Aimee.

'Listen, listen!' he said.

There was another scream, and another and still another, and a threshing and a pounding and a breaking, a rushing around and through the maze. There, there, wildly colliding and ricochetting, from mirror to mirror, shrieking hysterically and sobbing, tears on his face, mouth gasped open, came Mr Bigelow. He fell out in the blazing night air, glanced about wildly, wailed, and ran off down the pier.

'Ralph, what happened?'

Ralph sat laughing and slapping at his thighs.

She slapped his face. 'What'd you *do?*'

He didn't quite stop laughing. 'Come on. I'll show you!'

And then she was in the maze, rushed from white-hot mirror to mirror, seeing her lipstick all red fire a thousand times repeated on down a burning silver cavern where strange hysterical women much like herself followed a quick-moving, smiling man. 'Come on!' he cried. And they broke free into a dust-smelling tiny room.

'Ralph!' she said.

They both stood on the threshold of the little room where the Dwarf had come every night for a year. They both stood where the Dwarf had stood each night, before opening his eyes to see the miraculous image in front of him.

Aimee shuffled slowly, one hand out, into the dim room.

The mirror had been changed.

This new mirror made even normal people small, small, small; it made even tall people little and dark and twisted, smaller as you moved forward.

And Aimee stood before it thinking and thinking that if it made big people small, standing here, God, what would it do to a dwarf, a tiny dwarf, a dark dwarf, a startled and lonely dwarf?

She turned and almost fell. Ralph stood looking at her. 'Ralph,' she said. 'God, why did you do it?'

'Aimee, come back!'

She ran out through the mirrors, crying. Staring with blurred eyes, it was hard to find the way, but she found it. She stood blinking at the empty pier, started to run one way, then another, then still another, then stopped. Ralph came up behind her, talking, but it was like a voice heard behind a wall late at night, remote and foreign.

'Don't talk to me,' she said.

Someone came running up the pier. It was Mr Kelly from the shooting gallery. 'Hey, any you see a little guy just now? Little stiff swiped a pistol from my place, loaded, run off before I'd get a hand on him! You help me find him?'

And Kelly was gone, sprinting, turning his head to search between all the canvas sheds, on away under the hot blue and red and yellow strung bulbs.

Aimee rocked back and forth and took a step.

'Aimee, where you going?'

She looked at Ralph as if they had just turned a corner, strangers passing, and bumped into each other. 'I guess,' she said, 'I'm going to help search.'

'You won't be able to do nothing.'

'I got to try, anyway. Oh God, Ralph, this is all my fault! I shouldn't have phoned Billie Fine! I shouldn't've ordered a mirror and got you so mad you did this! It's *me* should've gone to Mr Big, not a crazy thing like I bought! I'm going to find him if it's the last thing I ever do in my life.'

Swinging about slowly, her cheeks wet, she saw the quivery mirrors that stood in front of the Maze, Ralph's reflection was in one of them. She could not take her eyes away from the image; it held her in a cool and trembling fascination, with her mouth open.

'Aimee, what's wrong? What're you –'

He sensed where she was looking and twisted about to see what was going on. His eyes widened.

He scowled at the blazing mirror.

A horrid, ugly little man, two feet high, with a pale, squashed face under an ancient straw hat, scowled back at him. Ralph stood there glaring at himself, his hands at his sides.

Aimee walked slowly and then began to walk fast and then began to run. She ran down the empty pier and the wind blew warm and it blew large drops of hot rain out of the sky on her all the time she was running.

The Portobello Road

Muriel Spark

One day in my young youth at high summer, lolling with my lovely companions upon a haystack, I found a needle. Already and privately for some years I had been guessing that I was set apart from the common run, but this of the needle attested the fact to my whole public, George, Kathleen, and Skinny. I sucked my thumb, for when I had thrust my idle hand deep into the hay, the thumb was where the needle had stuck.

When everyone had recovered George said, 'She put in her thumb and pulled out a plum.' Then away we were into our merciless hacking-hecking laughter again.

The needle had gone fairly deep into the thumb cushion, and a small red river flowed and spread from the tiny puncture. So that nothing of our joy should lag, George put in quickly:

'Mind your bloody thumb on my shirt.'

Then hac-hec-hoo, we shrieked into the hot Borderland afternoon. Really I should not care to be so young of heart again. That is my thought every time I turn over my old papers and come across the photograph. Skinny, Kathleen, and myself are in the photo atop the haystack. Skinny had just finished analysing the inwards of my find.

'It couldn't have been done by brains. You haven't much brains, but you're a lucky wee thing.'

Everyone agreed that the needle betokened extraordinary luck. As it was becoming a serious conversation, George said:

'I'll take a photo.'

I wrapped my hanky round my thumb and got myself organized. George pointed up from his camera and shouted:

'Look, there's a mouse!'

Kathleen screamed and I screamed, although I think we knew there was no mouse. But this gave us an extra session of squalling hee-hoos. Finally, we three composed ourselves for George's picture. We look lovely, and it was a great day at the time, but I would not care for it all over again. From that day I was known as Needle.

One Saturday in recent years I was mooching down the Portobello Road from the Ladbrooke Grove end, threading among the crowds of marketers on the narrow pavement, when I saw a woman. She had a haggard, careworn, wealthy look, thin but for the breasts forced-up high like a pigeon's. I had not seen her for nearly five years. How changed she was! But I recognized Kathleen my friend; her features had already begun to sink and protrude in the way that mouths and noses do in people destined always to be old for their years. When I had last seen her, nearly five years ago, Kathleen, barely thirty, had said:

'I've lost all my looks; it's in the family. All the women are handsome as girls, but we go off early, we go brown and nosey.'

I stood silently among the people, watching. As you will see, I wasn't in a position to speak to Kathleen. I saw her shoving in her avid manner from stall to stall. She was always fond of antique jewellery and of bargains. I wondered that I had not seen her before in the Portobello Road on my Saturday morning ambles. Her long stiff-crooked fingers pounced to select a jade ring from amongst the jumble of brooches and pendants, onyx, moonstone, and gold, set out on the stall.

'What d'you think of this?' she said.

I saw then who was with her. I had been half conscious of the huge man following several paces behind her, and now I noticed him.

'It looks all right,' he said. 'How much is it?'

'How much is it?' Kathleen asked the vendor.

I took a good look at this man accompanying Kathleen. It was her husband. The beard was unfamiliar, but I recognized beneath it his enormous mouth, the bright, sensuous lips, the large brown eyes for ever brimming with pathos.

It was not for me to speak to Kathleen, but I had a sudden inspiration which caused me to say quietly:

'Hallo, George.'

The giant of a man turned round to face the direction of my voice. There were so many people – but at length he saw me.

'Hallo, George,' I said again.

Kathleen had started to haggle with the stall owner, in her old way, over the price of the jade ring. George continued to stare at me, his big mouth slightly parted so that I could see a wide slit of red lips and white teeth between the fair grassy growths of beard and moustache.

'My God!' he said.

'What's the matter?' said Kathleen.

'Hallo, George!' I said again, quite loud this time and cheerfully.

'Look!' said George. 'Look who's there, over beside the fruit stall.'

Kathleen looked but didn't see.

'Who is it?' she said impatiently.

'It's Needle,' he said. 'She said "Hallo, George".'

'*Needle*,' said Kathleen. 'Who do you mean? You don't mean our old friend *Needle* who —'

'Yes. There she is. My God!'

He looked very ill, although when I had said 'Hallo, George', I had spoken friendly enough.

'I don't see anyone faintly resembling poor Needle,' said Kathleen, looking at him. She was worried.

George pointed straight at me. 'Look *there*. I tell you that is Needle.'

'You're ill, George. Heavens, you must be seeing things. Come on home. Needle isn't there. You know as well as I do, Needle is dead.'

I must explain that I departed this life nearly five years ago. But I did not altogether depart this world. There were those odd things still to be done which one's executors can never do properly. Papers to be looked over, even after the executors have torn them up. Lots of business except of course on Sundays and Holidays of Obligation, plenty to take an interest in for the time being. I take my recreation on Saturday mornings. If it is a wet Saturday, I wander up and down the substantial lanes of Woolworths as I did when I was young and visible. There is a pleasurable spread of objects on the counters which I now perceive and exploit with a certain detachment, since it suits with my condition of life. Creams, toothpastes, combs and hankies, cotton gloves, flimsy flowering scarves, writing paper and crayons, ice-cream cones and orangeade, screwdrivers, boxes of tacks, tins of paint, of glue, marmalade; I always liked them, but far more now that I have no need of any. When Saturdays are fine I go instead to the Portobello Road, where formerly I would jaunt with Kathleen in our grown-up days. The barrow loads do not change much, of apples and rayon vests in common blues and low-taste mauve, of silver plate, trays, and teapots long since changed hands from the bygone citizens to dealers, from shops to the new flats and breakable homes, and then over to the barrow stalls and the dealers again: Georgian spoons, rings, earrings of turquoise and opal set in the butterfly pattern or true-lovers' knot, patch boxes with miniature paintings of ladies on ivory, snuff boxes of silver with Scotch pebbles inset.

Sometimes as occasion arises on a Saturday morning, my friend

Kathleen who is a Catholic has a Mass said for my soul, and then I am in attendance as it were at the church. But most Saturdays I take my delight among the solemn crowds with their aimless purposes, their eternal life not far away, who push past the counters and stalls, who handle, buy, steal, touch, desire and ogle the merchandise. I hear the tinkling tills, I hear the jangle of loose change and tongues and children wanting to hold and have.

That is how I came to be in the Portobello Road that Saturday morning when I saw George and Kathleen. I would not have spoken had I not been inspired to it. Indeed, it is one of the things I can't do now – to speak out, unless inspired. And most extraordinary, on that morning as I spoke a degree of visibility set in. I suppose from poor George's point of view it was like seeing a ghost when he saw me standing by the fruit barrow repeating in so friendly a manner, 'Hallo, George!'

We were bound for the south. When our education, what we could get of it from the north, was thought to be finished, one by one we were sent for to London. John Skinner, whom we called Skinny, went to study more archaeology; George to join his uncle's tobacco firm; Kathleen to stay with her rich connections and to potter intermittently in the Mayfair hat shop which one of them owned. A little later I also went to London to see life, for it was my ambition to write about life, which first I had to see.

'We four must stick together,' George said very often in that yearning way of his. He was always desperately afraid of neglect. We four looked likely to shift off in different directions and George did not trust the other three of us not to forget all about him. More and more as the time came for him to depart for his uncle's tobacco farm in Africa he said:

'We four must keep in touch.'

And before he left he told each of us anxiously:

'I'll write regularly, once a month. We must keep together for the sake of the old times.' He had three prints taken from the negative of that photo on the haystack, wrote on the back of them, 'George took this the day that Needle found the needle', and gave us a copy each. I think we all wished he could become a bit more callous.

During my lifetime I was a drifter, nothing organized. It was difficult for my friends to follow the logic of my life. By the normal reckonings I should have come to starvation and ruin, which I never did. Of course I did not live to write about life as I wanted to do. Possibly that is why I am inspired to do so now in these peculiar circumstances.

I taught in a private school in Kensington for almost three months, very small children. I didn't know what to do with them, but I was kept fairly busy escorting incontinent little boys to the lavatory and telling the little girls to use their handkerchiefs. After that I lived a winter holiday in London on my small capital, and when that had run out I found a diamond bracelet in a cinema for which I received a reward of fifty pounds. When it was used up, I got a job with a publicity man, writing speeches for absorbed industrialists, in which the dictionary of quotations came in very useful. So it went on. I got engaged to Skinny, but shortly after that I was left a small legacy, enough to keep me for six months. This somehow decided me that I didn't love Skinny, so I gave him back the ring.

But it was through Skinny that I went to Africa. He was engaged with a party of researchers to investigate King Solomon's mines, that series of ancient workings ranging from the ancient port of Ophir, now called Beira, across Portuguese East Africa and Southern Rhodesia to the mighty jungle-city of Zimbabwe, whose temple walls still stand by the approach to an ancient and sacred mountain, where the rubble of that civilization scatters itself over the surrounding Rhodesian waste. I accompanied the party as a sort of secretary. Skinny vouched for me, he paid my fare, he sympathized by his action with my inconsequential life although when he spoke of it he disapproved. A life like mine annoys most people; they go to their jobs every day, attend to things, give orders, pummel typewriters, and get two or three weeks off every year, and it vexes them to see someone else not bothering to do these things and yet getting away with it, not starving, being lucky as they call it. Skinny, when I had broken off our engagement, lectured me about this, but still he took me to Africa knowing I should probably leave his unit within a few months.

We were there a few weeks before we began inquiring for George, who was farming about four hundred miles away to the north. We had not told him of our plans.

'If we tell George to expect us in his part of the world, he'll come rushing to pester us the first week. After all, we're going on business,' Skinny had said.

Before we left, Kathleen told us, 'Give George my love, and tell him not to send frantic cables every time I don't answer his letters right away. Tell him I'm busy in the hat shop and being presented. You would think he hadn't another friend in the world the way he carries on.'

We had settled first at Fort Victoria, our nearest place of access to the Zimbabwe ruins. There we made inquiries about George. It was clear he hadn't many friends. The older settlers were the most tolerant about the half-caste woman he was living with, as we learned, but they were furious about his methods of raising tobacco, which we learned were most unprofessional and in some mysterious way disloyal to the whites. We could never discover how it was that George's style of tobacco farming gave the blacks opinions about themselves, but that's what the older settlers claimed. The newer immigrants thought he was unsociable, and of course his living with that nig made visiting impossible.

I must say I was myself a bit offput by this news about the brown woman. I was brought up in a university town where there were Indian, African, and Asiatic students abounding in a variety of tints and hues. I was brought up to avoid them for reasons connected with local reputation and God's ordinances. You cannot easily go against what you were brought up to do unless you are a rebel by nature.

Anyhow, we visited George eventually, taking advantage of the offer of transport from some people bound north in search of game. He had heard of our arrival in Rhodesia, and though he was glad, almost relieved, to see us, he pursued a policy of sullenness for the first hour.

'We wanted to give you a surprise, George.'

'How were we to know that you'd get to hear of our arrival, George? News here must travel faster than light, George.'

'We did hope to give you a surprise, George.'

We flattered and 'Georged' him until at last he said, 'Well, I must say it's good to see you. All we need now is Kathleen. We four simply must stick together. You find when you're in a place like this, there's nothing like old friends.'

He showed us his drying sheds. He showed us a paddock where he was experimenting with a horse and a zebra mare, attempting to mate them. They were frolicking happily, but not together. They passed each other in their private play time and again, but without acknowledgement and without resentment.

'It's been done before,' George said. 'It makes a fine, strong beast, more intelligent than a mule and sturdier than a horse. But I'm not having any success with this pair; they won't look at each other.'

After a while he said, 'Come in for a drink and meet Matilda.'

She was dark brown, with a subservient hollow chest and round shoulders, a gawky woman, very snappy with the houseboys. We said pleasant things as we drank on the stoep before dinner, but we found George difficult. For some reason he began to rail me for breaking off my engagement to Skinny, saying what a dirty trick it was after all those good times in the old days. I diverted attention to Matilda. I supposed, I said, she knew this part of the country well?

'No,' said she, 'I been a-shellitered my life. I not put out to working.

Me nothing to go from place to place is allowed like dirty girls does.' In her speech she gave every syllable equal stress.

George explained. 'Her father was a white magistrate in Natal. She had a sheltered upbringing, different from the other coloureds, you realize.'

'Man, me no black-eyed Susan,' said Matilda, 'no, no.'

On the whole, George treated her as a servant. She was about four months advanced in pregnancy, but he made her get up and fetch for him many times. Soap: that was one of the things Matilda had to fetch. George made his own bath soap, showed it proudly, gave us the recipe which I did not trouble to remember; I was fond of nice soaps during my lifetime, and George's smelt of brilliantine and looked likely to soil one's skin.

'D'you brahn?' Matilda asked me.

George said, 'She is asking if you go brown in the sun.'

'No, I go freckled.'

'I got sister-in-law go freckles.'

She never spoke another word to Skinny nor to me, and we never saw her again.

Some months later I said to Skinny.

'I'm fed up with being a camp follower.'

He was not surprised that I was leaving his unit, but he hated my way of expressing it. He gave me a Presbyterian look.

'Don't talk like that. Are you going back to England or staying?'

'Staying for a while.'

'Well, don't wander too far off.'

I was able to live on the fee I got for writing a gossip column in a local weekly, which wasn't my idea of writing about life, of course. I made friends, more than I could cope with, after I left Skinny's exclusive little band of archaeologists. I had the attractions of being newly out from England and of wanting to see life. Of the countless young men and go-ahead families who purred me along the Rhodesian roads hundred after hundred miles, I only kept up with one family when I returned to my native land. I think that was because they were the most representative, they stood for all the rest; people in those parts are very typical of each other, as one group of standing stones in that wilderness is like the next.

I met George once more in an hotel in Bulawayo. We drank highballs and spoke of war. Skinny's party were just then deciding whether to remain in the country or return home. They had reached an exciting part of their research, and whenever I got a chance to visit Zimbabwe he would take me for a moonlight walk in the ruined temple, and try to make me see phantom Phoenicians flitting ahead of us or along the walls. I had half a mind to marry Skinny; perhaps, I thought, when his studies were finished. The impending war was in our bones; so I remarked to George as we sat drinking highballs on the hotel stoep in the hard, bright, sunny July winter of that year.

George was inquisitive about my relations with Skinny. He tried to pump me for about half an hour, and when at last I said, 'You are becoming aggressive, George,' he stopped. He became quite pathetic. He said, 'War or no war, I'm clearing out of this.'

'It's the heat does it,' I said.

'I'm clearing out, in any case. I've lost a fortune in tobacco. My uncle is making a fuss. It's the other bloody planters; once you get the wrong side of them you're finished in this wide land.'

'What about Matilda?' I asked.

He said, 'She'll be all right. She's got hundreds of relatives.'

I had already heard about the baby girl. Coal black, by repute, with George's features. And another on the way, they said.

'What about the child?'

He didn't say anything to that. He ordered more highballs, and when they arrived he swizzled his for a long time with a stick. 'Why didn't you ask me to your twenty-first?' he said then.

'I didn't have anything special, no party, George. We had a quiet drink among ourselves, George, just Skinny and the old professors and two of the wives and me, George.'

'You didn't ask me to your twenty-first,' he said. 'Kathleen writes to me regularly.'

This wasn't true. Kathleen sent me letters fairly often in which she said, 'Don't tell George I wrote to you, as he will be expecting word from me and I can't be bothered actually.'

'But you,' said George, 'don't seem to have any sense of old friendships, you and Skinny.'

'Oh, George!' I said.

'Remember the times we had,' George said. 'We used to have times.' His large brown eyes began to water.

'I'll have to be getting along,' I said.

'Please don't go. Don't leave me just yet. I've something to tell you.'

'Something nice?' I laid on an eager smile. All responses to George had to be overdone.

'You don't know how lucky you are,' George said.

'How?' I said. Sometimes I got tired of being called lucky by everybody. There were times when, privately practising my writings about life, I knew the bitter side of my fortune. When I failed again and again to reproduce life in some satisfactory and perfect form, I was the more imprisoned, for all my carefree living, within my craving for this satisfaction. Sometimes, in my impotence and need I secreted a venom which infected all my life for days on end, and which spurted out indiscriminately on Skinny or on anyone who crossed my path.

'You aren't bound by anyone,' George said. 'You come and go as you please. Something always turns up for you. You're free, and you don't know your luck.'

'You're a damn sight more free than I am,' I said sharply. 'You've got your rich uncle.'

'He's losing interest in me,' George said. 'He's had enough.'

'Oh well, you're young yet. What was it you wanted to tell me?'

'A secret,' George said. 'Remember we used to have those secrets!'

'Oh yes, we did.'

'Did you ever tell any of mine?'

'Oh no, George.' In reality, I couldn't remember any particular secret out of the dozens we must have exchanged from our schooldays onwards.

'Well, this is a secret, mind. Promise not to tell.'

'Promise.'

'I'm married.'

'Married, George! Oh, who to?'

'Matilda.'

'How dreadful!' I spoke before I could think, but he agreed with me.

'Yes, it's awful, but what could I do?'

'You might have asked my advice,' I said pompously.

'I'm two years older than you are. I don't ask advice from you, Needle, little beast.'

'Don't ask for sympathy, then.'

'A nice friend you are,' he said, 'I must say, after all these years.'

'Poor George,' I said.

'There are three white men to one white woman in this country,' said George. 'An isolated planter doesn't see a white woman, and if he sees one she doesn't see him. What could I do? I needed the woman.'

I was nearly sick. One, because of my Scottish upbringing. Two, because of my horror of corny phrases like 'I needed the woman', which George repeated twice again.

'And Matilda got tough,' said George, 'after you and Skinny came to visit us. She had some friends at the Mission, and she packed up and went to them.'

'You should have let her go,' I said.

'I went after her,' George said. 'She insisted on being married, so I married her.'

'That's not a proper secret, then,' I said. 'The news of a mixed marriage soon gets about.'

'I took care of that,' George said. 'Crazy as I was, I took her to the Congo and married her there. She promised to keep quiet about it.'

'Well, you can't clear off and leave her now, surely,' I said.

'I'm going to get out of this place. I can't stand the woman, and I can't stand the country. I didn't realize what it would be like. Two years of the country and three months of my wife has been enough.'

'Will you get a divorce?'

'No, Matilda's Catholic. She won't divorce.'

George was fairly getting through the highballs, and I wasn't far behind him. His brown eyes floated shiny and liquid as he told me how he had written to tell his uncle of his plight. 'Except of course, I didn't say we were married, that would have been too much for him. He's a prejudiced, hardened old colonial. I only said I'd had a child by a coloured woman and was expecting another, and he perfectly understood. He came at once by plane a few weeks ago. He's made a settlement on her, providing she keeps her mouth shut about her association with me.'

'Will she do that?'

'Oh yes, or she won't get the money.'

'But as your wife she has a claim on you, in any case.'

'If she claimed as my wife, she'd get far less. Matilda knows what she's doing, greedy bitch she is. She'll keep her mouth shut.'

'Only, you won't be able to marry again, will you, George?'

'Not unless she dies,' he said. 'And she's as strong as a trek ox.'

'Well, I'm sorry, George,' I said.

'Good of you to say so,' he said. 'But I can see by your chin that you disapprove of me. Even my old uncle understood.'

'Oh, George, I quite understand. You were lonely, I suppose.'

'You didn't even ask me to your twenty-first. If you and Skinny had been nicer to me, I would never have lost my head and married the woman, never.'

'You didn't ask me to your wedding,' I said.

'You're a catty bissom, Needle; not like what you were in the old times when you used to tell us your wee stories.'

'I'll have to be getting along,' I said.

'Mind you keep the secret,' George said.

'Can't I tell Skinny? He would be very sorry for you, George.'

'You mustn't tell anyone. Keep it a secret. Promise.'

'Promise,' I said. I understood that he wished to enforce some sort of bond between us with this secret, and I thought, 'Oh well, I suppose he's lonely. Keeping his secret won't do any harm.'

I returned to England with Skinny's party just before the war.

I did not see George again till just before my death, five years ago.

After the war Skinny returned to his studies. He had two more exams, over a period of eighteen months, and I thought I might marry him when the exams were over.

'You might do worse than Skinny,' Kathleen used to say to me on our Saturday morning excursions to the antique shops and the junk stalls.

She, too, was getting on in years. The remainder of our families in Scotland were hinting that it was time we settled down with husbands. Kathleen was a little younger than me, but looked much older. She knew her chances were diminishing, but at that time I did not think she cared very much. As for myself, the main attraction of marrying Skinny was his prospective expeditions in Mesopotamia. My desire to marry him had to be stimulated by the continual reading of books about Babylon and Assyria; perhaps Skinny felt this, because he supplied the books, and even started instructing me in the art of deciphering cuneiform tables.

Kathleen was more interested in marriage than I thought. Like me she had racketed around a good deal during the war; she had actually been engaged to an officer in the US navy, who was killed. Now she kept an antique shop near Lambeth, was doing very nicely, lived in a Chelsea square, but for all that she must have wanted to be married and have children. She would stop and look into all the prams which the mothers had left outside shops or area gates.

'The poet Swinburne used to do that,' I told her once.

'Really? Did he want children of his own?'

'I shouldn't think so. He simply liked babies.'

Before Skinny's final exam he fell ill and was sent to a sanatorium in Switzerland.

'You're fortunate, after all, not to be married to him,' Kathleen said. 'You might have caught TB.'

I was fortunate, I was lucky . . . so everyone kept telling me on different occasions. Although it annoyed me to hear, I knew they were right, but in a way that was different from what they meant. It took me very small effort to make a living; book reviews, odd jobs for Kathleen, a few months with the publicity man again, still getting up speeches about literature, art, and life for industrial tycoons. I was waiting to write about life, and it seemed to me that the good fortune lay in this whenever it should be. And until then I was assured of my charmed life, the necessities of existence always coming my way, and I with far more leisure than anyone else. I thought of my type of luck after I became a Catholic and was being confirmed. The bishop touches the candidate on the cheek, a symbolic reminder of the sufferings a Christian is supposed to undertake. I thought, how lucky, what a feathery symbol to stand for the hellish violence of its true meaning.

I visited Skinny twice in the two years that he was in the sanatorium. He was almost cured, and expected to be home within a few months. I told Kathleen after my last visit.

'Maybe I'll marry Skinny when he's well again.'

'Make it definite, Needle, and not so much of the maybe. You don't know when you're well off,' she said.

This was five years ago, in the last year of my life. Kathleen and I had become very close friends. We met several times each week, and after our Saturday morning excursions in the Portobello Road very often I would accompany Kathleen to her aunt's house in Kent for a long weekend.

One day in the June of that year I met Kathleen specially for lunch because she had phoned me to say she had news.

'Guess who came into the shop this afternoon,' she said.

'Who?'

'George.'

We had half imagined George was dead. We had received no letters in the past ten years. Early in the war we had heard rumours of his keeping a night club in Durban, but nothing after that. We could have made inquiries if we had felt moved to do so.

At one time, when we discussed him, Kathleen had said:

'I ought to get in touch with poor George. But, then, I think he would write back. He would demand a regular correspondence again.'

'We four must stick together,' I mimicked.

'I can visualize his reproachful limpid orbs,' Kathleen said.

Skinny said, 'He's probably gone native. With his coffee concubine and a dozen mahogany kids.'

'Perhaps he's dead,' Kathleen said.

I did not speak of George's marriage, nor any of his confidences in the hotel at Bulawayo. As the years passed, we ceased to mention him except in passing, as someone more or less dead so far as we were concerned.

Kathleen was excited about George's turning up. She had forgotten her impatience with him in former days; she said:

'It was so wonderful to see old George. He seems to need a friend, feels neglected, out of touch with things.'

'He needs mothering, I suppose.'

Kathleen didn't notice the malice. She declared, 'That's exactly the case with George. It always has been. I can see it now.'

She seemed ready to come to any rapid new and happy conclusion about George. In the course of the morning he had told her of his wartime night club in Durban, his game-shooting expeditions since. It was clear he had not mentioned Matilda. He had put on weight, Kathleen told me, but he could carry it.

I was curious to see this version of George, but I was leaving for Scotland next day and did not see him till September of that year just before my death.

While I was in Scotland I gathered from Kathleen's letters that she was seeing George very frequently, finding enjoyable company in him, looking after him. 'You'll be surprised to see how he has developed.' Apparently he would hang round Kathleen in her shop most days – 'it makes him feel useful' as she maternally expressed it. He had an old relative in Kent whom he visited at weekends; this old lady lived a few miles from Kathleen's aunt, which made it easy for them to travel down together on Saturdays and go for long country walks.

'You'll see such a difference in George,' Kathleen said on my return to London in September. I was to meet him that night, a Saturday. Kathleen's aunt was abroad, the maid on holiday, and I was to keep Kathleen company in the empty house.

George had left London for Kent a few days earlier. 'He's actually helping with the harvest down there!' Kathleen told me lovingly.

Kathleen and I had planned to travel down together, but on that Saturday she was unexpectedly delayed in London on some business. It was arranged that I should go ahead of her in the early afternoon to see to the provisions for our party; Kathleen had invited George to dinner at her aunt's house that night.

'I should be with you by seven,' she said. 'Sure you won't mind the empty house? I hate arriving at empty houses myself.'

I said no, I liked an empty house.

So I did, when I got there. I had never found the house more likeable. A large Georgian vicarage in about eight acres, most of the rooms shut and sheeted, there being only one servant. I discovered that I wouldn't need to go shopping, Kathleen's aunt had left many and delicate supplies with notes attached to them: 'Eat this up please do, see also fridge', and 'A treat for three hungry people, see also 2 bttles beaune for yr party on back kn table.' It was like a treasure hunt as I followed clue after clue through the cool, silent domestic quarters. A house in which there are no people – but with all the signs of tenancy – can be a most tranquil, good place. People take up space in a house out of proportion to their size. On my previous visits I had seen the rooms overflowing as it seemed, with Kathleen, her aunt, and the little fat maidservant; they were always on the move. As I wandered through that part of the house which was in use, opening windows to let in the pale yellow air of September, I was not conscious that I, Needle, was taking up any space at all, I might have been a ghost.

The only thing to be fetched was the milk. I waited till after four when the milking should be done, then set off for the farm which lay across two fields at the back of the orchard. There, when the byreman was handing me the bottle, I saw George.

'Hallo, George,' I said.

'Needle! What are you doing here?' he said.

'Fetching milk,' I said.

'So am I. Well, it's good to see you, I must say.'

As we paid the farmhand, George said, 'I'll walk back with you part of the way. But I mustn't stop, my old cousin's without any milk for her tea. How's Kathleen?'

'She was kept in London. She's coming on later, about seven, she expects.'

We had reached the end of the first field. George's way led to the left and on to the main road.

'We'll see you tonight, then?' I said.

'Yes, and talk about old times.'

'Grand,' I said.

But George got over the stile with me.

'Look here,' he said. 'I'd like to talk to you, Needle.'

'We'll talk tonight, George. Better not keep your cousin waiting for the milk.' I found myself speaking to him almost as if he were a child.

'No, I want to talk to you alone. This is a good opportunity.'

We began to cross the second field. I had been hoping to have the house to myself for a couple more hours, and I was rather petulant.

'See,' he said suddenly, 'that haystack.'

'Yes,' I said absently.

'Let's sit there and talk. I'd like to see you up on a haystack again. I still keep that photo. Remember that time when –?'

'I found the needle,' I said very quickly, to get it over.

But I was glad to rest. The stack had been broken up, but we managed to find a nest in it. I buried my bottle of milk in the hay for coolness. George placed his carefully at the foot of the stack.

'My old cousin is terribly vague, poor soul. A bit hazy in her head. She hasn't the least sense of time. If I tell her I've only been gone ten minutes, she'll believe it.'

I giggled and looked at him. His face had grown much larger, his lips full, wide, and with a ripe colour that is strange in a man. His brown eyes were abounding as before with some inarticulate plea.

'So you're going to marry Skinny after all these years?'

'I really don't know, George.'

'You played him up properly.'

'It isn't for you to judge. I have my own reasons for what I do.'

'Don't get sharp,' he said, 'I was only funning.' To prove it, he lifted a tuft of hay and brushed my face with it.

'D'you know,' he said next, 'I didn't think you and Skinny treated me very decently in Rhodesia.'

'Well, we were busy, George. And we were younger then; we had a lot to do and see. After all, we could see you any other time, George.'

'A touch of selfishness,' he said.

'I'll have to be getting along, George.' I made to get down from the stack.

He pulled me back. 'Wait, I've got something to tell you.'

'OK, George, tell me.'

'First promise not to tell Kathleen. She wants it kept a secret so that she can tell you herself.'

'All right. Promise.'

'I'm going to marry Kathleen.'

'But you're already married.'

Sometimes I heard news of Matilda from the one Rhodesian family with whom I still kept up. They referred to her as 'George's Dark Lady', and of course they did not know he was married to her. She had apparently made a good thing out of George, they said, for she minced around all tarted up, never did a stroke of work, and was always unsettling the respectable coloured girls in their neighbourhood. According to accounts, she was a living example of the folly of behaving as George did.

'I married Matilda in the Congo,' George was saying.

'It would still be bigamy,' I said.

He was furious when I used that word bigamy. He lifted a handful of hay as if he would throw it in my face, but controlling himself meanwhile, he fanned it at me playfully.

'I'm not sure that the Congo marriage was valid,' he continued. 'Anyway, as far as I'm concerned, it isn't.'

'You can't do a thing like that,' I said.

'I need Kathleen. She's been decent to me. I think we were always meant for each other, me and Kathleen.'

'I'll have to be going,' I said.

But he put his knee over my ankles so that I couldn't move. I sat still and gazed into space.

He tickled my face with a wisp of hay.

'Smile up, Needle,' he said; 'let's talk like old times.'

'Well?'

'No one knows about my marriage to Matilda except you and me.'

'And Matilda,' I said.

'She'll hold her tongue so long as she gets her payments. My uncle left an annuity for the purpose; his lawyers see to it.'

'Let me go, George.'

'You promised to keep it a secret,' he said, 'you promised.'

'Yes, I promised.'

'And now that you're going to marry Skinny, we'll be properly coupled off as we should have been years ago. We should have been, but youth – our youth – got in the way, didn't it?'

'Life got in the way,' I said.

'But everything's going to be all right now. You'll keep my secret, won't you? You promised.' He had released my feet. I edged a little farther from him.

I said, 'If Kathleen intends to marry you, I shall tell her that you're already married.'

'You wouldn't do a dirty trick like that, Needle? You're going to be happy with Skinny, you wouldn't stand in the way of my –'

'I must, Kathleen's my best friend,' I said swiftly.

He looked as if he would murder me, and he did; he stuffed hay into my mouth until it could hold no more, kneeling on my body to keep it prone, holding both my wrists tight in his huge left hand. I saw the red full lines of his mouth, and the white slit of his teeth last thing on earth. Not another soul passed by as he pressed my body into the stack, as he made a deep nest for me, tearing up the hay to make a groove the length of my corpse, and finally pulling the warm dry stuff in a mound over this concealment, so natural looking in a broken haystack. Then George climbed down, took up his bottle of milk and went his way. I suppose that was why he looked so unwell when I stood, nearly five years later, by the barrow in the Portobello Road and said in easy tones, 'Hallo, George!'

The Haystack Murder was one of the notorious crimes of that year.

My friends said, 'A girl who had everything to live for.'

After a search that lasted twenty hours, when my body was found, the evening papers said, ' "Needle" is found: in haystack!'

Kathleen, speaking from that Catholic point of view which takes some getting used to said, 'She was at Confession only the day before she died – wasn't she lucky?'

The poor byrehand who sold us the milk was grilled for hour after hour by the local police, and later by Scotland Yard. So was George. He admitted walking as far as the haystack with me, but he denied lingering there.

'You hadn't seen your friend for ten years?' the inspector asked him.

'That's right,' said George.

'And you didn't stop to have a chat?'

'No. We'd arranged to meet later at dinner. My cousin was waiting for the milk, I couldn't stop.'

The old soul, his cousin, swore that he hadn't been gone more than ten minutes in all, and she believed it to the day of her death a few months later. There was the microscopic evidence of hay on George's jacket, of course, but the same evidence was on every man's jacket in the district that fine harvest year. Unfortunately, the byreman's hands were even brawnier and mightier than George's. The marks on my wrists had been done by such hands, so the laboratory charts indicated when my postmortem was all completed. But the wristmarks weren't enough to pin down the crime to either man. If I hadn't been wearing my long-sleeved cardigan, it was said, the bruises might have matched up properly with someone's fingers.

Kathleen, to prove that George had absolutely no motive, told the police that she was engaged to him. George thought this a little foolish. They checked up on his life in Africa, right back to his living with Matilda. But the marriage didn't come out – who would think of looking up registers in the Congo? Not that this would have proved any motive for murder. All the same, George was relieved when the inquiries were over without the marriage to Matilda being disclosed. He was able to have his nervous breakdown at the same time as Kathleen had hers, and they recovered together and got married, long after the police had shifted their inquiries to an Air Force camp five miles from Kathleen's aunt's home. Only a lot of excitement and drinks came of those investigations. The Haystack Murder was one of the unsolved crimes that year.

Shortly afterwards the byrehand emigrated to Canada to start afresh, with the help of Skinny who felt sorry for him.

*

After seeing George taken away home by Kathleen that Saturday in the Portobello Road, I thought that perhaps I might be seeing more of him in similar circumstances. The next Saturday I looked out for him, and at last there he was, without Kathleen, half worried, half hopeful.

I dashed his hopes, I said, 'Hallo, George!'

He looked in my direction, rooted in the midst of the flowing market mongers in that convivial street. I thought to myself, 'He looks as if he had a mouthful of hay.' It was the new bristly maize-coloured beard and moustache surrounding his great mouth suggested the thought, gay and lyrical as life.

'Hallo, George!' I said again.

I might have been inspired to say more on that agreeable morning, but he didn't wait. He was away down a side street and along another street and down one more, zigzag, as far and as devious as he could take himself from the Portobello Road.

Nevertheless, he was back again next week. Poor Kathleen had brought him in her car. She left it at the top of the street, and got out with him, holding him tight by the arm. It grieved me to see Kathleen ignoring the spread of scintillations on the stalls. I had myself seen a charming Battersea box quite to her taste, also a pair of enamelled silver earrings. But she took no notice of these wares, clinging close to George, and, poor Kathleen – I hate to say how she looked.

And George was haggard. His eyes seemed to have got smaller as if he had been recently in pain. He advanced up the road with Kathleen on his arm, letting himself lurch from side to side with his wife bobbing beside him, as the crowds asserted their rights of way.

'Oh, George!' I said. 'You don't look at all well, George.'

'Look!' said George. 'Over there by the hardware barrow. That's Needle.'

Kathleen was crying. 'Come back home, dear,' she said.

'Oh, you don't look well, George!' I said.

They took him to a nursing home. He was fairly quiet, except on Saturday mornings when they had a hard time of it to keep him indoors and away from the Portobello Road.

But a couple of months later he did escape. It was a Monday.

They searched for him in the Portobello Road, but actually he had gone off to Kent to the village near the scene of the Haystack Murder. There he went to the police and gave himself up, but they could tell from the way he was talking that there was something wrong with the man.

'I saw Needle in the Portobello Road three Saturdays running,' he explained, 'and they put me in a private ward, but I got away while the nurses were seeing to the new patient. You remember the murder of Needle – well, I did it. Now you know the truth, and that will keep bloody Needle's mouth shut.'

Dozens of poor mad fellows confess to every murder. The police obtained an ambulance to take him back to the nursing home. He wasn't there long. Kathleen gave up her shop, and devoted herself to looking after him at home. But she found that the Saturday mornings were a strain. He insisted on going to see me in Portobello Road, and would come back to insist that he'd murdered Needle. Once he tried to tell her something about Matilda, but Kathleen was so kind and solicitous, I don't think he had the courage to remember what he had to say.

Skinny had always been rather reserved with George since the murder. But he was kind to Kathleen. It was he who persuaded them to emigrate to Canada so that George should be well out of reach of the Portobello Road.

George has recovered somewhat in Canada, but of course he will never be the old George again, as Kathleen writes to Skinny. 'That Haystack tragedy did for George,' she writes. 'I feel sorrier for George sometimes than I am for poor Needle. But I do often have Masses said for Needle's soul.'

I doubt if George will ever see me again in the Portobello Road. He broods much over the crumpled snapshot he took of us on the haystack. Kathleen does not like the photograph. I don't wonder. For my part, I consider it quite a jolly snap, but I don't think we were any of us so lovely as we look in it, gazing blatantly over the ripe cornfields – Skinny with his humorous expression, I secure in my difference from the rest, Kathleen with her head prettily perched on her hand, each reflecting fearlessly in the face of George's camera the glory of the world, as if it would never pass.

No Flies on Frank

John Lennon

There were no flies on Frank that morning – after all why not? He was a
responsible citizen with a wife and child, wasn't he? It was a typical Frank
morning and with an agility that defies description he leapt into the
barthroom on to the scales. To his great harold he discovered he was
twelve inches more tall heavy! He couldn't believe it and his blood raised
to his head causing a mighty red colouring.

'I carn't not believe this incredible fact of truth about my very body
which has not gained fat since mother begat me at childburn. Yea, though
I wart through the valet of thy shadowy hut I will feed no norman. What
grate qualmsy hath taken me thus into such a fatty hardbuckle.'

Again Frank looked down at the awful vision which clouded his eyes
with fearful weight. 'Twelve inches more heavy, Lo!, but am I not more
fatty than my brother Geoffery whose father Alec came from Kenneth –
through Leslies, who begat Arthur, son of Eric, by the house of Ronald
and April – keepers of James of Newcastle who ran Madeline at 2–1 by
Silver Flower, (10–2) past Wot-ro-Wot at 4s. 3d. a pound?'

He journeyed downstairs crestfallen and defective – a great wait on his
boulders – not even his wife's battered face could raise a smile on poor
Frank's head – who as you know had no flies on him. His wife, a former
beauty queer, regarded him with a strange but burly look.

'What ails thee, Frank?' she asked, stretching her prune. 'You look
dejected if not informal,' she addled.

''Tis nothing but wart I have gained but twelve inches more tall heavy
than at the very clock of yesterday at this time – am I not the most
miserable of men? Suffer ye not to spake to me or I might thrust you a
mortal injury; I must traddle this trial alone.'

'Lo! Frank – thou hast smote me harshly with such grave talk – am I to
blame for this vast burton?'

Frank looked sadly at his wife – forgetting for a moment the cause of his misery. Walking slowly but slowly towards her, he took his head in his hands and with a few swift blows had clubbed her mercifully to the ground dead.

'She shouldn't see me like this,' he mubbled, 'not all fat and on her thirty-second birthday.'

Frank had to get his own breakfast that morning and also on the following mornings.

Two, (or was it three?) weeks later Frank awake again to find that there were *still* no flies on him.

'No flies on this Frank boy,' he thought; but to his amazement there seemed to be a lot of flies on his wife – who was still lying about the kitchen floor.

'I carn't not partake of bread and that with her lying about the place,' he thought allowed, writing as he spoke. 'I must deliver her to her home where she will be made welcome.'

He gathered her in a small sack (for she was only four foot three) and headed for her rightful home. Frank knocked on the door of his wife's mother's house. She opened the door.

'I've brought Marian home, Mrs Sutherskill' (he could never call her Mum). He opened the sack and placed Marian on the doorstep.

'I'm not having all those flies in my home,' shouted Mrs Sutherskill (who was very house-proud), shutting the door. 'She could have at least offered me a cup of tea,' thought Frank lifting the problem back on his boulders.

Sister Coxall's Revenge

Dawn Muscillo

Sister Coxall had been in Violet Ward for many years. Her pride and joy was her own little office, scrupulously clean, its walls glistening with fresh white paint. A bowl of crisp daffodils stood on the middle of her desk exactly an inch away from the leather bound blotter. The arrangement of pens behind the blotter gave the impression of rigor mortis soldiers all in a row, their black caps tightly screwed on.

Sister Coxall sat at her desk, her eyes unseeing. She pondered deeply. Who was this new doctor, anyway? Some silly youth fresh from medical school? What right had he to interfere in the running of her ward? Her small hand tightened into a fist. What right had he to even voice an opinion?

She had met him yesterday. He had driven into the hospital grounds and almost driven over her. There were plenty of 'Go Slow' notices within sight. Besides, almost everybody who worked at the hospital knew she walked through the grounds at that time of day.

'Are you all right?' he had said, scrambling from his car. 'I really wasn't concentrating.'

His sombre eyes, glowing with concern, rested on her uniform. He seemed embarrassed. 'Er, Sister, I'm frightfully sorry.'

She couldn't help smiling. 'That's all right, Mr –' she paused politely.

'Doctor – Doctor Green. I've just arrived, as you can see,' he grinned. 'I'm to take over the running of D Block.'

Sister Coxall noticeably stiffened. 'D Block?' she echoed.

'Look, get into my car and I'll drive you to the Nurses' Home. I take it you do live in?'

They sat in silence and soon were mounting the dingy staircase leading to Sister Coxall's neat room. Once inside, she took off her cape and carefully folded it into straight pleats.

'Sit down, Doctor. I'll make some tea.'

Sitting drinking the sweet tea, Doctor Green explained how he had always been interested in the work amongst mentally disturbed people and how, when he had finished his studies, he had applied for this post in one of the country's largest psychiatric hospitals. He little thought he would be accepted, but he had, and without an interview. It seemed his references and commendations were sufficient.

He told her of the great changes and new ideas he hoped to introduce on his own block. 'For instance,' he said, 'the sister on Violet Ward has been in the same ward for ten years without ever circulating around the other wards and buildings. She surely must have lost her identity to some extent, nurse and patients fusing into one large family. Her patients are growing old with her; they must be more like children to her than sick people.' He leaned forward. 'You know, Sister, a person working with the mentally ill for any length of time without a change, is in great danger of illness herself. Tomorrow, when I begin my work, I intend to move that sister to a different ward. She may not realize it at the time, but the change will do her good.'

Sister Coxall listened, a faint pink flush tinged her ears. Reality bloomed in the shape of the lawn outside the window, her eyes taking in the neatness of its razor trimmed edges.

The day had arrived. She looked around her office. She was to be removed from this, her home, and cast among strangers.

'No,' she screamed, and her fist came heavily down upon the blotter, scattering the pens into sudden life.

Sister Coxall's mind began to work. Now it raced. Nobody knows he is here except me. He said he was staying at an hotel last night and would be coming straight to the ward this morning, before reporting to the General Office. He had no white coat or identity badge yet.

A diabolical smile drew back the corners of her thin straight mouth. 'There is only one thing to do,' she muttered, and rose and went to the door.

'Nurse,' she shrilled, 'a new patient is expected this morning, a Mr Green. When he arrives, bring him straight to my office.' She looked down at an empty report paper she held in her hand. 'It says here that he is paranoid and greatly deluded; he thinks he is a doctor. Humour him, Nurse. I'll prepare a strong sedative.'

Going to the cupboard, Sister Coxall took down a syringe and filled it with a cool amber liquid. She then took an empty file from a cabinet and began to prepare a written report on Mr Green.

She sighed. The ward was full of sedated men, all deluded, all insisting in their nightmare ravings that they were doctors. No one would ever take her ward and office away from her. No one.

Later that day in the General Office, the Hospital Secretary was speaking into the phone.

'It seems odd, Matron, this is the tenth doctor who has failed to report for duty in ten years. I must say though, that Sister Coxall manages admirably, a true devotee to her work. A doctor would find very little to do on her ward, anyway.'

Thou Shalt Not Suffer a Witch . . .

Dorothy K. Haynes

The child sat alone in her bedroom, weaving the fringe of the counterpane in and out of her fingers. It was a horrible room, the most neglected one of the house. The grate was narrow and rusty, cluttered up with dust and hair combings, and the floorboards creaked at every step. When the wind blew, the door rattled and banged, but the window was sealed tight, webbed, fly-spotted, a haven for everything black and creeping.

In and out went her fingers, the fringe pulled tight between nail and knuckle. Outside, the larches tossed and flurried, brilliant green under a blue sky. Sometimes the sun would go in, and rain would hit the window like a handful of nails thrown at the glass; then the world would lighten suddenly, the clouds would drift past in silver and white, and the larches would once more toss in the sunshine.

'Jinnot! Jinnot!' called a voice from the yard. 'Where've you got to, Jinnot?'

She did not answer. The voice went farther away, still calling. Jinnot sat on the bed, hearing nothing but the voice which had tormented her all week.

'You'll do it, Jinnot, eh? Eh, Jinnot? An' I'll give you a sixpence to spend. We've always got on well, Jinnot. You like me better than her. She never gave you ribbons for your hair, did she? She never bought you sweeties in the village? It's not much to ask of you, Jinnot, just to say she looked at you, an' it happened. It's not as if it was telling lies. It has happened before; it has, eh, Jinnot?'

She dragged herself over to the mirror, the cracked sheet of glass with the fawn fly-spots. The door on her left hand, the window on her right, neither a way of escape. Her face looked back at her, yellow in the reflected sunlight. Her hair was the colour of hay, her heavy eyes had no shine in them. Large teeth, wide mouth, the whole face was square and dull. She went back to the bed, and her fingers picked again at the fringe.

Had it happened before? Why could she not remember properly? Perhaps it was because they were all so kind to her after it happened, trying to wipe it out of her memory. 'You just came over faint, lassie. Just a wee sickness, like. Och, you don't need to cry, you'll be fine in a minute. Here's Minty to see to you . . .'

But Minty would not see to her this time.

The voice went on and on in her head, wheedling, in one ear and out of the other.

'Me and Jack will get married, see, Jinnot? And when we're married, you can come to our house whenever you like. You can come in, and I'll bake some scones for you, Jinnot, and sometimes we'll let you sleep in our wee upstairs room. You'll do it, Jinnot, will you not? For Jack as well as for me. You like Jack. Mind he mended your Dolly for you? And you'd like to see us married thegither, would you not?

'He'd never be happy married to her, Jinnot. You're a big girl now, you'll see that for yourself. She's good enough in her way, see, but she's not the right kind for him. She sits and sews and works all day, but she's never a bit of fun with him, never a word to say. But he's never been used to anyone better, see, Jinnot, and he'll not look at anybody else while she's there. It's for his own good, Jinnot, and for her sake as well. They'd never be happy married.

'And, Jinnot, you're not going to do her any harm. Someday you'll get married yourself, Jinnot, and you'll know. So it's just kindness . . . and she *is* like that, like what I said. Mebbe she's been the cause of the trouble you had before, you never know. So you'll do it, Jinnot, eh? You'll do it?'

She did not want to. The door rattled in the wind, and the sun shone through the dirt and the raindrops on the window. Why did she want to stay here, with the narrow bed, the choked grate, the mirror reflecting the flaked plaster of the opposite wall? The dust blew along the floor, and the chimney and the keyhole howled together. 'Jinnot! Jinnot!' went the voice again. She paid no attention. Pulling back the blankets, she climbed fully dressed into the bed, her square, suety face like a mask laid on the pillows. 'Jinnot! Jinnot!' went the voice, calling, coaxing through the height of the wind. She whimpered, and curled herself under the bedclothes, hiding from the daylight and the question that dinned at her even in the dark. 'You'll do it, Jinnot, eh? Will you? Eh, Jinnot?'

Next day, the weather had settled. A quiet, spent sun shone on the farm, the tumbledown dykes and the shabby thatch. Everything was still as a painting, the smoke suspended blue in the air, the ducks so quiet on the pond that the larches doubled themselves in the water. Jinnot stood at the door of the byre, watching Jack Hyslop at work. His brush went swish swish, swirling the muck along to the door. He was a handsome lad. No matter how dirty his work, he always looked clean. His boots were bright every morning, and his black hair glistened as he turned his head. He whistled as his broom spattered dung and dirty water, and Jinnot turned her face away. The strong, hot smell from the byre made something grip her stomach with a strong, relentless fist.

Now Minty came out of the kitchen, across the yard with a basin of pig-swill. With her arm raised, pouring out the slops, she looked at the byre door for a long minute. To the child, the world seemed to stop in space. The byreman's broom was poised in motion, his arms flexed for a forward push; his whistle went on on the same note, high and shrill; and Minty was a statue of mute condemnation, with the dish spilling its contents in a halted stream.

A moment later, Jinnot found that Jack Hyslop was holding her head on his knee. Minty had run up, her apron clutched in both hands. Beatrice, the dairymaid, was watching too, bending over her. There was a smell of the dairy on her clothes, a slight smell of sourness, of milk just on the turn, and her hair waved dark under her cap. 'There now,' she said. 'All right, dearie, all right! What made you go off like that, now?'

The child's face sweated all over, her lips shivered as the air blew cold on her skin. All she wanted now was to run away, but she could not get up to her feet. 'What was it, Jinnot?' said the voice, going on and on, cruel, kind, which was it? 'Tell me, Jinnot. Tell me.'

She could not answer. Her tongue seemed to swell and press back on her throat, so that she vomited. Afterwards, lying in bed, she remembered it all, the sense of relief when she had thrown up all she had eaten, the empty languor of the sleep which followed. Beatrice had put her to bed, and petted her and told her she was a good girl. 'It was easy done, eh, Jinnot? You'd have thought it was real.' She gave a high, uneasy laugh. 'Aye, you're a good wee thing, Jinnot. All the same, you fair frichted me at the beginning!'

She was glad to be left alone. After her sleep, strangely cold, she huddled her knees to her shoulders and tried to understand. Sometime, in a few months or a few years, it did not seem to matter, Minty and Jack Hyslop were to be married. Minty was kind. Since Jinnot's mother had died, she had been nurse and foster mother, attending to clothes and food and evening prayers. She had no time to do more. Her scoldings were frequent, but never unjust. Jinnot had loved her till Beatrice came to the dairy, handsome, gay and always ready with bribes.

'You're a nice wee girl, Jinnot. Look – will you do something for Jack and me – just a wee thing? You've done it before; I know you have. Some time, when Minty's there . . .'

And so she had done it, for the sake of sixpence, and the desire to be rid of the persistent pleading; but where she had meant to pretend to fall in a fit at Minty's glance, just to pretend, she had really lost her senses, merely thinking about it. She was afraid now of what she had done . . . was it true then, about Minty, that the way she looked at you was enough to bring down a curse?

It could not be true. Minty was kind, and would make a good wife. Beatrice was the bad one, with her frightening whispers – and yet, it wasn't really badness; it was wisdom. She knew all the terrible things that children would not understand.

Jinnot got up and put on her clothes. Down in the kitchen, there was firelight, and the steam of the evening meal. Her father was eating heartily, his broad shoulders stooped over his plate. 'All right again, lassie?' he asked, snuggling her to him with one arm. She nodded, her face still a little peaked with weakness. At the other side of the room, Minty was busy at the fireside, but she did not turn her head. Jinnot clung closer to her father.

All the air seemed to be filled with whispers.

From nowhere at all, the news spread that Jinnot was bewitched. She knew it herself. She was fascinated by the romance of her own affliction, but she was frightened as well. Sometimes she would have days with large blanks which memory could not fill. Where had she been? What had she done? And the times when the world seemed to shrivel to the size of a pin-head, with people moving like grains of sand, tiny, but much, much clearer, the farther away they seemed – who was behind it all? When had it started?

In time, however, the trouble seemed to right itself. But now, Jack Hyslop courted Beatrice instead of Minty. Once, following them, Jinnot saw them kiss behind a hayrick. They embraced passionately, arms clutching, bodies pressed together. It had never been like that with Minty, no laughter, no sighs. Their kisses had been mere respectful tokens, the concession to their betrothal.

Minty said nothing, but her sleek hair straggled, her once serene eyes glared under their straight brows. She began to be abrupt with the child. 'Out the road!' she would snap. 'How is it a bairn's aye at your elbow?'

Jinnot longed for the friendliness of the young dairymaid. But Beatrice wanted no third party to share her leisure, and Jinnot was more lonely than ever before.

Why had she no friends? She had never had young company, never played games with someone of her own age. Her pastimes were lonely imaginings, the dark pretence of a brain burdened with a dull body. She made a desperate bid to recover her audience. Eyes shut, her breathing hoarse and ragged, she let herself fall to the ground, and lay there until footsteps came running, and kind hands worked to revive her.

So now she was reinstated, her father once more mindful of her, and the household aware of her importance, a sick person in the house. The voices went on whispering around her, 'Sshh! It's wee Jinnot again. Fell away in a dead faint. Poor lassie, she'll need to be seen to . . . Jinnot – Jinnot . . . wee Jinnot . . .'

But this time, there was a difference. They waited till she waked, and then questioned her. Her father was there, blocking out the light from the window, and the doctor sat by the bedside, obviously displeased with his task. Who was to blame? Who was there when it happened? She knew what they wanted her to say; she knew herself what to tell them. 'Who was it?' pressed her father. 'This has been going on too long.' 'Who was it?' said the doctor. 'There's queer tales going around, you know, Jinnot!' 'You know who it was,' said the voice in her mind. 'You'll do it, Jinnot, eh?'

'I – I don't know,' she sighed, her eyes drooping, her mouth hot and dry. 'I . . . only . . .' she put her hand to her head, and sighed. She could almost believe she was really ill, she felt so tired and strange.

After that, the rumours started again. The voice came back to Jinnot, the urgent and convincing warning – 'She *is* like that, like what I said . . .' For her own peace of mind, she wanted to *know*, but there was no one she could ask. She could not trust her own judgement.

It was months before she found out, and the days had lengthened to a queer tarnished summer, full of stale yellow heat. The larches had burned out long ago, and their branches drooped in dull fringes over the pond. The fields were tangled with buttercups and tall moon daisies, but the flowers dried and shrivelled as soon as they blossomed. All the brooks were silent; and the nettles by the hedges had a curled, thirsty look. Jinnot kept away from the duckpond these days. With the water so low, the floating weeds and mud gave off a bad, stagnant smell.

Over the flowers, the bees hovered, coming and going endlessly, to and from the hives. One day, a large bumble, blundering home, tangled itself in the girl's collar, and stung her neck. She screamed out, running into the house, squealing that she had swallowed the insect, and that something with a sting was flying round in her stomach, torturing her most cruelly. They sent for the doctor, and grouped round her with advice. Later, they found the bee, dead, in the lace which had trapped it; but before that, she vomited up half her inside, with what was unmistakably yellow bees' bodies, and a quantity of waxy stuff all mixed up with wings and frail, crooked legs.

She looked at the watchers, and knew that the time had come. 'It was Minty Fraser!' she wailed. 'It was her! She *looked* at me!' She screamed, and hid her face as the sickness once more attacked her in heaving waves.

They went to the house, and found Minty on her knees, washing over the hearthstone. One of the farm-men hauled her to her feet, and held her wrists together. 'Witch! Witch! Witch!' shouted the crowd at the door.

'What – What –'

'Come on, witch! Out to the crowd!'

'No! No, I never –'

'Leave her a minute,' roared Jack Hyslop. 'Mebbe she – give her a chance to speak!' His mouth twitched a little. At one time, he was thinking, he had been betrothed to Minty, before Beatrice told him . . . he faltered at the thought of Beatrice. 'Well, don't be rough till you're sure,' he finished lamely, turning away and leaving the business to the others. Those who sympathized with witches, he remembered, were apt to share their fate.

The women were not so blate. 'Witch! Witch!' they shrilled. 'Burn the witch! Our bairns are no' safe when folks like her is let to live!'

She was on the doorstep now, her cap torn off, her eye bleeding, her dress ripped away at the shoulder. Jinnot's father, pushing through the mob, raised his hand for the sake of order. 'Look, men! Listen, there! This is my house; there'll be no violence done on the threshold.'

'Hang her! Burn her! A rope, there!'

'No hanging till you make sure. Swim her first. If the devil floats –'

'Jinnot! Here's Jinnot!'

The girl came through a lane in the throng, Beatrice holding her hand, clasping her round the waist. She did not want to see Minty, but her legs forced her on. Then she looked up. A witch . . . she saw the blood on her face, the torn clothes, the look of horror and terrible hurt. That was Minty, who cooked her meals and looked after her and did the work of a mother. She opened her mouth and screamed, till the foam dripped over her chin.

Her father's face was as white as her own spittle. 'Take the beast away,' he said, 'and if she floats, for God's sake get rid of her as quick as you can!'

It was horrible. They all louped at her, clutching and tearing and howling as they plucked at her and trussed her for ducking. She was down on the ground, her clothes flung indecently over her head, her legs kicking as she tried to escape. 'It wasna me!' she skirled. 'It wasna me! I'm no' a witch! Aaah!' The long scream cut the air like a blade. Someone had wrenched her leg and snapped the bone at the ankle, but her body still went flailing about in the dust, like a kitten held under a blanket.

They had her trussed now, wrists crossed, legs crossed, her body arched between them. She was dragged to the pond, blood from her cuts and grazes smearing the clothes of those who handled her. Her hair hung over her face and her broken foot scraped the ground. 'No! No!' she screamed. 'Ah, God . . . !' and once, 'Jinnot! Tell them it wasna me –'

A blow over the mouth silenced her, and she spat a tooth out with a mouthful of blood. She shrieked as they swung and hurtled her through the air. There was a heavy splash, and drops of green, slimy water spattered the watching faces. If Minty was a witch, she would float; and then they would haul her out and hang her, or burn her away, limb by limb.

She sank; the pond was shallow, but below the surface, green weed and clinging mud drew her down in a deadly clutch. The crowd on the bank watched her, fascinated. It was only when her yammering mouth was filled and silenced that they realized what had happened, and took slow steps to help her. By that time, it was too late.

What must it be like to be a witch? The idea seeped into her mind like ink, and all her thoughts were tinged with the black poison. She knew the dreadful aftermath; long after, her mind would be haunted by the sight she had seen. In her own nostrils, she felt the choke and snuffle of the pond slime; but what must it feel like, the knowledge of strange power, the difference from other people, the danger? Her imagination played with the thrilling pain of it, right down to the last agony.

She asked Beatrice about it. Beatrice was married now, with a baby coming, and Jinnot sat with her in the waning afternoons, talking with her, woman to woman.

'I didn't like to see them set on her like yon. She never done me any harm. If it hadn't been for me –'

'Are you sure, Jinnot? Are you sure? Mind the bees, Jinnot, an' yon time at the barn door? What about them?'

'I – I don't know.'

'Well, I'm telling you. She was a witch, that one, if anybody was.'

'Well, mebbe she couldn't help it.'

'No, they can't help the power. It just comes on them. Sometimes they don't want it, but it comes, just the same. It's hard, but you know what the Bible says: "Thou shalt not suffer a witch . . ." '

She had a vision of Minty, quiet, busy, struggling with a force she did not want to house in her body. Beside this, her own fits and vomitings seemed small things. She could forgive knowing that. 'How . . . how do they first know they're witches?' she asked.

'Mercy, I don't know! What questions you ask, Jinnot! How would I know, eh? I daresay they find out soon enough.'

So that was it; they knew themselves. Her mind dabbled and meddled uncomfortably with signs and hints. She wanted to curse Beatrice for putting the idea into her head; she would not believe it; but once there, the thought would not be removed. What if she was a witch? 'I'm not,' she said to herself. 'I'm too young,' she said; but there was no conviction in it. Long before she had been bewitched, she had known there was something different about her. Now it all fell into place. No wonder the village children would not call and play with her. No wonder her father was just rather than affectionate, shielding her only because she was his daughter. And no wonder Beatrice was so eager to keep in with her, with the incessant 'Eh, Jinnot?' always on her lips.

Well, then, she was a witch. As well to know it sooner as later, to accept the bothers with the benefits, the troubles and trances with the newfound sense of power. She had never wanted to kill or curse, never in her most unhappy moments, but now, given the means, would it not be as well to try? Did her power strengthen by being kept, or did it spring up fresh from some infernal reservoir? She did not know. She was a very new witch, uncertain of what was demanded of her. Week after week passed, and she was still no farther forward.

She continued her visits to Beatrice, though the thought of it all made her grue. It angered her to see the girl sitting stout and placid at the fireside, unhaunted, unafraid. 'You'll come and see the baby when it's born, eh, Jinnot?' she would say. 'Do you like babies? Do you?' Nothing mattered to her now, it seemed, but the baby. In the dark winter nights, Jinnot made a resolve to kill her. But for Beatrice, she might never have discovered this terrible fact about herself. Beatrice was to blame for everything, but a witch has means of revenge, and one witch may avenge another.

She had no idea how to cast a spell, and there was no one to help her. What had Minty done? She remembered the moment at the byre-door, the upraised arm, and the long, long look. It would be easy. Bide her time, and Beatrice would die when the spring came.

She sat up in the attic, twining her fingers in the fringe of the bedcover, in and out, under and over. Beatrice was in labour. It had been whispered in the kitchen, spreading from mouth to mouth. Now, Jinnot sat on the bed, watching the larches grow black in the dusk. She was not aware of cold, or dirt, or darkness. All her senses were fastened on the window of Beatrice's cottage, where a light burned, and women gathered round the bed. She fixed her will, sometimes almost praying in her effort to influence fate. 'Kill her! Kill her! Let her die!' Was she talking to God, or to the devil? The thoughts stared and screamed in her mind. She wanted Beatrice to suffer every agony, every pain, and wrench, to bear Minty's pain, and her own into the bargain. All night she sat, willing pain and death, and suffering it all in her own body. Her face was grey as the ceiling, her flesh sweated with a sour smell. Outside, an owl shrieked, and she wondered for a moment if it was Beatrice.

Suddenly, she knew it was all over. The strain passed out of her body, the lids relaxed over her eyes, her body seemed to melt and sprawl over the bed. When she woke, it was morning, and the maids were beaming with good news. 'Did you hear?' they said. 'Beatrice has a lovely wee boy! She's fair away wi' herself!'

Jinnot said nothing. She stopped her mouth and her disappointment with porridge. It did not cross her mind that perhaps, after all, she was no witch. All she thought was that the spell had not worked, and Beatrice was still alive. She left the table, and hurried over to the cottage. The door was ajar, the fire bright in the hearth, and Beatrice was awake in bed, smiling, the colour already flushed back into her cheeks.

'He's a bonny baby, Jinnot. He's lovely, eh? Eh, Jinnot?'

She crept reluctantly to the cradle. Why, he was no size at all, so crumpled, so new, a wee sliver of flesh in a bundle of white wool. She stared for a long time, half sorry for what she had to do. The baby was snuffling a little, its hands and feet twitching under the wrappings. He was so young, he would not have his mother's power to resist a witch.

She glared at him for a long minute, her eyes fixed, her lips firm over her big teeth. His face, no bigger than a lemon, turned black, and a drool of foam slavered from the mouth. When the twitching stopped, and the eyes finally uncrossed themselves, she walked out, and left the door again on the latch. She had not spoken one word.

It seemed a long time before they came for her, a long time of fuss and running about while she sat on the bed, shivering in the draught from the door. When she crossed to the window, her fingers probing the webs and pressing the guts from the plumpest insects, she saw them arguing and gesticulating in a black knot. Jack Hyslop was there, his polished hair ruffled, his face red. The women were shaking their heads, and Hyslop's voice rose clear in the pale air.

'Well, that's what she said. The wee thing had been dead for an hour. An' it was that bitch Jinnot came in an' glowered at it.'

'Och, man, it's a sick woman's fancy! A wee mite that age can easy take convulsions.'

'It wasna convulsions. My wife said Jinnot was in and out with a face like thunder. She was aye askin' about witches too, you can ask Beatrice if you like.'

'Well, she was in yon business o' Minty Fraser. Ye cannie blame her, a young lassie like that . . . mind, we sympathize about the bairn, Jacky, but –'

They went on placating him, mindful of the fact that Jinnot was the farmer's daughter. It would not do to accuse *her*; but one of the women went into the cottage, and came out wiping her eyes. 'My, it would make anybody greet. The wee lamb's lying there like a flower, that quiet! It's been a fair shock to the mother, pour soul. She gey faur through . . .'

They muttered, then, and drifted towards the house. Jinnot left the window, and sat again on the bed. She was not afraid, only resigned, and horribly tired of it all.

When they burst into her room, clumping over the bare boards, her father was with them. They allowed him to ask the questions. Was he angry with them, or with her? She could not guess.

'Jinnot,' he said sternly, 'what's this? What's all this?'

She stared at him.

'What's all this? Do you know what they're saying about you? They say you killed Beatrice Hyslop's bairn. Is that true, Jinnot?'

She did not answer. Her father held up his hand as the men began to growl.

'Come now, Jinnot, enough of this sulking! It's for your own good to answer, and clear yourself. Mind of what happened to Minty Fraser! Did you do anything to the baby?'

'I never touched it. I just looked at it.'

'Just looked?'

'Yes.'

A rough cry burst from Jack Hyslop. 'Is that not what Minty Fraser said? Was that not enough from her?'

'Hyslop, hold your tongue, or you lose your job.'

'Well, by God, I lose it then! There's been more trouble on this bloody farm –'

'Aye! Leave this to us!'

'We'll question the wench. If she's no witch, she's nothing to fear.'

The women had come in now, crowding up in angry curiosity. The farmer was pushed back against the wall. 'One word, and you'll swim along with her,' he was warned, and he knew them well enough to believe them. They gathered round Jinnot, barking questions at her, and snatching at the answers. Every time she paused to fidget with the fringe, they lammed her across the knuckles till her hands were swollen and blue.

'Tell the truth now; are you a witch?'

'No. No, I'm not!'

'Why did you kill the baby this morning?'

'I – I never. I can't kill folk. I –'

'You hear that? She can't kill folk! Have you ever tried?'

She cowered back from them, the faces leering at her like ugly pictures. She would tell the truth, as her father said, and be done with all this dreamlike horror. 'Leave me alone!' she said. 'Leave me, and I'll tell!'

'Hurry then. Out with it! Have you ever tried to kill anybody?'

'Yes. I tried, and – and I couldn't. It was her, she started telling me I was bewitched –'

'Who?'

'Beatrice – Mistress Hyslop.'

'My God!' said Jack and her father, starting forward together.

'Hold on, there! Let her speak.'

'She said I was bewitched, an' I thought I was. I don't know if it was right . . . it was all queer, and I didn't know . . . and then, when she said about witches, she put it in my head, and it came over me I might be one. I *had* to find out –'

'There you are. She's admitting it!'

'No!' She began to shout as they laid hold of her, screaming in fright and temper till her throat bled. 'No! *Leave* me alone! I never; I tried, and I couldn't do it! I couldn't, I tell you! She *wouldn't* die. She'd have died if I'd been a witch, wouldn't she? She's a witch herself; I don't care, Jack Hyslop, she is! It was her fault Minty Fraser – oh God, no! NO!'

She could not resist the rope round her, the crossing of her limbs, the tight pull of cord on wrists and ankles. When she knew it was hopeless, she dared not resist remembering Minty's broken leg, her cuts and blood and bruises, the tooth spinning out in red spittle. She was not afraid of death, but she was mortally afraid of pain. Now, if she went quietly, there would only be the drag to the pond, the muckle splash, and the slow silt and suffocation in slime . . .

She had no voice left to cry out when they threw her. Her throat filled with water, her nose filled, and her ears. She was tied too tightly to struggle. Down, down she went, till her head sang, and her brain nearly burst; but the pond was full with spring rains, and her body was full-fleshed and buoyant. Suddenly, the cries of the crowd burst upon her again, and she realized that she was floating. Someone jabbed at her, and pushed her under again with a long pole, but she bobbed up again a foot away, her mouth gulping, her eyes bulging under her dripping hair. The mob on the bank howled louder.

'See, see! She's floating!'

'Witch! Burn her! Fish her out and hang her!'

'There's proof now. What are you waiting for? Out with her. See, the besom'll *no* sink!'

So now they fished her out, untied her, and bound her again in a different fashion, hands by her side, feet together. She was too done to protest, or to wonder what they would do. She kept her eyes shut as they tied her to a stake, and she ignored the tickle of dead brushwood being piled round her feet and body. She could hardly realize that she was still alive, and she was neither glad nor sorry.

They were gentle with her now, sparing her senses for the last pain. At first, she hardly bothered when the smoke nipped her eyes and her nostrils; she hardly heard the first snap of the thin twigs. It was only when the flames lapped her feet and legs that she raised her head and tried to break free. As the wood became red hot, and the flames mounted to bite her body, she screamed and writhed and bit her tongue to mincemeat. When they could not see her body through the fire, the screams still went on.

The crowd drifted away when she lost consciousness. There was no more fun to be had; or perhaps, it wasn't such fun after all. The men went back to the fields, but they could not settle to work. Jinnot's father was gnawing his knuckles in the attic, and they did not know what would happen when he came down. Beatrice tossed in a muttering, feverish sleep; and beside the pond, a few veins and bones still sizzled and popped in the embers.

The Terrapin

Patricia Highsmith

Victor heard the elevator door open, his mother's quick footsteps in the hall, and he flipped his book shut. He shoved it under the sofa pillow out of sight, and winced as he heard it slip between sofa and wall and fall to the floor with a thud. Her key was in the lock.

'Hello, Vee-ector-r!' she cried, raising one arm in the air. Her other arm circled a big brown paper-bag, her hand held a cluster of little bags. 'I have been to my publisher and to the market and also to the fish market,' she told him. 'Why aren't you out playing? It's a lovely, lovely day!'

'I was out,' he said. 'For a little while. I got cold.'

'Ugh!' She was unloading the grocery bag in the tiny kitchen off the foyer. 'You are seeck, you know that? In the month of October, you are cold? I see all kinds of children playing on the sidewalk. Even, I think, that boy you like. What's his name?'

'I don't know,' Victor said. His mother wasn't really listening, anyway. He pushed his hands into the pockets of his short, too-small shorts, making them tighter than ever, and walked aimlessly around the living-room, looking down at his heavy, scuffed shoes. At least his mother had to buy him shoes that fitted him, and he rather liked these shoes, because they had the thickest soles of any he had ever owned, and they had heavy toes that rose up a little, like mountain climbers' shoes. Victor paused at the window and looked straight out at a toast-coloured apartment building across Third Avenue. He and his mother lived on the eighteenth floor, next to the top floor where the penthouses were. The building across the street was even taller than this one. Victor had liked their Riverside Drive apartment better. He had liked the school he had gone to there better. Here they laughed at his clothes. In the other school, they had finally got tired of laughing at them.

'You don't want to go out?' asked his mother, coming into the living-room, wiping her hands briskly on a paper bag. She sniffed her palms. 'Ugh! That stee-enk!'

'No, Mama,' Victor said patiently.

'Today is Saturday.'

'I know.'

'Can you say the days of the week?'

'Of course.'

'Say them.'

'I don't want to say them. I know them.' His eyes began to sting around the edges with tears. 'I've known them for years. Years and years. Kids five years old can say the days of the week.'

But his mother was not listening. She was bending over the drawing-table in the corner of the room. She had worked late on something last night. On his sofa bed in the opposite corner of the room, Victor had not been able to sleep until two in the morning, when his mother had gone to bed on the studio couch.

'Come here, Veector. Did you see this?'

Victor came on dragging feet, hands still in his pockets. No, he hadn't even glanced at her drawing-board this morning, hadn't wanted to.

'This is Pedro, the little donkey. I invented him last night. What do you think? And this is Miguel, the little Mexican boy who rides him. They ride and ride all over Mexico, and Miguel thinks they are lost, but Pedro knows the way home all the time, and . . .'

Victor did not listen. He deliberately shut his ears in a way he had learned to do from many years of practice, but boredom, frustration – he knew the word frustration, had read all about it – clamped his shoulders, weighed like a stone in his body, pressed hatred and tears up to his eyes, as if a volcano were churning in him. He had hoped his mother might take a hint from his saying that he was cold in his silly short shorts. He had hoped his mother might remember what he had told her, that the fellow he had wanted to get acquainted with downstairs, a fellow who looked about his own age, eleven, had laughed at his short pants on Monday afternoon. *They make you wear your kid brother's pants or something?* Victor had drifted away, mortified. What if the fellow knew he didn't even own any longer pants, not even a pair of knickers, much less *long* pants, even blue jeans! His mother, for some cock-eyed reason, wanted him to look 'French', and made him wear short shorts and stockings that came to just below his knees, and dopey shirts with round collars. His mother wanted him to stay about six years old, for ever, all his life. She liked to test out her drawings on him. *Veector is my sounding board*, she sometimes said to her friends. *I show my drawings to Veector and I know if children will like them.* Often Victor said he liked stories that he did not like, or drawings that he was indifferent to, because he felt sorry for his mother and because it put her in a better mood if he said he liked them. He was quite tired now of children's book illustrations, if he had ever in his life liked them – he really couldn't remember – and now he had two favourites: Howard Pyle's illustrations in some of Robert Louis Stevenson's books and Cruikshank's in Dickens. It was too bad, Victor thought, that he was absolutely the last person of whom his mother should have asked an opinion, because he simply *hated* children's illustrations. And it was a wonder his mother didn't see this, because she hadn't sold any illustrations for books for years and years, not since *Wimple-Dimple*, a book whose jacket was all torn and turning yellow now from age, which sat in the centre of the bookshelf in a little cleared spot, propped up against the back of the bookcase so everyone could see it. Victor had been seven years old when that book was printed. His mother liked to tell people and remind him, too, that he had told her what he wanted to see her draw, had watched her make every drawing, had shown his opinion by laughing or not, and that she had been absolutely guided by him. Victor doubted this very much, because first of all the story was somebody else's and had been written before his mother did the drawings, and her drawings had had to follow the story, naturally. Since then, his mother had done only a few illustrations now and then for magazines for children, how to make paper pumpkins and black paper cats for Hallowe'en and things like that, though she took her portfolio around to publishers all the time. Their income came from his father, who was a wealthy businessman in France, an exporter of perfumes. His mother said he was very wealthy and very handsome. But he had married again, he never wrote, and Victor had no interest in him, didn't even care if he never saw a picture of him, and he never had. His father was French with some Polish, and his mother was Hungarian with some French. The word Hungarian made Victor think of gypsies, but when he had asked his mother once, she had said emphatically that she hadn't any gypsy blood, and she had been annoyed that Victor brought the question up.

And now she was sounding him out again, poking him in the ribs to make him wake up, as she repeated:

'Listen to me! Which do you like better, Veector? "In all Mexico there was no bur-r-ro as wise as Miguel's Pedro", or "Miguel's Pedro was the wisest bur-r-ro in all Mexico"?'

'I think – I like it the first way better.'

'Which way is that?' demanded his mother, thumping her palm down on the illustration.

Victor tried to remember the wording, but realized he was only staring at the pencil smudges, the thumbprints on the edges of his mother's illustration board. The coloured drawing in the centre did not interest him at all. He was not-thinking. This was a frequent, familiar sensation to him now, there was something exciting and important about not-thinking, Victor felt, and he thought one day he would find something about it – perhaps under another name – in the public library or in the psychology books around the house that he browsed in when his mother was out.

'Veec-tor! What are you doing?'

'Nothing, Mama!'

'That is exactly it! Nothing! Can you not even *think*?'

A warm shame spread through him. It was as if his mother read his thoughts about not-thinking. 'I am thinking,' he protested. 'I'm thinking about *not*-thinking.' His tone was defiant. What could she do about it, after all?

'About what?' Her black, curly head tilted, her mascaraed eyes narrowed at him.

'Not-thinking.'

His mother put her jewelled hands on her hips. 'Do you know, Veec-tor, you are a little bit strange in the head?' She nodded. 'You are seeck. Psychologically seeck. And retarded, do you know that? You have the behaviour of a leetle boy five years old,' she said slowly and weightily. 'It is just as well you spend your Saturdays indoors. Who knows if you would not walk in front of a car, eh? But that is why I love you, little Veec-tor.' She put her arm around his shoulders, pulled him against her and for an instant Victor's nose pressed into her large, soft bosom. She was wearing her flesh-coloured dress, the one you could see through a little where her breast stretched it out.

Victor jerked his head away in a confusion of emotions. He did not know if he wanted to laugh or cry.

His mother was laughing gaily, her head back. 'Seeck you are! Look at you! My lee-tle boy still, lee-tle short pants – Ha! Ha!'

Now the tears showed in his eyes, he supposed, and his mother acted as if she were enjoying it! Victor turned his head away so she would not see his eyes. Then suddenly he faced her. 'Do you think I like these pants? *You* like them, not me, so why do you have to make fun of them?'

'A lee-tle boy who's crying!' she went on, laughing.

Victor made a dash for the bathroom, then swerved away and dived onto the sofa, his face towards the pillows. He shut his eyes tight and opened his mouth, crying but not-crying in a way he had learned through practice also. With his mouth open, his throat tight, not breathing for nearly a minute, he could somehow get the satisfaction of crying, screaming even, without anybody knowing it. He pushed his nose, his open mouth, his teeth, against the tomato-red sofa pillow, and though his mother's voice went on in a lazily mocking tone, and her laughter went on, he imagined that it was getting fainter and more distant from him. He imagined, rigid in every muscle, that he was suffering the absolute worst that any human being could suffer. He imagined that he was dying. But he did not think of death as an escape, only as a concentrated and painful incident. This was the climax of his not-crying. Then he breathed again, and his mother's voice intruded:

'Did you hear me? – *Did you hear me?* Mrs Badzerkian is coming for tea. I want you to wash your face and put on a clean shirt. I want you to recite something for her. Now what are you going to recite?'

' "In winter when I go to bed," ' said Victor. She was making him memorize every poem in *A Child's Garden of Verses*. He had said the first one that came into his head, and now there was an argument, because he had recited that one the last time. 'I said it, because I couldn't think of any other one right off the bat!' Victor shouted.

'Don't yell at me!' his mother cried, storming across the room at him. She slapped his face before he knew what was happening.

He was up on one elbow on the sofa, on his back, his long, knobbly-kneed legs splayed out in front of him. All right, he thought, if that's the way it is, that's the way it is. He looked at her with loathing. He would not show the slap had hurt, that it still stung. No more tears for today, he swore, no more even not-crying. He would finish the day, go through the tea, like a stone, like a soldier, not wincing. His mother paced around the room, turning one of her rings round and round, glancing at him from time to time, looking quickly away from him. But his eyes were steady on her. He was not afraid. She could even slap him again and he wouldn't care.

At last, she announced that she was going to wash her hair, and she went into the bathroom.

Victor got up from the sofa and wandered across the room. He wished he had a room of his own to go to. In the apartment on Riverside Drive, there had been three rooms, a living-room, and his and his mother's rooms. When she was in the living-room, he had been able to go into his bedroom and vice versa, but here . . . They were going to tear down the old building they had lived in on Riverside Drive. It was not a pleasant thing for Victor to think about. Suddenly remembering the book that had fallen, he pulled out the sofa and reached for it. It was Menninger's *The Human Mind*, full of fascinating case histories of people. Victor put it back on the bookshelf between an astrology book and *How to Draw*.

His mother did not like him to read psychology books, but Victor loved them, especially ones with case histories in them. The people in the case histories did what they wanted to do. They were natural. Nobody bossed them. At the local branch library, he spent hours browsing through the psychology shelves. They were in the adults' section, but the librarian did not mind his sitting at the tables there, because he was quiet.

Victor went into the kitchen and got a glass of water. As he was standing there drinking it, he heard a scratching noise coming from one of the paper bags on the counter. A mouse, he thought, but when he moved a couple of the bags, he didn't see any mouse. The scratching was coming from inside one of the bags. Gingerly, he opened the bag with his fingers and waited for something to jump out. Looking in, he saw a white paper carton. He pulled it out slowly. Its bottom was damp. It opened like a pastry box. Victor jumped in surprise. It was a turtle on its back, a live turtle. It was wriggling its legs in the air, trying to turn over. Victor moistened his lips, and frowning with concentration, took the turtle by its sides with both hands, turned him over and let him down gently into the box again. The turtle drew in its feet then, and its head stretched up a little and it looked straight at him. Victor smiled. Why hadn't his mother told him she'd brought him a present? A live turtle. Victor's eyes glazed with anticipation as he thought of taking the turtle down, maybe with a leash around its neck, to show the fellow who'd laughed at his short pants. He might change his mind about being friends with him, if he found he owned a turtle.

'Hey, Mama! Mama!' Victor yelled at the bathroom door. 'You brought me a tur-rtle?'

'A what?' The water shut off.

'A turtle! In the kitchen!' Victor had been jumping up and down in the hall. He stopped.

His mother had hesitated, too. The water came on again, and she said in a shrill tone, '*C'est une terrapène! Pour un ragoût!*'

Victor understood, and a small chill went over him because his mother had spoken in French. His mother addressed him in French when she was giving an order that had to be obeyed, or when she anticipated resistance from him. So the terrapin was for a stew. Victor nodded to himself with a stunned resignation, and went back to the kitchen. For a stew. Well, the terrapin was not long for this world, as they say. What did a terrapin like to eat? Lettuce? Raw bacon? Boiled potato? Victor peered into the refrigerator.

He held a piece of lettuce near the terrapin's horny mouth. The terrapin did not open its mouth, but it looked at him. Victor held the lettuce near the two little dots of its nostrils, but if the terrapin smelled it, it showed no interest. Victor looked under the sink and pulled out a large wash pan. He put two inches of water into it. Then he gently dumped the terrapin into the pan. The terrapin paddled for a few seconds, as if it had to swim, then finding that its stomach sat on the bottom of the pan, it stopped, and drew its feet in. Victor got down on his knees and studied the terrapin's face. Its upper lip overhung the lower, giving it a rather stubborn and unfriendly expression, but its eyes – they were bright and shining. Victor smiled when he looked hard at them.

'Okay, *monsieur terrapène*,' he said, 'just tell me what you'd like to eat and we'll get it for you! – Maybe some tuna?'

They had had tuna-fish salad yesterday for dinner, and there was a small bowl of it left over. Victor got a little chunk of it in his fingers and presented it to the terrapin. The terrapin was not interested. Victor looked around the kitchen, wondering, then seeing the sunlight on the floor of the living-room, he picked up the pan and carried it to the living-room and set it down so the sunlight would fall on the terrapin's back. All turtles liked sunlight, Victor thought. He lay down on the floor on his side, propped up on an elbow. The terrapin stared at him for a moment, then very slowly and with an air of forethought and caution, put out its legs and advanced, found the circular boundary of the pan, and moved to the right, half its body out of the shallow water. It wanted to get out, and Victor took it in one hand, by the sides, and said:

'You can come out and have a little walk.'

He smiled as the terrapin started to disappear under the sofa. He caught it easily, because it moved so slowly. When he put it down on the carpet, it was quite still, as if it had withdrawn a little to think what it should do next, where it should go. It was a brownish green. Looking at it, Victor thought of river bottoms, of river water flowing. Or maybe oceans. Where did terrapins come from? He jumped up and went to the dictionary on the bookshelf. The dictionary had a picture of a terrapin, but it was a dull, black and white drawing, not so pretty as the live one. He learned nothing except that the name was of Algonquian origin, that the terrapin lived in fresh or brackish water, and that it was edible. Edible. Well, that was bad luck. Victor thought. But he was not going to eat any *terrapène* tonight. It would be all for his mother, that *ragoût*, and even if she slapped him and made him learn an extra two or three poems, he would not eat any terrapin tonight.

His mother came out of the bathroom. 'What are you doing there? – Veec-tor?'

Victor put the dictionary back on the shelf. His mother had seen the pan. 'I'm looking at the terrapin,' he said, then realized the terrapin had disappeared. He got down on hands and knees and looked under the sofa.

'Don't put him on the furniture. He makes spots,' said his mother. She was standing in the foyer, rubbing her hair vigorously with a towel.

Victor found the terrapin between the wastebasket and the wall. He put him back in the pan.

'Have you changed your shirt?' asked his mother.

Victor changed his shirt, and then at his mother's order sat down on the sofa with *A Child's Garden of Verses* and tackled another poem, a brand-new one for Mrs Badzerkian. He learned two lines at a time, reading it aloud in a soft voice to himself, then repeating it, then putting two, four and six lines together, until he had the whole thing. He recited it to the terrapin. Then Victor asked his mother if he could play with the terrapin in the bathtub.

'No! And get your shirt all splashed?'

'I can put on my other shirt.'

'No! It's nearly four o'clock now. Get that pan out of the living-room!'

Victor carried the pan back to the kitchen. His mother took the terrapin quite fearlessly out of the pan, put it back into the white paper box, closed its lid, and stuck the box in the refrigerator. Victor jumped a little as the refrigerator door slammed. It would be awfully cold in there for the terrapin. But then, he supposed, fresh or brackish water was cold now and then, too.

'Veector, cut the lemon,' said his mother. She was preparing the big round tray with cups and saucers. The water was boiling in the kettle.

Mrs Badzerkian was prompt as usual, and his mother poured the tea as soon as she had deposited her coat and pocketbook on the foyer chair and sat down. Mrs Badzerkian smelled of cloves. She had a small, straight mouth and a thin moustache on her upper lip which fascinated Victor, as he had never seen one on a woman before, not one at such short range, anyway. He never had mentioned Mrs Badzerkian's moustache to his mother, knowing it was considered ugly, but in a strange way, her moustache was the thing he liked best about her. The rest of her was dull, uninteresting, and vaguely unfriendly. She always pretended to listen carefully to his poetry recitals, but he felt that she fidgeted, thought of other things while he spoke, and was glad when it was over. Today, Victor recited very well and without any hesitation, standing in the middle of the living-room floor and facing the two women, who were then having their second cups of tea.

'*Très bien*,' said his mother. 'Now you may have a cookie.'

Victor chose from the plate a small round cookie with a drop of orange goo in its centre. He kept his knees close together when he sat down. He always felt Mrs Badzerkian looked at his knees and with distaste. He often wished she would make some remark to his mother about his being old enough for long pants, but she never had, at least not within his hearing. Victor learned from his mother's conversation with Mrs Badzerkian that the Lorentzes were coming for dinner tomorrow evening. It was probably for them that the terrapin stew was going to be made. Victor was glad that he would have the terrapin one more day to play with. Tomorrow morning, he thought, he would ask his mother if he could take the terrapin down on the sidewalk for a while, either on a leash or in the paper box, if his mother insisted.

'– like a chi–ild!' his mother was saying, laughing, with a glance at him, and Mrs Badzerkian smiled shrewdly at him with her small, tight mouth.

Victor had been excused, and was sitting across the room with a book on the studio couch. His mother was telling Mrs Badzerkian how he had played with the terrapin. Victor frowned down at his book, pretending not to hear. His mother did not like him to open his mouth to her or her guests once he had been excused. But now she was calling him her 'lee–tle ba–aby Veec–tor . . .'

He stood up with his finger in the place in his book. 'I don't see why it's childish to look at a terrapin!' he said, flushing with sudden anger. 'They are very interesting animals, they –'

His mother interrupted him with a laugh, but at once the laugh disappeared and she said sternly, 'Veector, I thought I had excused you. Isn't that correct?'

He hesitated, seeing in a flash the scene that was going to take place when Mrs Badzerkian had left. 'Yes, Mama. I'm sorry,' he said. Then he sat down and bent over his book again.

Twenty minutes later, Mrs Badzerkian left. His mother scolded him for being rude, but it was not a five- or ten-minute scolding of the kind he had expected. It lasted hardly two minutes. She had forgotten to buy cream, and she wanted Victor to go downstairs and get some. Victor put on his grey woollen jacket and went out. He always felt embarrassed and conspicuous in the jacket, because it came just a little bit below his short pants, and he looked as if he had nothing on underneath the coat.

Victor looked around for Frank on the sidewalk, but he didn't see him. He crossed Third Avenue and went to a delicatessen in the big building that he could see from the living-room window. On his way back, he saw

Frank walking along the sidewalk, bouncing a ball. Now Victor went right up to him.

'Hey,' Victor said. 'I've got a terrapin upstairs.'

'A what?' Frank caught the ball and stopped.

'A terrapin. You know, like a turtle. I'll bring him down tomorrow morning and show you, if you're around. He's pretty big.'

'Yeah? – Why don't you bring him down now?'

'Because we're gonna eat now,' said Victor. 'See you.' He went into his building. He felt he had achieved something. Frank had looked really interested. Victor wished he could bring the terrapin down now, but his mother never liked him to go out after dark, and it was practically dark now.

When Victor got upstairs, his mother was still in the kitchen. Eggs were boiling and she had put a big pot of water on a back burner. 'You took him out again!' Victor said, seeing the terrapin's box on the counter.

'Yes, I prepare the stew tonight,' said his mother. 'That is why I need the cream.'

Victor looked at her. 'You're going to – You have to kill it tonight?'

'Yes, my little one. Tonight.' She jiggled the pot of eggs.

'Mama, can I take him downstairs to show Frank?' Victor asked quickly. 'Just for five minutes, Mama. Frank's down there now.'

'Who is Frank?'

'He's that fellow you asked me about today. The blond fellow we always see. Please, Mama.'

His mother's black eyebrows frowned. 'Take the *terrapène* downstairs? Certainly not. Don't be absurd, my baby! The *terrapène* is not a toy!'

Victor tried to think of some other lever of persuasion. He had not removed his coat. 'You wanted me to get acquainted with Frank –'

'Yes. What has that got to do with a terrapin?'

The water on the back burner began to boil.

'You see, I promised him I'd –' Victor watched his mother lift the terrapin from the box, and as she dropped it into the boiling water, his mouth fell open. '*Mama!*'

'What is this? What is this noise?'

Victor, open-mouthed, stared at the terrapin whose legs were now racing against the steep sides of the pot. The terrapin's mouth opened, its eyes looked directly at Victor for an instant, its head arched back in torture, the open mouth sank beneath the seething water – and that was the end. Victor blinked. It was dead. He came closer, saw the four legs and the tail stretched out in the water, its head. He looked at his mother.

She was drying her hands on a towel. She glanced at him, then said, 'Ugh!' She smelled her hands, then hung the towel back.

'Did you have to kill him like that?'

'How else? The same way you kill a lobster. Don't you know that? It doesn't hurt them.'

He stared at her. When she started to touch him, he stepped back. He thought of the terrapin's wide open mouth, and his eyes suddenly flooded with tears. Maybe the terrapin had been screaming and it hadn't been heard over the bubbling of the water. The terrapin had looked at him, wanting him to pull him out, and he hadn't moved to help him. His mother had tricked him, done it so fast, he couldn't save him. He stepped back again. 'No, don't touch me!'

His mother slapped his face, hard and quickly.

Victor set his jaw. Then he about-faced and went to the closet and threw his jacket onto a hanger and hung it up. He went into the living-room and fell down on the sofa. He was not crying now, but his mouth opened against the sofa pillow. Then he remembered the terrapin's mouth and he closed his lips. The terrapin had suffered, otherwise it would not have moved its legs so terribly fast to get out. Then he wept, soundlessly as the terrapin, his mouth open. He put both hands over his face, so as not to wet the sofa. After a long while, he got up. In the kitchen, his mother was humming, and every few minutes he heard her quick, firm steps as she went about her work. Victor had set his teeth again. He walked slowly to the kitchen doorway.

The terrapin was out on the wooden chopping board, and his mother, after a glance at him, still humming, took a knife and bore down on its blade, cutting off the terrapin's little nails. Victor half closed his eyes, but he watched steadily. The nails, with bits of skin attached to them, his mother scooped off the board into her palm and dumped into the garbage bag. Then she turned the terrapin onto its back and with the same sharp, pointed knife, she began to cut away the pale bottom shell. The terrapin's neck was bent sideways. Victor wanted to look away, but still he stared. Now the terrapin's insides were all exposed, red and white and greenish. Victor did not listen to what his mother was saying, about cooking terrapins in Europe, before he was born. Her voice was gentle and soothing, not at all like what she was doing.

'All right, don't look at me like that!' she suddenly threw at him, stomping her foot. 'What's the matter with you? Are you crazy? Yes, I think so! You are seeck, you know that?'

Victor could not touch any of his supper, and his mother could not force him to, even though she shook him by the shoulders and threatened to slap him. They had creamed chipped beef on toast. Victor did not say a word. He felt very remote from his mother, even when she screamed right into his face. He felt very odd, the way he did sometimes when he was sick at his stomach, but he was not sick at his stomach. When they went to bed, he felt afraid of the dark. He saw the terrapin's face very large, its mouth open, its eyes wide and full of pain. Victor wished he could walk out the window and float, go anywhere he wanted to, disappear, yet be everywhere. He imagined his mother's hands on his shoulders, jerking him back, if he tried to step out the window. He hated his mother.

He got up and went quietly into the kitchen. The kitchen was absolutely dark, as there was no window, but he put his hand accurately on the knife rack and felt gently for the knife he wanted. He thought of the terrapin, in little pieces now, all mixed up in the sauce of cream and egg yolks and sherry in the pot in the refrigerator.

His mother's cry was not silent; it seemed to tear his ears off. His second blow was in her body, and then he stabbed her throat again. Only tiredness made him stop, and by then people were trying to bump the door in. Victor at last walked to the door, pulled the chain bolt back, and opened it for them.

He was taken to a large, old building full of nurses and doctors. Victor was very quiet and did everything he was asked to do, and answered the questions they put to him, but only those questions, and since they didn't ask him anything about a terrapin, he did not bring it up.

Man from the South

Roald Dahl

It was getting on towards six o'clock so I thought I'd buy myself a beer and go out and sit in a deckchair by the swimming pool and have a little evening sun.

I went to the bar and got the beer and carried it outside and wandered down the garden towards the pool.

It was a fine garden with lawns and beds of azaleas and tall coconut palms, and the wind was blowing strongly through the tops of the palm trees, making the leaves hiss and crackle as though they were on fire. I could see the clusters of big brown nuts hanging down underneath the leaves.

There were plenty of deckchairs around the swimming pool and there were white tables and huge brightly coloured umbrellas and sunburned men and women sitting around in bathing suits. In the pool itself there were three or four girls and about a dozen boys, all splashing about and making a lot of noise and throwing a large rubber ball at one another.

I stood watching them. The girls were English girls from the hotel. The boys I didn't know about, but they sounded American, and I thought they were probably naval cadets who'd come ashore from the US naval training vessel which had arrived in harbour that morning.

I went over and sat down under a yellow umbrella where there were four empty seats, and I poured my beer and settled back comfortably with a cigarette.

It was very pleasant sitting there in the sunshine with beer and cigarette. It was pleasant to sit and watch the bathers splashing about in the green water.

The American sailors were getting on nicely with the English girls. They'd reached the stage where they were diving under the water and tipping them up by their legs.

Just then I noticed a small, oldish man walking briskly around the edge of the pool. He was immaculately dressed in a white suit and he walked very quickly with little bouncing strides, pushing himself high up on to his toes with each step. He had on a large creamy Panama hat, and he came bouncing along the side of the pool, looking at the people and the chairs.

He stopped beside me and smiled, showing two rows of very small, uneven teeth, slightly tarnished. I smiled back.

'Excuse pleess, but may I sit here?'

'Certainly,' I said. 'Go ahead.'

He bobbed around to the back of the chair and inspected it for safety, then he sat down and crossed his legs. His white buckskin shoes had little holes punched all over them for ventilation.

'A fine evening,' he said. 'They are all evenings fine here in Jamaica.' I couldn't tell if the accent were Italian or Spanish, but felt fairly sure he was some sort of a South American. And old too, when you saw him close. Probably around sixty-eight or seventy.

'Yes,' I said. 'It is wonderful here, isn't it.'

'And who, might I ask, are all dese? Dese is no hotel people.' He was pointing at the bathers in the pool.

'I think they're American sailors.' I told him. 'They're Americans who are learning to be sailors.'

'Of course dey are Americans. Who else in de world is going to make as much noise as dat? You are not American no?'

'No,' I said. 'I am not.'

Suddenly one of the American cadets was standing in front of us. He was dripping wet from the pool and one of the English girls was standing there with him.

'Are these chairs taken?' he said.

'No,' I answered.

'Mind if I sit down?'

'Go ahead.'

'Thanks,' he said. He had a towel in his hand and when he sat down he unrolled it and produced a pack of cigarettes and a lighter. He offered the cigarettes to the girl and she refused; then he offered them to me and I took one. The little man said, 'Tank you, no, but I tink I have a cigar.' He pulled out a crocodile case and got himself a cigar, then he produced a knife which had a small scissors in it and he snipped the end off the cigar.

'Here, let me give you a light.' The American boy held up his lighter.

'Dat will not work in dis wind.'

'Sure it'll work. It always works.'

The little man removed his unlighted cigar from his mouth, cocked his head on one side and looked at the boy.

'*All*-ways?' he said slowly.

'Sure, it never fails. Not with me anyway.'

The little man's head was still cocked over on one side and he was still watching the boy. 'Well, well. So you say dis famous lighter it never fails. Iss dat you say?'

'Sure,' the boy said. 'That's right.' He was about nineteen or twenty with a long freckled face and rather sharp birdlike nose. His chest was not very sunburned and there were freckles there too, and a few wisps of pale-reddish hair. He was holding the lighter in his right hand, ready to flip the wheel. 'It never fails,' he said, smiling now because he was purposely exaggerating his little boast. 'I promise you it never fails.'

'One momint, pleess.' The hand that held the cigar came up high, palm outward, as though it were stopping traffic. 'Now juss one momint.' He had a curiously soft, toneless voice and he kept looking at the boy all the time.

'Shall we not perhaps make a little bet on dat?' He smiled at the boy. 'Shall we not make a little bet whether your lighter lights?'

'Sure, I'll bet,' the boy said. 'Why not?'

'You like to bet?'

'Sure, I'll always bet.'

The man paused and examined his cigar, and I must say I didn't much like the way he was behaving. It seemed he was already trying to make something out of this, and to embarrass the boy, and at the same time I had the feeling he was relishing a private little secret all his own.

He looked up again at the boy and said slowly, 'I like to bet, too. Why we don't have a good bet on dis ting? A good big bet.'

'Now wait a minute,' the boy said. 'I can't do that. But I'll bet you a quarter. I'll even bet you a dollar, or whatever it is over here – some shillings, I guess.'

The little man waved his hand again. 'Listen to me. Now we have some fun. We make a bet. Den we go up to my room here in de hotel where iss no wind and I bet you you cannot light dis famous lighter of yours ten times running without missing once.'

'I'll bet I can,' the boy said.

'All right. Good. We make a bet, yes?'

'Sure. I'll bet you a buck.'

'No, no. I make you a very good bet. I am rich man and I am sporting man also. Listen to me. Outside de hotel iss my car. Iss very fine car. American car from your country. Cadillac –'

'Hey, now. Wait a minute.' The boy leaned back in his deckchair and he laughed. 'I can't put up that sort of property. This is crazy.'

'Not crazy at all. You strike lighter successfully ten times running and Cadillac is yours. You like to have dis Cadillac, yes?'

'Sure, I'd like to have a Cadillac.' The boy was still grinning.

'All right. Fine. We make a bet and I put up my Cadillac.'

'And what do I put up?'

The little man carefully removed the red band from his still unlighted cigar. 'I never ask you, my friend, to bet something you cannot afford. You understand?'

'Then what do I bet?'

'I make it very easy for you, yes?'

'Okay. You make it easy.'

'Some small ting you can afford to give away, and if you did happen to lose it you would not feel too bad. Right?'

'Such as what?'

'Such as, perhaps, de little finger on your left hand.'

'My what?' The boy stopped grinning.

'Yes. Why not? You win, you take de car. You looss, I take de finger.'

'I don't get it. How d'you mean, you take the finger?'

'I chop it off.'

'Jumping jeepers! That's a crazy bet. I think I'll just make it a dollar.'

The little man leaned back, spread out his hands palms upwards and gave a tiny contemptuous shrug of the shoulders. 'Well, well, well,' he said. 'I do not understand. You say it lights but you will not bet. Den we forget it, yes?'

The boy sat quite still, staring at the bathers in the pool. Then he remembered suddenly he hadn't lighted his cigarette. He put it between his lips, cupped his hands around the lighter and flipped the wheel. The wick lighted and burned with a small, steady, yellow flame and the wav he held his hands the wind didn't get to it at all.

'Could I have a light, too?' I said.

'God, I'm sorry, I forgot you didn't have one.'

I held out my hand for the lighter, but he stood up and came over to do it for me.

'Thank you,' I said, and he returned to his seat.

'You having a good time?' I asked.

'Fine,' he answered. 'It's pretty nice here.'

There was a silence then, and I could see that the little man had succeeded in disturbing the boy with his absurd proposal. He was sitting there very still, and it was obvious that a small tension was beginning to build up inside him. Then he started shifting about in his seat, and rubbing his chest, and stroking the back of his neck, and finally he placed both hands on his knees and began tap-tapping with his fingers against the knee-caps. Soon he was tapping with one of his feet as well.

'Now just let me check up on this bet of yours,' he said at last. 'You say we go up to your room and if I make this lighter light ten times running I win a Cadillac. If it misses just once then I forfeit the little finger of my left hand. Is that right?'

'Certainly. Dat is de bet. But I tink you are afraid.'

'What do we do if I lose? Do I have to hold my finger out while you chop it off?'

'Oh, no! Dat would be no good. And you might be tempted to refuse to hold it out. What I should do I should tie one of your hands to de table before we started and I should stand dere with a knife ready to go chop de momint your lighter missed.'

'What year is the Cadillac?' the boy asked.

'Excuse, I not understand.'

'What year – how old is the Cadillac?'

'Ah! How old? Yes. It is last year. Quite new car. But I see you are not betting man. Americans never are.'

The boy paused for just a moment and he glanced first at the English girl, then at me. 'Yes,' he said sharply. 'I'll bet you.'

'Good!' The little man clapped his hands together quietly, once. 'Fine,' he said. 'We do it now. And you, sir,' he turned to me, 'you would perhaps be good enough to, what you call it, to – to referee.' He had pale, almost colourless eyes with tiny bright black pupils.

'Well,' I said, 'I think it's a crazy bet. I don't think I like it very much.'

'Nor do I,' said the English girl. It was the first time she'd spoken. 'I think it's a stupid, ridiculous bet.'

'Are you serious about cutting off this boy's finger if he loses?' I said.

'Certainly I am. Also about giving him Cadillac if he win. Come now. We go to my room.'

He stood up. 'You like to put on some clothes first?' he said.

'No,' the boy answered. 'I'll come like this.' Then he turned to me. 'I'd consider it a favour if you'd come along and referee.'

'All right,' I said. 'I'll come along, but I don't like the bet.'

'You come too,' he said to the girl. 'You come and watch.'

The little man led the way back through the garden to the hotel. He was animated now, and excited, and that seemed to make him bounce up higher than ever on his toes as he walked along.

'I live in annexe,' he said. 'You like to see car first? Iss just here.'

He took us to where we could see the front driveway of the hotel and he stopped and pointed to a sleek pale green Cadillac parked close by.

'Dere she iss. De green one. You like?'

'Say, that's a nice car,' the boy said.

'All right. Now we go up and see if you can win her.'

We followed him into the annexe and up one flight of stairs. He unlocked his door and we all trooped into what was a large pleasant double bedroom. There was a woman's dressing-gown lying across the bottom of one of the beds.

'First,' he said, 'we 'ave a little Martini.'

The drinks were on a small table in the far corner, all ready to be mixed, and there was a shaker and ice and plenty of glasses. He began to make the Martini, but meanwhile he'd rung the bell and now there was a knock on the door and a coloured maid came in.

'Ah!' he said, putting down the bottle of gin, taking a wallet from his pocket and pulling out a pound note. 'You will do something for me now, pleess.' He gave the maid the pound.

'You keep dat,' he said. 'And now we are going to play a little game in here and I want you to go off and find for me two, no tree tings. I want some nails, I want a hammer, and I want a chopping knife, a butcher's chopping knife which you can borrow from de kitchen. You can get, yes?'

'A *chopping knife*!' The maid opened her eyes wide and clasped her hands in front of her. 'You mean a *real* chopping knife?'

'Yes, yes, of course, come on now, pleess. You can find dose tings surely for me.'

'Yes, sir, I'll try, sir. Surely I'll try to get them.' And she went.

The little man handed round the Martinis. We stood there and sipped them, the boy with the long freckled face and the pointed nose, bare-bodied except for a pair of faded brown bathing shorts; the English girl, a large-boned fair-haired girl wearing a pale blue bathing suit, who watched the boy over the top of her glass all the time; the little man with the colourless eyes standing there in his immaculate white suit drinking his Martini and looking at the girl in her pale blue bathing dress. I didn't know what to make of it all. The man seemed serious about the bet and he seemed serious about the business of cutting off the finger. But hell, what if the boy lost? Then we'd have to rush him to the hospital in the Cadillac that he hadn't won. That would be a fine thing. Now wouldn't that be a really fine thing? It would be a damn silly unnecessary thing so far as I could see.

'Don't you think this is rather a silly bet?' I said.

'I think it's a fine bet,' the boy answered. He had already downed one large Martini.

'I think it's a stupid, ridiculous bet,' the girl said. 'What'll happen if you lose?'

'It won't matter. Come to think of it, I can't remember ever in my life having had any use for this little finger on my left hand. Here he is.' The boy took hold of the finger. 'Here he is and he hasn't ever done a thing for me yet. So why shouldn't I bet him? I think it's a fine bet.'

The little man smiled and picked up the shaker and refilled our glasses.

'Before we begin,' he said, 'I will present to de – to de referee de key of de car.' He produced a car key from his pocket and gave it to me. 'De papers,' he said, 'de owning papers and insurance are in de pocket of de car.'

Then the coloured maid came in again. In one hand she carried a small chopper, the kind used by butchers for chopping meat bones, and in the other a hammer and a bag of nails.

'Good! You get dem all. Tank you, tank you. Now you can go.' He waited until the maid had closed the door, then he put the implements on one of the beds and said, 'Now we prepare ourselves, yes?' And to the boy, 'Help me, pleess, with dis table. We carry it out a little.'

It was the usual kind of hotel writing desk, just a plain rectangular table about four feet by three with a blotting pad, ink, pens and paper. They carried it out into the room away from the wall, and removed the writing things.

'And now,' he said, 'a chair.' He picked up a chair and placed it beside the table. He was very brisk and very animated, like a person organizing games at a children's party. 'And now de nails. I must put in de nails.' He fetched the nails and he began to hammer them into the top of the table.

We stood there, the boy, the girl, and I, holding Martinis in our hands, watching the little man at work. We watched him hammer two nails into the table, about six inches apart. He didn't hammer them right home; he allowed a small part of each one to stick up. Then he tested them for firmness with his fingers.

Anyone would think the son of a bitch had done this before, I told myself. He never hesitates. Table, nails, hammer, kitchen chopper. He knows exactly what he needs and how to arrange it.

'And now,' he said, 'all we want is some string.' He found some string.

'All right, at last we are ready. Will you pleess to sit here at de table?' he said to the boy.

The boy put his glass away and sat down.

'Now place de left hand between dese two nails. De nails are only so I can tie your hand in place. All right, good. Now I tie your hand secure to de table – so.'

He wound the string around the boy's wrist, then several times around the wide part of the hand, then he fastened it tight to the nails. He made a good job of it and when he'd finished there wasn't any question about the boy being able to draw his hand away. But he could move his fingers.

'Now pleess, clench de fist, all except for de little finger. You must leave de little finger sticking out, lying on de table.

'Ex-cellent! Ex-cellent! Now we are ready. Wid your right hand you manipulate de lighter. But one momint, pleess.'

He skipped over to the bed and picked up the chopper. He came back and stood beside the table with the chopper in his hand.

'We are all ready?' he said. 'Mister referee, you must say begin.'

The English girl was standing there in her pale blue bathing costume right behind the boy's chair. She was just standing there, not saying anything. The boy was sitting quite still, holding the lighter in his right hand, looking at the chopper. The little man was looking at me.

'Are you ready?' I asked the boy.

'I'm ready.'

'And you?' to the little man.

'Quite ready,' he said and he lifted the chopper up in the air and held it there about two feet above the boy's finger, ready to chop. The boy watched it, but he didn't flinch and his mouth didn't move at all. He merely raised his eyebrows and frowned.

'All right,' I said. 'Go ahead.'

The boy said, 'Will you please count aloud the number of times I light it.'

'Yes,' I said. 'I'll do that.'

With his thumb he raised the top of the lighter, and again with the thumb he gave the wheel a sharp flick. The flint sparked and the wick caught fire and burned with a small yellow flame.

'One!' I called.

He didn't blow the flame out; he closed the top of the lighter on it and he waited for perhaps five seconds before opening it again.

He flicked the wheel very strongly and once more there was a small flame burning on the wick.

'Two!'

No one else said anything. The boy kept his eyes on the lighter. The little man held the chopper up in the air and he too was watching the lighter.

'Three!'

'Four!'

'Five!'

'Six!'

'Seven!' Obviously it was one of those lighters that worked. The flint gave a big spark and the wick was the right length. I watched the thumb snapping the top down on to the flame. Then a pause. Then the thumb raising the top once more. This was an all-thumb operation. The thumb did everything. I took a breath, ready to say eight. The thumb flicked the wheel. The flint sparked. The little flame appeared.

'Eight!' I said, and as I said it the door opened. We all turned and we saw a woman standing in the doorway, a small, black-haired woman, rather old, who stood there for about two seconds then rushed forward, shouting, 'Carlos! Carlos!' She grabbed his wrist, took the chopper from him, threw it on the bed, took hold of the little man by the lapels of his white suit and began shaking him very vigorously, talking to him fast and loud and fiercely all the time in some Spanish-sounding language. She shook him so fast you couldn't see him any more. He became a faint, misty, quickly moving outline, like the spokes of a turning wheel.

Then she slowed down and the little man came into view again and she hauled him across the room and pushed him backwards on to one of the beds. He sat on the edge of it blinking his eyes and testing his head to see if it would still turn on his neck.

'I am sorry,' the woman said. 'I am so terribly sorry that this should happen.' She spoke almost perfect English.

'It is too bad,' she went on. 'I suppose it is really my fault. For ten minutes I leave him alone to go and have my hair washed and I come back and he is at it again.' She looked sorry and deeply concerned.

The boy was untying his hand from the table. The English girl and I stood there and said nothing.

'He is a menace,' the woman said. 'Down where we live at home he has taken altogether forty-seven fingers from different people, and he has lost eleven cars. In the end they threatened to have him put away somewhere. That's why I brought him up here.'

'We were only having a little bet,' mumbled the little man from the bed.

'I suppose he bet you a car,' the woman said.

'Yes,' the boy answered. 'A Cadillac.'

'He has no car. It's mine. And that makes it worse,' she said, 'that he should bet you when he has nothing to bet with. I am ashamed and very sorry about it.' She seemed an awfully nice woman.

'Well,' I said, 'then here's the key of your car.' I put it on the table.

'We were only having a little bet,' mumbled the little man.

'He hasn't anything left to bet with,' the woman said. 'He hasn't a thing in the world. Not a thing. As a matter of fact I myself won it all from him a long while ago. It took time, a lot of time and it was hard work, but I won it all in the end.' She looked up at the boy and she smiled, a slow sad smile, and she came over and put out a hand to take the key from the table.

I can see it now, that hand of hers; it had only one finger on it, and a thumb.

Uneasy Home-coming

Will F. Jenkins

Connie began to have the feeling of dread and uneasiness in the taxi but told herself it was not reasonable. She dismissed it decisively when she reached the part of town in which all her friends lived. She could stop and spend the evening with someone until Tom got home. But she didn't. She thrust away the feelings as the taxi rolled out across the neck of land beyond most of the houses. The red, dying sun cast long shadows across the road.

So far, their house was the only one that had been built on the other side of the bay. But she could see plenty of other houses as the taxi drew up before the door. Those other houses were across the bay, to be sure, but there was no reason to be upset. She was firm with herself.

The taxi stopped and the last thin sliver of crimson sun went down below the world's edge. Dusk was already here. But everything looked perfectly normal. The house looked neat and hospitable, and it was good to be back. She paid the taxi driver and he obligingly put her suitcases inside the door. The uneasy feeling intensified as he left. But she tried not to heed it.

It continued while she heard the taxi moving away and purring down the road. But it remained essentially the same – a sort of formless restlessness and apprehension – until she went into the kitchen. Then the feeling changed.

She was in the kitchen, with the close smell of a shut-up house about her, when she noticed the change. Her suitcases still lay in the hall where the taxi driver had piled them. The front door was still open to let in fresh air. And quite suddenly, she had an urgent conviction that there was something here that she should notice. Something quite inconspicuous. But this sensation was just as absurd as the feeling she'd had in the taxi.

There was a great silence outside the house. This was dusk, and bird and insect noises were growing fainter. There were no neighbours near to make other sounds.

She turned on the refrigerator, and it began to make a companionable, humming sound. She turned on the water, and it gushed. But there her queer sensation took a new form. It seemed that every movement produced a noise which advertised her presence, and she felt that there was some reason to be utterly still. And that really was nonsense too.

She glanced into the dining-room. She regarded her luggage still piled in the hall near the open front door. Everything looked exactly as everything should look when one returns from a two weeks' holiday and one's husband has been away on business at the same time. Tom would get home about midnight. She had spoken to him on the telephone yesterday. He would positively get back in a few hours. So it would be absurd not to stay here to greet him. The feeling she had, she decided firmly, was simply a normal dislike of being alone. And she would not be silly.

She glanced around the kitchen. Afterwards she remembered that she had looked straight at the back door without seeing what was there to be seen. She went firmly down the hall. Then she went out of doors to look at her flowers.

The garden looked only a little neglected. The west was a fading, already dim glory of red and gold. She could not see too many details, but the garden was fragrant and appealing in the dusk. She saw the garage – locked and empty, of course, since Tom had the car – and felt a minor urge to go over to it. But she did not. Afterwards the memory of that minor urge made her feel faint. But it was only an idea. She dismissed it.

She smelled the comfortable, weary smells of the late summer evening, which would presently give way to the sharper, fresher scents of night. There was the tiny darting shadow of a bat overhead, black against the dark sapphire sky. It was the time when, for a little space, peace seems to enfold all the world. But the nagging uneasiness persisted even out here.

There was a movement by the garage, but it failed to catch her eye. If she had looked – even if she failed to see the movement – she might still have seen the motor-cycle. It did not belong here, but it was leaning against the garage wall as if its owner had ridden it here and leaned it confidentially where it would be hidden from anyone looking across the bay. But Connie noticed nothing. She simply felt uneasy.

She found herself going nervously back towards the house. The sunset colours faded, and presently all would be darkness outside. She heard her footsteps on the gravelled walk. Occasional dry leaves brushed against her feet. It seemed to her that she hurried, which was ridiculous. So she forced herself to walk naturally and resisted an impulse to look about.

That was why she failed to notice the pantry window.

She came to the front of the house. Her heels made clicking sounds on the steps. She felt a need to be very quiet, to hide herself.

Yet she had no reason for fear in anything she actually had noticed. She hadn't seen anything odd about the back door or the pantry window, and she hadn't noticed the motor-cycle or the movement by the garage. The logical explanation for her feeling of terror was simply that it was dark and she was alone.

She repeated that explanation as she forced herself to enter the dark front doorway.

She wanted to gasp with relief as she felt for the switch and the lights came on. The dark rooms remaining were more terrifying then than the night outside. So she went all over the ground floor, turning on lights, and tried not to think of going upstairs. There was no one within call and no one but the taxi driver even knew that she was here. Anything could happen.

But she did not know of anything to cause danger either.

Connie had felt and fought occasional fear before. To bring her nameless frights into the light for scorn, she had talked lightly in the past of the imaginary Things towards which women feel such terror – the Things which nervous women believe are following them; the Things imagined to be hiding in cupboards and behind dark trees in deserted streets. But her past scorn failed to dispel her terror now. She tried to be angry with herself because she was being as silly as the neurotic female who cannot sleep unless she looks under the bed at night. But still, Connie could not drive herself to go upstairs or to look under her own bed right now.

It was an unfortunate omission.

In the lighted living-room she had the feeling of someone staring at her from the dark outside. It was unbearable. She went to the telephone, absolutely certain that there was nothing wrong. But if she talked to someone –

She called Mrs Winston. It was not a perfect choice. Mrs Winston was not nearly of Connie's own age, but Connie felt so sorry for the older woman that when she needed comfort she often instinctively called her. Talking to someone else who needed comforting always seemed to make one's own troubles go away.

Mrs Winston's voice was bright and cheery over the phone. 'My dear Connie! How nice it is that you're back with us!'

Connie felt better instantly. She felt herself relaxing, she heard her voice explaining that she'd had a lovely holiday and that Tom was coming back tonight and –'

Mrs Winston said anxiously, 'I do hope your house is all right, Connie. Is it? It's been dreadful here! Did you hear?'

'Not a word since I left,' said Connie. 'What's happened?'

She expected to hear about someone having been unkind to Charles, who was Mrs Winston's only son. He gave Connie the creeps, but she could feel very sorry for his mother. He had a talent for getting into trouble. There'd been a girl when he was only sixteen, he had been caught stealing in school when there was no excuse for it, and he'd been expelled from college and nowadays wore an apologetic air. Mrs Winston tried to believe that he was simply having a difficult time growing up. But he was already twenty, and at twenty a hulking young man with an apologetic air and a look of always thinking of something else – one could sympathize with his mother and still feel uncomfortable about him.

Mrs Winston's voice went on explaining. And the feeling of terror came back upon Connie like a blow.

There had been a series of burglaries in the town. The Hamiltons' house had been ransacked while they were out for an evening's bridge. The Blairs' house was looted while they were away. The Smithsons'. The Tourneys'. And Saddler's shop was robbed, and the burglars seemed to know exactly where Mr Saddler kept his day's receipts and took them and the tray of watches and fountain pens and the cameras. And poor Mr Field –

Mr Field was the ancient cashier at Saddler's. He had interrupted the burglars, and they had beaten him horribly, leaving him for dead. He never had regained consciousness, and it was not believed now at the hospital that he ever would.

Connie said from a dry throat, 'I wish you hadn't told me that tonight. I'm all alone. Tom won't be back until midnight.'

'But my dear,' Mrs Winston exclaimed, 'you mustn't. I'll locate Charles and have him come for you right away! You can spend the evening here, and he can take you back when –'

Connie shook her head at the telephone. 'Oh, no! That would be silly!'

She heard her voice refusing, and her mind protested the refusal. But Charles made her flesh crawl. She could not bear to think of him driving her through the darkness. Baseless terror was bad enough, she thought, without actual aversion besides.

'I'm quite all right!' she insisted. 'Quite! I do hope Mr Field gets better, but I'm all right . . .'

When she hung up the phone she was aware that she was sick. But it was startling to discover that her knees were physically weak when she started to move from the instrument. She could telephone someone else, and they would come for her. But Mrs Winston would be offended and take it as an affront. And Connie was still sure that her fear was quite meaningless. It was just a feeling.

She moved aimlessly away from the telephone, found herself at the foot of the stairs. Then she looked up at the dark above and wanted to whimper. But a saving fury came to her. She would not yield to groundless fear. She was in terror of – she called it burglars now, but actually it was of Them, the unknown men women are taught to fear as dangerous.

'Ridiculous!' Connie told herself.

She got a suitcase and started for the stairs. It was deep night now. If she looked out – say, at the garage – she would see nothing. Somewhere there was a dismal cooing. Doves.

She climbed the stairs into darkness. Nothing happened. She pressed a switch and the passage sprang into light. She breathed again. She went into Tom's and her bedroom. There was dust on the dressing table. There was an ash-tray. She put down the suitcase and was conscious of bravery because she was angry.

Then she saw cigarette ends on the rug. Scorched places. Someone had sat here in this bedroom, smoking and indifferently dropping cigarette ends on the rug and crushing them out.

Connie stood with every muscle in her body turned to stone.

A part of Connie's brain directed her eyes again to the bed. Someone had sat on it – only sat – and smoked at leisure. But a corner of the bed-spread was twitched aside. What was under the bed? She found herself backing away from it, into a chair which toppled over. The noise made her freeze.

But nothing happened. There was no change in the companionable hum of the refrigerator downstairs. No reaction to the sound of the overturned chair – which seemed incredible. If one of Them – the nameless Things of which she was in terror now – was under the bed, he would come out at the noise.

Presently – her breathing loud in her own ears – Connie bent and looked under the bed. She had to. None of Them was under it. Of course. But there was an object there which was strange.

A very long time later, Connie dragged it out. It was a bag with bulges in it. Her hands shook horribly, but she dumped its contents on the floor. There were cameras. Silver. Sally Hamilton's necklace and rings. There were watches and fountain pens. This must be what the burglars had taken from the Hamiltons' house and the Blairs' and the Smithsons' and the Tourneys'. The cameras and pens and watches came from Saddler's shop, where Mr Field had come upon the burglars and they had beaten him almost to death. The burglars had nearly killed him.

Connie went to the bedroom door. Her knees were water. Her house had been used as the hiding place for the loot of the burglaries that had taken place in her absence. But now if they found out she was back –

Without much rationalization, she could guess why Mr Field had been nearly killed. He must have recognized the burglars. And now they could look across the bay and see that Connie was home. Wouldn't they know instantly that she would soon find their loot? And that she then would telephone for the police . . .?

Unless they came and stopped her. Quickly.

Shivering, Connie turned out the light in her bedroom. And in the upstairs hall. Downstairs, she turned out the light in the living-room, went quickly to the front door and bolted it. She was leaving it when she thought to fumble her way across the room and make sure that the window was locked. It was. If the lights had been seen across the bay . . .

She hastened desperately to turn out the rest. The dining-room. Lights out. The windows were locked. The pantry. It was dark. Whimpering, she was afraid to enter it. She flashed on the light to make sure of the window.

The window was broken. A neat jagged section of glass was missing. It had been cracked and removed so that someone could reach in and unlock it. It was now impossible to lock; anyone could reach in and unfasten it again.

Connie snapped off the light and fled into the kitchen and made that dark. But as the bulb dimmed she realized what she had seen in the very act of snapping the light switch. The back door was not fully closed. Its key was missing. There was mud on the floor where someone had come in – more than once. The burglars must have made casual, constant use of the house.

She stood panting in the blackness. Somewhere outside, frogs croaked. There was a thump, and her heart stood still until she realized that a night-flying insect had bumped against the window.

The refrigerator cut off.

It was coincidence, of course, but it was shocking. The proper thing, the logical thing, was to go to the telephone now. She could not see to dial, but somehow she must.

She felt her way blindly to the instrument. Her fingers on the wall made whispering sounds that guided her and she became aware of the loud pounding sound her heart made.

Just as she reached the telephone there was a faint noise which might have been a footstep in the garden.

She waited, filled with such fear that her body did not seem to exist and she had no physical sensation at all.

But a part of her brain saw with infinite despair that if the burglars had been near the house at sunset, intending to enter it as soon as darkness fell, they would have seen the taxi deliver her. They would have known that sooner or later she would discover proof of their presence. And what she had just done told them of her discovery! The light in the bedroom where their loot was hidden turned out . . . Every other light turned out. They would know she had darkened the house to hide in it, to use the telephone.

There was a soft sound at the back door. It squeaked.

Connie stood rigid. The clicking of the dial would tell everything. She could not conceivably summon help.

There was the soft whisper of a foot on the kitchen linoleum. Connie's hands closed convulsively. The one thought that came to her now was that she must breathe quietly.

There was a grey glow somewhere. The figure in the kitchen was throwing a torch beam on the floor. Then it halted, waiting. He knew that she was hiding somewhere in the house.

He went almost soundlessly into the living-room. She saw the glow of the light there. Back into the kitchen. She heard him moving quietly — listening — towards the door through which she had come only a few seconds before to use the telephone.

He came through that door, within three feet of her. But when he was fully through the doorway she was behind him. Again he flashed the light downwards. But he did not think to look behind him. By just so much she was saved for the moment.

In the greyish light reflected from the floor she recognized him.

He went into the dining-room. He moved very quietly, but he bumped ever so slightly against a chair. The noise made her want to shriek. He was hunting her, and he knew that she was in the house and he had to kill her. He had to get his loot and get away, and she must not be able to tell anything about him.

He was back in the kitchen again. He stood there, listening, and Connie was aware of a new and added emotion which came of her recognition of him. She felt that she would lie down at any instant and scream — because she knew him!

He came towards the door again, but he went up the stairs. They creaked under his weight. He must have reasoned cunningly that she would want to hide, because she was afraid. So he would go into the bedroom and look under the bed . . .

Connie slipped her feet out of her slippers. He had not reached the top of the stairs before she stood in her stockinged feet in the blackness below.

The front door was impossible. She would have to unlock it, make a noise. But he had not closed the back door behind him.

She crept out of it, with a passionate care that almost vanished when she was in the blessed night. There were stars. She remembered that she must not step on the gravel on which her feet might make a noise, so she stepped on the grass. And she fled.

There were sounds inside the house. He was opening cupboards, deliberately making sounds to fill her with panic as he hunted her down. He hadn't guessed yet that she was outside.

There were shrubs by the garage, so she slowed her flight to avoid them. And then she came upon the motor-cycle. She smelled it, oil and petrol and rubber. It was useless to her. She had no idea how to operate it. But suddenly a wild escape occurred to her – the motor-cycle wasn't entirely useless.

Connie fumbled with the machine. She turned a little tap. The smell of petrol grew strong. There was a crash inside the house. But outside, the night was full of stars, and the air was cool and sweet – except that the smell of petrol was growing stronger in it.

Connie had a box of matches in her pocket. Quickly she got it out, and in one motion struck a match and dropped it and ran away into the darkness, with the strange feel of grass under her feet.

The petrol blazed fiercely. She hid herself in the shadows and watched, sobs trying to form in her throat. The fire would be seen across the bay. It would plainly be at Connie's house. People would come quickly – a lot of them. And fire engines.

As the flames grew higher, she saw the figure plunge from the house, run furiously towards the fire, try to flail it out. But it was impossible.

And he knew it. Even his twisted mind would tell him that nothing could hide his identity now. The motor-cycle would be identification enough, and there was the loot in the house.

Connie found herself weeping. It was partly relief. But it was also the unnerving realization that the fears she'd had about Them, the men who prey on others, were not entirely groundless.

The headlights of cars began to focus towards the house, along the road from the mainland. The bells of fire engines started tolling and grew louder. And in the leaping flames surrounding the motor-cycle, a hulking, desperate figure threw futile handfuls of earth upon the machine. Was he, Connie wondered, trying to create the hopeless pretence that he was the first to help?

Even so, she was quite safe now, Connie knew. She began to cry in reaction from her terror. But, also, she wept heartbrokenly for poor Mrs Winston. She, Connie, could have been murdered. She could have been the victim of one of those twisted men who prey on their fellow beings. But she wept for Mrs Winston.

She, Connie, would not now be one of the women They had killed. But Mrs Winston was the mother of one of Them.

The Aquarist

J. N. Allan

Perhaps the deities of the sea claim affinity with him, and carry him down into ocean depths; where, with the nobles of the sea and their attendant Nereids, he holds strange festivals in submarine palaces. Perhaps the Naiads of the river become enamoured of him, decoy him beneath the waves which they rule, and keep him, a very willing prisoner in their mysterious home, enchained by their beauty, and forgetful of his earthly love.

The Fresh and Salt Water Aquarium
Rev. J. G. Wood, 1867

I kept my first aquarium in our London flat. Thelma my wife didn't seem to mind, but our landlady didn't like it. One day a crack appeared in it, I didn't know where it came from and patched it up with tape. When I came back in the evening the place was flooded, the plate glass aquarium had fallen to pieces discharging sea-water over fashionable carpets, covering the fashionable furniture with sea-anemones, crabs and other inhabitants. The landlady didn't like crabs, or the sight of a small moray eel wriggling on her new carpet, reminding her of her husband's distended prick no doubt, as it lay sunning itself in front of the Parkray. So we moved. I worked overtime for two years to raise the money for a better one, working the night shift in a local factory. All I could think about was fish.

The aquarium is very large. Now that I open the door and move into it from the kitchen I find a feeling of solidarity, such as I forgot existed: to be on my own, just the fish and me with the steady hum, the burble of filter system and pump, the green half light coming out through the glass sides of the tank, pouring over the floor. It's as if there's a bright hallway of trees in front of me, the seaweed that is, all green, endless and beautiful. When move through into the aquarium like this I always see it. Looking out at me.

My face reflected in the glass, like a great warped, a tufted sphere; my mouth
a black slit like the wound from a knife. Behind this I can see the webby
shadow of an octopus. One of my octopuses. A reef octopus from South
East Asia. It keeps growing out of the coral, skull-like, a set of fantastic
antlers ending in myriads of long stringy tendrils that spread downwards
until they reach the bottom of the tank. Lepidotheuthis grimaldi, Loligo
opalescens, Todarodes pacificus; I remember looking down the list of
octopuses in the zoo, trying to decide which I should get. It was there that I
saw my first one, close up. Thelma and I had gone there on one of my
birthdays, I can't remember which. I don't remember much, to do with the
past that is. All I remember is that it was dark in there and the fish lay around
like bleached things. All streaky and weird.

They had different fish to mine which set up different feelings inside
of me. Or so it seemed to me at the time; or so it seems to me now, since
I must make note of these things. Through the windows the things
swam, or were suspended immobile. People murmuring, echoing black
against the windows. Like swimming silhouettes. In the first tank they
had some garfish, all bones and appetite and horny plates, with snouts
like an alligator's. The notice said that they were the nearest link between
the animal life of today and the reptilian period. In the same tank there
were some shovel-nosed scats, really a deformed kind of fresh-water
sturgeon which I'd read about, with great fan-shaped membraneous plates
jutting out from their noses. It was like being confronted by a row of
masks. Sometimes the scats just lay there, eyes still, fixed straight ahead.
Faces frozen into a round-mouthed expression. Malignant. Inescapable.
They might be dead for all I knew. Dead and stuffed. There was a
temptation to go over and feel for a pulse, tap the glass, hold a match up
before an open mouth to see if they breathed on it. A waxworks jury. A
dream. A nightmare of course. A nightmare sweeping over me. If I
tapped on the glass there was no response. You could shout. Nothing. Or
just the endless to and fro of anxious swimming. They seemed trapped
within themselves. Like my reflection.

It was in the next tank that they had the octopuses and small squid. I
remember that something snapped inside me when I saw them. They
were a variegated patchwork of rich browns and fawns, on which were
numerous shining blue spots and rings. The whole appearance of an
octopus gives the impression of head and arms, its body a soft, a very
muscular bag. Most of the time water is pumped in and out of that bag.
Quite slowly. The head is roundish and it has two large eyes. Underneath
the head is the mouth with the sharp beak inside. The only hard part of
an octopus is the beak. Surrounding the mouth are eight very flexible

arms, each with a single or double row of suckers. The suckers are on
stalks and can be moved in any direction it seems. Sometimes one would
make a rapid movement when it was within range of its prey. It would
then engulf a crab or a passing fish in a kind of soft flexible umbrella,
formed by the outstretched arms and the webs which connected them.
The notice said that when the octopus bit a crab with its powerful sharp
beak, it injected poisonous saliva into the flesh of its victim. The flesh was
then liquidized and sucked out in a kind of soup. The octopus's body
would ripple for a moment when it did this, before the folds of its arms
relaxed, dropping away like slow detaching bands of meat. As for the
giant squid, it said that there was no doubt a real danger of divers being
held in the eight clinging and very painful arms, nipped by the strong
beak and dissolved out of their skins.

They didn't have any giant squids. But in the next tank they had some
more octopuses. Smaller this time. It was a very large tank called
MARINE LIFE. There were morays in there as well. Scaleless slick
things, with corpsy dead eyes; a few poisonous fins like javelins, long
whiskers dangling from the sides of their cavernous heads. One was six
or seven feet long. It swam past me, one gigantic probing nerve. Looking
like me, I remember Thelma said at the time; its head a warped, a tufted
sphere, its mouth a black slit like the wound from a knife. Its skull sloped
back so abruptly that it could hardly be said to have a forehead at all, its
chin slanting off, right into nothing. Its eyes were black and strangely
intelligent. Set wide apart in its head. And they were unwinking and
staring. As it moved its head from side to side their gaze stayed fixed on
me. The effect was hypnotic. I felt it knew me. I felt ashamed.

As I looked through the glass I saw it eat one of the smaller octopuses.
It seized one of its arms, gripping it so firmly with its sharp teeth and
proceeded to dismember it. Slowly. Bit by bit. It stretched its body so
that it was quite straight, then twisted round and round until the octopus's
arm was wrenched off. After swallowing this wriggling arm the moray
repeated the action, until the octopus was left with no arms; just the
immobile bag of its body, like a pudding tipped out of its mould. As it
ate the bag, I remembered the octopus's trunk twisting distortedly when
it was first caught. Its legs twitching and kicking like the legs of a speared
frog. When I looked into the dark shells of its eyes, I noticed that they
were beginning to dry up and a chalky hardness like pumice creep over
them. It seemed to put my backbone out of place. I felt as if I'd done a bad
thing. I felt ashamed. It was as if something had spent a long time inside
of me and only at this point decided to surface, to become a part of me.

*

My aquarium has a tank much larger than any at the zoo. The fish swim about in it like gods, dressed in vaguely allegorical costumes, all spangled and glittered, some with cloaks to hide their divinity. Thelma never comes here. Thelma doesn't like looking into the aquarium. It deprives her of the anonymity of the group, forcing her into something more intimate that she doesn't understand. Fractions of time that the human eye and brain aren't meant to perceive can assume a significance of grotesque importance in here. Perhaps there's a risk that a person's mind might fragment into several parts. Maybe it's something that you must get used to, like a long illness. Maybe Thelma doesn't like fish because they don't breathe, don't blink like we do.

My mind runs more than ever on the fish these days. Sometimes they're like shadows conspiring to unfix me. A vibration of light in front of me, an endless drift of light and dark particles circling alone or in groups. So erratic. So devious. There is no way of knowing whether they belong to my own eyes. To the outside world. Or both. Then, for a split second against this background, I sometimes see myself as small to the point of deformity, thinking it's all bad bad bad, thinking how far away I am. But far from what? What makes me think so? As I stroke the salamander which lives in the aquarium, pecking it under the chin, I know I've never wanted more from life than moments like these. Yet is it fair to be separated from the world? Looking down at my notebook I find myself writing under my last entry on the octopuses that my life is just single days, small and bright. Yet is it too hard being alone in them, is this what being alone is like? I want to forget, not remember, otherwise the same things will happen and I'll be trapped. I can look back, but the past seems so short and worthless that it fuses into a whole. Just before this moment. And suddenly beyond it. Exactly as the parrot fish merge and move upwards from the masses of shiny anemones, with nothing beyond that movement. What is it I know? When I think I've caught a glimpse of it, it's not there anymore. When I come near to touch it, it's already going away, because I've taken something moving in my hands.

Again and again I go to the same places through the glass, to the corals which spill over and grow up the rocky ledges, to the tangles of anemones hanging down from them. But sometimes I feel they're only feelings, not real places at all, not far away places. Then I like to dream I'm William Beebe, or Otis Barton who made the first dive in a bathysphere somewhere in the Atlantic Ocean. I can imagine Beebe staring through the window of the bathysphere with the electricity cable one inch thick, creeping in through the ceiling and coiling round them like an umbilicus, as it was forced in by the pressure outside. I can imagine Beebe staring at the yellow lights of the lantern fish and the collars of the jellyfish carrying long strings of light. Below a thousand feet the temperature of the sea is a little above freezing point. In their tiny chamber Beebe and Barton would feel cold. Sometimes Beebe peering eagerly through the fused quartz window like the cornea of some eye, would see a deep-sea squid and feel numb in mind and body. This would be reinforced by the blackness of the lower levels, where only the body patterns of glowing colour identify friend from foe. Their whole beings must have felt pinpointed by danger into clarity. It would not seem important that they might die. The important thing was being, there, so deep, away from the disappointments of life, the misunderstandings, the jealousy. It must be so clear, so simple down there on a wire.

I sit alone in this room. In a sense I shall always lie within it, always, as if I was a word suspended on this page. There is no way of leaving it, unless I pass through the door, in which case I shall carry it with me in my head and all that will remain will be this point. And my departure. And Thelma just sleeps during the day when Frank is not here, so I'm usually left alone with these endless trains of thought in this corner of the house, with my notebooks and fish. After a while I may look at Willoughby's ichthyological work, or Halieutick's: *Of the Nature of Fishes*. It was written in the sixteenth century. The pictures hold me spellbound and would have excited the envy of Doré or Piranesi. I think that some of these things are supposed to depict men, at least a certain sort of man, though the creatures are shown swimming like fishes in the waters of some marine grotto, or paying homage to some monolithic shrine which appears under the waves as well. They are semi-grotesque, semi-human, semi-fish, human in general despite their webbed hands and feet.

Now Thelma's pounding on the door with her fist and fitting her eye to the keyhole.

'Tea I have and cheese. What are you doing in there?'

The door shifts back on its hinges. Like the great wing of a bird.

'What's the matter with you? Why do you keep locking the door? What are you afraid of? I can't keep tea waiting all this time. Why do you keep the door locked?'

'Eh?' I stand still and stare at her back.

'You never locked the door before. Only just recently. Why?'

I stop listening, Thelma's lips gone like sea creatures living a life of their own under water; her ears like gill slits behind her head. I continue to stare at her back. If I catch her dressing in the mornings I sometimes imagine my saliva trickling down the whiteness of that back. But if I brushed up against her she would stiffen layers of skin, curl up and harden like a sea-anemone. Sometimes I notice spots like a longitudinal row of pore-bearing scales forming a lateral line to the right of her spine. They could almost be the external manifestation of a sensory system. The pores in some species of fish are the openings which allow the disturbances in the water to be felt and recorded by sensitive devices in the canals joining the pores below the skin. At other times I imagine there's a groove on the outer and inner sides of her spine, along which lies a transparent gland full of poison. The whole thing is covered by the thin skin of her back. Pressure on the tip of her spine down by her coccyx, might cause it to break through the skin, buckle up the middle and the venom to run down the groove. But if I persist in these imaginings I get a little scared, because I realize that but for a twist in the evolutionary process, a sea-urchin or sea-cucumber might well be where I am at the moment. Sitting in my chair. Looking like me. I might even be a crown of thorns starfish with tube-feet, pushing its stomach out through its mouth to invest its prey. I might even hunt Thelma if she was a sea-urchin, for her ripe ovaries which are held to be a great delicacy by some. Her olive skin troubles me. Those female's eyes watch me. The line at the top of her shoulder blades crossing the spine. The tension there. Her body is quite alarming sometimes. Today is a particularly bad one because she is menstruating. Her body becoming angry at the least little thing.

I watch her face now which hangs like a moon over the kitchen table as it is chopping, skinning, peeling, plunging hands into flour; only a tiny distance below a quiet smile fish-scales scraped with a knife onto a marble slab. My hair is plastered down with water. I have put on a clean blue shirt through which I breathe in the knock at the door, behind which comes Frank, his fingers like great plant buds growing out from the ends of his arms. Thelma has put on a whole cauldron of water onto an electric ring. Is dropping in little fish from her hands, cupped hands. The bubbles rise in silver chains as Frank kisses her; the fish swimming through the cauldron with no heads, their severed heads strangely inanimate, lying in front of me on the marble slab, Thelma's and Frank's like lanterns swinging before me. Thelma is always ovo-viviparous at times like these, like my fish, Frank laying his tongue inside her head and letting it develop like an egg and hatch inside its mother. Thelma smiles as wrinkles like stretch-marks crisscross her skin and slowly but surely the lower rays of her tail fin begin to elongate and splay. Thelma inducing a kind of mouth-brooding. Her distensible mouth engulfing the head of this brooding male.

Frank comes around here every day. No explanations ever come from him. He never asks me about myself, just leaves his hat on the bed and never stays aloof from my Thelma's lickings and warblings.

'Pretty place,' he says at last, his voice not a voice but a mere clicking under the tongue. The pulse on his neck moving, a small creature ready to jump out and seize Thelma's neck that arches back and down where she feels the ache.

'First rate,' he says, straightening his shoulders, very male, very sure.

'Many days without you, Thelma,' he lies. 'How's life?'

'All right it is,' she laughs, shuffling her feet up and back, keeping time for him with her bird shoulders bunched together.

'And with you I see it's all right too,' the line at the top of her shoulder blades crossing the spine. The tension there. Expectation of his touch quickening the pulse, a hump of muscle rising in her neck. He closes his eyes on me as if a membrane was covering them and makes an odd clicking laugh. Looking into his eye I can see that he thinks there's something separate and arrogant about me, very different.

I cannot say when the idea first occurred to me that they were having an affair. There had been signs for the past month, suspicions, things like sea tides deep within me. Sometimes I dream about them in the aquarium, repelled and fascinated it's as if I was watching them, it's as if I'd taken my clothes off and was standing before them, watching them behind the glass of the tank. Their high-pitched cries disturb me then, the way they use their stomachs as an accessory lung, emitting a hissing sound, soft then savage, their faces flowers opening out into black centred suns.

The two of them are present now in the unlit room, stepping in and out of the shadows, their faces like glow-worms swimming in front of me. The whole place seems full of them and yet strangely empty as if things could be different; the room dark, empty, black like a moonless sky when I close my eyes. To reassure myself I turn round to look at the moon, which is not there until I open my eyes and put it back into space, this moment transparent, horribly soft. There is a strong smell of the sea in the room; dead flat sea trapped in walls, sea heavy with forms, speckled with the white bellies of fish. Or is it that I am bringing the sea in with me, bringing the fish in with me from the aquarium? Even they seem superimposed on the place, not quite solid, not quite clear, they're either here, behind things, or else on their way sending their mystery ahead to me, another way of life going on quietly separately the whole time. They seem the repositories of all the lively colours that seem to have been exiled from the place, vivid as a hot-house; but perhaps none of them exist, perhaps all are mute, are fictions, even their multitude of glass eyes which seem to congeal in turn.

Looking down I see its limp little balls tossing from side to side, over what must seem to it a smooth plateau of rock. Sometimes I see them lying on the tops of the wall outside, as though on display, like yellow globular eyes. At night sand lizards like this one come out and eat the roots in the garden so that the plants collapse on themselves mysteriously. You can't see anything wrong above ground, but when you lift the stalks up by the leaves you can see where their sharp little teeth have bitten through. This one seems to have wandered in from the garden outside so I take it into the aquarium for safety, leaving Thelma and Frank to themselves for the time being.

I hear the birds outside. Through the window I can see their eyes bright in the darkness between the leaves, their legs like sticks covered with harsh short hairs, their beaks like caterpillars curling in green rings. It seems to have grown darker after all, the day to have disappeared as we tilt away from the sun, the moon a white maggot growing stronger, more assured, raising its head above the tree line. My fingers are searching for something, I wish I could say fitting the world like a glove, quite complete in themselves once they come into contact with my pocket knife. Through the keyhole I can see both of them now. With my eye at the keyhole I can hear the hiss and slap of their bliss, as my skull bones creak and slip inside my head, my forehead creased on the handle I dare not twist. In the corner of my eye I can see the octopuses as well; I watch them mating in the aquarium, I watch the male extend his hectocotolyzed arm and touch the female very gently with its tip. Eventually he succeeds in placing the tip of his arm loaded with spermataphores inside the female, inside her bag-like form, impregnating the darker jellyfish fixed at the centre of a mass of tangled arms. The photopores round the rims of their eyes give off a blue light with a pearly sheen as I watch them; their eyes like great semi-circular canals set deep within their heads. It is with a sense of unreality that I return my gaze to the key hole, a black slit like the wound from a knife; it is with a sense of unreality that I gaze at the object my wife's fingers have revealed. It is unmistakably a plant bud of some sort, a strange corsage with involved and involuted folds of pale blue and bloody pink that seems to expand, that seems to exude a thin sanguineous fluid, making me shudder when I see its internal structure full of nerve-like filaments with a core that suggests cartilage.

After a time I turn away to the sea which arches and stretches itself like a grey animal outside, turning, making myself a protective hood, a bell-shaped cover for the small live thing swimming inside of me. The clouds that have been hugging the surface of the sea are now rolling towards me. I can feel the dampness and chill of them even though they are some way off. The smell of the sea. Clouds. Their naked backs caught by the light, made grey and fearsome. The octopuses smile and smile as they swim in their wake, the moonlight on my knife silvering everything.

I must have dozed a little.

My body keeps sinking through the surface on which it is supposedly sitting. I am lying on it somehow, as in water. I must have dozed a little; but I cannot remember dreaming, only that the walls became indistinct a while back, that the evening went clammy as if the whole sky had closed around me, sealing me in a hot wet envelope. Perhaps I dreamt, dreamt that I was seeing things for the last time, dreamt someone waving a knife. There were screams around the person, perhaps a single laugh; but the sound was so loud it swept the room away and in the silence afterwards the wind rushed in like a big black bird. I must have dreamt, dreamt the trembling as something rough-scaled brushed against my feet, dreamt the liquids in my body passing through me as if through a porous sponge. I remember that something made a call like a bird when it dropped down beside me, only to sit looking at the eddies on the ground with its legs drawn into it. The lizard perhaps, quivering with repulsive animations, as though it was breathing through its flesh which arched darkly on either side of a series of gill slits, as if it was breathing in, choking on something which had spent a long time in the depths and only at this point decided to surface, to breathe, to breathe out through a series of platter-shaped gaps, to breathe out a long reddish tongue, a monstrous amber bud that seemed to grow with preternatural rapidity, a loathsome stem quivering, pulsing, protruding and curling upwards; its tip like a prodigious blossom opening into a sort of fleshy disk, broad as a man's face. I must have dreamt this lizard, its forearms albino as it changed its colouration, white as leprosy, its fingers that twisted viperishly. The lizard perhaps; yes I must have put it with the others outside, black against the glare.

I must have dozed a little. The walls are now becoming more distinct, the window opposite becoming larger. I can see outside now, I can see the whole tree and the garden in which it stands. I should have known. I have seen it before, it looks so familiar. Now that I look into the garden I can see the lizards, they keep crawling, suck at the branches of the tree with small mouthing sounds, as if they found the taste of it agreeable. In other places their dismembered skeletons still stand upright in the earth like little crosses. Their rib cages exposed, or peer face down into the depths of the pond. It's grey weather, warm and damp. The evening seems to have grown darker, until only the anemones are glowing in the shadows, smears and blots of colour bursting by the path and tracing the tops of the broken walls outside. They cover the roofs of the houses, like cold fires of purple and crimson, lighting the ground everywhere, parting their black-button centres without the sun, smelling only of earth and rain.

Something heavy sits on my chest as I turn now and move through the room like a swimmer. How should I describe it to you, this tea towel that I'm holding, its texture, how its folds form, my feelings as I look at it standing in the kitchen wiping a glass. The very action seems foreign to me, my fingers clustering alongside, then in front of me. I can see them inside the glass, it's as if I was inside the glass, myself impossibly part of what seemed a minute landscape, with which I felt so unconnected a moment ago. It's as if I was back there, behind one of those windows in a dark corridor in the zoo, like a train under the sea. Instead of scenery streaming, people like fish, who lean and tap the glass and shiver as I scratch back. To me they seem like sea creatures that float with no support along the dark corridor.

A woman is standing amongst them, standing there as if drowned, the waves washing into her hair, her dress semi-transparent like a membrane; a woman, perhaps my wife. My wife, I stand close to her now, stand close to Thelma so that with the slightest movement of my hand I can stretch out a finger and touch her back. I keep staring at her, her eyes dim and unblinking, her skin seems glazed and clouded as though covered by a shell of powdered titian. When I look into her eyes, I notice that their glassy surface is not only dim, it is beginning to dry up and a chalky hardness like pumice creep over them.

Our bodies are close now. If she could hear me, she'd hear me breathe, she'd see the lizard too, carrying its balls in a sack as it runs this way then that way on the windowsill, so that even she would desire to watch it, as it extends its tongue. The head on the top of her spinal column changes position ever so slightly when I touch her, and from the pallor in her face, from the dead white shoulders and dead white arms, there seems to exhale and slowly creep a shudder as her mouth opens wide to receive my tongue which curls towards it, her long-boned hands lying there belly up as if they'd been filleted with a knife.

Evening is gathering in now. The day hasn't been all bad and this is the easy part, the waiting, the downhill run. I don't even have to turn the lights on, just let the room fill up with twilight and silence. I can see a blank space suspended in the frame of the mirror. It takes a moment for me to see another there, to see the moray reflected back at me as it sits like the corpse of a drowned man, occupying the space in my chair. It must have escaped from the zoo. Perhaps the smell of salt meat attracted it. He must have entered something between a river and a room when he arrived here, the surfaces crammed with currents, crackling like released footprints. The world must have seemed like a jewel when he arrived, hanging in black flesh and pulsing like a heart as his power slid off great faces of water, power in flat sheets rising. Against the flowery paper he must have seen them glide, before he opened his mouth wide and they were gone.

Yes, I remember now, I remember how it was. I stood over them a while back. They were pretending to drink tea when I came through the door of the aquarium and stood over them with my knife like a beak in my hand. Thelma began twisting inside her skinny body, as if there was another inside and separate. I could see her face which was always pale, but now drained of its colour right down to the bone. I observed her extreme slenderness, felt I could enclose the whole of her with one hand, even the rib-cage containing her heart which beat like a glass fish's in front of a silvery peritoneum. I remember that her arms like great rakes reached out at me as she tried to contain me, her fingers like traps shutting tight over my legs before her face seemed to explode like a paper bag. After a while she didn't move. Neither did Frank. I remember the first thing he did was to bend and sway, soften and go flaccid before he fell to the ground by the Parkray like a half-deflated inner tube, his little bead bright eyes gone dull and lacklustre. I remember that he made a call like a bird, only to sit looking at the eddies on the ground with his legs drawn into him. By the time I'd finished with him a circle of scaly coils like an umbilicus had emerged from him as something white like a worm pushed out from his stomach before going limp.

I continue to write in my notebook, writing down anything that seems of interest, but restrained, with a peculiar uncertainty as to what is real and what thought of, as if some other might be listening to my every word. I am waiting now, waiting for something else to happen, perhaps waiting for the self inside of me to come forward and take control, to come forward to the boundaries from which it has long ago withdrawn. Yes the waiting is pleasant. I can wait. I am used to waiting. Soon they will come for me and there will be no time to reflect, a moray's mind cannot reflect. Yes they will soon come and I will be left quite to myself after a little disturbance, me left after life to myself, left after this life, left after nothing, no life, no me existing after this end, no exit, no new beginning. Yes they will come for me, perhaps I will just have time to think of my aquarium somewhere back there, the plains of anemones sweeping back without plan or meaning in the neat little sea-world. The colours will seem old and restful back there, brown and gold and dark green; life will seem close to a dream in space like that, never to be seen or heard of again, with all its longings kept to itself.

Looking through the window I can see another police car like a great fin pull up and stop in the turn of the road. I can see the moon like a white maggot snagged in the branches of the tree outside, forming a halo round Frank's head, who dangles there like a great lizard with his arms collapsed around his knees. I wonder at the May-red clouds parting under the water outside, fantastic plumes and tapers that loom and boom, beyond them cloud worlds that seem deeper and wider still. I can see the policemen outside in the garden, I can hear them on the stairs like wild black birds, like a great migration of birds that thicken the air, a great rushing of wings that beat so dark so fast around me when they enter the room, beating for ever inside my head.

An Interview with M. Chakko

Vilas Sarang

Interviewer: Mr Chakko, you say that the island on which you spent so many years was named Lorzan, is that right?

Chakko: That's right.

Where exactly is it located?

I never learned that. When our ship went down, four of us drifted for several days in a lifeboat. Our food had all run out and we were nearly at death's door when we came upon Lorzan. All I can say is that the island lies somewhere to the far south in the Indian Ocean.

So four of you landed on Lorzan?

No, two men died at sea. Kuruvila was the only one who made it to Lorzan with me.

And, as you testified in court, all the women on this island had only half bodies. Not a single woman possessed a whole, normal human body?

No, they all came in halves. The upper half, or the lower half.

But the men were normal?

Yes, that's right.

How did that happen?

Apparently their genes had undergone some strange mutation.

And what about reproduction?

They had test-tube babies.

Which suggests a fairly advanced civilization.

Yes, indeed it does. In some respects they were far in advance of us.

What race were they?

I was told their ancestors had migrated centuries ago from somewhere in East Asia. Since that time they had avoided all contact with the outside world and developed their own civilization.

And they accepted you among them?

Well, yes, I can't say I had any problems fitting in. In fact, they wouldn't let me leave the island. They were afraid I'd tell the outside world about them if I left. After a while, I simply settled down there.

In spite of the peculiarity of the island women?

It didn't bother me all that much. One can get used to almost anything, you know. I got a job in an engineering firm. Once I had established myself, I applied for a wife at the government marriage bureau. Since the female population of the island was smaller than the male, there was a waiting list. Then one day I was allotted a wife. Her name was Ka Sirinom.

Did she have an upper body or the lower?

The lower. The women with lower bodies were referred to as the 'Ka' women, and those with the upper half as 'Lin'. The Lin women could speak of course; so they were more desirable as company. At the time, I didn't care much for company in that sense.

But tell me, was living with half a woman really satisfying?

Well, why not? Children in Lorzan were raised in government nurseries, and the family as an institution didn't exist in any real sense. What it came down to was men living by themselves in apartments, and they simply enjoyed having another person about the house, that's all. It didn't matter much if the woman had a whole body or only half of one. You must keep in mind that what one needs is simply *someone else* around. It doesn't matter who. I'm sure you know the difference it makes, if you're living by yourself, just to discover a spider or a mouse in the room, or even to have a fly buzzing about you! – let alone sharing the house with a cat or a dog. The point is, half a woman can fill the need quite well.

You lived happily with your wife, then?

Ka Sirinom became a part of my life in the course of time. At first, living with a half-woman was a strange experience. I often had the feeling that there was an invisible upper body floating above her waist like a ghost. Wandering about on heavy feet, she sometimes came and stood before me, and I felt that she was staring at me with invisible eyes. Once, when I was copulating with her in a standing position, I suddenly had the sensation of unseen arms embracing me, and I jumped back in fright.

Didn't experiences like that make your life miserable?

It was nothing but my mind playing tricks on me. They soon stopped. Besides, I was involved in a research project in engineering at the time which kept me occupied. I had little time for Ka Sirinom. She wandered about the house, or rested in bed. Whenever I felt the need, I went to her and tapped her on the legs – like tapping at a door, you might say. She had nice, large hips, and nice, soft legs.

Did you remain with Ka Sirinom for all your stay in Lorzan?

(Chakko, not having heard the question) Yes, she was really good . . . One thing was a nuisance, though. I had to pare her toe-nails every few days. Did you ask something?

Did she remain with you until you left Lorzan?

No, she lived at my house for about five years. Then things went wrong for me at work. I made a series of terrible blunders on a particular project. I used to come home very depressed in those days. Then I would fall wildly on Ka Sirinom. I sucked her toes so hard that the skin was raw. She put up with everything.

(Seeing Chakko lost in thought) *And then?*

I soon realized that it was no use. My frustration only became worse. If Ka Sirinom could have listened and talked, I would have spoken with her, would have told her about many things and unburdened myself to her. But she could neither listen nor speak. All she knew how to do was open her legs. So one day I returned her to the bureau, and got myself another woman – this time of the Lin class. Her name was Lin Rabaya.

But couldn't you get another wife without giving up Ka Sirinom?

No, I couldn't. Since there were fewer women than men, one was allowed to keep – to marry, that is – only one at a time. There was, however, a method which people sometimes resorted to. A man with a Ka wife would team up with one with a Lin wife. They'd tie their wives together with a rope, thus making 'one' woman out of them, and then take turns sleeping with 'her'. I tried this with Ka Sirinom a few times, but it really wasn't very satisfactory. In a way you could make one woman from the halves, but in your heart you knew it wasn't real, you were merely fooling yourself. Besides, the two half-women were never smooth and flat at the waist and therefore never joined perfectly, which was annoying. On one occasion I was heaving up and down on top of the bound bodies, when the rope suddenly slipped and the two halves began to slip apart. The Lin woman was embracing and kissing me passionately, while down below Ka Sirinom had clasped her legs tightly around me. They were sliding in opposite directions, pulling me apart. It was like the earth splitting beneath my feet.

Well, then did you get what you wanted from your second wife?

After I brought Lin Rabaya home, I used to talk to her a lot. There were times when we talked through the night. Lin Rabaya was an intelligent women. She had read a great deal. You might even call her an intellectual. In the course of time, I think I genuinely came to love her.

What about physical satisfaction, though?

Oh, there were her hands, her lips . . . you understand.
Yes, I do.
She had nice, full lips – and she knew how to use them. But in winter
they were chapped, and that was unpleasant. Then I gave her a salve for
her lips. We got along fine, on the whole. Once during the holidays we
went to a beach resort. I took her to the seashore on long excursions,
although it was tiring pushing her wheelchair in the sand. We used to sit
on the beach and watch the sunset. I told her about the country I came
from. When I said that the women there had whole bodies just like men,
she laughed and gave me a pat on the cheek. 'That's some fantasy of yours
– something you dreamed about,' she said.
*If the Lorzanians were as advanced as you say, they must have known about
the outside world?*
The government did. The common people were generally kept in the
dark. The government took pains to see that the people looked down on
the outside world.
I see. Please go on with Lin Rabaya's story.
After a while, I became disaffected with Lin Rabaya. I would whisper
to her, 'I love you, I love you', and she'd say, 'I love you, too'. But she
didn't really mean it. She showed little interest in any emotional
involvement. She was a sensualist, a pleasure-seeker. She fondled and
stroked me endlessly. Then I used to hold her hands and say, 'I love you,
Lin Rabaya', and she'd smile and say, 'I love you, too, Chakko'. But as
soon as I released her hands, they began moving all over my body again.
You'd think she was groping in darkness for something she had lost. Her
fingers became so avid that at times they seemed to be trying to penetrate
beneath my skin. Gradually we spoke less and less. I lay still as her lips
and fingers explored my whole body. It was like soft hail falling upon
me, burying me slowly. Then I started spending most of my time away
from home.
So you abandoned Lin Rabaya too?
I did. I returned her to the bureau.
And you brought another woman home?
Not right away. I lived for a year without anyone. Then I brought
home a Ka woman. Not Ka Sirinom, who had gone to someone else.
This one was called Ka Punnasarto.
Tell me about her.
Ka Punnasarto was different from Ka Sirinom. She wasn't as plump
and fleshy. She had long, tapering legs. You might call her thin. But she
had an attractive, delicate walk. I didn't pay much attention to her, at
first. I had taken her only because I thought I ought to have someone

about the house. Ka Punnasarto always got beaten in the women's games, and that put me off even more.

Women's games? What were they like?

We used to have these games in each residential block once in a while. Everybody brought his wife to the Community Centre hall. A few Ka women, along with an equal number of Lin women, were put inside a circular area. The Ka women, who couldn't see of course, groped about with their legs, and kicked when they came across a Lin woman. The Lin women tried to grab their legs and pull them down. The Lin women couldn't move swiftly; they could only crawl about on their hands. Defending themselves, they did their best to pull the Ka women to the ground. That was the nature of the game. Ka Punnasarto wasn't able to kick very powerfully; on the other hand, she was usually pulled to the ground fairly easily because of her long legs. That embarrassed me.

So you sent her back like the others?

No, I didn't. As time passed, I came to know her better. Whenever I drew her near, she clung to me and brushed herself against me affectionately. There was an intelligence, and a certain understanding, in everything she did. She didn't open her legs abruptly as Ka Sirinom did. She deliberately pressed her thighs together, and then parted them gradually and coyly. Sometimes she used to dance by herself. It was marvellous to watch – that dance of half a body! The intricate movement of her legs, so swift and yet so graceful, entranced me. When she had stopped dancing, I lifted her gently and placed her on the bed. I massaged her legs. She used to like that. She held my hand between her calves, and rubbed herself against it. She had a peculiar habit. She would press one of her toes on my body, lift the toe, then press again, then lift and press elsewhere, as you might test the softness of the ground. She once pressed the toe of her left foot at the very base of my spine, and instantly a strange sensation spread throughout my body. Eyes shut, I lay still for I don't know how long. I didn't stir even when she lifted her toe. At other times Ka Punnasarto placed her toes over mine, and pressed them alternately, as though she were sending a telegram. She pressed her toes passionately, as if she were desperately trying to tell me something. I too pressed my toes upon hers. This went on with increasing fervour. But it was never clear what she wanted to say. Then in despair she opened her legs and pulled me closer with her feet. But I would gently extricate myself and lie quietly beside her. Wearied, we lay still, clinging to each other. In this way I lived with Ka Punnasarto for several years. Then I noticed that she was becoming thinner. Her legs first became like dry sticks, and then they began to swell. I called in a doctor. He gave her a series of injections, but told me that her disease was incurable, and that she wouldn't live long. Ka Punnasarto's legs continued to swell. Her feet cracked and began to ooze a watery fluid. To me it seemed as though they were literally weeping – shedding tears. I caressed her cracked feet, and brushed my face against them. My tears mixed with the water oozing from her feet. She tried to move her feet, but they had become too heavy. In a few days she was dead.

(After a pause) *But tell me, Mr Chakko, how did the Lorzanian women manage to live?*

They were given injections of life-sustaining fluids at regular intervals. A medical van visited each house for this purpose.

You must have been very unhappy at the death of Ka Punnasarto?

For a few years after her death I lived alone. Then one day I took in Lin Maulafa. Lin Maulafa was a quiet, loving wife. But my relationship with her remained a superficial one. She stayed with me until I left Lorzan.

Tell me, Mr Chakko, in a country like Lorzan wasn't homosexuality widespread?

Not in the least. Homosexuality was commonly regarded as a great sin. Anyone indulging in it was sentenced to life imprisonment.

What happened to the other man you mentioned – the one who reached Lorzan with you?

Kuruvila met with a strange end. That wasn't in Lorzan, but in Amuraha. Did I tell you about Amuraha?

No, you didn't.

Some distance from Lorzan was the island of Amuraha. The situation on this island was exactly the opposite of that on Lorzan. Which is to say, the men there had half bodies, whereas the women were normal. The legend was that centuries ago Zem, a prince, and his sister Zemna, a princess, came there from the eastern regions of Asia. They had been driven out by their uncle, cast away on the ocean on a ship with a supply of food and water. Zemna, along with her seven husbands, landed at Lorzan, while Zem, along with his seven wives, reached Amuraha. What you find on the two islands is their respective progeny. The Amuraha women had normal bodies – you'll naturally wonder why Lorzanian men didn't marry Amurahan women. The answer is, that since time immemorial, relations between Lorzanians and Amurahans were taboo. They believed that if a Lorzanian man so much as touched an Amurahan woman the two would perish instantly. Any relations between them were, therefore, out of the question.

What became of Kuruvila?

Oh yes, I was telling you about Kuruvila. Now, Kuruvila too married a Lorzanian woman. But he wasn't happy. When he learned about Amuraha, he came to me and said, 'Look, Chakko, let's both go to Amuraha. Who wants to spend his life in a country of half-women? There's no harm in our going to Amuraha. The taboos of these people don't apply to us, since we don't belong to their race. Think of the great time we'll have in a country where the women have never seen a man with a normal body! I tell you they'll literally grovel before us. We'll live like kings over there!' The idea didn't appeal to me, in spite of Kuruvila's great enthusiasm. I didn't want to risk my life on the sea again. Things weren't so bad in Lorzan after all. I said no to Kuruvila. He said he'd go alone. We were both under surveillance, but one night Kuruvila stole a small boat and headed for Amuraha. For about a year after that, I had no news of him. Then one day I found out what had happened. Apparently, he reached the Amurahan shore, and the women in a coastal settlement there gathered about him. Every woman wanted him for herself. They began quarrelling over him. Seizing his arms and legs and head, they started pulling him in every direction. They tugged at him so ferociously that his limbs were almost torn off. He was screaming in the midst of irate, shrieking women. He was dead before the Amurahan policewomen arrived on the scene.

It was a good thing you didn't go with him, wasn't it?

Perhaps.

Were the conditions for Amurahan men the same as that of Lorzanian women?

They may have been. I don't know much about Amuraha.

So by and large you were happy in Lorzan? You didn't feel like returning to the world where you could see normal women?

Not particularly. Risking my life on the sea solely on that account didn't seem worthwhile. How would I know in which direction to sail? To set out on the sea simply trusting to luck seemed suicidal.

And yet, in the end, you returned. How did that happen?

Towards the end a change came over me. For one thing, I was getting on in years. I thought, am I going to die without ever holding a whole woman in my arms? But that wasn't the only thing. I was becoming homesick, too. I had spent the prime of my life in Lorzan. Now, with the prospect of old age before me, the desire to return to my homeland took hold of me. This sentimental yearning to return 'home' became stronger and stronger. One night I lay alone on the terrace of my house. The stars shone in the clear sky. A cool breeze blew in from the sea. Suddenly I said to myself, 'I've got to go back!' The government didn't keep a strict watch on me any longer. They didn't think I'd make an attempt to escape after all these years. Taking advantage of this, I piled as much food and

water as I could in a motorboat, and said good-bye to Lorzan. I drifted at
sea for several days, until at last a tanker picked me up. I was back.

Didn't you find it exciting to return after all those years?

Of course. I visited places I knew, saw some people. Things had
changed a great deal.

And how did you react to seeing women with normal bodies?

For the first few days, I simply stared at every woman I saw, whether
she was beautiful or not. Then I went to a whore. I told her to undress,
sat down and stared at her. Then I went nearer and stroked her all over
gently. She looked at me strangely. She must have thought it odd, a man
of my age behaving like a kid! Well, I *was* a kid in a way. When I landed
in Lorzan I was not yet twenty, and had never had a woman. The rest of
my years had passed in Lorzan. It was only now, in late middle age, that
I was touching a normal woman. Some time after my arrival, I married
Lakshmi. Lakshmi was an independent widow. She wanted company in
her declining years. Even in middle age, she had preserved her figure and
remained attractive. Her late husband had left her a sizeable estate, so
neither of us had to work. We stayed at home all day, spending hours in
bed petting or teasing one another. We went out whenever the mood
came on us. In spite of our ages, we lived like newlyweds. Lakshmi's late
husband had been a withdrawn person with little appetite for sensual
pleasures. Now, in my company, Lakshmi blossomed. She even said that
for the first time she felt she was married in the true sense. But then little
by little, I grew dissatisfied. Not that I had anything against Lakshmi. It
was just that I didn't like the idea of women with whole bodies. When I
returned from Lorzan, I was fascinated by the sight of normal women,
but now in a few months I had lost interest in them. Perhaps this wasn't
so very unusual. We sometimes desperately want to get somewhere, and
when we arrive we wonder why we're there. That kind of experience
isn't unusual, is it?

I must say it isn't.

So my attitude towards Lakshmi changed. I detested the sight of all
women. Lakshmi was greatly disturbed at this change in my behaviour
'Are you bored with me? Are you in love with someone else?' she kept
asking me. I said no.

*May we talk about this in some detail, Mr Chakko? I'm interested in finding
out why this change came over you. I wonder if, after all those years in the land
of half-women, you had got used to it, and couldn't accept women with whole
bodies?*

(After some thought) No, I don't think it was merely a question of habit,
or getting used to something. There was more to it than that.

Perhaps you believed that women should always be imperfect and inferior. You didn't like the idea of women being physically the same as men.

(After some thought) No, I don't think it was that either.

What was the reason for the change, then?

First I should admit that I'd never given it much thought. But it seems to me that the half, the partial, gives something that the whole, or what appears whole, doesn't.

Could you expand upon that a bit?

(Chakko throws up his hands.)

Never mind. Please go on with your story.

All I know is that day by day I grew more unhappy. I spent my time sulking, curled up in an armchair. Then one day I got up and went out. I went down to the blacksmiths' lane and bought myself an axe. I hid it under my bed. That night after Lakshmi had fallen asleep I brought the axe out, and, in the pale glow of the night-lamp, I aimed at her navel. In four or five blows I cut her exactly in two.

(Interviewer opens his mouth, but does not speak; Chakko remains silent) And then?

Then? Then there were the usual things. The police and everything.

You confessed to the crime, didn't you?

What else could I do? I assumed that I was going to hang. But the other day my lawyer came to see me and said that the psychiatrists had certified that I was mentally incompetent, and that the death sentence had been suspended. I'll remain here as long as the psychiatrist says I'm insane. I thought, fine, good for me. If that idiot thinks I'm nuts, and if it saves me from the hangman's noose, why should I complain?

(Looking at his watch) Mr Chakko, there were many more things I wanted to ask you, but there's not much time left now. Let me ask you a final question: do you have anything to say to our readers – I mean in general?

(Chakko, lost in thought.)

(Interviewer sees the Superintendent standing in the doorway) Sorry, Mr Chakko, I've got to go now. I wish you luck. Good-bye, Mr Chakko.

(Chakko remains silent.)